THE GRIFFIN
MAGE TRILOGY

THE GRIFFIN MAGE
TRILOGY

LORD OF THE CHANGING WINDS
LAND OF THE BURNING SANDS
LAW OF THE BROKEN EARTH

RACHEL NEUMEIER

FANTASY

LORD OF THE CHANGING WINDS Copyright © 2010 by Rachel Neumeier
    Publication History: Orbit mass market paperback, May 2010
LAND OF THE BURNING SANDS Copyright © 2010 by Rachel Neumeier
    Publication History: Orbit mass market paperback, June 2010
LAW OF THE BROKEN EARTH Copyright © 2010 by Rachel Neumeier
    Publication History: Orbit mass market paperback, November 2010

First Science Fiction Book Club Omnibus Edition: January 2011

Published by arrangement with
Orbit
Hachette Book Group
237 Park Avenue
New York, NY 10017

Visit The SFBC online at http://www.sfbc.com
Follow us on Facebook: http://www.facebook.com/ScienceFictionBookClub

ISBN 978-1-61129-073-8

Printed in the United States of America.

CONTENTS

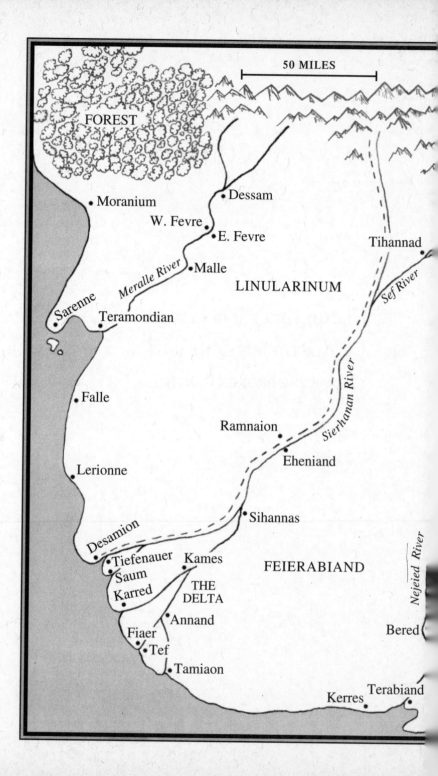

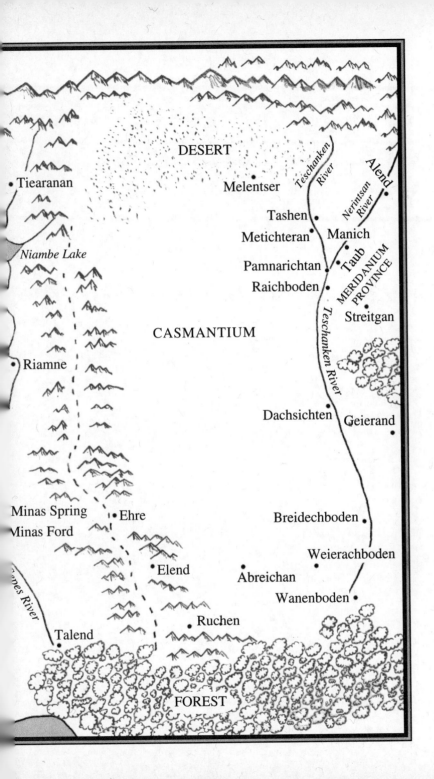

LORD OF THE
CHANGING WINDS

This one's for my brother Brett—without whose advice,
instructions, and long-distance consultation,
my Web sites would either not exist or
would crash on a regular basis!

CHAPTER 1

The griffins came to Feierabiand with the early summer warmth, riding the wind out of the heights down to the tender green pastures of the foothills. The wind they brought with them was a hard, hot wind, with nothing of the gentle Feierabiand summer about it. It tasted of red dust and hot brass.

Kes, gathering herbs in the high pastures above the village of Minas Ford, saw them come: great bronze wings shining in the sun, tawny pelts like molten gold, sunlight striking harshly off beaks and talons. One was a hard shining white, one red as the coals at the heart of a fire. The griffins rode their wind like soaring eagles, wings outstretched and still. The sky took on a fierce metallic tone as they passed. They turned around the shoulder of the mountain and disappeared, one and then another and another, until they had all passed out of sight. Behind them, the sky softened slowly to its accustomed gentle blue.

Kes stood in hills above the high pastures, barefoot, her hair tangled, her hands full of fresh-picked angelica, and watched until the last of the griffins slid out of view. They were the most beautiful creatures she had ever seen. She almost followed them, running around the curve of the mountain's shoulder, leaving her angelica and elecampane and goldenseal to wilt in the sun; she even took a step after them before she thought better of the idea.

But Tesme hated it when Kes did not come home by dusk; she hated it worse when her sister did not come home before dawn. So Kes hesitated one moment and then another, knowing that if she followed the griffins she would forget time and her sister's expectations. There would be noise and fuss, and then it would be days before Tesme once again gave reluctant leave for Kes to go up into the hills. So she stayed

where she was on the mountainside, only shading her eyes with her
hand as she tried to follow the griffins with her eyes and imagination
around the curve of the mountain.

Griffins, she thought. *Griffins*. . . . She walked slowly down from
the hills, crossed the stream to the highest of the pastures, and went on
downhill, her eyes filled with blazing wings and sunlight. She climbed
stone walls without really noticing them, one after another: high pasture
to hill pasture, hill pasture down to the midlands pasture. And then the
low pasture, nearest the barns and the house: the fence here was rail instead of stone. This meant Kes had no convenient flat-topped wall on
which to put her basket while climbing over. She balanced it awkwardly
against her hip and clambered over the fence with one hand.

Her sister, Tesme, spotted Kes as she walked past the nearest barn
and hurried to meet her. The griffins, it was plain, had not come down
so far as the house; Tesme's eyes held nothing of fire and splendor.
They were filled instead with thoughts of heavy mares and staggering
foals. And with worry. Kes saw that. It pulled her back toward the ordinary concerns of home and horse breeding.

"Kes!" said her sister. "Where have you been?" She glanced at the
basket of herbs and went on quickly, "At least, I see where you've been,
all right, fine, did you happen to get milk thistle while you were in the
hills?"

Kes, blinking away images of shining wings, shook her head and
made a questioning gesture toward the foaling stable.

"It's River," Tesme said tensely. "I think she's going to have a difficult time. I should never have bred her to that Delta stud. He was too
big for her, I knew he was, but oh, I want this foal!"

Kes nodded, taking a step toward the house.

"I got your things out for you—they're in the barn—along with your
shoes," Tesme added, her gaze dropping to Kes's bare feet. But her tone
was more worried than tart, the foaling mare distracting her from her
sister's lack of civilized manners. "You just want your ordinary kit,
don't you? Don't worry about those herbs—somebody can take them to
the house for you." Tesme took Kes by the shoulder and hurried her
toward the barn.

In the foaling barn, Kes absently handed her basket to one of the
boys and waved him off toward the house. Tesme hovered anxiously.
Kes saw that she could not tell Tesme about the griffins; not now. She
tried to make herself focus on the mare. Indeed, once she saw her, it
became less of an effort to forget sunlit magnificence and concentrate
instead on normal life. River, a stocky bay mare with bulging sides, was
clearly uncomfortable. And certainly very large. She looked to have

doubled her width since Kes had last looked at her, and that had only been a handful of days ago.

"Do you think she could be carrying twins?" Tesme asked apprehensively. She was actually wringing her hands.

"From the look of her, she could be carrying triplets," Meris commented, swinging through the wide barn doors. "I've been waiting for her to explode for the past month, and now look at her. Kes, glad to see you. Tesme, just how big was that stud?"

"Huge," Tesme said unhappily. "But I wanted size. River's not *that* small. I thought it would be a safe cross."

Kes shrugged. Usually crossing horses of different sizes worked all right, but sometimes it didn't. No one knew why. She looked at her kit, then back at the mare.

"Mugwort," she suggested. "Partridge berry."

"Good idea," said Meris. "Partridge berry to calm her down and help her labor at the beginning—mugwort later, I suppose, in case we need to help the strength of her contractions. I have water boiling. Want me to make the decoctions?"

Kes nodded.

Meris was a quick-moving little sparrow of a woman, plain and sensible and good-humored, equally at home with a foaling mare or a birthing woman. Kes was far more comfortable with her than with most other people; Meris never tried to draw Kes out or make her talk; when Kes did talk, Meris never seemed surprised at what she said. Meris was willing, as so few people seemed to be, to simply let a person or an animal be what it was. No wonder Tesme had sent for Meris. Even if River had no difficulty with her foal, just having Meris around would calm everyone's nerves. That would be good. Kes gave the older woman the packets of herbs and slipped into the stall to touch River's neck. The mare bent her neck around and snuffled down Kes's shirt. She was sweating, pawing at the stall floor nervously. Kes patted her again.

"What do you think?" Tesme asked, seeming almost as distressed as the mare. "Is she going to be all right, do you think?"

Kes shrugged. "Jos?" If they had to pull this foal, she wanted someone with the muscle to do it. Jos had been a drifter. Tesme had hired him for the season six years past, and he had just never seemed inclined to drift away again. He was very strong. And the horses liked him. Kes liked him too. He didn't *talk* at you all the time, or expect you to talk back.

"I'll get him," Tesme agreed, and hurried out.

Kes frowned at the mare, patting her in absent reassurance. River twitched her ears back and walked in a circle, dropping her head and shifting her weight. She was thinking of lying down but was too uncomfortable to do so; Tesme, with her affinity for horses, could have made the mare lie down. Kes neither held an affinity for any animal nor possessed any other special gift—if one did not count an unusual desire to abandon shoes and sister and walk up alone into the quiet of the hills. She did not usually envy Tesme her gift, but she would have liked to be able to make River lie down. She could only coax the mare down with a touch and a murmur.

Fortunately, that was enough. Kes stepped hastily out of the way when the mare folded up her legs and collapsed awkwardly onto the straw.

"How is she?" Tesme wanted to know, finally returning with Jos. Kes gave her sister a shrug and Jos a nod. He nodded back wordlessly and came to lean on the stall gate next to her.

Foals came fast, usually. There was normally no fuss about them. If there was trouble, it was likely to be serious trouble. But it would not help, in either case, to flutter around like so many broken-winged birds and disturb the mare further. Kes watched River, timing the contractions that rippled down the mare's sides, and thought there was not yet any need to do anything but wait.

Waiting, Kes found her mind drifting toward a hard pale sky, toward the memory of harsh light striking off fierce curved beaks and golden feathers. Tesme did not notice her bemusement. But Jos said, "Kes?"

Kes blinked at him, startled. The cool dimness of the foaling barn seemed strange to her, as though the fierce sun the griffins had brought with them had somehow become more real to her than the gentle summer of Minas Ford.

"Are you well?" Jos was frowning at her, curious. Even concerned. Did she seem so distracted? Kes nodded to him and made a dismissive "it's nothing" kind of gesture. He did not seem fully convinced.

Then Tesme called Kes's name sharply, and, pulling her attention back to the mare, Kes went back to lay a hand on River's flank and judge how she was progressing.

The foal *was* very big. But Kes found that, after all, once the birth began, there was not much trouble about the foaling. It had its front feet in the birth canal and its nose positioned properly forward. She nodded reassuringly at her sister and at Jos.

Tesme gave back a little relieved nod of her own, but it was Jos who was the happiest. The last time a foaling had gone badly, the foal had been turned the wrong way round, both front legs hung up on the mare's pelvis. Jos had not been able to push the foal back in enough to straighten the legs; he had had to break them to get the foal out. It had been born dead, which was as well. That had been a grim job that none of them had any desire to repeat, and the memory of it was probably what had wound Tesme up in nervous worry.

This time, Kes waited until the mare was well into labor. Then she simply tied a cord around each of the foal's front hooves, and while Tesme stood at the mare's head and soothed her, she and Jos added a smooth pull to the mare's next contraction. The foal slid right out, wet and dark with birthing liquids.

"A filly!" said Meris, bending to check.

"Wonderful," Tesme said fervently. "Wonderful. Good *girl*, River!"

The mare tipped her ears forward at Tesme, heaved herself to her feet, turned around in the straw, and nosed the baby, which thrashed itself to its feet and tottered. Jos steadied it when it would have fallen. It was sucking strongly only minutes later.

After that, it was only natural to go to the village inn to celebrate. Tesme changed into a clean skirt and braided her hair and gave Kes a string of polished wooden beads to braid into hers. Tesme was happy. She had her foal from the Delta stud—a filly—and all was right with the world. Jos stayed at the farm, keeping an eye on the baby foal; he rarely went to the village during the day, though he visited the inn nearly every evening to listen to the news that travelers brought and to have a mug of ale and a game of pian stones with the other men.

Kes was not so happy. She would as soon have stayed at the farm with Jos and had bread and cheese quietly. But Tesme would have been unhappy if she had refused to go. She was never happy when Kes seemed too solitary. She said Kes was more like a silent, wild creature of the hills than a girl, and when she said such things, she worried. Sometimes she worried for days, and that was hard on them both. So Kes made no objection to the beads or the shoes or the visit to the inn.

They walked. The road was dry and firm at the verge, and Tesme—oddly, for a woman who raised horses—liked to walk. Kes put one properly shod foot in front of another and thought about griffins. Bronze feathers caught by the sun, tawny flanks like gold. Beaks that gleamed like metal. Her steps slowed.

"Come on," Tesme said, and impatiently, "There's nothing to be afraid of, Kes!"

Kes blinked, recalled back to the ordinary road and the empty sky. She didn't say that she was not afraid, exactly. It had been a long time since she'd tried to explain to Tesme her feelings about people, about crowds, about the hard press of their expectations. From the time she had been little, everyone else had seemed to see the world from a different slant than Kes. To understand, without even trying, unspoken codes and rules that only baffled her. Talking to people, trying to shape herself into what they expected, was not exactly frightening. But it was exhausting and confusing and, in a way, the confusion itself was frightening. But Tesme did not seem able to understand any of this. Kes had long since given up trying to explain herself to her sister.

Nor did Kes mention griffins. There seemed no place for them in Tesme's eyes. Kes tried to forget the vision of heat and beauty, to see only the ordinary countryside that surrounded them. To please her sister, she walked a little faster.

But Tesme, who had been walking quickly and impatiently with her hands shoved into the pockets of her skirt, slowed in her turn. She said, "Kes—"

Kes looked at her inquiringly. The light of the sun slid across Tesme's face, revealing the small lines that had come into her face and set themselves permanently between her eyes and at the corners of her generous mouth. Her wheaten hair, braided with a strand of polished wooden beads and tucked up in a coil, held the first strands of gray.

She looked, Kes thought, startled, like the few faint memories she had of their mother. Left at nineteen to hold their father's farm and raise her much younger sister, married twice and twice quickly widowed, Tesme had never yet showed much sign of care or worry or even the passage of time. But she showed it now. Kes looked down again, ashamed to have worried her.

"Are you all right?" Tesme asked gently. She usually seemed a little distracted when she spoke to her sister, when she spoke to anyone; she was always thinking about a dozen different things—mostly practical things, things having to do with raising horses and running the farm.

But Kes thought she was paying attention now. That was uncomfortable: Kes preferred to slip gently around the edges of everyone else's awareness—even Tesme's. Close attention made her feel exposed. Worse than exposed: at risk. As though she stood in the shadows at the edge of brilliant, dangerous light, light that would burn her to ash if it fell on her. Kes always found it difficult to speak; she never knew what anyone expected her to say. But when pinned by the glare of close attention, the uncertainty she felt was much worse. She managed, in a voice that even to her own ears sounded faltering and unpersuasive. "I—I'm all right. I'm fine."

"You seem preoccupied, somehow."

Since Tesme frequently noted aloud that her sister seemed preoccupied, even when she was paying quite close attention, Kes did not know how to answer this.

"There's something . . . *Is* there something wrong?"

Kes could find no words to describe the magnificence of bronze wings in the sun. She would have tried, for Tesme. But the mere thought of trying to explain the griffins, the hard heat they had brought with them, the strange look of the sky when they crossed it in their brilliant flight . . . She shook her head, mute.

Tesme frowned at her. "No one has been, well, bothering you, have they?"

For a long moment, Kes didn't understand what her sister meant. Then, taken aback, she blushed fiercely and shook her head again.

Tesme had come to a full halt. She reached out as though to touch Kes on the arm, but then her hand fell. "Some of the boys can be, well, boys. And you're so quiet. Sometimes that can encourage them. And besides the boys . . ." She hesitated. Then she said, "I like Jos, and he's a wonderful help around the farm, but Kes, if he bothers you, you surely know I'll send him away immediately."

Kes said, startled, "Jos?"

"I know you wouldn't encourage him, Kes, but lately I've thought sometimes that he might be, well, watching you."

"*Jos* doesn't bother me," Kes said, and was startled by the vehemence of her tone. She moderated it. "I like Jos. He wouldn't . . . he isn't . . . and he's too old, anyway!"

"Oh, well, Kes! He's not *that* old, and he's not blind, and you're growing up and getting pretty, and if he notices you too much, there are other places he could get work." But Tesme looked somewhat reassured. She started walking again, if not as quickly.

Kes hurried the few steps necessary to catch up. "I like Jos," she said again. She did, she realized. His quiet, his calm, the competent way he handled the horses. The way he never pressed her to speak, or seemed to expect her to fit into some unexplained pattern of behavior she couldn't even recognize. He was comfortable to be around, as so few people were. He had been at the farm for . . . nearly half her life, Kes thought. She could not imagine it without him. "He doesn't bother me, Tesme. Really, he doesn't. Don't send him away."

"All right . . ." Tesme said doubtfully, and began to walk a little more quickly. "But let me know if you change your mind."

It was easier to nod than protest again.

They walked a little farther. But then Tesme gave Kes a sideways look and added, "Now, if there's a boy you *do* like, you'd let me know, Kes, wouldn't you? I remember what I was like at your age, and shy as you are, you *are* getting to be pretty. You know you don't need to slip off silently to meet somebody, don't you? If you want to walk out with

Kanne or Sef or somebody, that's different, but you would tell me, wouldn't you? There's a world of trouble for a girl who's too secretive, believe me."

Kes felt her face heat. "I don't like anyone!" she protested.

"That changes," Tesme said, her tone wry. "If it changes for you, Kes . . ."

"I'll tell you. I'll tell you," Kes said hastily, hoping to sound so firmly reassuring that Tesme would let the subject die. It was true anyway. Kanne? She suppressed an urge to roll her eyes, not wanting her sister to reopen the subject—but *Kanne*? Kanne was a baby, and too interested in himself to even notice a girl. Sef was almost as bad, all but welded to the smithy where he was apprenticed. Kes couldn't imagine either of them, or any other of the village boys, ever choosing to simply walk out across the hills and listen to the wind and the silence.

"All right . . ." Tesme said. She did sound somewhat reassured. "It's true you're not much like I was. On the whole, that's probably just as well." She glanced at Kes, half smiling and half worried.

Kes had no idea what to say to this, and so said nothing.

"You're yourself, that's all," Tesme concluded at last, smiling. She patted Kes on the shoulder and lengthened her stride once more.

The inn, set by the road near the river, right at the edge of the village, was all white stone and dark wooden beams. It had a dozen pretty little tables in its wide, walled courtyard, across from its stables, which were screened from the inn by small trees and beds of flowers. Jerreid and his wife, Edlin, and their daughters ran the inn, which was widely acknowledged to be the best of all the little country inns along the western river road that ran from Niambe Lake all the way down to Terabiand. The inn was not overlarge, but it was pleasant and very clean, and every window looked out onto one flower garden or another. And the food was good.

Many ordinary folk and even nobles broke their journey in Minas Ford as they traveled from the little jewel-pretty cities of the high north to the sprawling coastal town of Terabiand in the south—the Ford of the town's name had long ago been replaced by the best bridge anywhere along the river—and, as the saying went, everyone and everything passed along the coast at some time. And so a good proportion of everyone and everything traveled up from Terabiand and through Minas Ford eventually, and since Minas Ford was conveniently a long day's journey from Bered to the south and an easy day's journey from Riamne to the north, many travelers looked forward to a stay at Jerreid's pretty little inn.

Every upstairs room had a window, shutters open in this fine weather;

every table, outdoors or in, was graced by a slender vase of flowers. Edlin made the vases of fine white clay, glazing them with translucent glazes in blue and pink and white. She made them to keep cut flowers, and she had the gift of making in her hands: It was common knowledge that flowers stayed fresh in one of Edlin's vases twice as long as they lasted in an old cracked mug.

Edlin also made tableware that was both pretty and very hard to break. She sold bowls and plates and platters from a shop behind the inn, leaving the running of the inn almost entirely to her husband and their three daughters. Edlin grew the flowers herself, though, and picked them fresh every week to arrange in the vases. That was, famously, as close to the work of the inn as she would come. Jerreid, fortunately, seemed perfectly happy to leave his wife to her dishes and glazes and gardens.

"Tesme!" Jerreid said, as they came into the yard. He was a big, bluff, genial man with a talent for making his inn feel homey and all his visitors feel welcome. He'd been leaning against one of the outdoor tables, chatting with what looked like half the folk of the village—a big crowd for the middle of the day. There were no travelers present at the moment, although some would probably stop later in the day. But Chiad and his wife had torn themselves away from their farm to visit the inn, along with a dozen children and cousins and nephews. And Heste had abandoned her bakery for the moment—well, the morning bread was long out of the ovens, and perhaps she had a little time before she would start the pies and honey cakes for the evening. But Nehoen was also present, which was less usual. His big house with its sprawling lands lay well outside the village, and he did not usually come to the inn except on market day. And Caris had for some reason left her weaving to visit the inn, as well as Kanes and his apprentice Sef the smithy.

Kes looked at them all uneasily, wondering nervously whether she might guess what had drawn them all away from their ordinary business. She hoped she did not blush when she glanced at Kanne or Sef. How could Tesme possibly think—? Was Kanne even fourteen yet? And Sef! She looked hastily away from the smith's apprentice, aware that she probably *was* blushing, now.

"You seem happy," Jerreid was saying to Tesme. His smile, at least, seemed ordinarily cheerful. "How is your mare? River, wasn't it? She must have done well by you, yes?"

"Yes, yes, yes!" Tesme came across the yard, leaving Kes to follow more slowly. She took Jerreid's hands in hers and smiled at him. "A filly, healthy and big, and River's fine. We're celebrating. Have you any blackberry wine left, or did you drink it all yourself?"

"We've plenty—"

"But you might want to hold off on the celebrations," said Chiad. Dark as the earth he worked, serious by nature and not given to celebrations at even the best of times, he looked at the moment even more somber than usual. He slapped the table with one broad hand for emphasis as he spoke.

"Give the woman a chance to catch her breath!" exclaimed Jerreid, shaking his head in mild disapproval.

Chiad gave him a blink of incomprehension and instantly transferred his attention back to Tesme. "You've got your young foals down by the house, haven't you, Tesme? Do you know what Kanne saw this morning?" Kanne was Chiad's son, and he now sat up straight in his chair and looked important.

Kes knew. She heard it in Chiad's voice. She saw it in Kanne's eyes.

Tesme arched her eyebrows, still smiling, if a little less certainly. "If it wasn't someone underselling me with Delta-bred stock for cheap, I don't think I'll mind, whatever it was."

"You will," said Chiad, heavily, with a somber shake of his head. "Tell her, boy."

Kanne laid his hands down flat on the table and sat up even straighter, looking proud and important. "Griffins!" he said.

This had not been what Tesme expected, and she looked blank.

"Griffins!" Chiad said. He slapped the table, shaking his head again in heavy disapproval. "Of all things! Half lion, half eagle, and all killer! My barley is likely safe enough, but you'd best look after your stock, Tesme!"

Tesme still looked blank. She said after a moment, "Kanne, are you sure they weren't just eagles?"

"Now, that's what I said," Jerreid agreed, nodding.

"Sure, I'm sure," Kanne said importantly. "I *am* sure! I know what eagles look like, Jerreid! These weren't eagles or vultures or any bird!"

"Griffins never leave their desert," said Heste, frowning. Her attitude suggested that she had said this before, repeatedly.

"They do," said Nehoen, so patiently it was clear he'd said this before as well. "Griffins in the spring mean a hard summer." Nehoen was not sitting at the table. He had gotten to his feet when Tesme and Kes had entered the courtyard. Now he moved restlessly, leaning his hip against one of the tables and crossing his arms over his chest. He was old, nearly fifty, but he was one of the few gentlemen of the village and thus showed his age far less than a farmer or smith.

"What?" said Tesme, blinking at him.

Nehoen smiled at her. He owned all the land out on the west side of the village near the river, and he could not only read, but owned far more books than all the rest of Minas Ford put together. His grandmother had been an educated woman of the Delta, and had put great store by books and written learning. He explained now, "Griffins in the fall mean an easy winter, griffins in the spring a hard summer. They say that in Casmantium. There wouldn't be a saying about it if the griffins never left their country of fire to come into the country of earth."

"But why would they?" Tesme asked. "And why come so *far*? Not just so far south, either, but all the way across the mountains into Feierabiand?"

"Well, that I don't know. The mages of Casmantium keep them out of Casmantian lands—that's what their cold mages are for, isn't it?—so maybe if the griffins wanted to move, they had to cross the mountains. But why they left their own desert in the first place?" Nehoen shrugged. "Who can guess why such creatures do anything?"

"Griffins are bad for fire," said Kanes. The smith's deep voice rumbled, and everyone hushed to listen to him. "That's what I know. They're made of fire, and fire falls from the wind their wings stirs up. That's what smiths say. They're bad creatures to have about."

Smiths knew fire. Everyone was silent for a moment, thinking about that.

"Griffins," said Jerreid at last, shaking his head.

"Griffins," agreed Nehoen. He began a rough sketch on a sheet of paper somebody had given him.

Chiad's wife said, practically, as she was always practical, "Saying Kanne is right, as I think he is, then what? Fire and hard summers, maybe—and then maybe not. But it stands to reason a creature with eagle talons and lion claws will hunt."

"Surely—" Tesme began, and stopped, looking worried. "You don't think they would eat our horses, really?"

"Nellis stops wolves from eating livestock," said Chiad, laying a broad hand on his wife's hand.

She nodded to him and went on herself, "Jenned stops mountain cats. Perren stops hawks from coming after chicks." Perren was a falconer as well as a farmer, and gentled hawks and falcons for the hunt. Chiad's wife added, "I can keep foxes off the hens, and my little Seb stops weasels and stoats. But I don't know who's going to stop griffins eating your foals or my sheep, if that's what they want. What we need is a cold mage. I wonder why our mages in Feierabiand never thought to train up a youngster or two in cold magic?"

"We've never needed cold magecraft before," Chiad answered his wife, but not as though he found this argument persuasive.

His wife lifted her shoulders in a scornful shrug. "Well, and we don't need ice cellars until the summer heat, or a second lot of seed grain until a wet spring rots the first sowing; that's why we plan ahead, isn't it? They should have thought ahead, up there in Tihannad—"

"Now, now." Jerreid shook his head at Chiad's wife in mild reproof. "Summer we have every year, and wet springs often enough, but if griffins have ever come across the mountains before, it was so long ago none of our fathers or grandfathers remember it. Be fair, Nellis."

"Whoever thought or didn't think, it's my horses that are going to be eaten by griffins," said Tesme, sitting down rather abruptly at the table in the chair Nehoen had abandoned.

"They wouldn't eat them," Nehoen said, patting her shoulder. "Griffins don't eat. They may look part eagle and part lion, but they're wholly creatures of fire. They hunt to kill, but they don't eat what they bring down."

"That's even worse!" Tesme exclaimed, and rubbed her forehead.

Kes watched her sister work through the idea of griffins coming down on her horses. It clearly took her a moment. She wasn't used to thinking of the danger a big predator might pose if no one in the village could speak to it or control it.

In every country there were folk with each of the three common gifts. But just as Casmantian folk were famously dark and big-boned and stocky, Casmantian makers and builders were famously the best. There were makers everywhere, but more and better makers in Casmantium; to find makers with the strongest gifts and the deepest dedication to their craft, to find builders who could construct the strongest walls and best roads and tallest palaces, one went to Casmantium.

In the same way, one could recognize Linularinan people because they commonly had hair the color of light ale and narrow, secretive eyes, but also because they were clever and loved poetry. Everyone in Linularinum could write, they said, so probably it wasn't surprising that Linularinum had the cleverest legists. There were legists in Feierabiand, at least in the cities, but if you wanted a really unbreakable contract that would do exactly what you wanted, you hired a Linularinan legist to write it for you.

But everyone knew that if you needed someone with a really *strong* affinity for a particular sort of animal, you came to Feierabiand. As Tesme held an affinity to horses, others held affinities to crows or mice or deer or dogs. In Feierabiand, every town and village and tiny hamlet had one or two people who could call wolves and mountain cats—and more important, send them away. But griffins were creatures of fire, not earth. No matter how dangerous or destructive they might prove, no one, even in Feierabiand, would be able to send the griffins back across the mountains.

Tesme was looking more and more unhappy. "Maybe you and Edlin would let us borrow the use of your lower pasture for a while?" she said to Jerreid. "Mine isn't big enough for all the horses. Will I have to move all the horses, do you think? How big are griffins? How many did you see, Kanne?"

"Dozens," the boy said. He sounded pleased about it. "Big."

Nehoen silently held out a sketch he'd drawn. It showed an animal with a savage look: a creature half feathered and half furred, with the cruel hooked beak and talons of an eagle and the haunches of a cat. Everyone crowded forward to look. Kes, peering over Kanes's shoulder, winced a little. The monster in the drawing was a crude misshapen thing, neither bird nor beast; it looked clumsy and vicious.

"Yes," said Kanne triumphantly. "Griffins!"

Kanes nodded heavily. "We need king's soldiers. That's what we need. Clean the creatures out before they settle in to stay."

Kes continued to study the drawing for a moment longer, not listening as everyone else spoke at once. It was all wrong. And what she found, though she didn't understand why it mattered to her, was that she couldn't bear to have everyone believe Nehoen's drawing showed the truth. So she silently took the paper from Nehoen's hand and picked up the piece of charcoal he had used for his drawing. Nehoen looked startled, but he let her have the charcoal. Nellis stood up, giving Kes her place at the table, and waved for Kanne to move, too.

Kes turned the paper over to the blank side and sat down. She had already forgotten her audience. She was thinking of griffins. Her eyes filled with fire and beauty. She turned the charcoal over in her fingers and set it to the paper. The creature she drew was not like the one Nehoen had sketched. She had a surer hand with the charcoal than Nehoen, but that was not the difference. The difference was that she knew what she was drawing.

The griffin flowed out of the charcoal, out of Kes's eyes. It was eagle and lion, but not mismade, not wrong, as Nehoen's griffin had been wrong. She gave this griffin the beauty she had seen. She had seen griffins flying, but the one she drew was sitting, posed neatly like a cat. It was curled around a little, its head tilted at an inquisitive angle. It was fierce, but not vicious. The feathers around its eyes gave it a keen, hard look. Its sharp-edged beak was a smooth curve, exactly right for its eagle head. The feathers flowed down its forequarters and melted smoothly into a powerfully muscled lion rear. Its wings, half opened, poured through the sketch with the clean purity of flame.

Tesme, looking over Kes's shoulder, took a slow breath and let it out.

Nehoen took the finished drawing out of Kes' hands and looked at it silently. Kes looked steadily down at the table.

"When did you see them?" Nehoen asked gently.

Kes glanced up at him and looked down again. She moved her hand restlessly across the rough surface of the table. "This morning."

Tesme was staring at her. "You didn't say anything."

Kes traced the grain of the wood under her hand, running the tip of her finger around and around a small knot in the wood. "I didn't know how. To talk about them. They . . . are nothing I know words to describe."

"You—" Chiad said incredulously.

"Hush," said Nellis, laying a hand on her husband's arm. "Kes, love—"

At the gate of the inn yard, someone moved, and everyone jumped and stared. Then they stared some more.

The man at the gate was a stranger. But more than a stranger, he was himself strange. He wore fine clothing, but unusual in both cut and color. Red silk, red linen, red leather—all red, a dark color like drying blood, except for low black boots and a black cloak. He did not wear a sword, though even in Feierabiand nearly all men of good birth carried one. But this man did not carry even a knife at his belt. He held no horse, and that was surely strangest of all, for how had a gentleman come to Minas Ford if not by horse or carriage?

The man's hair was black and very thick, without a trace of gray—although it was somehow immediately clear that he was not a young man. The lines of his face were harsh and strong. His eyes were black, his gaze powerful. He had a proud look to him, as though he thought he owned all the land on which his gaze fell. His shadow, Kes saw, with a strange lack of astonishment, was not the shadow of a man. It was too large for a man's shadow, and the wrong shape, and feathered with fire. Kes glanced quickly into her sister's face, and then looked at Nehoen and Jerreid and Kanes, and realized that although everyone was startled by the stranger, no one else saw that his shadow was the shadow of a griffin.

The black-eyed stranger with the griffin's shadow did not speak. No one spoke, not even Jerreid, who liked everyone and was hard to put off. Everyone stared at the stranger, but he had attention only for Kes. And rather than speaking, he walked forward, straight to the table where she sat. He clearly assumed everyone would get out of his way, and everyone did, although Nehoen, getting abruptly to his feet, put a hand on Kes's shoulder as though he thought she might need protection.

Ignoring Nehoen, still without speaking, the man picked up the drawing Kes had made and looked at it. Then he looked at her.

Kes met his eyes, seeing without surprise that they were filled with fire. She took a breath of air that seemed stiff with heat and desert magic. She could not look away, and wondered what the man saw in her eyes.

"What is your name?" the man asked her. His voice was austere as barren stone, powerful as the sun.

After a moment, Nehoen cleared his throat and answered on her behalf. "Kes, lord," he said. "Kes. She doesn't talk much. And what is *your* name?"

The man transferred his gaze to Nehoen's face, and Nehoen stood very still. Then the man smiled suddenly, a taut hard smile that did not reach his eyes. "I am sometimes called Kairaithin. Anasakuse Sipiike Kairaithin. You may call me so, if that pleases you. And yours, man?"

Nehoen swallowed. He met the black stare of the stranger as though he was meeting a physical blow. He said slowly, reluctantly, "Nehoen. Nehoen, son of Rasas, lord."

"Nehoen, son of Rasas," said the stranger. "I am not your enemy." He did not say, I do not care about you at all, but Kes saw the merciless indifference in his eyes. When he turned his attention back to her, she looked down at the table. She said nothing. She did not dare speak, but beyond that, she simply had no idea what to say. The stranger seemed to see her exactly as she was, but she had no idea who, or what, he saw. In a way, she found this hard-edged perception more difficult to endure than the ordinary expectations of the townsfolk.

"Kes," said the man. He put down the drawing she had made. "My . . . people . . . have encountered difficulty. There are injured. We have need of a healer. You are a healer, are you not? My people are not far removed from this place. Will you come?" He asked this as though Kes had a choice.

Kanes rose to his considerable height, crossed his powerful smith's arms across his chest, and rumbled, "Who asked you to bring your . . . *difficulties* . . . here, stranger?"

The man did not even glance at the smith. But Kes flinched. She could not understand how Kanes, strong as he was, could possibly think he could challenge the stranger. She could not understand how the smith could miss his contained power.

But Kanes, it seemed, was not alone in that inclination. Nehoen shifted half a step forward and said in a tone edged with hostility, "She's needed at her home." He looked at Tesme.

Tesme blinked. She had been staring at the stranger, wordless.

Now she said in a breathless voice, "Kes. Come home," and held out her hand to her sister.

Kes did not move. She looked into the face of the stranger and whispered, "You are a mage. As well as—" she stopped.

A swift, fierce smile glinted in the black eyes.

"Are you—" Kes began, and stopped again.

"I am not your enemy," the man said, harsh and amused. "Do this for me, and perhaps I will be your friend." Fire flared in his eyes. He said patiently, holding out his hand, "I have no power to heal. I think you do. Will you come?"

"Kes—" said Tesme.

"Look, Kes—" said Nehoen.

"I—you should understand, lord," Kes whispered, "I only use herbs."

The man continued to hold out his hand expectantly. "You drew that. Yes?"

Kes, lowering her gaze, looked at the drawing that lay on the table between her hands. It seemed strange to her now, how smoothly that image had emerged from her eyes, from her memory. Her hands closed slowly into fists. "Yes."

"Then I hardly think you will need herbs. It was not a herb woman I sought. Searching, it was you I found. Will you come?"

Kes found she wanted to go with him. She knew he was not truly a man; she knew he was not any creature of the ordinary earth. But she longed, suddenly and intensely, to go with him and see what strangeness he might show her. Kes got to her feet, not looking at anyone but especially not at her sister, and laid her hand in his. His long fingers closed firmly around hers. The stranger's skin was dry, fever hot to the touch. He tilted his head to the side, meeting her eyes with his powerful black gaze. There was nothing remotely human in his eyes.

The world moved under their feet, rearranging itself. They stood high up on the slopes of the mountain. Kes caught her breath, blinking, and found the world had gone as strange and beautiful as she could ever have wished.

The sun poured down with ruthless clarity upon the rocks, which were red, all in twisted and broken shapes, nothing like the everyday rounded gray stone of the mountain. Griffins lounged all around them, inscrutable as cats, brazen as summer. They turned their heads to look at Kes out of fierce, inhuman eyes. Their feathers, ruffled by the wind that came down the mountain, looked like they had been poured out of light, their lion haunches like they had been fashioned out of gold. A white griffin, close at hand, looked like it had been made of alabaster and white marble and then lit from within by white fire. Its eyes were the pitiless blue white of the desert sky.

And, Kes realized, the griffins were not actually lounging. They were not relaxed. They lay on the sand or atop the twisted red stone ledges, tense and tight-coiled, looking at Kes with fierce and angry stares.

The man at her side moved a step, drawing her glance. The merciless sun threw his shadow out behind him, and here in the desert that shadow was clearly made of fire. It was more brilliant than even the molten sunlight. Flames tossed around the shadow's fierce eagle head like feathers moved by the wind. Its eyes were black.

The man said with harsh approval, "You knew, of course."

Kes nodded hesitantly.

"Of course. You see very clearly. You are such a gift as I had hardly hoped to find, woman, though it was for one such as you I searched. You are exactly what we need." He drew her forward, between gold and bronze griffins, into the shade cast by the shoulder of the mountain. His shadow paled in that relative dimness, like the edges of a clear flame, more sensed than seen.

A griffin lay there in the shade. It was, indeed, injured. A deep and bloody wound scored its golden lion flank, and blood speckled the bronze and black feathers of its chest. It lay with its mouth open, panting rapidly. Its tongue was narrow and barbed. Its eyes were open but blind, glazed with pain.

Kes stared at the wounded griffin in horror, as much at the ruin of its beautiful strength as at its pain. The stranger had said he needed a healer, but she had not imagined such desperate wounds and suffering. She had none of her things, not the sinews for sewing injuries nor the powders to keep infection from starting. And even if she had had those things, the griffin's wounds looked too serious for her skill anyway.

Another griffin crouched near the injured one like a friend or a brother: Something in this griffin's manner made Kes think of how Tesme would have hovered by her side if *she* had been hurt. She longed, suddenly and intensely, for Tesme; yet at the same time, she was fervently glad that her sister was not here. There was nothing in this place Tesme would have understood, and Kes felt, strongly if incoherently, that her sister's presence would only have offended the griffins and weakened Kes herself.

The guardian griffin had feathers of brilliant gold overlaid with a copper tracery. He sat up as they approached, tail wrapped neatly as a cat's around his feet, and fixed Kes with a brilliant copper-gold stare. She faltered, but Kairaithin drew her forward.

"There are others injured," Kairaithin said. He sounded . . . not concerned, precisely. Not like a man might sound, whose friend was injured. Kes did not understand what she heard in his voice, but it was nothing human. He went on, "But this is the worst. This is our . . . king. He must live. Far better for your people, as well as mine, if he should live."

Kes could not tell if he meant this as a threat, or merely as a statement. She moved forward hesitantly, kneeling by the wounded griffin. She put her hand to its chest, parting the feathers delicately. The injured griffin did not move; the other one shifted a foot, talons scraping across stone. Kes flinched back, but he did not move again. And Kairaithin was waiting.

The wound she found was a puncture, deep . . . she could not tell how deep . . . wide as well as deep. It was bleeding only a little, a slow welling of crimson droplets that ran, each in turn, along the lie of the feathers to fall, glittering and solid, to the sand. Tiny gemstones, rubies and garnets, sparkled in the sand under her knees. Kes blinked at them, fully understanding for the first time that these were truly not creatures of earth. That they were wholly foreign to this land and to her own nature. And she was expected to heal them? She cast Kairaithin a frightened glance.

"An arrow made of ice and ill intent," said the griffin mage, watching her face. "I drew the arrow and slowed the blood. But I have no power to heal. That is for you."

Kes laid her hand over the wound. She had no herbs, no needles, no clean water, nothing a healer would use at her craft . . . She touched the griffin's face, traced the delicate shadings of gold and bronze under the blind eye, moved her hand to rest on the rapid pulse beating under the fine feathers of the throat. She said, trying to sound helpless rather than defiant, "But . . . truly, lord, I know nothing but herbs."

"You know what you see. You know what we are. Are you not aware of your own power, poised to wake? Did you not know me at once?"

Kes did not know what the man meant by "your own power." True healers were mages, not mere herb women. She was not a mage. She knew very well she was not a mage. Mages were not simply gifted, as Tesme was gifted with her affinity for horses, as makers or legists might be variously gifted. There was always magic in making, in made things; everyone had that to at least a small degree. There was magic in spoken and, especially, written words—especially in Linularinum, where everybody learned to write. But the affinity to an animal, the ability to make or build, the legist's gift of setting truth down with quill and ink . . . all of those things were part of inborn, natural earth magic. Anybody could be gifted.

But mages were not merely gifted. They *were* gifted, but the gift wasn't enough to make a mage. Or so Kes had always believed. Mages studied for years and years, learning . . . Kes could not imagine what. And there were never many of them: the necessary combination of power and dedication were vanishingly rare.

It had never occurred to Kes to wonder how an old mage chose an apprentice, or how a young person, perhaps, found within herself the desire or capacity or . . . whatever it might be that might lead her to want to be chosen. Kes had never wanted anything like that. Kes had only wanted to be left alone, to walk in the hills and look at the sky and the pools and the growing things. Hadn't she? If the idea of being a mage had ever occurred to her . . . *would* she have wanted that? Did she want it now?

Now that the notion had occurred to her, Kes thought, uneasily, that she might almost want it. It would set her apart . . . but in a way that people could understand, or at least that they could be comfortable with not understanding. And she had always been set apart anyway, or set herself apart, somehow. Mage-skill would have made her . . . made her . . . she did not know what. Something different than she was now. Wouldn't it? And yet, this griffin-mage thought *she* might be a mage? Even trying now to look inside herself, she could find nothing whatsoever that seemed to her like *power.*

Kairaithin's power, on the other hand, beat against her skin like the heat of a bonfire. Kes closed her eyes and saw a black-and-red griffin move in the darkness behind the lids. *I have no power to heal,* he had said. What power *did* a griffin have, when he was also a mage? When she thought of the griffin, fire roared through the darkness. A voice like the hot wind of the desert said in her mind, *Anasakuse Sipiike Kairaithin.* She did not doubt Kairaithin's power. Was it possible the griffin mage had made a mistake about her?

"Searching, I found you, and so brought my people to this place," Kairaithin said to her, as though in answer to her unspoken question. With her eyes closed, it seemed to Kes that he spoke from a place very far away. "And so we are here; and so is Kiibaile Esterire Airaikeliu, Lord of Fire and Air. See him whole, woman, with insistent sight; pour through your heart and into him the fire that sustains him, and he will be whole."

Kes opened her eyes again and looked up at the griffin mage, baffled. *Insistent sight?* She laid her hand on the wounded griffin's chest and stared down at him, hoping for inspiration. His breath came rapidly.

His blood, liquid as it left his body, was hot against her fingers. The gold-and-copper griffin stared furiously at her. She did not ask what the griffins would do if she could not heal their king. She thought instead of the griffin mage saying in his austere voice, *I hardly think you will need herbs.*

Could he be right? What, then, would she need? *See him whole, and he will be whole.* She stared down at the bloody feathers under her hands, and found she did indeed want to heal that terrible wound and restore the griffin to health and wholeness. She wanted that. But even so, she did not know what to do. She drew her hands back and looked helplessly at Kairaithin, afraid he would be angry, but simply at a loss.

The griffin mage did not appear to be angry, although perhaps impatient. He took one of Kes's hands in both of his and held it firmly. Heat struck up her arm, racing from her hand up to her shoulder and then spreading down toward her heart. Kes gasped. It did not actually hurt. But it was a strange feeling, as though her own blood had been turned into a foreign substance within her veins.

"Creature of earth," said Kairaithin, letting her go but holding her eyes with his. "You may yet learn to understand fire. Reach for fire and it will follow the pathway your will lays down for it, as a fire follows tinder across stone."

"Reach for it?" Kes said, faltering.

"Make it a part of your nature. I will give you fire. Let the fire strike into your heart." The griffin mage bent forward, staring at her, willing her to understand.

Kes stared back at him. *Let the fire strike into your heart.* She pictured an arrow slanting down out of the sun at her, guided by Kairaithin's will: a burning arrow, a golden arrow trailing flames. She flinched from the image.

Beside her, the injured griffin shifted. His breath rattled in his throat. His eyes were blind, Kes thought, because they were filled with shadows.

She blinked, and blinked again, and then shut her eyes and turned her face up to the sky. Lord of Fire and Air. King of the griffins. His pulse beat under the tips of her fingers. His name beat in her own pulse. She said, not understanding her own certainty, "Why is he in the shade? He needs light."

The mage moved his hand and the rock above them shattered and fell away, raining far down the mountain in little pieces. The sun poured down. Kes thought about the fiery arrow coming down at her, and this time she didn't flinch. Instead, she did something that felt like calling out to it.

"Yes," said Kairaithin, his tone fierce and triumphant.

Mere image though it might be, the arrow seemed to blaze down and snap into Kes's body with an almost physical shock: The image in her mind of the arrow striking home was so vivid she gasped. She thought she could feel its sharp entry into her heart. There was a sharp-edged moment of agony, but then at once a sense of fierce satisfaction and a strange kind of wholeness, as though she had been waiting all her life for that arrow of light and heat to enter her. She felt filled with fire. It did not feel like power. It felt like completion.

Kes shut her eyes and held up her hands to the sunlight. She cupped the light in her hands, hot and heavy as gold, and then opened her hands to pour it out like liquid. She listened to the griffin's name in the beating of her blood. Kiibaile Esterire Airaikeliu. Creature of fire and blood. She stared into the sun, and then lowered her eyes to stare into his. She saw him whole, and blinked, and blinked again, her eyes filled with heat and light.

Beneath her hands, the pulse that had been so rapid steadied and slowed.

The king of the griffins moved his head and looked at her with eyes that were no longer blind, but clear and savage. The wounds were gone. When he rolled to crouch and then sit, his movements were fluid, effortless. When he struck at Kes with his savage eagle's beak, he moved fast as light pouring across stone.

Kes could never have ducked in time. But in fact she did not try to dodge the griffin's beak at all. She knelt in the sun and stared into fierce golden eyes, stunned as a rabbit by the gaze of an eagle, as much by what she had done as by the unexpected violence, watching light glance savagely off that curved beak as it slashed toward her face.

The gold-and-copper griffin interposed his own beak, blindingly quick, with a sound like bone striking bone. The king of the griffins turned his shoulder to the copper-traced one and stretched, muscles shifting powerfully under the tawny pelt of his haunches; he spread his great wings, shaking the feathers into place. They spread behind him, a tapestry of gold and bronze and black. He cried out, a hard high cry filled with something that seemed to Kes akin to joy, but not a human joy. Something stranger and harsher than any human emotion.

Kairaithin had not moved, but he was smiling. The copper-traced griffin swept his head back and cried out, the same cry as the king, but pitched half a tone higher. The king swept his wings forward and then down, catching the hot breeze, and leapt suddenly into the air. The hot wind from his wings blew Kes's hair around her face and drove up from the ground a whirling red dust that smelled of hot stone and fire.

Flickering wisps of fire were stirred to life in the wind of those wings; the fiery sparks turned to gold as they scattered across the sand.

The other griffin lingered a moment longer. *I am Eskainiane Escaile Sehaikiu*, he said to Kes, his voice flashing brilliantly around the edges of her mind. *When you would set a name to burn against the dark, think of me, human woman.* Then he said to Kairaithin, *I acknowledge your claim; you were right to bring us to the country of men and right to seek a young human with her magecraft on the very edge of waking.*

Kairaithin inclined his head in acknowledgment and satisfaction.

The coppery griffin spread wings like a blazing stroke of fire and swept into the sky, following the king. Kairaithin put his hand down to Kes. "There are other injured. I will show them to you."

Kes asked him shakily, "Will they all try to kill me?" She felt very strange, and not only because of the griffin king's unexpected savagery. She felt light and warm, but it was not, somehow, a comforting kind of warmth. It seemed to her that if she stood up she might fall into the hot desert wind and blow away across the red sand; she felt as though she had become, in some essential manner, detached from the very earth. But she took Kairaithin's hand and let him lift her to her feet.

"Perhaps some." The mage released her hand and tilted his head to look at her sidelong, a gesture curiously like that of a bird. He said after a slight pause, "Do not be offended, woman. These are not your own kind. Esterire Sehaikiu gave you his name, and he is not the least among us. Will you not then allow the king his pride? I will protect you if there is need. Will you come?" He offered her his hand again.

Kes got slowly to her feet, though this time she did not take the mage's offered hand. She looked at him wordlessly, meeting his eyes. She took a breath of hot desert air, tasting light like hot brass on her tongue. She thought of a red griffin with black eyes. Red wings heavily barred with black shifted across her sight. *Kairaithin*, she thought. *Anasakuse Sipiike Kairaithin.* His name beat in her blood like her own pulse.

"No," said the mage briefly, and moved his hand. A darkness fell across Kes's sight like the shadow of a great wing, and the rhythm in her blood faded with the light. His shadow looked at her; its black eyes laughed. "You could be powerful," Kairaithin said, that same harsh amusement in his voice. "But you are young. You would not be wise to challenge me, woman. Remember that I am not your enemy."

Kes looked at him. The black eyes met hers with absolute assurance. There was no trace of offense in his eyes, in his austere manner. She asked, her voice not quite steady, "Will you be my friend?"

He smiled slowly, a hard expression that was not like a human smile.

"Kairaithin," she said, tasting the word.

He shifted and glanced away, expression closing, and turned to show her the way he wanted her to go. "Come, woman. See the other injured."

Kes followed obediently. She wondered who in the world had had the temerity to attack griffins. With arrows of ice and ill intent. Had she not heard that, in Casmantium, some of the earth mages used a magecraft of cold and ice? And used it specifically against griffins, to keep them out of the lands of men? Such mages might, she supposed, make arrows of ice.

But griffins had always dwelled in the desert north of Casmantium; why would Casmantian mages now attack the griffins? Had the griffins first come south and threatened the cities of men? She wanted to ask Kairaithin. But she did not ask. She only threaded her way between stark stones, following the griffin mage. The sun rode its punishing track above. The griffins ignored their mage, but they turned their heads to watch Kes pass. Their eyes were the fierce hot eyes of desert eagles, unreadable. The griffins were beautiful, but Kes did not have the nerve to meet their stares.

The injured griffin Kairaithin brought Kes to was a slim dark creature, with feathers of rich dark brown only lightly barred with gold. The lion belly was cut across by a long terrible gash that had come near to disemboweling the griffin. Garnets lay strewn across the sand near it, some of them disturbingly large. The griffin lay half in the sun, half in the shade of a towering red rock shelf. Its beak was open as it panted; its eyes, dazed with pain and endurance, were half-lidded. It turned its head as Kairaithin stopped beside it, though, and looked at the mage, and then at Kes. Golden-brown eyes met hers. But this griffin did not seem savage. It seemed, more than anything, simply patient.

"Opailikiita Sehanaka Kiistaike," said Kairaithin.

There was something in his tone, something strong, but nothing Kes recognized. When she moved cautiously past the mage to put a hand on the leonine side of the griffin, it only turned its head away. She did not know if it was acquiescent to her touch, or simply refused to acknowledge her. Or whether it felt something else that she recognized even less. She was not absolutely certain she could heal it. She did not understand what she had done to heal the first griffin. But she wanted to heal it. The thought of the savage wound across its belly was like the thought of broken legs on a foal.

It was surprisingly hard to remember that the griffin was dangerous. That it would perhaps try to kill her. That she did not understand it. *Her*, she thought. She had not been paying particular attention, but she knew that this griffin was female. And young. Yes. The slimness of the haunches said this was a young griffin. She wondered if its composure was feminine in a griffin? Or was it part of just this griffin, an individual characteristic, like Jerreid's friendliness and Nellis's practicality and Tesme's slightly flurried kindness? She did not let herself think of Tesme for longer than an instant. Opailikiita. Opailikiita Sehanaka Kiistaike. Dark and slim and quick and graceful. Opailikiita. Yes.

Kes closed her eyes, then opened them, looking into the sunlight. The griffin's name beat through Kes's awareness. Through her blood. Kes stared into the dark, patient eyes, her own eyes blind with the fierce light of the sun, and groped for the memory of what she had done to heal the griffins' king. She seemed, in just those few steps it had taken to come to this griffin, to have lost the trick of it. She felt much like a child learning to walk, who could not keep his balance and fell every few steps. Of course, a child could cling to the hand of his father. What could Kes cling to?

She thought of fire and fiery arrows and put her hand out, blindly, to Kairaithin. His long angular fingers closed around hers, and again the half-familiar, not-quite-painful heat rushed up her arm. Her heart bloomed with fire.

It demanded no effort to see the griffin the way she should be, rather than the way she was. Opailikiita Sehanaka Kiistaike. Slim and young and beautiful, undamaged by malice or injury. It was more difficult to gather light and heat in her hands, as though half her mind had realized by this time that what she was doing was impossible and this realization interfered with her heart.

Kes blinked through the dazzle of heat, then closed her eyes and lifted a double handful of sand and gemstones. The sand was hot; the garnets rich even to the touch. Kes closed her hands around the grit, then opened her hands again, and looked down. Light pooled in her hands, molten and liquid, and she reached then to touch the injured griffin. And found, with no sense of surprise at all, that the griffin under her hands became whole.

This griffin stretched slowly and rose, and stretched again, fastidious as a cat. She did not strike at Kes, however. She angled her head to the side and regarded Kes from an eye that was unreadable, but not violent. Kes smiled, finding that her face felt stiff, as though it had been a long time since she had last smiled. The griffin leaped up to the top of the red rock that had sheltered her, stretched out in the sun, and began to ruffle her feathers into proper order with her beak, for all the world like a common garden songbird.

Kes looked at Kairaithin. He, too, was smiling. It was not a gentle expression on his harsh face, but he was clearly pleased. "Come," he said, and moved a hand to show her the way.

"She didn't try to kill me," Kes said tentatively.

"She would not," the griffin mage agreed without explanation. "This next one will try, I think. His name is Raihaisike Saipakale. He is quick in temper and embarrassed to have suffered injury. I will, however, protect you."

Kes believed he would. She followed the mage around broken rock and struggling parched grasses, thinking about wounds made with arrow and spear. Made with ice and steel. And ill intent . . . "Who makes such weapons?"

The mage gave her a severe look from his black eyes. "Mages."

This was singularly uninformative. Kes asked tentatively, "Cold mages? Casmantian mages?"

"Yes," said Kairaithin, but he said nothing else.

Kes wanted to ask him why the cold mages of Casmantium had done this, but she looked into Kairaithin's hard, spare face, into his black eyes that held fire and power, into the fiery dark-eyed shadow that shifted restless wings at his back, and did not quite dare.

Raihaisike Saipakale was lying in a patch of withered grass that had once been spring fed; Kes recognized the site, but the spring was dry. The mostly buried gray rock from which the water had seeped was cracked and broken, half-hidden by drifting sand. It was strange and disturbing to see a familiar place so altered; for a moment, Kes found herself wondering whether, if she went home now, she would find her home, too, half buried in desert sand, the bones of the horses wind-scoured, Tesme gone. This was a terrible image. Kes paused, horrified, unable to decide whether she thought it might be true.

"You may attend to the injured. The places of men remain untouched by the desert," Kairaithin said, watching her face. His black eyes held nothing she could recognize as sympathy, but neither did they hold deceit.

Kes took a shaky breath of hot desert air and turned back to the wounded griffin.

This griffin had dreadful injuries across his face and throat and chest; his blood had scattered garnets and carnelians generously through the dead grasses. Kes was surprised he was still alive. But she was confident, this time, that she could make him whole. She called light into her eyes and her blood; she poured light through her hands into the griffin and felt it shape itself into sinew and bone, into bronze feather and tawny pelt. His name ran through her mind, and an understanding of his fierce, quick temperament. She made him whole, unsurprised by the ferocious blaze of temper that accompanied his return to health.

There were many injured griffins. The mage brought her to one and then another, and another. He gave her their names, and she made them whole. The names of the griffins melted across her tongue, tasting of ash and copper, and settled uneasily to the back of her mind. She thought she would be able to recognize every griffin she had healed for the rest of her life, to recall each one's name like a line of poetry. Dazed with sun and the powerful names of griffins, she was startled to find at last that there were no others awaiting her touch and the healing light. She stood in the shadow of a red rock where Kairaithin had brought her and looked at him in mute bewilderment. The only griffin there was Opailikiita Sehanaka Kiistaike, and Kes knew the small brown griffin did not need further healing.

"Rest, *kereskiita*," Kairaithin suggested. Not gently, nor kindly. With something else in his tone. Not exactly sympathy, but perhaps . . . a strange kind of heedfulness.

It seemed, at the moment, enough like kindness. Opailikiita shifted, half-opening a wing in a gesture that looked like welcome, or something similar. *Come*, she said, a smooth touch against the borders of Kes's mind. The tone of her voice, too, suggested welcome.

Kes had not known how desperately weary she had grown until the opportunity to rest was offered. She did not answer the slim brown griffin. She did not think she was capable of putting words together with any lucidity. But she went forward and sank down in the shade where the heat was marginally less oppressive, leaned her head against Opailikiita's feathered foreleg when the griffin turned to offer her that pillow, and was instantly lost in fire-ridden darkness.

CHAPTER 2

On one particularly fine morning in late spring, Bertaud son of Boudan, Lord of the Delta, found himself standing in the courtyard of the king's winter house in Tihannad, watching the king of Feierabiand tease apart the delicate roots of young lilies so that they might be most aesthetically arranged in their waiting box. The morning was very fair, and Bertaud would rather, perhaps, have been hunting or hawking or even shooting at targets in the courtyard with the queen and her ladies to look on and applaud. But Iaor Safiad, in perhaps an excess of affection for his young wife, wished instead to wander through the gardens of his winter house, bury his hands in warm dark earth, and play with flowers. Bertaud shifted his weight, trying not to sigh.

The king finished with the lilies and washed his hands in a basin. Ignoring the towel Bertaud proffered, he shook his hands dry in the air and finally looked at Bertaud with a glint in his eyes. The king was not quite as tall as Bertaud and not quite as dark; though both men spent much time out of doors, the king's skin went golden in the sun rather than brown, and his dark hair, untouched as yet by any gray, picked up sun-bleached streaks and became almost tawny. In looks, Iaor resembled his mother far more than his great black bull of a father. But when he gave Bertaud a sidelong glance and observed, "You're bored," the mocking edge to his tone was very like the old king's.

Bertaud lifted his eyebrows. "Bored? How could I be?"

Iaor laughed—his own laugh. He was far less guarded in manner than his father had been, but with a wickedly sardonic edge to his humor, utterly unlike his mother.

The king's laugh pulled at uncomfortably deep places in Bertaud's heart. He couldn't help it; couldn't help that he admired and

honored—and, yes, loved—Iaor Safiad above any other man in Feierabiand. Bertaud would never have insulted Iaor by claiming to feel toward him as toward his father. But as toward an older brother . . . the
best and most admirable of older brothers . . . He might have admitted
to that.

Bertaud could still remember how splendid and kind Iaor had
seemed to him when he had first come to court from his own father's
huge cluttered house in the Delta, which had been always crowded and
yet never companionable. He had been only ten; Iaor more than twice
that. But Iaor had seen something in the awkward, silent boy Bertaud
had been, and had made him his own page, holding him at court long
past the time he had been due to return to his father's house. Bertaud
had tried to conceal his desperate fear of returning home, but Iaor had
known it, of course. So he had kept Bertaud at his side for eight years,
until Bertaud's father had suddenly died in a frenzy of rage and drink
and Bertaud himself, though barely grown, inherited title to the broad,
fertile lands of the Delta.

But when, only a few years later, Iaor's father too had suffered a
stroke and died, it had been Bertaud whom Iaor Safiad had summoned
to his side. And Bertaud had gladly left one of his many uncles to keep
his own lands in order and returned to Iaor's court. Lord of the Delta,
Bertaud hated the Delta; he had a hundred cousins but cared for none
of them; all that he valued lay in this court, and most of all, the friendship and trust of the king. But Iaor despised sycophancy, and Bertaud
would never risk giving any such impression. Now he waited a moment, until he was certain his voice would show nothing he didn't want
it to show. Then he said, matching Iaor's drily mocking tone, "How
could I possibly desire anything other than what you desire, my king?"

Iaor laughed again. "Of course!" he said. "And what I desire is to
enjoy the last of the spring and think, for a moment, of nothing more
complicated than lilies." Straightening his back, the king stretched ex-
travagantly and then turned and stood for a long moment, looking
around at the gardens and his house in palpable satisfaction.

The winter house of the king of Feierabiand nestled into the land at
a place where three hills came together, where the little wavelets of
Niambe Lake ran before the wind away from the rocky shore. A low,
sprawling building built of the native stone, set against the winter gray
of the lake, the king's house seemed a part of the land. Like the hills, it
might have simply grown there long ago. The Casmantian kings might
build magnificent palaces to impress both their own people and travelers with their grandeur and their skill as builders; the Linularinan
kings might raise delicate towers and airy balconies to the sky; but Iaor

Safiad was a true king of Feierabiand, and the kings of Feierabiand wanted a warm and comfortable house, one with small rooms that could each be heated by a single fireplace, with thick walls and soft hangings to keep in the warmth during the long winters.

The town of Tihannad had grown up around the king's winter house, or perhaps the king's house had been built by the lake because of the town; no one in these latter years remembered. But the town was like the king's house: low and plain and comfortable. Its homes were snugly built of stone, and its streets paved with more stone, with gutters to carry the spring's melting snow to the river that curved along one wall of the town. The wall went all around the town, a tall, thick barricade, though no one living remembered a time the wall had held back any enemy. The gates in the wall stood open day and night, and the wall itself, forgetful of the purpose it had originally been made to serve, did not present opposition to travelers.

In winter, the people of Tihannad dressed in warm coats of poppy red or gentian blue, put bells and ribbons on the harnesses of their horses, and went skating on Niambe Lake. They lit bonfires in the town square around which young men and women gathered to dance in the long evenings. They carved blocks of thick ice from the lake to store in deep cellars for summer, and then carved more blocks into flowers and swans and other fanciful shapes.

But though the people of Tihannad enjoyed winter, they loved spring. As soon as the west wind warmed and the snow melted, every house in Tihannad put out boxes and pots and half-barrels of flowers—blue and white pansies, pink kimee with huge fringed petals and delicate blue-green foliage, white trumpet-flowered moonglow, soft saffron-and-pink spring lilies. All the girls wore flowers in their hair, and children braided flowers into the manes of their families' horses on the slightest excuse.

The king's house was no exception to this joy in spring, for the king, too, took pleasure in the warming days and the bright flowers. The King of Feierabiand was a Safiad; his full name was Iaor Daveien Behanad Safiad. Safiads had ruled Feierabiand for three hundred years, and had generally ruled it well. Iaor Safiad had inherited his father's strong will along with his mother's self-possession, and this combination made some of his opponents uneasy. Nevertheless, Feierabiand was accustomed to Safiad rule, and even Iaor's most outspoken critics in his court did not truly expect to trouble his rule overmuch.

Iaor needed both assurance and determination, for no matter the season, he ordinarily had a good deal more to think about than lilies. As his father and grandfather had before him, Iaor Safiad kept a wary peace with Feierabiand's neighboring countries. To the west lay Linularinum—sophisticated, imperious, haughty Linularinum, always ready to believe that Feierabiand peasants would one day learn to accept the natural superiority of their western neighbor.

Linularinum was not exactly warlike. But a mere hundred years ago, King Lherriadd Kohorrian, high-handed and overbearing, had offended the Lord of the Delta and lost the allegiance of the Delta, which at that time had been one of Linularinum's more valuable coastal assets. And everyone also knew that if Linularinum's current king, Mariddeier Kohorrian, ever saw a way to force the issue, he would not necessarily care whether the Delta wished to switch allegiance once more. No, if the old Fox of Linularinum glimpsed a chance to bring the Delta into his grasp, he would consider it a matter of pride to reach out and take it.

But in some ways Casmantium, across the mountains in the dry country of the east, presented a greater threat. Barely eighty years ago, it had conquered the small country of Meridanium to its northeast. Now Meridanium had a Casmantian governor and its people paid taxes to the Casmantian king in Breidechboden. Worse—from Feierabiand's point of view—Meridanium had been more than conquered; it had been absorbed. As Meridanium no longer seemed restive under Casmantian rule, the kings of Casmantium were free to consider other projects. Everyone knew Brechen Glansent Arobern was ambitious to add another province to his possessions; everyone knew he did not necessarily consider the current border his country shared with Feierabiand to be the last word on the subject.

So Iaor Safiad kept the Feierabiand armies blatantly visible on both borders. And he encouraged trade and business, since prosperous merchants always preferred peace and were seldom much concerned with who claimed what chunk of territory as long as the trade moved briskly. The old Fox of Linularinum would press only subtly at the river border so long as all his wealthiest subjects preferred to use the bridges for peaceful—and lucrative—trade. Similarly, as long as roads and harbors yielded trade and wealth, even the restless young king of Casmantium seemed content to confine arguments over road tolls and harbor dues to strong words rather than flashing swords and spears.

Still, it was not astonishing that this spring Iaor Safiad would find a moment or two for flowers. He had married during the winter, his second marriage, and hardly before time, according to his court and kingdom. Iaor's first wife had died without issue three years past and, by most accounts, the king had not been half forward enough in seeking another. Everyone hoped for heirs from his new young queen.

The new queen, Niethe, was a beautiful young woman from a good Tiearanan family, graceful as a fawn and playful as a kitten, delighted with Iaor and her new life and still charmingly amazed by her good fortune. And the king was captivated by her. Once spring had arrived, Iaor spent more time arranging flowers to please his new bride than he did attending to the business of the kingdom, a propensity greeted with tolerant amusement by the town, and with displeasure only by those of his court who suspected that his preoccupation was merely a ruse and that they might be targets of it.

Niethe was in her early twenties, little more than half the king's age—her youth accounted fortuitous for the production of heirs. But, despite any calculation that had been involved in the match, Niethe seemed as pleased by Iaor himself as much as by her new royalty. Certainly she loved proof of his love for her. She loved flowers, and loved best of all the ones her lord brought to her with his own hands: She loved to be courted and made much of. And the king made much of her . . . a little overmuch for some of his court, who found themselves, this spring, somewhat displaced from his attention.

Bertaud tried hard not to feel jealous of the new queen; he knew it was neither just nor sensible to resent Niethe. But sometimes he found Iaor's focus on his new wife a little trying. He supposed he would view the matter more favorably if he found a wife of his own—but the Lord of the Delta would need to marry a woman of the Delta, and as Bertaud had no desire at all to return to his own lands, he was not eager to pursue the question. He said now, mildly, "I suppose we must enjoy the spring while it lasts; soon enough we will have the full heat of summer closing down upon us."

"And then we will need to contend with the bother of moving to the summer house," Iaor agreed, but still smiling. "Well, we shall ride out when we can and, as you wisely suggest, enjoy the spring while it remains to us! But I fear, much as I might desire otherwise, we'll have no time for either hunting or hawking this morning. One of my judges has appealed a case to me. No doubt it will be some strange, convoluted matter, or why else appeal to me?" He made a face, though to Bertaud it was clear he was actually looking forward to finding out what the problem involved.

Iaor went on, "However, I have hope this judgment will not take long. Perhaps this afternoon there will be time to take the hawks out. You know the Linularinan ambassador just gave my lady one of those miniature falcons they are so proud of. A pretty little thing, though I have a certain doubt as to its ability to take anything so large as a rabbit."

Of course Iaor's first thought was of Niethe. Bertaud would have died before allowing Iaor to glimpse any hint of jealousy, though sometimes he could not help but remember a time before the young queen had intruded into the closeness he had once shared with the king. He said smoothly, "I think they mostly hunt mice. Do you suppose the queen would like mice?"

"She might, if it was her falcon caught them. She thinks the bird is charming—well, so it is. We shall have to try it on young rabbits and see how it does. Or persuade the cooks to try what they might do with mice, hah? See if the judge is here, will you? I gave him the third hour."

They had arrived at the king's personal reception room, a small, cheerful chamber with broad windows, shutters thrown back this morning to let in the light and air. The king himself had a chair, set up on a low dais; there were no other furnishings.

The judge was, of course, already present in the antechamber—it would not do to risk keeping the king waiting, so the judge had come early, bringing with him the principal from his case. That proved to be a young man, about Bertaud's age, with bound wrists and—reasonably enough—a sober expression. The prisoner had a narrow face, brown hair, and long hands. From his dress, which was plain but good, he was likely the son of a tradesman or minor merchant. A guardsman was also present, standing behind the young man.

The judge was Ferris son of Tohanis, a man Bertaud knew a little. He inclined his head to the judge and said, "Esteemed sir." He did not glance at the other men, other than one swift look to be sure the guardsman looked professional and alert. The guardsman returned a small nod. The captain of the royal guards answered to Bertaud. That responsibility did not normally accrue to the Lord of the Delta, but so Iaor had granted it, despite Bertaud's youth. Bertaud was fiercely proud of the honor and strove to be worthy of Iaor's trust—though with the royal guard, his duty largely consisted of leaving Eles, their captain, a free hand.

"My lord," the judge answered formally. "If I may ask—"

Bertaud smiled. "He is curious what you may have for him. He is, I believe, rather in the mood for tangled thoughts, and looks forward to finding out what you have brought him."

The judge nodded and sighed, not returning Bertaud's smile. "I hope his majesty's mood is still inclined that way after he hears me. This matter is not so much complicated as provoking—or so I have found it. Well . . . well, thank you, my lord, and is his majesty ready to see me, then?"

"If you are ready to present your case, esteemed sir, his majesty is prepared to hear it."

The judge was, of course, ready. Bertaud let him lead the way down the hall and to the small reception room.

The king nodded as they entered. The young man, guided by the guardsman, came forward to the foot of the dais and, pressed down by firm hands on his shoulders, went awkwardly to his knees. The guardsman stood behind him. The judge clasped his hands together before his chest and bowed.

"Esteemed Ferris," said the king. "What does your diligence bring me?"

The judge bowed a second time and straightened. He said, his manner somewhat pedantic, "Your majesty, this man is Enned son of Lakas. He was brought before me on charges of mayhem and murder. He has not denied guilt—indeed, his guilt is not in question. The circumstances are these: A Linularinan merchant—a dealer in salt, linen, and metals, who has traded in Tihannad every spring for the past seven years, a respected and wealthy man—offended against the father of this young man, Lakas son of Timiad. This Lakas is a tradesman of Tihannad. He makes goods out of linen, buying the linen from Linularinum, of course."

"Of course," agreed the king. "An equitable arrangement, I expect. And?"

The judge tilted his head to one side. "In fact, the Linularinan merchant, one Mihenian son of Mihenian, had for several years been going to some effort to ensure that the arrangement was *not* equitable. Indeed, due to certain contracts drawn up by a Linularinan legist, Mihenian's fortunes had risen substantially, whereas Lakas son of Timiad was very close to being ruined."

"Ah."

"On this fact being discovered—having exhaustively investigated the matter, your majesty, I am satisfied that it is a fact—Lakas went to the merchant Mihenian and attempted to gain satisfaction. However, confident that Lakas would not be able to collect monies owed him legally, due to an interesting principle of Linularinan law, which—well, your majesty, to be brief, Mihenian refused to regularize his dealings with Lakas son of Timiad. He was, in fact, directly insulting. He went so far as to strike Lakas in the face."

Iaor nodded, interested but also a little impatient.

"It being clear that the monies would be impossible to collect, and severely offended at Mihenian's callous disregard of his father's ruin, this young man then laid an ambush for the merchant and killed him. Due to an exceptionally alert guardsman, whose name, my king, I have given to the captain of your guard for commendation, he did not succeed in doing so secretly. When this young man was approached by the guard, he surrendered without resistance and cast himself on the mercy of the court; that is to say, my mercy."

"Yes?" said the king.

Ferris inclined his head. "Well, your majesty, I would be inclined to grant it, except of course I have no way to do so, legally. The Linularinan merchant behaved in a most offensive manner. It's true, of course, that Lakas son of Timiad might have brought charges against Mihenian for assault, only the witnesses to the act were all employees of Mihenian. And, legally, Lakas had no recourse for the business dealings that Mihenian had employed against him. Evidently, he was prepared to accept his losses and the blow to his pride, but his son was not."

"Nevertheless, despite the lack of disinterested witnesses, you are satisfied as to what occurred."

"Yes, your majesty."

"Then I, too, am satisfied."

Ferris inclined his head, gratified, and continued. "In the strictest legal sense, Mihenian son of Mihenian was not at fault. The contract was, to even the closest reading, legally unassailable. However, from the standpoint of disinterested justice, Mihenian clearly acted without regard for just and proper dealing. On the other hand, he was a citizen of Linularinum, which broadens the scope of this matter in a most unfortunate way."

"Yes," agreed the king, with distaste. Linularinan opinion was often too inflexible for his taste, but impossible to take lightly. As the people of Feierabiand frequently held an affinity to one animal or another, as the people of Casmantium were famous for their making and building, so the people of Linularinum were well known for the magic many of them could weave with quill and ink. "When you sign a Linularinan contract," the saying went, "count your fingers afterward—and remember as the years pass to count the fingers of your children and grandchildren."

When a Linularinan legist set the magic of the binding word into his work, a contract might unroll its meaning in unexpected directions—and be very difficult to rewrite. Iaor would not want to give the old Fox of Linularinum any opening to claim that legal impropriety had been done. Dismissing a justified charge of murder done upon a Linularinan merchant, for example, might very well provide such an opening.

"So I appeal to your majesty," said Ferris, opening his hands. He inclined his head.

"Yes," said the king again. He surveyed the young man. Enned son of Lakas looked back steadily. He was rather pale. But he had too much pride to flinch from the king's searching gaze. Looking at him, Bertaud was not surprised that this young man had been willing to risk his own life to retrieve his father's pride and punish the man who had ruined him. And what would the father think of that? Surely any normal father would be appalled? If not at the murder, than at this aftermath?

"Have you anything to add?" the king asked him. "Do you concur with what the esteemed Ferris has recounted?"

Enned bowed his head over his bound hands. "No, your majesty. That is, yes. Everything he said is true."

"You understand that the penalty for murder is death?"

"Yes, your majesty," the young man answered. He was afraid, Bertaud saw, but not defiant; he looked bàck at the king frankly and honestly. His voice was not, however, quite as calm as his face.

"Do you think your father would regard the trade of your life for the death of his business rival as a fair and good trade?"

The young man shook his head, stiffly. "His grief will be hard. I didn't mean to get caught. I'm sorry I was. And I'm sorry if you think I was wrong. But I can't be sorry I killed the Linularinan. My family was not wealthy, your majesty, but we were not poor, and my father worked hard to build our business. And he is a good man, and no one to cast aside like a beggar!"

"As you cast aside my law?"

Enned looked startled. Color rose in his face. "I . . . confess I didn't think of it that way, your majesty."

The king tapped his fingers thoughtfully against the arm of his chair. "My law exists for a reason. My courts exist to give legal recourse to wronged men. *I* am here to hear appeals, where the courts cannot give satisfaction. And yet you did murder on your own account, on account of your own pride."

The young man could not, evidently, think of anything to say.

The king leaned forward. "I conclude you are a fool." He looked, and sounded, more and more severe. "If every man whose business associates bested or offended him drew a knife, if the law were disregarded every time a rash young man felt his pride touched, how would we all live? And in what disorder? Enned son of Lakas, the esteemed Ferris brought you to me because he felt you deserved mercy he could not give you. I don't know that I feel so. If the Linularinan merchant offended your father's pride and your family's well-being, how much more have you offended my pride, and the well-being of my kingdom?"

The young man swallowed, bowing his head.

Straightening, the king looked thoughtfully at the judge.

Ferris shrugged, opening his hands. "If every man who did business was upright in his dealings with his business associates, then their
business associates would not suffer through their actions and young
men would not be offended, however proud they might be. Though I
grant you, this one is proud. He is also the only son of his father. His
father came to me and begged for the life of his son, which I, of course,
have no authority to grant."

"But you would have *me* grant it."

"The law is stern, your majesty, but I serve it gladly. Except when
it is flouted by men who use sly cunning to slip its proper bounds. Then
I am unable to be glad in its service. Still, at such moments, as I am not
the final authority, I have recourse. Your majesty, of course, does not.
Forgive me if I was wrong to appeal to your majesty."

The king leaned back in his chair and stared for a long moment at
the young man, who flinched under that stare at last, his gaze dropping
to the floor.

The king's eyebrows lifted. He said severely, "My brother king
Mariddeier Kohorrian will be offended, and rightly, if he finds his merchants cannot travel to Feierabiand without being knifed in dark alleys
by proud young fools."

Enned son of Lakas said in a faint voice, "Yes, your majesty."

"Bertaud," said the king.

Bertaud straightened attentively. "My king?"

"Though he is without doubt a proud young fool, I am inclined to
spare this young man's life. But do you see a way I may do so that
would satisfy Linularinum?"

It was a reasonable question to throw to Bertaud. The Delta had
belonged to Linularinum as often, in the convoluted history of the two
countries, as it had belonged to Feierabiand. But a hundred or so years
ago, when the King of Linularinum had become a little too overbearing
in his attempts to force the Delta to comply with a handful of Linularinan laws that it did not favor, its allegiance had swung decisively toward Feierabiand. Even the cleverest threats devised by the most subtle
Linularinan legists had done nothing but make Keroen son of Be-
traunes order a Linularinan banner made so he could throw it down
under the hooves of his horse, trample it into the mud, and invite Da-
raod Safiad to make him an offer.

But more than any other region, the Delta still mingled the peoples
and customs of both Feierabiand and Linularinum. Bertaud considered
the king's likely intentions and desires against his own estimation of
Linularinan attitudes. He said after a moment, "The Linularinan people
respect, ah, creative interpretations of the law. This is not Casmantium:

We have neither the custom of the murderer's *geas* nor the cold mages who might inflict it, for which I suppose Enned son of Lakas may well be grateful. But what if we borrowed the general idea rather than the actual practice? Perhaps you might require this man's life, rather than his death. You might give the young man over to the army, my king, and thus take his life while not requiring his death. Military service is hardly as severe as the Casmantian *geas*, but perhaps it could be seen to satisfy the requirements of the moment."

The king rested his elbow on the arm of his chair and leaned his chin on his hand. "A worthy suggestion. And you think Jasand or Adries will take him among his soldiers? A hot-hearted fool like this?"

After a moment, Bertaud realized where Iaor was heading with this question. He didn't know whether to laugh or groan and in the end made a sound midway between the two. Iaor smiled.

"Oh, earth and iron," Bertaud said resignedly. "All right, then. Give him to your guard, if you must, and I will take him. I'm sure Eles will be delighted by the gift I'll bring him."

Enned looked from the king to Bertaud cautiously, bewildered, but beginning to hope that he might, in fact, not die this day.

"Will you take him, then?"

"If it please you, my king."

"Then he is yours," the king said briskly, and waved a hand to show the decision was made.

Bertaud gestured to the guardsman, who, face professionally blank, leaned forward to cut the young man's bonds and lift him to his feet. Bertaud said, "Enned, son of Lakas, do you understand what the king has decreed?"

"I—" stammered the young man, who clearly was not sure. "I know—I think he gave me to you, my lord—"

"I am Bertaud son of Boudan," Bertaud said, striving, with some success, he thought, for a severe tone. He tried for the tone Iaor himself used when displeased, and thought he copied it rather well. The young man seemed impressed, at any rate. "Among my other duties, I serve the king by overseeing the royal guard, to which you now belong. I think you will do well. You had better, because for you there is no return to your father's house. The mercy of the king, while considerable, is not endless. Do you understand me?"

"Yes," Enned said faintly. "My lord."

"You are fortunate to be alive. On your knees, and thank the esteemed Ferris son of Tohanis, who had no duty to seek mercy for you, for your life."

After the merest pause, Enned turned to the judge, dropped to his knees—still awkwardly; he would have to learn better grace—and said fervently, "Thank you, esteemed sir. Thank you very much."

The judge inclined his head. "I will inform your father."

"Thank you," the young man repeated, and looked nervously to Bertaud.

Bertaud crossed his arms forbiddingly over his chest and said, "Now, as you have not yet done so, thank the king."

Still on his knees, Enned turned back to the king and said humbly, bowing his head, "Thank you, your majesty. For your mercy."

Iaor inclined his head by a minute degree, effortlessly royal.

"Now, get up and present yourself to me," said Bertaud, and waited for Enned to find his feet. The young man was flushed, still disoriented by the suddenness and unexpectedness of the king's decision. He probably, Bertaud was aware, had very little idea what the duties of the guard even were. He looked Enned up and down, maintaining a stern visage, then glanced at the guardsman. "Annand."

"My lord," said the guardsman.

"Present this man to Eles. If the captain has any questions or reservations about this assignment, tell him he may apply to me." Bertaud gave the king an ironic glance on this last, and Iaor crooked a finger across his mouth to hide a smile.

"My lord," repeated the guardsman, and put a hand on the young man's elbow to escort him out. Enned went, not without a wide-eyed backward look over his shoulder at Bertaud and the king.

Bertaud waited until the door was closed behind the two men, gently, by the guardsman. Then he let himself laugh at last.

Iaor, too, was grinning. "You did that well. So stern! Anyone would quail." He stood up and clapped Bertaud on the shoulder. "I impose on you, I fear, my friend."

"How could I possibly desire anything other than what you desire, my king?" Bertaud was having a hard time finding a serious tone. "No, no. A hot-hearted proud young fool is meant for the guard—just ask Eles." Eles was not a man who suffered foolishness from any proud young men. The captain of the guard certainly hadn't ever been inclined to suffer it from Bertaud in years past, when he had already long been the captain and Bertaud merely Iaor's page and companion. Dour and emotionless, he had seemed to Bertaud then; only much later had Bertaud learned to catch the occasional gleam of unspoken humor in the captain's eye. He hoped Eles would be amused by this unexpected gift the king and Bertaud had sent his way.

"So I thought," agreed Iaor. He sounded pleased with himself, as well he might. It was a solution worthy of a Linularinan legist. No one, not even the old Fox, could say the king had passed lightly over the young man's crime; even without imposing an actual *geas*, Iaor might be said to have imposed a rather severe sentence. Or, by taking the young man into his own guard, he had done him honor. And giving him into the hand of the Lord of the Delta was a nice touch: that might be a slight concession toward Linularinan sensibility . . . or a slight insult to Linularinan conceit. Depending on how one regarded it.

Thus, both Feierabiand pride and the king's justice had been preserved, and without doing actionable violence to any legal understanding between Linularinum and Feierabiand. It was an excellent maneuver, worthy of a Safiad. Even so, the king's glance at Ferris was less amused, and less pleased.

The judge saw this change in manner, too. "Your majesty, of course the boy did, without question, offend your law—the law that I swore an oath to uphold. And yet I brought the matter to you. Justly might your majesty rebuke me."

"Am I not the proper authority to hear such appeals?"

"Your majesty cannot have hot-hearted young fools knifing merchants, honest or otherwise, in dark alleys."

"Not even if the young man in question broke my law in answer to a sly slipping of its intentions? Was that not your argument?"

"The misuse of the law to protect dishonest dealing offended me. The boy's honest crime, if I may call it so, offended me less. I did advise him he should rightly have come to me in the first place. It would have been a good deal easier to appeal the matter to your majesty before blood was shed. As you yourself pointed out."

"Mmm." The king was still frowning.

Ferris lowered his eyes. "I am rebuked, then," he said, and formally, "I ask your majesty's pardon."

"Ah. No. I do not rebuke you." Iaor lifted his chin decisively. "Find out the extent of the merchant's losses to the Linularinan merchant. I will pay him compensation for the loss of his son. Out of my own personal monies." He paused.

The judge, reading this pause correctly, bowed. "Perhaps your majesty will permit me to provide that compensation, as it was my decision that led to this expense."

The king smiled, satisfied. "You may pay half. That is only just, I think. Good." He stood, took the older man's arm, and turned with him toward the door. "Walk with me, esteemed sir. I do esteem your judgment, I assure you. I promise you, I have no rebuke to offer. I am glad you brought this to my attention. I am certain Eles desires nothing more than to gain a young hot-hearted fool for his command. Walk with me, if you please, and tell me about the particular intricacies of Linularinan law that allowed this Linularinan merchant to cheat—lawfully!—my honest Feierabiand tradesman."

The judge smiled and said, "Gladly." He appeared resigned to the unofficial fine the king was imposing. At that, Bertaud reflected, even a sizable fine was far less to be dreaded than a royal rebuke.

Bertaud trailed them, sighing. He knew the signs. Iaor had been drawn entirely into kingly concerns. It seemed unlikely he would find time now to ride out with hawks, no matter how tedious his companions might find the threatened intricacy of law. No, he thought, not even if Iaor's young wife greatly desired to try her little falcon.

The trace of jealousy—unworthy, even shameful—in that thought disturbed him at once, and Bertaud called himself to stern order and tried to fix his mind on law.

However, they had hardly got out into the hall before the ring of quick-striding boot heels brought them all to a startled halt. The king released the judge's arm and drew himself up. Ferris cocked his head to one side, looking curious and alarmed. Bertaud himself laid a hand on his sword, ready to draw: Generally, no one ran down the halls of the king's house.

However, this person proved to be a messenger—one of the king's own couriers: a young woman with the king's badge at her shoulder and her courier's wand thrust through her belt. Iaor preferred young women for his couriers, a custom his father had begun; the old king had famously declared that girls rode more lightly and were more careful of their horses than boys, which, as Iaor had once commented, among other effects had ensured that the young men became at least somewhat more careful as well. But the courier-master still accepted more girls than boys for the king's service.

This courier's name was Teien, daughter of Kanes. Bertaud knew that Teien was posted to the south of Tihannad; her rounds included many of the smaller villages and towns along the Nejeied River. She went to one knee and saluted the king carefully. Her breathing was fast, but not desperately so.

"Yes?" said Iaor impatiently.

The woman bowed her head briefly, sucked in air, and said rapidly, "Word from Minas Spring and Minas Ford, your majesty. This is the word: Griffins have come across the mountains. They despoil your country, your majesty, turning good land into sand and sending hot winds across the young barley; they are killing calves in the pasture and game in the forest. Your people ask you for help in their need."

"Griffins," said Ferris, without expression.

"Did you see these griffins yourself?" Bertaud asked the courier.

"Yes, lord: So I could report clearly, I went to Minas Spring and up into the high hills behind the village. There are indeed griffins there. The very rock of the hills has changed its character; it is all red stone and sand there, now. The wind comes the wrong way, from the east, off the mountains. Coming from the heights, it should be a cold wind, but it is hot, and so dry it pulls moisture from the earth—I saw good soil turn dry and crack under that wind. I saw griffins there. I spoke to the folk of Minas Spring and Minas Ford. They say there are many griffins in the hills there, hundreds maybe; that they make all that country their own."

"Hundreds, Teien?" Bertaud said, drily.

"I saw only two," confessed the courier.

"It's more than one or two, to bring the desert wind to this side of the mountains," Ferris observed.

"I would be surprised to learn that there are hundreds of griffins in all the world," said the king. "I much doubt there are hundreds at Minas Spring." He looked seriously at the courier. "Do they kill the people there? Or only calves?"

"So far, they say, only calves and the odd sheep."

"Still," said Bertaud, "we can hardly have griffins settling along in the hills on our side of the mountains, making a desert out of our good farmland. Aside from ruining the land, it would not do to show weakness of either arms or resolve."

The king made a small, impatient gesture of agreement. "Obviously not." He signaled to the courier to rise. "Go find General Jasand and send him to me. Then go and rest. In the morning, present yourself to your captain. I suspect he will have a task for you."

"Your majesty," said the young woman, pulling herself to her feet and departing quickly.

To Ferris, the king said, "Esteemed Ferris, forgive me, but if you will excuse us. Please write me an explanation of the legal matters that created the problem for, ah, Lakas, and send it to me. I assure you I will be interested."

The judge, restraining his interest and curiosity, bowed acknowledgment and withdrew.

Bertaud said, in wonder, "Griffins?"

Iaor began to walk, waving to Bertaud to accompany him. "Teien saw them herself. Do you doubt her veracity?"

"No," Bertaud said. "Of course not. But I don't understand why griffins would leave their own country—and I certainly don't understand why they would go as far south as Minas Spring! If they were

determined to cross the mountains, why not simply come straight west
through Niambe Pass? That, at least, would make some sense!"

Iaor gave a thoughtful nod. "Perhaps they did not like to fly near
Niambe Lake and were willing to go many miles south to the next pass
they could find. The natural magic of Niambe Lake would hardly be an
amicable magic for griffins. Well, that's a question for mages and we shall
pose it to them, but whatever the reason, it's just as well, or we might have
the griffins bringing their desert to the shores of Niambe, and all the way
to Tihannad, perhaps!"

Bertaud laughed, as his king intended. Feierabiand had never had
much to do with griffins, but they both knew it was inconceivable that
griffins, no matter how numerous or powerful, would dare trouble the
king himself in his own city.

CHAPTER 3

Kes woke as the first stars came out above the desert, harder and higher and brighter than they had ever seemed at home. She lifted her head and blinked up at them, still half gone in dreams and finding it hard to distinguish, in that first moment, the blank darkness of those dreams from the darkness of the swift dusk. She was not, at first, quite sure why the brightness of the stars seemed so like a forewarning of danger.

She did not at once remember where she was, or with whom. Heat surrounded her, a heavy pressure against her skin. She thought the heat should have been oppressive, but in fact it was not unpleasant. It was a little like coming in from a frosted winter morning into a kitchen, its iron stove pouring heat out into the room: The heat was overwhelming and yet comfortable.

Then, behind her, Opailikiita shifted, tilted her great head, and bumped Kes gently with the side of her fierce eagle's beak.

Kes caught her breath, remembering everything in a rush: Kairaithin and the desert and the griffins, drops of blood that turned to garnets and rubies as they struck the sand, sparks of fire that scattered from beating wings and turned to gold in the air . . . She jerked convulsively to her feet, gasping.

Long shadows stretched out from the red cliffs, sharp-edged black against the burning sand. The moon, high and hard as the stars, was not silver but tinted a luminescent red, like bloody glass.

Kereskiita, Opailikiita said. Her voice was not exactly gentle, but it curled comfortably around the borders of Kes's mind.

Kes jerked away from the young griffin, whirled, backed up a step and another. She was not exactly frightened—she was not frightened of

Opailikiita. Of the desert, perhaps. Of, at least, finding herself still in the desert; she was frightened of that. She caught her breath and said, "I need to go home!"

Her desire for the farm and for Tesme's familiar voice astonished her. Kes had always been glad to get away by herself, to walk in the hills, to listen to the silence the breeze carried as it brushed through the tall grasses of the meadows. She had seldom *minded* coming home, but she had never *longed* to climb the rail fence into the lowest pasture, or to see her sister watching out the window for Kes to come home. But she longed for those things now. And Tesme would be missing her, would think—Kes could hardly imagine what her sister might think. She said again, "I need to go home!"

Kereskiita, the slim brown griffin said again. *Wait for Kairaithin. It would be better so.*

Kes stared at her. "Where is he?"

The Lord of the Changing Wind is . . . attempting to change the course of the winds, answered Opailikiita.

There was a strange kind of humor to the griffin's voice, but it was not a familiar or comfortable humor and Kes did not understand it. She looked around, trying to find the lie of country she knew in the sweep of the shadowed desert. But she could not recognize anything. If she simply walked downhill, she supposed she would eventually find the edge of the desert . . . if it still had an edge, which now seemed somehow a little unlikely, as though Kes had watched the whole world change to desert in her dreams. Maybe she had; she could not remember her dreams. Only darkness shot through with fire . . .

Kereskiita—said the young brown griffin.

"My name is Kes!" Kes said, with unusual urgency, somehow doubting, in the back of her mind, that this was still true.

Yes, said Opailikiita. *But that is too little to call you. You should have more to your name. Kairaithin called you* kereskiita. *Shall I?*

"Well, but . . . *kereskiita*? What is that?"

It would be . . . "fire kitten," perhaps, Opailikiita said after a moment. And, with unexpected delicacy, *Do you mind?*

Kes supposed she didn't actually *mind*. She asked, "Opailikiita? That's *kiita*, too."

Glittering flashes of amusement flickered all around the borders of Kes's mind. *Yes. Opailikiita Sehanaka Kiistaike*, said the young griffin. *Opailikiita is my familiar name. It is . . . "little spark"? Something close to that. Kairaithin calls me by that name. I am his* kiinukaile. *It would be . . . "student," I think. If you wish*, you may call me *Opailikiita. As you are also Kairaithin's student.*

"I'm not!" Kes protested, shocked.

You assuredly will be, said another voice, hard and yet somehow amused, a voice that slid with frightening authority around the edges of Kes's mind. Kairaithin was there suddenly, not striding up as a man nor settling from the air on eagle's wings, but simply *there*. He was in his true form: a great eagle-headed griffin with a deadly curve to his beak, powerful feathered forequarters blending smoothly to a broad, muscled lion's rear. His pelt was red as smoldering coals, his wings black with only narrow flecks of red showing, like a banked fire flickering through a heavy iron grate. He sat like a cat, upright, his lion's tail curling around taloned eagle's forefeet. The tip of his tail flicked restlessly across the sand, the only movement he made.

You have made yourself acquainted with my kiinu-kaile? the griffin mage said to Kes. *It is well you should become acquainted with one another.*

"I am *not* your student!" Kes declared furiously, but then hesitated, a little shocked by the vehemence of her own declaration.

She is fierce, Opailikiita said to Kairaithin. *Someday this kitten will challenge even you.* She sounded like she approved.

Perhaps, Kairaithin said to the young griffin, *but not today.* There was neither approval nor disapproval in his powerful voice. He added, to Kes, *What will you do, a young fire mage fledging among creatures of earth? I will teach you to ride the fiery wind. Who else will? Who else could?*

Kes wanted to shout, I'm not a mage! Only she remembered holding the golden heat of the sunlight in her cupped hands, of tasting the names of griffins like ashes on her tongue. She could still recall every name now. She said stubbornly, "I want to go home. You never said you would keep me here! I healed your friends for you. Take me home!"

Kairaithin tilted his head in a gesture reminiscent of an eagle regarding a small animal below its perch; not threatening, exactly, but dangerous, even when he did not mean to threaten.

He melted suddenly from his great griffin form to the smaller, slighter shape of a man. But to Kes, he seemed no less a griffin in that form. The fire of his griffin's shadow glowed faintly in the dark. He said to Kes like a man quoting, "Fire will run like poetry through your blood."

"I don't care if it does!" Kes cried, taking a step toward him. "I healed all your people! I learned to use fire and I healed them for you! What else do you *want*?"

Kairaithin regarded her with a powerful, hard humor that was nothing like warm human amusement. He answered, "I hardly know. Events will determine that."

"Well, I know what *I* want! I want to go *home!*"

"Not yet," said Kairaithin, unmoved. "This is a night for patience. Do not rush forward toward the next dawn and the next again, human woman. Days of fire and blood will likely follow this night. Be patient and wait."

"Blood?" Kes thought of the griffins' terrible injuries, of Kairaithin saying *Arrows of ice and ill-intent.* She said, horrified, "Those cold mages won't come *here!*"

Harsh amusement touched Kairaithin's face. "One would not wish to predict the movements of men. But, no. As you say, I do not expect the cold mages of Casmantium to come here. Or not yet. We must wait to see what events determine."

Kes stared at him. "Events. What events?"

The amusement deepened. "If I could answer that, little *kereskiita*, I would be more than a mage. I may guess what the future will bring. But so may you. And neither of us will *know* until it unrolls at last before us."

Kes felt very uneasy about these *events*, whatever Kairaithin guessed they might entail. She said, trying for a commitment, suspecting she wouldn't get one, "But you'll let me go home later. You'll take me home. At dawn?"

The griffin mage regarded her with dispassionate intensity. "At dawn, I am to bring you before the regard of the Lord of Fire and Air."

The king of the griffins. Kes thought of the great bronze-and-gold king, not lying injured before her but staring down at her in implacable pride and strength. He had struck at her in offended pride, if it had not been simple hostility. Now *he* would make some judgment about her, come to some decision? She was terrified even to think of it.

She remembered the gold-and-copper griffin, Eskainiane Escaile Sehaikiu, saying to Kairaithin, *You were right to bring us to the country of men and right to seek a young human.* Maybe that was the question the king would judge: Whether Kairaithin had been right to bring her into the desert and teach her to use the fire, which belonged to griffins and was nothing to do with men? Escaile Sehaikiu had said Kairaithin was right. But she suspected the king would decide that Kairaithin had been wrong. She gave a small, involuntary shake of her head. "No . . ."

"Yes."

"I . . ."

"*Kereskiita.* Kes. You may be a human woman, but you are now become my *kiinukaile*, and that is nothing I had hoped to find here in this country of earth. You do not know how rare you are. I assure you, you have nothing to fear." Kairaithin did not speak kindly, nor gently, but with a kind of intense relief and satisfaction that rendered Kes speechless.

I will be with you. I will teach you, Opailikiita promised her.

In the young griffin's voice, too, Kes heard a similar emotion, but in her it went beyond satisfaction to something almost like joy. Kes found herself smiling in involuntary response, even lifting a hand to smooth the delicate brown-and-gold feathers below the griffin's eye. Opailikiita turned her head and brushed Kes's wrist very gently with the deadly edge of her beak in a caress of welcome and . . . if the slim griffin did not offer exactly friendship, it was something as strong, Kes felt, and not entirely dissimilar.

Kairaithin's satisfaction and Opailikiita's joy were deeply reassuring. But more than reassurance, their reactions implied to Kes that, to the griffins, her presence offered a desperately needed—what, reprieve?—which they had not truly looked to find. Kairaithin had said the cold mages would not come here. *Not yet*, he had said. But, then, some other time? Perhaps soon?

I have no power to heal, Kairaithin had said to her. But then he had taught *her* to heal. Kes hesitated. She still wanted to insist that the griffin mage take her home. Only she had no power to insist on anything, and she knew Kairaithin would not accede. And . . . was it not worth a little time in the griffins' desert to learn to pour sunlight from her hands and make whole even the most terrible injury? Especially if cold mages would come here and resume their attack on the griffins? She flinched from the thought of arrows of ice coming out of the dark, ruining all the fierce beauty of the griffins. If she did not heal them, who would?

Kairaithin held out his hand to her, his eyes brilliant with dark fire. "I will show you the desert. I will show you the paths that fire traces through the air. Few are the creatures of earth who ever become truly aware of fire. I will show you its swift beauty. Will you come?"

All her earlier longing for her home seemed . . . not gone, but somehow distant. Flames rose all around the edges of Kes's mind, but this was not actually disagreeable. It even felt . . . welcoming.

Kes took a step forward without thinking, caught herself, drew back. "I'm *not* your student," she declared. Or she *meant* to declare it. But the statement came out less firmly than she'd intended. Not exactly like a plea, but almost like a question. She said, trying again for forcefulness and this time managing at least to sound like she meant it, "My sister will be worried about me—"

"She will endure your absence," Kairaithin said indifferently. "Are you so young you require your sister's leave to come and go?"

"No! But she'll be *worried*!"

"She will endure. It will be better so. A scattering of hours, a cycle of days. Can you not absent yourself so long?" Kairaithin continued to hold out his hand. "You are become my student, and so you must be for yet some little time. Your sister will wait for you. Will you come?"

"Well . . ." Kes could not make her own way home. And if she had to depend on the griffin mage to take her home, then she didn't want to offend him. And if she had to stay in the desert for a little while anyway, she might as easily let him show her its wonders. Wasn't that so?

She was aware that she wanted to think of justifications for that decision. But *wasn't* it so?

Come, whispered Opailikiita around the edges of her mind. *We will show you what it means to be a mage of fire.*

Kes did not feel like any sort of mage. But she took the necessary step forward and let Kairaithin take her hand.

The griffin mage did not smile. But the expression in his eyes was like a smile. His strange, hot fingers closed hard around her hand, and the world tilted out from under them.

The desert at night was black and a strange madder-tinted silver; the sky was black, and the great contorted cliffs, and the vast expanses of sand that stretched out in all directions. But the red moon cast a pale, crimson-tinged luminescence over everything, and far above the stars were glittering points of silver fire. Now and again, in the distance, a coruscation of golden sparks scattered across the dark, and Kes knew a griffin had taken to the air.

Kes sat above the world, high atop stone, under the innumerable stars. Kairaithin, wearing the shape of a man as he might have worn a mask, stood at the very edge of the cliff, gazing out into the blackness. From time to time, he glanced momentarily toward Kes and Opailikiita, but he always turned again to look outward. Like a sentinel. But Kes could not decide whether he seemed to be waiting for a signal from a friend—though she wondered whether griffins exactly *had* friends—or from an enemy. She knew very well griffins had *those*.

Kairaithin's arms were crossed over his chest, and now and again when he glanced her way, he smiled slightly—not a human smile. It was even less a human smile, Kes had decided, than his shadow was a human shadow. But she could not decide exactly where the difference lay.

Kes was sitting cross-legged on the stone, leaning back against Opailikiita's feathered shoulder. The young griffin was teaching Kes how to summon fire into the palm of her hand, and how to let it sink down into her blood. *Fire will run like poetry through your blood*, Kairaithin had said to Kes, and she now understood, at least a little, what the griffin-mage had meant. She called the fire out of her body again, set it dancing once more in her hand, and grinned swiftly up at Opailikiita.

Good, said the young griffin, bending her head down to look at the little flame. She clicked her beak gently in satisfaction or pleasure or approval—something at least akin to those things. *Fire becomes part of your nature.*

"Yes, I suppose," agreed Kes. The little flame in her hand was a pleasant warmth. It felt oddly familiar, as though she had spent her life holding fire in her hands—it felt as comfortable as holding an egg, only more lively. More like holding a kitten, maybe. Something small and alive. Something that might scratch, but not seriously. She closed her hand carefully around the flame. For a moment it flickered at her past the cage of her fingers. Then it was gone.

Could you call it back? Opailikiita asked.

Kes looked up at the slim griffin, then down at her closed fist. She opened her hand again, palm up, and drew fire from Opailikiita, from the stone, from the desert air. The flame bloomed again in her palm. "It's not even hard," Kes said, smiling.

It is always easy to follow your nature, agreed Opailikiita.

"I never knew . . ."

Opailikiita began to answer, but Kairaithin said first, "Every man, and every griffin, believes he possesses a fixed and singular nature. But sometimes our distinctive self proves more mutable than we might suppose possible." He was not smiling now, but Kes did not understand the expression she saw in his eyes. But she did not have time to wonder about it, for then he straightened away from the pillar he'd leaned against and glanced away, toward the east. "The sun rises," he said.

It did. There was nothing of the pearl-gray and lavender dawn Kes might have watched from her window at home. Here, the return of the sun seemed altogether a wilder and fiercer phenomenon. First the merest edge of gold touched the sky over the tips of the mountains, and then the sunrise piled up behind the black teeth of the mountains in towering gold and purple, and then the burning sun itself seemed somehow almost to leap away from the mountains and into the desert sky, fiercer and larger here than it ever seemed in the gentler country of men.

The light was probably gentle and warm in the cold heights, but there was nothing gentle about the sunlight that poured heavily across the desert. Kes thought she could almost *hear* it come, as she might have heard floodwaters roar down from the mountain heights. Heat, thick as honey, filled the air. It was not exactly unpleasant, but it was very powerful. Kes swayed under its force, let the fire she held flicker out, and put her hands over her face to shield her eyes. She blinked hard, expecting her eyes to water in the brilliance, but there were no tears.

"Opailikiita," said Kairaithin in edged reproof, "that is not entirely a creature of fire."

Yes, answered the young griffin, though in a faintly uncertain tone. She stretched out a wing to shelter Kes from the fierceness of the sun. Light glowed through the feathers above Kes's head, but the brilliance was much attenuated.

"Useful as a momentary solution. However, as a permanent resolution of the difficulty, it lacks elegance," Kairaithin said drily. He put out a hand, and stone shuddered around them. A hot wind came up, driving sand whirling about the plateau where they stood exposed to the sky. Opailikiita reached out hastily with her other wing, enclosing Kes entirely in a sweep of rich brown and gold.

Then the wind died. Opailikiita drew her wings away, and Kes, blinking around, saw that tall twisting pillars now stood all around the edge of the flat top of the cliff, crowned with a slab of red stone. The rough hall that was thus formed was nothing at all like anything men would have built. She had not exactly understood before that *making* was truly a thing of men. But this hall—rough, but blatantly powerful—was, she realized, probably as close to making or building as griffins ever came.

She had no time to think about this, however, for into the stone hall, riding on the wind and the light, came Kiibaile Esterire Airaikeliu, Lord of Fire and Air. His name beat like poetry or fire through Kes's blood, overwhelming as the desert sun itself. He seemed huge, much bigger than she remembered; his wings seemed to close out half the sky. The wind roared through his wings; his talons flashed like polished bronze; his eyes were gold as the sun.

To the king's left flew the copper-and-gold griffin, Eskainiane Escaile Sehaikiu, who had told Kes, *When you would set a name to burn against the dark, think of me. Escaile Sehaikiu would burn against the dark like a conflagration*, Kes thought; he blazed with such brilliance that he might almost have been feathered in fire even now. To the king's right flew a female griffin—whose name Kes did not know, as she had never healed her—her red wings heavily barred with gold, lion body gold as the pure metal.

The king came down at the edge of the cliff, tucking his wings in close to fit between the narrow stone pillars and stalking forward with lion grace. He turned his head one way to stare at Kairaithin, then as his companions came under the roof after him, he turned that fierce golden stare on Kes.

His gaze, she found, was less readable than even the regard of an eagle or a lion. Kes wanted to cower down like a rabbit before that proud, incomprehensible stare. But Opailikiita nudged her gently in the back and said softly, her voice creeping delicately around the outermost edge of Kes's mind, *Remember you are Kairaithin's kiinukaile and my iskarianere, and remember your pride.*

Kes had no idea what *iskarianere* meant—except she did, in a way, even though Opailikiita had not exactly explained it to her. When the slim brown griffin said it to her, something of the sense of the word unfolded like a spark blooming into a flame. Kes put a hand out almost blindly, burying her fingers in the fine feathers of Opailikiita's throat and whispering, "Sister." And though it might not be exactly true in familiar human terms, though she did not really understand what the griffin meant by the word or what it encompassed, Kes was comforted and found the courage to stand up straight.

Human woman, said the Lord of Fire and Air. The king's voice slammed down across Kes's mind like a blow, so that she staggered under it and had to brace herself against Opailikiita's shoulder. The king's voice did not exactly hurt her—not exactly—but it came down on her with the heavy power of the desert sun. He said implacably, *Human mage. And will you become a mage of fire?*

Kes had no idea how to answer.

It seems a small creature, the king said to Kairaithin.

"Esterire Airaikeliu, it will grow," Kairaithin answered, sounding drily amused.

The king mantled his wings restlessly. *Perhaps. But soon enough?*

She made you whole, Eskainiane Escaile Sehaikiu reminded the king. *She found your name in the light and perceived you insistently whole. She is not so small as that.*

The coppery griffin's voice was not at all like the king's: It rang all around Kes's mind as though a brazen gong had been struck, singing with vivid joy. Kes understood that Escaile Sehaikiu had expected the king to die and was passionately glad Kes had saved him—but she thought the copper-and-gold griffin was also by nature expansively joyful.

She will never stand against the cold mages, when they come, said the red-and-gold female griffin. Her voice was swift and hot and bitterly angry, so that Kes stopped herself only with difficulty from taking a step backward.

"*I* will stand against the Casmantian mages," Kairaithin said flatly. His black gaze passed without pity or fear across the red female and met the king's. "This young *kiinukaile* of mine need merely call into her mind and heart the names of our people and see them whole and uninjured. This she will do, as she has already done."

You will do this, the king said to Kes. It was not a question.

"Yes," Kes said softly. But she was surprised by the certainty she felt. "Yes, lord. If the cold mages come with their arrows. I would not want . . . I would not let them injure your people. Kairaithin says he has no power to heal. I would heal your people."

Indeed. Not so very *small*, said the king, bending low to gaze hard into Kes's face.

Kes longed to back away, but instead she pressed her hand hard against Opailikiita's shoulder and stayed exactly where she was, staring back into those fiery golden eyes.

Your name is Kes? said the king. *That is what they call you, among men? It is too small a name.*

"Kereskiita," said Kairaithin, sounding amused.

For her familiar name? That will do.

Eskainiane Escaile Sehaikiu said, fierce laughter edging his voice, *Kereskiita Keskainiane Raikaisipiike.*

That is not fitting! said the red-and-gold female griffin, with no laughter at all in her voice. She glared at Kes, so fiercely that it almost seemed her stare could scorch the very air.

The king did not exactly say anything to this, but a forceful, if silent, blow seemed to shake the whole cliff—maybe the whole desert. The female griffin crouched down, snapping her razor beak shut with a deadly sound. But she did not say anything else.

It will do, said the king, and to Kes, *Keskainiane Raikaisipiike.* He flung himself back and away off the cliff, his great wings snapping open to catch the desert wind. Little flames scattered from his wings, sparks that glittered into delicate fragments of gold and settled to the sand far below. The other two griffins followed him, Eskainiane Escaile Sehaikiu blazing with glorious abandon and the red female furiously silent.

"She hates me," Kes said shakily, and leaned gratefully against the hot solidity of Opailikiita's shoulder. She stretched her arm as far as she could around the small griffin's neck and pressed her face into the soft feathers. "Why isn't it fitting? The name the king gave me?"

"It draws upon the name of Eskainiane, and upon one of my own names. Nehaistiane Esterikiu Anahaikuuanse objects to both, though especially to the former," said Kairaithin. His tone was distracted; he did not look at Kes but stared after the departing griffins, into the red reaches of the desert. "She is the mate of the Lord of Fire and Air and also of Escaile Sehaikiu."

"Both?"

"Both," said Kairaithin, lifting an amused and impatient eyebrow at Kes's surprise. "She was once wise. But she lost three *iskairianere* to the Casmantian assault and is in no mood to be patient with men."

"Oh . . ." Kes pulled away from Opailikiita again to follow Kairaithin's gaze. "I'm sorry . . ."

That was a night for grief, said Opailikiita, and declared fiercely, *But on the night that comes, my sister, you will burn back the cold.*

Kes wondered if she would.

Kairaithin turned the hard force of his attention back toward Kes at once. His shadow rippled with flame; its black eyes blazed with a fiery dark like the desert sky at night. He said forcefully, "You must learn the ways of fire. You will have days to do this. It will take days. Do you understand? Thus I hold you here in the country of fire."

"If I do this for you," Kes said slowly, meeting his eyes, "you will be my friend."

"Assuredly not your enemy," said Kairaithin, amused.

But Kes thought he also meant what he said. "You won't harm my people. Or allow your people to harm them?"

"So long as you are my *kiinukaile,* I will see to it that neither your sister nor any of the people of your little town come to harm from fire."

"Then I'll stay," Kes said, and found she felt both glad that she had an unshakable excuse to stop arguing and guilty for the very gladness. She knew she ought to want nothing but to escape the desert and the griffins' dangerous attention. She knew she ought to want to go home— she knew Tesme must truly be desperately worried for her, that everyone would be desperately worried, that their worry would only grow worse if she stayed in the desert for days. But she remembered the strangely comfortable flame dancing in her palm, and there was nothing she wanted more than to stay in the desert and learn the ways of fire.

CHAPTER 4

Reports came in over the course of the next few days, some brought by couriers and some by ordinary folk: Griffins in the countryside around Minas Spring and Minas Ford; griffins settling all through those hills. Hundreds, some of the reports claimed. At least a thousand, asserted the most hysterical.

"Dozens," said General Jasand. "Dozens, I will grant you. A hundred is unlikely. A thousand is beyond any possibility. I doubt there are so many griffins as that in all the world."

The senior of Feierabiand's three generals, Jasand was a tall, grizzled man, broad-built and powerful, twenty years older than Iaor. He was not a personal friend of the king—he had been a friend of Iaor's father. These days, Jasand rarely took the field personally. But his whole career had been spent along the mountain border, and in his dealings with Casmantium he had picked up a good deal of griffin-lore. That was why Iaor had sent for him in particular.

Now the general tapped the table impatiently and added, "Not that we want even a few dozen griffins making themselves at home over by Minas Spring and Minas Ford. They're dangerous creatures, and it's said it takes years to recover decent land from the desert they make where they lie up."

Though no one asked him, Bertaud agreed with Jasand that there could not be hundreds of griffins down at Minas. No one had made a clear count. It seemed that no one, villager or courier or even soldier, quite dared go far enough into the hills to try. But it was clearly unlikely that there should be more than a few dozen of the creatures. All the sweep of history recorded no such invasion. Griffins belonged not to Feierabiand but to the dry eastern slopes of the mountains, the desert north of Casmantium, where rain never fell. They were creatures of fire and air, not earth and certainly not water.

The court mage Diene, the other person Iaor had asked to be present, tented her thin fingers and looked thoughtfully down the length of the table at the king. "As Beremnan Anweierchen of Casmantium famously put it, 'The desert is a garden that blooms with time and silence.' Griffins tend that garden," she observed. "Why have they left it and come to this side of the mountains? The west wind is filled with the smell of the sea: It must work against the wind they bring with them. They cannot be comfortable here."

"Why ever they came, they must not be allowed to become comfortable," the king said firmly. "Let us send them back to their desert. General?"

"A hundred men should suffice to send them off," said Jasand. He sounded confident, as well he might: Those were *his* men, and he had every right to be confident of their capability after years of withstanding the Casmantian brigands that sometimes slipped across the mountains—defying their own king, or so they claimed—to test the defenses of Feierabiand.

"Bowmen," said the general now. "With spears to use up close and swords we'll hope they needn't use at all. But it's surely bow work against griffins. Keep them at a distance and they should hardly be worse than mountain cats or bulls."

"They've magic of their own," countered Diene, putting up a severe eyebrow at this confidence. "They are creatures of fire and air, rather than the good solid earth of men. You've never put your soldiers against such as that, Jasand, and you might find griffins a surprise to men used to fighting other men. Well-made steel-tipped arrows may be—should be—hard for griffins to turn. However, they are *not* mountain cats or bulls. Someone should go to them before Jasand's men and ask them to withdraw."

"*Ask* them," said Bertaud, startled.

The mage turned her powerful gaze to him. Her eyes were the dark color of fresh-turned loam. Her strength was of the earth, to bring forth growing things and coax rich harvests from the land. She was old—the oldest of any of the king's habitual councilors, though not quite the eldest of the mages in Tihannad. Iaor was the third king she had advised. She had taught him his love of flowers, and sometimes regarded Bertaud with disfavor because he had never cared much for her gardens. As a boy, Bertaud had been frightened of her acerbic turn of phrase and stern frown. It had taken him years to learn to see the humor hidden behind both.

She said now, "Griffins are foreign to the nature of men, but they have a wisdom of their own, and they are powerful. Yes, someone should go to them before a hundred young men with bows and spears set foot in their desert."

The king folded his hands on the table and studied the mage. "Someone may indeed go to them. With a hundred young men with bows and spears at her back, to command respect from these creatures of fire and air. I ask you to go, esteemed Diene."

"I?" the mage folded her hands upon the table and judiciously considered this request. She glanced up after a moment. "Men are not meant to intrude into the country of fire, Iaor. But it is said that earth mages find the desert particularly inimical."

The king tapped his fingers restlessly on the table. But he responded at last, "Diene, I confess I had looked for you to bend your wisdom and knowledge to deal with these matters. You do not wish to go? Or you do not find it advisable to go?"

"On the contrary." Diene half smiled. "I would be most interested to study the desert and associated phenomena. I am confident I will be able to endure the desert, however hostile an environment it may prove. I am at least certain that a visit to the country of fire will be a fascinating experience. But I am bound by duty to warn you, your majesty, of the reputed difficulties involved."

Iaor waved a hand, dismissing this warning. "If you are willing to go, esteemed Diene, I wish you to go. One would expect a mage's learning and power to be of particular use in this sort of matter. Or do you feel yourself likely to suffer physically from the task? Perhaps someone more, ah, vigorous might be less troubled by the difficulties to which you refer?"

Diene tilted her head, considering, and Bertaud knew she was telling over the tally of younger mages in Tihannad, and coming up short: Though many people were gifted in one way or another, very few possessed the potential for true magecraft, and of those, fewer still wished to spend years of their lives developing the deep understanding of magic that underlay that craft—and the scholar-mages of high Tiearanan did not accept even all of those for training. "A magical gift isn't sufficient," Diene had commented once to Bertaud. "Gifts are narrow things, though under the proper circumstances and with sufficient effort the right sort of gift may be, hmm, *stretched*, shall we say. But blind desire isn't sufficient, and nor is dedication, though that's important. Magecraft requires a most unusual *breadth* of power."

Bertaud had not understood precisely what Diene meant, but what it came to in practical terms was a general lack of mages upon whom the king might call. There *were* a few young mages in Tihannad, but one was too young and one too rash and one too timid. The only mage more experienced and more powerful than Diene herself was also frail as a wisp of winter-dried barley, and blind besides. Diene frowned, and sighed. "Youthful vigor is all very well, Iaor, but I suspect mature wisdom will be more to the point. I have never encountered a griffin. I believe I would be interested to meet one now. And in any case, you would surely not wish to wait for a younger person to come down from Tiearanan. If it please you, your majesty, I will go."

"Thank you." The king gave a little nod. He turned to Jasand. "General. Select your men. Esteemed Diene, are you able to make yourself ready by the morning after tomorrow?" He accepted their nods and dismissed both general and mage, keeping Bertaud behind with a glance.

Bertaud leaned back in his chair and waited.

"The esteemed mage will go, to lend her learning and wisdom to the task, as I said," Iaor said. "But considering her warning, it is you I would have go, to speak for me."

Bertaud glanced down, then back up, hoping he had not visibly flushed. He turned a hand up on the table. "I am honored that you would send me, Iaor. But General Jasand is far more experienced than I."

"He will guide your judgment. But it is your judgment I trust." The king's voice was grave, measured: This was not an impulsive decision. Even when Iaor decided quickly, his decisions were considered. "I don't know what instruction to give you. So I must ask you to do as I would do, and speak my words to these creatures as I would speak them. Will you do this for me?"

Bertaud hesitated a bare instant longer, then answered, "It will be my honor to try."

Iaor smiled briefly, his father's ruthless smile. But it was also his own, with a quick warmth that the old king had never possessed. Both warmth and ruthlessness were quite real. That, Bertaud thought, was what made Iaor a good king. "Good. I will inform Jasand and Diene of my decision. Thus I will, as ever, take advantage of your loyalty, my friend."

Bertaud answered lightly, but with truth behind the light tone, "That is not possible, my king."

The broad road from Tihannad, paved with great flat stones, crossed a bridge where the little Sef flowed out of Niambe Lake. On the other side of the Sef, the road was merely packed earth, but it was still broad. Six men could walk comfortably abreast, or four men ride, or one man ride beside a carriage, not that there were any carriages in this company. All the men were mounted, though: General Jasand had selected his men carefully and almost a fifth of them had an affinity for horses. There was no chance, then, that the horses would refuse to go into the desert if Jasand decided that a mounted attack was best, or that they would shy or bolt under the shadow of griffins' wings.

"I much doubt we'll want to take the horses into the desert, but I like to keep plenty of options available," Jasand had commented to Bertaud, and Bertaud had agreed and waited patiently for the general to sort out the men he thought best for this little foray. Three of the men had the much rarer affinities to eagles or falcons and carried birds on their shoulders or on perches behind their saddles. "Even better than dogs for scouting," Jasand had said, and thoughtfully added a man with an affinity for crows because, he said, he wanted at least one bird with brains in the company.

So it had taken longer than Bertaud had expected to put the company together, but they traveled more quickly than he'd anticipated once they got underway. Even Diene rode astride with no thought for a carriage. The hoofbeats on the hard earth of the road seemed to hold muffled words in their rhythm, words that could not quite be made out but held a nameless threat: Peril, they said. Danger. Hazard ahead. Bertaud cast an uneasy glance at Diene, but the mage had her face set sternly forward and did not seem to hear anything amiss in the beat of the earth.

The road past the Sef had been raised above the land, so that snow-melt drained away to either side and left the surface of the road dry. Casmantian builders had been hired to guide the work on the road. With the magic those builders had set deeply into it, the road shed the rains of spring and summer as though it had been oiled. Thus it was a road on which a company could swing along at a great pace, in good heart, with energy left for the men to sing—which they did: Rude songs that Jasand pretended not to hear, and Diene not to understand. Spearheads flashed and swung above the ranks of soldiers like silver birds; each seemed to call out a single word as it flashed, and the word was *battle*. Most of the men also carried bows, unstrung for travel in damp weather, and the smooth curve of each bow whispered a long, low word of arrow's flight and fall.

Feierabiand was much longer from north to south than it was wide, as though it had long ago been squeezed thin between its larger and more aggressive neighbors. The road from Tihannad ran east along the shore of the lake to the much larger Nejeied River and then turned south along the river; it was raised and broad all the way to the bridge at Minas Ford and then south to Terabiand on the coast, for a good deal of traffic flowed along that route. If one followed the smaller Sepes River straight south from Minas Ford, one would find a narrower, rougher road leading to Talend at the edge of the southern forest. But the forest was not a welcoming place for men, and Talend, perhaps drawing some of its nature from the forest, liked to keep to itself, so that rough track was sufficient for the small amount of traffic that moved along the Sepes.

Bertaud wondered whether anyone in the north would yet have heard a whisper of their coming, if the griffins had crossed the mountains farther south and encroached upon Talend. But then, there was no good pass south of Minas Ford; the mountains near Talend were tall and rugged. And besides, he could not imagine that griffin magic would accord well with the natural magic of the great forest.

There was some traffic here, both on the road and the river, merchants and farmers and ordinary folk about their ordinary business. A courier went past riding north at a collected gallop, her white wand held high in her hand to claim priority on the road. Jasand held up his hand and his men pressed to the left side of the road to let her pass.

"What news, I wonder?" Bertaud said to the general.

Jasand shrugged. "We might have stopped her and asked. But we'll be at Minas Ford soon enough and find out for ourselves."

"You don't want to turn off toward Minas Spring?" Diene inquired, guiding her tall gelding nearer the men.

"Minas Ford is hardly farther. And we can stay on the main road all the way," said Jasand. "Good roads are not to be disregarded, esteemed mage."

"Certainly not by me," Diene said equably.

Jasand grinned at her, so that Bertaud realized the old general was happy to be on campaign again, even a little campaign against griffins rather than a proper company of Casmantian raiders. An open road before him and a hundred spears behind . . . for Jasand, this was a simple vacation from the sometimes tedious court life in Tihannad. His confidence was catching, so that Bertaud felt some of his own tension ease away into the pleasant day. Maybe dealing with the griffins would indeed be that simple; maybe there would be nothing difficult or confusing or controversial about it. He could hope for that, at least.

It was about sixty miles to Minas Ford from Tihannad. Still, if they pressed fairly hard, they should come to the town of Riamne by evening. Then it would be an easy enough day's ride tomorrow to Minas Ford, leaving the men with energy for fighting. If it came to fighting. With luck, it would not. Better if Diene could speak to the griffins. And if Bertaud was called on to speak to them himself, in the king's voice? What, he wondered, would he say? Probably Jasand had the right of it; probably better to enjoy the ride and let the coming days arrive at their own pace.

Riamne was a town of timber and brick with cobbled streets and tall, narrow houses. They reached it just as the last light failed. It had two inns, both of which were filled to capacity. Jasand had his men set up their small tents in a field outside the town, which they had to do by the light of lantern and moon. The general had his own tent set up among them. Bertaud displaced a well-to-do farmer and his family from the best room of the nearer inn and installed Diene there instead.

"Though I shall go back to the fields myself," he said, smiling. "Jasand's tent is large enough for two, and if he will stay with his men, I hardly think I should set myself up here. Fortunate woman, you are affected by no such concerns. You will be comfortable here?"

The old mage touched the mattress with one fragile hand and glanced around at the spare furnishings. She gave Bertaud a caustic glance at his question, though he had made sure his tone was entirely innocent. "Yes. Certainly. Or, if not, I should hardly dare to say so after your comment, young man."

She had been a tutor to both the king and then later to Bertaud himself, when he had been a boy at the court of the old king. Then, Bertaud would never have dared predict the familiarity with which he spoke to her now. He grinned and offered a slight bow.

Diene lifted an eyebrow at him, moved slowly across the room, and sank with a sigh into the sole chair it contained. "It needs a cushion," she remarked judiciously. "But it will do, since it is not a saddle. It has been years since I traveled even so far as this, you know."

"I know." Bertaud collected a pillow from the bed and offered it, with courtesy only a shade exaggerated. "Do you need assistance to stand, esteemed Diene?"

The glance this time was even more acerbic, but the old mage suffered him to help her to her feet. Bertaud arranged the pillow in the chair, and she settled back down with a nod of satisfaction.

"I will do very well. Will you join me for supper here? Or do you feel constrained to join the men for that, as well?"

"I think I need not go so far as that." The men carried rations that were adequate, but hardly up to the standards of a good inn. "I shall have the staff serve us here."

"To avoid the curiosity of men," said the mage, her dark eyes sliding sideways to meet his.

Bertaud inclined his head, quite seriously this time. "To avoid the crowd and the noise. You may tell me more about griffins, esteemed Diene, as we in fortunate Feierabiand have never been plagued with the creatures. You may advise me on what the king's voice should say to them, if we should speak."

The mage half-smiled. "I hardly know what advice to give. I will tell you the lines of poetry I know that hold fire and red dust and the desert wind—I hardly expect you will remember anything of your youthful studies, hmm?"

Bertaud flushed and laughed. "Little enough, esteemed Diene, begging the pardon of my esteemed tutor!"

Diene nodded in disapproving resignation. "Young men so seldom care for the poetry and history we so painstakingly draw out for them. Well, I will tell you poetry, then, and you may tell me what intentions the king should have toward griffins."

"Other than that they depart?"

"I hope," said Diene, "that it proves so simple."

So did Bertaud. Fervently.

The village of Minas Ford, when they arrived there, hoped so, too. There was an inn, small but pleasant, and perhaps half a hundred families who lived within a day's walk. Some, wary of griffins, had evidently gone north to Riamne, and others south to Talend or west to Sihannas at the edge of the Delta. But many had stayed. They were happy to see a troop of soldiers with the king's standard flying before them. This was clear even though they refrained from pressing forward toward the new arrivals.

"But a hundred men aren't enough, young lord," the innkeeper said earnestly, holding the bridle of Bertaud's horse with his own hands. "There are a good many griffins in those hills, lord, begging your pardon, and they're big, dangerous creatures."

Red dust stirred under the hooves of the horse as it shifted its feet. It was nervous. Its ears flicked back and forth, listening to sounds a man could not hear. The breeze that moved through the courtyard of the inn had an odd, harsh feel to it.

"The king hopes there are not so many," Bertaud said neutrally, dismounting with a nod of thanks for the innkeeper's assistance. "And we all hope not to fight them, however many there may be. Have you seen them yourself?"

"Not I, lord—that is to say, just as they fly over now and again. But Nehoen and Jos and even Tesme have all been up there looking for Kes, and they say there're a gracious plenty of them up there." The innkeeper gave the horse to a boy to take to the stable. The boy had to weave a path past the onlookers to get it there.

Bertaud tilted his head in interest, glancing out at the crowd. "Nehoen? Jos, Tesme, Kes?" Jasand and Diene had come up silently to listen.

The innkeeper bobbed a quick bow. "Kes was . . . Kes is just a girl, lord. She had . . . she has some skill with herbs, and she can stitch a cut or set a bone. A man came and asked her to come, and she went up into the desert to help somebody who'd been hurt. Before we even knew there was a desert."

Bertaud marked the past tense uncomfortably avoided in this answer. "And she has not returned?"

"No, lord. So we went looking, some of us. All of us, at the first. Tesme—that's Kes's sister, lord—Tesme kept searching. For days. And Nehoen. Nehoen is a gentleman of this district, lord, an educated man, not the kind to stretch the truth out thin, if you understand me. If he says *at least fifty*, he doesn't mean *five and their shadows*, lord. He . . . well, lord, I think he promised Tesme he'd keep looking, so as she wouldn't keep going up there herself. And Tesme's hired man, Jos, he stayed out a long time and went up a long way, but even he, well, I think he maybe doesn't expect to find her, anymore."

"I see." What might pass for educated in a little village like Minas Ford, Bertaud did not inquire. But the innkeeper seemed honest. Bertaud said, "Can you find these good folk for me? We would greatly desire to speak to them before we ourselves go up into the mountains. Which we shall, early tomorrow, I expect. Ah, and I trust there is indeed room in your inn for us?"

"For the lady and some few of your men more, lord, if you please; we've little enough business just now, but, as you see, it's not a large inn. And I'll send my girls out with word you'd like to speak with those as have seen the griffins."

Bertaud nodded his thanks and headed for the welcome comfort of the inn, not forgetting to offer his arm to Diene, who was finding it difficult to walk after two days on horseback but was trying not to show it.

"Fifty?" Jasand muttered on his other side. He shook his grizzled head in doubt. "Do you find that likely, my lord?"

Bertaud shrugged. "Likely? I want to see the men making the claim. You should ask, is it possible? And of course it is *possible*. And if it is true, General?"

"Then I would wish for more soldiers. Though come to it—" Jasand said consideringly, "—even in the worst case . . . I would set the men I brought against even a *hundred* griffins, my lord, if necessary."

Bertaud knew Jasand was right to be confident. The soldiers of Feierabiand had never been able to afford the luxury of incompetence in either their ranks or their officers. Only a clear and continual demonstration of Feierabiand skill in the field, along both the river border with Linularinum and the mountain border with Casmantium, made room for the central of the three countries to remain untroubled. And Jasand did not need to mention his own record or reputation. Though Bertaud might have wished some part of the general's experience had been against griffins. Or that they had, aside from mage's poetry, a Casmantian advisor handy to offer counsel on the creatures. But he said merely, "We shall hope these townsfolk can give us a clear idea of what we shall meet."

And, indeed, the men who came that evening to tell what they had seen in the mountains, Bertaud judged, might, in fact, be credible witnesses. The woman Tesme had not come, but Nehoen and Jos had evidently been close by the inn.

The hired man, Jos, was a plainspoken man who did not seem given to exaggeration or flights of imagination. And by his dress and manner, Nehoen was undoubtedly a wealthy man by the standards of the region and probably an even more creditable witness. Both men were clearly seriously worried about the missing girl and the griffins.

"Kes went up the mountain to assist someone who had been injured," Nehoen said, giving Bertaud the respectful nod due his rank, but with the straight look of a confident man. "The same day the griffins were first spotted, lord. A man came to find her. Seemed to know she has a talent with healing, for all he was a stranger to the district. No knowing who he really was."

"A mage, or so they say," Jos put in grimly, with a wary glance at Diene. "*I* didn't see him." And blamed himself for his absence, by his harsh tone. Or everyone else, for letting her go.

"A mage?" repeated Diene, startled. The innkeeper had not said this.

"Yes, esteemed mage—clearly so," Nehoen agreed, but the emphasis in his voice was clearly for Jos; he was obviously continuing a longstanding argument. "I saw him, and spoke to him, and he was *surely* a mage. A strange, dangerous sort, I would guess. Well, clearly so, or we'd not be missing a girl, would we? Middling age, a hard sort of face, a thin mouth. Black eyes. Hard-hearted, I would say—if I were guessing." The landowner paused, visibly bracing himself. Expecting condemnation, Bertaud realized, for having allowed this stranger to take away one of the Minas Ford girls on some weak pretext. Nehoen added, as much to Jos as to them, "He took her and they just went, like that." He snapped his fingers. "I *swear* to you, it was too quick for any of us to think twice about stopping it! They were just *gone*, right into the air."

Jos set his jaw and looked grim, as though only the presence of the king's servants kept him from a sharp retort.

"Neither of you could have prevented him, if the man was a mage," Diene said firmly. Her mouth had tightened. "You think this man, this mage, took the girl into the desert? To the griffins?"

"Well, esteemed mage," Nehoen said reasonably, "it's a striking coincidence if he didn't, isn't it?"

Diene inclined her head. "By your description, the man is no one I know. And a mage taking a healer girl to the griffins? This is a puzzle."

"I should say so. The *griffins* wanted a human healer? And this mage came and got them one?" Jasand said skeptically—Bertaud could not tell whether he was skeptical of the suggested connection, or skeptical of the whole story. The general frowned at the townsmen. "So you went looking for this girl?"

"A dozen or so folk of this district, yes, esteemed sir. We found . . . we found the desert. It's grown since," Nehoen said, with a simplicity Bertaud found very persuasive.

Jasand continued to frown. "And you've seen these griffins? You, personally?"

The man gave Jasand a nod. "Yes, lord. More than one or two. I'd guess fifty or more. But Jos went farther up than I." He looked at the other man.

"There are certainly dozens of the creatures up there," the hired man said, his tone still grim. "Fifty is a near-enough guess. Not many more than that, I'd say. I walked as close to them as I stand to you, and they did not even seem to notice I was there. They ought never be allowed to rest there on our land."

"They lie in the sun like cats," Nehoen put in. He spoke steadily, but his eyes had gone wide, abstracted with memory. "They ride the still air like eagles. Their eyes are filled with the sun. The shadows they cast are made of light. They are more beautiful . . . I have no words to describe them."

Jos said, even more harshly, "Beautiful they may be, those creatures, but they took Kes and we did not find her."

"I made Tesme stop looking lest we come across her bones," Nehoen said quietly, to Jasand rather than to Jos. "But . . . we didn't find those either. But if there are fifty griffins up there . . . You brought only a hundred men?" He seemed to become suddenly aware of his own temerity in offering criticism to officers of the king, and stopped. Then he said, "Forgive me if I speak out of turn, lord. But It seems to me it would be better to have more."

"A hundred soldiers should do well enough," Jos said roughly. "You clean those creatures out, lord, and you might bid your men, if they find a girl's dry bones in the red sand, they might bring them out of the desert for her sister."

Nehoen bowed his head in agreement, looking from Jasand to Ber-

taud and then settling on Diene. "If you . . . if you do go into the desert
lords, esteemed mage, if you should find her . . . maybe she's still all
right . . ."

Jos made a grim, wordless sound that made clear his opinion of this
chance. He said, "Destroy them all, lord. That's all you can do for her
now."

Bertaud did not know whether he believed a mage had taken the
girl—still less whether the mage had been working somehow with the
griffins. But he said, "We will certainly bring her out if we find her,
even if we find only bones. But we will hope for better." And better still,
though he did not say this, if they did not, in fact, require to do battle
with the griffins. Whether or not there was a mage, and whatever had
happened to the girl.

After the townsmen had gone, Bertaud, Jasand, and Diene discussed the
griffins and the proper approach to them by the light of lanterns that
threw shadows like half-seen glyphs across the walls of Diene's room.

"A *mage* working with the griffins?" Jasand said, skeptical.

Diene gazed thoughtfully into the air. "One does not expect any
earth mage to work with creatures of fire. However . . . there was a
mage once, Cheienas of Terabiand, who loved the desert and spoke to
fire and creatures of fire. He wanted to ride the hot wind, to catch fire
in his eyes and understand it. He vanished from our ken, and it is said
he gave away the earth of his nature and became a creature of fire. I
wonder if he would strike a man as hard-hearted?"

"Would he be the sort to work against us?" Jasand asked practically. "And if he is, or if any fire mage is up there and set against us,
can you deal with that, esteemed Diene? I've many men with animal
affinities . . . but I've no one I'd set against a hostile mage. Mages were
not something I expected to encounter."

Diene raised her eyebrows, with an air of faint opprobrium, as
though she found this showed an unfortunate lack of foresight. Not that
she had suggested any preparations for this eventuality herself before
they had left, Bertaud did not point out.

"Then it is fortunate I am here," the mage said. "I expect I would
indeed be able to handle Cheienas, if this is he."

Bertaud asked, "And other possibilities?"

Diene considered. "There was a man named Milenne, originally
from Linularinum, who lived in the high forest north of Tiearanan.
One day he found a golden egg in the forest. Of the creature that
hatched from that egg, he wrote only that it was a creature of fire, with

wings of fire. What became of it, he did not write. But he left Feierabi-
and because, he said, it made him want to seek a deeper silence than
that found in even the deepest forest."

Jasand waved a disgusted hand. "Poetry and riddles. Golden eggs
and wings of fire! Esteemed Diene, if you can handle this mage, whom-
ever he may be, then I'm satisfied. What matters then is how many griffins there are, and how they can be made to go back across the mountains."

"And your ideas about this?" Bertaud asked him.

"Well . . . well, Lord Bertaud, that man Jos only said *dozens*, and he
seems to have had as good a look as any. Even the other man guessed
only fifty or so. I think maybe we don't need to worry about a hundred
of the creatures after all. And then, we brought archers. Arrows are
proof against any creature that walks or swims or flies through the air,
whether it's a creature of fire or air or good plain earth." Jasand paused,
thinking. "We must be certain of our ground. I do not want my men
shooting uphill into the sun. If we leave the road—if we divide the men
into two companies, say, and go up across the slant, in afternoon so the
sun is at our backs—we can set up a killing field between the companies. That should do well enough. At least griffins can't draw bows of
their own."

Bertaud nodded. "We might send back to Tihannad for more men
if you think that best."

"No," the general answered, consideringly. "No, I think that should
not be necessary. It would take time, and what if these griffins begin to
do more harm to more than calves while we delay? The core of this
company is Anesnen's fifth cavalry."

Bertaud knew Anesnen's reputation. He nodded. "If we must bring
the griffins to battle, that is indeed good to know," he agreed. "Especially if there are only a few dozen up there. Still, we shall hope for
better than battle. Esteemed Diene, have you given thought to our ini-
tial approach?"

The mage glanced up, an abstracted look in her dark eyes. "What
is there to consider? We shall be straightforward."

"But prepared to be otherwise," said Jasand.

They were straightforward. But prepared to be otherwise. They left
their horses in Minas Ford; neither griffins nor the desert itself would
likely be kind to horses. They marched on foot out of the village and up
into the hills. The village folk turned out to watch them go, but no one
but some of the younger boys ventured to follow. Their mothers called
them back before they could follow very far.

"That's as well," General Jasand observed. "In case any of the creatures get past our lines."

Bertaud nodded. The last thing they wanted was to stir up the griffins and then allow one or two to escape to ravage the countryside. "If there must be a battle, we shall hope they are willing to mass and meet us."

Diene gave him a reassuring nod. "You needn't fear they'll avoid us, I think. Indeed, they'll meet us quickly enough, if we walk into their desert. *Griffins* are not likely to avoid conflict, I assure you."

Bertaud supposed that was true enough. He did not find it especially reassuring, however.

They turned around a curve of a hill and, for the first time, found a handful of villagers waiting to watch them pass. Jos, whom Bertaud recognized, and a scattering of grim-looking men and excited older boys. A couple of the men lifted their hands in recognition and salute. Some of the soldiers, pleased to be recognized, returned solemn nods. As Bertaud passed the villagers, he offered a deep nod that was almost a bow, acknowledging their presence and concern.

He remarked to Jasand, "They'll follow, I'm sure, and watch from a safe distance. I trust it will be a safe distance. In fact, I'd send a man to make sure of it, if necessary."

"I hope we'll have plenty of men to spare for all sorts of minor functions," the general answered drily. But he also gave one of his men a glance, and the soldier peeled off from the column and went to speak to the village folk.

The edge of the desert was a remarkably clean line: On one side, the gentle green of the ordinary Feierabiand countryside; on the other, the empty desert. They halted on the ordinary side of the line. General Jasand, with a nominal glance at Bertaud for approval, divided his men and began to arrange a company to either side of the approach he thought most promising for battle. But for the first hopeful approach, Diene and Bertaud simply walked straight up the mountain to see what they might meet. Bertaud gave the mage his arm, which she leaned on gratefully.

"I'm far too old for such nonsense," she grumbled. She flinched as they crossed into the heat and drought of the desert, muttering in dismay and discomfort. Bertaud found the pounding heat uncomfortable, but from Diene's suddenly labored steps and difficult breathing, he thought that the elderly mage was indeed experiencing something more than mere discomfort. There was a wind off the mountains that blew into their faces. It was a strange, hot wind, carrying scents of rock and dust and hot metal—nothing familiar to a man born on the sea side of these mountains. There was an unfamiliar taste to it. A taste of fire, Bertaud thought.

Sand gritted underfoot, on slopes where there never had been sand before. Red rock pierced the sand in thin twisted spires and strange flat-topped columns, nothing like the smooth gray stone native to these hills. Bertaud glanced over his shoulder to where the men waited, drawn up in the green pasture at the edge of the desert, and shook his head incredulously.

A shape moved ahead of them. Not a griffin, Bertaud saw, after the first startled lurch of his stomach. A man, seated on a low red rock, fingers laced around one drawn-up knee. He sat there as though the rock were a throne, watching them approach with no appearance of either surprise or alarm. His face was harsh, with a strong nose and high cheekbones. There was a hard, stark patience in those eyes, and also a kind of humor that had nothing to do with kindness. He looked neither old nor young. He looked like nothing Bertaud had ever seen.

"That," said Diene, "is surely the stranger that the man spoke of. And quite clearly a mage." Her voice was flat with dislike. She shaded her eyes with her hand, as though against light.

Bertaud said nothing. He took a step, and then another, feeling heat against his face as though he walked into a fire. The feeling was so vivid he was faintly surprised not to hear the roar of leaping flames before him. He glanced at Diene, but her expression was set and calm. He could not tell what she was thinking or feeling.

The man rose as they approached, and inclined his head. "You were looking for me, I believe," he said. His voice, pitiless as the desert, nevertheless held the same strange, hard humor Bertaud saw in his eyes. "Kes told me I might look for lords of Feierabiand on this road. Your soldiers I saw for myself."

Bertaud tried to focus his thoughts. But a hot wind blew through his mind, shredding his focus. The wind seemed to contain words; it seemed to speak a language he might, if he strained hard enough, learn eventually to comprehend. At the moment . . . it only confused his wits and his nerve. He tried to work out whether this was something the man was doing purposefully or merely a strange effect of the desert, but he could not decide.

"You are a griffin," Diene stated. The familiar human words seemed somehow surprising; they seemed to hold a meaning beyond what Bertaud grasped. The woman stood straight, but there was more than straightness to her posture. She had gone rigid with a hostility that alarmed Bertaud. It was not fear. That, he would have understood. Her feeling appeared stronger and more dangerous.

But the mage's hostility did not appear to be returned. A smile glinted in the powerful eyes; curved, after a moment, the thin mouth. "I have no desire to be your enemy, earth mage. Restrain your sensibility.

Have you never before experienced the antipathy between earth and fire? It's compelling, I know, but you need not give way to it, if you will not. I assure you, it *is* possible to rule your instincts—"

Diene shook her head. She broke in, her voice harsh with strain. "I know you are unalterably opposed to creatures of earth. I *know* that. If you would not be our enemies, go back to your own country of fire."

"We cannot."

The woman stared into the austere face. "Then we will be enemies."

Wait, Bertaud wanted to say. Wait. This is moving far too fast. But he could not find his voice. He thought if he tried to speak, the voice of the desert wind would come out of his mouth.

The taut smile became fierce. "If you will it so, then we will be enemies," said the man. The griffin.

"Wait," Bertaud managed, but lost his voice again. The potent stare moved to catch his, and he found he could not look away.

"Man," said the griffin. It was acknowledgment, and something more. "What is your name?"

For a stark moment Bertaud thought he might have lost the ability to speak. But a reflex of pride stiffened his back and let him, at last, find his voice. "Bertaud. Son of Boudan." His tone became, with an effort, wry. "Lord of Feierabiand, Lord of the Delta." And the title that was most precious to him: "Advisor to Iaor Daveien Behanad Safiad, King of Feierabiand. And yours?"

"Kairaithin," said the griffin, with that ferocious hard humor that was nothing like the humor of a man. "If you like. Sipiike Kairaithin. Anasakuse, to those who presume themselves my intimates. Shall we be enemies, man?"

Speaking, Bertaud found, became easier after the first words. A little easier. He shook his head sharply, trying to hear past the high, hot wind that blew through his mind. "Are you . . . are you doing this to me?"

The intensity of that black gaze shaded off toward curiosity. The man tipped his head to the side inquiringly, a gesture oddly inhuman. "I am doing nothing to you. I assure you. Your earth mage would know if fire overreached itself in her presence. But I did not approach you to take hostile action. I put myself in your way only to speak."

"Is something troubling you? Something *else*? What's wrong?" Diene was studying Bertaud with narrow-eyed concentration and an attitude that said, *Whatever it is, it is the griffin's fault and he is lying.*

But Bertaud thought that the griffin spoke the truth. So this strange blurring of his mind was surely an effect of the desert. He shook his head again, stopping Diene when she would have asked again. He tried to think clearly. "You cannot go back to your own desert. Cannot. Why not?"

The griffin mage—Kairaithin—lifted his shoulders in a minimal shrug. "Because we were driven from the desert into the mountain heights, man, and that is no world of ours; because we had no choice but to come down into this humid land where the sea wind combats our own wind. And have no choice but to remain, at least for a time. This country is not ours, but it can be made to serve. We will not give way. We have no way to give. Go back to your king, man, and tell him we have no desire to be enemies of the men here. Tell him he would be wise to make room for our desert."

Bertaud shook his head, drew a difficult breath. Blinked against a haze of hot, red dust. Tried to focus. Asked at last, "Driven by what?"

The griffin's lip curled.

"Driven by whom?" Bertaud asked him. He drew a breath of hot air and tried to think. "Why?"

The griffin held out a hand, a sharp commanding gesture. Bertaud blinked, took a step forward. He almost extended his own hand, as the other seemed to expect. But Diene struck his hand down. The griffin lowered his, slowly. He said to her, "Earth mage, you are unwise. You were unwise to put yourself in my way, and you are unwise now to yield to your dislike for fire."

"Wiser than to trust you." The look in Diene's dark eyes was hostile. "You are a mage. But what else are you?"

"I have been patient," the griffin answered curtly. "You exhaust my patience, earth mage." He shifted his weight restlessly, glancing up the slope toward the cliffs, as though he would go.

"Wait," said Bertaud, faintly. He tried to imagine what an impatient griffin would be like, if this was patience. But the griffin mage, to his surprise, turned back. He was restless, catching Bertaud's eyes again with his as a hawk might catch a hare. But he turned. To meet that hard stare was almost physical pain. Bertaud sustained it with an effort; asking again, "Driven by whom?"

"Casmantium." The expression in those black eyes had gone hard, savage. "Who else?"

Bertaud closed his eyes, trying to think. He breathed the metallic air, listened to the desert wind. The taste of hot copper slid across his tongue. Casmantium. "Casmantium," he said aloud, and opened his eyes again. "Why?"

The griffin's shrug this time was indifferent, edged with a restlessness like fire. "Perhaps Casmantium tired of having our red desert crowd her fair cities." But once again he seemed willing to speak. He took a step forward, holding Bertaud's eyes with his own, and spoke more intensely. "Man, there are some who declare that desert ours, and argue for our return to it. Others say we should make this land ours, and stay. Our . . . king . . . is of the first mind. Therefore, I advise you, go. Leave the desert we make here to the wind of our wings. We will withdraw in time, and then you may reclaim it."

"You have no right to dictate terms to us!" Diene snapped, glaring at the griffin.

"Be *quiet*," Bertaud commanded her desperately. He felt he had been on the edge of an important understanding, and had lost it. He had been so glad Diene had come. He had not wanted to meet the griffins alone, and he had agreed with Iaor that the learning and wisdom of a mage would be valuable in this meeting. But now he would have given almost anything to be rid of her.

"Earth mages," the griffin mage said to him, with an impatient little movement of his head, oddly birdlike. "She should not have come into this desert. Do you not know earth magic is antithetical to fire? All mages experience the aversion, but the stronger the mage, the stronger the aversion. One may make allowances for the effect," he added, his tone edged with contempt, "but your mage does not seem inclined to try."

Diene began to speak, clearly a hostile answer to this statement. Bertaud held up a hand in a gesture so sharp she desisted. He shook his head, trying to shake sense back into his mind, and looked back at the griffin. Kairaithin. "If Casmantium drove you out of your desert, what makes you confident we cannot?"

That strange, harsh amusement moved in the black eyes. "You have no cold mages. Your earth mages here do not study to become cold. Nor, even did you find cold magecraft at your fingers, do we now sleep unaware of human aggression."

Well, that was certainly true. Bertaud drew a breath, let it go. "If you would withdraw into the hills. Leave the pastures. If you would hunt deer and leave be the cattle, I would be prepared to take that as a gesture of goodwill."

"And your king?"

"Will expect some recompense for his generosity to allow your sojourn in his lands. Nevertheless, he will be guided by my opinion."

"Will he? And is your opinion sound, man? We have not hunted *men*. You may take *that* as a measure of our goodwill."

"Yes," said Bertaud. He thought it was. He stared into the austere face. "I will need more than that to take to my king."

"Will you? Then come." The griffin took a step forward, lifted his hand a second time. Not a commanding gesture, this time. Nor the appeal of the suppliant. This gesture held invitation. Or perhaps challenge.

"No!" said Diene.

Bertaud shut his eyes, opened them, and said patiently, "Esteemed Diene—"

"No!" snapped the mage. "Young fool! This creature is nothing you can trust! Put yourself in its power and you may well find it's no power you can put off again. Fool! And you!" She spoke directly to the griffin mage. "Be clear, creature! You say I should trust *you*? What nonsense! Explain what you intend and what you will do, if you will have us trust you!"

The griffin stood with stark patience, waiting, his hand still extended. He did not so much as glance at Diene. His attention, furnace hot, was all for Bertaud.

Diene glared at him, transferred her glare to Bertaud, and drew herself up to her best small height. She was furious, and furiously hostile. But did he, Bertaud asked himself, think his own judgment superior to hers? The heat of the desert seemed to beat against his face like the power of the sun. He knew he could not think clearly. Had not been able to think clearly since he had first found red sand under his boots and looked into the fierce human face of the griffin. If the mage so vehemently distrusted fire, maybe she was right; if earth mages hated the desert, maybe that was a sign it was wise for men to hate it . . .

Young fool, Diene had called him. Bertaud feared that she was right, whether Kairaithin had done this to him purposefully or whether it was merely some strange effect of the desert.

The griffin lowered his hand. He said, with savage humor and no sign of either disappointment or anger, "Then go. And go, man. Go. Out of this country, you and yours, and back to your king. You may tell him, if he is wise, he will leave well alone. If he is wise, he will heed *that* opinion."

And he was gone. Red dust blew across the place where he had been.

Bertaud was halfway down the mountain before he was aware that he was moving, and farther than that before he remembered Diene.

The mage was with him, struggling to walk over the rough ground, her face set hard as a mask.

Bertaud stopped, offering her his arm. She stopped, too, breathing harshly, and looked him in the face. He did not know what she saw there.

"If you had gone into that power," she said, "I think you would not have come out of it."

Breath hissed through his teeth. But he did not give her the answer that first leaped to mind. He said instead, deliberately, "It's possible you saved my life, esteemed Diene."

The mage blinked, waited.

"Or it's possible you threw it away! We came here to talk to them! Now we will have no choice but to fight. Was that the antipathy? You expected it; did you control it, or did it control you?"

"I expected it—I'd read about it—Meriemne reminded me about it, but I confess it was a stronger effect in the event than I'd anticipated." The lines in Diene's face had deepened; she looked drawn and exhausted and ten years older than she had that morning. "But, believe me, Lord Bertaud, mages' antipathy to fire or no, it's not possible to make peace with those creatures. I know that now, very clearly. Does the wolf lie down beside the fawn?"

Bertaud shook his head, not exactly disagreeing but wanting to disagree. And he did not even know why. He glanced up the mountain, irresolute, ready on that thought to turn on his heel, go back up the mountain, and leave the mage to make her own way down.

Her hand on his arm stopped him. She said, "Lord Bertaud, from the first moment, there was no possibility of avoiding battle. I had hoped—I had thought—but I knew it was impossible when first I saw that . . . when I saw that creature and the shape it had put on. You must surely have known it, too. There is no possible *way* to yield to it! You are not blind. Or I would have said not."

Bertaud wondered if she was right. He said nothing.

Diene waved her hand to indicate the mountains, the heat haze that moved in the silence—a silence vaster and harsher than any that belonged by rights to Feierabiand. "I thought *I* understood what we would face up on this mountain. And I saw nothing any creature of earth will ever understand. Antipathy? How could there ever be anything else between fire and earth?" She was shivering. Even in the heat. She looked small and old and frightened. Despite himself, Bertaud was moved. He let out his breath. Offered her his arm.

This time she took it.

General Jasand, it was clear, was not entirely displeased by the outcome of their first venture up the mountain.

"They must be aware of our numbers," Bertaud warned him. "They can fly—they will know what dispositions we make of our men."

"So? What will they do? Griffins do not use bow or shield. They can retreat, or they can come down to us. Even if there are a hundred, we'll claim victory. As Casmantium did, by what you say. And we'll then have soldiers blooded against griffins, which can only be useful if we are to have these creatures coming across the mountains once and again."

"Mmm." Bertaud did not feel at all comfortable with that thought. What, would griffins come again and again down from the mountains, and Feierabiand slaughter them over and over? He did not like the idea of Feierabiand being used by Casmantium for any such purpose, if Casmantium had, in fact, decided to rid itself of the desert on its northern border.

But the general did not notice Bertaud's discomfort, or else he attributed it to a different cause. "You may trust our men's training, my lord, and our weaponsmiths. Arrows properly made fly true; spears properly made strike hard. Griffins can hardly be better armed than boar or bear. When all's said, beak and talon are no match for well-crafted steel. With the esteemed Diene to stop any mage from interfering, my men can handle this."

Bertaud, for all his lack of enthusiasm for Jasand's plan, could see no honest reason to disagree with his assessment. Nor did Diene contradict the general's words. The men, drawn up in two orderly companies, looked dangerously competent. The spears and arrows knew what they had been made for; the deadly magic of their making glittered along their edges.

The plan of battle was simple. Bertaud thought the griffins would attack, and he thought there was every chance they would indeed be slaughtered like the animals Jasand was evidently so willing to consider them. He said bleakly, "If they were boar or bear, any man born with an affinity for boar or bear could turn them and send them into the wild, far from settled land. Would that earth magic ruled these creatures also!"

Jasand only shrugged. "We'll go up there, and there. With your approval, my lord," he added absently. "The griffins are straight up that way." There was no question of that: One could tell by the way the light lay on the land and the taste of the air where the griffins had made the country their own. "If they come straight down, that's fine. If they go after each company separately, that's not as neat, but it will still do. Archers on the inside, you know, and spears on the edge. I can see nothing the griffins can do that will give the men enough trouble to matter. We'll be back at Minas Ford in time for a late supper."

"Yes," said Bertaud. He tilted his head back and stared into the sky. It was blank, giving nothing back. Foreign heat poured out of it. The sun, lowering in the west, cast its light across the face of the hills. He wanted to say, No. He wanted to go back up into the red desert the griffins had made of this country, to find the griffin mage and speak with

him again, find some other option. Anything but take Feierabiand soldiers into that desert. Whether it was the men or the griffins who would
die of it.

Diene stood to one side, thin arms crossed across her chest, mouth
a thin, straight line. Looking at her, Bertaud doubted himself. He could
put his judgment above hers, except how could he trust his own judgment? She might have been instantly hostile to the griffin mage, but she
had at least been coherent. Fool, she had called him. Perhaps she had
been right. He thought of the griffin mage and shut his eyes at the
memory of how tongue-tied he had suddenly become in that creature's
presence. He was dismayed by his own irresolution. In retrospect, it
seemed more and more likely that that had been some subtle form of
attack. If it had been, it had worked. How could a man blinded by the
power of the desert possibly see what he should do to serve his king?

He said again, reluctantly, "Yes."

Jasand gave a satisfied nod and signaled, and the horns sounded,
bright clear notes in the golden afternoon.

The men strode forward, in step. The Feierabiand banner flew above
each company: golden barley sheaf and blue river. Spear points glittered and threw back the light. *War*, they said. *War. War.* Bows of horn
and wood, light sliding down their sinew strings, were in the hands of
the men protected by those spears. Most of the archers already had arrows nocked, ready to draw. Some, those who made their own arrows,
were already speaking to the shafts they had crafted, heads bent over
their bows, whispering of true flight and blood. General Jasand led one
company, one of his captains the other; Bertaud, who might have
claimed the honor, stood with the mage Diene on a rock outcropping
and left it to the captain, who was a good deal more experienced in
military matters.

"If something goes wrong," Jasand had said, "the king will need to
learn of it. I certainly won't trust villagers to carry proper word! And
we can't leave the mage unprotected." He had given Bertaud a horn, in
case a man standing apart might see some urgent necessity those in the
thick of battle might have missed. He had not had to say that he expected Bertaud not to use it. Leave the fighting to the soldiers, and keep
well out of it—that was the expectation.

Bertaud had taken the horn, and he had not argued. Both points
were good. And he thought, though he did not say, that if he went up
into this desert, he might find himself unable to think or speak. Where
would the men be then? He set his face in the blank expression he had
first used to deal with his father and then found useful for tedious or
unpleasant court functions. He did not allow himself to pace.

"They'll be perfectly fine," said Diene, tense and straight beside him. He had suggested she sit. She would not.

"Of course," Bertaud said, but wondered whether his tone rang as false as hers.

And the griffins came down. They came straight down the red mountain, straight into the killing field between the two companies, as though they had no fear of bows, or no knowledge men used such things. They flew in irregular formation, some alone and some by threes or fours. Two dozen. Four dozen. Six.

"Earth and iron," Diene breathed. Bertaud was speechless. They were huge, big as the white bulls bred in the Delta, but nothing so tame. They flew out of the light as though the light itself had formed them. Red dust drove before their wind, stinging, whipping into a blinding veil. Bertaud, shielding his eyes with upraised hands, could nonetheless see that fire fell on the wind from their wings and tongues of flame leaped up from the sand beneath them. The griffins, wreathed in dust and fire, stooped like hunting falcons, talons shining. They screamed as they fell, savage high cries that cut through the air like knives.

Men cried out in answer. Bertaud could not blame them. Precious seconds were lost before the soldiers remembered discipline and drew their bows. Arrows rose; the light that struck off the steel tips was red as flame, and flame fell past the arrows as they mounted. Some of the griffins were surely struck; Bertaud could not tell, but well-made arrows would seek living flesh and turn to find it. Even so, a vicious rain of fire fell into the companies of men, which became suddenly ragged. Spears rose, almost in order despite the flames, and he caught his breath: If the men held, Jasand would be proved right, because even with fire and wind, the griffins would not be able to breach that curtain of steel—not without spilling their own blood out onto the sand. And the men would hold. He was sure the men would hold.

Then griffins came past the rock where Bertaud stood with the mage—griffins with wings folded, moving with great bounds like running lions. Diene cried out, thinly. A passing griffin, powerful muscles rolling under the dark bronze hide of its haunches, turned its head and fixed her with one fierce coppery eye. It went past without pausing.

They would take the men from behind, Bertaud understood at once. The griffins on the ground would come against the soldiers like scythes striking barley stems; hidden by the dust and by the terror of their brethren aloft, they would come and strike below the lifted spears. He found the military horn in his hand with a feeling of surprise, and lifted it to his mouth.

A great white griffin, gleaming even through the veils of whipping dust, cleared the rock where they stood in a bound that was half flight. Talons white as bone closed on Bertaud's arm; a wing like a hammer struck him in the chest. He would have screamed with pain except he could not get the breath to cry out. The griffin's other wing struck Diene and flung her from the rock; she fell without a sound, like a child's crumpled doll.

The griffin struck at Bertaud's face with a beak like a blade, but somehow Bertaud's sword was in the way; he had no notion how it had come into his hand—his left hand, for the white griffin had his right pinned in its grip. He cut at its head, so close to his own, and it flung him away. He fell hard, to sand that flickered with little ripples of fire; he rolled fast to get up, beating at a charred patch of cloth over his thigh, but he made it only so far as his knees. He could not move the arm the griffin had torn. White agony lanced through his chest: Ribs were broken. He could not get his breath, did not yet know if broken bones had pierced his lungs, could not imagine the pain would be worse if they had. He had lost his sword in the fall. The loss did not seem likely to matter. The griffin, above him on the rock, wings spread wide, seemed immense as the sky. It stared at him with fierce eyes of a hard fiery blue, and sprang like a cat.

"No," he cried at it without breath, without sound. He found himself more furious than terrified. He tried to fling himself to his feet, but his right leg would not hold, and he was falling already as the white griffin came down upon him. Darkness rose up like heat, or he fell into it, and it filled his eyes and his mind.

CHAPTER 5

Despite everything Kairaithin had said about mages and battle, Kes had hoped that perhaps no one would come against the griffins. She had spent days playing with flames, learning to love fire, and if sometimes she thought of Tesme, she found it easier, as measureless time passed, to turn her thoughts away from home, back again toward the fire Opailikiita showed her. But she hoped no one would come. The Casmantian mages would stay in Casmantium, and the griffins would linger here in Feierabiand for a little while and then go home, and Kes would go home as well . . .

But then an army came after all. Word of it came flickering from mind to mind like beacon fires lighting one after another, and Kes spent a tense, anxious afternoon pacing around the edges of the great, high hall Kairaithin had made upon the cliff of the plateau. But the griffins won their fight, so all was well, after all. That was what Kes thought, when Kairaithin came at last to bring her to the field of battle.

But there is little enough for you to do, the griffin mage told her with grim satisfaction. He was in his true form, beautiful and terrible as the embers at the heart of a great bonfire. *Our enemies here do not know how to do battle against us: This time, they came openly rather than in stealth, in the high heat of the day rather than in the dark reaches of the night, and without cold magecraft to shield them or strike at us. Thus, the blood that was poured out upon the sand was theirs and not ours.*

Kes thought, *Our enemies here?* And she wondered why men so little prepared had come against the griffins. But she did not understand exactly what Kairaithin meant until the griffin mage shifted them across the desert and brought her to the place where the few wounded griffins waited for her, and she saw the innumerable dead men lying where they had fallen, all across the burning sand.

They were not Casmantian soldiers. They were soldiers of Feierabiand, and they were all dead. Kes stared out across the red desert where they lay, speechless.

They died well, Kairaithin told her, in a tone of reassurance, as though he thought that this would make it all right that they were dead.

Kes slowly turned her head to stare at him. Looking at the griffin was much easier than looking out at the dead soldiers. She fixed her attention on his fiery black gaze, trying to see nothing else. She found she was trembling, but she couldn't stop.

The worst of our injured lies there. Kairaithin indicated the first of the wounded griffins, a bronze-and-black female who lay beside a low, sharp ridge of stone quite close to the edge of the battlefield.

Kes glanced that way, found her gaze caught by the abandoned dead, flinched from the sight of the twisted bodies of men, and closed her eyes. She had not previously met the injured griffin. But her name sang through Kes's awareness even from that brief glance: Riihaikuse Aranuurai Kimiistariu. Kes knew she was badly wounded—she already knew that there was a deep cut across her chest and belly. But she did not move. She whispered, "Why didn't you tell me?"

Kairaithin tilted his eagle's head, puzzled. *Did I not tell you?*

"Days of fire and blood, you said!" Kes was not whispering now. She was nearly shouting. "But you didn't say—you didn't tell me—" she gestured blindly toward the men who lay scattered across the sand.

The griffin mage was silent for a moment. He said at last, *I did not mean to do you harm by this. Indeed, I sought to turn the day, for I think it wiser to reserve our strength for use against Casmantium. The King of Feierabiand sent an emissary, which was wise. But the emissary brought an earth mage to advise him, which was not wise at all, for she feared me and loathed the desert and thus he would not speak to me. Thus, the day became a day for blood and fire, and their deaths came upon them.*

Kes stared at him.

But they died well, Kairaithin assured her. *And there is still a need for your gift of healing.*

Kes didn't move. She didn't think she *could* move. She was still trembling. She knew she definitely could not approach the field of battle—no matter how many wounded griffins lay there. And anyway— she asked Kairaithin, hearing her voice shake and not caring, "Should I heal your people? When you kill mine?"

There was a silence. Kes thought that the griffin-mage was not ashamed or even disturbed at what his people had done, that he didn't understand why she was upset, that when he said *It was a day for death*, he meant something other than, and more than, what she heard. She realized that when she did not understand him, he did not know how else to answer her.

But he said at last, *The emissary of your king yet lives. He may die. But it would please me if he lives. I cannot heal his wounds. I do not know whether even you might heal human injuries with fire. But perhaps you may find a way to save this man. Will you try?*

"Of course!" Kes looked around at once, as though she might find the man lying near at hand. She even made herself look across at the field of battle, but flinched again from it—anyway, she could not believe anyone lying there might live. The sand and overpowering heat were already claiming the dead men, who no longer looked as though they'd ever really been alive.

He is not there, said Kairaithin. *I will take you to him. I think you should first remind yourself of fire and of healing. Aranuurai Kimiistariu will die if you do not see her whole. Will you let her die?*

Kes hesitated, looking once more toward the battlefield. She took a step toward the wounded griffin, but stopped. "I can't go over there!"

Kairaithin regarded Kes from the fierce, impenetrable eyes of an eagle. Then he stretched out his wings and brought the wounded female griffin from where she lay, shifting her through the desert afternoon to lie close by Kes's feet.

Riihaikuse Aranuurai Kimiistariu lay almost upright, in a near-normal couchant position, but her head was angled oddly downward and she panted rapidly. Her eyes were glazed with pain, or even possibly with approaching death. Crimson blood rolled down from savage wounds, scattering as rubies and garnets across the sand.

See her whole, Kairaithin said, *or she will surely die.*

Kes wanted to weep like a child. But weeping would not bring back the dead, and anyway, she found, despite the pressure behind her eyes, that she had no tears. Nor would the death of Aranuurai Kimiistariu bring back the dead. It would be wrong to let her die. Wouldn't it be wrong? Kes hesitated one more moment. Then she let the wounded griffin's name run through her mind and her blood and held up her cupped hands to gather the hot afternoon light. But she did not at once kneel down by the bronze-and-black female, but glared instead at Kairaithin. "You'll take me to the injured man after this? *Next* after this? If he dies before I come to him," she said fiercely, "I won't heal any other of your people! Do you hear?" Even Kes herself did not know whether she meant this threat. But she tried very hard to sound as though she meant it.

Little kitten, you are grown fierce, said Kairaithin. His tone was amused and ironic, but he also spoke as though he approved. *No other of my people are so badly injured that they cannot wait. Make Aranu-urai Kimiistariu whole, and I will take you to the man of your own kind. Though it is, in all truth, a day for death, I, too, wish this man to live. An emissary to send to your king is precisely what I desire.*

Kes stared at the griffin mage for another moment. Then she knelt down to pour the rich light she held in her hands out across the griffin's injuries.

The injured man lay high atop the red cliffs, within the pillared hall. The stone roof blocked the direct sun, but the heat even in the shade was heavy—it seemed somehow more oppressive than it had been out in the open light. Opailikiita lay near the man but had, so far as Kes could see, done nothing at all to help him. Kes spared the slim young griffin hardly a glance before falling to her knees beside the man; she was barely aware that Kairaithin followed her, or that he had once more taken the shape of a man so that he would not crowd her when he looked over her shoulder. Her attention was all for the man.

She saw at once that he was badly injured. His arm had been gashed as though by knives; he was still bleeding from those wounds, though fortunately the blood flowed only slowly. Kes thought that his arm was also broken, though she was not sure. She was nearly sure the ankle was broken, though, from the swelling and the black bruising. Worse, the man's breathing sounded shallow and difficult, and there was a bubbling sound to it that suggested to Kes that probably ribs, too, had been broken, and that at least one had pierced a lung.

No one, so far as Kes could see, had done anything to help the injured man. But then, as far as Kes could see they hardly did anything to help one another either, except for lending an injured griffin their company. And Opailikiita had done that, at least. And he was still alive, so maybe the young griffin was actually doing something to help him after all . . .

Opailikiita bent her neck around and down to watch Kes as she opened the man's shirt and touched the terrible spongy bruising across his chest. *I have no power to heal*, she said, not quite apologetically. *I slowed the loss of blood. That seemed the same as for one of my own people.*

"Oh," said Kes, startled and remembering at last that the griffins could at least do that. "Thank you . . ."

"That was well done," Kairaithin said, glancing down at the injured man's arm with a strange kind of indifferent approval. "Another time, you will find that you might also block our desert from drawing the strength of earth from a wounded human. This is possible. One makes the barrier of one's own self."

Yes, said the young griffin, in a tone of surprised comprehension.

"One does not use fire to heal a creature of earth," Kairaithin said to Kes. "But you are uniquely poised between earth and fire. I do not know what you might find to do—either with fire or with earth."

Kes did not really hear him. She was frowning down at the man. She ran her hand across the stone, gathering a little red dust; then she let the dust turn to light within her hand. She knelt, then, holding light cupped in her palm and wondering what, precisely, she could do with it. Nothing of the man spoke to her; though she listened, she could not hear his name in the beat of her blood. She had known that griffins were creatures of fire and that they were nothing to do with earth; she had known that the fire magic Kairaithin had taught her to use was nothing to do with men. But she had somehow forgotten, during these few days in the desert, how very unlike men and griffins truly were. Now she did not know what to do.

The man's breathing had grown more labored, even in this small time. Bubbles of blood formed at his nostrils; blood ran slowly down from the corner of his mouth. He was going to die. If Kes might save him, she would have to do it swiftly; there was no time to think and think again, or to hesitate—and if she tried and failed, he would be no more dead than if she did not try.

Kes took a sharp breath and set her hands on his chest, both her empty hand and the hand holding light. She shut her eyes, listening for his name, for his heartbeat. But no matter how she listened, she heard nothing except his difficult breathing. It was worse still; it worsened every moment. He was surely going to die. Unless Kes could save him.

His blood did not turn to rubies as it fell in droplets to the hot stone; it flowed. There was no fire in his blood. Kes bit her lip and poured fire into his blood, as she had learned so recently to take it into hers. At first, his body fought the intrusion of the fire; he did not wake, but convulsed, and he made horrible, hoarse sounds. Kes flinched. But at least, she thought, he could still *make* sounds. So his lungs were not altogether ruined . . . Opailikiita put out a wide feathered eagle's foot and pinned the man down against the stone so that he would not injure himself further in his agony.

Kes almost stopped, almost drew back. But she knew sometimes a healer has to cause pain in order to heal; and though she hurt this man, she hoped healing might follow. She could not use fire to heal a creature of earth—so he had to stop being entirely a creature of earth, at least for a moment; and if *she* could take on something of both natures, then why not this man? And so she poured fire into him and through him, though he fought it; she made fire run through his blood as she had learned to allow it to run through hers. She altered his very nature, and though his body fought her, she persisted. And he had been much weakened. She felt his resistance break under the relentless assault of fire.

She could feel very clearly that if she persisted he would die, and that if she stopped he would reject the fire and revert entirely to earth, and then he would still die. But for just a moment, caught between those choices, the man held fire as well as earth. And in that moment, Kes poured light over him and through him and pulled him hard toward the wholeness she saw behind the broken body. And, under the touch of her hands and the insistent gaze of her eyes and the fierce pressure of the light, he became whole.

As he became whole, his true nature reasserted itself with violent force, and the fire poured out of him in a fierce blaze that, as Kes lost control of it, might have burned him badly. But Kairaithin reached past her and caught the fire, and sent it elsewhere before it could so much as singe the man's clothing.

The man took a long shuddering breath, but it was a deep and steady breath and there was no blood in it. The wounds were gone; there were not even scars to show where his arm had been torn, nor any shadow of bruises across his chest where his ribs had been broken. He did not open his eyes, not yet. But, Kes knew, he was no longer unconscious. He merely slept.

She stood up, shakily, and put a hand out to Opailikiita. The slim griffin was there, her wing tucking itself under Kes's hand, quietly supportive.

"Remarkable," Kairaithin said. His tone was more thoughtful than approving, and Kes looked at him sharply, but he said nothing else.

Yet he is, in truth, wholly a creature of earth, is he not? Opailikiita said, sounding a little uncertain.

"Yes," said Kairaithin. "Now." His bent a considering glance on Kes. "Will you see the other wounded? There are not so many, and none other so seriously injured. Still, they would benefit from your care. Will you come?"

"Yes . . ." But Kes gave the sleeping man an uncertain look, reluctant to leave him.

"He will live," Kairaithin said. "He will sleep for some time, I think. It is difficult rest you will have given him, *kereskiita*, teaching him to dream of a fire he cannot touch. But I think that will not harm him. You are safe to leave him for a little."

I will stay near him, Opailikiita volunteered, and stretched out like a cat on the hot stone. *I will watch him for you, little sister. I will block the desert from drawing his strength. I think I understand now the way to do that.*

"All right," Kes agreed. She was still reluctant, but she trusted Opailikiita. More, she found, than she trusted Kairaithin. She gave the griffin mage a wary look. "You'll bring me back here?"

"I will assuredly bring you back to this place," Kairaithin told her. "Kiibaile Esterire Airaikeliu will come soon enough to speak to this man. I think when our king speaks to the emissary of the King of Feierabiand, it might be as well if you were here, little fire kitten."

"Oh . . ." Kes winced a little at the idea of standing between the Lord of Fire and Air and the man; only . . . only she liked even less the idea that the man might wake here in the griffins' hall to find himself entirely alone, surrounded by griffins. *That* would be hard. Especially after he had watched the griffins kill all his companions . . . "All right," she said at last. "But I don't know how to speak to . . . to emissaries and great lords."

"You will do well enough," Kairaithin assured her drily. "Am I not your teacher?" He held out his hand.

Kes cast one more glance at the sleeping man and then stepped toward the griffin mage and let him take her hand.

There were indeed not many injured griffins this time. And, as Kairaithin had told her, they were not so badly injured, most of them. They were much, much easier to heal than the man had been; Kes found she barely had to think about what she did. This did not exactly surprise her. It seemed very reasonable that she should find healing the people of fire easy, after the struggle to heal a man of earth.

What did surprise Kes was how many of the griffins greeted her by name—by her fire-name. This time, they did not look through her, nor did any of them strike at her. They were not embarrassed, this time, for her to see them injured and weak—or Kes thought that perhaps that was the difference, or something like it, as nearly as a human woman could understand it. This time, the injured griffins knew her and spoke to her; not only the injured ones, but their *iskarianere* as well. They called her Keskainiane Raikaisipiike in fierce, joyful voices. Kes wondered what *exactly* that name meant. She did not, somehow, like to ask Kairaithin—if it drew partially on his own name, maybe it was too personal a question somehow? Maybe she would ask Opailikiita, later . . .

"When is Esterire Airaikeliu going to go to the hall?" she asked

Kairaithin nervously. "Will it be much later than this? Are there many other griffins to heal?"

Kairaithin glanced up at the sun, which still blazed hot and high above the desert, well above the western edge of the desert. "Not so much later," he conceded. "But that was the last."

Around them, the world tilted and shifted. Fiery winds whipped sand through the air, then settled. They once more stood in the hall of stone and sand, high above the desert. The man still lay where they had left him, though now his head was pillowed on Opailikiita's foot. The young griffin had stretched not only a wing above the man, but also a different kind of protection; Kes could see that the desert heat beat less harshly upon the shadowed stone where the man lay.

Along one edge of the hall, with here a foot or there a wing dangling casually above the height, rested the Lord of Fire and Air and his *iskarianere* Eskainiane Escaile Sehaikiu, and the red griffin who was their mate, Esterikiu Anahaikuuanse, and a griffin of pure shining white whose name Kes did not know. They had all been studying the human man. Kes thought Opailikiita was very brave to stay by the man and shield him not merely from the forceful heat of the desert, but also from those powerful stares, which, at least from Anahaikuuanse and from the white griffin held considerable hostility.

Now the king and all three of his companions turned their heads and regarded Kairaithin for a long moment, and then as one bent that implacable regard on Kes. She resisted an almost overpowering urge to step backward and hide in Kairaithin's shadow.

Keskainiane Raikaisipiike, said the king.

"Lord," Kes answered hesitantly, after she found a quick glance at Kairaithin did not yield any guidance.

What is this here? demanded the king, the power of his voice ringing through the hot air. *Do I understand you bent the nature of fire to repair injury to this creature of earth?*

Kes was too startled by what seemed a rebuke to answer at once. But then she was, to her own surprise, angry. She said, "I bent *his* nature, lord. Since it was fire that injured him in the first place, it seems only fair that fire should repair his wounds!"

The king and the red female both looked angry at this, though whether because Kes had used fire in such a way or merely because of her boldness, she could not tell. The white griffin looked savagely hostile. But Escaile Sehaikiu tipped his head back and laughed—silent, joyful griffin laughter that made Kes want to smile, though she was still angry. It occurred to her that in griffins, anger and laughter might not be so separate as they were in men, but then she did not know what to make of this realization or whether the insight might be important.

The white griffin said in a ferocious, deadly voice, *That is rightfully my prey, and nothing to give to a human woman.*

Kes flinched from its hostility, but Kairaithin said in his driest tone, "If one will make a fire mage of a human, it is hardly just to be astonished when occasionally she acts according to the nature of a human. You may well give up your prey to her and to me, Tastairiane Apailika. Why not? You may surely afford the luxury."

You claim this man, then, said the king, in a hard tone that silenced any response the white griffin might have made.

"I do. Will anyone challenge my decision?" Kairaithin walked across the hall and stood over the man Kes had healed, looking back aggressively at the other griffins.

Opailikiita folded her protective wing and drew away from the man, coming to join Kes. But her withdrawal was somehow nothing like a retreat; from her fierce stare, it was clear she would willingly take on all four of the larger and greater griffins to protect the human man—for Kes's sake, because Kes had left him with her. Kes buried a hand in the fine feathers of Opailikiita's throat, trying to draw bravery of her own from the brilliant courage of the slim griffin.

"He will wake soon," observed Kairaithin, not glancing down at the man. "And what shall we say to him when he wakes, O Lord of Fire and Air?" He returned the hot stare of the king with effortless power of his own. "Will any here declare that I was wrong to seek out this human woman and raise the fire in her blood?"

You remind us all of your prior right decision, said the king harshly. *Shall we believe that all your decisions are right?*

Kairaithin smiled, a thin, fierce smile with nothing of yielding in it.

At his feet, the man moved at last, groaned, and opened his eyes, blinking against the flooding light, powerful even under the shelter of the stone hall, staring around with a dazed, helpless expression. Without thinking, Kes stepped forward as the man pushed himself up. She knelt to touch his shoulder, that he should not find himself in this place altogether alone.

CHAPTER 6

In the dream, Bertaud had wings . . . cleverly feathered wings that could feel the most subtle shift of wind. He stared into the wind and saw it layered with warmth and greater warmth, heat rising where red stone underlay it. He turned, fire limning each feather of his wings as he curved them to catch the air. Below him, the red desert spread out in all directions: rock and sand, dust and silence; nothing moved upon it but the wind. Both the desert and the wind were his, and he loved them with a fierce possessive love. . . .

He lay upon red stone, in rich sunlight that pooled on the stone like molten gold; he stared into the hot brilliant light with eyes that were not dazzled. The heat struck up from the rock like a furnace, and he found it good. His wings were spread, turned to catch the sun. There could never be too much heat, too much light. . . .

He rode through a storm. The wind roared through his wings. He was flung upward by the violence of the wind; a wing tip, delicately extended, was enough to send him spinning sideways into a loop that carried him, at last, above the storm into clear air. He cried aloud with exaltation. His voice struck through the air like a blade, but against the bellow of the storm he could hardly hear even his own cry; yet somehow both his cry and the roar of the storm were part of the great silence of the desert. It was a silence that encompassed all sound, just as the violence of the storm itself was encompassed by the greater stillness of the desert . . .

He woke slowly. He did not hurt and that seemed strange, though he did not understand why he expected pain. Trying to move, he could not understand the response of his own body. It seemed the wrong body. He could not understand why he did not have wings and talons.

His . . . hands . . . yes, *his* hands . . . moved, flinching from unexpected grit and stone, but he did not know what he had expected. He opened his eyes, with some difficulty. The lids were gummy, sticky with . . . blood, he thought. Blood? There had been . . . there had been . . . an accident? A . . . fight?

He got his eyes open at last, scrubbed his arm across them, and looked up. Memory crashed back so hard it stopped his breath.

He was lying on stone, high above the world. Pillars of twisted red stone stood all about, supporting a roof of stone so that he lay in shade—a hot shade, so hot the very air seemed like the breath of a living animal. The great hall surrounded by these pillars was floored with sand; the desert breeze wandered in and stroked the sand into patterns on the floor. It was not a human place. He did not have to be told that it was a place for griffins, which they had somehow drawn out of fire and the desert.

And there were griffins in it: one that caught his eye immediately though it was not the nearest, dark bronze eagle forequarters merging seamlessly into lion rear, relentless golden eyes staring into his. Anger poured off it, like heat against his face. The anger frightened him. Yet Bertaud did not feel as . . . stifled, as stunned, as when he had first met Kairaithin before the battle. He could think, now. He thought he would be able to speak, if he came up with something worth saying.

Even so, it took an effort to tear his gaze away, to get himself up on one elbow and look around. A gold-and-copper griffin was there, bright as the sun, close by the side of the first. Another griffin, dark red, her feathers heavily barred with gold, lay couchant behind those two males. That one, too, seemed angry. Angry and fierce and ready to kill for any provocation, or no provocation. And a white griffin, quite near, far more terrifying, a griffin from whom Bertaud flinched reflexively before he even remembered why.

Then he remembered. He froze, trying to deal with that memory. The white griffin did not move. Its fiery blue eyes held his, utterly inhuman.

A hand touched his shoulder, and he flinched, turning his head. A woman knelt at his side. No. A girl. Hardly more than a child. *Kes*, he thought. Of course, this would be the girl Kes, who had frightened her family and friends by vanishing into the desert with an unknown mage and had not returned.

The girl's eyes met his with a strange openness, as though she had no secrets in all the world, and yet there was a silent reserve at the back of them that he could not see through at all. A heavy golden light moved in her eyes, a light that held fiery wings and red desert sand, so that it took him a moment to see that those eyes were actually a grayed blue, like Niambe Lake under a stormy sky; the color seemed very strange. He had expected her eyes to be the color of fire.

Then her gaze dropped. Untidy pale hair fell across her delicate face, and she drew back against the . . . shelter, he thought, odd though that seemed . . . the shelter of a slim brown griffin that curved its body behind the girl and curved a wing across her shoulder.

Behind the girl stood Kairaithin. Anasakuse Sipiike Kairaithin. The name slid through Bertaud's mind with a strange familiarity. Kairaithin still wore the shape of a man, yet he did not look like anything human. He stared back at Bertaud with pitiless calm, as though the stillness of the desert had settled in his eyes. He looked . . . satisfied. As well he might, Bertaud thought bitterly. But the griffin mage did not, at least, seem angry.

Bertaud got to his feet, slowly. But not painfully. Recalling his battle, if one could so describe it, with the white griffin, this seemed miraculous. He looked around again, incredulously, at the stone hall, at the waiting griffins, at the girl leaning against the griffin at her back, petting it as though it were a cat . . . at Kairaithin.

"Man," said Kairaithin, and waited, starkly patient.

Bertaud met his eyes with what pride he could find. The griffin mage stared back, something strange and not human in his eyes . . . a kind of hard, fierce humor that was not the humor of a man. Bertaud bent his head slightly before that black stare, acknowledging the griffin's power. "Lord."

Kairaithin tilted his head in satisfaction. "I would have brought you to this place without spilling blood out on the sand."

"And what place is this?" Bertaud steadied his voice with an effort.

"The hall of the Lord of Fire and Air." Kairaithin walked past Bertaud toward the bronze-and-gold griffin Bertaud had seen first. As he moved, he changed: rising, swelling, extending in all directions, the true form of the griffin emerging from the shape of the man.

He made a splendid griffin: large and heavy, with powerful shoulders and eyes blacker than the desert sky at night. His dark coloring made him yet more impressive: His wings, so heavily barred with black that little red showed through, mantled above a body the color of the dark embers at the heart of a fire. He said to Bertaud, *But here you are come, in the end, are you not, man?*

His voice as a griffin was very much like the voice he had as a man. It had the same hard humor to it. It slid into Bertaud's mind like a lion slipping through the dark.

Bertaud thought of too many things to say, and thought better of saying any of them.

The lord of the griffins stirred, hardly more than a slight ruffling of bronze feathers, an infinitesimal shift of his head. But he drew all eyes. His strength and anger beat through the hot air. He said, in a voice like the sun slamming down at noon, *Bertaud, son of Boudan. Do you serve the King of Feierabiand?*

Bertaud closed his eyes for a moment. He said carefully, "Yes." And added, "Lord."

The griffin tipped his head to one side, unreadable eyes fixed on Bertaud's. *Sipiike Kairaithin considers you might usefully bear a message from me to the King of Feierabiand.*

"I might," agreed Bertaud and, because he did not care to be taken lightly, "If *I* judged it useful; I am my king's servant, and none of yours."

The gold-and-copper griffin tossed its head back in what seemed a silent shout of intermingled laughter and anger; the red-and-gold one was merely angry. So was the griffin king, hard hot anger like a gust from a desert sandstorm.

His own pride held Bertaud still. The girl was not so proud. She drew aside, the brown griffin with her, and tucked herself down into a small space at the foot of one of the twisted pillars. Bertaud was sorry he had frightened her, and at the same time, incredulous that she should be in this place, in this company. He wanted badly to take her aside and ask her a thousand questions. He wished he was certain he would survive long enough to speak to the girl. He was not even confident he would survive the next moment.

Peace. Peace, said Kairaithin, sounding harshly amused, and all the griffins settled, slowly. *Man, take more care.*

"Do you take care for *my* pride?" retorted Bertaud, a little more sharply than he had intended, and made himself stare back without giving ground.

Are you free to come and go in this hall? The griffin waited a heartbeat, pitiless eyes holding the man's. *Then take more care.*

After a moment, Bertaud bowed his head. "Lord."

Your folk died well, said the gold-and-copper griffin by the king. His voice was swift as fire, fierce, proud . . . not kind, precisely. Generous, perhaps. Bertaud stared at him, wondering what death a griffin might find good.

It was a day of blood and fire, said the griffin. He seemed to mean, in some odd way, to offer comfort. *Though they were overmatched, your people fought bravely. You may have my name, to speak as you choose: It is Eskainiane Escaile Sehaikiu.*

"Thank you," said Bertaud, which seemed due. "Did you . . . are they all . . . do any still live?"

Certainly not, said the griffin. Eskainiane . . . Eskainiane Escaile Sehaikiu. His quick fiery voice held surprise, somehow even reproof. *We would not so offend their courage as to leave them living on such a day.*

"What?"

The griffin blinked, a slow sliding of feathered eyelids across amber-colored eyes. *Their dishonored blood would cry out of the sand that drank it in. We would hear their names in our dreams, in the voice of the wind through our wings.*

"Men are not griffins," Bertaud protested. He wanted to shout it. He managed a calm tone, somehow.

The coppery griffin looked at him with unhuman eyes that might have meant well, yet failed entirely to comprehend him. *Blood is blood.*

We have no need to take our counsels with men, the white griffin said, breaking in with angry impatience. His voice came like a knife edge against Bertaud's mind, like fire whipping through the dark— nothing like the blatant power of the king's voice nor the subtlety of Kairaithin's nor the brightness of Eskainiane's.

To Bertaud, this griffin's voice was like a physical assault. He shut his eyes to keep from flinching from it, found his physical balance compromised, and shamed himself by staggering. He steadied himself only with difficulty because there was nothing close enough to catch hold of. It was very nearly as disorienting as his first encounter with Kairaithin, and he had believed himself past that strong a reaction.

We shall do as we please and as we must, and let this human king send men against us if he does not care for what we do, said the white griffin, and again his voice seemed to Bertaud like a blow, although the griffin was not even looking at him.

We would do better, Tastairiane Apailika, to have a care for what men might do, said Kairaithin. *Or why are we here building a desert in this foreign land?*

Peace. The king's powerful voice slammed down across the whole hall, silencing all dissent. Bertaud swayed with the force of it. *Man. Bertaud, son of Boudan. Will you bear a word from me to the ear of your king?*

"Certainly," Bertaud said, staring at him, trying to keep his voice steadier than his undependable body. "If you ask me. What word, O Lord of Fire and Air, would you have me take to my king?"

We forbid men from our desert. We will tolerate no intrusion into the country we have made. In return, we will not hunt men. What will your king say to this word?

Bertaud said honestly, "He will not accept it. He will bring a thousand men against you, or hire Casmantian mercenaries if he must, and drive you back across the mountains."

He expected anger, hotter and more dangerous than before. Strangely, it did not come. The griffins spoke among themselves . . . He could distinguish words and phrases and the odd uninterpretable image. But it was like listening to a quick interchange in a foreign language one barely knew: He knew he missed far more than he understood.

The griffin king said, *What then will he offer?*

It dawned on Bertaud that he was, in fact, negotiating with the griffins . . . just as Iaor had desired, although not from the position of strength they had both expected. But negotiating. He saw that the griffins had made, not an ultimatum, but a first offer. Like merchants bargaining over a length of cloth or a jeweled ring. He was astonished. He said instantly, "My king will forgive your incursion into his land, if you go at once. You may depart in peace."

That is not acceptable, said the griffin king. *We will hold this country hereabout for four seasons, until the heat of the summer rises again, and hunt as we please among the pastures of men and the woodlands of these hills.*

The overwhelming power of his voice made it seem, again, like an ultimatum or a threat. Forcing himself to disregard this impression, Bertaud countered, "You must go south, to the lowlands beyond Talend, where there is little farmland to be ruined. You may stay in that country until the leaves turn, provided you hunt only in the forest and the hills, leaving be the pastured beasts."

There was a short pause.

We will stay in this desert we have made, stated the griffin king. *But we will stay only three seasons, until the light dies and then quickens anew in the rising year. But we must hunt, and there are no desert creatures here for us.*

Unexpectedly, the girl stood up. The slim brown griffin rose with her, gazing at the larger griffins over the girl's shoulder. It seemed the girl, unlike Bertaud, had been able to follow the speech of the griffins, for she said in a low voice that was hardly more than a whisper, "Kiibaile Esterire Airaikeliu, Minas Ford and Minas Spring and Talend—and Bered—all the small towns and villages will give your people a dozen cattle. Two dozen. We will drive them into the high desert you have made and give them to you. So you can leave be the animals we value more." She glanced quickly and nervously at Bertaud. "Lord, it would be better so."

Bertaud stared at her. So did the griffins, but though Kes blushed and dropped her eyes away from his, she did not seem to mind their savage attention.

Six for each month that we stay, said the king of the griffins, to the girl. *And we will not withdraw until the light quickens in the next year.* He swung his fierce head around and stared at Bertaud out of fierce black eyes. *Agree, man, if you are wise.*

The memory of a hundred men butchered like oxen suggested a stiff refusal, followed by a punitive expedition—even if Iaor had to hire Casmantian mercenaries to help deal with the griffins Casmantium understood better than Feierabiand. But the sober knowledge that it was they themselves and none others who had been responsible for leading their men against a foe they had calamitously underestimated, argued otherwise. And he, who might have overruled Jasand, was most to blame.

Kairaithin had tried to bring him here, before the . . . battle. The attempted battle. If he had come—if he had not let Diene's fears overrule his own inclinations—Bertaud deliberately shut down that thought. It was one to endure on sleepless nights. Not, by any means, one to entertain while in the midst of serious negotiations.

He said, "There are small villages and homesteads through all this country."

We will not trouble them, said the griffin king.

"And you have ruined enough land. Your desert is wide enough."

The griffins stirred. The red-and-gold female opened her beak and made a low, aggressive sound. The king did something that was like a silent, motionless hammer blow, and she was suddenly still. All the griffins were still.

We shall contain the desert as we can, said Kairaithin. *It is a considerable concession, man,* he added impatiently. *Agree, if you would be wise.*

Bertaud inclined his head. "Subject to my king's approval, I do agree. However, the king's honor will demand suitable recompense for the damage and trouble you have caused him."

The honor of men, said the white griffin, contemptuously.

"If you seek peace with Feierabiand," Bertaud said flatly, "you will recognize that we have our own honor, even if it is not the same as yours."

Kiibaile Esterire Airaikeliu did not, at least, strike him down immediately where he stood for his temerity. Bertaud thought the white griffin would have liked to. But the griffin king did not move, and Kairaithin said, *We shall consider what you say. Perhaps you may have a suggestion regarding what your king might find suitable remuneration.*

For a moment Bertaud's mind went entirely blank. He could think of absolutely nothing Iaor might consider acceptable that griffins might supply. It seemed, in fact, a question for mages. If a mage could be found who did not despise the desert and actually knew something of its creatures. He said temperately, "I shall inquire. When I bring your word to him."

"Rubies," said Kes, again breaking in unexpectedly. "Fire opals. Sparks of gold."

Bertaud stared at her. But Kairaithin said, *We might indeed part with these echoes of blood and fire, if these would please your king. If he is wise, he will indeed ask for such small tokens. Will you permit me to take you to him? Will you give him this word?*

"Yes," said Bertaud.

At sunset, then. Kairaithin stood and stretched himself like a great cat. He shook his feathers into order. He was suddenly gone: The hot, close air seemed to hesitate an instant before closing into the space where he had been.

One by one the other griffins rose and paced to the edge of the open hall and dropped off the edge of the cliff into the wind. The white griffin went first. Bertaud found himself surprised by the strength of his own relief at that creature's departure. Then the red-and-gold griffin, and the gold-and-copper one, and last the king.

Their departure left Bertaud alone in a hall of twisted red stone and sand, with a girl who spoke to griffins with amazing familiarity and a slim-bodied brown-and-bronze griffin. The relief of the departure of the other griffins was so great that it took him a moment to realize the brown one was still present, for all it was the size of a small horse and undoubtedly capable of tearing an unarmed man in half, if it wished. Which it did not seem to. It stood by the girl like a dog, or a friend. She had her hand on its neck, as though for comfort and support—in fact, precisely as though it were a dog. Or a friend.

The girl did not *look* like a mage. Nor like the kind of vile, treacherous, death-loving creature who would deliberately let a hundred men go to be slaughtered by griffin savagery and desert fire. In fact . . . in fact, if Bertaud had passed her on the streets of Tihannad, he thought he would not have so much as glanced her way. Though, to closer inspection, she was not without a certain waiflike attractiveness.

She ducked her head as he studied her, closing in upon herself. Her hair fell forward and hid her eyes. The griffin with her stared at Bertaud with pale, fierce eyes, startling in its dark face.

He said, "Kes. Am I right?"

"Yes," she whispered, not looking up.

She was shy. She looked timid as a fawn. And yet she stood in a stone hall above the world with a griffin at her back and had spoken to the powerful, dangerous king of griffins by name.

"Why are you here?" he asked her directly.

The girl glanced up, and dropped her gaze again immediately.

She is a powerful . . . healer, said the small griffin. Its voice was subtle, soft; it came unobtrusively around the edges of Bertaud's mind. *She made you whole.*

Bertaud flashed on the shining white griffin, leaping down from the rock above to come against him after it had cast him down from that height. He had known he was going to die. The memory was vivid enough that he was forced to sit down rather suddenly and lean his head on his hand. He had been badly hurt. He knew that. He remembered a blow that he thought had crushed his ribs, and put a hand involuntarily to his chest. It seemed momentarily beyond belief that he could draw breath, that the bone and flesh under his hand was not even bruised.

And this girl had healed him. So she was a mage, then, after all.

The girl lifted her eyes again, tentatively. "Kairaithin said he wanted you whole. He told me I might use fire to heal you, even though you are a creature of earth. I thought at first I would not find a way to do that. Then I did. It was hard. I thought you might . . . might die of it. But if I hadn't done it, you would have died anyway. And then it worked after all."

"Yes." Bertaud touched his chest again. "Thank you."

The girl gave him a tiny nod. "I was afraid for you. Even after you were whole. Tastairiane Apailika said . . . He said you were his prey. But then Kairaithin made him give you to me."

"He's very powerful," Bertaud said, trying for a neutral tone. "Kairaithin. Isn't he?"

"Yes, lord," the girl answered faintly. "But he has no power for healing. So he told me. He brought me to see the battlefield after the battle was done." She met his eyes with what seemed to be an effort of will. "It was terrible to see everyone dead. I was afraid you would die, too."

But she had healed him. He could not even decide whether he should be grateful. He asked again, trying to sound gentle, "But why are you here?"

She looked at him with a trapped expression. "It would have been wrong to let them *die.* Wouldn't it?"

She was asking *him?* Then it dawned on him what she was saying. "You came up here to heal the *griffins?*"

The girl nodded.

"And now they will not let you leave them?"

"Kairaithin said he thought there would be a battle. I thought he meant with the Casmantian mages. I was . . . I didn't know . . . I think I didn't *want* to know he meant with you. And then he brought me to the place where everyone was already dead. Then I understood. But then it was too late."

"I see."

"All the men were already dead! What good would it have done to let the griffins die, too? How could I let them die?"

Bertaud did not try to answer this.

The girl went on, hesitantly, "Kairaithin told me he tried to talk to you, lord. He said the mage you brought with you hated him. He said you shouldn't have brought a mage. He said she feared him, so that he could not speak to you. Or he would have. I think he would, truly. He brought me to heal you, though he did not know whether I would find a way to do it." She stopped and glanced at him and then away again, seeming afraid that he might be angry.

Bertaud said with difficulty, not knowing whether he believed it or not, "It's not your fault." He walked away, stood at the edge of the hall, looked out over the red desert, and thought about what the girl had said. And what he had answered. He thought it was the truth—both times. What had happened *hadn't* been her fault. He knew whose fault it had been. He should have left Diene with the men outside the desert and walked back into it himself . . . He had not. And so. One dealt with the choices one made. And the consequence they carried with them.

Bertaud sat down next to a pillar at the edge of the cliff, laced his fingers around his knee, and stared out into the air. There were no griffins in sight. Except the one with the girl. The girl . . . "You're from Minas Ford?" It seemed very strange that a powerful mage should also be a timid little girl from a small mountain village.

She nodded.

"Who's your friend? I presume it *is* your friend?"

"Opailikiita Sehanaka Kiistaike. She is my friend." The girl stroked the rich brown feathers of the griffin's neck, and the griffin curved its head around and nibbled Kes's hair gently.

"And Kairaithin?"

"Anasakuse Sipiike Kairaithin . . . is not my enemy."

"No?" He glanced at her sidelong. "You . . . do you speak their tongue, Kes?"

The girl was seeming calmer at last. She came over and sat down near him, her back against the striated surface of the next pillar over. "I understand it a little. Opailikiita is teaching me. She says it is a good language for fire magecraft. Part of it is the language of fire."

"I didn't know that human mages could be fire mages."

Neither had the girl, or so her quick downward glance seemed to suggest. She glanced up again, though, and said cautiously, "Kairaithin said I would have been an earth mage. Only he showed me fire instead. He said he could do that because the earth magecraft hadn't woken in me yet. He was looking for someone like me, but he said he didn't expect to find anyone. Only he found me, after all. He says I have both natures, now. I suppose . . . no." She met his eyes. "I know that is true, lord. I feel it is true."

Bertaud nodded slowly. He thought he, too, could simply look at the girl and see it was true; he could see the fire in her eyes. "Well, Kes. So what should I tell my king?"

"That they will do as they say," the girl answered at once. "Or . . . as Kiibaile Esterire Airaikeliu says they will. Kairaithin says they would fly in all directions if their king did not choose their direction and call them all to ride the same wind. That's why . . . I don't know. I think that's why he told me it was important to heal the king."

Yes, said the small griffin. Opailikiita. *The people of fire follow the fire. The Lord of Fire and Air and the Lord of the Changing Wind guide the flight of the people of fire.*

"The Lord of the Changing Wind?"

"Kairaithin," explained the girl. "He is the only fire mage they have left. I think mages are as rare among the griffins as among men. And Kairaithin was always the strongest. So he is very important. I wish . . . I wish you had listened to him." She added hastily, "But of course you would trust the mage you brought with you. Kairaithin told me earth mages can't bear fire mages—I suppose he has trouble enduring the presence of earth mages, too, only he's too proud to show it. But if your mage told you not to listen to the griffins, it's not your fault."

It most certainly was. Bertaud did not say so. It was a truth that would return, he was certain, to whisper in his ear in the days to come. "Casmantian soldiers attacked the griffins in their desert and drove them across the mountains. Is that right?"

Yes, said Opailikiita.

"And that is why you have only one mage left?" Bertaud asked the griffin directly.

Yes, she said. *The Casmantian mages of cold earth were very strong. We did not know they came until they were upon us. Our fire mages stood against them to give the people time to fly. The halls broke behind us. The cliffs fell. The wind blew cold where our desert had once burned.* She spoke with a simple directness that somehow evoked the terror and grief of that night . . . Bertaud could almost see it, in the dark behind his eyelids: red cliffs crumbling in a cold gale, griffins pitting the strength of their fire against the violent cold . . . He blinked, imagining men cloaked in black walking toward him across sand that froze beneath their feet, hurling darts tipped with ice at blazing griffin mages. Fires going out in the dark, one by one. He blinked again, shaking his head, and found both Kes and the griffin looking at him curiously.

"But you will go back across the mountains," he said to the griffin, not quite a question. "And face those cold mages. What *is* a cold mage? A kind of earth mage, isn't that right?"

Yes, said Opailiikita. *Earth magecraft is always opposed to fire magecraft, and a human mage who truly sets himself against fire can turn cold. But we must strike fire through the cold, so Kairaithin says, or perish in the end. So we will do as we must.* The griffin spoke very simply, though Bertaud only understood a little of what she said.

Bertaud thought he recalled one or two glancing references he'd seen or heard to earth mages who specialized in a strange winter magic and drew power from the dormant earth. It had seemed strange to him at the time. But if an earth mage should happen to want to fight griffin magic, the specialty suddenly made sense. And if cold mages were so strong, he wondered at the griffin's optimism. But he said only, "I will tell my king what you say."

"Tell him," the girl said earnestly, "that we can spare the cattle. The griffins need to hunt. It's part of . . . part of being a predator of fire."

"He'll make good your loss." Iaor would, in fact, feel bound to, for the sake of his royal honor, if he allowed the folk of this region to feed the griffins until next spring. If he did not decide instead that his pride could not bear them in his country even for so long. Which he might. It was his pride more than any that would be offended by the destruction of his soldiers. "I *wish* it had not come to battle!"

It was a day for death, said the griffin, in a tone that suggested she meant this to be comforting.

Both Bertaud and Kes looked at her. Kes said to him, "Sometimes I don't understand them, either. Most of the time. Almost all the time."

Bertaud nodded.

"But . . . she has a good heart."

He understood what the girl meant, and felt, strangely, that she was even right. But he was not sure why he thought so. He was uneasily aware that this feeling was akin to the impulse he had felt to go with Kairaithin during their first meeting. To trust a creature that he knew was not a man, was nothing like a man . . . a creature of fire, alien to the shape he wore. But then he had doubted all his impulses. And now . . . he doubted them more than ever.

It would not be long until sunset, he thought, looking out into mountains that rose red and dusty in the near distance. He shut his eyes and leaned against a red pillar. And tried to keep images of blood and death from invading the darkness behind his eyes. But the images were persistent, so that eventually he gave up and opened his eyes again. "Why sunset?" he asked, not even knowing whether it was the griffin he asked or the girl, or why he thought either of them would know. Or care to answer.

"Because the shadows are longest then," Kes answered. Her soft voice sounded distracted. She was gazing out over the desert. "Because the wind dies in the evening. The direction of the wind is easiest to change when the air is still."

Bertaud studied her. "Come with me, Kes. Speak to the king yourself. You . . . I think you would be very persuasive."

The suggestion shocked her. Her eyes widened. "I could never . . . oh, no. No, lord. I am sorry. I could never . . . You must understand, lord," she said earnestly, "I could never speak very . . . well."

And if she would change her mind, what would Kairaithin permit? Bertaud frowned at her and leaned back against his pillar. Before them, shadows stretched out across rock and sand. The lower slopes were already in darkness, though the mountains themselves still glowed with a red light, as though lit from within.

Kairaithin returned to the hall on that thought. He came out of the lowering light: a griffin the color of glowing embers, face and wings black as char. The stroke of his wings across the empty desert sky drew fierce music from the wind, which seemed to rise to meet him.

As the griffin mage came down, he dwindled. His wings beat one last stroke, wind singing like a bell through the open stone hall, and closed round him like a cloak. The wind he had brought with him died, leaving behind a silence that felt like the silence after music. Kairaithin, black cloaked, turned his human face to them. His shadow stretched out long and low behind him, molten as a banked fire. Its eyes gleamed with fire-haunted darkness.

The griffin mage's own eyes were the same: black, secretive, opaque. Bertaud could see nothing in them. Yet he could meet them only with difficulty. He got slowly to his feet.

Kes stood also, with a shy downward glance. Bertaud was shaken by the idea that a girl so fragile and timid should somehow own power. He could not imagine her defying Kairaithin or the griffin king; indeed, Bertaud could not imagine her defying anyone who so much as shouted at her. She would never be able to use her strength for Feierabiand. She would stay meekly in the griffins' desert, and the griffins would rule her.

He said urgently, "Kes. Please come with me to Tihannad. I swear to you, Iaor will be kind to you. We will need you so badly. Who else is there to explain the griffins to us? Please come." He thought perhaps Kairaithin would say something to him then, or to her: a threat, a warning, a simple refusal.

But the griffin mage said nothing. He turned his powerful gaze on the girl and lifted an ironic eyebrow.

Kes only shook her head, leaning back against the dark bulk of her griffin friend.

"She would not be comfortable to do as you ask," Kairaithin said to him, matter-of-factly. And to the girl, "Would you, *kereskiita*? Would you go to the king of Feierabiand, as this lord suggests?"

Kes shook her head, still not speaking.

"You keep her here against her will. To act in your service, against her own people." Bertaud tried to keep anger out of his tone, to speak as calmly as the griffin.

"We refrain from hunting men here. So," said Kairaithin, tone dry, while Kes looked steadfastly down at the stone where she sat, "do we establish partiality toward our *kereskiita*." The mage held out his hand to Bertaud. It might have been a command, or an invitation. This time, there was no earth mage to warn him against griffin intentions. And nothing to do but yield to them, whatever warnings his own rationality might suggest. Bertaud slowly came forward and took the offered hand.

Kairaithin's thin mouth crooked in austere amusement, or approval, or . . . something else less recognizable. He closed a hand on Bertaud's shoulder, his grip powerful as an eagle's talons, and around them the world moved.

Bertaud staggered. Only the mage's grip on his shoulder kept him on his feet. The air was suddenly much colder; it smelled of moisture and growing things. Even though the sun was not quite below the horizon, it was much darker without the mountains to cast back the late sunlight. Loose water-rounded pebbles made treacherous footing. The gray waters of Niambe Lake washed over the pebbles, running nearly up to their feet, with a low murmur entirely different from any sound of the desert. The unguarded wall of Tihannad rose against the sky less than a bowshot from where they stood.

Kairaithin let him go. Bertaud backed up involuntarily, realized what he was doing, and stood still with an effort. The mage tilted his head slightly. His expression was impossible to read. Bertaud thought that even if the sun had been full on his face, the griffin mage's expression would have been impenetrable.

"Will you think well of us, man?" asked the griffin. His tone, astonishingly, might almost have been wistful.

Bertaud stared at him, taken utterly aback. "How can I?"

"Try," Kairaithin advised. He turned his head toward the west, looked into the last light of the sun, and was gone.

CHAPTER 7

The young lord stepped freely forward into Kairaithin's grip, going to carry word of the griffins to his king. Kes admired him: He was, she thought, not really *so* many years older than she was. But *he* was brave. She knew he was afraid of Kairaithin and she thought that, in his place, she would not have been able to come forward with such courage.

Though she understood that, she did not understand *him*.

He would go to his king . . . her king, too, Kes supposed, but this was so strange an idea that she dismissed it almost at once. He would take to the king his memory of Tastairiane Apailika as well as Kairaithin, and the great Lord of Fire and Air . . . of her, even. And what image of her would he carry to his king? She wondered about that distant king—what was he like? Was he proud? Violent? Did he fear battle, or long for it? Was he clever, or wise? Or neither?

What would this king say to the lord who came to him from this airy hall? Would the king even listen to a man whom he had sent here, who had lost all his companions and returned alone?

And if he did listen, what would the lord tell him?

If she had gone there, what would she have told the king? Kes sighed. If she had known what to say, perhaps she would have found the courage to go. If Kairaithin had permitted her to go. Kes stared out into the desert night. The wind smelled of hot stone and silence.

Opailikiita's voice slid into her awareness, oddly tentative. *Are you well?*

"Yes," said Kes, quite automatically. Then she asked herself the same question and did not know the answer. She sighed again and stroked the slim griffin's neck, ruffling the feathers gently against the grain so that she could feel them settle back. In the darkness, Opailikiita was perceptible mainly as a stirring of heat, a puff of breath. "Would you take me home?" Kes asked her.

Kairaithin has forbidden it.

Kes hesitated. Yet, somehow . . . she did not feel that this statement, plain as it was, carried quite the force it might have. "Yes," she said. "But would you do it anyway?"

Opailikiita curled her neck around and touched Kes lightly on the cheek with the tip of her deadly beak; it was a caress, and Kes smiled and moved to lean against the griffin's shoulder.

Kairaithin is my siipikaile, said the griffin. *But you are my sister, and I would not hold you here if you did not want to stay. But is the desert not your home? And is Kairaithin not your* siipikaile *as well?*

Kes shook her head, but not exactly in denial. Perhaps griffin mages never asked whether you were interested in becoming an apprentice, whether you wanted to learn how to make the fire and the rising wind part of your soul, whether you wanted to belong to the desert. Perhaps a griffin only saw that you could hold the power he needed even when you did not know it yourself, and made sure you would learn to use it according to his needs.

Are you angry? Opailikiita sounded curious, but not disturbed by the prospect.

Kes wasn't angry. But longing rose in her, for the simple human house she had shared with Tesme, for the whicker of mares in the low pasture and the homey smells of cut hay and new bread instead of hot stone and dust. She shut her eyes against the heavy darkness and whispered, "I want to go home."

Then I will take you, said Opailikiita. *As far as it is possible to go.*

Riding the griffin was not like sitting on a horse. There was no saddle, no stirrups, but the difference was more than that. The feathers under Kes's knees were soft and fragile. Kes found herself afraid to hold the feathers of the griffin's neck too tightly, lest she harm her.

You may grip tightly, Opailikiita said, and leaped from the rock with a great leonine bound, sudden enough that Kes bit her tongue.

It was not like riding a horse at *all*. The jarring lurch when the griffin opened her wings to the wind nearly threw Kes off. She swallowed a gasp and held tightly with hands and legs.

The high pasture above the house had become desert. The trees that had been there were gone—not dead, but gone, as though they had never grown there. The grass had withered and blown away; even in the lower part of the hill pastures the grass had become sparse and thin. But on the other side of the creek that ran through the midlands pasture, the grass grew thick and green, as abrupt a change in the landscape as though the little creek separated countries that lay a thousand miles apart.

Opailikiita did not cross the creek into that cooler country, but came down to the ground on its desert side. Kes swung her leg across the griffin's neck and slid off her back onto legs that seemed inclined not to hold her; she put an arm over Opailikiita's neck for balance and support.

Can you cross into the country of earth? asked the griffin.

Kes looked at her without comprehension. She straightened gingerly away from Opailikiita's support and walked carefully, then more quickly, to the creek; before she quite came to it, it occurred to her that Opailikiita was not with her, and she turned her head to look inquiringly over her shoulder.

That was perhaps why, when she struck the barrier of cold air at the edge of the creek, it was so unexpected that it knocked her entirely off her feet. She sat, dazed, on parched ground at the edge of the desert and stared, mute with bewilderment, at the water lying inches from her feet.

Kairaithin has put a binding on you, that you shall not leave the desert, said Opailikiita. She did not sound precisely sympathetic. Her tone held something more akin to the satisfaction of someone who has had a shrewd guess confirmed. *You will be angry now. Do not fight him. You do not have the strength.*

Kes was not angry. But she wanted to weep in frustration and disappointment. Looking down the hill, she could see the lights in the windows of the house, small at this distance. She should have been able to walk to it in minutes. It was utterly out of reach. Kes stood up and put out a hand toward the creek. She found that she could not even reach out over the water. The barrier she could not see prevented her.

I will take you to the heights, said Opailikiita. *I will bear you so high you feel the starlight on your shoulders, so high the air shatters and fire comes down to scatter through your feathers. It is very beautiful.*

Kes barely heard her. She looked at her own hand, stretched out toward the creek, unable to reach further. She was aware, faintly, that she was shaking.

Sister, said Opailikiita.

"*You* aren't my sister." Kes turned her back to the griffin and walked away from her, away from loss and confusion, into the stillness of the desert night. When she felt Opailikiita move to come after her, she began to run. She found she *was* angry—angry with Opailikiita, with Kairaithin, with all the griffins, with herself; she hardly knew. Rage, bright and unfamiliar, ran through her in a quick hot wave, like a fire cracking through the dark. The strength of it frightened her. She did not want Opailikiita's company, but it was terror of her own anger that made Kes find a way to shift herself through the world, far from the banks of the creek, into the endless desert silence.

Kes had not known she could do this until she did it, but after it was done it felt as inevitable as taking a step. It was only a matter of understanding the movement of fire. The shifting endless movement of flame through air. That knowledge, which should have been foreign to her, felt as familiar as her own breath. And she found a sure knowledge of what she wanted, which was solitude and quiet.

Solitude Kes found at once. Quiet was longer in coming. The desert itself was quiet; it was within herself that Kes carried a clamor of rage, bewilderment, longing, and terror. She could step from one edge of the griffins' desert to the other; she could step away from the element of earth into the element of fire; but she could not find her way from this emotional storm into calm.

Thoughts of Tesme, of Minas Ford, of the creek she could not cross all beat painfully at her attention. Kes tucked herself down against the base of a great twisted spire of rock and pressed her face against her knees. Her eyes felt hot; she wanted to weep. But tears would not come. Perhaps she was too angry to weep. She wanted Tesme to hold her, to rock her in her arms like a little child. But Tesme was not here. Tesme was at home. Where Kes should be.

Except that, surrounded now by the silence of the desert, Kes felt the storm of anger and longing slowly subside. She thought that all trouble, all emotion, might fade at last into that great silence; that the desert stillness might encompass all things. Kes found in herself a great longing for that silence, and welcomed it as it closed around her. The silence of the desert muted memory and unhappiness. She thought, *The desert is a garden that blooms with time and silence*, but then could not remember where she might once have heard that line, or whether it was from a history or a work of poetry or a story that Tesme, perhaps, had told her long ago. Except it did not sound like it could have belonged to the kind of stories Tesme told.

Time and silence. Time and silence grew through the dark and flowered with a bodiless beauty that seemed almost to have physical presence. Kes stared into the stark desert night and waited to see what would blossom out of it.

That was where the cold mages of Casmantium found her, in the soft pre-dawn grayness that preceded the powerful sun.

The first Kes knew of the Casmantian mages was a darkening of the desert, a shadow that stretched suddenly across the sand, a colder and stranger darkness than the night itself had brought. Then, startled, she saw frost run across the sand at her feet and spangle the stone by her hand.

She scrambled to her feet. Space seemed to close in around her, as though the infinite reaches of the desert had suddenly become bounded. She shuddered and groped at her back for the steadiness of rock, but flinched from the chill of the stone she found under her hand.

A voice out of the dimness spoke words Kes could not understand. Kes could not see the speaker, but turned her head blindly toward him. It was not, to her ear, a pleasant voice. It seemed to her to contain ice and ill will.

Another voice, deeper and harsher and yet not so unpleasant, answered the first. Men loomed suddenly out of the grayed light, closer than Kes had expected. Frightened, it occurred, at last, to Kes to move herself through the world; yet when she reached for that way of movement, for the heat and stillness that balanced motion, she could find nothing. A coldness lay between her and that way of movement. She tried to call out in the manner of a griffin, silently, for Opailikiita or for Kairaithin, but her call echoed back into her own mind unanswered.

The first voice spoke again and laughed. The sound made Kes shiver. She understood suddenly that the cold voice belonged to a mage, and understood as well that she was terrified of him. He was nothing like Kairaithin; though he was a man and her kind, she thought the man infinitely more frightening than the griffin.

The harsh voice answered, and a man, his dark form bulking large against the sky, came forward and laid a hand on her arm. Kes flinched, terrified, from that touch, and at this the grip eased; the harsh voice spoke again, but this time there was reassurance in its tone. Kes could not stop shivering, but her fear also eased and she stopped trying to pull away. When the man put his hand under her chin and tipped her head up, though she shut her eyes, she did not resist. The man spoke, curtly, not to her; then again to Kes. His was the harsh voice, and yet he seemed to be trying to speak gently. He shook her a little, not hard, and repeated himself. She realized, slowly, that the sounds of the language he spoke were not entirely strange, and understood at last that the language the man spoke was the harsh, choppy Prechen of Casmantium, and that he was Casmantian. That all these men were Casmantian.

Other men, farther back in the dimness, spoke—to the man who held her, or to one another, she did not know. The cold one said something, and Kes flinched again and quickly opened her eyes, afraid that she would find the cold man close by her in the dark. But, though dimly visible, he was not too near.

The man who held her answered the cold one, but absently. His eyes were on Kes's face. He gestured abruptly, and torches were lit and brought forward; Kes found her heart leaping up at the friendly brightness of the fire, though she knew her relief was not reasonable. Her shivering eased, and she found herself able to look at her captor more steadily.

He was a large man, not tall, but broad. His hand on her arm was twice the span of hers. He was clearly a soldier. He wore armor—rings of steel showed under his shirt, which was of finer cloth than a common soldier would own, surely. His features were strong, as powerful as his deep voice. He wore a short beard, grizzled with gray where his hair was dark, which made him look somehow harsher still. But his eyes held only interest and a little anger, not cruelty. And the anger faded as he studied her.

He said to her, speaking this time in the language of Feierabiand, "What is your name? How old are you?" He spoke carefully, awkwardly, with a strong accent, so that at first Kes did not understand him. But he repeated himself patiently. She was surprised, even in her fear, at his patience.

"Kes," she whispered at last. "Fifteen, lord. Fifteen this spring."

Heavy brows lifted, and the man said something in Prechen, sounding surprised. Then he said to her, speaking carefully, "A girl. A child." And something again to the cold mage at his back.

"She is a mage, my lord, no matter her age; make no mistake about it," said the mage. He spoke quickly and easily, his Terheien effortless. The light of the torches showed that he was an unusually small man; indeed, he was hardly taller than Kes herself. Yet he did not seem young—nor precisely old. Kes thought he seemed somehow ageless, as though passing years had touched him only lightly. He might have been forty or fifty years old—or a hundred, or a thousand. Kes would have believed he had lived a thousand years; there was a depth in his pale eyes that whispered of long years and hard-won power. His features were fine, almost delicate; his hair, worn much longer than the soldiers wore theirs, was frost white.

Despite his small size, the cold mage seemed very much assured. He was smiling. Kes would have shied away from that smile, only the other man held her so she could not. "A fire mage," said the mage. "So they found a child on the cusp of power who might be turned from earth to fire. Who would have thought it?" He reached to touch her face.

Kes shrank with a gasp against her captor, hiding her face against his chest from the threatened violation of that touch.

The lord of soldiers held still an instant in clear astonishment. Then he closed a powerful arm around her shoulders, gently, and said something terse in Prechen to the cold mage that stopped the other man in his tracks.

The mage spoke in Prechen.

The big man shook his head at whatever the mage had said, then shook it once more, a curt gesture, when the mage spoke again. He said something to the mage in his turn, and then again to the other men in a tone of command. The men fell back and turned away, making ready to go . . . somewhere.

"Come," the man said to her, but kindly. His grip on her arm eased and finally fell away. "Will you come? Not try to run? I not—I will not hurt you." He added as an afterthought, "My name is Festellech Anweiechen. My honor would broke, would be broken, to hurt little girls."

His clumsy Terheien was oddly reassuring. Or perhaps, Kes thought, it was the careful way he tried to reassure her.

"All right," she whispered, and took a step as he directed.

They took her high into the mountains, out of the desert. Her promise notwithstanding, Kes looked for a chance to break away from the men and flee into the desert, but her captors were careful and no chance came. There were horses waiting with more men a little distance away. Kes thought she might be able to get away when she saw the horses, but she was not given one of her own. She was lifted instead to sit in front of the lord. Kes did not protest, but inwardly she felt despair; she knew she was trapped as surely as any rabbit in a snare. She would never be able to leap from the horse without the lord catching her, and even if she did jump all the way down to the sand, she would never be able to flee on foot from men on horseback. She could do nothing but make herself small and quiet and hope to see the bright, clean flight of a griffin across the brightening sky. But she saw nothing.

It seemed to Kes that they rode for a long time, always up and farther up, but she thought afterward that it could not have been so long, for the dawn had not yet fully arrived when they reached the place where the desert border lay against the mountain country. The cold boundaries around her mind seemed to close her in upon herself, so that she found it hard to think. But she knew that the binding Kairaithin had put on her must have been broken, and this cold binding put in its place. She knew the little mage must be very powerful, and she was more afraid than ever.

When the hoof falls of the horses changed from the soft muffled thud of hooves falling on sand to the sharper metallic ring of shod hooves on stone, she looked up. The air had seemed cold to her since the men had found her in the shadow of the red cliff. But the cold was different now, seeming deeper, more a true part of the world. The cold mage sat back in his saddle, small hands letting the reins fall loose on his horse's neck, seeming to relax from a tight-held tension Kes had not recognized until it vanished. Everyone seemed relieved. Men all around her laughed and spoke among themselves. They took cloaks from their saddles and put them on. Festellech Anweiechen threw his cloak around Kes without a word, riding bare-armed himself. Kes slowly pulled the cloak around herself. One kind of cold eased. The other kind did not.

They had come much higher into the mountains, she understood, and had crossed beyond the farthest edge of the griffins' desert into country no one, neither griffin nor man, claimed. There was even snow, glimmering white in the pale morning light. Kes had longed to wrench herself free of the desert, but she had wanted to go home, not be forced to ride up to a snowy pass in the high mountains. Now she longed for the desert, but it was behind her, and felt miles farther with each step the horses took.

At last they came to a camp. They rode past rank after rank of tents without slowing, and she saw that it was very large. The tent they came to at last was three times the size of the others and had men standing before its door, which was folded open to the night. They stopped in front of this tent. Lord Anweiechen dismounted and held up his hands for Kes as though she was a much younger child. She bit her lip and took his hands carefully, allowing him to catch her as she slid down the horse's shoulder. He took her into the tent, seeming oblivious to her nervousness.

More men came in—some who had come with them on the ride, and others, she thought, who had not. The cold mage was one who came in. Kes recoiled from him, but he did not approach her. She found herself whisked instead to one side, to a pile of cushions thrown across a thick carpet on the floor of the tent. Someone went around the tent lighting lanterns. Someone else passed around mugs of hot spiced wine, giving Kes a mug with a matter-of-factness that made her take it. She sipped it carefully. The spices were not the ones her sister would have used, and a sharp homesickness, distinct from the fear that had begun to ease, went through her. She bent her head over her mug, blinking hard. Men spoke among themselves and to Lord Anweiechen, who answered them cheerfully.

Then another man came in, and Lord Anweiechen rose to greet him with a quick attentiveness that caught Kes's attention. In fact, everyone rose, orienting to this man as naturally as flowers turn toward the sun. He was younger than Anweiechen, but not a young man: There was no gray in his beard, but he was thickset and powerful. He was clearly a soldier, metal showing at wrist and throat; he was tall as well as broad, with a heavy, rugged face that nevertheless did not seem cruel. Anweiechen spoke to him, and he answered in a friendly tone and clapped the man on the shoulder. So they were friends, Kes thought, and this newcomer was also surely a lord; indeed, everything about him proclaimed it. The cold mage inclined his head and said something to him, and again the man answered cheerfully, this time glancing aside at Kes where she sat among the cushions.

She could not understand them, and found herself looking down at the carpet on the floor. Except then nervousness made her look back up to make sure the little mage was not coming near. He was not. He had taken one of the chairs to one side of the tent, near a long table, and sat there, imperturbably smiling, with a mug of hot wine in his hand. He was not even looking at her. He laughed at something one of the other men said to him. Kes could not help shrinking from the sound of his voice.

The new lord noticed. He came over to her and stood frowning. Kes looked down. He said abruptly, in harshly accented Terheien, "I am Brechen Glansent Arobern. Do you know me?"

Kes mutely shook her head.

The lord tossed a wry look to Festellech Anweiechen and said something in Prechen. The older man grinned. Then the lord said to Kes, speaking slowly, "I am King of Casmantium. Do you understand me?"

Kes nodded cautiously, staring at him. He looked, she thought, like a king. There was a power to him like the power of the king of griffins. The other men in the tent moved around him with the same kind of awareness the griffins had for the Lord of Fire and Air.

"This *child* is a fire mage?" another man said, in slightly better Terheien. He also wore a beard—rare in Feierabiand—but his was brown verging on red, and considerably thicker than those of the other men. As though to balance the beard, his head was bald. Then Kes, blinking, saw that he did have hair, but that it was shaved very short all over his head. She realized she was staring, blushed, and looked down.

"So Beguchren assures me," said the king.

The man made an incredulous sound.

"She is indeed a fire mage," said the small mage, coolly, in his smooth Terheien. "Though new to it, I judge, and with nothing of the customary mage's training. The human training. A griffin mage must have woken fire in her when she was just on the verge of coming into her proper magecraft. He preempted the magecraft of earth before it could rise properly. Look at her shadow."

They all looked. Kes looked also. Her shadow, dim in the light, had been thrown out in several different directions because of all the lanterns. It swayed and flickered as the lanterns moved. Yet even Kes saw that it was edged with flame, that it stared back at the cold mage with eyes more fiery than lantern light. She blinked in surprise.

"So," said the king, in a thoughtful tone.

"I thought the griffins had no mages left," said Lord Anweiechen, his tone faintly accusatory.

"I, also," the frost-haired mage said mildly. He said to Kes, regarding her with composed curiosity, "Whoever he was, the griffin mage did you no favors, child. Did he tell you what would happen to your shadow if you reached out your hand to the fire?"

Kes did not try to answer. She looked helplessly down at the carpet, feeling very small, like a rabbit surrounded by wolves.

The king said something to the mage.

"Of course," he answered the king, but in Terheien. "I am not merely an earth mage, but a cold mage. Mages of fire and earth have a natural aversion toward one another at the best of times, but this girl has a greater antipathy toward me than she would even toward an ordinary mage of earth. She would fear and dislike me under far kinder circumstances than these, lord king." He hesitated, and then shifted to Prechen and spoke again.

The king frowned. He said to Kes, quite kindly, "Rest, child. Sleep a little, if you can. No one will hurt you. Certainly Beguchren will not." Then he turned away and went to the table, where some of the men joined him. Anweiechen took another of the chairs. Some of the other men did the same. Other men received orders from the king—that was clear from his tone and attitude—and left the tent.

One man came and stood near Kes. Like many of the other men, he wore a brown shirt with a black badge on the shoulder; metal links showed where the shirt laced up at the throat. He had a short sword at his side. He rested his hand on its pommel absently, but he did not look threatening when Kes glanced at him timidly. He gave her a brief smile, crossed his arms over his chest, and looked away. The understanding that he was a guard set on her by the king dawned on Kes slowly. But he did not seem unkind. Ignored by all the men, she even began to relax a little. Later still, she slept, and dreamed of flying through brilliant skies on pale wings that flung fire into the air with each downstroke.

CHAPTER 8

Bertaud found Iaor in his private parlor with his queen and only the barest handful of attendants.

The king gave Bertaud one assessing, incredulous stare and rose from his couch. Eles, behind him, cocked his head to one side and looked warily interested. Bertaud waited as the king murmured a word of apology to his little queen. He whispered something to her that made her blush and giggle, and she went out happily. She smiled at Bertaud as she left the room, a smile untouched by any faintest shadow of worry. She looked very young.

Keenly aware of his own youth and inexperience, Bertaud glanced after her. He found himself faintly aware of surprise that he had ever managed to be jealous of this girl, whom Iaor petted and reassured and dismissed like a child; the king had never treated him so—even when he had been a child. Now, far worse than the intrusion of the new young queen into Iaor's life was the new question of how much of Iaor's favor had ever been merited by a man incompetent enough to lose a hundred men and a mage in a single day's disastrous campaign. How much would be left, after this?

Gathering his courage, Bertaud told the king, in a few terse words, what had occurred in the griffins' desert, and how he had come to return to Tihannad alone. Eles, standing stolidly behind the king, jerked his head at a guardsman, who went out quickly. Eles folded his arms and looked grim.

The king, schooled from childhood not to wear his thoughts on his face, nevertheless looked stricken, to a man who knew him well. He slowly sat back down on the couch. Leaning his elbow on its arm, he looked at nothing for a long moment.

Bertaud hesitated, ashamed to ask for reassurance and yet unable to keep still. "Iaor . . . this isn't news I wanted to bring you."

The king glanced up. "Bertaud," he said after a moment. "I don't think you, or poor Jasand, can justly be held responsible for failing to anticipate what happened. It was I who sent a hundred men with spears and a mage, when it appears I would have perhaps done better to send you alone."

This was a far kinder judgment than Bertaud had expected, or was due. "I could have overruled both Jasand and Diene. I should have done."

"Why didn't you?" The king's tone still did not hold condemnation, only query.

"Iaor . . . I did not trust my own judgment in the matter." Bertaud hesitated, not knowing how to explain the confusion that had afflicted him in the griffins' desert. Not certain he wanted to try. No. He was certain he did not want to try. What he wanted to believe was that he wasn't obligated to try. But . . . Iaor would need to know what he faced.

After a moment, he said reluctantly, "That is not a comfortable desert for men. It is hard to think clearly with the red wind blowing. I mean that literally. I felt—I thought—this isn't easy to describe, but I didn't trust my own thoughts or feelings. The problem seemed—it seemed worse for me than for Jasand. And worse, or at least different, for me than for Diene. And as Jasand and Diene were in accord, it seemed better to trust their opinion than my own."

Iaor nodded slowly. "I will send you to Meriemne. She may understand the affliction you describe. Will you go to her?"

Bertaud hesitated. Diene had been . . . implacably hostile to the desert and the griffins. He found in himself a strong reluctance to face the eldest mage of Feierabiand and see in her seamed face the same hostility. But . . . the suggestion was only one step from a command, and if he didn't comply willingly with the one, he had no doubt the other would follow. He bowed his head obediently. "Of course, Iaor."

The guardsman returned, escorting General Adries, who had clearly been told the news. The general nodded grimly to Eles and took a quiet place to one side. The king acknowledged Adries with a glance, but spoke to Bertaud. "And so, now? What do you advise me to do?"

Alarmed, Bertaud shook his head. "Please. Don't ask me. I don't . . . I don't trust my own judgment even now. Truly, Iaor."

The king's eyes narrowed.

"You know what I will advise you," Eles said to the king, and asked Bertaud, "How many men would it take to do the job right and have it done?"

Bertaud felt a strong reluctance to even address this question. But he had no choice, and answered slowly, "I certainly saw more than a hundred griffins. I would not be surprised if there were several hundred there. If we expected them to be clever as well as big . . . a dozen companies ought to be able do it, with mages to keep the fire and wind away from the men. If your majesty," he added to the king, "thought that wise."

Iaor propped his chin in his hand and gazed at them both. "Bertaud," he asked again, deliberately, "what is it that *you* advise me to do?"

In a way, this insistence could only be seen as flattering. But Bertaud dropped his eyes, for once uncomfortable with the trust Iaor showed in him. Since the king demanded an answer, however, he tried to form one. He thought of Kairaithin saying, *Agree, man, if you would be wise.* He thought of the great force contained, barely, within the powerful griffin king. He thought of fire falling from the air like hail, and the flame-edged flight of griffins across the dust-veiled sky.

He thought of Kes, her hand on the shoulder of her friend, saying, *I don't understand her, but she has a good heart.* He thought of Kairaithin asking, oddly wistful, *Will you think well of us?*

He asked, "What will your honor endure?"

The king, relentless, returned the question. "What should it endure? What will you advise me?"

Bertaud let his breath out and spread his hands. "Leave them be for their year. That desert can be reclaimed by time and rain. The land won't be lost forever."

"Is that what you advise me? Shall I take the rubies I am offered and let men say I traded the blood of my men for a handful of gemstones?"

Bertaud winced, though he had expected precisely this reaction. He thought of the blood of a hundred men poured out on the red sand. He thought of a frail, elderly mage, flung through the air by a careless blow from a great white wing.

He thought also of Feierabiand, with sly Linularinum on one side and aggressive Casmantium on the other, and how both neighbors would surely think, *How strong can Feierabiand be, if Iaor Safiad makes accommodation with invading monsters and will not fight them even when they take his land? If Feierabiand will not guard its borders from griffins, perhaps it will not guard its borders from us?*

He thought of the rumors that must already have run to the Fox of Linularinum and Brechen Arobern of Casmantium, and knew Feierabiand was endangered by the presence of the griffins in the heart of their country, even aside from the damage done by the desert they had brought with them.

Against this there was nothing but the voice of an unlettered village child, saying helplessly, *But it would be wrong to let them* die.

Bertaud pressed the heels of his hands over his eyes, sighing. Then he dropped his hands and looked up. "My king . . . I see that you have no choice but to drive them out. But *I* wish you would let them be."

The king sat back in his chair, looking subtly dissatisfied.

"Iaor . . . I understand that Feierabiand must not appear weak, lest Casmantium or even Linularinum become overexcited. But I don't . . . I don't think you should take what happened with the griffins as provocation, or see their simple presence as affront, or necessarily go to great trouble to be rid of them. It was our fault. My fault. It's no reason to spill living blood after dead."

"Theirs was the provocation."

"They couldn't help it, Iaor."

"They could certainly have acted with greater restraint once they arrived in our lands. *We* are not the ones who drove them from their own country. Their arrogance here does them no credit."

Bertaud made a frustrated gesture. "You asked my opinion, Iaor. I told you I did not trust it. But I would not wish . . . if you will permit me . . . I would not wish to make the desert our enemy."

"Is it not our enemy now?"

"Not yet."

The king conceded this possibility with a slight tilt of his head.

"I am sorry to disagree with the esteemed Bertaud, but if these creatures make desert of our lands or kill the cattle of our people, then they are our enemies. And if we permit them their depredations, we will look weak," Adries argued, contributing to this debate for the first time. Adries was a younger man than Jasand, a quieter man, less experienced in the field, not given to braggadocio or showy gestures. But he had a gift for keeping a great number of details in mind at once, and so was trusted by Iaor to keep track of all the military matters that concerned both borders. He added now, "Save if they yield a great tribute to your hand, my king; and even if they did, could we trust them? They are not creatures of earth. They are foreign by their very nature."

Iaor Safiad glanced at Bertaud and turned a hand palm up. "My friend, you must know this is true."

Bertaud nodded. He did know it. Bitterness filled his mouth; he did not even clearly understand why. "I never guaranteed them peace from you."

The corner of Iaor's mouth twitched up. "I should think not."

"I had simply hoped for it."

"I am sorry, then, that I cannot follow that course. I will send

General Adries south. I must. Nor, though I regret this as well, will I ask you to accompany him when he goes."

And Bertaud knew that the king's regret was real. Not that it made the slightest difference. As a true Safiad, once decided on a course, Iaor committed himself fully. General Jasand was dead, but Adries remained. Iaor would send the younger general south, and spill blood once more to water the thirsty desert sands. Adries, warned by Jasand's example, would be cautious, but he would be determined: it was not likely to be only human blood spilled, next time.

Bertaud was grateful not to be asked to lead, even nominally, this second force. Grateful not to even be accompanying it. He *was* grateful, most determinedly. He would not allow his exclusion to feel like a slap; had he not repeatedly questioned his own judgment? How then could he blame Iaor for questioning it, too?

So he pretended to a calm he could not feel, and outlined the weapons of the griffins for Adries. Wind and fire; dust that stung and blinded . . . surprise.

"We shall have to summon a mage or two from Tiearanan," Adries said, acknowledging this warning with a serious nod. "And I shall ask several of the mages here to accompany us. I think that will reduce the effects of wind and sand. And surprise is a weapon you yourself give to your opponent. We shall endeavor not to give the griffins that weapon a second time."

Bertaud tried not to read this last comment as yet another judgment on his own recent performance. He knew Adries did not mean it so. He was simply a straightforward, quietly competent man who was determined to redeem the honor of Feierabiand. Bertaud understood perfectly. That he could not desire the general's success with a whole heart was not Adries's fault.

Bertaud understood very well whose fault it was. He was furious with himself for allowing the singing clarity of a griffin's flight across a lucent sky to echo in his memory. But that night, he dreamed that he rode on out-swept wings across fiery winds. In his dreams, he let exultant storms of sand and wind sweep him up to crystalline heights so dark and pure that even fire froze and shattered like glass . . . He woke in the morning startled by the earthbound heaviness of his own humanity.

Meriemne, eldest of all mages of Feierabiand, found his stumbling descriptions of the desert and the griffin and his dreams both interesting and troubling. She gave him tea and made him sit on the floor by her feet so she could rest the tips of her thin fingers on his cheek. Bertaud sat patiently, leaning his head against her knee. He felt as though time had scrolled backward and he had returned to this court as a boy of ten. Or as though that boy sat next to him, filled with fear and despair and barely acknowledged hope, not yet confident of the strength and constancy of Prince Iaor's protection. But in time, powerful bonds of loyalty and trust had grown between them . . . Had the man finally lost the trust with which Iaor had honored that boy? He tried not to even think about that question, focusing rather on the details of his encounter with the griffins.

Meriemne listened intently to Bertaud's recounting of what had happened in the desert, her blind old eyes aimed at his face as though she could see. She acknowledged, when Bertaud asked her, that a budding earth mage might, if caught just as her power began to flower, be twisted into other channels. "At least in theory," Meriemne said thoughtfully. "One can see how such a thing might be possible. That is technically quite interesting, but it *is* hard on the poor child. Does she know what long-term effects this, ah, alteration of her nature is likely to have?"

Bertaud had no idea what Kes knew, and could only guess what Meriemne meant. He shook his head. "I don't know, esteemed Meriemne. If it's true that earth and fire mages have a strong aversion to one another, then one would imagine it might be uncomfortable for a girl to be made into a fire mage when she ought to have been an earth mage?"

"Oh, the aversion is real enough," Meriemne agreed absently. "Natural affinities and antipathies are not unusual, you know. As the aversion of a songbird to a serpent, or the affinity of a raven to a wolf: There is a similar affinity between earth mages and young people growing into a gift for magecraft, you know; that's often the first hint of the coming gift. And then there is this deep aversion between mages of earth and those of fire. But no, I don't believe it will be uncomfortable, as you say, for the girl herself. More for those who love her, who find she has become something they cannot recognize . . . and a shame to lose her," the mage added more prosaically. "We can always use another earth mage."

But what had happened to Bertaud in the desert, Meriemne did not recognize.

"Not a deliberate attack," she said thoughtfully. Her fingers, cool and dry, moved across his face and drew away as she straightened in her chair. "Or I think not. It seems more an intrinsic response in you to the fire of the griffin. As the antipathy poor Diene experienced was intrinsic in her, and a mercy it is that only mages suffer such an aversion."

"I saw no sign that the griffin mage returned Diene's aversion," Bertaud said, suddenly realizing that this was true. "Or is it only earth mages who suffer it, and not mages of fire?"

"Oh, no, young man—the antipathy is a knife with two edges." Meriemne paused. "Hmm. This was an experienced mage, then, to rule his own reaction so well you did not even perceive it. Well, you say he took on human form. I wonder whether he is very experienced indeed with moving through the country of earth? Perhaps he has learned to recognize and compensate for the aversion? I would almost," she said thoughtfully, "wish to meet this creature. Though, on further consideration, perhaps not . . . You yourself did not suffer from the classic mage's aversion? No, indeed, what you describe is entirely distinct. Tell me, esteemed Bertaud, are you gifted at all? Have you an affinity for an animal? Or are you a maker? A legist?"

"No, esteemed Meriemne. Those of my family are rarely gifted." Though his father had held an affinity to hawks and falcons, and had been furiously angry when Bertaud showed not the slightest trace of any affinity of his own. Bertaud, wincing from the memory, did not mention that.

"Hmm." Turning her head, the mage stared into his shadow with her blind eyes. What she saw in it, if anything, she did not say.

"But the dreams?" Bertaud pressed her.

"Certainly the dreams you describe are unusual," the mage conceded. "I shall search in my books for such reactions."

With no guarantee she would find anything this year or next. And in the meantime—"What shall I tell Iaor?" Bertaud asked her.

"Hmm. Well, child . . . do you love the king better than you love the desert?"

"Of course!" he snapped, and then wondered at the instant offense he'd felt. Was it too sudden? Too sharp? A defense, perhaps, against his own heart? He dismissed the doubt at once, yet it returned, slipping uncomfortably around the edges of his thoughts.

"Then trust yourself," Meriemne advised serenely, either missing or ignoring this uncertainty, and he could not bring himself to give it voice and ask her advice. A baseless concern, anyway. An impossible doubt. Surely.

And so Bertaud went through the next days, and attended his king, and tried not to find the fixed stolidity of stone walls disturbing.

Three days after Bertaud's return from the disastrous field of battle, Iaor Safiad declared himself satisfied with the preparations for the second attempt to clear the desert from Feierabiand. But on that third day,

Bertaud found, to his astonishment, that the griffins had not waited for soldiers to come to their desert. Kairaithin came to Tihannad.

Kairaithin came, unannounced, into the large conference chamber where Iaor and his advisors and General Adries and Meriemne and one of the younger mages in Tihannad were all gathered, discussing last-minute details of the impending military exercise.

It was dusk. The desert wind, Bertaud thought, had no doubt died . . . From the heart of that stillness, Kairaithin stepped into human time. His black eyes, pitiless as fire, swept across all of them, checked for the space of a breath on Bertaud's face, and settled on the king.

"Iaor Daveien Behanad Safiad," he said, and took a short step farther into the chamber. He bowed his head infinitesimally. "May I speak?"

The king was startled, but not, Bertaud saw, afraid or angry. He said, "You should have given your name to my steward. Did no one stop you as you looked for me? This is a private meeting. You should have been told the proper day and manner in which to seek an audience."

At first bewildered, Bertaud finally understood that the king did not understand that the man who had come so precipitously into this conference was not a man. He could not see, or had not yet seen, the fire in those inhuman eyes; he had not yet noticed that the shadow the lanterns cast back from his visitor was made of fire . . . He was blind.

It slowly occurred to Bertaud that all the men in this room were similarly blind; even the mages were blind. The younger was looking with growing dislike at the stranger who had come into their presence, but Bertaud saw no sign in his face that he understood what he saw or felt. Only Meriemne, for all she was truly sightless, turned her head toward the griffin with a slow awareness in her old face. *She* looked, as yet, less hostile than simply distressed.

Rising so sharply his chair fell backward onto the stone floor, Bertaud found himself standing between his king and the griffin mage with no clear memory of having moved and no notion at all what he would do if Kairaithin intended harm to Iaor, or to any of them.

"Son of Boudan," Kairaithin said to him, pitiless amusement moving in his unhuman eyes. "So you have regained your place."

"Anasakuse Sipiike Kairaithin," Bertaud answered, and was surprised to find his own voice steady. "Why are you here out of yours?"

"Peace, man," the griffin mage said, turning empty hands forward. "I followed the path you made for me to speak to your king, if he will hear me."

Iaor had not risen, but his whole body had tightened. General Adries was on his feet, as were several of his officers. They were armed, and

Bertaud could only hope they did not draw their swords and, with that, Kairaithin's enmity.

"The path I . . ." Bertaud cut that startled question off short, and said instead, "Iaor, this is the greatest of the griffin mages come to speak to you. I would suggest—"

The young mage, his face twisted in an expression of fear and aversion, rose suddenly and flung a binding of stone and earth at Kairaithin.

Kairaithin, not even blinking, sent the binding awry in a shower of sparks. He said patiently to the king, ignoring the mage, "King of Feierabiand, I have come to this place to speak to you on a matter of importance to us both. If you are wise, you will hear me."

Iaor gripped the arms of his chair hard. He was meeting Kairaithin's eyes, and even if he did not see the griffin behind the man, he would have had to be dead not to feel the power rolling through the air around him. He drew breath to speak.

Before he could frame a word, Meriemne shut her sightless eyes and turned her frail hands palm up on the table. The full gathered weight of the earth fell down upon Kairaithin as irresistibly as a landslide.

The griffin, evidently taken by surprise, had only a fraction of a second to react, and it was not enough. Then the stolid power of the earth rolled over him and crushed him to the floor. Even his fiery shadow was pressed out; it went out like a snuffed candle. Helpless, bound by the power of stone and earth, his restless shadow quenched and his black eyes closed, Kairaithin had never looked more human.

"Meriemne?" the king inquired.

"That," said the oldest mage, "is an unbearably dangerous creature, Iaor. Even from the esteemed Bertaud's descriptions, I had no idea . . . Do you not perceive it?" Her voice was the husk of a voice, barely audible. She had turned her face toward Kairaithin as though she could see him.

"He only wished to speak to you!" Bertaud exclaimed.

Meriemne turned her blind gaze toward him. A line appeared between her brows; she tilted her head intently to one side. She whispered, "I would not wish to . . . Iaor, I might bind this creature. Then you might speak to him safely . . ." her voice trailed thinly off as though she had simply lost the strength to speak.

Iaor looked from the mage to him. "He may speak to me," he answered at last. "Once he is bound. Bertaud—would you expect me to leave this powerful creature unbound in my presence? In this company? In this house? Will you say Meriemne was unwise to do as she did?"

"Not unwise," whispered Bertaud, and added more strongly, almost despite himself, "but wrong."

The king hesitated. "Do you trust your own judgment in this? Shall I trust it?"

Bertaud could not prevent a slight flinch that said as clearly as a shout that he did not know.

The king shifted his attention to Meriemne. "Will you release this creature from your hold without binding him? What is your advice?"

The mage opened a frail hand. "This creature is opposed to earth, Iaor. It cannot help but be opposed. I am afraid it would pull every stone of this hall down on every other stone, and burn your hall to ash. The stones want to fall just for its presence here. The very air wants to ignite. Can you not feel this?"

Her fragile voice held conviction. Bertaud shook his head. "That's the aversion speaking—she can't help but feel that way, Iaor—"

"Do you advise me from uncontrollable antagonism?" the king asked Meriemne. "Is your advice sound?"

The mage hesitated. "I think it is sound," she whispered at last. "I think so, Iaor. I know this creature is horribly powerful—and unalterably opposed to earth. I *know* that."

Bertaud stood wordless and helpless when his king looked deliberately back at him. What could he say? That the oldest and wisest mage in Feierabiand was wrong even in her certainty? What possible reason could he give Iaor to think so? He tried, nevertheless, to find words that might persuade him, persuade them all. None came to him.

The king looked back at Meriemne. "You can bind him?"

"Oh, yes," the mage whispered. "I will make you a chain with the power of earth and of made things in it; it will not be broken by anything that is not of earth. It will bind fire and air and the changing wind. With that chain, you may hold this creature safely in your hand."

The king nodded. "Make your chain."

She made it. She shaped the chain link by link out of a sword one of the guardsmen gave her, and out of the stone table itself. She made a link out of a delicate porcelain cup and another from a copper bangle one of the soldiers gave her, and another from a string of polished wooden beads. Into each link she put a power of solidity, of holding, of weight.

The younger mage took the chain reverently from Meriemne's hands when she was finished making it. It looked like an ordinary chain, but from the manner in which the young man lifted it, it contained the weight of the world. He fastened it around Kairaithin's wrists and stood back.

With a tiny gesture of her hand, Meriemne released the griffin mage from her hold. Then she leaned back in her chair and tucked her hands in her lap, trembling in exhaustion or in the sudden chill that seemed to invade the room.

Kairaithin lifted his head and got his hands underneath his body, drawing himself slowly to his knees. He looked at the chain that bound his wrists without expression, almost as though he could not actually see it. But when he got to his feet, he moved as though he felt its weight dragging at him. His shadow was . . . gone. Though the lanterns threw light across the room, and all the rest of them cast shadows . . . Kairaithin's shadow was not among the rest. Bertaud could not have said why he found this so deeply disturbing.

Kairaithin did not look at Bertaud. Nor did he look, even for an instant, at Meriemne. He turned his head slowly and looked straight at Iaor.

"If you have something to say to me," said the king, "say it."

Kairaithin's mouth crooked in an expression that might have been humor. "Now? Now I have nothing to say."

The king stared at him. "Griffin. Fire mage. Kairaithin—is that your name? What greeting was it you looked for from me?"

His answer was a slight lift of austere brows, and a dry, "You have there a man who has seen the heart of fire. You should listen to him."

"Bertaud?"

Bertaud gave his king a helpless shrug, unable to find words to express his belief that his king had made a terrible mistake in his—surely perfectly reasonable—defense of his own person and his people. He could ask only, "Let me take the chain off, Iaor."

He knew this was out of the question when he asked it, and was unsurprised by the judicious tilt of the king's head, No. It might even have meant, *I'm sorry, but no.* But it did not offer any yielding.

Bertaud turned to Kairaithin instead. "If you came here to speak to the king, then speak! Is your pride worth sacrificing the chance?"

Kairaithin returned him only a blank, incredulous stare.

"Take him," the king said to General Adries, "to the tower room; hold him there." And to the griffin mage, he said, "When you would speak to me, I will hear you."

Kairaithin stopped the general in his first step with merely his fierce stare. He said to the king, "Very soon you will have no choice but to hear me. But, I warn you, by then it will do you no good to listen."

Iaor's mouth tightened, and he waved sharply to Adries.

"Didn't you *hear* him?" Bertaud cried in frustration and inexplicable terror.

"Yes," the king said. "Tell me clearly what I should do to make him speak. Or do you truly believe I should release this dangerous creature in my hall? Everything he has said to me so far has had the tone of a threat."

I don't know! Bertaud wanted to shout.

He did not shout. He merely plucked the nearest soldier's sword from the man's hands, stepped forward, and brought the blade slashing down between Kairaithin's wrists, where it cut the mage-wrought chain that bound him as though the links had been made of grass stems. They spilled away in all directions, shattering into bits of metal and stone and porcelain.

Kairaithin did not watch the descent of the blade, but had stood quite still and gazed at Bertaud instead. His eyes held an odd expression, as though he had, for once, been taken by surprise and was having difficulty deciding on a reaction to the experience.

It seemed to Bertaud that everything was happening very slowly: That it had taken an hour to lift the sword and step forward, that it had taken a day for the sword to fall and free the griffin mage, that it had taken a year for Kairaithin to lower his arms to his sides. The eyes of the griffin mage held his, so that his vision swam with fire, its black heat all he could see. It filled his mind: a fiery silence as perfectly free of thought or emotion as the sun.

Then Iaor shouted and that odd sense of timelessness was shattered: Meriemne bent slowly forward in her seat and rested her forehead against her fragile hands. She did not try to renew any attack on Kairaithin. Neither did the young mage; he stepped back, and back again, face white.

Adries drew his own sword and lunged forward to put his own body before that of the king. All the officers had their swords out. Bertaud shut his eyes for a moment, his mouth dry. He let the sword he held fall from fingers that had gone suddenly numb. It rang on the stone like the stroke of an iron warning bell, sending echoes all through the room.

"Stop," the griffin mage advised them all, his tone not loud, but deadly serious. The general flung up his hand and all the movement of his officers halted, men stopping where they stood.

Iaor's eyes were on Bertaud's face. He did not speak. He looked far more astonished than angry.

For his own part, Bertaud did not think he *could* speak. He certainly could not think of anything to say.

"Ask me for protection," Kairaithin advised Bertaud. "I will grant it, if you ask me."

Bertaud moved his gaze from Iaor's face and stared at the griffin.

"Ask," said Kairaithin.

Bertaud swallowed. He looked again at Iaor. The king's face had gone stony, impossible to read. He looked at Adries, and the general's face was very easy to read. He shut his eyes, but nothing came to his mind save the desert and the brilliant sky.

"Yes," he whispered.

And the world tilted and widened; the walls fell away to an immense distance, and the fierce living heat of the desert crashed down around him.

Heat beat up from the stone underfoot, into a darkness ornamented but not brightened by stars: A desert darkness that had nothing to do with the lantern-lit halls of men. Kairaithin's strong hand caught Bertaud's elbow when, disoriented, he staggered. The grip steadied Bertaud until he had regained his balance, then released him.

Kairaithin, disembodied in the powerful darkness, said quietly, "I have been surprised many times by the unpredictable actions of men; not least tonight."

"Yes," Bertaud said, his throat tight. "I, as well." He wanted to weep, not for fear of the griffin, but for loss and grief. Iaor's face came before him in the blind darkness, set and hard; but the king's eyes were not angry, only astonished. Iaor had simply not believed Bertaud's treachery.

For, though Bertaud had not thought of it that way in the moment—he could hardly have been said to be thinking at all, in that moment—how else could his actions be described, save as betrayal? Bertaud thought he might dream of that look in Iaor's eyes for the rest of his life. He turned sharply away from the griffin, lifting his hand to his face to hide the shine of tears.

There was a short, tense silence. The griffin said finally, "I did not ask you to free me. I admit I expected you to speak for me to your king. I judged him by you and did not expect him to be a fool."

"He is not." Bertaud took a breath and tried to think past what he supposed, with some dispassionate part of his mind, to be shock. He said at last, "He did not trust you—your intentions, or your power. What man would?"

"You, evidently," Kairaithin answered drily. "I find that curious."

Bertaud said, "You've surely given no reason for trust. To Iaor, or to me." He turned and walked blindly several paces, until a sense of space and shape he had not known he possessed told him suddenly that the stone before his feet fell away into emptiness. He could not even find room in his heart for wonder at this strange perception. He asked the night, not turning, knowing the griffin mage watched him patiently from the powerful darkness, "Why did you go there?"

Kairaithin said, "I would have told your king that Casmantium has come into his kingdom. The Arobern of Casmantium waits in the hills just there, above our desert."

Bertaud, incredulous, turned. He took a step back toward the griffin. "What?"

"Brechen Glansent Arobern of Casmantium," Kairaithin said patiently. "And five thousand soldiers. Just there." He nodded to a point in the mountains, visible as a bulk against the stars. "It is as well the Safiad did not hold me, as I think he will have enough to trouble his days without my people striking as the mood takes them all through his lands, as Airaikeliu and Eskainiane would not be able to prevent them without my support. So you did well to free me, man."

Bertaud took a deep breath, let it out in a slow trickle. Then, unable to contain himself, he drew a second breath and shouted, "And you did not *tell* him about Casmantium?"

The griffin did not answer. He was not visible in the darkness, and yet Bertaud knew where he stood, even knew the hard, pitiless look that would be in his eyes, if he had been able to look into them. Bertaud shut his own eyes. He whispered, "You did not even tell me?"

The quality of the silence changed in some indefinable way. "I should have come to you, perhaps, man, and asked you to speak for me to your king," said Kairaithin. "That did not occur to me. And then your king offended me. I am sorry for that."

"Sorry!"

"Yes," said the griffin. "I am sorry for it, because my young *kereskiita* has gone into the cold hand of Casmantium, and I do not know now how I may get her out of it."

It took Bertaud a long moment to understand this. He said at last, "Kes?"

"Kes. Yes," said Kairaithin, and there was something in his voice that was not exactly grief, not precisely fear. "I did not know in time that she had come to the attention of the cold mages, and then it was too late. Now she is beyond my reach." He came forward and stood near Bertaud at the edge of the cliff, gazing out into the dark and up at the bulk of the mountains that rose above the desert.

"What . . . will that mean?"

"I hardly care to guess what it may mean." But the griffin's voice was weary, shadowed by something that sounded very close to despair. There was a short pause, and then Kairaithin touched Bertaud's shoulder—a light touch, oddly tentative. "You are tired." A low sound, not quite a laugh. "As are we all. Rest, then. Perhaps the light of the sun will bring clarity."

Bertaud could only hope it would. He had little hope of it.

CHAPTER 9

Kes woke, confused and afraid, nestled into a bed of cushions, with shadows swinging dizzyingly around her as quiet-footed men took down the lanterns and carried them away. She had slept, she understood, though surely not for very many hours. But the tent was filled with daylight. It was also nearly empty of men: Her guard was there, and the king, sitting in a chair with his long legs thrust out before him and a scattering of papers across the table at his side. The door of the tent was open, light and cold air spilling in across the carpeted floor. The light was nothing like the hammering brilliance of the desert. Kes looked at it, feeling lost and somehow bereft.

The king looked up as Kes straightened in her nest of cushions. He smiled, shoved some of the papers out of the way, and held out a powerful hand to her, indicating a chair near his. "Come," he said in Terheien.

The King of Casmantium looked younger in daylight, and yet somehow larger than ever, even though he was sitting down. He had clearly not slept himself, but energy radiated from him as heat from the sun: When he looked at Kes, his attention was powerful as a griffin's.

He was no longer wearing mail. His shirt was a soft ivory color that made the blackness of his hair and beard more stark by contrast. His hair was very short, but his head was not, at least, shaved completely, as some of the Casmantian soldiers seemed to do. He was not wearing any kind of crown, but he had a thick-linked chain of gold about his throat. It seemed somehow to suit his heavy features.

Kes climbed stiffly to her feet, brushing wrinkles out of her clothing as well as she could with her hands. She wanted a bath, a comb, and a change of clothing. There was no sign that she was to be given any of these things, at least not immediately. But it seemed the King of Casmantium did mean to offer her breakfast. Kes looked at the platters of rolls and sliced fruit on the table without interest and settled gingerly into a chair a little farther from the king than the one he had clearly meant her to take. She folded her hands in her lap and looked at the table.

"Kes," the king said affably. His voice was still harsh and guttural, but he could not help that, and he seemed to want to be kind. "Where is your home?"

Kes found her voice after a moment and whispered, "Minas Ford."

"You are fifteen, Festellech Anweiechen informs me?"

She nodded.

The king grunted and shoved a platter of rolls her way. "You look twelve," he said bluntly. "It is the shy way about you, I suppose. My mage Beguchren Teshrichten says you are becoming a fire mage. He says you are half fire now. I suppose that is true."

Kes supposed it was.

"Eat," ordered the king, frowning at her. "You are all bone. That makes you look young also."

Kes obediently took a roll, nibbling it without appetite.

The king took one also and ate it in two bites, continuing to frown. He asked abruptly, "Why were you alone in the desert?"

Kes had no easy answer for this. But she was afraid not to answer. She said, ashamed of the timidity of her voice, "I . . . I was walking. And . . . and thinking."

"Walking and thinking," repeated the king. His eyebrows had gone up a little, but he did not seem to find this answer incomprehensible. "Humph. Minas Ford . . . are there king's men at Minas Ford? Feierabianden soldiers? I hear there was a battle and many soldiers of Feierabiand were killed, yes? Did any survive, do you know? Or did some stay in Minas Ford, or others come after?"

Kes blinked at him and shook her head.

"Humph." The king continued to study her. "Is Iaor Safiad content to have *malacteir* in his land, then? Griffins, yes?"

Kes did not know what to say, or whether she should say anything at all. It seemed best perhaps to say nothing, but she was afraid silence would make the king angry. Besides, he looked at her so expectantly and so forcefully that she felt she had to find some kind of answer. At last she answered cautiously, "There . . . there was a battle. Yes. I saw the place, after. It was . . . it was horrible. I suppose there might be more soldiers there now. I don't know."

The king's eyebrows went up again. "Huh." He did not say anything more for a little while, gesturing instead for Kes to eat.

Kes was not hungry. She made herself eat part of the roll, to make the king happy, and a small slice of white cheese. She did not want even that. Because the king did not seem unfriendly, she nerved herself to ask, "What . . . what is it that you want . . . in Feierabiand . . . lord?"

"A port city with a good harbor," he answered promptly, taking Kes utterly by surprise. "And if I can win one, perhaps a new province for Casmantium, hah? Terabiand has a good harbor. Your kings have always charged very high to use it. And the tolls on the mountain road are, ah, an insult, you know? Always the tolls go up, and the road is not even good."

Kes stared at him. "You can't . . . you can't just *take* Terabiand."

"I think I can," said the king mildly, or as mildly as his heavy voice would allow him to say anything. "And all that country between Tera- biand and Casmantium, maybe all the way up to Bered and Talend. That would make a very good province. It would rival Meridanium, which my great-grandfather won, hah? You, well, you may be a prob- lem, yes."

Kes looked down at the table, at the bread she had been slowly pulling to pieces with her fingers.

"Do you know . . . *did* you know that the *wanenteir*—the fires- mages of the griffins, you understand? — were making you into a *san- dicteir*, a creature of fire? Did you know you must stop being a *sandichboden*, a creature of earth, to become a creature of fire? You would lose your *festechanken*, your human-ness, the part of you that is part of the earth. You would not be able to get it back." The king had tilted his powerful head to the side, frowning again, angry . . . on *her* behalf, Kes understood suddenly. She remembered being angry herself and wondered if she should be again, but the anger was dim now. Fear of the cold mage suffocated even the memory of anger. She only felt cold. She said nothing.

"My mage, Beguchren Teshrichten, you know? He says you are not all the way *sandicteir*. Not yet. He says he could clean the fire from you, he and my other cold mages. But you would fight him, very hard. So hard you might die of it."

Kes stared at him, horrified. The thought of that small, white- haired mage touching her in any way whatsoever made her feel ill.

The king propped his head on one hand, looking at her closely. "You would fight him, yes," he concluded. "You do not like my cold mage, yes? He does not like you either, little fire mage. He says it is a natural . . . what is the word . . . dislike, but stronger. Yes? So Begu- chren is wise enough to leave you to me, which is best. I am not a mage at all. I like you, little *festechanenteir*. I do not like what the *wanenteir* did to you. Do you like it?"

Kes hardly knew. She knew that what the king said was true, that Kairaithin had indeed made her into something other than she had been. It felt natural to be as she was, to long for the sun and the clean desert, to reach for the stillness that lay at the heart of the flame . . . She reached out, on that thought, and flinched away from the cold barriers the Casmantian mage had put around her mind. She huddled instead into her chair.

"You should help me," the king said persuasively. "Against the *malacteir*, not against your own people; I would not ask that. But against the *malacteir*, why not? You have family, yes? A lover waiting for you, maybe? The *malacteir* would take those things from you. Did the *wanenteir*, the mages who began this change, did they warn you what they did? Help me against the *wanenteir* and at least the change will not go further. If you wish, if you want enough to be human, my mages can give you back your *festechanken*. They could take the fire out of you. You could endure their touch if you wanted it enough. Yes? I think you could. I think you are very brave."

Kes did not know what to say. She was afraid that everything the king said was true, and she did not want it to be true. She did not feel brave at all.

"Yes?" the king urged her.

Kes thought of Kairaithin, of the sweep of powerful wings against the hot blaze of the desert, the griffin mage's mastery of fire and air. His power. His austere voice, saying, *You are a gift I had hardly hoped to find.* He had made her feel . . . had made her know . . . had made her understand . . . her thoughts stuttered to a confused halt. Kairaithin was too difficult to think about. He had bound her so she could not go home, so she had to stay in the desert. She had been so angry.

Now she was too frightened to be angry. The cold binding Beguchren had put on her seemed so much worse than anything the griffins had done, even if it hurt her only because of what Kairaithin had done to her first. It might not be sensible to be more frightened of the cold mage than of Kairaithin; in fact, it might be *sensible* to do as the King of Casmantium said and ask his mages to tear the fire out of her blood—but it wasn't a matter for sense and Kes couldn't help what she felt. And what she felt, she realized bleakly, was that she would rather die than let Beguchren touch her. Except, if she could never go home again, that would be *like* death, wouldn't it? And would she *truly* rather accept that than let the cold mage take the fire out of her blood?

She did not even know. She whispered, almost blindly, "Why did you have to drive the griffins into Feierabiand?"

The King of Casmantium regarded her through narrowed eyes and did not answer.

Kes answered her own question. "Because you *wanted* them to make their desert in Feierabiand. So we would worry about them and not see you. But you thought you had killed all their mages. No wonder . . . no wonder you want me to help you. And then stop being . . . being a mage myself." She stopped, looking suddenly and fearfully at the king.

He had his chin propped on his hand, and he was smiling. That smile would have looked threatening, except for the rueful expression in his eyes. "Well," he said. "Not so much a child, are you? So you think behind those fire-lit eyes, yes? So, Kes, you must understand . . . if you will help me against the *malacteir*, that would be good, but I can do without this." He paused, and his expressive eyes hardened. "If you will not, well, I must have my own mages free to help me and not spend all their attention to guard me against *you*. So if you will not do as I ask, I will have Beguchren take the fire out of you. I think that is what I must do. Do you understand?"

Kes understood. She shrank into her chair.

"I am sorry," the king told her.

Kes knew that he meant it. And that he had meant the threat he had made as well. She could not move. She longed, suddenly and desperately, for the brilliant silence and layered time of the desert—and then realized that she ought to have longed for her own home. But all she saw when she closed her eyes was the stark beauty of the desert. She tried again to cry out within her mind for Kairaithin, for Opailikiita. But her voice echoed within the barriers the cold mage had closed around her and she knew they would never hear.

"All your choices are hard," the king said, and sighed sympathetically, but with no suggestion he would change his mind. He stood up and gestured curtly toward the soldier who still guarded her. "That is Andenken Errich. He will stay with you, yes? He will not harm you. He speaks Terheien, a little. He will bring you water to wash, food if this does not please you. You may stay here or go out of the tent, walk around—Andenken Errich will go with you, you understand? No one will harm you."

"Except you," Kes whispered.

"Except me," the king agreed. "So think hard, little *festechanenteir*. Walk and think. I will send for you at dusk and ask you again. You understand?"

Kes nodded. Her throat felt thick, her eyes dry and barren of tears, yet she thought if she tried to speak she might weep like a child.

The king, frowning again, shook his head. Then he went out.

Kes looked cautiously at her guard.

The soldier looked sympathetic. He said in bad Terheien, "Would go out? Would walk? Is cold."

Kes thought of all the tents in this camp, of all the Casmantian soldiers there. Of how they would all look at her if she went out. They would all know she was the human fire mage their king had caught—the king's mage had caught, netted like a fish out of a stream. She felt as much out of her element as that fish. She wanted to cry. Her throat swelled; she blinked hard and shook her head.

But then the confines of the tent seemed suddenly as unbearable, and she jumped to her feet after all. She took a step toward the door and, hesitating, turned back to the safety of the tent—knowing it was not safe, that nothing was safe, but it felt safer than the outside world. She could hear the voices of men, the clatter of activity all around her. It frightened her. Yet she could not bear to stay still. She looked in appeal at her guard.

He seemed to understand what she felt, although Kes did not understand how he could. He went to the door of the tent and held the flap back for her. "Come," he said—not a command, but an invitation.

The guard took her first to his tent—she thought it must be his own, from the way the soldiers there greeted him. They called him Errich and laughed at him for being so lucky as to escort a pretty girl—Kes did not have to understand their language to understand that. He blushed, looking younger than she had thought him, and they teased him harder. But when Kes also blushed, they stopped teasing and became very solemn, although their eyes still laughed.

There were four of them besides her guard. They were all young, all earnest, and all very polite. Young men in Minas Ford would never have been kind enough to stop teasing just because a girl blushed—that would only have made them tease harder. Or, well, maybe they, too, would be gentler, with a girl they did not know, a prisoner whose language they did not speak.

Either way, because they had hardly any language in common, Kes didn't need to speak, and the young soldiers couldn't think her strange for her silence. *They* did not know she had been made into something not entirely human, Kes realized, and on the heels of that thought found it surprising that they couldn't see the fire in her eyes. She could see the earth in theirs.

They offered her bits of dried fruit, clearly the choicest food they had, so that she blushed again and, although she wasn't hungry, made herself nibble what they gave her. They brought her water to bathe, which was wonderful, and stood careful guard over her privacy while she washed. Kes washed very quickly, but though she half expected one or another of the young men to peek in at her past the cloth they'd hung up, none of them did. One of them had given her a clean brown shirt to wear after she'd washed. The shirt was much too big for her, coming down past her knees, making a kind of short dress. Kes looked doubtfully down at herself after she put on the shirt. It was certainly a *strange* kind of dress. She knew she must look ridiculous wearing it. Gathering enough courage to put back the cloth took longer than the bath itself. But what choice did she have? She couldn't hide in this tiny corner of the tent for the rest of the day. Could she? The idea was tempting. But, no, Kes decided reluctantly. Really she couldn't.

But when she at last came out into the tent, the young men didn't seem to think Kes looked ridiculous. They hid smiles at how far she had to roll up the shirt's sleeves, but that wasn't the same, and their glances were admiring as well. Although she blushed again, they didn't make Kes want to hide. One of them—the tallest—found a thin strip of leather and gave it to her for a belt, because all their belts were too big. Then all the young men went off somewhere, with much teasing back and forth, except Errich, who watched them leave and then gathered up his sword and a spear—Kes could not imagine he thought he would need them, but he took them anyway—and led her to the edge of the camp.

It took a surprisingly long time to go all the way to the edge. It was hard for Kes to guess how many soldiers there might be in this company. A lot, she thought, but she had no clear idea how many that might really be. The camp was far larger than Minas Ford. Most of the men had gone somewhere else—Kes could hear them in the distance, a shout of command and roar of response, and supposed they were doing something soldierly and probably violent. So there was no crowd of soldiers in the camp. That made it easier to look curiously around, to examine in wonder the neat rows of tents—for everything was neat and orderly, despite the rugged land in which the soldiers had been forced to camp.

From the edge of the camp, she could just see the desert. She longed for its heavy golden light. But of course Errich wouldn't let her go that way. She sat on a rock and just looked at it, as a little crippled sparrow might have looked at the wide sky it could not reach. Errich stood nearby and gazed down at the desert as well, a slight worried crease between his eyebrows: Was he thinking of marching down into it to face the griffins? Or of coming out the other side to strike into Feierabiand? What did simple soldiers think about when their king took them off into battle? Kes couldn't imagine what that might be like. She shivered.

Think hard, the king of Casmantium had advised her. Kes found it hard to think at all. She sat on the gray stone with her arms wrapped around her drawn-up knees, the sleeves of her borrowed clothing rolled up around her wrists, and stared at the boundary between the human world and the world of the desert.

Errich leaned on his spear a few paces away and waited patiently. Occasionally a soldier jogged past about some fathomless errand. None of them even seemed to notice Kes. They all looked the same to her— large young men in brown and black, with metal showing at neck and wrist, carrying swords or spears or bows. None of them looked worried. They all looked depressingly like they knew exactly what they were doing and what their place was in the world. Maybe Errich had only been thinking about Kes, who had been found in the desert and who so clearly wanted to return to it—was it clear to him? Probably. She hadn't tried to hide her longing.

The sun climbed higher, shedding little warmth across the mountain heights. Errich had found a place near Kes to sit down. He still seemed patient. He simply rested, his spear leaning against the rock where he sat, his hand casually resting on the hilt of his sword. But he was alert enough. Kes knew that if she got to her feet and started to walk down the mountain, he would stop her.

Men came and went in the camp at their backs, sometimes many men and sometimes only a few, according to some pattern of activity that doubtless made sense to Errich but that seemed completely random to Kes.

A soldier came up during one of the quiet periods, a big man like any of the others; Kes did not look at him. He said something to Errich, and her guard laughed and agreed. The soldier smiled. He started to go, turned back, said something else, and both men laughed. Then, leaning smoothly forward with a casual air, the soldier drew a knife swiftly and competently across Errich's throat.

Kes, shocked, leaped to her feet.

Errich, his eyes wide with horror and amazement, made it to his knees before the other soldier thrust him back and down. He could not cry out; with his throat cut, he could not even whisper. The blood ran down his chest. He made an awful choking sound as the life went out of his eyes.

The soldier bent down and closed the young man's open eyes, speaking again, a low phrase in Prechen. At that moment, the Casmantian language did not sound coarse or harsh at all. It sounded like a language meant for grieving, for sorrow. For loss.

Kes had not made a sound. She stood with her hands clenched in front of her mouth, her eyes wide, staring.

The soldier who had killed Errich straightened and turned toward her. She thought he would kill her next and knew she should run away, except he would catch her, and besides she couldn't move. Then their eyes met. For a long moment she did not know him, even then. But then she did. The big soldier—wearing the clothing of a Casmantian soldier as though perfectly familiar with it, with a sword at his side like it belonged there and a shirt of metal chain under the one of brown cloth—was Jos.

He said, "There is a horse," and nodded back the way he had come.

For another long moment, Kes was completely incapable of movement. Or speech.

He said impatiently, almost harshly, "We must be quick."

She shaped his name, without sound. But then she took the hand he held out to her and went the way he indicated.

There was indeed a horse, a very good one, black with three white feet and a narrow white blaze. It waited, ground-tethered, around the curve of the mountain, not forty feet from where Kes had sat with Errich to look at the desert. Jos gathered up its reins and mounted, and held down a hand to help Kes up in front of him. He was clearly tense, but also clearly far from panic. He had a plan. He meant to fold her up into it and . . . what? Take her back to Minas Ford and Tesme? She should want that.

Kes glanced over her shoulder at the camp, which was stirring briskly. No one, as far as she could tell, had yet noticed . . . anything amiss. She said, barely above a whisper, but clearly, "The desert. The desert is close, Jos."

Jos put the horse into a brisk trot north and west, angling down and across the slope, not quite parallel to the distant edge of the desert, but nearly. "We'll cut around above Minas Spring, avoid the desert—they'll be sure you went straight down into it. They won't think so quickly to search this way."

Kes rested her hands on the neck of the horse; its muscles moved smoothly under her palms. She had a strange feeling it should be feathers under her hands. "They will . . . will they not see us?"

"Men see what they expect to see," Jos said, his tone grim. "I have given them a thing they think they understand, and so they do not see anything else."

Kes didn't understand, but she nodded. She thought of Beguchren, waiting with his imperturbable smile and ice-pale eyes to take the fire out of her heart, and whispered, "I want to go to the desert."

"You don't," Jos answered flatly. His arms around her were tense. She felt him move to look back over his shoulder, then shift to face forward again. "You must not go back into the desert; I know it looks like the quickest way, but the *malacteir* will only find you again if you go there. They'll take you back into their power. You need to get home. You and Tesme—you can take horses, ride west. All the way to Sihannas, if necessary. You'll be safe there."

Safe, thought Kes. *Sihannas?* It took a moment for her to understand what Jos had said, as though he had expressed an idea so strange she could not wrap her mind around it. She opened her eyes at last, turned her head warily. The camp was still there, on their right, stretching on—a little farther away, but only a little. There were men moving briskly about, and yet no one had challenged them. She did not understand how they could slip so invisibly by the camp. She looked at Jos's mailed wrist, at his Casmantian uniform shirt. But if he looked like he belonged to this camp, surely she did not? But she did not ask. She only reached out to take the reins in her own hands and turned the horse firmly south, straight toward the desert.

Jos started to speak, a muffled exclamation.

"The desert," Kes said tensely. "The desert. Beguchren—Beguchren put a cold binding on me. The sentries don't matter—the men don't matter. Only Beguchren. Only the desert. Please. I have to go into the desert. The griffins—they will not harm me. You—you don't have to come. But I have to go."

He started to shake his head, a movement she sensed rather than saw.

"Jos," she said.

He stilled, his hands quiet on the reins, not fighting her. Then he shifted in the saddle. "What are you to the *malacteir*, Kes? You were a prisoner there! Were you not? Shall I not take you home?"

Kes started to say that she had not been a prisoner of the griffins. But she could not say that. It was not true. And yet it *felt* true. She knew perfectly well that she felt this way only because of what Kairaithin had done to her, teaching her to use fire, making her into a fire mage. But even though she *knew* this, she still felt, all through her bones, that fire was a natural and normal element for her, and that Beguchren's cold magecraft would destroy her. And besides—

She whispered, "They need me. They need me so much. And besides—" she touched her chest—"The cold. *Whatever* else is true or might be true, I can't bear it, Jos. I need Kairaithin to break the cold binding. Or Beguchren will find me. He'll know as soon as he begins to look for me where I am—" She shuddered helplessly. "I couldn't stand that. I couldn't. Please. *Please,* Jos."

Jos muttered a curse under his breath, turned to look carefully behind them, and nudged the horse into a slightly faster gait. Down the mountain this time, along a rough path that led almost straight for the desert. Kes shuddered again, in an agony of anxiety lest someone should shout behind them. No one did.

They came around a turn in the rugged path they were following and a man—two men—rose to stand in their way. One of the men had a bow, with an arrow already nocked, though not pointed at them. Kes uttered a small scream, but Jos seemed perfectly unmoved. He drew the horse up and spoke briefly to the men in Prechen, his tone matter-of-fact.

The men looked at Kes with covert interest, but their answers seemed respectful and somehow perfunctory. The one with the bow slipped his arrow from the string. Jos said something else, and the men laughed. Then, nudging the horse, Jos sent it on past them.

"Why—why don't they stop us?" Kes asked him, when she thought she might be able to speak without her voice shaking.

It took Jos long enough to answer that she thought he was not going to. But he said at last, "This is Lord Anweiechen's horse. Men know this horse. And I am wearing his badge. So they think I am his man, on his errand, and that is what they see."

Anweiechen's horse. The lord who had come into the desert with Beguchren to capture her. Hadn't that been Lord Anweiechen? Kes said doubtfully, "You stole Lord Anweiechen's horse?" After a moment, she added, her tone rising incredulously, "You knew his horse, to steal it? You knew his badge, to wear it? You have a Casmantian uniform. And you speak—you speak Prechen. I don't—I think I don't understand anything."

There was a silence, long enough for the desert to grow measurably nearer. But finally Jos said, harshly, "I am Casmantian."

"Yes," said Kes. That much was obvious, though inexplicable. "But . . ."

The horse tossed its head as Jos's grip on the reins tightened. Jos muttered a word under his breath, but he eased his hands and the horse pricked its ears forward again and quickened its pace. Jos said, in a tone flat and hard as the gray mountain stone, "I am—I was a Casmantian spy."

This didn't make sense. Kes blinked. She turned her head, trying to look at his face. She didn't understand what she saw: The glimpse she got of his expression was . . . different. It didn't even look like him, but like some bleak stranger. She said tentatively, "But . . . you worked for us. For Tesme. For years."

"Minas Ford," Jos said, in that precise hard voice that seemed so little like his, "boasts one of the finest inns between Terabiand and Tihannad. A small inn, but still. Men stop there. Merchants, petty lords, everyone. And they talk. To one another, to Jerreid. Jerreid can draw out anyone. He doesn't really listen to their private business when travelers confide in him. But I do. Did. Minas Ford is a good place for a spy."

Kes, unable to think of anything to say, said nothing.

"I knew when the Arobern brought his army across from Casmantium. I encouraged that young lord from Tihannad to do battle with the griffins; I watched the battle and saw that little army destroyed, exactly as the Arobern wished. I meant to bring the news of that battle to Anweiechen, who is master of the Arobern's spies. I did bring that news. But once I came here, I also heard of you."

And had freed her. Killing a man to do it. A countryman, impossible though that seemed. Kes shook her head slightly, incredulous.

"I—" said Jos, and stopped.

Kes could not imagine what he might say. Apparently, neither could he, because he did not finish his thought, but only pressed the horse to greater speed. When Kes looked cautiously back, she found that the Casmantian camp was no longer visible; it had been lost behind them among the gray stones and snow. She relaxed a little. For a few moments, there was nothing but the sound of hooves on stone and rough ground, the feel of the horse between her thighs, the solidity of the man behind her. Whom she had thought she'd known.

Jos had never pressed Kes to speak; silences between them had always been easy. Companionable. But this time, his discomfort seemed to radiate outward from his body like heat. He fidgeted in the saddle, turning his head to look behind them—there was still no sign of pursuit—then turning again a moment later. His hands shifted on the reins, then shifted again, until the horse tossed its head uncomfortably.

"You came for me," Kes said, not turning. And he was taking her toward the desert, even though he didn't want to go there or take her there, even though he couldn't understand why she insisted that she must go there. She had never understood gratitude, she thought, until this moment. She said again, "When I was a prisoner, and alone, you found me and freed me, when I thought no one would."

The quality of the silence behind her eased.

Before them, the red desert grew closer, until she thought she could feel its presence like a hot wind against her face, though the air was still.

CHAPTER 10

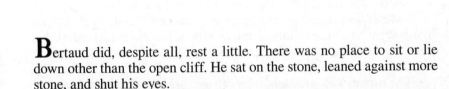

Bertaud did, despite all, rest a little. There was no place to sit or lie down other than the open cliff. He sat on the stone, leaned against more stone, and shut his eyes.

He did not dream of Iaor, which was a mercy and yet dismayed him even as he welcomed the fierce griffin dreams that came to him. He dreamed of rivers of burning liquid rock that ran across a jagged iron-dark land and cast droplets of fire into the air where it broke against stone. The air smelled of hot brass and burning stone. Soaring across a last ridge of broken black rock, he found before him a lake of molten fire; a violent joy consumed him, although he did not know why. Sweeping back his wings, he plunged into a steep, fierce dive straight for the heart of the fiery lake, knowing that when he entered it . . . when he entered it . . .

Bertaud woke, heart pounding, with red light in his eyes. He moved, startled, murmuring, and a hand closed on his shoulder. It took him a moment to understand that the hand belonged to Kairaithin, and that the griffin mage had stopped him from moving too near the edge of the cliff where he had slept. The red light was the dawn, the sun burning down across the slopes where the red desert rose to the heights.

He was, Bertaud realized as he pulled himself slowly out of his dreams, stiff and hungry and desperately thirsty.

Kairaithin did not look like *he* was stiff or hungry. He stood on the edge of the cliff, his face toward the rising sun, light and heat seeming to pour out of him as much as out of the sun. His shadow, the shadow of a griffin, molten and hot, shifted like a live thing across the stone, and fixed Bertaud with fiery black eyes.

Kairaithin turned, and his eyes were the same as his shadow's; he gazed at Bertaud with an air of surprise, as though taken aback to find a human man here beside him on this red desert cliff.

"You are thirsty," he said then, and a wry look came into his eyes. "I am not accustomed to providing for the needs of men."

"Is there—surely there is no water in this desert?"

"No." Kairaithin did not quite smile. The sunlight poured across the desert and lit an aureole behind him. His outline seemed to shift, or his shadow had risen up and stood beside him; he seemed now man, now griffin. He said, and Bertaud was not certain whether he heard his voice in the ordinary fashion or merely within his mind, *There is no water nor hope of water in this desert.*

Bertaud suddenly felt twice as thirsty. He shut his eyes.

Come, said Kairaithin, and the world tilted and moved.

The air was suddenly much colder—cold and fresh, with a clean living scent to it utterly unlike the smells of hot stone and metal that filled the desert. It struck Bertaud like a bucket of icy water. He gasped, opening his eyes.

The stone was gray and smooth underfoot rather than jagged. Twisted mountain trees clung to the thin soil captured by hollows and pockets of stone. Snow lay tucked into shadows and crevices. A thin trickle of clean water ran down a sheer stone face and gathered at its foot into a small pool.

Bertaud blinked at this startling, chilly world, and turned his head.

Kairaithin, in griffin form, lounged in pouring golden light not twenty paces away. Red sand flickering with delicate tongues of flame spilled out from the shadow of his wings. The desert stretched out behind him, running down the lower slopes of the mountain and vanishing in a bright hot horizon.

Bertaud looked back at the icy pool, and then lifted his gaze, following the sweep of the mountains up to the cold heights where the edges of gray stone blurred into a pale sky. He shook his head, bemused, and went forward to drink. The water from the pool was so cold it hurt his teeth. It tasted of the living earth and the promise of growing things.

Bertaud straightened, feeling that he might never thirst again. He dipped his hands in the water idly once more, and walked back toward the griffin and the desert with droplets of icy water spiraling around his fingers and sparkling as they fell to the stone.

Quite deliberately, Bertaud stepped from the pale light of the mountains into molten summer. The water on his hands evaporated instantly.

Kairaithin waited. His taloned front feet were crossed lazily, one over the other; his haunches were tucked to one side like a great indolent cat. A slow breeze stirred the fine feathers of his neck and the longer ones across his shoulders. He looked very much part of the desert, as though it had brought him forth from red stone and golden light and the blackness of the desert night. His head turned to fix Bertaud with the quick unhuman movement of an eagle. But his black eyes were exactly the same.

Bertaud cleared his throat and gestured up the mountain. "Is that where the Casmantian troops are?"

Kairaithin tilted his head a little to the south. Light slid across his beak as over a sword blade. *There.*

Bertaud eyed the steep land the griffin had indicated. It did not look like it hid thousands of men. A close inspection yielded a suggestion of haze in that area that might have been the smoke of cooking fires. Or might have been simply haze. "The *King* of Casmantium is there? The Arobern himself?"

Do you doubt me?

Bertaud looked back at the elegant form of the griffin, at the fierce eyes. They were harder to read, set in the face of an eagle. He thought he saw a familiar hard humor in them. He did not see deception. He could not imagine a reason for this particular deception. "No."

You should not. Shall I send you back to your king to tell him so?

Bertaud thought of the look on Iaor's face when he had brought his stolen blade down across Kairaithin's chains and winced. And he had left his friend and his king for the desert, at the urgent demand of a griffin. "I don't . . . I doubt . . ." He did not know how to finish his thought, and fell silent.

If I sent you to speak for me to the King of Feierabiand as my *agent . . . as the agent of the Lord of Fire and Air, if you would prefer . . . the human king could not lift his hand against you. And then you might speak to him of Casmantium. I might suggest such a course of action. Would he hear you?*

"He did not hesitate to raise his hand against *you*."

He would not perceive you as a threat.

That was certainly true. Bertaud let his breath out slowly. He did not want to go back to Tihannad to face Iaor. He very passionately did not want that. He turned the idea over in his mind, and said at last, "If I go back to Iaor, it will most certainly not be as your vassal. Or as the vassal of any griffin. Meaning no offense, O Lord of the Changing Wind." On the other hand . . . he could not help but realize that the griffins did most desperately need an emissary. He winced slightly, thinking about that.

Kairaithin merely watched him, without sign of either offense or understanding. Waiting, Bertaud understood, for something more: something, perhaps, that he would be able to understand.

He sat down on the hot sand and wrapped his arms around his knees. "Perhaps . . . I don't know. Perhaps I might agree to speak for you. As your . . . I don't know. Not your vassal. I should never have let you give me your protection. Potent though it undoubtedly is."

It seemed expedient at the time, Kairaithin said. *If I misjudged and did you harm, I regret it. That was not my intention.*

"You are not at fault," answered Bertaud, and sighed, feeling the weight of guilt. He tried to think. "Maybe as your advocate."

Casmantium is dangerous to my people; Feierabiand is dangerous. Kairaithin turned his head, stared out across the reaches of the desert as though he tried to gaze through possibility and chance to see what he should do. For all the griffin's undoubted power, Bertaud understood that he, too, felt the press of limited, difficult options.

I must reclaim my little kereskiita, said the griffin, in the tone of one acknowledging stark necessity. *With her, we have choices; without her, we have nothing. You must help me regain her, man, and then we will talk further of human kings and armies.* Kairaithin rose to his feet, scattering sand; when he shook himself, the movement of feathers settling into place made a sound like the hissing of fire.

Bertaud, too, stood. He said, "But—"

He did not know what he might have said. A horse bearing a rider came at that moment around the curve of the mountain, checked nervously at the sight of sand and griffin, and then came on slowly.

The feathers on the back of Kairaithin's neck rose into a stiff mane; he opened his fierce beak a little and clicked it shut again, with a noise of bone against bone. He said, *Kes.*

"What?" Bertaud was startled. It was obvious to him that the rider on the horse was far too big to be Kes—too big to be any woman.

Kes, said the griffin. *And a Casmantian soldier.* His beak clicked again, a sharp aggressive sound.

"What?" said Bertaud, in an entirely different tone, finding this hard to credit.

But, as the horse drew closer, he saw that Kairaithin was right. A Casmantian soldier sat in the saddle, with Kes, in an outlandish brown dress rather too short for decency, perched on the animal's withers in front of him. She sat with her hands resting on the horse's neck, leaning forward eagerly, like she might at any moment slip from the saddle and run to the desert.

Though she did not hold the reins, it became clear as they neared the desert boundary that it was Kes who chose their direction. When the soldier eyed Kairaithin and even Bertaud askance, it was Kes who touched his arm and spoke to him, and he—reluctantly, Bertaud thought—directed the horse directly toward them. And when the animal tossed up its head and balked at the searing, dangerous scent of the griffin, it was Kes who slid down to the ground, Kes whose word to the soldier drew him to dismount after her.

The soldier released the horse, which backed nervously, spun, and cantered back the way it had come. The soldier cast a glance after it as though he thought of following its example, but then he looked down at the girl at his side and followed her instead.

Kes showed no uncertainty at all. She ran forward, crossing the border between natural mountain and desert with the urgency of a drowning swimmer coming to the surface of the water and a lifesaving mouthful of air. She was barefoot, but showed no sign of discomfort, though the sand should have burned her feet. Barely seeming to notice Bertaud, she went straight to Kairaithin. Her pale hair was tangled and her eyes huge in her small, delicate face; she looked like a tiny child next to the griffin. Kairaithin bent his head down to her like a falcon bending over a mouse. Their shadows lay across each other on the sand, the griffin's made of fire, the girl's fire-edged.

The Casmantian soldier crossed the desert boundary more slowly, with far less enthusiasm. He looked at Bertaud, oddly, with more trepidation than he seemed to hold for the griffin. His face, coarse featured and broad, was perfectly inexpressive. Passing him in the streets of a town, one would perhaps think him simple. Bertaud sincerely doubted this was the case.

Kereskiita, said Kairaithin, ignoring the soldier completely, and stroked her face lightly with his beak.

"Anasakuse Sipiike Kairaithin," answered Kes, in her timid little voice, and reached, not timid after all, to lay her hand on the griffin's face just behind that dangerous beak. Then she drew back. "This is my friend Jos," she said simply, indicating the soldier, who glanced uncomfortably away from the searching look Bertaud gave him. Again, he seemed less worried about Kairaithin.

Bertaud found it difficult to imagine what Kes was doing, running from the Casmantian army in the company of a *Casmantian* soldier. Even if he could have thought of a way to ask, he doubted he would get an answer.

If he brought you out of the grip of Casmantium and back to me, I am grateful to him, said Kairaithin. The look he bent on the man was severe, dangerous, forcefully attentive. The soldier—Jos, if that was his right name—swayed under the force of it, going ashen. He did not look away from the griffin's stare; perhaps could not. For the first time, he appeared more impressed by the griffin than by Bertaud.

"He did."

Then I am grateful. The griffin had not glanced back at Kes, but continued to fix the soldier with his hard, black stare. He said to him directly, *I am in your debt. What will you ask of me?*

"Nothing," said the man, in a deep, quiet voice. "Lord."

Wise. Kairaithin's voice glinted with humor. He turned again to Kes. *You are well? I see you are bound.*

"Free me," whispered Kes.

Whose binding? Do you know his name?

"The little one. The white-haired one, with ice in his eyes and his blood. Beguchren, Beguchren Tesh—Teshrichten, I think."

Yes, said Kairaithin. *Beguchren. I know him. I know his work. He is very powerful, but now that you are come back to me, I can break his binding. Come here to me.* He lifted his head, his wings; fire ran suddenly across his wings and filled his eyes, his open beak. Fire ran down the fine feathers of his throat and fell, like the petals of some strange flower, to the sand. It burned bright and clean, without smoke; it made a sound like the hissing of wind-caught sand.

The Casmantian soldier stepped back hastily. Bertaud, too, backed away.

But Kes lifted her hands to the griffin's fire. She took fire into her hands, into her mouth; fire ran across her skin like water, blossomed in her eyes. There was a hissing sound, as fire meeting frost might hiss: Mist rose around the girl in a thin, drifting veil. She made a small sound that might have been surprise or fear or even anger, though Bertaud had never seen Kes angry.

The air chilled suddenly. Frost ran across the sand at the girl's feet, flashing brilliantly white in the stark desert sun. Kairaithin leaned forward and reached deliberately into the cold air with a feathered eagle's leg. He touched Kes's face with a single talon. The sunlight that surrounded him seemed to gain body and spill from the air like liquid; it roared like a bonfire. Both Bertaud and the Casmantian soldier took another step back.

Again, Kes made a wordless sound, this one definitely both angry and frightened. She had crouched a little, and now sank down to her hands and knees and buried her hands in the red sand. Fire hissed across the sand and rippled up along her wrists. She bowed her head over the flames as a normal girl might bend over a friendly little campfire. Kairaithin made a sharp gesture with his head and flexible eagle's neck as though he were throwing something into the air from his beak. He *had* thrown something, something small and bright and—Bertaud thought—deadly. Whatever it was, it left a delicate trail of tiny sparks as it flashed away, back the way Kes had come. Sparks fell glittering to the ground, sparkling now as they became—Bertaud looked more closely—minute fire opals and specks of gold. He took a deep breath of the hot air and looked up again.

Kairaithin was standing perfectly still, looking not after the thing he had cast away, but at Kes. The girl was still kneeling on the ground, her face tilted up to the sunlight. Light poured over her, thick and golden as honey. She swayed suddenly and shut her eyes, then opened them. They were filled with light; tears of fire ran down her cheeks, but she did not seem to be in distress. In fact, she shivered all over and then smiled and sat back on her heels.

Beguchren has lost his binding, said Kairaithin. He folded his black-barred wings and sat down on the sand with a satisfied air.

"I know," answered Kes. She looked away, up the mountain, gray and cold, to where the snow lay on heights. "He will know it, too."

Oh, yes. The griffin's tail lashed across the sand, one quick motion.

"Soldiers," the Casmantian said suddenly, jerking a hand toward the boundary between the normal mountain chill and the desert.

There were: To his chagrin, Bertaud had not seen them until the Casmantian had pointed them out. They were far away, but coming fast. Quite a few men. *That* was not good. And neither he nor—he looked quickly—Jos had anything more than a knife.

Beguchren Teshrichten is among them, said Kairaithin.

"Then why are we still here?" Bertaud asked urgently. The Casmantians had put their horses into a gallop; he saw arrowheads glitter in the pale morning light. The first arrows arched high and began to fall.

There will be an accounting between us, said the griffin. *But you are correct, man. It cannot be yet.* The world tilted dizzyingly around them—then tilted back. Bertaud flung a hand out for balance, staggering. He had expected Kairaithin to move them far back into the desert, but when his sight cleared he found that they were still at its very edge. And the Casmantian soldiers were moving even faster now, if that was possible.

Beguchren prevents me, said Kairaithin.

An arrow whipped past Bertaud's face and buried itself for a third of its length in the sand at his feet. He took an involuntary step backward and cursed, shaken. Nearby, the Casmantian, Jos, drew his knife as though he seriously meant to face down several dozen Casmantian horsemen with nothing but that. Other arrows fell around them, though

none so close as the first. Then arrows started bursting into flame as
they flew, burning to ash and blowing away on the hot wind.

Well done, Kairaithin said to Kes.

"Five minutes and they'll be on us," said Bertaud to the griffin
mage, drawing his own knife. "Or less."

"Less," said Jos, tersely.

Kairaithin half spread his immense wings. Flames rose, pale in the
brilliant sunlight, at the edge of the desert. The racing horses, almost
too close to the fire to stop, shied away to either side so violently that
two of their riders fell. One fell into the flames and sprang up instantly,
running blindly toward them, his clothing on fire, screaming in a horrible high-pitched voice. Kes covered her eyes, crying out herself, and
the man crumpled almost at their feet, no longer burning.

Jos, without a word, took the man's sword. There was no sign now
that the man had ever been burned, though his uniform was charred.
Kes knelt on the sand near Kairaithin, eyes wide with terror, looking
tiny and young and entirely helpless.

Kairaithin said, *Beguchren is trying to smother my fire.* The griffin
had ringed them with fire, a towering but thin circle of wavering flames.
As Bertaud watched, the circle narrowed perceptibly. The heat pouring
off it was incredible. If they hid behind its protection for very long, he
doubted either he or Jos would survive the experience.

"Who is stronger? You or Beguchren?" Bertaud asked Kairaithin.

*In this desert, I. But if I set myself against the cold mage and break
his hold, I will not have sufficient attention to spare to prevent the men
from coming against you. And I will be too busy with Beguchren to
defend either you or myself from them.*

"Then you'll have to let them past and hope we can keep them off
you long enough. It would be nice if you didn't take too long with Beguchren." Bertaud stepped forward to put himself shoulder to shoulder
with Kes's Casmantian friend, in front of Kes and Kairaithin. He
added, "I'll need a sword."

"Yes," said Jos.

The circle of fire died. Bertaud could tell which of the men outside
that circle was Beguchren, not only because the cold mage, small and
white haired and finely dressed, looked nothing like a soldier, but also
because he stopped in midstep and put his hands over his face, looking
like a man under a terrible strain.

Besides, he wasn't carrying a sword. Well, so slight a man wasn't
likely to do well in a sword fight, but he wasn't carrying even a bow. No
doubt being weaponless was less of a handicap for the cold mage than
for Bertaud.

The first three Casmantian soldiers came in at them in a rush: Swords, not arrows, which was good; so Kes had done that much for them by burning the earlier arrows.

Bertaud threw his knife at the first man, and a handful of sand at the second—Jos lunged forward and killed the first man as he ducked away from the flung knife, and engaged the other two while Bertaud got the first one's sword; Bertaud flung himself down, rolling under a stroke from a fourth soldier and barely making it back to his feet in time to block a slashing blow from a fifth.

The fifth soldier was a heavily built bald man with tremendous reach and plenty of weight to put behind his attacks. He also proved to be, unfortunately, extremely fast on his feet and uncommonly good with a sword. Bertaud backed up rapidly, half running, trying to prevent the rest of the Casmantian soldiers from coming at his back while he worked to keep his opponent from eviscerating him, and also tried to draw the soldiers away from Kairaithin. He was peripherally aware of Jos at the center of a knot of Casmantian soldiers, he had lost track of Kes entirely, and what *was* Kairaithin *doing*? The griffin mage seemed to be taking an unconscionable time about getting them all out of this.

The attempt to draw off the Casmantian soldier had certainly worked . . . a little too well. The bald soldier was backed up by two others, both uncomfortably skilled. The bald man aimed a slashing blow at Bertaud's face, then brought his sword around in a smooth arc, terribly fast, in a reversed cut at his chest while his companions circled in either direction around Bertaud. Bertaud blocked both attacks, the second one just by a hair, and attacked straight ahead to get out from between the other two soldiers. The bald Casmantian met his attack without giving back more than a step or two; the force of their swords clashing together reverberated through Bertaud's whole body.

He feinted at his opponent's lightly armored legs, tried a real thrust at his belly, and was forced to leap sideways to avoid the aggressive attack of one of the others, a much younger man with silver-chased armor—he dropped to one knee under a wickedly fast attack of the young one, swept his sword in a circle to force all his attackers back, lunged to get to his feet, and the bald Casmantian made a quick sideways rush, and this time Bertaud did not manage either to block or avoid the blow.

It was like a kick from a horse against his side: There was no sense at first of being cut. That would, Bertaud knew, come. He felt no pain, yet. That would come, too. He tried to get back to his feet and found no opposition—a measure of how badly he was hurt, that his opponents backed away and did not try to re-engage. Another, that he could not after all manage to get up. He found, to his surprise, that he no longer seemed to be holding his sword. He touched his side and felt moisture; he could not bring himself to look down, and looked up instead.

He saw Kairaithin, surprisingly close, rearing up, his red-chased black wings immense against the brilliant sky. He was aware of Kes, huddled by the griffin's leonine feet, looking tinier than ever. He thought Jos was still fighting—good for him—although he was aware of a faint and foolish embarrassment that he'd gone down before the other man. As though that mattered. He wondered whether Kairaithin was still too much engaged with Beguchren to protect himself from the soldiers. Bertaud had not managed to do much to reduce that danger. Nor would Jos, probably. Bertaud could not see the cold mage anywhere. Was that a good sign? It was obvious that neither Bertaud nor, soon, Jos was going to be able to protect the griffin or Kes much longer.

He thought he saw Kairaithin come down to all fours, wings spreading out to cover the whole sky, darkness blotting out sun and light and heat alike . . . and then the light returned, pouring across him with an intensity that was almost pain. He was blind with light, filled with light and heat, he felt his very bones had turned to light and burned through his body. Gasping, he lunged upward and found himself caught and held. For an instant, remembering battle, he tried to fight. A voice, soft and delicate, spoke words he did not at once understand, and the constraint disappeared. So he got an elbow under himself and pried himself up at least far enough to look around.

Kes, sitting back on her heels beside him, sighed, relaxed, stretched, and got to her feet.

Bertaud blinked, and blinked again, trying to clear his eyes of light enough that he could see. The measureless desert stretched out in all directions. Red cliffs and spires twisted upward all around them, reaching narrow jagged fingers to the hard sky. Heat poured down upon them so forcefully that it might have possessed weight and body.

If Bertaud was disoriented, Kes was not. She now stood poised, looking at once timid and confident, close by Kairaithin's side. Her fine soft hair fell around her face, sun glowing through it; it might have been spun of pale light. A warm light seemed to glow through her skin, as though it contained fire rather than flesh. Possibly she would have been an earth mage save for Kairaithin's intervention, but she looked now as though she had always been meant to be a mage of fire. She looked, in fact, as Kairaithin did when he wore the form of a man: like nothing that had ever been human.

Jos sat on the sand near Bertaud, in the shadow of a twisted red rock, not looking at any of them, but outward at the desert. Bertaud followed his gaze.

All around them, among the spires of rock, lounging on the hot sand or on rugged ledges, were griffins. Golden and bronze, warm rich brown and copper red; pale as the edges of a candle flame or darkly red as the last coals of a smoldering fire, they sprawled in the sun like cats and stared into the brilliant light with eyes that were not blinded. Only a few appeared to acknowledge the arrival of Kairaithin or Kes or human men in their midst.

Kes looked at Bertaud, glanced at Jos, shook her head, and raked her fingers absently through her hair. They moved again, the world tilting around them. Bertaud realized with a shock that it was the girl and not the griffin mage who had moved them this time. That she had done it as a griffin mage would: With a thought, with a shifting of the stillness of the desert. They stood suddenly in the stark black shadow of a broken cliff. The contrast of the shadow with the relentless pounding sun out in the open was dizzying.

Bertaud gasped, catching his balance with an outflung hand against the stone wall. He did not try to get up, but leaned his head back against the cliff wall and shut his eyes.

The Casmantian soldier, who had gotten to his feet, sat back down as well, with slow, careful movements.

Kairaithin lay down, stretching out like a cat. He appeared amused, although Bertaud could not have said why he had such an impression. Bertaud asked him, "Beguchren?"

Retreated, answered the griffin, with obvious satisfaction. *This day was mine.* And, after a moment, with a little tip of his fierce eagle's head, *Ours.*

Bertaud nodded back to him and said to Kes, "That's twice you've saved my life, I think. Thank you."

Kes gave him a quick shy smile, but she seemed more edgy and nervous now than she had during the fight. She paced hurriedly from one edge of the shadow to the other, unable to settle. She said, "I used fire. It was much easier this time."

Of course, Kairaithin told her. *You do very well,* kereskiita. *You are quick to learn and powerful in your gifts.*

Kes turned to the griffin. "The Casmantian king said I was—was—I don't know the word—*festech*-something."

"*Festechanenteir,*" said Jos, not looking up.

"Yes—*festechanenteir.* That means a fire-mage who is also human. Isn't that what it means?"

Yes, agreed the griffin.

Near Bertaud, Jos glanced up at Kes and then looked away again. Her friend, she had said, with no explanation of how she had made a friend of any Casmantian soldier. The man did not seem inclined to explain.

"My heart is turning to fire, my bones to red stone. Why didn't you *tell* me?" Kes asked Kairaithin. Her voice rose; she might have been happy to get away from Beguchren and back to the desert, but now that she felt herself safe, and despite her apparent shy timidity, she was clearly angry. "I knew you were teaching me to love fire. But I didn't know you were teaching me to forget earth! Why didn't you *tell* me what you were doing to me?"

Jos turned his head away and shut his eyes. Bertaud, though most of his attention was on the girl and on Kairaithin, studied the Casmantian curiously.

Should I have? Should I have said, "You should be an earth mage, you would wake into your power at a touch, but if you reach for fire now, you will become fire? Your heart will become fire, your breath will become desert wind?"

"Yes!" Kes cried. "Shouldn't you? Why should you not?"

Think, said Kairaithin, patient and pitiless as the sun. *I might have told you, "Take what I give you, do as I teach you, and you will lose what you are and become something other." You would have fled me and fought me and wasted your strength struggling against the fire, until I would have been forced to compel you by threat to obey me. I would have killed your sister's horses, one by one. And then I would have killed your sister's servants. And then I would have killed your sister. Would you have withstood all that I would have done?*

Kes stared at him, her anger smothered by shock and fear. She should have been weeping. Her eyes were dry as the desert. She whispered, "I would not even have been able to bear the horses."

So. And then you would have become fire all the same.

Bowing her head, the girl whispered, "I would rather have known what it was I was losing."

You do know, now. Does this knowledge please you? Kereskiita, you will become other than human. Already fire rather than earth sustains you. You have no thirst, no hunger; though you may be weary, it is not with the weariness of men. Does it profit you to know this?

Kes did not answer. Perhaps she could not. She looked down at the sand beneath her feet, her breath catching. Tears fell at last, flashing in the sun and rolling in the sand, fire opals and carnelians. Kes dashed jewels away from her face and turned her back on them all.

I would give you a choice, if I could.

Unexpectedly, Jos moved. He got up and took a step forward, coming up close behind the girl. With startling familiarity, he laid his broad hands on her shoulders and turned her to face him, giving her a little shake to make her lift her head. With unexpected eloquence he said, "Kes, this *wanenteir* would have you believe you have already given up your humanity. But you have not. You use fire; fire flows through your hands and your eyes and your heart and you think you are made of fire. But you are not. You were born to use the magecraft of earth. You should gather earth into your hands; you should use earth and metal and human magecraft until there is no room left in your heart for fire. You can do this. Would you abandon earth? Forget Tesme? She certainly won't forget you. She thinks of you all the time, she watches the hills all the time, she still hopes you will come back to her. What you choose now is what you will become. But it is still your choice. Won't you come back?"

Kes stared up at him.

Kairaithin said, *You are mistaken, man. Have you not been listening? She has no choice, for I will give her none.*

Jos didn't even look at the griffin, but only at Kes. He said, "You need her. You need her goodwill, lord *malacteir.* Or how should your people stand against even Feierabiand, far less Casmantium? You found her and you made her and you intend her now to be your weapon, but if she will not, then you are lost. I know this, and you know it, and if *Kes* understands it, she will be proof against any threat you can make—"

Be quiet. Or it is you I will kill, said the griffin.

"No," said Kes. Her voice was thin and shaky, but she turned quickly to stare at Kairaithin, and her eyes, though enormous in her delicate face, held in them a resolve that Bertaud had not expected.

Kairaithin tipped his head to the side, studying the girl out of one fierce black eye. His expression was not readable. But he did not threaten Jos again. He said to Kes, *In a hundred years perhaps you will have the strength to challenge me. But I assure you, you do not have that power today, and you will do as I choose and not as you would choose.*

"I trusted you," Kes whispered.

Do you not understand that my need is too great to allow me to be trustworthy? I will permit neither Casmantium nor Feierabiand to destroy what remains of my people. The choice you have is whether to suit your power to my need by your own choice or by mine. That is all the freedom you have. Kairaithin paused. No one spoke. The desert wind brought the dry scents of dust and stone and heat into the dark shadow of the cliff.

It is not a terrible thing, to be a creature of fire, the griffin added, his tone almost wistful. He angled his head sharply downward; his beak opened and clicked cleanly shut. Fire ran through his eyes, and he went suddenly elsewhere, leaving three humans who should never have been in this foreign desert to stand alone in the shadow.

Kes sighed sharply and sat down rather suddenly, her legs folding under her. Her thin hands trembled. She closed them into fists and stared blindly at the sand. The Casmantian soldier sat down more slowly next to her, and she leaned against him and turned her face into his shoulder.

"Who *are* you?" Bertaud asked him, bewildered anew by the familiarity between the soldier and the girl.

The soldier sighed. "No one," he said.

Kes straightened and wrapped her arms about her drawn-up knees. She said, in a small, weary voice, "He . . . he works for Tesme. My sister. But . . ." Her voice trailed off.

"I was once a soldier of Casmantium," the man said. He met Bertaud's eyes, flatly refusing anything further. Then his eyes dropped back to rest on the girl's face, and he shook his head. "Better I had left you with the Arobern. He would not have harmed you."

"He would have," Kes whispered. "Don't you understand? His need would have been too great to allow him to be kind." She shut her eyes.

"I—" said Bertaud. "You—"

Neither of them even glanced at him. Jos touched her chin with a fingertip, turned her face up toward his. The girl opened her eyes again, surprised. Jos said gently, "He would have made you human again, and that would have been a good thing. Kes, that creature was trying to frighten you, and I suppose he did—he frightened me—but, look, he can't force you to use fire. To become a creature of fire. Either you will or you won't, and truly, the griffin's need is a weapon in *your* hand. Why else should he have tried to silence me? All you require is the courage to use your own strength."

Kes gazed at him wordlessly.

Jos dropped his hand to rest on his knee. But he spoke with even more intensity. "You've always been braver than anyone would think, to look at you. Braver than you've thought yourself. You can make them believe no threat will move you, if you try. The *malacteir* need you. You don't need them. The sword is in *your* hand."

"But threats can move me," whispered Kes, "if they are the right threats." She sounded very tired. "And, Jos . . . what if I want the fire? I ought to want to go home, and sometimes I do want that, but the fire is so beautiful. What if I forget to want anything but fire?" She closed her eyes and tipped her head up toward the hard sky. Again Bertaud thought there should be tears; he heard them in her voice. But this time no tears glittered into jewels down her face.

The man gripped her shoulder, giving her a tiny shake. "And Tesme? Meris? Nehoen? All those who searched for you when you vanished into the desert? *They* are your people. Minas Ford is your home. Would you turn away from them forever?"

"I don't know," the girl whispered. She paused and then confessed in an even smaller voice, "Sometimes I forget even *Tesme*. I'm sorry, I'm sorry she's worried for me, I knew she would worry, I don't know how I can forget, but sometimes . . ."

"Then I'm sorry, too." Jos touched her cheek with the tips of two fingers, then dropped his hand again, slowly.

Bertaud came a step forward, dropped to one knee to put himself at the girl's level, and asked her quietly, "And Casmantium?"

Kes opened her eyes. Both she and Jos looked at Bertaud as though he had spoken words in a foreign language neither of them understood.

"An army of Casmantian soldiers in the mountains, poised to come down across Minas Ford and all Feierabiand? Is this not a matter of concern? Do you not wonder about Casmantium's intentions?"

"Oh," said Kes. And answered very simply, "No, I know what Casmantium wants. The king told me. He wants a new province. He wants a port city with a good harbor."

"Terabiand," said Bertaud, appalled.

Kes nodded. "And not to pay the toll on the road. And he says the road is bad. But I think really what he wants most is Terabiand. And as much other land as he can take."

"And all Iaor knows is that griffins have made a desert here. He will come down from Tihannad, expecting nothing but griffins, and he will find the desert on one side and Casmantium on the other."

"You can warn him," the girl said, not understanding. "Kairaithin would take you to him, I think. He would . . . surely he would rather soldiers of Feierabiand fought Casmantian soldiers than came against his own people. Or I . . . I could ask Opailikiita to take you to him, if Kairaithin will not. I think she would, if I asked her."

"I think," Bertaud said bitterly, "that probably if I have the temerity to approach Iaor after the way I left him, he will have me arrested."

The Casmantian soldier gave Bertaud a narrow look at this, but Bertaud did not care. He was consumed suddenly by a disbelief in all the events of the past hours. It seemed incredible that a griffin should have come to Tihannad, that in order to free him, Bertaud should have renounced the loyalty that meant more to him than life itself. Again, the image of Iaor's face in that moment of betrayal came before his eyes. He flinched from that image, staring instead out into the desert, trying to let the brilliance drive that memory away. Despite everything he could do, it lingered.

Though . . . if he had not freed Kairaithin . . . he would still be in Tihannad, and no one in Feierabiand would know yet that Casmantium had come across the mountains. It was clear what Brechen Glansent Arobern intended: to let Feierabiand commit its strength against the griffins and then come hard against them from behind when they were exhausted with fighting fire. Was not the chance to prevent that worth anything? Bertaud pressed a hand over his eyes and tried to believe this.

Kes, too, rubbed her thin hands across her face. Then she asked, "But won't he listen to you before he arrests you?"

Bertaud sighed and stood up. He stared out across the stark, beautiful desert, where light pulled fire out of the sand and spilled fire down the red spires of rock until the brilliance of it became painful to gaze upon. He said, reluctantly, because it was not arrest he feared but the look in Iaor's eyes, "Yes. Yes, I suppose he will." He looked back at the girl, incredulous all over again at her smallness against the strength and power of the desert. "And what shall I tell him you will do?"

"I don't know," she whispered.

"You must do as *you* choose," said Jos, his deep, slow voice sounding very certain.

Bertaud answered him sharply, "Sometimes circumstances choose for us." He turned urgently back to the girl. "I shall go to Iaor and hope he will hear me. And you . . . Kes, the griffins must support Feierabiand against Casmantium. Is not Casmantium inexorably their enemy? Have they not proven so? *We* need not be their enemies. We might even be allies. Do you understand?"

"Yes," the girl whispered.

The Casmantian soldier had a grim look to him; he, too, understood what Bertaud was saying. He said nothing.

"Can you make Kairaithin understand? And the rest of them?"

She only shook her head, clearly not knowing.

"You must," he said intensely. "You must. We must not allow Casmantium a free hand here. That will be no benefit to the griffins or to us." He gave Jos a hard look. "Will you say otherwise? Whom do you support in this?"

The soldier only shook his head. "I chose . . . when I killed that boy and took Kes out of the Arobern's hands; again when I fought against the king's mage and his men. That was my choice then, lord. Do you think I can go back now?"

Bertaud gave a slight nod, not really satisfied. But it was all the assurance he was going to get, clearly. He said to Kes, "Then will you get your friend to take me to the edge of the desert? As far north as she can?"

And so Kes called Opailikiita.

CHAPTER 11

Bertaud found Iaor, this time, in the better of the two inns in Riamne, with a very respectable army spread out in an encampment half a mile below the town, along the Sepes where the smaller stream divided from the larger Nejeied and quickened its flow between steepening banks. That Kes's griffin friend had known where the king of Feierabiand rested this night . . . that carried its own uncomfortable message.

Opailikiita had brought him to Riamne by that strange folding through air and time that the griffin mages seemed able to do, but Opailikiita did not linger in Riamne; she brought him to its walls and immediately took herself away again. Back to Kes, who was her friend? Back to Kairaithin, who was, Bertaud understood, her master? If she went to Kairaithin, would she tell him where she had taken Bertaud? If she did, and if he was angry, it would be a problem for Kes to deal with. Could she?

Whether or not, there was nothing he could do about it. Standing outside the town's open gates, Bertaud gazed at the diverging rivers that ran past the walls. He wanted, suddenly and intensely, to walk away again and never turn his head to see what he was leaving. The water slid steadily past on its way south to the sea. He might follow it south to the coast. Or he might go west to his own estates in the Delta. That would certainly surprise his uncles and cousins there.

He turned back to the town instead, deliberately, and went through the gates, threading his way through its streets to the inn.

The inn was a brick edifice, three stories tall, with balconies outside the highest rooms and flowers on the balconies. Bertaud knew where the king would be: The best suite the inn offered was on that top floor, with rich furnishings and a private bath and rooms for servants the lord who guested there would bring. Iaor would have taken that whole floor for himself and his military advisors and senior officers, and for Meriemne if he had brought her with him, as seemed likely. Possibly the king's entourage was ensconced all through the lower floors as well.

What Bertaud did not know was how best he might now approach the king. His own nervousness appalled him, but he couldn't help it. The thought of Iaor's face when Bertaud had defied him came back to him again, starkly. And if he had lost the king's trust and regard, perhaps forever? What would be left for him then? His father's house in the Delta? He grimaced.

Deliberately, he put that thought aside. If he'd lost the king's esteem . . . at least, Bertaud thought, surely Iaor would listen to him before he sent him away, or had him arrested. And so the king would know that a Casmantian army was in the mountains behind the griffins' desert, with Brechen Glansent Arobern at its head. That news would surely buy forgiveness. But, Bertaud thought, probably not a return of the easy trust, the certainty that he and Iaor had once had between them.

He sighed and stepped toward the inn's main door, wanting now primarily to get this whole encounter behind him.

A soldier was posted there, not a guardsman whom Bertaud would have known, but a man in the colors of some western-border company whom Bertaud had not, to his knowledge, ever seen before. Bertaud began to speak to him, but the soldier unexpectedly laid a hand to his sword without waiting, moving quickly to block the door to the inn and raising his voice in a shout.

Startled, Bertaud began to protest, then paused. He might not know this young man, but surely there was no chance that the soldier did not know him. Had his captain set orders that Bertaud was to be arrested on sight? Had a general given such orders? Adries, perhaps?

Had Iaor given that command himself? Bertaud thought, heart cold, that after the way he had fled Tihannad with the griffin mage, this was all too possible. He wondered now why he had not expected it; why he had imagined to be able to walk straight into the king's presence. Perhaps, indeed, Iaor would refuse to speak with him.

Or if this command had been given by some general or courtier who had been his rival in the court, perhaps Iaor would not even be told that he had come back.

It was this last thought that sent Bertaud's hand to catch and hold the soldier's before the young man could quite clear his sword from its scabbard. The soldier tried to break his grip, so Bertaud caught the man's wrist in his other hand, even knowing how stupid this was, knowing that he had lost this encounter the moment he'd allowed it to become a physical contest. Other soldiers were coming . . . He saw no guardsmen, no one he could expect to listen to him over whatever order they'd been given. He could not fight the soldiers; he could not command them. What else was left? Bertaud let go of the soldier's wrist and stepped back, hoping for inspiration. It did not come.

Another soldier, some lieutenant he didn't know, as he did not know any of these men, grabbed Bertaud's arm and stepped behind him to pinion him. For a moment there was quiet. Bertaud opened his mouth to speak, but found he did not know what to say.

A young guardsman, undoubtedly drawn by the commotion, came out of the inn. He looked curious and half alarmed. The young man was faintly familiar . . . Bertaud had thought he knew all his guardsmen well, but this one . . . He recognized him, then, and was all but overcome with a sudden unlikely desire to laugh. It was Enned son of Lakas, whom he had reluctantly accepted as a guardsman . . . what, seven days ago, eight? Enned recognized him, too. The young man's eyes widened.

Bertaud started to call out, but the lieutenant jerked his arm sharply upward and he desisted, trying not to gasp in obvious pain. "If you please, my lord," said the lieutenant, like an order. "You'll come with me, quietly now, my lord."

Enned ducked silently back into the inn.

"I must see the king," Bertaud began.

"That's for my captain to decide, my lord."

"I'll take him," said a new voice, much deeper. Eles came out through the doorway of the inn, having to duck his head slightly to clear the lintel. The guard captain turned a grim stare on the lieutenant, who looked unhappy. There were a dozen soldiers in the yard of the inn, now, but three or four guardsmen pressed out of the inn after their captain. Though, with Eles present, the numbers would not matter: The captain would not likely allow this encounter to become a physical confrontation between soldiers and guardsmen . . .

The lieutenant tightened his grip. He looked as though he would have liked to countermand Eles's order, but knew he did not have the authority to do so. He said, "His lordship is to be brought to my captain, sir, and smartly. That's my orders."

"I'll take it up with your captain," Eles said curtly, and the lieutenant hesitated. The man might not have served in Tihannad, but everyone knew Eles. Indeed, sometimes Eles's reputation served him better than his actual presence. Although Bertaud was glad of his presence at this moment.

"You'd best come along with me, my lord, according to my orders," the lieutenant said at last, and shoved. Bertaud set himself and resisted.

Eles shook his head and sighed, a slow exhalation that carried a startling menace. "Lieutenant. Mennad, is it?"

The lieutenant stopped again, looking uncomfortable.

"I," said Eles, "will take this up with your captain, lieutenant. Sebes," he said to one of his own aides, "if you would escort his lordship."

Sebes, a dark, thin man with an even more dour look than the guard captain, came forward and laid a matter-of-fact hand on Bertaud's arm. "If you will come with me, my lord?"

"My *orders* . . ." began the lieutenant, weakly.

"The responsibility is mine," said Eles, without any special emphasis. Bertaud would have liked to be able to create that quality of grim certainty with so little effort, but it did not seem to be reproducible.

The lieutenant, yielding at last to the inevitable, opened his hands.

The second floor of the inn, it was evident, belonged to the guardsmen. At least they all came up the stairs with their captain and Bertaud, and none of the soldiers followed. No one laid a hand on Bertaud once they were clear of the soldiers. But once they were up the stairs, Eles himself turned back to face Bertaud, who perforce came to a halt. For a moment, the two men regarded one another in silence. Around them, the other guardsmen were uncomfortably silent.

"Lord Bertaud," Eles said at last, with a hard look. "And have you brought . . . anyone . . . with you?"

"No."

Eles studied him. Bertaud had never been confident of his own ability to read the guard captain's face: When he had been a boy, he had thought there were no emotions behind the captain's inexpressive face to be read. He did not know what he saw there now.

"You want to see the king?" Eles asked Bertaud at last.

"Yes," said Bertaud. Neither demanding nor pleading. Just a neutral statement. "It's urgent that I should, esteemed captain."

"Urgent," repeated the captain. "Is it?" He regarded Bertaud for another moment. "Are you armed?"

"No, esteemed captain."

Eles gestured. One of his men—Sebes again—came forward, expression neutral, and with a murmur of apology proceeded to search Bertaud. Bertaud felt his face heat. But he lifted his arms and stood still, suffering the search without comment.

Finding nothing, Sebes took a step back and glanced at Eles.

"Wait there, if you please, my lord," Eles said briefly, tilting his head to indicate the nearest room. "I will speak to his majesty and find out whether he will see you."

"Thank you," said Bertaud. And added after the slightest hesitation,

"If he will not, Eles . . . esteemed captain . . . I ask you: Speak to me yourself. It is indeed extremely urgent information that I bring you. His majesty must hear it, from you if he will not hear it from me."

The guard captain nodded briefly, and Bertaud relaxed a little.

"If you would care to sit, my lord," said Sebes, once they had gone into the room to wait. Bertaud obediently sat down in the closest chair, folded his hands across his knee, and waited. Sebes stood behind him with two other guardsmen, including, Bertaud saw, Enned. They all waited, as patiently as was possible.

Bertaud said, after a moment, to Enned, "Well done, to go for the captain. Thank you."

Enned looked uncomfortable. "I . . ." he glanced at Sebes, hesitating. The older man lifted an eyebrow but did not rebuke the young man for speaking to Bertaud. So Enned continued. "It was my duty, my lord, but also my pleasure. I think . . . I did not thank you, my lord, that day. I never . . . and then, later, I thought I would be glad of the chance to do so."

"You have well repaid me," Bertaud assured him. He was again half inclined to laugh. Then the thought of Iaor made the inclination die a quick death. For all he feared what the king's reception of him might be, he could hardly bear to wait.

But, in fact, the wait was not very long at all. Eles returned mere moments after he had left, and, Bertaud saw, discomfited, Iaor himself accompanied the captain.

Bertaud first stood, startled, then quickly dropped to one knee and bowed his head. He glanced up covertly from beneath lowered lashes, trying to discern Iaor's mind behind the mask of his face, but found that he could not.

"Bertaud," the king said. Bare acknowledgment.

That coolness was hard to face; as hard as Bertaud had feared, surely. A dozen apologies and justifications, explanations, and excuses battled suddenly for primacy within him. He set his teeth, fixed his mind on the needs of the moment, and said, as crisply and cleanly and briefly as he knew how, "Brechen Glansent Arobern has five thousand men in the mountains above the griffins' desert, poised to come down upon you like a hammer against the griffins' anvil. The Arobern has been heard to say he wants Terabiand as the cornerstone of a new province, but I doubt he expects to get it without taking a certain amount of trouble."

The king stood very still. He said at last, "Valuable word. Well done, to bring it to me." He hesitated, then asked in a warmer tone, "Was it for this purpose . . . was it to get from the griffins the word they would not give me that you went with their mage?"

Yes! Bertaud wanted to cry. It would have been the best possible explanation, indeed: a noble risk, undertaken for loyalty and duty. But . . . it would be a lie. And where would loyalty and duty be then? He gave Iaor the truth instead, painfully. "I did not know why I did anything I did that night. I still don't know." He looked up to meet the king's eyes, afraid of what he would see there . . . Doubt? Mistrust?

What he saw was . . . both of those, he estimated, and bowed his head again in pain.

"You told me you did not trust your own judgment," the king said quietly. "I did not understand then what you were trying to tell me. Perhaps I understand it better now."

Bertaud looked at him helplessly.

The king came forward, laid a hand on Bertaud's shoulder with unexpected sympathy, urging him to stand. "Up," he said softly. "Up. All aside . . . I am glad you have come back to me. I confess I did not know whether to expect it. Up, I say. I am grateful for the warning you have brought me. But are *you* well?"

Unable to find an answer to that question, Bertaud only shook his head. He got to his feet rather shakily, finding Iaor's hand under his elbow in swift support.

"Sit," said the king, indicating the nearest chair. "Sebes . . . wine. Eles."

The guard captain came forward a step. "Your majesty."

"Go confer with Adries and Uol. Begin to develop alternate plans we might use in this exigency. Frontal attacks up into the teeth of the mountains are probably not the tactic of choice. Do think of some alternatives."

Eles bowed and went out. The king waved the other guardsmen out after him and dropped into a chair of his own. He picked up his cup of wine, though he did not drink. He looked instead at Bertaud. "Well? Tell me everything. Begin . . . try to begin with why you freed the griffin in my hall, if you can. And then go on from there."

And was this, then, forgiveness? It was not, Bertaud judged reluctantly. Not quite forgiveness and not quite absolution, though it might perhaps grow into either. It was better, even so, than he had had any right to expect.

He drank off his own wine in one quick draught and set the cup down on the arm of his chair with a small decisive click. And groped slowly after impressions he had been trying for a long night and a day to pull into some coherent order. He found, with some surprise, that stumble though he might, it did not actually take all that long to lay out the events of the prior hours. Not days. Only hours, though that seemed unbelievable. So little time to go from knowing your own place in the world to . . . knowing very little with certainty, it seemed.

Iaor was silent, thinking. Of many things, probably: deserts and fire, Casmantium and cold . . .

"I think . . . that Kairaithin sincerely does not want battle with you. With us. And that if he is not with his people, his opinion is not likely to carry the moment. I think that without strong leadership, the griffins will take all courses of action instead of just one, and become very dangerous. Kairaithin told me . . . that he came to Tihannad to warn you of Casmantium."

"But he changed his mind."

Bertaud spread his hands. He was baffled by the griffin mage's behavior himself, and had no idea how to explain it to Iaor. He said tentatively, "You hurt his pride, I think. I don't know! I don't know. He seemed . . . I believe he was honestly distressed to leave you uninformed. For his own purposes, if not for your sake . . . I think he meant to use Feierabiand to try to get his little fire mage back from the Arobern."

Iaor put his cup down again, still untasted. He shook his head, incredulous perhaps at the shape of the world, so different than it had seemed so few days earlier.

Bertaud found himself tapping his fingers nervously on the arm of his chair and folded his hands firmly in his lap. He glanced at the king, and away. And, reluctantly, back, gathering his courage. "Iaor?"

The king glanced up.

Bertaud met his eyes, with an effort. "Iaor . . . I'm sorry."

"I am not certain you have reason to be. The news you have brought me has great value."

Bertaud shook his head. "All else aside . . . I asked protection from another lord, against you. That was . . . I don't know what I was thinking. At the time, I don't suppose I *was* thinking; not clearly. I . . . well. I am sorry, Iaor. My king. I most earnestly beg your pardon."

Iaor was still for a moment. Then he nodded. He said nothing, but . . . Bertaud thought some of the edge had gone from the king's manner. The king said, "I was also at fault. Another time I will listen more closely to what you try to tell me. As I have tried to listen tonight. I ask for your advice. If I go south, can I depend on your Kairaithin to hold back his people? It should be Casmantium against which the griffins rage, not Feierabiand. What say you? Is there a way to speak to the griffins, to win their quiescence, if not their aid? Or if they should aid us, they may have their desert, and welcome. Would they be amenable to this suggestion? Can I find this Kes, could she perhaps make my desire clear to them?"

"Kes would be the one who might well go between you and the desert," Bertaud agreed slowly. "I have told her so, and told her to seek you out, though . . . I don't know that she would have the nerve. She is a timid creature, and herself half fire, now. Or, failing the girl, you might try to speak to Kairaithin yourself. If he will speak to you. I do not know what to advise you, my king. Except, do not send a mage to speak to the griffins. I don't think earth mages understand how strong the antipathy will be until they experience it. I am the last person who should speak, I know, but . . . I truly, truly do not think you should trust the opinions of a mage when it comes to dealing with griffins."

"I might send you," Iaor suggested. "If you thought you might trust yourself."

That question, not quite asked, was hard to face. Bertaud thought of Kairaithin saying, *I could send you as* my *agent* . . . He had instantly rejected that idea. But neither was he confident that he could act as Iaor's agent against the griffins.

"Shall I trust you?" Iaor asked him. He asked as a friend. And as a king. "You chose the griffin over me in Tihannad. If it came to that a second time, whom would you choose? If your Kairaithin bids you against me . . . are you certain what choice you would make? Can I be certain?"

Bertaud knew, to his dismay, that he could not answer this question.

It was Iaor, his friend, who looked at him with sympathy. But it was the Safiad, King of Feierabiand, who said, "I will consult with Meriemne. I will take counsel of my generals and my advisors. But, my friend, I think we will be riding south tomorrow, and I think that you will stay here, under guard. I beg you will not think less of me."

"No," Bertaud whispered.

The top floor of the inn held five rooms. The best of these was actually a suite, containing a sitting room and servants' quarters as well as a bed chamber. Soft rugs covered the wooden floors, chairs with scrolled arms stood by small decorative tables, and a rather good painting of the town hung opposite the curtained bed. The walls were white, the wood bleached pale, the rugs and curtains the color of pale ivory; the effect was one of spacious light, though none of the rooms was large.

Wide windows, shutters thrown open, offered an impressive view over Riamne's low walls to the river. The afternoon sun struck the water to gold, as though it were molten fire that flowed there. Bertaud shifted uneasily and tried to see the river as simply water. On the road that ran alongside that river, a long column of two thousand men was slowly passing away to the south.

The king, with his banners and his retinue, was already out of sight. It would take an hour, probably, for the tail end of the column to pass out of view. Bertaud, his hands resting on the broad sill, watched their slow movement. For a very little, he would have gone out the window, found a horse, and followed them.

He knew what he wanted: to ride after the king, ask for a different decision, for leave to ride with the army. He understood there was no point. He had not remonstrated with the king's decision. He had not allowed a whisper of resentment, of bitterness, to inform his manner or his leave-taking with his king. If that leave-taking had been strained . . . that was nothing for which Iaor could be faulted. He believed that.

And now there was this window, with guards below—Bertaud did not have to look for them to know they were there—and the slow procession, of which he was not part. He paced unhappily from the window to the door and back to the window: Both would be guarded. By men who kept him here by order of the king they all served, whom he did not wish to defy.

He paced again, from window to door, from sitting room to bed chamber, back to the window. The column of soldiers was still in sight, and still moving so slowly a brisk stride might well carry a man to its head before the last of its baggage tail was well in motion.

Which, of course, he could not prove himself. In disgust, Bertaud flung himself into one of the fine chairs and stared sightlessly at the wall, refusing to look again out the window.

The quality of the light flooding the room changed slowly, so that the plaster of the walls turned from white to cream to the palest gold and then to a more luminescent gold, tinged with the red of the lowering sun. Shadows crept slowly into the room, dimming its light, and the breeze that wandered through the window became uncomfortably cool . . . time passing, carrying them all forward with it, he feared: The king riding endlessly through this suspended moment into the south and the new desert; and the Arobern, hidden with his army in the stillness of the mountains above that desert; and the griffins contained within it, building it out of themselves. All, all of them, separated by distance, but all contained in the identical moment. Until the moment should break, and they all crash together into disaster . . . He could all but see it, a fast-approaching moment toward which the inexorable wind of time carried them all . . .

A hand was set firmly on his shoulder, so that Bertaud jerked upright and spun sharply. Yet he was somehow not surprised to find it was Kairaithin who stood over him, in the form of a man, with his shadow the shadow of a griffin. "Earth and iron," he breathed, and dropped back into the chair.

"You called me," Kairaithin said, rather harshly. His face was not clearly visible in the dim light, but his eyes blazed with fire that made their blackness somehow only the more absolute.

"I?" Bertaud said blankly.

"You." Kairaithin gave him a long stare. "Well? Will you tell me you had no intention to call?"

Ignoring this baffling question, Bertaud instead leaned forward and said urgently, "Kairaithin, when Feierabiand comes into your desert, you must pretend to do battle. *Tell* Iaor what you will do. Go to him—or take me to him and I will speak for you. We can arrange it all. Then you and he can *both* turn against the Arobern when he comes down out of the mountains, and all will be well!" And the disaster toward which the wind carried them all would fail, and Feierabiand remain as it should be: Peaceful and green and in no way broken by griffin fire or Casmantian ambition.

The griffin mage turned his fierce, proud face toward the window and the sky beyond.

"Well?" Bertaud asked him urgently. "Well?"

"Tastairiane Apailika has persuaded Eskainiane Escaile Sehaikiu of the efficacy of a different course," Kairaithin said. His black eyes shifted from the window to Bertaud's face. "And Escaile Sehaikiu has persuaded the Lord of Fire and Air. We shall draw both Feierabiand and Casmantium into our desert, Feierabiand by pretended aggression and Casmantium by the hope of easy victory; yet both shall be illusion. Thus, once the Casmantian force has destroyed the soldiers of Feierabiand, we shall come down upon it in its turn, and Casmantium will not be able to stand before us. Thus the men of Casmantium will follow those of Feierabiand into the red silence, and my people shall be secure."

Bertaud stared at him, appalled. He got to his feet, took a single step forward. "Is this what you want?" he whispered.

The fierce eyes held his, without a shadow of apology or regret. "I argued for the calling up of a different wind. But no one has more influence with Kiibaile Esterire Airaikeliu than Escaile Sehaikiu; they are *iskarianere*, closer than brothers. The argument did not go my way. And, in truth, man, this plan will do well enough."

"Not for Feierabiand," Bertaud said sharply. "Not for Iaor."

"No," agreed the griffin, but not with sympathy. Only with frightening indifference.

Bertaud moved to the window and looked sightlessly out into the dusk for a moment. Then he turned back toward Kairaithin. "Casmantium beat you before, drove you from your own desert, destroyed all your mages but one. Why should you believe you can face the Arobern now? Even wearied by battle against Feierabiand?"

"I have no power for healing," stated the griffin. "But Kes does."

The implication stood starkly in the silence between them. Bertaud said at last, "Then you should not need to blunt the Casmantian spear against a Feierabiand shield."

Kairaithin tilted his head to the side, a slight gesture somehow more like the movement of an eagle than of a man. Fire seemed to burn just out of sight beneath his skin; his black eyes were filled with pitiless fire. He said, "While Casmantium battles Feierabiand, I shall hunt the cold mages. They will discover that the roused desert is more powerful than they had imagined. Thus when the battle of men is over, my little *kereskiita* will be neither wearied nor opposed. Thus she may do her work well during the battle between Casmantium and my people. Thus will the Arobern learn that the People of Fire and Air are not to be lightly offended."

"No," Bertaud whispered, without strength.

Kairaithin's stare held . . . regret, possibly. But still no hint of apology, or yielding. He said, "You will not need to call me again." The world shifted, tilted . . .

"No!" Bertaud shouted, not disbelief this time, but out of desperate need and horror. And found, to his astonishment, that that strange shift of space and time did not continue, that the world and the room steadied, that the griffin had stayed after all.

Kairaithin seemed exasperated, but he remained. "Cease," he said sharply.

Bertaud stared at him. The fire shone just below the surface of the griffin; for a moment, he saw neither the man-shape Kairaithin wore, nor the true griffin beneath that shape, but only fire—contained and channeled and ruled by will, but fundamentally wild.

He seemed to hear it, roaring high in its burning; he felt its searing heat against his face. It was fierce and merciless, wild and beautiful, passionate and joyous. It spoke, and its voice was the voice of the griffin. It spoke of the hot wind, of the desert storm, of stone that melted and flowed like water.

He was not, Bertaud knew distantly, dreaming. Though his eyes, it occurred to him, were closed. He opened them.

Kairaithin was standing very still in the center of the room, watching him. His proud, austere face showed very little. And yet Bertaud knew that the griffin was afraid. And he knew why. Impossible though it had seemed. Impossible though it seemed still.

He said, "You came when I called you. Can you go, though I refuse you leave?"

"You would not be wise to challenge me," Kairaithin said. He did not move, did not even blink, but a hot wind sang tensely through the confines of the room; sand hissed across the plaster walls and drifted on the rugs.

"Stop," Bertaud commanded him.

The wind died.

"Man," said Kairaithin, "I warn you plainly. You do not know what you are doing. Cease this foolishness. I *will* go. Be wise, and do not challenge me." The room shifted, tilting underfoot.

"Stop it!" snapped Bertaud, catching his balance on a windowsill that seemed, under his hand, to want to become twisted red stone.

And the room stilled, with both of them still within it.

"I do know what I am doing." Bertaud tried to steady his voice, which kept wanting to rise into a shout of incredulity. He tried to steady his hands, which were trembling. "Though I . . . did not know it was possible for a man to hold the affinity to griffins."

"It is not possible." Kairaithin blazed into griffin form and then into fire, a savage red fire that cast its own shadow, which was golden and shaped like a griffin. The fire roared up, red and gold, flames running along wooden tables and thick rugs, across the wooden floor and up the plaster walls. Somewhere, distantly, there were shouts.

"No," said Bertaud, and fought the fire. It only roared the more passionately until he stopped fighting it and let himself love it: its passion, its fierceness. "No," he whispered, and quieted it.

His eyes were shut again. He drew a breath of air that tasted of fire, and opened them.

Kairaithin stood in the center of the charred room, in the form of a man. His eyes, filled with fire and rage and a bleak awareness of his own helplessness, were fixed on Bertaud. It hurt to see that bleakness where there should be exultant power. It took a wrenching effort of the heart not to cry *Go, then!* and free the griffin of all constraint. Even knowing that, freed, Kairaithin's first act would certainly be to strike down the man who had constrained him. That knowledge alone would not have been enough to hold Bertaud back. But his own safety was far from the most important consideration, now.

"I offer you a new plan," Bertaud said.

"You do not command me."

Bertaud paused. He took a breath, made his heart iron, and said, carefully and ruthlessly, "Kneel to me."

The griffin's human face tightened. He fought the command. Bertaud simply waited; there was no effort in the compulsion he imposed on Kairaithin. It was not like a mage using the power of the earth to overcome the power of fire; it might have been something more akin to the compulsion of the Casmantian *geas*. Bertaud had always found the idea of the *geas* repellent. But the reality of this affinity was worse. The compulsion it let him impose did not require a battle of skill or strength. For Bertaud, though it twisted his heart, it was not a battle at all.

Kairaithin, with a low sound of effort, went to his knees on the charred floor. His quick breaths hissed like blowing sand.

"I do command you. You do not have the power to resist me. So you will do as I choose and not as you would choose."

Kairaithin brought his gaze up to meet Bertaud's. He said in a harsh, level tone, "I acknowledge your power, man. I acknowledge your strength. You are wrong to use it."

Bertaud agreed completely. It felt normal and right to understand the fierce mind and heart and will of the griffin. It felt horribly, devastatingly wrong to coerce that fierceness. He truly understood for the first time in his life why a man who could command the deer would not call them to the huntsman; why a man who could compel wolves to leave a village's flocks alone would slaughter his own sheep for them in a hard winter. He hated what he did. And yet . . . he lifted his hands, palms up. "Is not my need too great to allow me to choose what is right? I must choose what I must have. You *will* yield to me."

There was a pounding, sudden and loud, on the smoke-stained door. Both of them, startled, flinched. Kairaithin also used the moment of startlement to try to break Bertaud's hold, to fray into wind and fire and try to fly back to the desert.

Bertaud, after the first instant of surprise, stopped him. It did not even take a word. Only a thought. Only a thought to force the griffin back into human shape, to pin him to the charred boards, to force that proud face to the floor. As a man with the gift to speak to cattle might bring an enraged bull to instant docility, so he forced compliance from a creature not meant to yield to any compulsion.

Kairaithin fought him. To no effect.

"Yield to me," Bertaud insisted, furious and frightened and sickened all at once. And, as the pounding at the door suddenly took on a threatening force, "Keep them out!"

On that, they were in perfect accord. A blazing sheet of fire sprang up all around them. Without the room, there were sudden cries and then silence. The fire died. Kairaithin, as though obedience to the one command carried a yielding to both, slowly and deliberately relaxed the muscles in his back, in his neck, in his arms. He said, muffled against the floor, "I acknowledge that you are stronger than I. I could not possibly mistake it."

Bertaud eased the compulsion. He was shaking. Kairaithin, gathering himself slowly to his knees and then to his feet, was not. He was angry, with an anger deep and unrelenting as molten stone. Shamed and frightened and angry. Bertaud knew everything the other felt, recognized the shame and fear and anger, understood the source of those emotions and their power.

Kairaithin bowed his head, brought one long hand up, touched his own human face, his own eyelids. He looked, with that gesture, very human. Seeing past all outward appearances into his heart, Bertaud saw the griffin behind the human form and the fire behind the griffin.

Looking up, Kairaithin met Bertaud's eyes. "You are wrong to do to me what you have done."

"I know," Bertaud whispered. And then, more strongly, "I could not possibly mistake it. Were you right to cast Kes into the fire and make her your tool? Is my necessity less dire than yours?"

Kairaithin did not look away, but neither did he answer.

"Tonight," Bertaud said, "or tomorrow, Iaor will lead his two thousand into your desert. And . . . everything will go as it will go, from there. You have told me what your king expects. Here is the new plan: Your people will pretend to engage mine in battle, but both sides will understand this is pretense. Iaor will affect to be hard-pressed and ignorant; he will set his men with their backs to the Arobern. When the Casmantian army is lured down from the mountains, both your people and mine will fall upon them and destroy them."

Kairaithin heard this without expression. Inwardly, he was raging still, and afraid, and in neither his rage nor his fear was he human. He was something other, that should have been incomprehensible. And yet Bertaud looked past his form and understood his heart.

The face the griffin showed outwardly was calm. "This is not the intention of the Lord of Fire and Air."

"*Make* it his intention!" Bertaud said, his voice rising with anger and self-loathing. He caught himself, and continued more quietly. "You say you did not favor the current plan, that's all very well, but did you care enough to fight against it with all your strength? Now you must. Remind your king that it is Casmantium that is his enemy, that Feierabiand and your people have a common enemy in this. Suggest to him that if the Arobern's ambition is not curtailed now, Casmantium will only become more aggressive and more dangerous. Is that what your lord would desire? Is there not natural reason for alliance between your people and mine? Can there not be lasting advantage in an understanding between Feierabiand and the desert?"

Kairaithin did not answer. But at least he did not instantly decry these suggestions.

Bertaud warned him, "Or we shall see whether I am strong enough to force all your people at once to my will. I have never heard that there is a limit to how many animals a man can rule, who has the affinity for that animal."

"The People of Fire and Air are not to be called to heel like dogs."

Bertaud stared into the griffin's fiery eyes. "To me, you are."

Kairaithin closed his eyes against a visible leap of fury, clenched his teeth against the first violent words that came to his tongue. A moment passed. Another. Mastering his own rage, the griffin said, forcing his tone to a temperance and restraint with an effort Bertaud felt wrench his own heart, "You must not do that, man. Lord. You must not reveal to any other of my people even the merest shadow of the power you have shown to me." His black eyes met Bertaud's with a caution foreign to his nature, a trepidation that hurt them both. He said, harshly, "Do you not know what you would do to them? I will beg, if you demand it. I will kneel willingly."

Bertaud was so horrified by this suggestion he actually recoiled backward. "I have no desire whatsoever to, to . . . command *any* of your people. I promise you. *You* must see to it that my necessity does not encompass any such act. I want only what I have said."

Another pause. Kairaithin bowed his head, again with that clear effort. "And if I am not able to persuade him? Lord, you must not set such a penalty on my failure—"

"You will persuade him. You *must*."

Another moment. "Let me go, then," the griffin said harshly. "And I will see to it that all occurs as you require."

Bertaud nodded. "I will follow you in my own time, and expect to see that you have. You won't fail. I have," he said quite sincerely, "great faith in your strength and cleverness, once you put everything you have of each into this effort."

Bitterness shifted through Kairaithin's heart, hidden behind the mask of his face, but clear to Bertaud. Turning toward the window, the griffin let go of his human seeming and reached after the desert wind. It came to meet him, the world tilting as it came, and Kairaithin touched the boundaries of the desert. He made as he did so one last effort to reach also for freedom.

He did not succeed. Bertaud contained the griffin's shifting form, his tilting location, his fast flight into the dark and his fierce, sudden lunge against the binding that held him. It did not break. Distance thinned it to a thread. But if he called Kairaithin again, Bertaud knew, the griffin would have no choice but to come. And he knew Kairaithin knew it, too.

This awareness was both reassuring and deeply disturbing.

Bertaud stood for a long moment, his mind following Kairaithin south. Then he collapsed in the fire-damaged chair and put his face in his hands, struggling against overwhelming reaction: He wanted both to laugh hysterically and sob like a child; he wanted to spread great wings with feathers made of fire, to turn his body into fire and blaze like a torch through the sky. All those dreams, explained. And the explanation was nothing he had ever imagined or desired. An affinity for griffins! He felt as though the affinity, woken at last—undoubtedly by Kes, when she used fire to heal him—well, however it had happened, the affinity completed something in his heart that he had never even recognized was missing. A new depth informed the whole world. It felt wonderful. It was horrifying. If Kairaithin was again before him, he knew he would constrain the griffin exactly as he had done before; yet he could hardly believe even now that he had ever twisted the affinity to such a use.

He found that he understood far better than he ever had just how divided Iaor was between his two roles, both man and king. Of course, Bertaud had always understood this. But he understood it much better now. He understood it *intimately*. He had known that power requires to be used; that the world compels the exercise of power if one possesses it. And that necessity constrains what one may do with power.

The last shreds of resentment he had harbored against Iaor shredded in the face of this understanding; *of course* the king had left him in Riamne. What else could the king have done? This, too, though Bertaud had already understood, he understood much better now.

Even so, Bertaud knew that he could not possibly stay in Riamne now. He got to his feet . . . stiffly. He felt stiff all over, as though he'd pressed his body to its limits, rather than his heart. But stiff or not, he made his way across the fire-scarred floor to the door. How long would it take to get a horse and start after Iaor? Longer, he supposed, if men felt required to try to prevent him . . . He laid his hand on the door, took a breath, and shoved it open upon charred boards and the smells of smoke and burning.

CHAPTER 12

Kes watched the King of Feierabiand approach the desert from a high perch on an outcropping of red stone. She had one arm thrown lightly over Opailikiita's neck. Jos sat uneasily some distance away on her other side. It was not the height that made him uneasy, Kes knew. It was Opailikiita. Or perhaps it was Kes herself. She would not have blamed him.

At the edge of sight, where the northwestern border of the griffin's desert met the gentle country of river and field, lay the road that ran past Riamne, which Kes had never seen, all the way north to Tihannad, where she had never even imagined going. The King of Feierabiand was on that road. The dust of his army made a haze in that direction. So she knew he was there, approaching the country the griffins had made theirs.

And to her other side, beyond the desert, hidden within the smooth gray stone of the mountains, was Brechen Glansent Arobern and Beguchren and thousands of Casmantian soldiers. When the Feierabiand soldiers had met the griffins in the desert, they had all died. And when more soldiers of Feierabiand met that Casmantian army? They would all die. The griffins would let that happen. Even Kairaithin, though he had argued against it. Even Opailikiita, though she would be unhappy to make Kes unhappy.

Kes rested her face against her drawn-up knees, wanting to hide from the world, from her own thoughts, from everything she knew. She no longer exactly wanted to run home to Tesme. She could neither imagine leaving the fierce desert nor wishing to leave it. But at the same time, grief shadowed the brilliance of the desert. She longed for a simpler, gentler time, for the girl she had been and the life she had owned before the griffins had come. A time when the only choices she had to make were simple, because they did not *matter.*

Nothing was simple, now. She wished she could be angry about that. She should be angry—with Kairaithin; with the Lord of Fire and Air; with Brechen Glansent Arobern, the ambitious King of Casmantium, who had driven the griffins out of their high desert as a tactic against Feierabiand. And she *was* angry. But her anger only flickered around the edges of her fear.

Against her side, Opailikiita stirred. The griffin turned her head to look at Kes out of one golden-brown eye, a fierce attention that drew Kes all but involuntarily back into the immediate present. The stroke of gold through the feathers above the griffin's eye gave her a ferocious look. And she *was* ferocious. But . . .

"Sister," said Kes, and smoothed those soft feathers with the tip of one finger.

The griffin closed her eyes and tilted her head against the delicate caress; if she had been a cat, she would have purred.

Kes stared into the desert and thought about fire, and earth, and sisters. What, she wondered, would Tesme make of the red desert? Of the fire-eyed griffin? Tesme would be horrified by both, Kes was nearly certain. She would be afraid of both. And either might kill her, the griffin almost as indifferently as the desert. Though Opailikiita would not want to make Kes *unhappy.* But she might kill Tesme anyway and say in surprise when Kes protested, *But it was a day for blood.*

A day for blood.

Blood would surely water the desert, soon. It would flood forth abundantly. And what would bloom of this gathering storm? And what would it cost to turn that storm? If she could. Could she?

And if she could, would she be glad afterward? Perhaps she would say, *But was this not a day for blood?* and wonder why she had troubled herself. Kes pressed her hands over her eyes, trying not to think about losing herself to the desert, of letting it change her not only into a different person but into an entirely different kind of creature. But even if she refused to think about this, she knew it was possible. More than possible. She almost longed to pour fire through her heart to her hands, to scatter fire across the wind right now, just so that change would *happen,* would be *done* with, so she could stop agonizing over the prospect. Afterward . . . afterward, what would she think? Or feel?

Did it matter what she thought afterward? Or felt? Did it matter, what she might lose by what she chose, when she had no choice, really? Did it matter what she might gain?

Kes said to Opailikiita, "You know the binding Kairaithin put around me."

I know, the slim griffin said.

"I can't leave the desert. But you could help me. You could push the desert . . . out." Kes gestured vaguely.

The griffin turned her head, closed delicately feathered eyelids half across her golden-tawny eyes. *Where would you go?*

In a way, Kes wanted to say, Home. She shut her eyes, trying to think about the comfortable house where Tesme would be waiting for her. Worrying for her. Wondering where Kes was, what she might be doing, whether she was safe. But images of the desert intruded on memories of her home: flames rippling in the wind and licking out of the sand; the merciless sun blazing above red cliffs, stark shadows stretching out beneath . . .

She blinked, and blinked again, and stared away north and west, toward the dust haze that marked the road and the king. "There."

At her side, Jos stilled attentively.

What would you do there? asked the griffin.

"Find the king. And tell him . . . tell him . . . everything, I suppose." Kes contemplated this feat, now that it was laid out plainly in words, with extreme disquiet. She shivered. *Could* she walk into the presence of the King of Feierabiand and tell him anything at all?

Tears pressed at her eyes, or a pressure and heat that should have been tears. If she wept, she knew that fire opals would scatter across the sand. She blinked fiercely, not wanting to see jewels where there should be tears. She had bravely enough declared what she wanted to do. But when she stood in the midst of a crowd of soldiers and courtiers and strangers, she knew she would stand mute and helpless until, defeated by her own inability to speak, she was forced to retreat again to the silence of the desert.

And yet, if she could not believe she would find the courage to stand and speak, could she not at least find the courage to try for the first small step in that direction?

Opailikiita, fearless herself, did not understand fear and would not have comprehended Kes's anxiety even had she tried to put it into words. But she understood peril and prudence. She said, *The Lord of Fire and Air would be very angry.*

Kes knew this was so. She asked cautiously, "But . . . do you care?"

And it seemed she correctly understood the heart of the griffin, because where a human woman—or a human soldier—would have cared, and cared deeply, Opailikiita said simply, *No.*

Jos stared at her. At them both.

Kairaithin would also be angry, said Opailikiita. *His opinion, I do care for.*

Kes looked into her fierce tawny eyes, and beyond them into the ferociously independent, unconquerable heart of the griffin that would not bear any kind of mastery. "Kairaithin has imprisoned me here. He leaves me to choose only what he would have me choose. Is that right?"

No, said the griffin, definitely.

"Then," Kes asked her, "would you not help me choose as I would choose?"

Yes. If you ask me. You may ask.

Kes rose to her feet, standing on the edge of the cliff, at the edge of space; she blinked and stared into it, looking for the layers of heat and motion that a griffin would see. She perceived only space, however fire-touched her eyes. And, to the west, the haze of rising dust. Where the king would be. She did not let herself think of him. She thought only of the desert and the red cliff and the dizzying drop into space. And of Opailikiita, who was her friend and her sister and who understood space and movement.

Jos stood up and moved a step closer to her. "And me."

"Of course," said Kes, surprised, and put out a hand for his.

And the world shifted around them.

The edge of the desert was a sharp, clean break. Red sand and heat lay at their backs, an austere splendor ruled by a merciless sun set in a sky that was a hard and brilliant white. But before them, soft greens and grays and browns ran down the gentle hills into the more verdant green where the river ran. The light itself lay tenderly on the young green of pastures and woodlands, and the sky before them was a soft, delicate blue.

The king's camp was not in sight. Kes could see where the road must be, from the shape of the land; she knew there was a great host strung out along it from the dust and the distant sounds of many men.

And she knew, without even needing to put it to a test, that she could not step from one land to the other. Kairaithin had set the desert's boundary in her mind, or her heart. She could not pass through it.

Even if she found him, probably the king would not listen to her—why should he? He was not her friend, as Jos was. There was not, Kes thought, really much point to trying to speak to him. She could go back into the silent reaches of the desert and sit with Opailikiita and Jos on a high cliff and watch events unfold and there would really be nothing, nothing at all, she could ever have done about any of it.

She sighed. Then she said to Opailikiita, "I can't leave the desert, but you could move it." She gestured outward with both hands as though shooing the desert forward. "If the desert comes to the king, then I can speak to him and yet not break past Kairaithin's boundary."

Opailikiita said, *Yes.*

"I know it will be hard," Kes said apologetically. The griffins spun the desert out of their own hearts; the desert wind came into the world through their own souls. She did not quite know how she had such temerity as to ask Opailikiita to spend her own self and strength on a task that the griffin did not even value—that might even be dangerous for her. She started to say, No, never mind, don't worry about it, let's go back to the high desert and listen to the sun striking the red stone— whatever will happen, let it happen.

Before she could, Opailikiita half opened her wings and leaned forward. A hot wind blew past her, or out of her; it came from the shadow under her wings and stirred the green grasses of the pasture. The grasses withered at that sere touch, an alarming thing to watch. Sand blew gently across them, catching in the yellowing blades. The strength of the sun came down, and the grasses dried and crumbled and blew away on the parched wind.

Opailikiita took a step forward. And another.

Behind her, Jos swore softly and fervently.

Kes closed her eyes and followed Opailikiita blindly. She did not need to look where she walked: She walked in the desert and her path was always the same no matter where she set her foot.

A Feierabiand soldier spotted them before the camp itself came into their view; his shout of amazement and alarm made Kes open her eyes. She stretched her stride to come up beside Opailikiita and put a hand on the griffin's slim neck, hard-muscled under its soft feathers. She said worriedly, "If there are arrows—"

You must catch them, said Opailikiita, a little breathlessly. *They move in the air, they fly, they belong to the air. You can catch them with fire if you are quick, or turn them with wind. Remember, men make them so they will try to strike you. A wind must be very strong to turn them aside.*

Kes had burned arrows before; she knew she could be quick enough to catch them with fire. If there were not too *many* arrows. But what if there were too many? If an arrow struck Opailikiita, she thought she would be able to heal her. But what if an arrow struck her own body? Or Jos? Her steps slowed. It would be so much easier just to go back . . .

"They are not shooting," Jos said, and laid a hand on her shoulder. He meant the touch for reassurance, she knew. It felt like a pressure at her back, shoving her forward.

The one soldier had been joined by others, a few at first and then more. But the shouts ceased. Men drew aside into two companies, one to either side of the path Opailikiita was making; they were close enough now that Kes could make out bows in some hands and spears in others.

"You can see they will let us come right in among them," Jos said. Again in his deep voice Kes heard not reassurance, but warning.

She said worriedly, "Is the king there?" She did not know what she would do if the king was not there. Who else should she speak to? Who might carry her words to the king, and would they sound persuasive in someone else's mouth?

Would they, in hers?

Jos peered ahead. "Just there, I think."

Kes looked at the man he indicated: Standing between the two armed ranks of soldiers, with others close by him. He looked grim and authoritative and sure of himself, thoroughly intimidating. He was like a lion, she thought, with a broad, assured face and muscled arms and sun-bleached streaks in his thick tawny-colored hair. He wore no crown, but nevertheless he looked very much a king.

And what would this man see when he looked at her?

Closer yet, and the nearest soldiers were close enough to have almost touched Opailikiita with their spears. They didn't, however, but stood still, in straight ranks, with their spears grounded on the earth at their feet and their eyes straight ahead, except for little covert fascinated glances at the griffin, and at Kes and Jos.

The king, close now, was also standing patiently. There was a man at his side—not Bertaud, and Kes was sorry, she would have trusted Lord Bertaud far more than these strangers. There was a very old woman seated in a chair, with woman attendants about her. Her eyes were closed, but she turned her face toward Kes with an awareness that went beyond sight. Kes knew by the sudden twist of dislike she felt that this woman must be a mage and flinched uneasily away from her strong awareness.

Opailikiita stopped and sank down couchant upon the sand she had brought with her; her beak was slightly open and she panted with rapid shallow breaths. Kes laid an apologetic hand on her shoulder, cast one despairing glance back along the narrow tongue of desert they had made, and turned slowly and reluctantly to face the king.

He looked stern, she thought. Forbidding. She wondered if he ever smiled. Now that she was so close, she could see that his eyes were dark: not measurelessly black like Kairaithin's eyes, but dark as fresh-turned earth, with a power to them as the earth possessed. He did not have the presence of the Lord of Fire and Air. But he had a presence of his own.

Words deserted her. Just as Kes had feared, she did not know what to say, and stood tongue-tied and clumsy in the midst of a hundred men. She edged closer to Opailikiita, trying to draw strength and courage from the griffin, who possessed both in such generous measure. But Kes still felt neither herself. She was horrified by the possibility that she would not be able to speak after all, that the day for blood and death would come and she would not even have been able to *try* to prevent it.

The king came forward one step, and another, waving away the concern of the men who pressed forward anxiously at his back. His dark eyes looked into hers, and Kes wondered what he saw in them, and thought that if he was perceptive he would see fire. His own were filled with curiosity.

Then he brought his attention back to her face, looking her over quickly from the top of her head to her bare toes. "Kes, I presume," he said, and the laughter she had not seen in his face was suddenly perceptible at the edges of his voice.

Kes blinked. She nodded hesitantly.

"And who is this?" The king was looking in open wonder at Opailikiita.

Kes followed his gaze, and managed to smile, because the griffin was so magnificently unimpressed by men with spears, no matter how numerous, or by kings, no matter they were kings. Opailikiita arched her neck a little so her feathers ruffled into almost a mane; sun glinted off her feathers as though each one had been pounded separately out of bronze and had fine gold scrollwork inlaid across it. The muscles in her slim lion rear shifted powerfully as she eased herself to a sitting posture, and her tail, wrapping neatly around her talons, tapped gently on the sand.

"Opailikiita Sehanaka Kiistaike," said Kes, finding her voice after all. "She is my friend, and brought me here because I asked her to. She is not—well, she is dangerous, but not to you, um, your majesty, unless you try to shoot her. She only came because I asked her to make a path for me."

"She is welcome," said the king, and looked curiously at Jos.

"That is—"

"No one," Jos interrupted harshly. "Except her friend."

Kes looked at him in surprise.

"That is a Casmantian uniform," noted the king, in a mild tone.

Jos shrugged.

Kes did not want to say anything about Jos to the King of Feierabiand. She asked instead, "Did, um, did Bertaud, did Lord Bertaud, did he tell you . . . about the Casmantian army?" Her heart sank: What if, for whatever reason, Bertaud had *not* told his king about Casmantium? Why ever should the king then believe anything *she* should say about that threat?

"He told me," the king said reassuringly.

"Well," Kes said, and nervously stroked Opailikiita's neck, trying to draw courage from the griffin's hot presence under her hand. She tried to look only at the king, to pretend that no one else was there, only she and the king. Who was not, after all, a very frightening man. Not nearly so frightening as Kanes the smith, really, she told herself. He hadn't shouted even once, yet. She took a shallow breath and looked at her feet, trying to think what to say.

"Bertaud advised me very strongly that I should listen to you, if I was lucky enough to meet you," the king said gently. "What is it you came to tell me?"

Kes glanced up to meet his eyes, glanced down again. She said unhappily, "Kiibaile Esterire Airaikeliu—that is, the Lord of Fire and Air, the king of the griffins, you know—he has decided to, to . . . make you come into the desert and fight Casmantium there. And when Casmantium has destroyed you, he will bring his people down against Casmantium while they are still in the desert, and destroy *them*. It is," she explained earnestly, "a very simple plan, because you have to fight the griffins. And the King of Casmantium has to fight *you*, or why did he bring his army here? And he won't know the griffins are as dangerous to his men as to yours because he thinks his cold mages can keep the griffins from harming his men. He doesn't know—he doesn't know about me. Or . . . he knows I am here, but he doesn't know . . . we think he doesn't know what I can do."

The king stood very still, his eyes on her face. But Kes thought that he was seeing, not her face, but battles hidden just around the next corner of time. He said at last, "And if we will not fight this battle to please the griffins?"

Kes nodded hopefully—maybe he could find a way not to fight— but Opailikiita said, *The Lord of Fire and Air will see to it that you must fight*. Her graceful, unobtrusive voice slid delicately around the corners of the mind, but many of the men still flinched in surprise. Some swore, though quietly. The old earth mage recoiled slightly, looking like she was struggling between offense and fascination. The king's eyes widened briefly. He said to the griffin, with careful courtesy, "How would he do this?"

This land knows us, now. The desert we have made out of our hearts is ours. Your earth mage will not break its power, though she may try. The King of Casmantium does not yet understand that his mages cannot break its power, either. So you will understand you must fight within the reaches of our desert.

The king stared at her. His face tightened; he looked suddenly stern again. "And if I take my people back up the road to the north?"

If you retreat, you will cede all this country to Casmantium; if you go south to block his move there, my people will put the desert under your feet and hold you. If you stay where you are, then the Arobern will press you against our desert and destroy you and still claim all this land.

"And what do you suggest I do to preserve my people against destruction, then?" the king asked her.

There is nothing you can do, Opailikiita said, with a strange griffin satisfaction.

"Split your force," suggested Jos. His deep voice carried an odd, reluctant kind of assurance. "If you must take part of it into the desert, do so, and use those men as well as you can. You will lose most of them, probably. But also send men to cut around through the mountains and come down on the Arobern from above. Even a small force can have a great impact if it's used well. That way you may save something from this battle. If you send word to the west and the south now, at once, then what you do here may at least hold the Casmantian army long enough for the rest of Feierabiand to prepare."

Everyone looked at him. He shrugged, looking half apologetic and half defiant.

"You're a soldier," the king said at last. "To be plain, a *Casmantian* soldier."

"Not any longer."

"No? Then where is your loyalty now?" the king asked him.

Jos grimaced, nothing that could be called a smile, though he might have intended it that way. He tilted his head toward Kes. "With her."

"You were a spy," said one of the men with the king, his expression neutral but his tone flat with distaste. The man turned a hand palm up when they looked at him, and shrugged. "Or so I surmise." He seemed to consider this for a moment and then added to his king, with sudden urgency, "We need this man."

Kes flung a worried glance up at Jos's face and put a hand anxiously on his arm.

Jos looked down at her, touched her cheek with the tips of two fingers, and took his hand away in a gesture like a farewell.

"No," said Kes.

He said, "It was a choice . . . to come here. It was for this I made that choice."

"No!" said Kes, sure, if she was sure of nothing else, that she could not let Jos go into the hands of men who . . . men who . . . She did not know what soldiers might do to a captured spy, and she did not want to find out. Opailikiita, probably understanding nothing of the specific accusation, nevertheless understood that Kes was upset. She stood up, half lifting her great wings, fire limning the brown feathers with gold. Half the soldiers present lifted their bows, steel arrowheads flashing like ice in the sun.

The king flung out his hands in urgent command, compelling all to stillness; remarkably, all were still. Even Opailikiita.

It was to Kes the king spoke. "No one will harm him, you know—for your sake, if there were no other reason. Is it not his choice? Did he not make it when he suggested a plan against his own people?"

Kes, struck mute by her own words in this king's mouth, could not find an answer.

Jos could. He stepped off the narrow line of desert Opailikiita had made for them, walked the few paces necessary to come to the king, gave him a brief nod, and turned toward the officer. He was pale. But no one could miss the deliberation of what he did.

"He is yours," the king said to the officer.

Jos bowed his head and allowed the officer to lay a hand on his arm.

Opailikiita, perhaps baffled by these strong human emotions, or perhaps merely disliking the way the arrowheads caught the light, said, *We should go back to the desert. Are you satisfied with the warning you have given, sister? Do you not desire to return to the heart of fire?*

Kes blinked. She looked at the king, who gave her a brief bow and a murmur of gratitude. A brief worried glance at Jos saw him stolid and uncomplaining, with a stubborn look on his face that she knew was meant for her. She took a small step toward him, though she could not leave the desert. "But I don't understand," she whispered. "Why would you want to do this?"

Jos said gently, "Kes . . . you are still partially a creature of earth. But if this battle takes place as your friend describes, what will you do?"

Kes said helplessly, "You know I can't let them die."

"Which? Your people . . . or the griffins?"

Either. Both. Kes could not speak.

"If I help your king against mine, there is a chance . . . a poor one, yes, but a *chance* . . . that Feierabiand will be able to turn Casmantium back without the griffins coming in at all. That, even if the griffins come in, they will not need you to keep them in the battle. However poor, this is the one chance that the griffins will not after all carry you with them into their world. If you do not use fire, you will still have a way back to earth."

Kes shook her head.

"A poor chance, I said. Can you see any other?"

They looked at each other, Kes tongue-tied and silent, Jos stubborn. He said at last, "Don't use fire, Kes. Don't let that Kairaithin force you to it. Don't be drawn into this battle. It will burn out your humanity. You know that is true. This is the griffins' battle, and a battle for men. It's nothing for you."

"I think—Jos, I think it's not so simple—" Kes turned and put her hand almost blindly on Opailikiita's shoulder. She thought of the exaltation of flight when the slim griffin carried her, the warmth of Opailikiita's voice when she said *sister*. It occurred to Kes that she had ceased questioning the word. It was a truth, now. But she thought it could not be a truth unless she lost *Tesme* as a sister. Learning to love the desert would mean turning away, once and for all, from human love. And she realized she couldn't bear to give up either her earth nature or her fire nature. "Maybe I can keep them both," she whispered. "Can't I just stay in between? Can't I keep both worlds?"

Jos, his mouth set in a hard line, started to come back toward her.

"If you will all please wait," cut in an austere voice that Kes knew instantly, and everyone turned hurriedly: Arrowheads and spear points flashed again, light striking off metal in quick, hard glints.

Kairaithin was there, in a little space that cleared about him instantly simply because of the barely leashed force that seemed to radiate outward from him like heat from the desert sun. He was in human form, but he had never looked less like a man. The harsh features of his human face barely hid the eagle's fierce eyes and savage, predatory beak; his long hands might as well have been talons. His shadow was entirely that of the griffin: Insubstantial feathers ruffled in the wind, and the shadow stared out upon them all with fiery eyes.

The slim bar of sand and heat Opailikiita had made swept out in both directions to make a much wider extension of the desert; a hot wind carried red dust whispering across the earth. Kairaithin stood on sand; the wind stirred his clothing and whipped with sudden strength through his hair. It reached the king, and the king blinked and lifted a hand to shield his eyes against the dust; men all through the company were doing the same as the desert suddenly encompassed the land on which they all stood. The air smelled of hot metal and molten stone. Opailikiita shook herself, stretched, and lay down on the sand, looking much more comfortable. Kes understood how she felt. It seemed to her also as though the world itself had suddenly widened.

The old mage with the king shifted in her chair.

Kairaithin rounded on her instantly, small flames springing from the ground at his feet and ruffling his black hair. His power, grounded in the desert, thundered soundless and potent through the air; the very air tasted of fire. "Do *not* press me!" he snapped at her. "This is *not* the time. Fire and *air*, cannot you earth-mages rule your own inclinations?"

"Yes," answered the woman without apparent offense. "If we have sensible reason to do so. I am not challenging you. Can you not tone *your* power down a little, griffin mage?"

The taut line of Kairaithin's mouth did not ease, but the wind died slowly and the fire at his feet ebbed like water back into the sand. He turned his back to the woman and the king, came to Kes in three long strides, and took her by the shoulders. Some of the men shifted—Jos clearly wanted to come back to her side—but the king lifted a forbidding hand and none of them moved to interfere.

Kairaithin was, Kes understood, very angry. Very angry. She wanted to shrink away, and could not. She wanted to hide herself away in any small shadow that might offer sanctuary, and could not. She stared into the griffin's fierce eyes and tried not to flinch visibly.

"You are everything," the griffin told her harshly. "You are my hope of deliverance for all my people. And I find you here! Within the reach of powerful earth magic; within the reach of human kings! What would you have done if this earth mage had cut across your little strip of desert and trapped you here in the cold?"

Unable to speak, Kes only shook her head.

The tight line of Kairaithin's mouth eased unexpectedly. He released her and shifted back a step, giving her a little space. She was shaking. He frowned at her and half turned, to take in the king as well. But most of his attention was still for her. "If you would have men and griffins together lay an ambush for our common enemy, we shall do so. Do you understand me?"

"I had been told," said the king warily, "that this was not your intention." He, too, must have felt the barely contained rage that burned within the griffin, but he met his eyes steadily.

"Your man Bertaud son of Boudan persuaded me of the justice of your cause," Kairaithin snapped. "Do *not* press me, king of men; I am not yours to rule. I will tell you what you will do: Go into the desert when the opportunity is offered, and the Lord of Fire and Air will make a pretense of battle; both your men and my people will bring the Arobern down into the desert and there destroy them, and them alone."

The king studied him; one sun-streaked eyebrow lifted. "Is that how it will be?"

Kairaithin's thin mouth tilted into a hard smile; he looked taut and dangerous and like nothing human. He said to Kes, "If you face Esterire Airaikeliu and tell him that you will make whole no injuries of griffin-kind, save if he and his protect and aid your people, he will have no choice but to do as you require or else give way before the armies of men. And he will not give way, nor would he long rule my people if he attempted it. Yours is indeed the will that may rule here, *kereskiita*. Our need for your goodwill is greater than your need for ours."

Among the Feierabiand soldiers, Jos gave Kes a slow nod, meaning, *Is that not what I said? Do you see now that you do in truth hold the sword in your own hand?*

"But—" whispered Kes. "Tesme? And everyone?"

"The Lord of Fire and Air will be angry," Kairaithin acknowledged, meeting her eyes. "His mate Esterikiu Anahaikuuanse will be angry; Tastairiane Apailika will be very angry. You must withstand all their anger, all their threats. I suspect that Eskainiane Escaile Sehaikiu will support you. But it does not matter. If they would carry out their threats, *I* will prevent them, and you must trust me for that. I promise you, no harm will come to your sister, nor to your little village of men. Will you trust me to do as I say?"

"Isn't your need too great to allow you to be trustworthy?"

"You will have to decide whom you will trust."

Kes nodded, slowly.

"You taxed me previously with unjustly withholding choice from you. I give it to you now. There is a cost. You will pay it either way. You will ride the fiery wind and be changed by it, and achieve triumph for us all. Or you will refuse to become fire, and your people will be crushed by the strength of Casmantium. You wished me to be clear with you. Am I clear?"

He had unbound her. Kes could feel the difference, as though her awareness of the desert had suddenly expanded and clarified. She whispered, "Yes."

Among the men, Jos came half a step forward and then stopped as he met an officer's forbidding hand. He said furiously, "No! How dare you steal her from earth, how dare you make her a fire mage and force her to do the work *you* ought to do—"

"If she will be a fire mage, it's not in the way a griffin is a mage!" snapped Kairaithin. "*I* have no power to heal. It's not your choice, man!

Nor even mine." Kairaithin turned his proud stare upon the king, who met it and did not even visibly flinch. "And you, king of men? You are the other one here to have a choice: to battle griffins in the desert, and then Casmantium when the Arobern comes down from the heights, or to trust my intentions and my skill and reserve your strength for Casmantium alone. Do you understand what it is I will do for you?"

"I think I do," said the king. He looked deliberately at Kes. "Shall I trust this creature? What say you?"

Kes shook her head, found her voice, and whispered, "You should trust me." She looked at Jos. "You . . . you told me that the . . . the sword was in my hand. I didn't think so. But it is. You were right. I see that, now. I won't let them harm you. But you know I will have to use fire. I will have to, Jos."

He started to answer, to come back to her, but the king shook his head, and the officer stopped him with a hard grip. Then the king glanced at the woman in the chair. "Meriemne?"

The woman's strange clouded eyes might be blind, but they still saw more, Kes thought, than the surface of men; she looked down, feeling exposed and very small.

"She has given her heart to the fire," the woman said to the king, her fragile voice nevertheless perfectly clear in the quiet. "But she has not yet forgotten how to love the earth. She will try hard to do what she has said she will do."

"And the griffin?"

"Ah." Ruthless discipline struggled with dislike in those old eyes. "There I can't well judge."

"Wise," Kairaithin said to her, at once harshly furious and amused. He looked at the king, waiting.

"I am inclined," said the king, "to follow your script, griffin mage."

"Wisdom is showered like fire across the earth!" exclaimed Kairaithin, with more bitterness than humor. And laid a hand on Kes's shoulder, and moved them all, Kes and Opailikiita and himself, back into the heart of the desert.

CHAPTER 13

The Lord of Fire and Air was very angry. His anger beat through the air as though the sun itself raged across the desert. He was angry with Kes, but he was angrier still with Kairaithin.

This is your kiinukaile, he said to Kairaithin, his powerful voice slamming down around them like silent thunder. *This is* your *little kitten. You set yourself against me—you set this little earth-creature before you and set yourself in its shadow!*

Do you believe so? For this battle, Kairaithin had taken his true form. He matched the king glare for glare, but he sat poised and still, like a cat, ostentatiously unconcerned with any threat. He said, with a disdainful, contained fury of his own, *Will you say that I keep to the shadow of any creature? Of earth or fire or both at once? Do you declare so?*

Shall I? demanded the king.

Little flames licked up and down Kairaithin's black wings. *I declare your intention is ill-conceived. And will you nevertheless hold to it, in the face of the necessity I perceive?*

Lord of the Changing Wind, will you claim to be Lord of Fire and Air?

There was a short pause. Kairaithin did not drop his gaze as a man would have before his king; he did not look away or bow himself down or make any gesture that recognized the griffin king's threat or challenge or reprimand or whatever it had been. He merely said, *No.* Just that, flatly.

Having considered the direction of the wind, I decide how the People of Wind and Fire shall follow it, the king said, and the whole desert seemed to shudder with the force of that assertion.

Having found the direction of the wind unsustainable, I alter its direction, Kairaithin answered, still in that flat tone.

You are influenced by your little kiinukaile, said Tastairiane Apailika. The white griffin lounged in a pose that mimicked relaxation, but he was not relaxed. Kes heard the tension in his voice; it sang in the wind that ruffled the shining feathers around his fierce eagle's head and neck and shoulders. When he shifted a forefoot, he tore deep gouges through the red stone with his eagle's talons. He said contemptuously, *Your* kereskiita *maintains attachment to its mud-people, and you are influenced by its attachment. There comes a wind of blood and fire; we may mount the heights to ride this storm. We have this chance to rid ourselves of both kinds of human creatures and claim this land. And you would* change *this wind, Sipiike Kairaithin?*

It is an error to set trust or good regard into the keeping of any human, added Nehaistiane Esterikiu Anahaikuuanse, mantling her red-and-gold wings and glaring at Kes. *You would distinguish between the human creatures here and those who came into our great desert to destroy us, but this is a false distinction. We had much better destroy them all. Have you not fashioned this human woman into a creature of fire for this exact purpose?*

Kes, horrified, said, "I won't!"

For a terrible moment, all the griffins stared at her. The combined ferocious power of their regard nearly drove her to cower away from them. Kes closed her hands into fists, shut her eyes so she would not have to try to meet all those furious unhuman glares, and concentrated on standing up straight. She said again, "I won't! You want to *kill* everyone? You say the—the Lord of the Changing Wind made me into a creature of fire to *destroy all my people*? Well, maybe I've learned to love fire, but I remember my people and it doesn't matter what you do! I won't ride *any* wind of death that comes against my people!" Then she had to open her eyes again, trying not to flinch.

Esterikiu Anahaikuuanse, glaring more ferociously than ever, began to answer.

Eskainiane Escaile Sehaikiu interrupted the red female. *It's a brave little kitten*, he declared approvingly, *and it knows its own mind and heart.* He turned to the king. *I watched this little one make you whole, my brother, when she was still almost entirely a human woman and hardly knew fire. Even then, that was nothing any of us could do, and who but her teacher might guess what she might have become since?*

Exactly so, said the red female sharply. *Thus—*

She's not of our kind, said Eskainiane, and turned to nudge Kes with the tip of his beak, a gesture that was not *exactly* friendly, but something very like. He said to the other griffins, *If she was, what reason would Sipiike Kairaithin have had to seek her out? If she casts herself free of one wind for another, then if the wind changes, I might let slip the one wind from beneath my wings and ride the other.*

There was a pause. Esterikiu Anahaikuuanse still looked furious, but the king now seemed more thoughtful than angry. It was his decision that mattered, and he did not speak.

She is determined on her course, Kairaithin said in a hard voice. *She is adamant. She will yield to no threat.*

If you would begin to carry out *the threats you have made so liberally, she would cower at your feet*, Tastairiane Apailika said, his voice whipping through Kes' mind like a thrown knife.

I am satisfied you are mistaken, said Kairaithin. *And who perceives the hearts of men more clearly, you or I?*

The white griffin had no answer for that.

And if you are wrong, said Kairaithin, *and no threat nor punishment will move her, and we lose her gift and her skill, then what will we do when at last a more powerful Casmantium settles its strength and strikes against us? As it will. Do not mistake the Arobern's intention: He will not suffer a desert to exist in the midst of his new lands. And Feierabiand, though weakened and angry, will in the end join with Casmantium against us, for all human peoples are natural allies when fire strikes against earth. You believe that with my* kiinukaile's *skill and gift, we can destroy anything of humankind that comes against us, but the strength of earth is far less exhaustible than you imagine. And who would know better than I?*

A deadly pause spun itself out. Tastairiane Apailika began to answer.

Kes drew courage from Kairaithin's strength, from Opailikiita's warm support, from bright Eskainiane's amused approval. Eskainiane Escaile Sehaikiu was wrong: She was not brave. She did not know how to make powerful speeches. She was too afraid of the white griffin to even look at him. But she said swiftly to the Lord of Air and Fire, before the white griffin could speak, "I might cower at your feet. Maybe I will. But I won't . . . I *won't* make right any harm that comes to any griffin. If you harm people of Feierabiand. I won't. Nobody of Feierabiand has harmed *you*. What business is it of yours to do them harm?"

Eskainiane Escaile Sehaikiu laughed, quick and confident and brilliant and pleased by courage wherever he found it—even in her. Even when she opposed his own plan.

And the king, always inclined to be swayed by his *iskarianere's* opinions more than any other, allowed himself, at last, to be amused as well. He said, *We will consider this new wind you propose. Sipiike Kairaithin, you may make it plain to us, and we shall consider it.*

Kairaithin inclined his proud head at last, small flames rippling through the delicate black feathers of his throat. He said, *It will please you well enough, O Lord of Fire and Air—or so I believe. And if it will also please my little* kinukaile, *shall we not be generous to please her?*

Perhaps we shall, said the king, and Kes knew they had won after all—won a changed direction for the wind, and life for her people, and a chance for safety for all of Feierabiand. She moved quietly to one side, joined Opailikiita, and leaned against the young griffin, catching her breath and trying to believe that they had won and that everything would be all right.

Iaor Safiad of Feierabiand engaged Casmantium in the midst of the desert, as everyone, Kes supposed, had at one time or another intended, although for wildly differing purposes. But they did so under conditions designed to favor Feierabiand. Or Kes hoped that was so. Kairaithin said it was. Opailikiita said so, too, an assurance Kes trusted more than the griffin mage's.

When the army of Feierabiand came bravely into the desert, the griffins flew to meet them with every appearance of violent intent, but without harboring such intent in their fierce unhuman hearts—or so Opailikiita assured Kes.

Kes tucked herself between Opailikiita's wings when the young griffin took to the wind: She clung hard to handfuls of feathers, trying not to think about how far below the sand lay. Opailikiita turned in slow spirals through the hot air, above even most of the larger griffins, and slowly Kes relaxed a little. Opailikiita lay so still on the wind, with only the slightest shift of feathered wings to adjust her course, that it began to be easy to feel safe. Kes leaned what seemed perilously far over to peer across the griffin's shoulder.

The griffins rode the hot winds below Opailikiita. They soared in small groups or alone, forming slow patterns in the air as groups overlapped and parted and merged and parted again: bronze and gold, red and brown, and copper and black. White Tastairiane flew fiercely alone, sliding through the patterns other griffins made, and the rest made way for him. The only griffin Kes could not find below her in the sky was Kairaithin, and she knew where *he* was and why he was not with the rest.

She followed one griffin and then another with her gaze. She knew all their proud, violent names. She knew the feel of each one's voice, fierce or subtle or sharp as wind-honed stone. She would have known

each from all the others just from the tilt of a head or the fiery glance
of an eye. Their names thundered in her blood and rolled across her
tongue, each one distinct. She knew she would feel injury to any one of
them as a break in the natural flow of fire through this desert. She
knew that she would be able to channel fire into such injuries and make
them whole.

And she knew that doing so would mold her own body and soul
into the shapes of fire. She would fly with Opailikiita and call fire
through the air, pour it through her hands; fire would run through her
veins like blood and she would become a creature of fire. She knew
this. She thought, briefly, of shifting herself off Opailikiita's back and
far away. Of leaving this war between men and men, between men and
griffins, between earth and fire to be fought by someone else, its cost
borne by someone else. Anyone else. She could do that. Kairaithin did
not bind her. Nothing bound her. She might find herself outside Tesme's
house, with her sister's voice calling to her . . . What would Tesme be
saying? She found she could not imagine any possible words.

Far below stood the men, far away and small, impossible to tell one
from another. The heads of their spears flashed like silver droplets of
water in the desert; the strings of their bows and the heads of their arrows flashed silver. They stood in precise ranks, lines of men and more
lines beyond them: Kairaithin had said the King of Feierabiand had
brought only a small army with him into the desert, but to Kes it looked
like a very large army. She wondered whether they might actually turn
against the griffins, and if they did, what would happen.

*They have a magic of their own, which they bear with them, even
into our desert*, Opailikiita commented. *Those arrows are not earthbound. They, if not their makers, may fly to meet a griffin in the air.
Men are very dangerous. And the spears make it hard to come against
men on the ground.*

"You did not . . . the last time, you did not seem worried about the
spears?"

*There are many times as many men here now. And this time they
would expect blinding dust and sand, and falling fire, and attacks from
any direction. See how they have angled their companies to guard one
another.*

Kes could see nothing of the sort. She asked tentatively, "What
would you do if I were not here?"

Were you not with us, said Opailikiita, *we would have a difficult
battle, so few of us against so many men. Though the desert itself is
our element and will fight for us and carry our power, still there are
earth mages to hinder us. Even so, you will see today, when the Arobern*

comes onto the sand, how the desert is our ally and our tool, we who have no other gift for making. She sounded fierce and joyful and proud; she sounded like she was looking forward to it.

"You are sure the . . . the Casmantians will come into the desert?"

Are you not? Yes, little sister, they will come. You see how the Safiad sets his people so that they would be vulnerable to attack from out of the mountains. The Casmantians will see it also, and they will come to that opportunity, as an arrow in flight would be drawn to its target. Well you are with us, my beautiful sister, for if not my people would be as vulnerable as the men of Feierabiand.

Below, men lifted twisted horns of brass; long golden notes rolled out over the desert. Soldiers halted and turned; spear points dipped and rose again, flashing. Men in the center of each formation lifted bows, strings flashing silver, and nocked arrows. Horns rang out again, rich and mellow and sounding to Kes like slow summer days and harvest festivals and not like war at all.

Above the men, bright Eskainiane Escaile Sehaikiu swept a long, fierce trail of fire through the hot air. Esterire Airaikeliu, Lord of Fire and Air, darker and more terrible than his companion, curved suddenly out of a spiral and fell after his *iskarianere*, with a shrill piercing cry like a stooping falcon: His cry struck fire from the air. Above him, other griffins shrieked and flung back their wings and stooped, and fire fell from the wind that roared past the long feathers of their wings.

Below the griffins, men cried out in fear and shouted urgent commands: Arrows rose suddenly in a silver rain.

Kes covered her eyes and bowed low over Opailikiita's neck.

No. Look, said Opailikiita, and Kes peeked timorously from between her fingers. Arrows did not reach their targets but burst into flame in midflight. Griffins, striking, came down savagely upon the . . . sand, between companies of men, outside of spear's reach. The beating of their wings flung up red dust and sand until Kes could see nothing clearly. Men shouted. Metal crashed against metal, with a horrible clatter of ringing and shrieking.

But spears did not strike griffins, nor did griffins strike men. The fire that burned across the sand guttered in the stiff wind and went out.

Good, said Opailikiita. *They are brave.*

Kes did not know whether she spoke of the griffins or of the men. But she thought the men were very brave. Their horns sang through the thick dust, and the long notes were valiant and clear.

Casmantium, Opailikiita said, in a tone of satisfaction.

Startled, Kes followed the direction of the griffin's gaze. There, where the mountains came down and met the edge of the desert, men

were coming out from around a corner of smooth gray stone onto the
red sand. Men and more men, and then more yet, in ranks that formed
quickly and instantly broke into motion: brown and black, with silver
spears and bows that caught the light like griffins' beaks.

See, said Opailikiita, still with satisfaction, *they think the Safiad is
ignorant of them still. Possibly they even believe* we *are ignorant of
them.*

"Yes," Kes said nervously. It seemed to her to be taking a very long
time for the Casmantian army to cross the sand and close up behind the
Feierabiand soldiers. And, if she could trust Kairaithin and Opailikiita,
they would find themselves in a terrible trap. Of their own making. Yet
she could not watch, and covered her eyes.

Then she could not bear to be blind, and looked after all.

The first part of the Casmantian army struck the rear of the Feierabiand army, and there was suddenly a vast confusion all through that
region: Kes could find no order to any of it.

But Opailikiita said fiercely, *Thus we strike down those who would
destroy us.*

Kes said nothing. A griffin's name rolled through her mind suddenly: Esheteriu Nepuukai, a young griffin, copper-bright wings and
golden lion pelt, bright and passionate. She knew as though she stood
beside him that he lay in the sand with a terrible wound across his chest
and a spear through his foot, blood pouring out of him, shattering into
garnets and rubies as the sun struck it. She knew when the spear was
wrenched out and drawn back for another thrust. She thought of Tesme,
fleetingly, but there was not time to think or worry or be frightened,
because the spear was already stabbing out once more. Before the
strike could be made, Kes made the young griffin's body whole, and
watched with her mind's eye as he hurled himself forward. She felt as
though she flung herself forward with him, exaltation spilling like fire
through her own wings.

Shaistairai Kaihastaikiita fell through the brilliant air, arrows in
her side and flank; the arrows were tipped with ice and ill-intent. Kes
burned through them with clean fire and closed the wounds with fire;
the griffin fell through sheets of fire, caught the wind with powerful
wings, and flung herself straight down in an explosion of joy and fury,
an explosion that burned through Kes as well.

The Lord of Fire and Air himself took an arrow in the throat. Kes
burned it out and left him surging forward straight into a thicket of
spears. They tore him open, face and chest and sides, and Kes, his
name pounding like the sun through her blood, made him whole again.
And again. Until the wounds ceased to come.

Is it hard, my sister? asked Opailikiita, turning in her slow spiral path to carry Kes back across the battleground.

"No," whispered Kes. It was not hard. But it swept Kes's attention inward, where griffin names sang like poetry in her blood.

She had no attention to spare any longer to look from above at the battle. She felt she was in it herself: a battle to repair tears in the natural order of the world, to weave wholeness through ragged injuries. Once or twice a cold malaise seemed to touch her, crept like ice across her fingers where she gripped Opailikiita's feathers in her hands. But each time the cold fell away almost before she knew it was there, and she forgot it instantly in the rolling thunder of fire that filled her eyes and her heart. At last all she saw was fire, until she became fire and burned with Opailikiita, who turned to fire beneath her and laughed with fierce joy.

Kes did not notice right away when the frequency of injuries pressing themselves upon her attention slowed, and slowed . . . Eventually she found she had time to find herself riding the wind, griffin back, in human form again, uncertain whether she had ever truly left it. She had time to lean over Opailikiita's shoulder and stare into the burning dust below, time to try to see the shapes of men and griffins hidden by that red dust. She did not fear to fall, now. She thought that if she leaned too far and fell, she would simply fall into fire, turn into fire and blowing sand. But she did not fall. Nor did she speak. It seemed to her that she had forgotten the sounds of human language—that if she spoke, flames would fall like jewels from her tongue.

Opailikiita, too, seemed disinclined to speak. An awareness of her filled Kes, because she was so near or because she was so closely allied: She seemed not only a slim brown griffin, but also equally a streak of bodiless fire falling out of the molten sky.

Below, the dust was settling. Sunlight poured through the dust and turned the air the color of blood or fire. Small griffin fires burned here and there in the sand, leaving flecks of gold and fire opals and carnelians to glitter where they burned out. The darker garnets and rubies of griffin blood sparkled in the sand where the griffins had fought and bled for this victory.

The griffins themselves had drawn aside, going up into the red spires that were their halls and their homes. Few remained among the men, and those were reaching out with immense wings and pulling themselves, one after another, back into the sky.

Weary men moved slowly across the sand, heavy earthbound creatures, nothing that belonged to the desert, though some of them were gathering the jewels that blood and fire had spilled out across the sand.

Kes understood: Thus they would keep a small piece of the desert with them when they departed, as was only right. Their own blood had flowed like water and left only stains little redder than the sand.

The victors wore the undyed linen of Feierabiand uniform and the vanquished wore the brown and black of Casmantium, so she could tell the difference between them. Men were putting up awnings to shield the wounded from the hammer of the desert sun, and passing out skins of water and watered wine. Men of both countries bore injuries, but these did not call themselves to Kes's attention as griffin wounds would have done. There were not many men in brown left alive, Kes saw, which was only as it should have been: It had been a day for death, and their deaths had been good. The exaltation of the fire had ebbed, but she was still very happy.

She looked for the King of Casmantium among those who had survived, but she could not find him. She found the King of Feierabiand, however, in the shade of a great twisted tower of stone. She slipped down from Opailikiita's back and went toward him.

He was limping, she saw, and he looked very tired, but also deeply satisfied. He clapped another man on the shoulder as Kes approached, sending him off with a word that made the man laugh, though wearily. Then he turned to Kes with a quick nod of greeting and satisfaction. "Well done!" he said. "Your griffins turned the day handily, young Kes. We, now—we have wounded, though nothing like so many as we might have had facing the Casmantians alone. Can you heal them as you healed the griffins?"

"I could heal them, I think," Kes answered, feeling fire roll within her blood, desiring to spill flames across the world. She could loose it, she thought, and stitch with flames ragged patterns that should be smooth. She wanted to. It would be pleasant to run fire through her hands. Even for men.

"I don't think that would be wise," Meriemne answered, from a cushioned chair in the shade where Kes had not noticed her. "Men are not meant to be filled with fire."

Kes looked at the mage, whom she had not realized was there, first with startlement and then with dislike and confusion. Meriemne did not seem as unpleasant and frightening as Beguchren had when he had caught her in the desert and trapped her with his cold bindings. But she simply did not *like* her. The instant warmth of the smile the king turned toward the old woman confused and upset her.

"Fortunately," added the old mage, "I can heal them myself. Once they are out of this atrocious desert. No offense, fire child," she added to Kes, who only blinked at her in a confused muddle of aversion.

"Yes," the king began to say to the mage, but interrupted himself at the shout of one of his men and looked out across the desert where the man was pointing.

Kes backed quickly around Opailikiita to put the griffin between herself and Meriemne, and looked too. *Can you see?* she asked her.

A feather's weight of men, Opailikiita answered. She tilted her eagle's head and studied the approaching riders. *One of them is the lord of men who is beholden to Kairaithin—Bertaud son of Boudan.*

"Bertaud?" said the king, in a pleased tone. "Well, and timely arrived, for all I left him sternly in Riamne. Still, of course, he would know I would welcome him now. Well, well . . . he can join us at least for the ride out of this terrible desert. No offense," he added to Kes, who gazed at him in confusion.

They come in haste, Opailikiita observed, her attention still on the handful of approaching riders.

"Do they?" the king shaded his eyes and stared hard at the approaching riders. "So they do. They are not pursued? You see them in no difficulty?"

I see only those men, King of Feierabiand. If there is difficulty, I do not see it.

"Well, we shall discover the reason for their haste soon enough," the king said, faint unease in his tone, and turned to speak to officers of his men. Kes did not listen. She was looking across the desert at the men. They came slowly, slowly, until she wanted to blaze a path for them through the sand that would bring them directly to this one point of sand in all the vastness of the desert. It seemed momentarily strange to her that she should be impatient, she who had always been by nature patient; but then Opailikiita called to her and she turned back to the griffin.

Kairaithin summons me.

Then go, Kes said. *But listen for me.*

Your voice is in my blood, said the griffin, and shifted herself away through the desert in the manner of griffin mages.

The men came at last into the Feierabiand company and were temporarily lost from sight behind the awnings set up for the wounded men. The king turned expectantly, smiling, to greet the new arrivals; his smile faded as they came back into view and rode up. Kes, her eyes on the distressed, blowing horses, did not at once look at the men. But then the king's attention pulled hers after it at last, and she lifted her eyes to the strained face of the riders.

"Bertaud!" The king strode forward to greet them.

One of the men murmured something about water and took the

young lord's horse as he dismounted, leading it and the other animals away to be walked and watered.

Lord Bertaud strode rapidly to the king. He said sharply, urgently, "I could not stay in Riamne."

"No, I understand so—your friend Kairaithin found me and said, what was it, something about how you had persuaded him of the justice of our cause. Well done, well done, my friend! I would have sent for you then, but there seemed no time—we would have had a hard time of it without griffin assistance—"

Lord Bertaud seized the king's arm, fierce as a griffin in his urgency. "Iaor. I might not have been in time for the battle, but I saw part of it from a high cliff. Answer me this. Where is the Arobern? Captured? Killed?"

The king shook his head, studying the other man in obvious concern. "No, no—we did not see him. A griffin took him, I suppose. The Casmantian army was a good deal smaller than I'd feared—it seems your report was overanxious—"

"Overanxious?" Lord Bertaud gave a short, harsh laugh, looking more tense and strained than Kes had ever seen him. "Overanxious! No, Iaor! The rest of the Casmantian army is simply somewhere else. *And* the Arobern. I will lay any wager for it. And where else would he be but slipping down the edge of this terrible desert to strike unopposed as he sees fit?"

The king stared at him. He, too, clearly saw the truth of it at once—now that he had the leisure to think on it. "I should have realized."

"You were occupied."

"Yes, as the Arobern intended. Earth and iron! That man is far too bold. And now we shall all pay the cost of our own lack of imagination. How many men do you suppose he has with him? Three thousand? More?" He turned, shouting for his officers—one came up hastily from somewhere and said rapidly, not waiting for the king to speak, "Your majesty, that spy who came to us—he tells us we should have faced twice as many men here."

"So we have been discovering," said the king, and he gripped the man's arm, giving him a small shake. "Go get the best information you can about the number that should have been here. See if the man has any guess about what the Arobern might have done with the rest."

Bertaud, for his part, shouted for Kairaithin while Kes was still distracted by the mention of Jos.

The griffin arrived even before the officers, falling out of the red sky, half fire and half griffin: He reared up as he struck the ground and his wings, streaming behind him, were sheets of flame. Men fell back from him, shouting in alarm. Horses reared and wanted to scatter in panic; horse speakers ran to take lead lines and bridles, calming them and holding them still. Kes thought it was a pity no one could do the same for the men, but at least none so forgot themselves as to loose arrows at the griffin.

What? the griffin flung at Bertaud, rage blazing within as he burned with fire without. *Well? And do you not find this outcome satisfactory, man?*

Kes stared, shocked at the naked violence of Kairaithin's manner, of his voice; so much more ferocious than even when he had been angry at her for defying him to go to the king.

"Where is the Arobern?" Bertaud shouted back at him, appearing, to Kes's astonishment, neither surprised nor cowed by Kairaithin's violence.

Kairaithin stared hard into the man's eyes. His own were filled with rage and, strangely, something stronger, which might have been despair. But a more rational thought crept into them as Kes watched, and she was no longer certain what she had seen at first.

He gathered himself into a form winged with feathers rather than flames, and settled more solidly to the sand. *Is he not here?*

"No!"

"Nor is Beguchren," Kes added.

I will seek the cold mage, said Kairaithin, and flung himself back into the sky.

"But what about the Arobern?" Bertaud shouted after him.

Wincing at his shout, Kes shook her head and laid her hand on the lord's arm. "Let him go. Let him go. He will look for Beguchren."

"Forget about the cold mage," snapped the king, leaning forward intensely. He had the reins of a horse in his hand and was clearly preparing to mount. "Bertaud is right—it's the Arobern who concerns us now!"

Kes shook her head again, but she also called into the silence of the desert, so little disturbed by the shouts of men, *Eskainiane! Eskainiane?*

And the copper-and-gold griffin, riding the winds of the burning heights and resting as griffins rest, answered. He plunged from the wind to the red sand, from the side of the Lord of Fire and Air to Kes's side, so that the king's horse reared and had to be calmed by a horse speaker who ran hastily to it.

Kereskiita, Eskainiane said joyfully, ignoring man and horse and king. *Well flown, on a fierce wind! Do you call me? I declare I will hear you!*

Kes laughed and lifted her hand to touch the side of his beak, a gesture he returned by turning his head to brush her palm lightly with the cutting edge. He was still exultant from flight and battle, passionately joyful with victory and the speed of the wind. And he had come, as he said, to answer her call, though he was brother and more than brother to the Lord of Fire and Air.

Kes had known that he would. After this day's battle, where she had come to know them all, she loved this griffin above any other save only Opailikiita. Powerful and brilliant and generous, she trusted Eskainiane Escaile Sehaikiu to come to her call out of that open-hearted generosity and listen to her. *Eskainiane*, she said. And aloud, after the manner of humankind, "Eskainiane, where is the King of Casmantium? Would you ride the wind and search for an army that did not come into the desert? Would you send your people to look to the north and the east and the south, beyond the sand, where men might have gone and we not known?"

For you, kereskiita, *we will fly beyond the powerful sun and search*, answered Eskainiane, and touched her face with his beak in a griffin caress. *All will search: I will ask Kiibaile Esterire Airaikeliu to send all save Kairaithin, who is about business of his own, and after this day, I tell you, Kiibaile will hear your name in the wind through his wings.* The griffin flung himself back into the sky.

"Kiibaile—what?" asked the king, bemused.

"Kiibaile Esterire Airaikeliu," Kes said absently. "The Lord of Fire and Air. *You* shouldn't call him by his first name. That's for his *iskarianere*—his intimate . . ." she began to say *friends*, but that wasn't quite right and she stopped, frowning.

"Well, whatever his name, if he will set his people to searching, that will do," said the king, reaching again for his horse's reins once the griffin was gone. "Thank you, Kes. We will not wait. I want out of this desert, and if the Arobern did not watch from above and take himself back off across the mountains, it's to the east he'll be. Where is your horse, Bertaud? Has the creature a run left in it? How fast do you suppose we can make it out of this savage desert? And be in decent shape to fight? If we can find the Arobern to give him a fight! How can I have been so blind?" He paused. "I wonder if Eles found him? Earth and iron! I didn't give Eles half enough men to face any such threat!"

Lord Bertaud took a step forward, looking surprised and cautiously relieved. "Eles?"

The king frowned at him. "Well, what else was I to do when I must ride into a trap but make provision? It did not seem wise to leave all Feierabiand to depend only on my army. Eles was to get me another, as many men as he could, and to come south on his own, and on any account to stay out of the desert. I meant to keep him safe from the griffins and safe from the first thrust of the Arobern, but now I do not know where he is or what he may have met on his road."

For the first time, the tension that had tightened the lord's face and manner eased. He laughed and clapped the king on the shoulder. "My horse will have to do," he said, and beckoned to the man who had taken it away.

CHAPTER 14

The desert was as cleanly and elegantly beautiful as any airy palace or many-towered citadel built by men, Bertaud thought. But it was not a place meant for men, or for any creature of earth. Its starkness invited meditations on mortality and on the silence that lay behind life; the voice of the wind that sang across its twisted sharp-angled spires offered a suggestion of that greater music that lay behind the ordinary melodies of men. Its fierceness encompassed the fierceness of the griffins that made it; the passionate beat of its light and heat echoed the passion of griffin nature. Bertaud could imagine griffins emerging directly from the red silence of sand and stone, engendered by that powerful light, carved into shape by that ceaseless wind.

But it was not a place meant for men. It was drawing the very life out of them as they stood within its boundaries, as the sand might absorb blood spilled out upon it. And, it was clear, not even the earth mages, not even Meriemne, could resist that power. Not while it surrounded her, binding her strength and cutting her off from the living earth.

So there was a confusion and a haste that seemed utterly out of place in the patient desert: haste to load wounded men into litters and shaded carts, to cover dead men and lay their bodies out in other carts; haste to form men already fainting with heat and dazed by light into company ranks and send them east toward the cool country that waited so little distance away. Haste to lay plans for what they might find when they came there.

Iaor rode back and forth, with the vanguard for a short length and then back to the rear to check on the slowest of the carts. Here, he leaped down from his horse to lend a hand with an awning that would not stay up; there, he gave watered wine from his own supply to a wounded man.

That was a king's task: to be seen everywhere, to inspire. Bertaud left him to it and made his own slow way through the company, studying the men.

Two thousand and more men, he knew, had ridden south with the king from Riamne. Some, probably, had gone with Eles when Iaor had divided the army. Most had followed the king into the desert, and though Casmantium had not broken them, nor the griffins flung fire down upon them, still the battle, and even more the desert, had taken a toll. For every man struck down by spear or sword or arrow, Bertaud estimated, likely two had collapsed from heat and lack of water— though the army had carried a great deal of water, a man could not fight and drink simultaneously, and exertion under the pounding sun had sucked the moisture out of them.

Of whatever number had come into this desert with the king, perhaps a thousand remained strong enough and with heart enough for battle . . . if they should get out of the desert and into the green country and have time to rest and recover a little from the desert.

Kes rode with the army, perched high on the shoulders of the slim brown griffin who was her constant companion. Of them all, Kes rode with her face turned up to the sky as though she could not get enough light. She still wore the short brown dress she had made out of a Casmantian soldier's shirt, and with her skin ruddy with sun and her tangled hair down her back like a fall of pale light, she looked little more human than the griffin. And yet in a strange way her very unearthliness seemed to suit her, as though she had somehow always been meant for fire.

Kes brought her gaze down from the brilliant sky when Bertaud looked at her. She smiled at him, a sweet, perfectly human smile, but her eyes were edged and lit with fire. When she slid down from the griffin's back and ran across the sand to Bertaud's horse, men shied out of her way. She did not seem to notice this, either, but turned to walk beside his horse and lift trusting, unhuman eyes to his. If she had not clearly been able to see, he would have thought her blind.

"Yes?"

Bertaud strove for a neutral tone. "Eskainiane Escaile Sehaikiu?"

"Yes—Eskainiane." Her voice lingered over the name as though she spoke poetry. Her voice was not really a human voice any longer, although Bertaud could not have said precisely where the difference lay. Even the girl's steps seemed to have lightened, as though at the next step, or the next, she might walk right off the ground and into the air. "Eskainiane Escaile Sehaikiu . . . he will find them. Indeed, I think he has found them. You know," she said earnestly, patting the horse's neck, "you can trust Eskainiane. He is open-hearted and . . . not kind, exactly . . ."

"Generous," said Bertaud.

"Yes—generous. He will send . . . ah." She said then, in a different tone, "He has sent Kairaithin, I think."

The griffin mage came this time in a long, slow, smooth flight that carried him easily over the column of men and left him walking, in the shape of a man, beside Iaor's horse. He did not even glance at Bertaud, who was forced to take a moment to put down a violent and extremely stupid surge of jealousy.

"Esteemed mage," Iaor said to Kairaithin, with a nod.

Kairaithin gave the king a taut smile. "There is battle," he said. "Beguchren Teshrichten is with the Arobern, and both are with the main part of their army outside the town called Minas Ford."

"Minas Ford?" said Kes, much like someone told that the town of her childhood, distantly remembered, lies just beyond the next turn in the road.

"Eles *engaged* him?" Iaor said, in a completely different tone. "There is battle *now*?"

"The griffins must aid us again, then," Bertaud said, trying for no tone at all.

Kairaithin turned to him swiftly. "I have destroyed the cold mages sent against us here. But outside this desert, I cannot match Beguchren. And would you have us come down outside our place of power, with our fire turned all to ash, upon soldiers armed with cold steel? Bows made with purpose to kill creatures of fire? No, man. We would be destroyed, and is that your desire?"

Iaor said, "We haven't enough men to face down another army the size of the first—and our men spent with heat, and his men near fresh? Esteemed mage—"

"They *will* help us, my king," said Bertaud with resolve, and stared into fiery black eyes.

Kes gazed, clearly curious and alarmed, from him to Kairaithin.

Kairaithin did not glance at her. His attention, hot as the savage desert, was narrowed to Bertaud. "I will find a way," he said, straight to Bertaud, "if you will trust me for that, and do nothing on your own account." There was no anger in the griffin's voice, belying the anger in his eyes and his heart: He was, Bertaud understood, making a fierce effort to keep his tone neutral. It was, perhaps, the closest Kairaithin could publicly come to a plea.

Bertaud hesitated. He could imagine no greater dereliction of his duty to Iaor and Feierabiand than to allow the Arobern to strike through Minas Ford and then, unopposed, for Terabiand on the coast. Nor did he believe Iaor had any real chance of turning the Arobern from that purpose with a bare thousand sunstruck soldiers.

Yet at the same time he could imagine no greater wrong than to compel the wild, brilliant-hearted griffins to the service of men. No matter how desperately Feierabiand needed their service. He had dreamed of violent winds and lakes of molten stone: What would his dreams contain if he broke the griffins to harness like oxen? Or if he drove them all to their deaths in a cool green country where their fire could not burn?

He said at last, "Who could do so better than you, esteemed mage?"

Kairaithin inclined his head, backed up a step—waiting, Bertaud saw, to see that he would indeed be allowed to go—and then folded himself through space into the far heart of the desert.

Bertaud let his breath out. He said casually to Iaor, just as though nothing untoward had taken place, "He will do his best, I think, if only to humble the pride of Casmantium. I think he resents how his people were used as tools against us."

The king nodded sharply. "I should certainly think so." He glanced ahead and added with a good deal more interest, "Earth and iron, is there no *end* to this cursed desert?"

Kes, who had been gazing at Bertaud with alarming intensity, shifted her attention to the king. "You see that flat-topped spire? That one, with the double arch on the eastern side? The boundary is just there." She added at the king's raised-eyebrow look, "I always know." Her tone was almost wistful. "But cannot you see it? It is dark, like the edge of night against the day."

Bertaud thought he could. Iaor only shook his head.

"It is not far," said Kes, and walked away toward her griffin as though simply forgetful of the king, or of his rank. But she moved with that odd lighter-than-air grace, and Bertaud thought she had not so much forgotten Iaor's rank, as become, griffinlike, disinclined to care for it.

The creature had waited for Kes patiently. She lowered her beak to brush the girl's hair and turned for her to mount, then spread dark wings and reached for the heights. Bertaud watched them go. He knew, uneasily, precisely what it was like to spread wings and mount the sweeping stair of the wind. Precisely what it was like.

"I wish we might fly, and spare our feet," grumbled Iaor. "Or that the horses might, and spare their strength. Just there, is it? Well, I suppose I do see it, as the girl said. About time. Pass the word, Bertaud— men to form up once we cross that line. Water all around, and we'll try to get the sun-dazed men back on their feet, but with Eles possibly pressed by whatever the Arobern has with him, we cannot delay."

"Leave the sunstruck to guard the Casmantian prisoners," Bertaud advised.

The king nodded sharply. "Yes, that will do. That's a duty for which they should be fit. The horses—I think they will have done what they can merely to get us to the boundary. You have ridden this recently. How far from the boundary to Minas Ford?"

"Half an hour's ride, no more."

"And the griffins? *Will* they aid us?"

"Yes," Bertaud said fiercely, but then more moderately, "I think they will, my king."

"Well, we must not depend upon it. We must have surprise, if we can keep it—find Uol and have scouts sent ahead to see what waits for us—if we can find the disposition of men, that at least may favor us— earth and stone, Bertaud," Iaor added in a different tone, "how can a worn and paltry thousand stand against all the Arobern undoubtedly has brought to this war? Who ever heard of such a war as this, pulled out of a peaceful summer without a whisper of warning? *Can* the griffins aid us when we stand on good earth and not on their burning sand?"

Bertaud opened his mouth to say that he was sure they could, and closed it again. He did not know. He said at last, "I think they will try. As we will. The men know what this battle is for."

Iaor lifted one hand and rubbed his face; he looked suddenly as though the past days had suddenly caught him up. Then he let his breath out, dropped his hand to his horse's neck, and straightened in the saddle. "Well, if we dare not lose, then we must win, griffins or no," he answered his own question, and pressed the horse into a canter.

Bertaud did not follow. He, too, looked along the slow-footed column of Feierabiand soldiers and wondered what these men would be able to do at the end of a day such as they had had.

The leading edge of the column turned around the spire that Kes had pointed out, and suddenly the pace picked up; the men in front did not spare breath for shouting, but nonetheless as they found the desert boundary in sight before them, their weary relief was transmitted instantly straight through to the men at the very rear. Even the Casmantian prisoners matched that pace; even the horses drawing the carts of the wounded and dead stepped out with a will. Bertaud's horse lifted its head and flared red-rimmed nostrils, sensing that ahead lay air that did not burn with fire; it wanted to run, and after the briefest moment he gave the animal its head. It leaped forward over the sand as though flung like a spear.

The line between desert and ordinary land was sharp and clear as though lain down by a deliberate hand. On the other side of that line, it was raining.

Bertaud stared at the rain, coming down slantwise and heavy through the air; at the heavy skies above; at the water washing downhill past living trees and over living earth, and he laughed out loud as his horse broke from a canter to a stretched-out gallop. It shot across the boundary and tossed its head up, shying sideways as the rain came down against it. It was, after the desert, like charging into an icehouse and being pelted with sleet. Bertaud flung back his own head and opened his mouth, eyes closed, rain running down his face like tears. But he could not have said himself whether they were tears of grief or joy. Both, perhaps.

Probably no soldiers anywhere had ever been so glad to form up in the rain. Men shouted with the first shock of cold—then adjusted to the coolness that was, after all, no colder than usual for summer rain, and stripped off their helmets to let rain pour down their necks. The awnings on the carts suddenly became useful for keeping rain off the wounded, while Meriemne swept back the curtains of her litter to let the rain fall on her wrinkled face. She was already sending her bearers straight for the carts, and Iaor rode past and dipped to take her hand and kiss it, laughing: one more worry off his mind. Bertaud only hoped the earth mage could help the sunstruck also.

General Adries rode by at a smart pace, causing scattered soldiers to leap to order by his mere presence. The men should have had an hour to rest, hot food, wine—but there was no time, or so Iaor clearly feared. Bertaud feared it too. There were great holes in the ranks. Officers were working hastily to merge tattered companies into solid units; sergeants moved through the lines, taking out a man here or moving one to fill a hole there, making sure bowmen were protecting their strings, issuing orders for the men to sit down right in their ranks and get what rest they could. Baskets of hard bread and dried fruit were being passed down the ranks. It was raining harder now, hard enough for the drops to sting, but no one complained about the rain soaking the food. They were too glad for the extra moisture in their parched mouths.

Bertaud found Iaor speaking with his senior officers at the edge of the small army, all of them looking off down the hill as though they expected to see the Casmantian army right down there.

"Ah, Bertaud," Iaor said, catching sight of him. "We'll move out on the quarter hour. We'll cross through the pastures, come down the hills through that wood over there. If the Arobern has men posted to watch for us, that's where they'll be; at least, that's where I'd put them if it were me, so I'll want a dozen or so men to go down quietly in front of us and see what there might be waiting. This rain is luck for us."

Bertaud nodded. The rain would kill alertness, mute sound, restrict visibility.

Iaor frowned in thought. "We've got about eight hundred men fit to march—that'll have to do, no matter if the Arobern has two or even three thousand, as the spy tells us. We can hope Eles has blunted his teeth a little." He did not put into words what they both knew: that if Eles had put whatever force he had gathered against the Arobern, probably he and all his men had already been butchered.

"So . . ." Bertaud said instead, "we captured a Casmantian spy?"

"Not captured, precisely. He came with the girl and put himself in our hands—gone over to her side, I gather, if not precisely to ours. I gave him to Emend, you know, one of Moutres's people."

"Ah." Moutres was Iaor's master of spies. And the man, then, was the Casmantian soldier who had brought Kes out of the Casmantian camp. That he'd been a spy was very believable. That he'd entirely thrown over his own people for Kes . . . that, also, remembering him with her, was perhaps believable. Though one trusted turned spies not at all, and depended on their information as little as possible—but Iaor would know that, and at least there was little doubt he'd truly turned.

Iaor ran a distracted hand through his wet hair and glanced at the sky. "Luck for us, as this rain is—luck comes in threes, or we shall hope it does. I know what I want from it: quickness and surprise. Time?" he asked one of the officers.

"Twelve minutes, your majesty," said the man.

Iaor gave a curt nod and strode urgently off with a handful of officers trailing him.

Bertaud watched them go and then walked away, to the edge of the woods and then in among the trees. Rain beat down on the leaves overhead, a comforting sound that quickly muffled the noise of soldiers and horses behind him, until he might almost have been alone in this countryside. His shirt was soaked through . . . not unpleasant, after the desiccating wind of the desert. He stopped at last, his hand against the bole of a slim tree, and called into the rain, "Kairaithin."

As though he had been waiting for that call, the griffin mage was there. Maybe he *had* been waiting; he had come so quickly. He stood in the shadows of the trees with his shadow smoldering dimly behind him, as banked coals may glow faintly through thick ash. His eyes, Bertaud fancied, smoldered as well.

Bertaud said, "This rain—"

"My people cannot fly in this wet," said the griffin harshly. "Do you understand, man?"

Bertaud said nothing.

"You must not call us. If you call, we shall be compelled to come. And in this rain, we shall be helpless against Beguchren—against the cold arrows the Casmantian archers possess. Do you understand?"

The griffin's tone was abrupt, just short of savage; his face rigid. He was trying, Bertaud thought, to overcome his vast pride enough to plead. He was going to manage it in another moment. Bertaud said quickly, to forestall him, "Do *you* understand what will happen to my people, if yours will not aid us? You are asking me to sacrifice my people for yours—perhaps more: Perhaps my king. Perhaps Feierabiand entire." His voice fell to a whisper. "How can I fail to use all the weapons I possess, when the alternative is such profound betrayal? Do you deny that your griffins would still be a useful weapon in our need, even pulled out of the desert and weakened by rain? That your people might still help me save mine?"

Kairaithin came forward a step and half lifted a hand, only to let it fall with whatever gesture he had begun unfinished. He said nothing, perhaps because he could not fathom what argument might move a weary human heart in this exigency. Even silent, the griffin's presence beat against Bertaud like the heat of a great fire, though one banked and dim.

Bertaud ran his hand slowly down the smooth bark of the tree and tried to think, through the distraction of the rain—heavier now—and the fierce pressure of the griffin's presence so near at hand. He could not.

Distantly, he heard the shouts that told him the Feierabiand soldiers, what poor remnants of them remained, were forming up into ranks and prepared to march. They would move quickly, he knew, coming into this wood: There was not yet any need for stealth. He need not rush back to join the Feierabiand army. It would come here, to him. Indeed, he thought he could already hear the sounds of its approach.

He said harshly, hardly knowing what he said, "I won't call you."

Kairaithin met his eyes, waiting, expressionless.

Bertaud thought—knew—that the griffin did not yet believe him. Kairaithin expected some impossible demand to be laid on him, on his people, which they would not be able to refuse and which would destroy them. He repeated simply, not knowing of any complicated oath that would create belief, "I won't call you."

The griffin mage tilted his head to one side, a gesture startlingly like that of a bird. He started to speak.

Behind them, a voice called urgently, "My lord!" A young man came through the trees, riding a horse of his own and leading Bertaud's. "The king is asking for you," said the man.

Bertaud took the reins and turned back to look for Kairaithin. But the griffin was gone. A sharp sense of loss went through Bertaud like an arrow, and a sense of release; he understood that the griffin mage was gone, indeed, and would not return. This would be a battle between men. There was every chance Feierabiand would lose. But the griffins would not, at least, be pulled down with Feierabiand. Bertaud swung up into the saddle without a word to the young man—he felt wholly unsuited, just now, for speaking to men—and went, as directed, to find his king.

There were Casmantian sentries in the wood. "Three of them," Adries reported. "I hope that was all there were, for that's all we found."

By that time, the sounds of battle were faintly audible even over the sounds of rain and wind coming through the trees.

"Eles is holding?" Iaor wondered aloud. "How?" He sent Bertaud a sharp look. "Could your griffins have come there before us and reinforced him?"

Bertaud shrugged. He could hardly explain why he was certain they had not. So he said nothing, and wondered bleakly how he had come to keep such secrets from his king and his friend.

Minas Ford was not, of course, walled. It was far too small to bother defending, and all its wealth—in land and crops and livestock—would have lain outside any wall anyway. There were no more than a few dozen cottages in the village proper, all made of white stone and dark timber, with a single cobbled street and a broad green in the center. The Arobern's army pressed close on all sides. But the army had not yet entered the village: It had been stopped at its edges.

Defenders used the cottages themselves to fill out their lines: They had ranked themselves between ready-made walls. Even so, their lines were frighteningly thin, and growing thinner as Bertaud watched. They were mostly using swords, and mostly against spears, a desperately uneven match, especially with the vastly disparate numbers. Grunts of effort were audible, panting cries of anger or pain from both sides, the ring and scrape and crash of metal against metal . . . Orders, shouted in sharp, high voices to carry above the clamor. The scream, somewhere, of an injured horse, piercing and innocent as the cry of a child. And over all, the constant steady rush of the rain, pouring and pouring out of the heavy sky . . .

Men also were within the houses, shutters thrown wide so they could shoot out at the Casmantians. At first, Bertaud thought those within the buildings were all soldiers, but then he saw, from the way they cast back the dim watery light, that the arrowheads were the slim copper-tipped ones used for hunting and not war, and after that he saw that many of the defenders shooting from the windows were simply villagers. Of course, the Casmantians were shooting back, though it was harder for them, out in the weather as they were, to keep their bowstrings dry. But some of them were clearly managing the trick. When a defender, struck, cried out, it was a woman's high voice Bertaud heard. He flinched from the sound of it.

"Eles did well, and does well," Adries commented, coming up beside Bertaud. "That's more than a hundred men he has there, I expect— more nearly two, if you count the civilians. Women, too—yes, you heard that, too, did you? He might hold another quarter hour, even half, before the Casmantians break through that line somewhere. Then it'd be all over, of course . . . Well, we'll see if we can't beat that moment."

Adries did not put into words the obvious, which was that whatever they might do to relieve Eles and his men for a moment or an hour, it would nevertheless not be possible to win. Unless the griffins came in. *Kairaithin*, Bertaud thought, longing for the power of the griffin to reinforce the men of Feierabiand, but he did not call. The rain fell steadily, as though it had always fallen and always would, as though rain was an intrinsic quality of the air on this side of the boundary. Earth magic brought it, he was increasingly certain: the cold earth magic used by Casmantium, utterly antithetical to griffin fire . . . If he forced the griffins to fight, Bertaud thought, they would only come to be slaughtered, and what good would that do any of them? He did not call.

"We won't be sounding horns. You'd best take your position, my lord."

Bertaud, mouth dry despite the rain, nodded and reined his horse back to look for Iaor.

The king, helmed and armored, held a spear across his knee; his sword was sheathed, ready for a quick grab. He held no bow: He would not hang back in the rear to shoot, but ride with the vanguard. As would Bertaud, of course, to guard him as he might during the crush. He said, for Iaor's ears alone, "If we broke off and pressed hard for Terabiand, we could organize a welcome there that might be more a match for the Arobern than anything we can manage here."

The king gave him a quick edged smile. "Buying that chance with Minas Ford and the blood of all its defenders? Is that a price you would willingly pay? Or one you would expect me to pay?"

"No," Bertaud admitted.

"Of course not. I did," added the king, "send men south. The Arobern will have his welcome even so. If we bleed him heavily enough here, it may even be enough. And your griffins?" the king asked again, not with much hope.

Bertaud shrugged. "In this rain? It's a mage-crafted rain, I think—meant expressly to keep the griffins away."

The king smiled again, fierce as a griffin himself. "There can't be more there than three thousand or so. We need only kill three of them for every one of us that falls."

"An even match," Bertaud said, in a deliberately serious tone, finding himself despite everything falling back, at last, into the manner they had always had between them.

"Exactly," said the king with a brief grin, and turned his horse to ride quickly across the ranks, gathering the attention of all his men. He did not cry out the words of any fine speech: Such would only be heard by the men below and give everything away. He only met the eyes of one man, and another, and another. Then he turned his horse, gathered it, and sent it suddenly racing down the hill straight at the rear of the Casmantian force. Which turned, awkwardly at first but then more smoothly, to face them: The Arobern, clearly, had posted men to watch for such an attack. Or sentries had gotten away from the Feierabiand scouts. Or the Arobern was just that able, and watched all directions at once, rain or no rain.

There might have been a thousand Casmantian soldiers on the east side of Minas Ford: They were strung out more widely than the Feierabiand column, but until the armies should crash together that was an advantage to the Casmantians, who could shoot from both ends of their line into the Feierabiand advance. The arrows did not fall as thickly as they might; the rain thinned the volleys. The hundred or so Feierabiand bowmen who still had both dry strings and arrows fell back, halted their advance, and began to provide covering fire. The rest pressed forward as quickly as they could. The small horse contingent, including the king with Bertaud at his back, went before the foot soldiers, meaning to open a gap in the Casmantian line if they could.

Casmantian horns called, called again, and mounted Casmantian soldiers swept around from the other side of Minas Ford since they could not go through, rushing to reinforce their lines. From Minas Ford itself, a small force surged forward suddenly, trying to weaken the Casmantian line so the Feierabiand horse could break it. Rain fell, harder now, and colder.

The Arobern himself, marked by his sheer presence as much as by his banner, flung forward to meet the Feierabiand charge, and suddenly Bertaud was battling madly, his sword crashing against defending swords—he cut at a man on foot, did not know whether he hit the man

or not—cut at a horse, which reared, screaming—fended off a spear
that might have taken him in the side and sent his horse leaping to
cover Iaor's side, where another spear threatened the king. He had lost
sight of the Arobern. He tossed his head to clear rain from his eyes and
pressed his horse sideways to stay with Iaor, and they were no longer
moving forward; they were halted, or nearly, and that was not good—an
open space appeared before them, and he shouted and sent his horse for
it, Iaor right beside him—and they were jolting forward again, men at
their backs—Feierabiand men, Bertaud fervently hoped—and men before them, and Iaor shouted and flung up his sword, and everyone swept
sideways and forward again, and the hooves of the horses rang suddenly
on cobbles.

They were *in* Minas Ford, on its one street. They had gone right
through the Casmantian line—Bertaud understood suddenly that the
Arobern had let them through, the better to have all his opponents
bottled up in one trap. Iaor, he saw, had understood this at once; beside
him, the king was cursing steadily.

"He let you through," Eles snapped at Iaor, coming suddenly from
among the defenders of Minas Ford to set a hand on the bridle of the
king's horse. He and all his men, guardsmen and soldiers and townsfolk alike, looked as hollow-eyed and desperate as though they'd
been under siege for a week rather than, at very most, a few hours.
And those who had meant to be their saviors looked very nearly as
badly off.

"I know it," Iaor agreed, and gave up cursing in favor of a swift examination of the village and its defenders. A dismayingly small number,
they seemed to Bertaud, to hold ground against the Casmantian army
outside the village. And too many of them wounded already, and all of
them exhausted. Soldiers and guardsmen had quietly gathered around
Iaor, rivalry forgotten in this moment, looking to the king to come up
with some miraculous deliverance for them all. A village woman with a
hunting bow and a drawn expression had a place with archers in the uniform of regular soldiers; men in rough-spun village clothing had found
swords and filled out ranks of infantry. Bertaud spotted Enned son of
Lakas among the rest and was absurdly pleased the boy yet lived. Though
that was no guarantee he, or any of them, would see the coming dusk or
the dawn that followed it.

"Well, well . . . Minas Ford may be a trap, but it may still close in
both directions," said the king. "He daren't leave this town unsecured
at his rear. With the men I brought, we can hold it a while yet, I should
think, and I've sent men to raise the south. Eles, man . . . you did very
well to pin him down here."

The guard captain gave him a dour nod. "I sent men west to Sihannas and Eheniand. And Keoun of Sihannas does have a brain. He'll have a thousand men on the road by tomorrow afternoon at the latest. Much good it will do *us*," he added, with a glance back toward the Casmantian lines.

"In the end, the Arobern will have to come to terms. And he'll have to do it with me, and he must know that by this time. He won't take Terabiand with three thousand men, and we may thank the griffins he so kindly sent us he does not have more. For all the griffins' absence now, they have saved us by what they did in the desert." Iaor, too, sat back in his saddle, stretched, and turned to study the Casmantians.

"How about . . . more nearly seven, perhaps?" Bertaud asked, and jerked his head toward a great dark mass moving slowly down the distant slopes of the mountains. It was hard to see through the rain-hazed air . . . but the glitter of thousands of spear points was unmistakable.

Eles drew a slow breath between his teeth. Iaor did not make a sound, but his face, grimly satisfied a moment earlier, went still.

The Casmantians, too, had seen that force: Their shouts rang like horns, hailing their victory.

"He knew he would need more than five thousand men to take Terabiand, of course," the king said after a moment. "And so kept his force divided. To keep some of his people out of the desert, perhaps. Or to get me to underestimate him and commit myself to an indefensible position. Either way . . . well. How long, do you suppose, for him to get those men around the desert?"

"If they force the pace . . . they will be here before dawn, certainly."

"They won't stop here," said Adries, riding up and drawing rein near them. He looked perfectly disgusted. His wet hair stuck to his neck and clung to his mail. He stripped off his helmet and rubbed a hand impatiently across his face. "They'll go straight south, while the force already here holds us in place. I would lay odds. They could be in Bered by midnight, and in Terabiand by noon the next day, long before anyone there expects them. Meanwhile, the Arobern will finish us off this afternoon, rest tonight in Minas Ford, and take his men with him, come the new dawn, to meet any men coming east from Sihannas or Eheniand. Or so I would do, in his place."

The king looked at Bertaud. "We must have the griffins. And that girl to keep them flying."

"Yes," said Bertaud. He thought, *no*. He had made his decision earlier, and he kept to it now, desperately: There was no possible way to demand that of them. He said after a moment, "Only, outside their desert, my king . . . I think they will find themselves unable to be the weapon that turns this tide for us. And I can't think why they should fly to their own deaths in an attempt to protect us. Especially when they must ultimately fail."

"They could take word for us south to Terabiand. They could take word all across the south and the west. Would they do that for us?" Iaor asked. He glanced around as though half expecting Kairaithin or Opailikiita to suddenly loom up out of the rain and then glanced, frustrated, at Bertaud. "Or they could, if they would and if they were *here*. But we have no way to even ask them to do this for us."

Bertaud said nothing. He could call Kairaithin, breaking his word; he would even have done that, in this extremity. Except he knew, he was *sure* that this rain had been brought by the cold mages—by Beguchren. If he called Kairaithin into this mage-crafted rain, the griffin would surely fall to the cold mage, and what would be the good of that to any of them? Under these conditions, he could not, *must* not call. He thought, briefly, of trying to set a compulsion on all the griffins to fight Casmantian forces, not here at Minas Ford, but rather as and where they could . . . only he knew *exactly* how compulsion would ruin them, and in any case the compulsion would cease at his death. So he could not do that, either. Which was, in its way, a vast relief.

"Then if we have no help from the griffins, we are lost," Adries summed up, eerily as though he had been listening to Bertaud's thoughts. But the general went on with heavy decisiveness. "And I cannot imagine we will have such aid. That second Casmantian force will stay well clear of the desert, depend upon it, and I think we may be sure that there will be more cold mages accompanying it." He looked to the king. "Your majesty . . . despite everything we have done here, I doubt we can weaken this force enough to give the griffins a chance against that one, even if they should trouble themselves for our sake. Nevertheless, we could fight here as long as we can stand to battle. If you ask it. Or we could break a path through the Casmantian lines for you. You could get out and away toward Eheniand and so keep out of Casmantian hands yourself. Or," he added, his voice dropping, "you could ask the Arobern for terms. You will have to deal with him in the end, and he'll know that you will know that by this time."

Iaor's hands had tightened on the reins; his horse twitched its ears back and mouthed the bit uncomfortably. The king's grip eased, and he patted its neck in absent thought. Rain blew through the air, cold against their faces.

"Form up the men," Iaor said to Adries. And to Eles, "Integrate yours with his, if you please, my friend. Wounded . . . we have no earth mages with us here. Have you?"

"No," Eles said quietly.

"Casmantium is a civilized nation, at least," said Iaor. "And the Arobern, by all accounts, a generous man." He, too, took off his helm and ran a hand through his wet hair. His look was bleak. "Well, Bertaud? Shall I break out toward the west and run like a stag before the hunters' horns? Or form up the men and bravely make a stand? Or go out to face the Arobern of Casmantium and see what terms he will give me?"

The secret Bertaud was concealing seemed in this moment an enormity. He wanted to drop his own gaze; he wanted to blurt out, *I have an affinity for griffins, I can call them whether they will or no, and even now we may turn back the Arobern.* But he knew, he *knew* that summoning the griffins would do nothing but destroy them, and without saving anything from the wreckage of this day. He met Iaor's eyes steadily and, unable to find any honest advice to offer, said nothing. He wondered what the king was thinking: of his own pride, and failure? Of Feierabiand, which all the Safiad kings had always kept safe and independent, and a large piece of which he might be losing at last to Casmantium? With a sudden startling pang, Bertaud thought of the pretty young queen waiting with confidence in Tihannad. It seemed incredible now that he had ever been in the least jealous of her. Looking into the king's set face, he wondered whether Iaor was thinking of her, too.

He wanted to say, *Go, get out. How can you think of surrender? How do we know what the Arobern will do with a Safiad king once he gets one in his hands?* If Bertaud could not lay a victory at Iaor's feet, he might furnish at least momentary hope. But what he said, at last, was, "I certainly . . . can desire nothing but what you desire. My king."

"Yes," said Iaor, and tried to smile. He took a deep breath. He started to speak again, and stopped. He asked instead, "The griffins will not come, you think? They can do nothing for us?"

"I don't see how they possibly could, my king."

"No," said Iaor, and sighed again. "Well—" he said, and turned his horse toward the end of Minas Ford's one street.

The Arobern of Casmantium had drawn most of his men up in close order there, barely out of bowshot from the houses. He was there himself. Not inclined to press an attack, evidently. Waiting, rather. Bertaud could see him, sitting a big bay horse before his men, the banner at his side limp in the rain his mage had made. His face was turned toward Minas Ford. His whole attitude, even from this distance, was clearly one of patience.

Iaor rode as far as the last house and halted his horse there. Bertaud rode at his side, and Adries at the other. They halted with him.

"Well?" said the king to them.

"The decision," his general said without looking at the king, "is yours, your majesty."

"Bertaud?"

"I will bear your word to him, Iaor. Whether that is a gauntlet flung into his face, or . . . or the other."

"Yes," said the king, and let his breath out slowly. He straightened his back. "Tell him . . . tell him . . . My friend, you must tell him that I understand that continuing this battle now will do nothing but spend all the lives of my men, and to no purpose. Ask him . . . ask him for—"

The rain stopped. It did not slow or taper gently to a halt, but stopped all at once.

The wind turned. It had been blowing in ragged gusts from the west, a heavy moisture-laden wind. It turned now to come from the south, and it carried with it scents of sand and fire. This wind was so dry that it sucked moisture from the air and from the slick cobbles and from the very clothing men wore. Bertaud lifted a suddenly unsteady hand to touch his hair, which, cropped short, was already dry.

The clouds shredded on that wind, not blowing away so much as simply disappearing. The sky turned a deep sweet blue . . . then paled, and paled further, taking on a hard metallic tone. Heat came down across Minas Ford like a hammer dropping on an anvil; Bertaud almost thought he could hear the ringing blow as it struck.

And the griffins came. They rode their desert wind out of the south, their wings flashing gold or copper or bronze. The Lord of Fire and Air led them, fire falling from the wind of his wings; on one side of the griffin king flew white Tastairiane and on the other the blazing copper-and-gold Eskainiane. Bertaud looked for Kairaithin among that host, but could not find him. Men shouted, with joy in Minas Ford and with dismay among the ranks of the Casmantian army. Bertaud, too much stunned for words, made no sound. He could not imagine the power it had taken the griffins to force their desert through the rain and the cold. He could not imagine the cost they had taken on themselves to bring it here to this field of battle.

And then he found he could indeed imagine that cost. Because, as the griffins approached, it became possible to see the increasing raggedness of their flight. Where a formation of five griffins flew, fiercely splendid, one and then perhaps another would suddenly rip apart into a blast of fire and red sand. The desert wind came from this, Bertaud understood. They made the desert out of themselves. He had never before realized that if a griffin gave too much strength to the desert, it might unmake itself. But that was what they were doing. He could not bear to watch, but equally he could not look away.

The new desert, following the harsh dry wind, struck across Minas Ford and an instant later across the Casmantian army. Sand hissed across the cobbles. Red dust rode the wind, tinting the air the color of blood. The griffins flew low, well within bowshot, directly over the Casmantian ranks. Men cried out in alarm, lifting their bows. Arrows rose, striking griffin after griffin. Griffin after griffin faltered . . . then caught its balance and regained its place in the sky. Far above the battle, far out of bowshot, Bertaud found a single dark griffin wheeling in slow circles, and knew that though a griffin might tear apart into fire and air, no griffin would die by arrow or spear this day.

At the forefront of the Casmantian soldiers, the Arobern turned to the small figure beside him. The cold mage Beguchren, for it could be no one else, lifted his hands, fighting the desert. Bertaud did not know whether he truly felt the man's cold power struggle against the fire or whether he only imagined he felt it.

From the first ranks of the griffins, Eskainiane suddenly cast back his bright wings and stooped like an eagle. Bertaud thought the griffin meant to strike down the mage bodily, but he did not. Instead, he cried out, the long piercing shriek of a hunting eagle, and burst violently into flaming wind.

The cold mage put his hands over his face and staggered; if he made a sound, it was lost beneath the cries of the griffins. The Arobern supported his mage, and though Bertaud could not see his expression, the Arobern's attitude had now become one of furious acknowledgment of defeat. He turned and shouted to his men, waving his arm in urgent command, and as his officers picked up and repeated that command, the flights of arrows ceased.

The griffins wheeled slowly above the Casmantian army. They did not descend to strike, but slid through the hot air to spiral around Minas Ford, coming lower still, sunlight flashing from their savage beaks and pooling in their molten eyes. Griffins landed on rooftops, talons and claws tearing gouges through wooden shingles, their outspread wings tilting for balance. Others stayed in the air, sweeping slowly in a wide spiral out across the village and back over the Casmantian army; a long narrow line of fire followed their curving flight, leaping up all around that army and then dying back, leaving little tongues of flames flickering in the red sand.

A single griffin, gold and red, slanted down across the light toward the Arobern. It landed, light as a cat, directly before him. The King of Casmantium, as any of his opponents knew, did not lack boldness. He stepped forward to face it.

"Nehaistiane Esterikiu Anahaikuuanse," said Kairaithin, suddenly standing beside Bertaud's horse. The horse shied; all the horses were suddenly shying and trying to rear, and Iaor and Adries and Bertaud found it simplest to dismount and send them away.

"She was the mate of Eskainiane Escaile Sehaikiu and of our king," continued Kairaithin as though he had not noticed the disruption. "She has lost yet another *iskarianere* today. Now that Escaile Sehaikiu is no more, it falls to her to carry our word to the King of Casmantium. He had best be courteous. She will bitterly mourn her mate."

"And what is that word?" Iaor asked him. He was pale, but his tone was bland. He had clasped his hands behind his back, Bertaud saw, and thought probably they were shaking. He knew his own were.

Kairaithin's smile had nothing human about it: It was like the smile of the desert, utterly pitiless. "We will not be lightly offended," he said, and his smile tautened. "We will *ring* his army—both his armies—with desert sand, if we must; we will lay the desert beneath his boots and beneath the boots of his men and hunt them like earthbound cattle across the red sand. Let Beguchren Teshrichten challenge *this* working. He has already found it is beyond him."

"Why did you do it?" Bertaud asked in hushed tones.

"Many of us ceased to exist," the griffin said, and harshly, "*But we will not be the tools or playthings of men.*"

It was to Bertaud that the griffin directed that furious statement, he knew. But Iaor did not know that. The king said quietly, "For breaking the Arobern's power, I thank you, even if you did not do it for us."

Kairaithin's lip curled. He barely glanced at the king. "It was well done, to show Casmantium our strength . . . so. Esterikiu Anahai-kuuanse has given the Arobern our terms. He will deliver himself and all his men into your hands, Safiad king—for men to deal with men—or we will go to whatever lengths we must to destroy them ourselves." His black eyes glanced sideways at Bertaud. "What will he choose?"

"You ask me?"

"A man to judge what men will do. Well?"

"He will yield," Iaor said quietly. "When he sees that continuing this battle now will do nothing but spend all the lives of his men, and to no purpose. He will yield."

CHAPTER 15

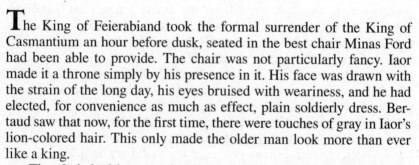

The King of Feierabiand took the formal surrender of the King of Casmantium an hour before dusk, seated in the best chair Minas Ford had been able to provide. The chair was not particularly fancy. Iaor made it a throne simply by his presence in it. His face was drawn with the strain of the long day, his eyes bruised with weariness, and he had elected, for convenience as much as effect, plain soldierly dress. Bertaud saw that now, for the first time, there were touches of gray in Iaor's lion-colored hair. This only made the older man look more than ever like a king.

The chair had been set beneath a hastily erected pavilion by the bank of the river, with the lowering sun at the king's back. This was not the harsh sun of the desert. The red desert had engulfed Minas Ford, but it had not quite come down to the river. Thus the pavilion, set out of the sand in the cool evening.

Iaor's small army had been drawn up to his left; Eles's guardsmen and the people of Minas Ford had a place of honor before the pavilion. The Casmantian soldiers, those who had been with the Arobern, stood in their ranks, disarmed and under a light guard, to the right. The other Casmantian army, receiving a messenger the Arobern had sent to them, had not come farther into Feierabiand, but rather had held its place on the far side of the desert.

Kairaithin, in griffin form, sat near Iaor's chair on one side, and Bertaud himself stood on the other.

The king of the griffins was not present, but the savage white griffin, Tastairiane Apailika, sat a little beyond Kairaithin. Bertaud did not know what the attendance of these particular griffins signified. Kes probably knew why Tastairiane Apailika in particular had been sent to watch these proceedings, but she sat on the ground between Opailikii-ta's feathered forelegs, her own arms around up-drawn knees, and looked not at all approachable.

The girl's hair had been brushed out—it was the first time Bertaud had ever seen it free of tangles and knots—and braided with a strand of honey-colored beads. And she had finally changed out of her makeshift Casmantian dress. She wore a plain pale-yellow gown that had no adornment at all. Bertaud suspected that Kairaithin had found, or perhaps made, the clothing for her; it seemed to him a detail that would matter to the griffin mage, though he could not have said why.

Kes looked older and less waiflike, but still not very human. Her feet were bare, her skin nearly transparent; she seemed barely to contain an internal light. She had not shown any desire to put herself in the company of the Minas Ford people. Most of those folk looked at Kes, quick anxious astonished looks, with a great deal more intensity than they spared for the king. She did not look back. She had her head tilted against Opailikiita's leg, and her own attention seemed reserved for the Arobern.

Brechen Glansent Arobern walked forward between the two armies, past the townsfolk and the griffins, and stopped before Iaor's chair. He had not been bound—"No," Iaor had said, undoubtedly thinking how nearly this moment had gone the other way, "let him keep his pride. We will see how little else we can leave him." So the Arobern was not chained. He had only been disarmed. He looked intent, energetic, not in the least humbled; his focus was not inward, on his own defeat and humiliation, as one might have expected, but outward, on Iaor.

He walked forward quite steadily, a big man with powerful shoulders and a face that was strong, even harsh. His dark beard accentuated the strength of his jaw and made him look stubborn, which he probably was; his eyes were quick and brilliant and utterly redeemed his heavy features from any appearance of dullness. When he got to Iaor, he did not kneel, but bowed, and then studied his conqueror with every appearance of lively curiosity as he straightened. He was tall enough, and arrogant enough, to make it seem by his attitude alone that his was the pre-dominant will in all this company.

Iaor smiled. It was not an amused smile. He had not wanted to humble the Arobern, but, Bertaud thought, he had rather expected the Arobern to show a certain humility of his own accord. That was lacking. Iaor did not demand it. He only said, with a mildness Bertaud recognized as his father's, signalling dangerous temper, "Brechen Glansent Arobern. Your country and mine were not, I thought, at war. And yet here we are. Why is this?"

The Arobern lifted powerful shoulders in a shrug. "Well. I thought it would work. Yes?" His Terheien was harshly accented, but perfectly understandable. "I thought I would come across the mountains and take your Bered and Terabiand, yes, and all that country to the east of the river, and make a new province for Casmantium. Then the road through the mountains might be made better, and Casmantium could profit from Terabiand's harbor. You understand, I did not think the *malacteir*, the griffins, I did not think they would fight for you. I thought the other way: That you would fight them and so be made weak."

His eyes went to Kes, where she sat at the feet of her griffin friend. She looked back at him with eyes that were filled with fire and the memories of the desert.

"I did not expect the *malacteir* to find a girl like that one. And then when I caught her, I did not think the little *festechanenteir* would slip my hand. And then she came into her power. So all I meant to do turned and went another way, yes? The *festechanenteir* turned the weapon I thought I had set against you so that it came against me instead. So I was wrong," he finished simply, and turned his attention back to Iaor. "So you have the day, yes? What will you do, Iaor Safiad?"

It might have been a humble question. The Arobern did not ask it humbly.

Iaor tapped the arm of his chair in a gentle rhythm. He said, even more mildly than before, "Naturally, I wish to restore relations between Feierabiand and Casmantium to their former amicability. I am certain you share this desire, Brechen Glansent Arobern. A reasonable indemnity will do. I presume your brother will pay it. Of course, it is one of your brothers you left holding your throne?"

"Yes. He will pay. For me. For them." The Arobern nodded over his shoulder toward his men.

"You are fortunate in your brothers."

"Yes," agreed the Arobern, very simply.

"And when next you conceive a plan to acquire a new province? I wonder whether your brother is perhaps less ambitious than you are, Brechen Glansent Arobern. I wonder if perhaps I would be wiser not to send you back to Casmantium, whatever price your brother offers me for you?"

The Arobern tilted his head back, assured and arrogant. "It would offend Casmantium if Feierabiand held her king beyond the time it takes to gather the indemnity. I do not think you should do that, Iaor Safiad."

"Don't you? Well, I will accept an indemnity for the damage you did to my lands and my people, and an indemnity for your men. But I think it only just to give your own person to the griffins, whom you wronged first and more grievously. And your remaining cold mages, of course."

This was a surprise. Bertaud blinked, wondering whether Iaor had come up with this idea on the instant. It was not, perhaps, a terrible idea. It would be impossible for Casmantium to argue that the griffins did not have a claim. And certainly no one would expect an offense against griffins to be paid off with gold; no, if they were to collect an indemnity, in what other coin would they take it but in blood? And Iaor might very reasonably be thinking of ways to keep the griffins well-disposed to Feierabiand. *That* would set Casmantium well back. *And* Linularinum. Both countries respected ruthlessness. They would no doubt be very impressed if Iaor could persuade the griffins to become Feierabiand's allies. Especially if he purchased this alliance with the blood of a rival king.

The Arobern, taken initially by surprise, quite obviously also concluded that this was a course of action Iaor might reasonably pursue. He glanced at the griffins, then back at Iaor. Iaor merely looked blandly courteous, an expression he did extremely well. The griffins were hard to read, but they certainly did not look courteous. Tastairiane Apailika opened his beak and clicked it shut again, producing a small deadly sound. Kairaithin tilted his head, a gesture that expressed, Bertaud thought, perhaps a kind of humor. Kes, tucked against Opailikiita's legs, looked very small, very young, and not at all human. She, Bertaud was disturbed to see, was smiling.

The Arobern said slowly, "You will do what you will, Safiad king." He looked faintly nonplussed, as though he had thought he had known how this interview would go and was taken aback to find his predictions overset. Bertaud might have told him that Iaor, when truly angry, was likely to become both quiet and creative. The King of Casmantium went on, slowly, choosing his words with care, "But I will ask you do it to me and not to my people, yes? My mages only did as I bade them, you understand?"

"The People of Fire and Air spent themselves recklessly this day. Shall I not acknowledge their cost?"

Kes stood up. All eyes went to her, though she did not appear to be trying to draw attention. A woman among the Minas Ford folk edged out toward her and then hesitated—her sister, Bertaud realized, though he could see no resemblance between them whatsoever.

Though she left one hand on Opailikiita's neck, Kes edged forward a step. She did not glance toward her sister, but said to the kings, in a small voice that was nevertheless surprisingly audible, "They don't want him. Or even Beguchren."

Iaor, clearly taken aback, lifted his eyebrows. His hands stilled on the arms of his chair as he tensed, waiting to hear what the girl would say so that he could try to fit it into his own plans. The Casmantian king tilted his head quizzically to the side. Even Bertaud was startled. But he felt Kes was right as soon as she had spoken.

"They don't want vengeance, you know," Kes said, glancing from one man to the other. "They don't . . . they don't think that way. They kill things, too, you know. They don't hold it against the King of Casmantium that he was fierce. Ferocity is something they understand. It's not vengeance they want."

Iaor gave her a questioning glance, not wanting to ask out loud what they did want and thus admit that he was as surprised as anyone else at what Kes had said.

Kes looked quickly at the griffins. Neither Kairaithin nor Tastairiane Apailika spoke, but only regarded her from fierce eagle's eyes. They were both sitting very still. They looked massive and powerful and thoroughly ferocious themselves, although neither of them moved. Kes turned her gaze back to the king, and then to the Arobern. "They want Melentser."

"They want what?" said the Arobern, in a startled tone.

Kes repeated, "They want Melentser."

Melentser was not merely a town. It was a small city near the edge of Casmantium's border with the desert.

"Melentser is ours." The Arobern now sounded rather blank. "My mother's mother was from there. It has been part of Casmantium for more than a hundred years."

"Well, before that, it was part of the desert," said Kes. She stroked her hand through the feathers on Opailikiita's shoulder, and the slim griffin bent her head around and brushed Kes's face with her beak. Kes smiled. She said, "The desert will take it again, King of Casmantium. That is what the People of Fire and Air want."

"I will not agree, *festechanenteir*. My brother will not agree. You set your indemnity too high."

"King of Casmantium," said Kes, "the desert here is new and it cost the lives of many griffins to make. But sending the great northern desert to take back Melentser will cost less, because no one will be fighting the desert when it comes. And no one will fight it. You will yield it. Or the Lord of Fire and Air will ask the King of Feierabiand to give all your people to the desert, those here and those in the mountains. And the King of Feierabiand will do it."

Kes paused, giving the Arobern a careful, assessing look. Then she added, deliberately, "Tastairiane Apailika wants to kill you all. He says he could do it by himself, if I am there to keep him whole. I would do that, if I had to. And then the desert will reach out to Melentser all the same, and your brother will find he is not wise to fight against sand and stone. Because I can defend the People of Fire and Air against anything he can do, and Feierabiand will be here at his flank, and Casmantium will be weak after losing all those men."

The Arobern regarded her with patent astonishment. He took a breath.

"Or you may simply yield Melentser as a proper indemnity," Iaor interrupted him easily, his tone perfectly matter-of-fact, just as though he had known all along what the girl was going to say. It sounded very smooth. "Casmantium can afford it."

The Arobern transferred his attention to Iaor.

"Melentser to the desert, a suitable indemnity to Feierabiand, and we may all go on with our lives," Iaor said to him. "With, of course, some form of reassurance that you will not think again of fashioning new Casmantian provinces out of my country. I believe you have a son, do you not, Brechen Glansent Arobern? Twelve years old, is he not?"

"You want my son as hostage?" The Arobern hesitated, now clearly off his balance. He ran a hand through his black hair, a frustrated gesture that made him look suddenly younger and much less arrogant. "No. I may yield Melentser. But not my son. What else would you take instead?"

"I am not negotiating." Iaor leaned forward in his chair. "I am telling you what I require. Melentser to the desert. An appropriate indemnity for the trouble to which you have put Feierabiand. And your son, as a guarantee of your future restraint. All this before I will return you to your kingdom, King of Casmantium."

The Arobern listened to him carefully. He nodded, not in agreement, Bertaud thought, but only to show he understood the terms demanded. Then he came forward a step and sank down to one knee in front of Iaor. His harsh features were not made for humility, but he was now clearly trying. "But I will ask you not to do this, Safiad. I acknowledge you have won everything. You have won, yes? Casmantium will yield everything. As you have said, yes? I know you have made alliance with the *malacteir*. I know your little *festechanenteir* gives the *malacteir* a strength I cannot challenge. Is that not enough assurance?"

"No," said Iaor. He sat back in his chair, hands relaxing. His chin tipped up in satisfaction. He had wanted the Arobern to humble himself, to ask for mercy. But now, having forced the other king to submit, he was willing to be kind. He said, "I will hold your son only eight years. Then he may return to Casmantium."

The Arobern did not rise. Evidently perceiving the satisfaction but not the inclination toward generosity, he said harshly, "You will not take vengeance on my son for your offense at me. I will not put him in the way of Safiad anger in a hostile court."

Iaor, startled, cast a brief involuntary glance at Bertaud, who lifted an eyebrow, trying to keep his face expressionless. Then the king said violently to the Arobern, "Do you think such things of me, Brechen Glansent Arobern? Your son will serve me as is appropriate for a young lord—he will be well-schooled at my court and treated as befits a prince. I assure you. Then he may return to you."

Some of the Arobern's tension eased. He nodded, and hesitated. "The years from twelve to twenty are long years. Yes? You will take a boy and teach him to be a man. At your court. If not to fear you, you will teach him to love you. Will you not? To love Feierabiand. That is what you mean."

"That is exactly what I mean," Iaor agreed.

"Yes." The Arobern bent his head, accepting this assurance because he had no choice. "The Safiad kings are clever. I knew this, but I thought I was more clever. Very well. I will take your word and do as you say."

"I was lucky," Iaor admitted. He paused, and Bertaud knew that the other king's submission had again inclined Iaor to generosity. He said slowly, "If Feierabiand was confident of Casmantium's intentions, there would be no intrinsic reason why mutually beneficial terms might not be worked out regarding the harbor at Terabiand and the eastern road. I find no compelling reason to reconsider the harbor dues. But we might discuss improvements to the road."

"Hah." The Arobern stared at Iaor. "Well." He got to his feet, managing a smile. "Mutually beneficial. Yes. If Casmantium is not beggared by the indemnity you set, Safiad king, we might well wish to make improvements to the mountain road. Our builders would be pleased by the challenge, I think. Maybe it might be widened. Maybe to twice its present width. It might even be paved, yes? And bridges put in, yes? Then the toll ended to compensate Casmantium for the expense. That would be fair, if Casmantium provides the builders."

"We will discuss these matters," said Iaor, and lifted his hand a little. General Adries gestured to the Arobern, and the Arobern bowed, rather more profoundly than he had initially, and suffered himself to be led away.

Iaor sighed, and leaned back in his chair. He glanced at the griffins, who did not now seem very interested. Kairaithin tilted his head, and was gone, with Tastairiane Apailika. Kes, not glancing around, appearing utterly unconcerned about anything creatures of earth might choose to do, put an arm around Opailikiita's neck and also vanished. She left behind only a breath of stone-scented wind and a scattering of sand. Her sister took a hesitant step toward the empty place where she had been, looking bereft.

Bertaud glanced away, reluctant to intrude on such personal grief. But then he found his eye caught by Iaor. "Well?" asked the king, making a private moment out of the general movement of men all around them scattering about evening duties and business.

Bertaud let his breath out. He shook his head. "What do you mean, well? Are you asking my opinion? I don't think . . . I don't think I would dare offer one."

"I will stop the toll on the eastern road," Iaor declared. "And Brechen Glansent Arobern will put an end to Casmantian tariffs on our goods. *And* he'll pay the harbor dues, and like it."

"I've no doubt you'll teach the Arobern not to bite," Bertaud agreed.

The king gave a satisfied little nod. "I doubt I can make a personal friend of the man, but perhaps I can do something with his son. Perhaps I'll reduce the dues in eight years, as a going-home gift for the boy."

"Well," Bertaud conceded, "I admit, that would be a good thing, if you could make an ally of Casmantium for a generation or two. And . . . I, of all men, don't underestimate your ability to make boys into your friends, Iaor."

Their eyes met, and after a moment the king said gently, "This has been hardest on you, perhaps. You seemed to me . . . You dealt well enough with the desert, this time, did you not, my friend?"

"Yes," Bertaud agreed without explanation. "I think my . . . susceptibility to the desert was a temporary problem. It seems to have passed off."

Satisfied, Iaor clapped him on the shoulder. "And so we have an agreeable end to the day, after all," he declared. "Earth and stone, I at least am glad for dusk and an end to this particular day, though I suppose we had luck riding our shoulders throughout it."

Bertaud met his king's eyes. "You made your own luck, Iaor."

"The griffins made it for me. Through your good governance, not mine, as I well know." The king shook his head in wonder. "You will have to tell me someday how you persuaded that terrifying mage of theirs to come in on our side. Well, and yet we have everything we could desire. With the possible exception of being rid of this desert on our doorstep. Though there are compensations, to be sure." He cast a wry glance over the displaced people of Minas Ford. "Some of the indemnity must go to these folk."

Then something about the quality of Bertaud's silence caught at the king's attention. "And you?"

"My king?"

"I am asking," Iaor said patiently, "whether you, too, are satisfied, my friend. Or whether there is perhaps something I have missed?"

Bertaud produced a smile that was, unexpectedly, almost genuine. "Iaor. What could I possibly desire, save what you desire?"

Iaor grinned suddenly and clapped Bertaud on the shoulder. "If something occurs to you, you must certainly let me know."

But what Bertaud wanted, he knew, was nothing Iaor could give him. This was a new thought, for he had always depended on Iaor to give him . . . everything. But now . . . the fire in his heart had burned high during the course of that last battle, as the griffins had unmade themselves to defeat the Casmantians. Now, when he longed for its heat, it was all but guttered out to ash. Yet he knew, with an odd, unaccustomed assurance, what he must do. Not to bring the fire back to life, but to . . . bank it properly.

The camp settled, Feierabiand soldiers and Casmantian prisoners housed alike, with few amenities and far too weary to care. Fires sparked in the twilight, friendly little fires that seemed to have nothing whatsoever in common with the red desert. Some impulse led Bertaud to look for Kes's sister, but the people of Minas Ford had all gone away somewhere—certainly not back to their lost village. Probably to some outlying farm they knew and strangers to this district did not. Likely they wanted the comfort of familiar walls and of one another's company, and no blame to them.

Bertaud did not want company, nor walls. He walked slowly up the road away from the river, toward the new desert, and then left the road and struck more directly up the sloping ground, welcoming the effort, the numbness of exhaustion that clung to him. The damp grasses yielded gently under his step, and he passed the small close-pruned trees of someone's orchard. Stripped of fruit now, he guessed, by soldiers only too glad to supplement their hard bread and dried meat with better. He would give long odds someone had found the energy for that.

Beneath his feet, the soft grasses suddenly gave way to sand. A heartbeat later the heat hit him, forceful even in the dusk, striking upward from the sand. Bertaud hesitated. Then he went on, walking more slowly still. He came to a low wall made of flat, rounded stones, tumbled and cracked now as though time and sun and the power of the desert had worked on them for many years rather than a single afternoon. He put a hand on top of the wall and clambered stiffly over. He felt as though he'd aged a score of years in this one night, and might have rested on the wall for a moment. But in the end, he couldn't settle: When he tried to sit still, he had too much time for thought. For the slow creeping terror to press through his weariness. So he went on quickly, looking for . . . he hardly knew what, or why one place would be better than another, for what he had in mind. Perhaps he was simply searching for a certain slant to the lengthening shadows. Or for an excuse to delay the closing moments of this interminable day.

In the end, he found himself walking down Minas Ford's one street, its cottages bulking to either side. Sand had covered the cobbles. The houses that had stood so bravely against the Casmantian army had been broken by the desert the griffins had made with their last effort: Here a wall had buckled as stone shifted beneath it, there a roof had fallen . . . Bertaud walked slowly through the village and at last discovered the gate to the inn's yard. He went through the gate. Tables still stood in the abandoned yard. Several had vases still poised on them, all their flowers dead and dried, at once absurd and desolate.

Bertaud sat down at a table. The light had nearly gone, now. The ageless stars shone overhead, hard and brilliant, with little of the trembling sparkle they would have had in a gentler sky. Bertaud looked up at them, somehow comforted by their timelessness. He found himself thinking of the stars above the lake at Tihannad and then, for some reason, of the wide sky of the Delta where he had spent those grim years of his early childhood. He had not thought of the Delta much at all in these latter years; he had quite deliberately refused to think of the Delta or his father's house. Even after his father's death, somehow even then he had not let his thoughts turn that way. Now he found he regretted that studied indifference. He wondered, for nearly the first time in his life, what he might have made of his inheritance if he had devoted himself to the Delta and not to Iaor's court, and it seemed both amazing and reason for grief that now he would never have the chance to find out.

It was perhaps a little late to entertain such thoughts. And he could hardly regret the place he had made for himself with the king—or Iaor had made for him—or they had made together. In the end, that place had survived . . . everything. *That* awareness, for all he had been compelled at last to walk out alone into the desert, was surely of infinite worth. Bertaud looked deliberately down from the sky, focused on the surface of the table between his hands. He called, "Kairaithin?"

Then he waited.

The griffin came. He was hardly visible in the night, and yet his wings seemed to reach across the sky. Starlight slid off his beak, his talons; his eyes, filled with fire, shone more brightly than the stars. The rush of air through the great feathers of his wings made a sound like sand across stone.

As he came down, he took on human form so smoothly that at no point was Bertaud certain where griffin became man. But it was as a man that he walked forward, and as a man that he faced Bertaud.

"Anasakuse Sipiike Kairaithin," Bertaud said softly.

The griffin considered him in silence for a moment. He said at last, "You did not call us to your battle. As you promised. Though you were defeated and faced death, or worse than death."

Bertaud did not ask him what a griffin would consider worse than death. He already knew that it was the defeat, and the shame attending that defeat. He understood how a griffin might flee before superior force, but would never yield. This seemed perfectly natural. The griffin heart informed his own, so that it had become difficult to distinguish one from the other.

"I have been surprised many times by the actions of men," Kairaithin said softly. "Not least this past day. Why, in your extremity, did you choose to loose my people from your hand?"

"If I had known that your people might have saved us, I might have called you," Bertaud admitted. "But I thought it would cause your destruction for, probably, nothing . . . I did not know you could bring the desert with you through all that cold rain, not with any sacrifice. So it seemed insupportable to demand your help."

Kairaithin lifted one narrow eyebrow. "And now?"

"Now . . . it seems still more insupportable to do anything whatsoever. I called you . . . to assure you that I will not call again. Not you nor any of your people."

"What?" said Kairaithin drily. "In no exigency?" He paused. "Do you know, man, what will happen to my kind if they discover that for you they are only animals? That they may be commanded as easily as dogs or horses?"

"Yes," Bertaud said.

"They would fight you to their deaths, if not to yours."

"I know."

"And if by some chance any of them survived it, and you not, they would spend every remaining spark of their lives doubting their own hearts and souls, which might be compelled to the will of another. Unlikely though it might be that another man with so unusual an affinity would have it woken by fire as yours was, they would fear that. So they would turn to hunting men, to their own eventual destruction."

"I know. You must make very certain Kes does not heal any other men. Just to be sure no one else with this peculiar affinity is brought to this . . ." He hesitated. It hardly seemed a gift. "Power."

"I shall. You may be quite confident. I shall tell her the truth, I think. That will constrain her more strictly than any limitation I might otherwise employ."

Bertaud nodded. "I called only you. I constrained only you. None other guessed?" he asked, to be sure.

"No, man. So you may be easy," the griffin said, with some irony. "Only I have been brought to heel by the strength of your command."

Bertaud tried not to flinch visibly. He said after a moment, "It's in the nature of a horse to yield to its rider. It's even in the nature of a wolf to respect the limits a man may put on its hunting. But I know . . . to submit to anyone's rule is utterly against the nature of your kind. Do *you* understand . . . how terrible a thing it is for a man to force against its nature a creature of his calling?"

"Is it?"

"It would break my heart," said Bertaud, very simply.

Kairaithin's proud face tightened. "So I should be glad to trust my freedom and the freedom of the People of Fire and Air to your gentle sensibilities, man? Is that what you expect of me?"

"No," said Bertaud. "I don't expect that at all. I know very well that you would spend the long years of your life doubting your own heart and soul." He met the griffin's fiery black eyes. "You should take your true form," he added after a moment. "I think you would be quicker so. You will need to be quick. Because if I . . . if I feel the blow coming, I don't think I will be able to let you deliver it."

Kairaithin stared at him.

Bertaud shut his eyes and waited.

A long moment passed. Far longer than should have been necessary. Bertaud opened his eyes.

Kairaithin sat before him in griffin form, like a great cat, lion tail wrapped neatly around taloned front feet. His neck was arched, his head tucked in toward his chest, his ferocious beak pointed at the ground. The feathers behind his head ruffled in the desert breeze. He looked massive and dangerous and heraldic and, somehow, indecisive.

"Do you think," Bertaud asked him, "that this is an offer I will make twice? Do you think I have endless nerve? Because I promise you, you are mistaken." His voice shook; he bit the last word off sharply.

No, said Kairaithin, softly. His voice slid delicately around the edges of Bertaud's mind. *I do not expect that at all.*

Bertaud stared into the griffin's eyes, then looked away. His hands, lying empty on the table, moved slowly across its gritty surface. He gathered up a small handful of red dust and let it run through his fingers. For a moment, he looked only at the faint glitter of dust in the starlight. He did not speak. He could not think of anything to say. The infinite sky arched over them both.

I will trust your sensibility, man, Kairaithin said. His tone was harsh and proud, as though it was defiance he expressed. *You will not call. You will not put your will upon me. Upon any of my kind.*

"No," said Bertaud.

I will spend the years studying ways to kill you, in the case you should prove false.

"I'm sure you will."

The griffin said, more gently, *I will not expect you to call. I will not wait for the moment. I will not live in dread of the sound of your voice speaking my name.*

Bertaud bowed his head. Then he looked up. "I won't speak it. I swear to you. I won't see you again."

No.

"That will break my heart. But in . . . in a better way." Bertaud opened his hands, a gesture of release.

Kairaithin was gone. The night seemed suddenly, bitterly, empty.

But Bertaud still lived to endure it. So even the bitterness, he thought, was something to cherish. And the promise of years to come during which the bitter loss might—would surely—transmute to a gentler memory. He took a slow, deep breath of the dry desert air, and left the ruined inn to the sand and the sleepless wind, to go back to life and to his king.

CHAPTER 16

Jos found her sitting on a twisted red rock where the highest pasture had once been. There had been a tree where the rock now stood; there had been a spring that had welled from the earth and spilled away toward the lower pastures. Neither tree nor spring remained.

Kes was sitting with her knees tucked up and her arms wrapped around them, looking into the desert sky. Its beauty pierced her like a spear; she wanted to mount the heights and fly through air so crystalline and pure that the light of the myriad stars might shatter it. She wanted to fly west until she overtook the sun, then pour herself into its molten light; she wanted to shred her body into fire and wind and dissolve into the desert. But she stayed where she was. She had not known why she waited, until Jos came to her.

He came forward and stood at the base of the rock. He was tall enough, and the rock short enough, that their faces were nearly at a level. His eyes shone with starlight. Kes knew that her own glimmered with fire.

"You always liked this place." Jos glanced around, sighed, and leaned against the twisted rock where Kes sat. "Now only the lie of the land is the same. You can't even tell where the spring used to be."

"I still like it."

"Do you? Is it the same in your eyes?"

"No. Not the same."

"No." He paused. "I have brought your sister to see you. I thought . . . it seemed like a good idea. She doesn't . . . You know, Kes, she hasn't seen you since, well. Not from the time you went into the desert, till the Safiad's little play this evening. You might . . . try to be kind."

Kes slipped off the rock, blurring through the little distance that separated its top from the sand. She noticed only afterward that Jos had put a hand up to help her down; he lowered it slowly.

Then Tesme came forward out of the dark, walking carefully over the unfamiliar ground, and Kes had attention only for her.

"Kes?" Tesme said. She did not run forward to embrace her sister. Her tone was tentative, almost doubtful. She was wearing a plain un-dyed dress, the sort of thing she might have worn to visit the horses and would not normally have put on to go away from the house; her hair was bound back with a simple twist of wooden beads. Her face was thinner than Kes remembered, with faint new lines at the corners of her eyes. There was a bandage around her left wrist, and she moved stiffly. She did not smile. "Kes?"

"Yes," Kes said. But she did not step forward.

"Kes?"

"Yes," said Kes patiently.

"You look . . . so different."

"Do I?" Kes thought about this. She thought she did feel different, within herself. But it was hard to think about what she had been like, before. When she reached after memories of herself, she could find nothing but fading echoes of a person who seemed only vaguely famil-iar. A shy but laughing child, a shyer and more silent girl . . . loves and sorrows and memories that seemed, now, to have little to do with her. The person she remembered had been a creature of earth, a person whose needs and desires and emotions she could not now readily un-derstand. When she reached after memories of Tesme . . . those memo-ries carried regret, even something like grief, though she did not really understand why they should. "I think I am different."

"Can you . . . can you . . . change back?"

"No."

Jos, watching them both, asked, "Do you want to change back to what you were before?"

Kes glanced at him, surprised. "No."

Tesme bowed her head a little.

"I'm sorry if you are hurt," Kes told her. "I do remember you. I haven't forgotten anything. It's just . . . it's different when I think about things now. I remember you. But it's like remembering a language I used to speak and have forgotten: What I remember doesn't feel . . . real. I'm sorry," she added, because an expression of regret seemed somehow appropriate.

Tesme's tears were real, and fell like drops of rain to the sand. She said in a low voice, "Jos told me. But I didn't understand what he said."

"I'm glad he brought you to see me," Kes said. "I see now I should have come to see you. I didn't think of it."

"I see you didn't," Tesme answered. Her head was still bowed, her shoulders rounded.

"You should probably go back to your own kind."

"Yes," Tesme whispered. She came forward suddenly and reached out, quickly at first but then more tentatively, to take Kes by the shoulders. She folded her into an embrace, fierce and longing and sorrowful all at once. After the first startled moment, Kes returned the embrace, bending her head against Tesme's shoulder as she had when she was a child needing comfort; it felt very strange.

"Are you happy?" Tesme asked. She eased back so that she could look into Kes's face.

This was not the sort of question a griffin would ask. Kes had to think about the answer. But she said at last, "Yes. I am happy. I don't think there was any other choice to make. But it was a right choice, all the same."

"I love you. But you'll never come home again."

"I will be glad to remember you. But the desert is my home now."

Tesme nodded, and let her go. She was trying to smile. "I know you're not alone. I hear you have a new sister."

"Opailikiita."

"I hear she's very beautiful. Does she love you?"

Kes could not even think about the question in those terms. But she said, "We are *iskarianere*—I think that is like love, for a griffin."

"You aren't a griffin, Kes."

"But I'm like a griffin now," Kes said, trying to make her tone kind, trying to remember exactly what kindness was, so that she might be kind to this human woman who had been her sister. She remembered that men valued kindness, that once she herself had needed people to be kind to her.

Tesme looked searchingly into her eyes. "Are you? Are you?"

"Yes."

Tesme's shoulders slumped again, and then squared as her head came up. "All right," she said. She might have meant to speak firmly— her attitude was firm—but the words came out in a thread of sound. "Be well, Kes. Wherever you go, into whatever strange country. Be happy."

"I will be," said Kes, and watched the woman who had been her sister walk away. Tesme looked back once. Then she turned her face forward and disappeared into the darkness.

"You did not ask how *she* was," Jos commented.

It had not occurred to Kes to do so. She looked at him wordlessly.

"She went to Nehoen's house. Everyone from Minas Ford did, except the badly injured. His house and most of his lands are still outside the desert, you know."

Kes did know this, when she thought of it. She knew where the boundary of the desert lay, and though everything beyond that boundary seemed dim and distant, her memory of the land told her where Nehoen's property lay.

"He has been courting her. Ever since you . . . left. I think he had her in his eye before that. He's been a great oak for her to lean on, this summer. I imagine that when everyone else leaves his house, she will stay."

"Oh," said Kes. She was glad, in a distant sort of way. She thought she had once liked Nehoen. He seemed old for Tesme. But then . . . perhaps Tesme was not so young as all that, really. "Good."

"You should be pleased." Jos regarded her with an expression she could not read. "The match will be good for both of them. Especially Tesme. She wore herself out with worry about you. Nehoen is the romantic sort. He'll be just what she needs now."

Kes had no feel for such matters, but she presumed he was right.

"They won't stay around here, you know," Jos added. "Tesme . . . well, Tesme hates the very sight of the desert. She was talking about Sihannas. That's good country for horses, and she and Nehoen will easily be able to afford the move, what with the king directing a good chunk of the indemnity to the folk of Minas Ford."

Sihannas. Sihannas, at the edge of the Delta. Kes had never even dreamed of going so far from home. And now she had gone so much farther, even standing in this high pasture so near the ruined village. She smiled slightly, feeling the desert wind tug at the edges of her soul.

"You don't mind that she will go so far?"

Kes blinked, recalled to the moment. "Everything in the country of earth is far, for me." Then she asked, the question slowly welling up in her mind, "But where will you go?"

Jos regarded her with an odd, intent expression. He said at last, "Not to Sihannas. The Safiad wants me either under his eye or out of his country, and who can blame him? Not to Casmantium: How could I face the Arobern? Not to Linularinum: I hate all the sly maneuvering that's lifeblood to everyone on that side of the river."

It had not occurred to Kes that Jos, of them all, faced the greatest dislocation. For her, there was the desert; for the folk of Minas Ford, all of Feierabiand; everyone else could hope to return eventually to their homes and their people. But she could not imagine where Jos would go.

"I thought," he said, his eyes on her face, "that I might go with you, Kes. That I might remind you, from time to time, what it means to be human."

Kes did not understand him. "There is no place in the desert for a creature of earth."

"There are places where earth borders fire, Kes. Where the mountains meet the desert, north of Casmantium . . . there are places there a man might live. Or—" and he took a deep breath—"for you it was different, I know. But maybe your friend Kairaithin might find a way to make an ordinary man into a creature of fire."

Kes stared at him, taken utterly by surprise. "Why would you want to do that?"

Jos took a step toward her, took a breath, started to speak, and stopped. Then he said, with careful restraint, "What is there for me in any of the countries of men? Hear me out, Kes. You may no longer be human, but among the griffins you will still be alone; you are not one of them, either. Think of that. You may learn to take the shape of a griffin, but you won't ever really be one, any more than Kairaithin is a man when he takes the form of a man. Will you endure a lifetime of loneliness? Of being one alone among many?" His voice had quickened as he continued, until his words tumbled over one another at the last and choked him silent; he was still, then, his eyes on her face.

Kes said slowly, "I would have been an earth mage. Kairaithin redirected what I should have been and made me a creature of fire. You are not a mage of any kind."

"He'll find a way. Or you will. If you want to."

Kes took a step forward and lifted her hand to touch his face. She found she was smiling. She did not know what a creature of earth would feel at such a moment. But what *she* felt was a kind of fierce possessive pleasure, something like the *iskairianaika* she shared with Opailikiita, but not the same. She was pleased Jos had made this unanticipated offer. Loneliness was not something she feared; she feared very little, now. But even so . . . "Yes," she said. "I would like your company in the country of fire. I think I would like that. Yes, I would. Yes." And she folded both of them into a sweep of shifting time and silence and took Jos away with her into the heart of the desert.

LAND OF THE
BURNING SANDS

*This one is for my mother, from whom I absorbed
a "feel" for grammar—so much easier than actually
having to learn the rules!*

CHAPTER 1

Gereint Enseichen sat on a narrow pallet in the lowest cellar of the Anteirden townhouse, waiting. He leaned against the rough stones of the wall, stretched his legs out before him, and listened to fierce sand-filled winds over his head pare the cobbles of the street down to bare earth. He could hear the savage wind, the scouring sand, faint crashes that marked the explosions of distant windows, the cracking of wooden beams, the collapse of stone walls: the destruction of the city under the ruthless wind and heat. Sometimes the very earth that surrounded him seemed to tremble in sympathy with the storm above.

Of course, the house's cellar was deep. Maybe Gereint only imagined he heard those sounds. Maybe he only imagined the occasional faint shaking of the earth. But if he went up the first flight of stairs to the upper cellar and then up the second flight to the door to the kitchens . . . If he did that, he would surely find the storm. Surely it had by now raked down from the north and fallen across Melentser. If it filled the world outside, it would be dangerous to go up those stairs.

Or if he imagined the faint sounds of destruction, if the storm hadn't yet arrived . . . it might be, for Gereint, more dangerous still.

Only if the storm had already come and destroyed Melentser and blown itself out would it be safe for him to leave the safety of the deep cellar. Gereint tilted his head, listening. Maybe the faint screaming of the wind, the raking hiss of blown sand, was his imagination. Maybe those sounds were not his imagination at all. Either way, he had no intention of going up those stairs. Not until he was *certain* the Fellesteden household was well away—and until he had given the storm ample time to arrive, rake across the city, and die.

According to Andreikan Warichteier's *Principia*, distance alone would break a *geas*. On the other hand, Pechorichen held, along with most other authorities, that only death could do that. How Warichteier had tested his idea was not clear, as no one *geas* bound could walk away from the man who "held the other end of the chain" unless he was given leave to go. But Gereint had not walked away from Perech Fellesteden. He had simply allowed Fellesteden to walk away from him.

If the *geas* actually broke, that would be best. If it merely became quiescent, that would do. Just so long as Gereint was not driven to follow the road south after his master, he should do very well. At the moment, he felt merely uneasy. He knew Fellesteden must be furious with him. But, sealed away beneath stone and earth, he was unable to hear his master's call, blind to the man's undoubted fury. The *geas* could not compel him to follow a man who was not *there*.

Or so Gereint fervently hoped.

The desert's coming had driven everyone in Melentser into chaotic retreat southward, on roads never meant to accommodate such a massive number of refugees. Or . . . probably not quite everyone. Gereint wondered how many others might be tucked away in cellars and wellhouses, waiting for the desert to drive the upstanding citizens of Melentser out of the city. The desperate, the stupid, the mad, those unfortunates both crippled and destitute: Probably few of her last inhabitants would survive Melentser's fall by more than a day or so.

Gereint counted himself among the desperate rather than the stupid or the mad, and hoped he would find no reason to change his mind. He had made good use of the scant days of preparation. No one had been able to keep careful count of supplies in those last days: Pilfering had been easy and nearly safe. Here in the cellar, he had a bottle of the Fellesteden's best wine, two rare books from the Fellesteden library, a change of clothing, decent boots a little loose in the ankle, a few coins, nine fat candles, two lanterns and four jars of oil, a twelve-hour sand timer, a bag of apples, some fresh bread and soft cheese, plenty of the hard cracker and dried beef that travelers carried, and six skins of clean water. He had not had time to make the waterskins himself, but these were the best he had been able to find. They should keep the water clean and cool; they wouldn't leak or spoil. They were for later. For the present, he had a small barrel, which had once held ale and that he had refilled with water before lugging it, with some difficulty, down to this cellar.

Aside from his own stolen supplies, there was nothing in this low cellar but empty racks where wine had been stored. It was a pity that all the racks were empty. The Anteirdens had been renowned for the quality of their wines. But they had left nothing behind when they closed their house, which they had done quickly: Berent Anteirden, head of the Anteirden household, was a decisive man and not inclined to risk his family by dithering. Unlike Perech Fellesteden, who had indeed dithered and let his own household's flight become . . . usefully chaotic.

Was he hearing the sound of sand scraping against stone overhead? Or was the sound merely in his mind? Gereint squinted up at the close-fitted stones of the ceiling and decided the sound was real. Probably.

To drive back the dark and his too ready imagination, he lit the second lantern as well as the first. This was profligate, but he had plenty of oil. He had made the lanterns himself and stolen only quality oil for them; the light was luxuriously clean and clear. There was nothing to do but wait for the dry storm to blow itself out. He did not intend to go up those stairs until enough time had passed to reasonably suspect it had. He picked up one of the books, Gestechan Wanastich's history of Meridanium, and let it fall open at random. Illuminations picked out in gold and powdered pearl glittered around the measured stanzas that marched down the page: *On this night, my friends, on this night of fire and iron / On this dark night of fire and rage / When we leave our wives weeping behind us / To play the game of death among the broken stones where the deadly wind cries . . .*

Gereint closed the book and set it aside. All his masters had been men of learning, or at least had wished to pass themselves off as such. Inclined toward old beautiful books even as a child, Gereint had learned early that a slave's best comfort and surest escape was to be found in black ink and painted illuminations, in philosophy and history and poetry. But perhaps not Wanastich's poetry, just at this moment when all his hope was bent on a more literal and far more dangerous kind of escape.

The other book was also a history, Berusent's great *Casmant Historica*. At least it contained no grim poetry, Berusent not being of a particularly dour temperament. Gereint picked it up, opened it to an account of the founding of Breidechboden, and read a few lines. But he found he could not concentrate. He put this book, too, aside, folded his arms across his chest, and stared at the ceiling.

How long *would* it take the storm of wind and sand to consume a city? A day, a night, and another day? That was how long Anteirch's account gave for the destruction of Sarachren. But then, Anteirch had fancied himself a poet. "A day, a night, and another day" was a poetical convention if Gereint had ever heard one. How long had it really taken? One day, three days, ten? Sarachren's destruction had happened too long ago, been recounted by too many unreliable historians. No one

knew how long it would take for Melentser to disappear into the red
desert. But if the storm took longer than three or four days to settle,
Gereint would surely wish he'd stolen more food.

The sand timer ran down three times—counting off, as it happened, a day, a night, and another day—before Gereint lost patience
and allowed himself to go up the first flight of stairs and open the
heavy, close-fitted door that led to the upper cellar. He paused, then,
listening. There was no sound at all. The air was different: not cool and
moist. It was light and dry, with an unfamiliar scent to it. Like . . . hot
iron, hot stone. Maybe. Or maybe that was his imagination again. But a
haze of dust glittered and moved in the light of his lantern. That was
not imagination.

He went up the second flight of stairs. Red dust had sifted under
the kitchen door and down the steps. It gritted underfoot; it puffed into
the air when he scuffed it with his foot. When he gripped the stair railing, his hand left pale prints in the dust. He touched the door. But then
he merely stood there for a long, long moment. He told himself there
was nothing to fear. He heard nothing, even when he pressed his ear to
the door. The storm . . . probably the storm had subsided. And if that
was so, then there was nothing to fear. No one would be in the kitchens.
No one would be in the house. No one would be in the city—certainly
no one important. Probably nothing would move in the broad streets of
Melentser but wind and sand and one desperate man willing to risk losing his life in the desert if he could only lose the *geas* as well . . . Lifting
his hand, Gereint rubbed his thumb across the brand on his face. The
smooth scar of the brand still felt strange to his touch, though it had
been there nearly half his life.

The door's brass knob was warm to the touch. Gereint turned it and
pushed. The door did not budge. It was not locked: Gereint could feel
the latch move. He shoved harder. To no avail.

He knew at once that sand had drifted across the door. Perhaps a
lot of sand. Perhaps the kitchen was filled with it; perhaps the house
was buried in it . . . Terror smelled like hot metal and hot stone: Fear
lived in a handful of red dust. Gereint shoved frantically.

The door gave. Not much. But enough to suggest it could be forced
open. Enough to let him push back panic, breathe deeply, stop fighting,
and think.

The pressure was against the lower part of the door. He set his back
against the stone wall of the stair landing and his feet against the door
right at the base and pushed steadily.

The door opened a crack, heavily. Heat and light poured through
the crack, and sand, and plenty of red dust. If there had been more than

a few inches of sand on the other side of the door, Gereint would not have been able to open it. He couldn't quite block out this realization, though he tried. It was a well-made, sturdy door: Strong as he was, he probably would not have been able to break it. Clever fool: clever enough to hide in a nice, cool, secret death-trap . . . Anger as well as fear loaned him the strength to shove harder on the door, against the sand that had piled up against it.

The crack widened. Light and heat, dust and sand, and through it all that strange dry smell to the air, as though heat itself had a scent. Red sand and silence . . . He found the kitchen empty and silent when he finally had a gap wide enough to force himself through. The shutters on the windows were not merely broken, but missing. Splinters clung to the twisted brass hinges. The door that had led to the kitchen garden was missing as well. And the garden, itself: gone. Buried under sand, which had drifted much more deeply outside than in. Dust eddied in the corner where a white-barked birch had stood. No trace of the tree remained. Gereint could see the Fellesteden townhouse, but . . . ruined, nearly unrecognizable—half the roof and part of the wall broken, the brick deeply etched by blowing sand. The house looked a hundred years old. Two hundred.

Everything outside the house was drowned in heavy light and red sand.

By the angle of the sun, it was late afternoon. Gereint scooped sand away from the kitchen door and retreated back down into the cellars. It seemed to him that even the deeper cellar was drier and warmer now; that the smell of hot stone was perceptible even here. He shut the heavy cellar door, looked down at the red dust that had settled on the floor, and wondered how far the desert now extended.

His supplies . . . He had never thought himself generously supplied. But he had thought his supplies at least adequate. Now he thought of the powerful heat and red sand and tried not to doubt it.

That evening, as the powerful sun sank low in the west, Gereint sat in the shade of a broken wall, waiting for sundown and looking out across the ruins of Melentser. The sun was blood red and huge; its crimson light poured across broken stone and brick, across streets drifted with sand. Dust hazed the air, which smelled of hot stone and hot brass. Scattered narrow fingers of jagged red stone had grown somehow out of this new desert: a new inhuman architecture of twisted knife-edged towers. These strange cliffs were like nothing Gereint had ever seen. They pierced the streets, shattered townhouses, reached sharp fingers toward the sky. If one had torn its way out of the earth beneath the Anteirden house . . . But, though he flinched from the images that presented themselves to his mind, none had. Now the red towers cast long shadows across the shattered city.

Nothing moved among those towers but the creeping shadows and the drifting sand. And the griffins. A dozen or so were in sight at any given moment, though rarely close. But three of them passed overhead as the sky darkened, so near that Gereint imagined he could hear the harsh rush of the wind through the feathers of their wings. He stared upward, trying to stay very small and still against the dubious shelter of his wall. If the griffins saw him, they did not care: They flew straight as spears across the sky and vanished.

The griffins were larger than he had expected, and . . . different in other ways from the creatures he'd imagined, but he could not quite count off those differences in his mind. They looked to him like creatures made by some great metalsmith: feathers of bronze and copper, pelts of gold . . . Gereint had heard they bled garnets and rubies. He doubted this. How would anyone find that out? Stick one with a spear and wait around to watch it bleed? That did not seem like something one would be able to write an account of afterward.

Spreading shadows hid the red cliffs, the streets, the kitchen yard where once the garden had grown. Overhead, stars came out. The stars looked oddly hard and distant, but the constellations, thankfully, had not changed. And he thought there was enough light from the stars and the sliver of the moon to see his way, if he was careful.

Gereint stood up. His imagination populated the darkness around him with predatory griffins waiting to pounce like cats after a careless rabbit. But when he stepped cautiously away from the wall, he found nothing but sand and darkness.

He had already drunk as much water as he could from the barrel. Now he picked up his travel sack, slung its strap across his shoulder, and walked out into the empty streets. He carried very little: the candles and a flint to light them, the travel food, one change of clothing and a handful of coins, and the six skins of water. More than he had truly owned for years.

The hot-brass smell of the desert seemed stronger now that he was moving. Heat pressed down from the unseen sky and hammered upward from the barely seen sand under his boots. He had read that the desert was cold at night. Though the furnace heat of the day had eased, this night was far from cold. The heat seemed to weigh down the air in his lungs and drag at his feet. The sand, drifted deep across the streets, was hard to walk through. Both the heat and the sand bothered him far more than he had expected.

He did not head south nor straight east toward the river. Those were the ways the people of Melentser had gone, and above all he did not want to walk up on the heels of any refugees from the city. He walked north and east instead, toward the unpeopled mountains. His greatest fear seemed unfounded: The *geas* did not stop him choosing his own direction. He could tell that it was still alive, but it was not active. He felt no pull from it at all.

Casmantium did not claim the country to the north, the mountains beyond the desert—no one claimed that land. Rugged and barren, snow capped and dragon haunted, men did not find enough of value in the great mountains to draw them into the far north. But a single determined man might make his way quietly through those mountains, meeting no men and disturbing no sleeping monsters, all two hundred miles or more to the border Casmantium shared with Feierabiand. The cold magecraft that shaped *geas* bonds was not a discipline of gentle Feierabiand: When a *geas*-bound man crossed into that other country, the *geas* should . . . not merely break. It should vanish. It should be as though it had never been set.

Or so Warichteier said, and Fenescheiren's *Analects* agreed. Gereint was very interested in testing that claim.

Maps suggested that the foothills of the mountains should be little more than forty miles from Melentser. On a good road in fair weather, a strong man should be able to walk that far in one night. Two at the outside. Across trackless sand, through pounding heat . . . three, perhaps? Four? Surely not more than four. How far did the desert now extend around Melentser? All the way to those foothills? He had planned for each skin of water to last for one whole night and day. Now, surrounded by the lingering heat, he suspected that they might not last so long.

While in the ruins of the city, he found it impossible to walk a straight line for any distance: Not only did the streets twist about, but sometimes they were blocked by fallen rubble or by stark red cliffs. Then Gereint had to pick his way through the fallen brick and timbers, or else find a way around, or sometimes actually double back and find a different route through the ruins of the city. He could not go quickly even when the road was clear; there was not enough light. Yet he did not dare light a candle for fear of the attention its glow might draw.

So it took a long time to get out of Melentser; a long time to clamber over and around one last pile of rubble and find himself outside the city walls. A distance that should have taken no more than two hours had required three times that, and how long *were* the nights at this time of year? Not long, not yet. They were nowhere close to the lengthening nights of autumn. How quickly would the heat mount when the sun rose? Gereint studied the constellations once more, took a deep breath of the dry air, drank a mouthful of water, and walked into the desert.

The stars moved across the sky; the thin moon drew a high arc among them. The arrowhead in the constellation of the Bow showed Gereint true east. He set his course well north of east and walked fast. The night had never grown cool. There was a breeze, but it was hot and blew grit against his face. Sometimes he walked with his eyes closed. It was so dark that this made little difference.

Already tired, he found that the heat rising from the sand seemed to lay a glaze across his mind, so that he walked much of the time in a half-blind trance. Twisted pillars and tilted walls of stone sometimes barred his way. Twice, he almost walked straight into such a wall. Each time he was warned at the last moment by the heat radiating into the dark from the stone. Each time he fought himself alert, turned well out of his way to clear the barrier, and then looked for the Bow again. Usually the ground was level, but once, after Gereint had been walking for a long time, he stumbled over rough ground and fell to his knees; the shock woke him from a blank stupor and, blinking at the sky, he realized he had let himself turn west of north, straight into the deep desert. He had no idea how long he had been walking the wrong way.

Then he realized that he could see a tracery of rose gray in the east. And then he realized that he was carrying a waterskin in his hand, and that it was empty. It had not even lasted one entire night.

The sun rose quickly, surely peeking over the horizon more quickly than it would have in a more reasonable land. Its first strong rays ran across the desert sands and fell across Gereint, and as they did, he felt the *geas* bond to Perech Fellesteden fail. It snapped all at once, like the links of a chain finally parting under relentless strain. Gereint staggered. Stood still for a moment, incredulous joy running through him like fire.

Then the sun came fully above the horizon, and Gereint immediately discovered that he'd been wrong to believe the desert hot at night. Out here in the open, the power of the sun was overwhelming. Unimaginable. No wonder the sunlight had broken the *geas*; Gereint could well believe the sun's power might melt any ordinary human magic. Once well up in the sky, the sun seemed smaller and yet far more fierce than any sun he'd ever known; the sky was a strange metallic shade: not blue, not exactly white. The very light that blazed down around him was implacably hostile to men and all their works. Indeed, hostility was layered all through this desert. It was not an ordinary desert, but a country of fire and stone where nothing of the gentler earth was meant to live. The great poet Anweierchen had written, "The desert is a garden that blooms with time and silence." Gereint would not have called it a garden of any kind. It was a place of death, and it wanted him to die.

He had hoped he might be able to walk for some of the morning. But, faced with the hammer-fierce sun, he did not even try. He went instead to the nearest red cliff and flung himself down in its shade.

The day was unendurable. Gereint endured it only because he had no other option. As the sun moved through its slow arc, he moved with it, shifting around the great twisting pillar of stone to stay in its shade. But even in the shade, heat radiated from the sand underfoot and blazed from the stone. He could not lie down, for the heat from the ground drove him up; he sat instead and bowed his head against his knees. The sleep he managed was more like short periods of unconsciousness; the twin torments of heat and thirst woke him again and again.

He stayed as far from the stone as he could get and yet remain in its shade, but the short shadows of midday drove him within an arm's length of the cliff and then he thought he might simply bake like bread in an oven. The occasional breeze of the night was gone; the air hung heavy and still, very much as it must within an oven. If there were griffins, Gereint did not see them. He saw something else, once, or thought he did: a trio of long-necked animals, like deer, with pelts of gold and long black scimitar horns that flickered with fire. They ran lightly across the sand near him, flames blooming from the ground where their hooves struck the sand. As they came upon Gereint, the deer paused and turned their heads, gazing at him from huge molten eyes, as though utterly amazed to find a human man in their fiery desert. As well they might be, he supposed.

Then the deer startled, enormous ears tilting in response to some sound Gereint could not hear, and flung themselves away in long urgent leaps. They left behind only little tongues of fire dancing in their hoof prints.

But perhaps he only hallucinated the flames. Or the deer. The heat was surely sufficiently intense to create hallucinations. Though he would rather have seen a vision of a quiet lake where graceful willows trailed their leaves . . .

He could not eat. The thought of food nauseated him. But Gereint longed for water. His lips had already cracked and swollen. Berentser Gereimarn, poet and natural philosopher, had written that, in a desert, the best place to carry water was in the body; that if a man tried to ration his water, he would weaken himself while the water simply evaporated right from the waterskin and was lost entirely. Gereint wanted very badly to believe this. That would give him every reason to drink all the water in his second waterskin. But Gereimarn had been a better poet than philosopher: His assertions were often unreliable. And the thought of emptying yet another skin of water in his first day, of being trapped in the desert with no water left, was terrifying. Gereint measured the slow movement of the sun and allowed himself three mouthfuls every hour.

Even at midsummer, even in the desert, the sun did have to retreat eventually. Shadows lengthened. The hammering heat eased—not enough, never enough. But it eased. Gereint got to his feet before the sun was quite down and walked away from the stone that had, all day, both sheltered and threatened to kill him. He walked quickly, because now that the heat was not so desperately unendurable, what he really wanted to do was collapse into an exhausted sleep. But if he did that, if he did not use every possible hour for walking, he knew he would never reach the end of the desert.

How long had he estimated for a man to walk forty miles? Fifty, if he could not keep a straight course? He worked out the sums again laboriously in his head. He felt he was trying to think with a mind as thick and slow as molasses, but it helped him stay awake enough to keep his direction clear. He worked the sums a second time, doubting his conclusion, and then a third. How quickly was he walking? Not fast, not once his first burst of speed had been exhausted. Not four miles an hour. As fast as two? That would make it sixteen miles in eight hours. Sixteen? Yes, of course, sixteen. Or if he managed *three* miles in an hour, wouldn't that be . . . twenty-four miles? That would surely take him clear of the desert by dawn. Wait, *were* the nights eight hours long at this time of year? He should know the answer to that . . . Anyone would know that . . . He could not remember. If he could get to the mountains by morning . . . He had to. How fast was he walking?

Gereint stopped, sat down, and finished all the water in the second skin and half the water in the third. He made himself eat some of the cracker and dried beef. He had lived through one day in the desert; he doubted he would survive another. So he needed to walk fast and not let himself fall into a heat-induced trance, and to walk fast he needed strength.

He did feel stronger when he got back to his feet. He found the arrow's head in the Bow and set his direction. Then he counted his steps. He allowed himself a mouthful of water every two hundred steps. He counted in a rhythm to keep himself from slowing down. When he stumbled and caught himself and realized he'd once again been walking in a daze, he began to count by threes. Then by sevens. Then backward from five thousand, by elevens. He told himself that if he lost count, he'd have to start over and forfeit his mouthful of water. That self-imposed threat helped him keep alert.

He finished the third skin of water and began on the fourth. He tried to suck on a pebble, but the pebbles of this desert neither felt nor tasted right in his mouth; they tasted of heat and hot copper and fire. He spat one out quickly, drank an extra mouthful of water, and tried to fix his thoughts on the northern mountains. There would be streams running down from the heights; it might be raining. He could hardly imagine rain.

It crossed his mind that it might be raining in the south. Perech Fellesteden had intended to take his family all the way south to the luxurious southern city of Abreichan: He had property there. Well, Fellesteden had property everywhere, but his holdings in Abreichan were among the largest.

If Gereint had gone with his master, he would be in the south. Maybe walking through the rain. But . . . he would still be with Perech Fellesteden.

Lifting a hand, Gereint traced the brand on his face with the ball of his thumb. Traced it again. Lowered his hand and lengthened his stride.

It occurred to him some time later that the ground was tending somewhat upward.

Then the sun sent its first deceptively gentle rose glow above the eastern horizon.

Gereint stopped and waited, straining his eyes for the first glimpse ahead of the mountains. He felt he was poised at the tip of a moment; that though the sun was rising, time was not actually passing; that the whole desert waited with him for the answer to the question of time and distance.

Then the sun rose, blazing. Heat slammed down across the desert like a smith's hammer on a glowing anvil. Ahead of him, dim in the distance, Gereint saw the first high foothills that led up to the great mountains. As far as he could see, the hills were red with fiery sand. Heat shimmered across them.

Gereint stared at the hills for a long moment. Then he laughed—it was not much of a laugh, but he *meant* to laugh. He drank the rest of the water in the fourth skin in one draught. Then he threw the skin aside and strode forward, straight into the teeth of the sun.

That burst of defiance lasted only very few minutes. Then, from striding, Gereint found himself suddenly on his hands and knees, with no memory of falling. For a moment he thought he might simply lie down and let the heat finish killing him. But the desert was too profoundly inimical; he could not bring himself simply to give way to it. He crawled instead into the shadow of a narrow bladelike spire that pierced the hot air and collapsed in its meager protection. Red heat beat up through him from the sand and closed down around him from the air, but he did not know it.

He woke in cool mist, surrounded by green light that filtered through branches dripping with water. A blanket guarded him from falling drops. A fire crackled an arm's length away, its tiny warmth a comfort rather than a threat. He was not thirsty. In fact, he felt a languid sense of well-being that at first was too foreign to recognize. Fragrant steam rose from a pot on the fire . . . Soup, he recognized eventually. The recognition drifted through the languor without urgency.

"Are you hungry?" a voice asked.

Gereint thought about this question. He did not quite know the answer, nor did it seem important. The voice was unfamiliar. A faint uneasiness made its way through the clinging vagueness.

"Can you sit up?" the voice asked him. "Come, now. Try."

Gereint did try, the uneasiness biting more sharply. He found himself weak, but less so than he had expected. A hand on his shoulder supported his effort . . . He turned his head, trying to focus his gaze on the owner of that hand. His vision faded oddly in and out.

"That will pass," the voice reassured him. "You need food; that'll get you back in proper order. Can you hold this mug? Try. Drink."

Gereint closed his eyes and sipped. It was a rich broth, thick with bits of meat, not beef . . . not mutton . . . venison, maybe. He drank the broth and found his attention sharpening, the languor receding. Strength seemed to pour outward from his belly through all his limbs. A recollection of the desert came back to him, the long walk and the final glimpse of the red desert going right up into the distant hills. The memory was vivid and yet seemed somehow long ago. It held little horror, and no terror.

Then he remembered the reason he had walked into the desert, and terror went through him like the crack of a whip. He put the mug down sharply—the handle broke off in his hand, he was dimly aware—and looked for his . . . benefactor.

The man wore the sort of good, tough, well-made clothing that any ordinarily prosperous man might wear for traveling, though the ring on his left hand looked more than ordinarily valuable. He was plump, round faced, older than Gereint . . . maybe in his fifties. Not tall. Not intimidating. He even looked kind, for what little that impression might be worth. But he was not meeting Gereint's eyes.

Then he did. And that was worse. There was a knowledge in that gaze that Gereint had desperately hoped he would never see again.

Gereint tossed the blanket back, got to his feet, and stared down at his own bare feet. His boots were gone. Fellesteden's little silver chains were no longer woven through the steel rings that pierced his ankles between bone and tendon. Instead, each ring was woven through by a neat little cord.

This was not exactly a surprise. Gereint had not needed to see those cords to feel the renewed bite of the *geas*. He lifted his gaze again, slowly.

The other man looked nervous, as a man might who was alone in the mountains with another, stronger man of dubious character and temper. But he also looked self-assured. He didn't seem wealthy enough to have owned *geas*-bound . . . servants. Even so, Gereint was sure the man knew exactly what he'd done with those cords.

Gereint made his voice soft. An easy, quiet voice. Not defiant, not angry, not frightened. Just . . . soft. Coaxing. "Let me go. You're kind . . . I can see that. There's no risk to you in letting me go. You don't even need to cut those cords. You can just tell me to walk away, not to come back. And I will. I promise you, that's all I want: a chance to walk away into the mountains . . ."

"Be quiet," said the man.

So he wasn't intimately familiar with the limits of the *geas* after all. That was, on the whole, rather more reassuring than not. Gereint did not point out his mistake, but obediently shut his mouth and waited.

"Kneel," ordered the man.

Gereint dropped immediately to his knees, not waiting for the bite of the *geas* to enforce the command. He bowed his head, though his new master hadn't commanded that. They had to try their power; it meant nothing. There was no reason to take it personally. It was what they did later that mattered, after they discovered they could do anything.

"All right," said the man. "Get up."

He sounded uneasy, which might be good . . . or otherwise. Some of the worst masters were the ones who felt guilty about the power they held over you. A man like this, prosperous but not noble, might well be one of that sort. Gereint got to his feet. Glancing covertly at his master, he said gently, "You don't need to do this, honored sir. It's not required. You can simply command me to walk away."

The man looked uncomfortable, but he shook his head. "I need you, you see. My—my companion died, in the desert. And then my poor burro . . . You were really much too heavy for her." He glanced regretfully at the pot simmering over the fire, a glance that suggested the final fate of the burro. "Everything was so much more difficult than I expected . . ."

Gereint could believe that, at least. He said softly, even knowing the effort was hopeless, "I'll help you with anything you need, sir. You saved my life, didn't you? You don't need the *geas*, I promise you. Or I'll help you now, and then, later, all you need to do is tell me to walk away . . ."

The man shook his head. "What did you do?" he asked abruptly.

"Nothing. I was not guilty," Gereint declared without hesitation. "I had powerful enemies, the judge made a mistake, I was condemned unjustly. Will you compound the injustice?"

Surprise gave way to disbelief and then to a kind of wry humor. "Yes, I recall Andreikan Warichteier says in his *Principia Magicoria* that the *geas* gives no control over the tongue, the eyes, or the thoughts. What did you really do?"

A first glance had definitely not suggested such perceptiveness. Nor had Gereint expected any random traveler to have read Warichteier's difficult and often abstruse *Principia*. He should have remembered that the man had known he could use a plain cord. Most people thought you needed the little silver chains mandated by custom. This man was more acute than he looked. Gereint let his face show something of his surprise and dismay and exclaimed without hesitation, "Nothing, honored sir! That *is* the truth."

The man tilted his head to one side, regarding Gereint with something that might almost have been sympathy. "I need your help," he declared. "And I won't release a dangerous criminal." He glanced around at the damp woods that surrounded them. "Even here, though I admit it seems unlikely you could do any harm here. You were in Melentser, I suppose? Where did you mean to go? Feierabiand? It's a long way. Even so . . ." His brows arched interrogatively.

There was no reason to deny it. Gereint shrugged. "Feierabiand, yes. But the desert was much worse than I'd expected. But why were you . . . ?" He cut the question off short, bowing his head.

But the man did not seem to notice the impudence. "Collecting some things from a private residence. I see you brought a few books out with you, too." He gestured at Gereint's small pack, lying beside his own. Then he shook his head, apparently in wonder at Gereint's folly. Or maybe at his own. Said, with obvious pain and grief, "A few hours in, it was supposed to be; a few hours out. How difficult could that be?"

Gereint would have offered fervent agreement, only it wasn't his place.

The man sighed and glanced around at the woods, green and dripping even though the mist had cleared. Then he looked sharply at Gereint. "What's your name? How do you feel? You should be quite recovered. Are you?"

"Gereint," Gereint said. "Yes . . . master. I think so."

A second sharp look, this one distinctly uncomfortable. "I'm Eben Amnachudran. Call me by my name, please." He glanced around once more. "There's plenty of time left in the day. Put your boots on. Have another mug of soup. There's some cracker in a pouch by the fire. Have some of that if you like." He walked away, began putting things away in a good-quality traveler's pack.

Gereint put his boots on, binding the steel rings flat against his ankles with strips of cloth so they wouldn't chafe. He had another mug of soup and some of the hard cracker. He felt . . . well. Amazingly well. Too well. He wanted to ask the man . . . his master . . . he wanted to ask if he had done something, what he had done. But those questions might be dangerous, and anyway the answers were tolerably obvious. So his new master was a mage of some sort, and with at least a little skill in healing. Likely he would not care to have Gereint asking about such things. Better to test his new master's temper with simpler questions.

Along with the ordinary pack, there were saddlebags. Four of them. Heavy, as though they'd been loaded with bricks. Gereint tried to picture the plump, soft-handed Amnachudran carrying even two of them for any distance, and failed. No wonder he'd brought a burro. And a companion. A friend, from the grief in his voice when he spoke of the man. Killed by the desert. That was certainly believable. The desert was visible from the woods: a straight line that cut across the hills. Behind that line was brilliant furnace heat blazing down on red sand and stone. On this side, trees dripping with moisture and a rain-fed stream racing its way down the mountainside across gray rocks. The stream ran straight into the desert and vanished; even the old streambed was barely discernable on the other side of the line. A long dimple in the sand, and then nothing.

"I think I can manage the pack and one of the saddlebags," Amnachudran said, coming briskly over to Gereint. "Do you think you can carry the other three?"

Gereint gave him a sidelong glance. "What if I said no?"

"I would tell you to try."

"I could probably carry all four."

"Try three for now." The plump man hefted the fourth, grunting, along with the two light packs. He glanced at the sky, heaved a resigned breath, and plodded away, east and south. Toward the Teschanken River, Gereint surmised. And then south along the river, toward Metichteran? Or across the river toward Tashen? He didn't ask. That was a good example of a question that patience would answer.

Three saddlebags, none of them made to sling properly from a man's back, were an awkward load. On the other hand, compared to walking unburdened through the griffins' terrible desert . . . there was no comparison. Even carrying three bags to Amnachudran's one, Gereint found he had to slow his stride to match his . . . master's. At first, he followed the other man. Then, seeing it made Amnachudran uncomfortable to have him at his back, he came up unbidden to walk beside him. The man gave him a grunt of acknowledgment and for a time they walked in silence. The woods dripped. Birds sang. Somewhere high overhead, a hawk cried. Gnats whined, but fortunately did not seem inclined to bite.

Amnachudran called a halt after about two hours. He dropped his saddlebag and the packs heavily to the ground beside another of the many little streams and stood for a moment with his hands braced on his knees. At last he straightened slowly, with a groan. He looked older now. The plump softness gave him a young sort of face, but Gereint revised his estimate of the man's true age upward.

Gereint dropped his three heavy bags beside the one. He wondered what was in them. Nothing that rattled or clanked or chimed. Unless it was packed so as not to rattle or clank or chime. Maybe he would find a chance to look through a bag later. Maybe Amnachudran would catch him at it. Maybe the things in those bags were secret and important, mages' things. Exactly the wrong kinds of things to be caught examining. He measured Amnachudran with a covert glance. Then he made a fire, found the small pot, filled it with water, and got out the packet of tea and a mug.

Amnachudran watched all this, frowning. "I didn't tell you to do that."

"I have to do everything you say." Gereint measured out tea. "That doesn't mean I can't do anything without your command. Do you not want tea . . . master? Ah, forgive me. Amnachudran, sir."

Amnachudran ignored this small provocation. He asked, "Why did you get out only one mug?"

Gereint was honestly surprised. He sat back on his heels, regarding the other man. "You expected me to get out two? That *would* be presumptuous."

"But you seem—" The other man stopped.

"Ah." Gereint felt a tug of reluctant amusement. He kept forgetting

Amnachudran's perceptiveness. Or wanting to trust his kindness. Or
even both. Worse than foolish: dangerous. And surprising. He said after
a moment, "Yes, but carefully. Nothing quite so blatant as . . . ah . . . getting out two mugs."

"Get another out," said Amnachudran. He sat down on a rock beside the stream.

Gereint found the mug with the broken handle and measured out
more tea.

"How long have you been . . . ?"

Gereint didn't look up. "Nineteen years."

A short pause. Then, "How old are you?"

Gereint brought his master a mug, kneeling to hand it to him so he
wouldn't loom over the smaller man. "Forty-two."

"Almost half your life . . . What *did* you do?"

"Murdered the governor of Breidechboden."

Amnachudran choked on a mouthful of tea, coughed, caught his
breath, stared at Gereint, and at last laughed incredulously. "You
didn't!"

"Well, no, I didn't," agreed Gereint. He went back to the fire,
folded his hands around the other mug. Sipped, watching Amnachudran carefully over the edge of the mug. "I was caught plotting to as-
sassinate the king himself, which he should have expected after he
forbade public houses to serve ale after midnight. What does he expect
young louts to get up to if they're thrown out on the streets while still
sober enough to stagger?"

Amnachudran, undoubtedly remembering the uproar about that
short-lived law, laughed again.

"No," Gereint conceded. "Not that either. I told you, I didn't do
anything. I had the wrong enemies and not enough friends." Not enough
friends and too many cousins, and too many of those had turned out to
be among his enemies . . . He hadn't intended to speak truth to this
man, and paused for a moment, hearing bitter truth echo unexpectedly
in those last words.

Trying to shake off a sudden surge of bitterness—not a helpful
emotion, for a slave—he said, just a little too harshly, "I'll carry these
bags wherever you require. Please . . . once I have, let me go. You don't
need to trust me. Do you think I'll stay anywhere in Casmantium?" He
traced the brand on his face with one thumb. "Believe me, honored sir,
my whole ambition would be to avoid meeting anyone at all until I was
well into Feierabiand."

Amnachudran held up one finger. "You murdered someone." Another
finger. "Or you raped a girl." He opened his hand again, shrugging.

"Those are the two crimes for which a man is put under the *geas*. There aren't any others. I don't see how I can let you go. I don't think girls in Feierabiand ought to be raped, any more than the ones here."

Gereint said tightly, "I did not rape a girl."

"I'm glad to hear it. Whom did you murder?"

"I told you—"

"I don't believe you."

"Neither did anyone else," Gereint said tightly. "Why should you?" He swung away and stamped out the fire. He also picked up all four saddlebags, leaving only the two packs for Amnachudran.

"I can . . ." the other man began.

"Four balance better than three," Gereint snapped. He strode away, south and east.

They did make better time with Gereint carrying all the bags. He was too proud to let the pace slacken; an odd vanity, for a man who ought to have had every vestige of pride beaten out of him years ago. But there it was. He let Amnachudran call the halts, which the other man did every few hours. But he was glad to have them. Ten years ago, even five, he would not have needed those breaks. He had hoped, briefly, that he might grow old a free man in Feierabiand. Now that seemed unlikely.

A little before dusk, they came to the Teschanken. This far north, the river was narrow, quick, and cheerfully violent: It flung itself down from the great mountains and raced through the hills. Far below it would meet the Nerintsan and turn into the stately, broad river that watered the south.

"We'll follow the river south tomorrow," Amnachudran declared. He walked out onto the pebbly shore and stared downstream. "If we're where I think we are, we should cross it about noon, be home before supper—" He stopped suddenly.

A griffin flew past not a spearcast away, fast and straight, flinging itself through the air northward along the path of the river. The late sunlight blazed off it, striking ruddy gold and bronze highlights from its pelt and feathers. The light seemed somehow a far more brilliant light than seemed to fall across the rest of the world. The griffin's feathers seemed to slice the air like knives, its beak flashed like a blade, flickers of fire scattered from the wind of its wings. Gereint could not speak; Eben Amnachudran seemed struck as silent as he.

There was no time to be afraid, and, it appeared, no reason. The griffin did not seem to see them at all, though they stood so close to the path of its flight. Its eyes, fiery copper, were intent on its own course. Before they could breathe twice, it had flashed by and was gone. Though the sunset still painted the sky in carmine and violet, all the colors of sky and earth seemed somehow muted for its passing. The whole world seemed caught for a moment in a subdued quiet. Not a single bird rustled in the woods around them, and even the river seemed to run more quietly along its swift course.

At last, Amnachudran cleared his throat. "I believe that may have been one of the most terrifying things I have ever seen. Beautiful, but terrifying. But what was it doing on the wrong side of the border between fire and earth?"

"It was flying north," Gereint said tentatively. "Maybe it was trying to get back to the desert before full dark. Doesn't Beremnan Anweierchen write that griffins hate the dark and cling to the day, on the rare occasion that they venture into the country of earth?"

"But he doesn't explain why they ever do so venture," Amnachudran pointed out. "Besides, it would need to turn west of north to return to its desert. Though perhaps it intends to." Then he hesitated, turning to study Gereint. "*You've* read Anweierchen?"

The question shook Gereint out of the memory of fire. He shrugged, said shortly, "My old master had a good library," and set the saddlebags down in a row, then began to collect wood for a fire. The wood was drier here, at least. The swift-moving little river might yield something better than dried beef. He looked through Amnachudran's pack for hooks and line, with a careful eye on his new master in case the man resented his rummaging.

But Amnachudran did not seem to care. He watched Gereint for a moment and then said, "There aren't any hooks. We didn't think there would be much opportunity to use them."

Gereint nodded, picked up Amnachudran's knife, selected a bit of wood, and began to make a hook. He turned over the question before he asked it, but guessed Amnachudran wanted to talk about simple things, nothing to do with griffins or fire. So he asked, "We?"

The man's face tightened in grief, but he answered readily. "A friend. The man who owned the house that's now in the desert. He was older than I, but neither of us thought . . . It was his heart, I think. The desert was worse than we'd . . . We had reached Brerich's house, but I wasn't in the same room when he was stricken. If I had been, perhaps . . ."

That was not simple, after all. And it recalled the desert far too vividly. But Amnachudran seemed to wish to speak of his friend. So perhaps it was as well Gereint had asked, after all. He set the hook aside, found a length of cord, and delicately unraveled it to make a finer thread. He rolled the thread between his fingers as he worked, coaxing it toward strength and lightness, feeling it become supple under his touch. "I'm sorry about your friend," he said sincerely. "But how did you . . . If you don't mind, how did you find me?"

"Ah. That was luck. And poor little Fearn. You had one of your waterskins open, did you know? I think she smelled the water." Amnachudran, apparently not having much confidence in Gereint's efforts, dipped water out of the river, put the pot over the fire, and began to cut up dried beef. But he didn't order Gereint to stop making fishing line. Picking up where he'd left off, he added in a quiet voice, "But she couldn't carry both you and the bags. Even with me carrying two of the bags, she didn't quite . . ." His voice trailed off.

Gereint carefully tied the line he'd made to the hook. Tested his knot. Glanced up. "You could have left me there." He touched the brand on his face. "It would only have been the death of a murderer or rapist."

Amnachudran shrugged. "You were face down. I didn't see the brand at once. By the time I did see it, I knew you might live. Once I knew that, I couldn't leave you." He didn't ask, *Are you glad or sorry I saved your life?* But his eyes posed that question.

Gereint stared back at him for a moment in silence. He said at last, "That desert is not the place I would choose to leave my bones." Gathering up his line and hook, he went down to the river.

By full dark, the soup was boiling and two small fish were grilling over coals.

"I didn't think you'd catch any," Amnachudran admitted, turning one of the fish with a pair of twigs.

"I was lucky."

"That was a good hook. Nor would I have thought you could make decent line out of that cord."

"It's a knack." Gereint turned the other fish.

"You're a maker."

And Amnachudran was far too perceptive, and far too difficult to lie to. It hadn't been a question. Gereint said merely, not looking up, "It makes me a valuable slave, yes."

There was a pause. Then Amnachudran began uncomfortably, "How many . . . ? That is, how many men . . . ?"

This time, Gereint did glance up. "How many masters have I had? Is that what you would ask? Five, in all. Each worse than the last."

"Your family . . ." Amnachudran hesitated. "They couldn't protect you?"

"Protect a murderer?" Gereint asked bitterly. The older man looked down. Gereint, observing the flinch, paused, lowered his voice. "You could be the last of my masters. You saved my life: You might save it again in a different way . . ."

"Stop asking me for that," Amnachudran ordered in a low voice.

"You can't command my tongue," Gereint reminded him, waited a beat, and added, "Of course, you *could* order me to kneel and hold still, then beat me unconscious. Or at least until your arm was too tired to lift. You haven't got a whip, but"—he gestured at the woods around them—"there's plenty of springy wood. That would probably work. Shall I cut you a—"

"Be quiet!" Amnachudran commanded him, his tone much sharper.

"If you don't wish to own a *geas* slave, you could simply tell me to walk away—"

"You *want* me to lose my temper," Amnachudran said suddenly.

Gereint stopped.

The other man studied him. "Of course you do. Because you want to know what I'll do if I'm angry. You need to find out how far you can push me—and what will happen if you push me too far."

Gereint didn't try to deny this. He'd never had a master more intelligent than he was. It occurred to him now that Amnachudran might be the first.

For a long moment, the other man only continued to look at him. His plain, round face was difficult to read. He said at last, "Gereint. Get up."

Gereint got to his feet.

"Walk that way"—Amnachudran pointed into the woods—"fifty paces. Sit down with your back to the fire. Stay there till I call you. Go."

Gereint turned immediately and walked into the woods. Carefully, because it was dark under the trees. And chilly. He counted off fifty paces, found a rock, sat down. Wrapped his arms around himself for warmth. His imagination populated the darkness with wolves. Griffins—no, griffins would, like the one they'd seen, have headed for the desert as dusk fell. If it *had* been headed back to the desert. But surely it had been.

Dragons, then. Did dragons hunt by night? Would fire keep a dragon away or draw it? He knew there was almost no chance of dragons this far south, but he nevertheless half believed he heard some vast creature shift its weight away off in the dark.

Probably there was a better chance of wolves. Fire would definitely keep wolves away. Though not from fifty paces behind him. He tried to think about poetry instead of wolves. Gestechan Wanastich's measured cadences came to mind, unfortunately. Fire and the dark and women weeping: not what he wanted in his mind at this moment. And hadn't

Wanastich actually written something about wolves? Ah, yes: the part
of the Teranbichken epic with the snow and the black trees and the
wolves' eyes glowing in a circle . . . Imagination was a curse, Gereint
decided, and closed his own eyes. He knew perfectly well there were
no wolves.

He wished he'd had a chance to eat that fish. He might have picked
up a blanket, at least, if he'd been quick. Amnachudran might have let
him keep it. He wondered whether the man meant to leave him out here
all night. Probably not. Maybe. The command had been *sit*. Gereint
would not be able to lie down. Though he probably would not have
found a dry spot to stretch out, if he was going to be left out here all
night, he was going to regret his inability to try.

Behind him, Amnachudran shouted his name.

Gereint jumped to his feet and, despite the darkness, walked back
to the fire much more quickly than he had left it. Once he stepped out
into the light, the idea of wolves seemed ridiculous. He walked more
slowly back to the fire and stopped, facing his master.

"Well?" asked Amnachudran, looking shrewdly up at him.

Gereint dropped at once to his knees. "Pardon my insolent tongue,
master—sorry. Forgive me, sir. I won't—"

"Stop it!" Amnachudran stopped, took a breath, and continued
more mildly: "I don't want you to, um. Grovel. What I was asking for
was simply your *opinion*."

Taken aback—again!—Gereint asked cautiously, "May I get up?"

"Yes!" Amnachudran gestured toward the blanket on the other side
of the fire. "Sit down, get warm, eat your fish. Tell me, are you going to
stop prodding me for a reaction? Are you satisfied?"

Gereint settled by the fire, poked at the fish. Ate a bite. Amnachudran had boned the fish for him and had a mug of hot tea waiting along
with the beef broth. Gereint had more than half expected his master to
call him back to the fire. But this additional small kindness was so far
outside anything he had expected that he did not even know what to
feel about it.

He looked up, met the other man's eyes. "You asked for my opinion
and whether I'm satisfied. Very well. You certainly haven't lost your
temper. I'm satisfied you won't, or not easily. Or did you wish my opinion about the punishment itself? Very well: It was effective. I don't
want you to do that again, for all you avoided brutality very neatly.
Thank you for calling me back to the fire."

"What you said. About being made to kneel while someone beat
you unconscious. Someone did that to you?"

Amnachudran might be a clever man. A perceptive man. But judging by his tone on that question, he was in some ways surprisingly innocent. Gereint controlled an impulse to laugh. He answered, with considerable restraint, "Oh, yes."

Amnachudran looked revolted. "I'd thought . . . You're right that I don't want a *geas* slave. Now less than ever. I'd thought, once we get back to my home, I might find out your old master's name, send you—"

Cold struck through Gereint's body like death. There could not be many *geas*-bound men of his size and general description. Even if he refused to give Amnachudran his old master's name, the man could easily find it out. He put the mug of tea down, stood up, came back around the fire to where Amnachudran sat, and knelt. Put his palms flat on the ground. Bent to touch his forehead to the earth.

"Gereint—"

"I know you don't want me to grovel." Gereint straightened his back, looking the other man deliberately in the face. "My most recent master, now. He likes a man to grovel. I'm sure he was very angry when he realized he would have to leave me behind. He would be very grateful to you if you returned me to him. He's a powerful man; his patronage could probably be useful to you. Me . . . he would expect me to plead for mercy. He would expect me to eat the dirt in front of his boots. I would do that for you, except you wouldn't like it. If you were searching for an effective threat, you've found one. Don't send me back to him. Please, don't. Just tell me to walk—"

"Away into the mountains, I know—"

"—back to Melentser. I would rather that than go back into that man's house."

There was a pause.

"What did he do to you?" Amnachudran asked, his tone hushed.

Gereint said gently, "Eben Amnachudran. You're a decent man. You don't want to know."

This time the pause was longer.

Gereint bowed his head, drew a slow breath, let it out. He didn't get to his feet, but said instead, "I know you won't free me. You've made that clear. I won't ask again. I'll ask this instead: What can I do to persuade you to keep me yourself? Not sell me, nor give me away, nor above all send me back to my old master?"

Amnachudran stared at him.

"You were right, of course: I have been pushing at you. I'll stop. I'll be respectful—I *can* be respectful. I'll call you by name, if you prefer. I won't grovel, since you don't like that. You can treat me as a hired man rather than a slave, if you wish. I can play that role. I can play any role that pleases you. You were right: I'm a maker. I could be useful to you—"

"Stop!" said Amnachudran, rather desperately.

Gereint shut his mouth. Rested his hands on his thighs, deliberately open and easy. Waited.

"What was it that you *did*?"

Gereint flinched, he hoped not noticeably. He began to speak, hesitated. Said at last, "If I tell you again I did nothing, you'll think I'm lying and be angry. I don't want that."

"Just tell me the truth!"

"You're waiting for me to lie to you. Are you so certain you would recognize truth, when you're listening for lies?"

Silence. Finally, Amnachudran made a disgusted gesture. "Eat your supper. Go to sleep. I'll think about your request . . . later. When we've gotten to my house."

The *geas* could compel Gereint to eat the rest of the fish and drink the tea. But even the *geas* couldn't force him to sleep, though it could make him lie quietly with his eyes closed.

The morning came watery and pale through the mist that rose from the river and the damp woods. There had been no sign of wolves or griffins or dragons. Or if there had been, it must have been in the small hours near dawn, when Gereint had finally slept a little.

Amnachudran had coaxed the fire back to life and made tea. He glanced up as Gereint got to his feet. "There's plenty of cracker. I'm sorry there's not time for you to catch more fish. But we should be home by evening."

Home. His, of course. Did he mean that it would be Gereint's home as well? Probably not. Gereint didn't ask. He went down to the river and washed his face and hands. Came back and began to roll up the blankets and stow away the little pot and other things. Ate a piece of cracker. Drank the tea. He couldn't tell what Amnachudran was thinking. If he was thinking about anything other than his home.

"I know you're much stronger than I am. But I think I could carry—" Amnachudran began.

"No, sir. That's not necessary. Just carry the packs," Gereint said. But respectfully. He inspected the straps on the saddlebags and spent a few minutes lengthening some and shortening the others. "We're crossing the river, are we? How waterproof are these bags? I brought some tallow candles. If you have a little oil, I can probably improve them."

"Thank you, Gereint. Yes. When we stop."

Gereint nodded, slung the straps over his shoulders, and straightened. The bags seemed to have grown heavier. He didn't let himself groan, but only glanced politely at the other man, waiting for him to lead the way.

The sun came out. The mist lifted. The river dashed cheerfully down the hill beside them. There was even a deer trail to follow. All in all, a pleasant morning. Gereint only wished he was alone, less burdened, and heading the other way.

On the other hand . . . on the other hand, he could be in Breidechboden. In Perech Fellesteden's house. Compared to that, Amnachudran's house, whatever it was like, would surely prove a perfect haven. Probably the man hadn't yet decided whether to grant Gereint's plea. Gereint glanced at him, a cautious sidelong glance. He did not want to annoy him. But he did not seem easy to annoy . . . Gereint asked, "Is it Tashen? Where your house is?"

"Near Tashen," Amnachudran agreed. "My house is out in the country, between the mountains and the city. Near the river, in fact. After the ford, we'll turn almost due east, walk fewer than ten miles. My house is at the base of some low hills, where a stream comes down year-round. It's easy country there, open and level, good for orchards and wheat and pasture. The apples are just beginning to ripen now. My wife loves apples; she's collected dozens of varieties . . ."

Gereint made an interested sound, listening with half an ear to descriptions of orchards and gardens and the new pond they'd just built and stocked with fish. Amnachudran was clearly wealthier than Gereint had guessed. And there was a wife. Gereint wondered whether she would object to the presence of a *geas*-bound servant. Would it be possible to win her over, make himself so immediately useful that she would object if her husband wanted to get rid of him?

But there were grown children, too, he gathered. With children of their own, in and out of their grandparents' house. *Geas* bound or not, Amnachudran or his wife might reasonably hesitate to bring a murderer into the house where their grandchildren played. Or a rapist.

Gereint's thoughts tended darker and darker. He doubted he could persuade Amnachudran to release him, but the more he thought about it, the less likely it seemed that the man would keep him either. Even if he did not send him back to Fellesteden . . . If he sold him, what were the odds Gereint's next master would be kind? Kind men did not buy *geas* slaves.

What were the odds, if he was sold, that it would be to someone from the city? The court nobles and the lesser nobles, the rich men angling for power and influence . . . Those were the men who liked to own *geas*-bound slaves. He might very well be sold and re-sold until he found himself in Breidechboden after all. If he were sold to anyone in the king's city, Perech Fellesteden would almost certainly learn of it eventually.

Gereint was very silent by the time they reached the ford, about an hour past noon. The river was wider here, still fast but not deep. Rocks thrust up through the water. A man would not be able to walk from one bank to the other without getting his feet wet, but he might come closer to that than Gereint had expected. In the spring, the river might be impassable. But now, only one thirty-foot channel looked difficult, and even that did not look actually dangerous.

And on the other side, fewer than ten miles away, Amnachudran's house. Perhaps forty miles from Melentser as the falcon flies. It seemed both infinitely farther than that and, at the same time, hardly any distance at all.

Amnachudran stared at the river and grunted. "Could be worse. I thought it would be worse, in fact. That's lower than we'd usually see, even this time of year."

Gereint, not very interested, nodded politely.

"I'll make tea," Amnachudran said, "if you'll see what you can do about the saddlebags?"

Gereint got out two of the tallow candles and found Amnachudran's jar of oil. And the broken mug, since his master was using the pan for the tea. He melted the candles with the oil over low flames, rubbed the hot tallow between his palms, and nodded toward the first of the saddlebags. "It would be easier if they were empty."

Amnachudran opened the first bag without a word. It contained books. Maskeirien's eclogues, Teirenchoden's epic about the nineteenth war between Ceirinium and Feresdechodan. Histories and poetry, natural philosophy and political philosophy. Leather embossed with gold; fine heavy paper illuminated with dragons and griffins and storm eagles and slender sea creatures with the tails of fishes and the proud, fine-boned faces of men. Nothing common. Not a single volume that was not beautiful and rare and precious. They made the two books he'd stolen look almost common.

Gereint wondered why he had not guessed. Heavy and valuable, but not breakable; valuable for themselves and not merely for their market price. Exactly the sort of riches a man might risk the new desert to recover. Especially if he'd thought, *A few hours in and a few hours out, how difficult can it be?*

No wonder Amnachudran was willing to wait in order to enhance the waterproofing on the bags before he carried those books across the river. Gereint rubbed the tallow across the leather. He gazed dreamily into the air while he rubbed it in, thinking about waterproof leather, about tight seams, about straps that closed tight and firm. He tried not to let himself be distracted by the books themselves, although he couldn't resist a glance or two as Amnachudran unloaded the second bag.

"The oil won't stain the books?" Amnachudran asked. He touched the first cautiously, inspected the tips of his fingers.

"It might if someone else did this," Gereint answered. "Not when I do it."

"A knack."

"It's a matter of knowing exactly what I want the oil to do and not do. And yes, it's a knack."

Amnachudran grunted and, finding his fingers clean and dry, began to replace the contents of the first bag and unload the third. "Just how waterproof can you make these?"

Gereint, massaging melted tallow into leather, shrugged. "It would probably be better not to actually drop a bag midriver."

Amnachudran grunted again and went to get the fourth bag.

Midchannel, the river was chest deep. And very fast. Gereint took his boots off and waded out cautiously, leaving the books behind while he tested the footing and the strength of the current. He came out shaking his head. "I don't like it . . . It's not too bad when you've got your hands free and no weight to carry . . ."

"I have rope," Amnachudran offered.

They slung the rope from shore to shore; it just reached. Then Gereint took the packs and his boots, and Amnachudran's boots, across first. The technique seemed sound. He could brace an awkward weight on his shoulder with one hand and cling to the rope with his other. He took three bags across, one after another, while Amnachudran watched anxiously. Then he came back for the last, standing back to allow Amnachudran to precede him into the water.

"Be careful," Gereint warned him as they came to the deepest part of the channel. "Chest deep on me is—"

"Just about over my head. Yes, I know. Even so, it's the nearest thing to an easy crossing anywhere above the bridge at Metichteran. I admit, it looks easier when you're ahorse than it does when you're on foot."

Gereint shrugged. "Keep hold of the rope. I'll be right behind you."

Amnachudran went ahead of Gereint, hand over hand along the rope, gasping with cold and sputtering as the racing water dashed into his face. He made it to the first of the broad stones on the other side of the channel and began to pull himself out of the water.

Gereint, ten feet behind the older man, saw the log come spinning down the river just too late to shout a warning. It hit Amnachudran's legs with a *thud* Gereint could hear even from that distance, tearing the man away from the rope. He cried out, falling, but the cry was choked off as the water closed over his head; Gereint, appalled, saw him come back to the surface in time to smash against one stone and then another and then go under once more.

Gereint heaved the last saddlebag toward the rocks without watching to see where it landed and flung himself into the current. He fended off a rock with his hands, followed the rushing current by instinct and luck, glimpsed the log, hurled himself after it, found himself in a great sucking undertow, went down. Found cloth under his hands. An arm. Stone beneath: He kicked hard and broke into the air, rolled to drag Amnachudran up as well, slammed back first into stone. Cried out with pain and at the same time clutched for any handhold he could find. The current pinned them against the stone. Gereint got an arm around the other man's chest, dashed water out of his own face, and found pebbles rolling under his toes. The river was fierce, here, but not much more than shoulder deep. And he could see where another stone offered support against the current.

Amnachudran was limp. Gereint tightened his hold, got his feet against the rock that supported them, and lunged for the other stone. Made it, and now the water was only chest deep. He dug his toes into the river's rough bed, heaved Amnachudran up onto the stone, made his way around it to where the water was still shallower, grabbed the man's arm, dragged him across his shoulder, and slogged for the shore. Dropped him—not as gently as he'd meant—on a shallow shelf of pebbles and sand. Fell to his knees beside him and felt for a pulse in his throat. Found one. Rolled him over and pressed to get the water out of his lungs; made sure he was breathing on his own. And only then realized what he'd done.

Gereint climbed to his feet. Everything had happened so fast; too fast. He felt dizzy and ill. His back and hip hurt, his knee hurt with a deep ache that told him it was at least wrenched, maybe sprained. The palms of his hands were raw—how had that happened?

But Amnachudran had suffered much worse. But he was still breathing, though the sound had a rattle to it that suggested water in the lungs. His pulse was rapid and thready with shock. There was a lump the size of a small egg above and behind his ear. Gereint thought one of his legs was probably broken.

Letting the other man drown hadn't occurred to Gereint fast enough. But now . . . an unconscious man could not command his help. Without care now, Amnachudran would probably die. Gereint stared down at him. He could not kick the man back into the river; even without the *geas* he didn't think he could have done that. But . . . he wouldn't have to do anything so active, would he?

The situation at this moment was too uncertain for the *geas* to bite hard. His master was too near death, maybe. Too deathly. Interesting word, "deathly." The *geas* seemed to accept it as nearly the same as "dead." Gereint was fairly certain he could simply walk away. His hip hurt; his knee hurt like fire. But it didn't seem to be sprained. He could walk well enough. He didn't even need a stick.

Judging from his previous experience, when Fellesteden had left him behind in Melentser, distance alone would suffice to keep the *geas* quiet. And now Gereint knew, as he hadn't then, that if he could step into direct desert sunlight, it would break the *geas*—and he could step back out immediately. He'd made a slight detour, yes. But the mountains still waited, and Feierabiand, and final freedom from the *geas*.

If Gereint walked away and, against all likelihood, Amnachudran did wake . . . well, then, he would be hurt and cold, with the chill of the night coming and no fire. It would not take wolves to kill a man left hurt and alone in the dark. He would die . . . alone and abandoned . . . fewer than ten miles from his home . . . Gereint cursed.

Then he heaved the smaller man up into his arms, grunting as his back and hip flared with pain. He limped back to clear ground near the saddlebags and put the man down there. Found out the blankets, and laid one out on the ground for a bed. Stripped away the wet clothing. A great spreading black bruise showed where ribs were probably broken. The leg was gashed as well as broken, but there wasn't much blood. Gereint bound up the gash and covered the injured man with the other blanket. Made a fire, afraid all the time that Amnachudran might wake after all. But he did not stir. Gereint glanced at the sun. Hours yet till dusk. And Amnachudran's breathing already sounded better. The pulse in his throat beat more strongly. If Gereint left him now, he might be all right. Though the leg . . . But surely his family was waiting for him. They must surely expect him to be on his way home. Someone would come down to the river soon to look for him.

Gereint went back to where he'd left the bags and packs. Absently collected the fourth saddlebag from the shallow water where it had fallen and put it with the others. The books it held were dry, he found. Then he looked at the book he held blankly, wondering why he'd bothered to check. He put it back and did up the straps.

He changed into dry clothing. Found his boots and put them on. Did not look back at Amnachudran. Most carefully did not look. If he looked, he might find himself compelled to go back to him. If he didn't look . . . If he fixed his mind firmly on the sky and the river and the sound the wind made in the leaves . . . why, then, he could swing a pack over his shoulder and walk away, upriver. He didn't look back.

The *geas* didn't stop him. He'd thought it might, at this last moment of abandonment: an act of defiance more active than merely letting Perech Fellesteden walk away from him had been. But the *geas* did not stop him. It wasn't gone. He knew by this that Amnachudran still lived. But it did not bite hard. An unconscious master, a master who was dying, was not something, perhaps, that the *geas* magic understood very well. He walked on.

Amnachudran was already too far away to call him back.

But Gereint hadn't even gone a mile when he saw the griffins. This time, there were three of them: one bronze and brown, one copper and gold, and one—the one leading—a hard, pure white, like the flames at the very heart of a fire. The air surrounding them was dense with light, so that Gereint had to squint against it to see them. It smelled of fire and hot brass; the air shimmered with heat.

As the other griffin had done, these were flying along the river—only these were heading south, downriver. Unlike that other griffin, these very clearly knew he was present: The white one tilted its head and looked down at him as it passed, a flashing sapphire glance of such hot contempt that Gereint swayed and took an involuntary step back. But they did not hesitate in their course or drop toward him, for which he was fervently grateful.

The griffins flew low, so low that their wingtips nearly brushed the topmost branches of the trees, so low that Gereint was gripped by a compelling illusion, as the last one soared past, that he might have touched its feathers if he'd reached out his hand. He wondered if those feathers could be as sharp edged and metallic as they seemed—probably not. But the light flashed off their beaks, and off talons as long as his fingers and as sharp as knives. It came to him, vividly, what those talons might do to a man . . . to a defenseless man, say, who had been left abandoned and injured on the riverbank . . . He shut his eyes, trying to close out the images his imagination suggested to him, as well as the too-brilliant light.

When he opened them again, the griffins were past, out of sight. The light was only ordinary sunlight, and the river and woodlands seemingly untroubled by any memory of fire.

The griffins surely would not stop to trouble Eben Amnachudran. They did not seem inclined to stop for any reason. The other one had not paid any attention to them; these three hadn't stopped to tear Gereint to pieces, though they'd clearly seen him. Why would they pause to kill a man who was, after all, already dying?

They wouldn't. Gereint was certain of it. Almost certain. He took a few steps along the river, northward.

Then he stopped again. What if the griffins passed Amnachudran by? They probably would not pause to kill him. The scholar had thought them beautiful as well as terrible. Maybe he was awake now. Maybe he would see them pass. Helpless as he was, he would be frightened. He would watch the griffins pass by—surely they would pass by. And then he would wait. And for what? How long would it take for the injured man to give up hope? How long might he linger, in pain and growing despair, until he finally died quietly there by that fire? While his wife and children and grandchildren waited for him not ten miles away?

Gereint could not put that image out of his mind. It was worse than imagining griffins tearing the scholar to ribbons. How long *would* it be before someone came down to the ford looking for the man? Who would it be: His wife? One of the grandchildren?

So it wasn't fear of the griffins that made Gereint turn back south. After all, if they wanted to kill Amnachudran, Gereint could never stop them, even if he was there. But the image of that kind, civilized, cultured man waiting in slowly dying hope, while the hours passed, maybe days, and no one came . . . that was what made Gereint turn back.

It took about a quarter of an hour to get back to the ford. Everything was exactly as Gereint had left it; there was no sign that griffins had stopped there. This was almost a shock, even though he had thought it unlikely that they would. Nor was Amnachudran awake. But he was still alive. Gereint stood for a moment, gazing down at him, and wondering if he wished the man had died. He did not know. But he knew he could not simply leave him a second time.

It took another quarter of an hour, maybe, to make a litter with green saplings and the blankets. Longer than seemed likely to get Amnachudran on the litter and the saddlebags arranged. Gereint discarded the packs, only tucking his own books into one of the saddlebags. He would not need tallow candles or a cooking pot now.

Then he picked up the stripped ends of the saplings and leaned into the weight.

His knee screamed as he took the weight. But the leg held. Blades of pain lanced down his back and stabbed into his hip, but he still thought nothing was actually broken. His hands hurt when he gripped the poles, though next to the knee and hip that seemed a minor distraction. Less than ten miles, Amnachudran had said. How much less? It had better be a lot less, Gereint thought grimly, or he would never manage it.

The ground might be easy compared to the high mountains, but soon enough Gereint doubted whether he'd manage this last leg of his journey after all. Merrich Berchandren had famously declared that the last mile of any journey was always the hardest. If the last mile was harder than the one he was currently traveling, Gereint did not look forward to it.

Now, though, rather than trying to coax the *geas* to sleep, he could actually use it. He pretended Amnachudran had ordered him to get him home. He imagined the man's pain-filled eyes and strained tone: *Gereint, get me home.* The *geas* couldn't really be fooled, but then, getting his badly injured master to his home *was* a desperately important service. There was no pretense about that. He glanced over his shoulder at Amnachudran's white face, thought hard of getting the man to shelter and safety, and felt the *geas* shiver awake at last and bite down hard. After that there was no question of stopping: Next to the compulsion of the *geas*, neither his hip nor his knee nor his bleeding palms mattered at all.

Gereint had been tall, big all through, all his life: He had been big for his age as a child and a boy and a youth, and once he'd got his growth he'd seldom met a stronger man. And much good it had done him. But his strength served him now. And hard-trained endurance. And sheer doggedness . . . The sun slid lower in the sky behind him. Shadows stretched out. The countryside opened out, patches of open meadows and woods replacing forest and then pastures replacing the woodlands. Gereint watched the shadows to keep his direction. He tried to remember to glance up sometimes, look for apple orchards and a house set against hills where a stream came down. He was thirsty . . . Thirst became a torment as soon as he thought of it. He had not thought to fill waterskins at the river. He put one foot in front of the other, though half his steps were short; he could no longer bend his right knee very well. But that was all right because the pain of his hip would have shortened his steps anyway.

Dusk, and shadows stretching out to cover the countryside, and no house with candles in its windows to light home a late traveler . . . He had missed the house. He knew he had missed it. Every little rough place in the ground made him stumble. He should just stop, wait for dawn. But he *couldn't* stop, not now, no matter how unreasonable pressing forward might be. Not until the last shreds of his strength had been spent and he just fell where he stood . . . He realized, dimly, that he was no longer going straight east, and for a long moment could not understand why. Then the breeze shifted, and he blinked. Apples. It was too dark now to see the trees, but he could smell the fruit on the gentle breeze. He lifted his head, turned his face toward that sweet fragrance . . . There was a light. There was a lantern, after all: a lantern in a high window, and beyond the light, dark rolling hills that cut across the starry sky.

Gereint made it through the orchard and right up to the gates of the house's yard. The gates were closed. He stood for some time, too dazed to understand why he had stopped. Then a voice called out from within the gate, and another voice answered. Gereint did not understand anything he heard, but he let go of the litter poles. His hands, cramped from hours of gripping, could not open. But he could hammer his fists against the gate. He could not form coherent words. But he could shout, hoarsely.

There were more voices, then. And the ringing sounds of boots against flagstones. And the scraping sound of wood against wood as the gates were unbarred. Lantern light spilled out as the gates were opened, and incomprehensible voices exclaimed. Gereint barely heard them. He was aware only of the *geas* relaxing within and around him. He did not even feel himself fall.

CHAPTER 2

Gereint dreamed of the hot iron. It traced a circle across his cheek, burning.

When the branding had actually happened, they had warned him against struggling. He might lose an eye, they warned, if the iron slipped. Gereint had been horrified by the threat. He had not fought them.

This time, he knew what the hot iron meant. He knew there were worse things than risking the loss of an eye. He fought desperately.

Weight pinned him. Hands gripped his arms, his shoulders, his body. Hands clamped around his head, holding him still no matter how he fought. The iron was slow, this time, tracing its deliberate path around its circle. Its path was agony, and the scar it left would be a torment forever, but he was held too tightly and could not stop them. He screamed . . . He had not screamed at the time, but he did this time, because he knew what kind of life the iron would leave him. And he screamed because he had nothing left but his voice; the *geas* would take his body and his hands, but it would leave his voice . . . Darkness and fire and the hot iron, and screaming in the dark . . .

Gereint jerked awake, shaking.

He was lying in a bed in a large, airy chamber with a pale-yellow ceiling and delicate yellow curtains fluttering at the window. He understood that almost at once. He was not in pain; he understood that almost as quickly. His face did not hurt. The iron had only been a dream; the branding was years in the past. But he dimly felt that he had been injured, that he should have been in some pain. He wasn't. He felt . . . well. Confused. But well.

His wrists were tied to the sides of the bed, and his ankles to tall ornate posts at its foot. Gereint realized this only gradually, when he tried to sit up. He did not immediately understand why he couldn't. Then he lifted his head as well as he could and squinted at the bonds, which were soft cloth. Nothing to cut or chafe. No wonder he hadn't understood at first that he was bound. He couldn't think why he should be tied to the bed . . . Well, he could think of one or two reasons a *geas* slave might be tied to a bed, but they seemed unlikely . . . Why unlikely? Ah. Eben Amnachudran. Some of the immediate past began to settle back into order. Yes. This was Amnachudran's house, surely. And those reasons did not seem very likely, if he was still *his* slave.

But he *was* bound . . .

Someone opened the door and came in. Gereint could not lift his head enough to see who it was. It occurred to him only too late that perhaps he might have been wiser to pretend to be asleep, but he did not think of that until the person made a little sound of surprise and hurried out again.

Gereint lowered his head back to the pillow and tried to think. It was hard. He felt strangely adrift. Thoughts came slowly and faded before he could quite grasp them . . .

The door opened again, and this time Amnachudran himself came in. He walked quickly to the head of the bed and stood frowning down at Gereint. His round, mild face did not seem meant for frowning. Gereint stared back at him in confusion, feeling the internal shift of the *geas*. Was the man angry? He had not meant to do anything to anger Amnachudran . . . Had he? But it must have been Amnachudran himself who had ordered him tied down . . . but the man could simply have commanded him to lie down and stay in the bed . . . Gereint looked away in confusion, feeling weak and somehow ashamed. He *was* weak, but he didn't understand the shame.

"How do you feel?" Amnachudran asked. He held up one hand. "How many fingers am I holding up? What's your name? What's *my* name?"

Gereint turned his head back, stared up at him. "I think I could manage . . . three out of four, maybe."

"Which one seems doubtful?"

"I feel . . . very odd."

The other man laughed, sounding relieved. He was no longer frowning. "Gereint . . ." he said, and shook his head.

"Why am I . . . ?" Gereint moved his hands illustratively.

"You fought us. Very hard."

"The *geas* didn't stop me?"

"Nothing stopped you. You were out of your mind. I don't think you recognized me. It was a lesson to me about desperation and the limitations

of the *geas*." Amnachudran produced a small knife and began to cut Gereint loose, very carefully. The knife did not want to cut the soft cloth. If
Gereint had made the knife, it would have done a much better job.

Gereint watched the knife. He watched the other man's hand working carefully to cut the cloth bonds. He said tentatively, "I was . . . you
were . . . is my memory right?"

"I don't know. What do you think you remember?"

"Didn't you have a broken leg? Among other things."

"Among other things, yes." Amnachudran finished cutting Gereint's hands free and stepped down to the foot of the bed. "My wife is
a skilled healer-mage; fortunately she is skilled especially with trau-
matic injuries. I . . . um. I'm more of a specialist, myself." He finished
cutting Gereint's feet free, reached to a table by the bed, and handed
Gereint a small hand mirror. The kind a lady would use, with an ornate
brass frame and little birds etched in the corners of the glass.

Gereint took it wonderingly. Looked in it, since that was what his
master clearly intended.

He almost did not recognize the face that looked back at him. Oh,
the *face* was the same: The forehead with untidy hair falling across it;
the wide cheekbones were the same, the nose, the line of the jaw . . .
but there was no broad circular scar from the branding. Gereint stared
hard, not understanding what he was seeing. Or not seeing. There was
nothing there. He lifted a hand, traced with his thumb the path of the
brand. But he had to trace it from memory: He could not find the
smooth raised scar by touch. He began to put the mirror down, snatched
it back upright and stared again. Tried to speak and found his throat
closed—and besides, he had no idea what to say.

"I'll be, um. Around," Amnachudran said quickly. "Come find me
when you, um. Feel up to it." He gestured rather randomly around the
room. "There's food—be sure and eat something. I think the clothing
should fit. Um—" He retreated.

For a little while, Gereint thought he might weep like a child, as
Amnachudran had clearly feared. He didn't, in the end. He ate a piece
of bread while standing in front of a full-length mirror, staring at his
unmarked face. The *geas* rings still pierced his ankles, but he had
known they must. The cords Amnachudran had used to bind him were
still woven through those rings. He had known that, too. But the face . . .
Did Amnachudran *know* what he had done?

The man was clever. And perceptive. And kind, with a depth of
honest kindness Gereint had almost come to believe could not truly exist. At least, not for him. Gereint stared at his own face in the mirror
and decided that Amnachudran had known *exactly* what he was doing.

Gereint touched the unblemished skin of his cheek and went to get another piece of bread. And some thin-sliced beef to layer on it. The food did help. He felt more solid and grounded every moment. The clarity of his thoughts showed him how vague and blurred he had been earlier. He thought he might need all the acuity he could own, soon. He went back to the mirror, chewing.

It was a lady's mirror, as the graceful table and pretty curtains were clearly the appointments of a lady's room. He wondered whose bed he had awoken in. And whose clothing had been provided for him. Someone big: The shirt was only a little too tight across the shoulders, the sleeves only a little too short. It was a good shirt. All the clothing was good. Better than anything Gereint had worn for a long time.

There were boots. And cloth to bind around the *geas* rings so they would not chafe. Gereint put on the boots and went back again to the mirror. The man that looked back at him could have been any man. Could walk through any town and never collect a second glance, save for his size.

Gereint went to find Amnachudran. It wasn't difficult. A servant, clearly posted in the hallway to wait, led him down the hall. The servant wore good clothing. Brown and pale yellow. Livery, by the look of it. Yes, hadn't Amnachudran said that his wife was nobly born? Gereint thoughtfully followed the man.

Eben Amnachudran was waiting in a room that seemed both an office and a music room. A delicate, graceful ladies' spinet stood in pride of place; a tall floor harp occupied one corner. But a desk cluttered with papers sat at the other end of the room, and books as well as scrolls of musical scores were shelved along the walls. Amnachudran stood by the desk, sorting the fine books he'd brought back from the desert. The collection was even more impressive spread out like that.

A woman, not beautiful, but plump and comfortable, sat at the spinet. She was not facing the instrument, but one of her hands rested on the keys. She had struck a note: just one. The sound lingered in the air, clean and clear and beautiful.

Amnachudran turned as Gereint came in. He did not speak. His wife—or so Gereint surmised—turned her head and smiled: a surprisingly warm, unconstrained smile.

Gereint nodded to her, faced Amnachudran, and lifted one hand to sketch the brand that wasn't there. "I know thanks are inadequate. But I do thank you, sir. Most earnestly."

Amnachudran looked uncomfortable. "You still bear the *geas*—"

Gereint held up a hand to stop him. "You've made it possible for me to walk unrecognized anywhere among men. As long as I wear boots, no one will covet me or guess he ought to. No one will know I was condemned; no one will wonder what crime I committed. You've given me back a kind of privacy I never—" His voice failed. He did not let himself look away, but met the other man's eyes and said quietly, "And you know you have. You meant to do this. Don't make little of it. I would kiss your feet for what you have done. Willingly. Except you wouldn't like it."

Amnachudran shook his head. "You saved my life. Should I not even have noticed?"

"I'm *geas* bound," Gereint reminded him.

But Amnachudran surprised him again. "The *geas* can force a man to do a great many things, I'm sure. But it can't force him to leap instantly into a river to drag out a drowning fool, when he hasn't been ordered to do anything of the sort. Andreikan Warichteier spends three entire chapters detailing the uses and limitations of the *geas*."

"He gets most of it right," Gereint admitted. "As one would expect from Warichteier. But you'd already saved my life."

Amnachudran replied patiently, "You didn't value your life. I valued mine very much."

The woman's mouth crooked. She leaned an elbow on the spinet, cupping her chin in her hand and regarding her husband with affection and humor.

Gereint glanced at her, bowed his head respectfully.

Amnachudran followed that glance. He said wryly, "You probably wondered why I had no men to help me. Why there was no one to meet me at the ford. It's complicated—"

"Not complicated in the least," murmured the woman, raising her eyebrows.

Amnachudran sighed. "Embarrassing, then." He said to Gereint, "This is, as you have surmised, my lady wife, Emre Tanshan. One of *those* Tanshans, yes. She married down, when she agreed to marry me."

Lady Emre lifted an eyebrow.

"What she is graciously not saying, among other things, is that I foolishly slipped away with just my friend, telling no one else, because I knew my wife would—quite reasonably—object to the whole venture."

"Just a few hours in and back out," said Gereint. "How difficult could that be?"

"Exactly." Amnachudran hesitated, then said. "You even brought the books. That surprised me."

"By the time I needed to abandon them, I wasn't thinking very clearly. But I'm glad they are safe." It was Gereint's turn to hesitate. He said slowly, watching the other man carefully, "You wouldn't have done this"—again, he ran a thumb across his unmarked cheek—"if you meant to send me back to my old master. Nor even if you'd just meant to sell me. I'm extremely grateful. But I wonder whether you do in fact mean to keep me. Or—or whether you might free me after all. I don't want to anger you, sir. I know I'm presuming on your kindness to me. I said I wouldn't ask again. But I beg you will permit me to ask just once more whether you might—"

It was Amnachudran's turn to hold up a hand. He said in a crisp, firm tone, "I won't sell you or give you away, whatever you tell me. I won't let anyone take you from me, either. You are safe here. Do you understand?" His tone gentled. "I would like to free you, in fact. I think I owe you that, and besides . . . well. But I will ask you one more time: What did you do?"

Gereint knew he shouldn't have been surprised. But he was. He felt badly off balance. Nothing in this house seemed to follow ordinary paths; all the things he would ordinarily do or say seemed . . . impossible.

He had never intended to answer that question. He had to answer it.

He did not dare lie to Amnachudran. He did not even *want* to lie to him, exactly. He wanted to turn the question aside, somehow. He couldn't do that, either.

Gereint braced himself. Tried to make himself meet the other man's eyes. Could not support the effort. He stared instead at the wall. Said, in his flattest tone, "When I was twenty, I married a lovely girl of good family. We were very happy. I thought we were. When I was twenty-three, I found her . . . with a man. A friend of mine, I thought. I picked up a chair, broke it to make a club. I meant to kill him. I swear I did not mean to kill her. I didn't hit her with the club. I slapped her." He stopped, glanced at Emre Tanshan. She did not look away, and after a moment Gereint bowed his head. "I knew my strength. I don't claim otherwise. Maybe I did mean to kill her. She died. So did he." He gazed down, then, at his hands. Closed them into fists. Opened them again. Made himself look up to meet Amnachudran's eyes. He couldn't read the other man's expression. "It's not a glamorous tale. Not exciting. It's common and stupid and petty and ugly."

"And true."

"Yes."

"Usually they don't bind a man under the *geas* for such an . . . impulsive crime."

Gereint nodded. "Her father was an important man. So was his. I told you I had powerful enemies. That part was true. My own father was dead; my cousins could not—didn't care to—protect me." He cut

that off, didn't explain that his cousin Gescheichan had been a rival for
his wife, that he'd been young enough and stupid enough to find that
amusing, until he'd found Gescheichan doing everything in his power
to make sure Gereint was *geas* bound. None of his other cousins had
tried to intercede. If his mother had been alive—if his sister had still
been in Breidechboden and not far away in Abreichan—but no one had
even tried to help him.

He drew a deep breath. Looked again into his master's face. Amnachudran's expression was hard to read. So was his wife's. Gereint
said with some intensity, "It was nineteen years ago. When I was still
young enough to believe a woman was worth dying for. Even then, I
hope I wasn't stupid enough to believe any woman was worth . . ." He
touched his face. Traced the path of the iron. Repeated, "It was nineteen years ago."

"They're still dead," Lady Emre said quietly.

Gereint dropped his hand. He didn't look at the lady. But he said,
"Yes, that's true." Then he drew a breath. Faced Amnachudran again.
"I'm no longer that stupid boy. An impulsive crime, you said. It was
that. I'm . . . about as far from impulsive, now, as any man you'll ever
meet. Sir. Master." Promises about future behavior were pointless:
Amnachudran was not a fool. Gereint said with low, passionate intensity, "You didn't ask to be my judge. I know that. I just . . . fell into your
hands. But you could free me. No one else can. No one else will. Please
free me."

"In fact . . ." Amnachudran began, but then stopped. He looked at
his wife. She raised her eyebrows, but said nothing. Amnachudran nodded as though she had spoken. He turned back to Gereint, frowning.

Gereint bowed his head under that stern regard. He fought to clear
all signs of recent emotion from his face. He was shaking; he couldn't
help that. He tried desperately to recapture a proper slave's resignation—he would have done anything to be this man's slave when he'd
belonged to Perech Fellesteden. The worse thing, the very worst, would
be for Amnachudran to decide that, after all, he was too much trouble
to keep . . . He tried to think of something to say, anything, to prevent
that. It was important to remember that Eben Amnachudran was more
intelligent than he was . . .

"Take off your boots," Amnachudran ordered.

For a long moment, Gereint did not believe he could have heard
that command properly. The *geas* believed it, however. His body moved
without conscious direction; he had his first boot off before he could
actually believe the man had said those words. If Fellesteden had given
that order—but if *Amnachudran* gave it, he meant to—he actually

meant—Gereint fumbled off the second boot with clumsy hands and looked up, hardly breathing, in terror that he might have somehow misunderstood.

But Amnachudran had a knife out and was beckoning for Gereint to put his foot up on the edge of a chair. He cut the first cord. Gereint thought he could feel the strands part. The entire *geas* trembled, poised on the edge of that knife.

Then the other foot. The other cord. As quickly and easily as if it was any cord.

The *geas*, defanged, settled quietly to the back of Gereint's awareness to wait for a new master's claim. Gereint stared down at his feet, at the plain silver rings, at the bits of cord scattered on the floor.

Amnachudran went back behind his desk and put the knife away with fussy precision. His wife nodded in calm approval, rose to her feet, smiled at Gereint—he was far too stunned to smile back—and went out of the room.

Gereint put his boots back on, hiding the rings. Then he stood up, turned, and deliberately dropped to his knees.

Amnachudran looked up sharply.

"Tell me to get up," Gereint suggested.

Amnachudran half smiled. "Stand up!" he commanded.

"No," said Gereint, and laughed. "I didn't expect you to do it. I never for one moment thought you would do it! Ah!" He flung his head back in extravagant joy, lifting his hands. "Do you doubt you've repaid me for your life? Don't doubt it!"

Amnachudran did smile this time, but shook his head. "Gereint—"

"You won't regret it," Gereint promised him. "Not by anything I do."

"I trust that I won't. Please get up, as a kindness to me? Yes, thank you, much better," he added, smiling, as Gereint climbed once more to his feet. "What will you do now? Head for Feierabiand by the fastest road?"

"I suppose so. I hardly know."

"You need rest, more food, time to think. We have supper an hour after dusk. If you're still here, I'd like to talk to you then, yes?"

Gereint hadn't expected this. He didn't quite know what he'd expected. But he said, "If you wish me to stay, I'll stay. Or if there's something you want me to do, you can tell me now."

Amnachudran shook his head again. "I don't think so. No. You need to, um, accustom yourself to the idea that you can choose your own course. No. Go for a walk. That's a suggestion, not an order, yes? Do what you like. And if I see you at supper, good."

Gereint stared at him for a moment. "I have—it was—it's been—"

He stopped. Turned without another word, since coherence was clearly beyond him at the moment, and went out.

He found a traveling pack in his room. A small hunting bow lay beside the pack, the kind meant for squirrels or birds. A dozen little arrows filled a small quiver. Gereint stood for a long moment, looking at the things. He didn't wonder who had brought him a traveler's kit: He knew it had been Amnachudran's wife.

He went quickly through the pack. A change of clothing, a blanket, a belt knife, cord. Travel food. A small bag of meal. A little oil. Flints. Candles. He laid a fingertip against one of the arrowheads and nodded. Squirrel and rabbit.

At the bottom of the pack, he found the two books he'd brought away from Fellesteden's house. Gereint looked at those for a long moment. Then he put everything back in the pack except the knife. He slid the knife's sheath onto his belt, drew the knife, looked at it. Ran the tip of one finger down its length. Turned it over in his hand, trying the hilt. Touched its blade briefly to his lips.

It was a good knife. Meant for nothing more dramatic than cutting meat or cord, slicing apples or green wood, but well made. Gereint gave it a little shove, pushing it toward the balance a fighting knife ought to have. To really alter it, he'd need tools and a forge. But he could do a little just by letting the knife know his preference.

The frilly lady's bed looked inviting. Gereint ignored it. *Go for a walk*, Amnachudran had said. He'd meant, *Test your freedom.* It was, of course, a perceptive suggestion. Gereint slung the pack over his shoulder, hung the little bow and quiver in their places, and walked out of the room. Down the hall. Down some stairs. It was a big house . . . down the largest hall he could find. He passed servants, who nodded. A pair of shaven-headed men-at-arms in livery, with swords at their hips, who also nodded politely but turned to watch as he passed. Cold ran down Gereint's spine, prickled at the back of his neck. He forced himself not to look over his shoulder, and after a moment breathed again when he found that the men had not followed. He turned the corner and found the main door of the house in front of him. It led out into the courtyard, filled with people . . . hurrying about their business. Some of them glanced up at Gereint, a few with enough interest to make his skin prickle.

But the courtyard gates were open. No one stopped Gereint from walking through them. In the light, with a clear mind, he could see how the road unrolled gently south and west through a pleasant patchwork of orchards and pastures.

Gereint followed the road through the nearest orchard, nodding to the people he passed. He didn't look back. He picked two apples—no one objected; one woman even looked up with a grin and a wave—splashed across a stream, put a gentle hill between him and the orchard, and turned across country, heading north. Glanced at the sun for his direction, turned east, and came back to the house from the northeast, where the quiet hills offered concealment. From this angle the house lay far below, a gracious presence at the heart of a gracious countryside. He found a decent rock to sit on and padded it with the blanket. He ate the apples and a strip of dried beef. Watched the house.

There was no unusual bustle that he could see. People moved around, going about the ordinary business of the day. A shepherd and two dogs brought in a small flock of sheep; a boy chased and caught a goose; women carried baskets of apples in from the orchard. No one hurried; no one seemed to feel any urgency about their chores. No one, as far as Gereint could tell, had followed him or tried to track him into the hills. There was no sign that the freedom Eben Amnachudran had offered had been any sort of deceit or trap.

The sun slid across the sky. Gereint dozed. Woke. Read some of Berusent's *Historica*. Dozed again. At dusk he finally stood up and stretched. Folded up the blanket and put it back in his pack, along with the book. Picked his way down the hill alongside the little stream, skirted the new pond with its raw-clay bank, and came back to the courtyard gates. The gates were standing open. He went through them.

A man-at-arms posted by the gates moved in the dimness. Gereint stopped.

The man-at-arms looked Gereint up and down. Said, expressionless, "The honored Amnachudran said he's expecting you. I am to ask, do you wish the gates left open tonight?"

Gereint stared back at him. "Not if your custom is to close them."

The man-at-arms shrugged. He said, "There's a man to show you where to go."

There was in fact a servant woman, who looked Gereint up and down in quite a different manner than the man-at-arms had, smiling in appreciation of his height. Being looked at by a woman was an entirely different experience without the brand. The woman said cheerfully, "The family is dining in the little hall. I'll take you there. May I take your pack? I'll put it safe in your room . . ."

Gereint let her take it.

The little hall turned out to be a spacious room with a single table and long sideboard, appointed in rich wood and dark, quiet colors. The table was covered with dishes of sliced beef and bread, late carrots and early parsnips, beans with bits of crisp pork . . . Gereint's mouth watered, despite the apples he'd eaten earlier.

Amnachudran was at the head of the table. The "family" consisted of Amnachudran, Lady Emre, a dark-bearded man of about
thirty—one of their sons, Gereint assumed—and, at least tonight, no
one else. The family evidently served itself; there were no servants in
the room. The son glanced up at Gereint with friendly curiosity; Gereint guessed his father hadn't told him every detail of his recent adventures. Lady Emre smiled a welcome. Amnachudran himself
smiled in welcome and what seemed relief. So the man had not been
as confident of Gereint's return as he'd seemed. That was, in a way,
reassuring.

An extra place was set at the table. Amnachudran gestured an invitation that was not merely kindness, Gereint understood. It *was* kindness;
he didn't doubt the man's natural sympathy. But it was also a test, of sorts.
Of whether he could use tableware like a civilized man? Or, no. More of
whether he could put off a slave's manner and behave not merely like a
civilized man but like a free man. He did not even know the answer to
that question himself.

Gereint nodded to Emre Tanshan and again to the son, walked forward and took the offered chair. Lady Emre passed him a platter of
beef; the son shifted a bowl of carrots to make room for it.

"Your day was pleasant?" Amnachudran asked politely.

"Very restful, honored sir," said Gereint. He took a slice of the beef
and a few carrots.

"Take more beef," Lady Emre urged him. "One needs food after
hard healing."

Gereint took another slice of beef, nodding polite thanks when
Lady Emre handed him the bowl of beans, and said courteously, "You
are yourself, like your husband, a healing mage, lady?" Yes, he remembered Amnachudran saying something like that . . .

Emre Tanshan waved a casual hand. "Oh, well . . . more or less."

"My lady wife is a true healing mage," Amnachudran explained.
"She is the one who healed us both. Not like me at all; I couldn't have
managed anything as difficult as your knee. I am, ah. More of a scholar
than a practitioner, you understand? My skill lies with, hmm. With injuries that are . . . symbolic or . . . one might say, those that have a
philosophical element."

Like scars from a *geas* brand, evidently. Gereint couldn't remember ever having heard of any such surgical specialty, but he nodded.

Amnachudran made a small, disparaging gesture. "Philosophically, I have some skill, I think. My practical ability . . . I removed the
scar, but I didn't guess the procedure would cause you such terrible
pain. And then it was too late to stop. I'm very sorry—"

Without even thinking about it, Gereint set his hands flat on the table and leaned forward. "Eben Amnachudran. I beg you will not apologize to me for anything."

The scholar stopped, reddening.

His son said earnestly, "But after you rescued my father from the river and dragged him all the way to our doorstep, I'd think it would be my father in your debt, honored sir, and not the other way 'round, whatever old and symbolic injury he eased for you."

The son wasn't much younger than Gereint himself. Standing, he would likely be taller than his father, broader in the shoulder, a good deal less plump. The shape of his face was his mother's, but his cheekbones were more prominent and his jaw more angular. His black hair was cropped very short, short enough to suggest he had recently shaved his head in the common soldier's style. His beard was also like a soldier's; maybe he had recently been with the army. Either way, his honest curiosity was hard to answer. Gereint said after a moment, "I suppose it's a debt that cuts both ways," and took some parsnips.

"Not from the account I heard," the young man declared enthusiastically. "Though I suppose we always feel our own debts most keenly. Still, it's a great service you did our household, honored sir; never doubt it."

Gereint felt his own face heat. He muttered, "You're kind to say so." He dipped a piece of bread in gravy and ate the bread to give himself an excuse to let the conversation go on without him.

"My eldest son, Sicheir," Amnachudran said to Gereint. "Sicheir is a more practical man than I. He is an engineer. He will be leaving for Dachsichten in the morning. The Arobern is gathering engineers there, you may know."

Gereint had not known, though he was grateful for the change of topic. He nodded. It made sense that the Arobern, King of Casmantium, would command his engineers to gather in Dachsichten, crossroads of the whole country. There, the great east-west road met the river road that ran the whole length of the country from north to south. Everything and everyone passed through Dachsichten.

"We're to head west from Dachsichten," Sicheir explained, as Gereint had already surmised. The young man leaned forward, speaking rapidly in his enthusiasm. "We are to widen and improve that rough little mountain road from Ehre across the mountains into Feierabiand. It's part of the settlement the Arobern made with the Safiad king. He"—meaning the Arobern, Gereint understood—"wants a road a spear-cast wide, paved with great stones, with bridges running straight across all the chasms. It will be a great undertaking. We'll have to lay down massive buttresses to support the road through the mountain passes, and devise wholly new bridge designs, and new methods of grading—there's never been another road so ambitious in Casmantium, probably not *anywhere*."

It surprised Gereint that the Arobern had gotten any concessions at all out of the Feierabianden king, under the circumstances. But that the Arobern would then design a massive, hugely ambitious road—*that* wasn't surprising. He nodded.

Eben Amnachudran cleared his throat. "You might go west with Sicheir. If you wish. It's the long way 'round, to be sure, going so far south before you head west—I'd understand if you preferred to make your own way through the mountains after all. But in these troubled days a man puts himself at risk traveling alone. A good many brigands have appeared, far more than usual—preying on the refugees heading south from Melentser, you know. Besides, a good road under your feet cuts miles off the journey, as they say." He offered Gereint a platter. "More bread?"

Eben Amnachudran came to find Gereint later, long after the household had retired for the night, after even most of the servants were abed. Gereint was still awake. He was standing, fully dressed, in front of the long mirror in his room, studying his unmarked face and thinking about the advice Merrich Berchandren suggested for travelers in his book on customs and courtesy. Among other recommendations, Berchandren suggested that "an uncertain guest might best speak quietly, smile frequently, and depart discreetly." The line did not make clear whether this advice was meant to apply when the guest or the situation was uncertain. Or, considering Berchandren's subtlety, both.

Gereint twitched when the knock came. But it was a quiet knock, the sort of circumspect rap that a man on the edge of sleep might ignore. Nothing aggressive or alarming. Gereint swung the door wide, found—of course—Amnachudran waiting there, and stepped back, inviting the scholar to enter with a gesture.

Amnachudran came in and stood for a moment, looking around. "This is my daughter's room," he commented. "I have four sons, but only one daughter; youngest of the lot. She hasn't stayed here for several years, but we keep the room for her—unless we have a guest, of course. It may perhaps be," the older man glanced around doubtfully, "a little feminine."

Gereint assured him solemnly that the room was the very essence of perfection, adding, "According to the precepts of Entechsan Terichsekiun, who declares for us that aesthetic perfection lies both in the flawless detail and the eye that appreciates it, and which of us would dare argue with the greatest of philosophers?"

Amnachudran laughed. "Any other philosopher, as I'm sure you know very well! But, you know, that you would quote Terichsekiun makes me wonder . . . My daughter lives in Breidechboden. Tehre. She's a maker, like you. Or, maybe not quite like you. She works on these, ah"—he gestured broadly—"these abstruse philosophical things. Nothing as practical as waterproof saddlebags. I may be something of a philosopher myself, if hardly in Terichsekiun's class, but I can't say I understand my daughter's work."

Gereint, wondering where Amnachudran was going with this digression, made a polite sound to show he was listening.

"Well, you see . . . I know my daughter's been searching for another maker who might help her do something or other. Someone intelligent and experienced, with a powerful, flexible gift. It's important to her, but she hasn't found anyone who suits her."

Gereint wanted to say, *You want me to go to* Breidechboden? *You do know there's no city I want to visit less?* Instead, he made another politely attentive sound, *Hmm?*

"Yes, well she *will* tell fools they're fools. I've advised her to keep her tongue behind her teeth, but she can't seem to. She's not precisely rude—well, she can be, I suppose. My wife says she would have an easier time of it if she were married, though I don't know . . ."

Gereint said *hmm* again. He could easily believe that any man a wealthy, well-born woman maker approached would take her unmarried status as an opportunity or a challenge. Especially if she told him he was a fool. Especially if she was pretty. If she followed after her mother, Tehre would be small and pretty and plump—the sort of girl a man might well take too lightly. Until she called him a fool and proved she was more intelligent than he was. Then he would be angry and embarrassed and probably twice a fool. That seemed likely enough.

He had known Amnachudran wanted something from him. This particular suggestion surprised him. The scholar wanted *Gereint* to go meet his *own cherished daughter* in, of all places, *Breidechboden*? He hesitated, trying to find a polite way to express his hesitation. A pointblank refusal would be churlish. He owed Amnachudran a great deal, not only for removing the brand, but also . . . In a way, he realized, he also owed the scholar for simply reminding Gereint that true, profound kindness existed, when, in Fellesteden's house, he'd come to doubt it. It was as though . . . as though Amnachudran's act had redeemed all his memories of kindness and compassion and generosity, limned all those memories with brilliance that cast years of horror into shadow.

That was what he owed Amnachudran. But . . . Breidechboden?

"Of course, I know you didn't intend to go to Breidechboden,"

Amnachudran said apologetically. "I'm sure you'd be concerned about meeting someone who might recognize you. But I also have a friend in the capital. A surgeon mage, a true master with the knife." He made a vague gesture. "There's—theoretically—a way to remove those, um, rings. They can't be cut, you know, except by the cold magecraft that made them. But any sufficiently skilled surgeon mage ought to be able to detach the tendon from the bone, do you see? Remove the rings whole, reattach the tendons . . ." He trailed off, caught by the intensity of Gereint's stillness.

Gereint did not speak. He couldn't have spoken to save his life. He only stared at Amnachudran.

The scholar dipped his head apologetically. "The difficult part is reattaching the tendons. If the surgeon isn't sufficiently skilled, the, um, patient would, well. You see."

Gereint did, vividly. Fellesteden had driven him to risk death in the desert. But not even to escape Fellesteden had Gereint ever considered crippling himself.

"I wouldn't dare attempt it," Amnachudran explained. "But my friend could manage that sort of surgical mage-craft." He hesitated and then added, "I'm fairly certain."

"Would he?" Gereint asked after a moment. "He would do that for me?" His tone had gone husky. He cleared his throat. It didn't help.

"Ah, well . . . I can't say that my friend has done any such surgery in the past." Amnachudran's tone implied that although he couldn't *say* it, it was true. "But I think it's possible he might be willing. As a favor to me, and for, ah, other reasons. I'd write a letter for you to take to him, of course. If you were willing to go to Breidechboden."

Gereint said nothing. Interfering with a *geas* was thoroughly illegal. But Amnachudran had already done it himself, and it seemed clear he knew very well that this friend of his had done the same and would be willing to do it again.

"You're a strongly gifted maker. Aren't you? Modesty aside?"

"Well," Gereint managed, still trying to wrap his mind around the possibility of true freedom, "Yes, but—"

"And if you did go to Breidechboden, you'd need a place to stay and a respectable person to vouch for you. Tehre could provide you with both of those. And," he gave Gereint a faintly apologetic, faintly defiant look, "Tehre really does seem to require the services of a really good maker, or so I gather from her most recent letter."

"Your daughter . . . you . . ."

Amnachudran tilted his head, regarding Gereint shrewdly. "Should I mistrust you? I don't assume my judgment is infallible. But as the

Arobern's appointed judge for the district north of Tanshen, I've had a good deal of experience assessing men's characters, and so has my wife, and in this case we're both fairly confident—"

"You're a judge?" Gereint was startled, almost shocked. But . . . at the same time, perhaps that explained why the scholar had felt himself able to interfere with the *geas*. He didn't exactly have the right; no one had the right to interfere with a legally set *geas*. And in fact the king famously held any of his judges to stricter account for breaking any law than an ordinary man. But still . . . a judge might feel he *ought* to have that right.

Amnachudran looked at him, puzzled. "Yes, I petitioned for the position some years past. Having to run down to Tashen every time we wanted a judge was so inconvenient. Everyone seems to prefer to simply come to me. Ah—does it make a difference? I can't see why it should."

It did make a difference, if not to Amnachudran then to Gereint. In some strange way, Amnachudran's generosity seemed to negate that other, long-ago judge's harshness. Gereint didn't know how to put this feeling into words, however.

After a moment, the scholar shrugged. "Trustworthiness, like soundness of design, can only be proved in the test. If you choose to go to Breidechboden, I think we will both find our best hopes proved out. I've a letter of introduction for you." He took a stiff, leather envelope out of his belt pouch and held it out to Gereint. "The man's name isn't on it. I'll tell you his name. It's Reichteier Andlauban. Anybody in Breidechboden could direct you to his house." He hesitated, studying Gereint. "You needn't decide right away. Or even before leaving this house, whether heading south or west or north."

Gereint had heard of Andlauban. Everybody had. If there were two better surgeon mages in all of Casmantium, there were not three. He said, a touch drily, "I think I can decide right away. I'll take your letter and go to Breidechboden. If your daughter will offer me a place to stay in the city, I'll take that, too, of course. I'm sure I'll find her work interesting."

Amnachudran gave Gereint a long, searching stare. "I'm not trying to coerce you," he said earnestly.

"Save perhaps with generosity."

Amnachudran gave a faintly surprised nod, perhaps not having quite realized this himself. "Yes, perhaps." He hesitated another moment, then merely nodded a good night and went out.

Gereint stared down at the envelope in his hand.

Andreikan Warichteier said that the cold magecraft that made the *geas* should break in Feierabiand, where no cold mages practiced their craft. He claimed that the gentle earth mages of the west forbade *geas* bonds to be imposed on any man, and laid down a powerful magic of breaking and loosing at the border to see their proscription was carried out. A contemporary and rival philosopher, Entechsan Terichsekiun, agreed that a *geas* could not be carried into Feierabiand, but argued that the limitation was a natural quality of the other kingdom. Feirlach Fenescheiren, not so widely read in the modern day, but a careful scholar whom Gereint had generally found reliable, disagreed with them both. Instead, he credited the Safiad kings with the proscription of every kind of cold magecraft—and warned that the Safiads would regret that proscription if they ever found themselves opposing the desert of fire and silence, as Casmantium was always required to oppose it.

Of course, Berentser Gereimarn, writing a hundred years later than any of the three, said that was all nonsense and that nothing whatsoever prevented cold magecraft and all its sorcery from working perfectly in Feierabiand or Linularinum or any country, however far west one went. Gereimarn was not the most reliable of natural philosophers, but Pareirechan Lenfarnan said the same thing, and he had been a more careful scholar.

But every single philosopher Gereint had ever read agreed that if the *geas* rings could be removed, the *geas* would come off with them. And Reichteier Andlauban, with his skill in surgery and magecraft, could surely detach and reattach tendon from bone if any man could. Eben Amnachudran had clearly implied the man had done so in the past.

At last, Gereint opened the envelope and slipped out the folded letter within. It seemed to be exactly what it should be: a personal letter, asking—as a personal favor—for an unnamed man to provide an unnamed service to the bearer of the letter. There was a clear indication, reading behind the ink, that both men agreed a favor was owed—and that, in any case, the man asked was not likely to object to the particular service requested. Gereint put the letter back into its envelope. When he finally undressed and lay down on the bed, he kept the envelope under his hand, as though there were some risk it might vanish before dawn if not constantly guarded.

In the morning, an hour after dawn, Gereint found Lady Emre in the breakfast room before her husband. It was a small room, very feminine, with delicately carved furnishings all in pale colors. Emre Tanshan, at the head of the graceful breakfast table, looked very much at home in it. Gereint said, "Ah—you were aware—that is, your husband *did* tell you—"

Lady Emre smiled with uncomplicated satisfaction. "Oh, yes. My daughter will be so pleased if you can help her make sense of whatever it is she's trying to work out," she assured Gereint. She nodded graciously toward the chair across from hers. "Have some eggs. You're too thin, you know. I suggested, in fact, that Eben should ask you to go meet Tehre."

Gereint could not quite find an appropriate response to this. But he did fill his plate.

"My daughter will appreciate you, I think," Lady Emre continued comfortably. "Especially if you quote Entechsan Terichsekiun to her at frequent intervals. Have you read his *On the Strength of Materials* as well as his *Nomenclature*? She *will* quote all this natural philosophy about materials and structures and the compulsion of tension compared with the persuasion of compression, or perhaps it's the other way around. Have some of this apple cake."

The apple cake was heavy, moist with the sweet liquor the cook had drizzled over it, and redolent of summer. Gereint let himself be persuaded to have a second slice. He *had* read *Materials*, but he could not at the moment recall what Terichsekiun had had to say about tension and compression.

"Now, my son is, as you know, going south to Dachsichten. He'll travel with half a dozen men-at-arms. There's some risk on the road south, you know; not everyone from Melentser departed in good order. You might go with Sicheir as far as Dachsichten, if you chose. He does know all the good inns along the way, though you're not likely to get anything better than mutton stew or boiled beef until you reach Breidechboden, I suppose."

Gereint nodded noncommittally. He did not say that buying mutton stew or boiled beef in any inn, and eating it in the common room like any free man, was a luxury he hadn't dreamed of for nineteen years.

"Good morning," said the architect of his new freedom from the doorway. Eben Amnachudran gave his lady wife a fond smile and Gereint a searching look.

Gereint got to his feet with a deference ingrained by long habit, then flushed, unable for a confusing moment to tell whether he'd shown a guest's proper regard for his host or a slave's shameful obsequiousness to his master.

Amnachudran, with characteristic kindness, showed no sign of noticing Gereint's uncertainty. He said cheerfully, hefting a large pouch bound up with a leather thong, "I have several books I'm sending to Tehre; you can show them to any patrol officer who asks." He set the pouch on the table at Gereint's elbow.

Thus furnishing a legitimate reason for Gereint's presence in the capital; the city patrol routinely turned indigents away at the gate. Only travelers who could show either some means of support or proof of legitimate business in the city were welcome in Breidechboden.

"A copy of Garaneirdich's *The Properties of Materials* and Dachse-chreier's *Making with Wood*," Amnachudran went on. "And a copy of Wareierchen's *Philosophy of Making*. She has that, but this copy has all the appendices, not just the first. I know you'll take great care of them. And I'm including a letter for Tehre, covering them. And explaining, ah—"

"Me," Gereint said, recovering his composure. He sat down again at the table, shifting the platter of apple cake and one of sausages toward Eben Amnachudran's place.

"Not in great detail," Amnachudran assured him, sitting down and regarding the cake with enthusiasm. "Emre, my dear—"

"Summer Gold apples, and that's the last of the berry liquor," Lady Emre answered. "Have a slice, and be sure to tell the cook how nicely the liquor sets off the apples; you know how he frets."

Amnachudran cut himself a generous slice, tasted it, and closed his eyes briefly in bliss. "Mmm. I'll be certain to reassure him. The last of the liquor, do you say? My dear, shouldn't the brambles be bearing soon? Let's remember to send the children berrying as soon as possible, yes? Now, Gereint, do you mean to travel with Sicheir as far as Dachsichten, or make your own way south?"

"I'd think travel between Tashen and Dachsichten must be a little hazardous just now, for a man on his own."

Amnachudran gave a serious nod. "It is, unfortunately. We really must do something soon about all the brigands. So you'll go with Sicheir, then? Good, then. I do hope you will find yourself able to work with my daughter."

Gereint let his mouth crook. "I'm sure it will be impossible for her to offend me."

Lady Emre smiled at him warmly, and Amnachudran laughed. He waved his fork in the air. " 'Three imperturbable things there be: the indifferent sky, the sums of mathematics, and a man too wise to be proud.' Though I always thought that *pride* was not quite the concept Teirench-oden wanted there."

"Vanity, perhaps," Lady Emre offered. Her wry glance Gereint's way suggested her suspicion that life had taught him the dispensability of vanity. Gereint lowered his eyes before her too-perceptive gaze.

"Very likely," agreed Amnachudran. He leaned back in his chair. "Now, Gereint, I have some coin for you; enough for you to get to Breidechboden and then through the gates. Breidechboden is not a kind city to the indigent; if you do any work for Tehre, make sure she remembers to pay you what it's worth."

"You've already been very generous—"

" 'My friend, if I am too generous, I can only hope you will forgive me and believe I don't intend to compel you with the bonds of gratitude.' "

Gereint blinked. He said at last, "Banrichte Maskeirien. Some epic or other . . ."

"Yes, the Engeieresgen cycle; very good." Amnachudran paused. Then he said kindly, "I would not dare try to improve upon Maskeirien's words."

Gereint considered the older man. "If I am compelled by the bonds of gratitude, it is because I choose to be."

Amnachudran was silent for a moment. Then he stood up, came to Gereint, and laid two fingers on Gereint's cheek where the scar of the brand had been. "As long as I do not regret this. I think I can trust you for that."

"You can," Gereint promised him. He met Lady Emre's wry gaze, including her in that promise.

CHAPTER 3

Gereint traveled with Sicheir Amnachudran and half a dozen men-at-arms. From Amnachudran's house, it was twelve miles south to Tashen. Because they did not leave the scholar's house until noon and were not pressed by any need for haste, they stayed the night at an inn in the town. No one paid Gereint any attention: Travelers passing through Tashen were nothing worth comment, no doubt especially after the flood of refugees from Melentser had passed through. That perfect lack of interest was even more to be treasured than a comfortable bed.

From Tashen, it was only about fifteen miles south to Metichteran, all on a good road. There, the northernmost bridge across the Teschanken River led from East Metichteran to West Metichteran. Gereint looked down with interest at the bridge as they crossed the river.

This bridge had been built so that that Casmantium, invading Meridanium, could send half its army down from the north upon the Meridanian forces. Casmantian builders had flung the bridge across the river in a single night and a day, according to Sichan Meiregen's epic, and the Casmantian soldiers had come down upon the armies of Meridanium like reapers upon wheat. Meridanium had lost its king and its independence and had become merely one Casmantian province among many. Then, in the more peaceful era that followed, there had been time for towns to grow up and roads to be built . . . but nothing that had been built in the north had stood longer or more solidly than Metichteran's bridge. Though Gereint sincerely doubted any account that claimed a night and a day sufficient for its building, no matter how great the general or how gifted his builders. It was a very solid-looking bridge.

Then they headed south again through the low, rocky hills along the river road. Here the road was narrow and rough, and though there were obvious signs of large numbers of recent travelers, there were few now on the road. This was a stretch of farmless backcountry where brigands might well wait for vulnerable travelers, but theirs was too large a party to tempt any brigands who might have been watching the road. They passed other travelers, slow-moving refugees who had left Melentser only right at the deadline. Those travelers had also been warned about the brigands, clearly. Very few of them traveled in parties smaller than Sicheir's, and those that did looked decidedly anxious.

From Metichteran, they traveled thirty miles south along the Teschanken River to Pamnarichtan, where the swift little Nerintsan River came out of the hills to join the wider Teschanken. The inn at the confluence was not very impressive, but the confluence itself was a great sight. The upper Teschanken flowed clear and swift from the north, and the Nerintsan came down in a quick, cheerful dash from the steep hills, but the lower Teschanken that resulted from their joining was very different in character from either northern stretch of river. It was broad and deep, colored a rich brown with sediment, seemingly lazy but treacherous, its currents running in unexpected directions. No one would try to build a bridge across the South Teschanken, but there was a ferry to Raichboden, southernmost town in the once independent province of Meridanium. Riverboats appeared here where the Teschanken was navigable; inns were crowded with boat crews as well as accommodating travelers off the road.

"Can't we try a boat?" asked the youngest of the men-at-arms, Bechten, craning wistfully to look after one that floated past.

"Oh, to be sure. The price will be high with all those folk crowding south from Melentser. But you can sell your horse for passage and walk on your own legs from Dachsichten back home," one of his elders answered, not unkindly. "No, boy; the road's a good one and the weather's fine, so don't tempt the sky with a grumble, eh? Besides, see, the river's running low. You wouldn't think it, looking at the water here, but once they get farther down, those boats will be snagging up and pressing even their paying passengers to get them over the bars."

So they rode at an easy pace, and the weather held fair; they came to Dachsichten six days after leaving Eben Amnachudran's house.

Dachsichten collected important roads that ran from the north and the south and the west. It was not a pretty town, but it was crowded and busy; the roads around Dachsichten thronged with respectable carters and farm wagons, with drovers and merchants' convoys, with the slow-moving wagons of families resettling from Melentser, and the carriages of the wealthy, and swift-horsed couriers.

"There won't be trouble with brigands from here," Sicheir commented to Gereint. He was standing on the tiny balcony of their room at the inn, looking out over the crowded city streets. It was not a good inn, but the only one they had found with rooms still to let: Many of the refugees from Melentser still lingered in Dachsichten while they decided where to go. Some would stay, probably. Especially the less well-to-do. Dachsichten was not a pretty town, but it was prosperous; folk looking for work might well find it here.

But it left the inns crowded. With Sicheir on the balcony, there wasn't room for Gereint to even set a foot on it. That was well enough; it was, no doubt, extremely unlikely that anyone from Melentser would happen to glance up and recognize him, but why take the chance?

"The men can all go back north in the morning, and we'll part company," Sicheir added. The young man looked over his shoulder at Gereint. "I'll be sorry for that. You've a good memory for the odd tale out of the histories. I see why my father thought you might work well with Tehre."

Gereint murmured something appropriate. He was distracted by a sudden desperate temptation to declare that he'd changed his mind, that Breidechboden was no longer his destination. He could head west to the pass at Ehre with Sicheir, test once and for all the notion that crossing the border would break the *geas* magic, avoid any possible encounter with any previous master or cousin or anyone else in Breidechboden who might recognize him.

Of course, if he did that, he would never find Reichteier Andlauban, never have the opportunity to ask the surgeon mage to remove the *geas* rings. Even if the *geas* itself broke crossing the border, Gereint knew that the physical presence of the rings would fret him for the rest of his life. He could endure that. There were far worse things than carrying merely the *symbol* of bondage. Even so . . . Gereint wanted the rings gone with an intensity that ached through all his bones.

And he had promised Amnachudran he would go to his daughter's house.

Gereint had spent years learning to disbelieve in the existence of true kindness. And then Eben Amnachudran and his family had effortlessly demonstrated that all the painful lessons he'd worked so hard to learn had been wrong. It had been as though the world had suddenly expanded before him, reclaiming all the generous width he remembered from his distant childhood. And Gereint had realized, gradually— was still realizing—that he'd spent all those years wanting nothing more than a reason to believe in that generosity. And Amnachudran had given him that reason.

So in the morning Gereint said nothing, but swung up on his borrowed horse and rode with Sicheir only so far as the western gate of Dachsichten. Then he left the younger man with a handclasp and a nod and rode south without looking back, through a pearly morning mist that drifted across the city and glittered on the slate roofs of the houses and cobblestones of the streets.

The mist turned into a cold rain before he even reached Dachsichten's southern gate, and then the rain stayed with him as he rode south. The road was too well made to go to sloppy mud; water simply beaded on its surface and ran away down its sloping edges. But the persistent rain got down the collar of his shirt and made the reins slippery in his hands, and he rode with his shoulders hunched and his head bowed. He tried not to take the rain as a sign of things to come.

The character of the countryside changed south of Dachsichten, becoming flatter and richer. Gereint rode now through a tight and tidy patchwork of fields and pastures and orchards, with woodlots few and much prized. The river rolled along on his left, the color of muddy slate, rain dimpling its surface. Boats with brightly painted trim slid past him, running downstream at a pace no horse could sustain. But as the man-at-arms had suggested, Gereint not infrequently saw one or another boat snagged up, the men of their crews cursing as they worked to free it.

There were few inns south of Dachsichten, but far more farms that offered travelers meals in their huge, busy kitchens, and the hospitality of a clean, hay-sweet barn or an extra room for those who wished to barter coin or labor for a night's comfortable rest. Gereint, disgusted by the continuing bad weather, halted early his first evening out from Dachsichten, when he came to a particularly pleasant-looking farm. He stayed there an entire extra day, watching the rain fall and setting his hands to small tasks of mending and making that had proven beyond the limited skill of local makers. He even borrowed the small portable forge the farmer owned and showed the farmer's twin sons, both moderately gifted, how to repair worn pots and skillets.

It occurred to Gereint for the first time that even bearing the *geas* rings, he might not need to go to Feierabiand to find a new life; that he might trade his skill as a maker for a place at almost any normal, peaceful farm and disappear from the sight of anyone who might wish to find him. Unless, of course, someone someday caught sight of the rings. Then that new life would vanish in a heartbeat . . . No. He set his face south when the rain finally stopped and went on.

The sun came out at last, and Gereint's horse strode out with a will in the clean air, happy with its rest and with the generous measure of grain the farmer's sons had measured out for it. The most common travelers on the road were now farmers with small dog-carts and teams of wagonners with six-horse teams of enormous horses. The carts were for local travel, but the wagons were heading, loaded, to Breidechboden, or returning empty to their farms.

It had been years since Gereint had lived in Breidechboden, and he had neither intended nor wished to return. Nevertheless, a strange feeling went through him when, two days later, he finally saw the Emnerechke Gates rise up before him: great stone pillars that marked the beginning of the city proper. It was foolish to feel he'd come home. Breidechboden was not, could never again be, his home. But even so, the feeling was there, surprising him with its intensity.

A wall had once run between each of the four hills that framed the city, encircling the valley that lay in their midst. That wall had been two spear-casts thick and six high, faced with stone and huge timbers from the heart of the great forest, heavy with builders' magic so that it would stand against even the most powerful siege engines.

Berusent described the great wall of Breidechboden in his *Historica*, when he described the founding of the capital. Tauchen Breidech, one of the early kings of the original, smaller Casmantium, had built this city on a base of seven wide roads linking eight concentric circles; the outermost circle comprised the wall and its famous gates. But successive iterations of war and conquest and peace and growth had thoroughly disguised the great king's original plan. The wall had been first absorbed into the widening city and finally, after a century or so, torn down completely. Its great stones had been incorporated into the innumerable tenements and apartments and private houses that now ascended the hills, rising rank above rank, pink and creamy gold in the soft morning light. Gereint wondered whether any of those residences might possibly prove impervious to siege engines, if a catapult happened to fire against them: Berusent had not commented on whether the builders' magic might have stayed in the stones and timbers when the walls were taken apart for their materials.

The Amnachudran townhouse was set on the lee side of Seven Son Hill, which lay to the right hand of the Emnerechke Gates. Gereint gave his name—not his real name, of course—and the townhouse address to the city patrol at the Gates, explained he was a maker, showed the patrol officer the books he carried, and at last gained the necessary month's pass to the city.

"Keep this pass with you at all times," the patrol officer told him. "You're from the north? Melentser would that be? There's too many of you lot wanting into Breidechboden." His suspicious look made it clear that if not for the books and the Amnachudran name, he'd have thought Gereint might be looking not for work but for a big city in which he could profitably beg or steal.

"I'm from Meridanium," Gereint lied, and added, in order to show normal curiosity, "So a lot of Melentser refugees have come here, then?"

"All of 'em, I sometimes think," the patrol officer said sourly. "I suppose we can be grateful those cursed griffins didn't demand Tashen as well as Melentser, or we'd be flooded to the gates. Even as it is, most days there're shortages of bread and meat in the markets. You'll move on, if you take my advice. Wanenboden might be better."

Anywhere not here, was the clear subtext of that suggestion. Gereint said, "I'll likely be heading west."

"Good. But if you do decide to stay in Breidechboden, apply for a permanent residence pass as soon as you qualify. Clear? Go on, then." And he waved Gereint into the city.

The public roads were wide near the Gates, the apartments tall and well built, faced with bright-painted plaster. Only specially licensed wagons and carts were allowed into Breidechboden between dawn and dusk, so the streets offered plenty of room for people ahorse or riding in sedan chairs or walking on their own feet. Wagons and riders kept to the middle of each roadway; pedestrians and sedan chairs traveled on raised pavement walks that ran on each side of the streets, clear of the refuse that littered the roadways. Gereint headed right, toward Seven Son Hill.

The street led in an arc around the curve of the hill. The apartment blocks here were less tall but considerably finer, faced with white limestone and plaster painted to resemble marble. Then these gave way in turn to private houses with small walled gardens. Wealthy merchants and men of business lived here. If one continued around the circle, one would come eventually to the Hill of Iron, where the king's palace rose up above the common city.

The lee side of Seven Son Hill—the side that faced away from the center of Breidechboden—was a place where the private houses were large and the gardens generous. Here the facades were real marble, the doors carved and polished, and the gates decorated with the figures of dogs or horses or falcons or grotesques. The public street was much cleaner, and the private walkways that ran to each house were lined with tubs of flowers.

Tehre Amnachudran lived in one of these houses. Gereint had

known more or less what the Amnachudran townhouse must be like when her father had told him where she lived, but he was surprised again, studying it now, at the family's wealth.

The house had leaping deer figures by its gate. More deer held round porcelain lanterns on either side of its walkway; at night, each stag must seem to carry a small glowing moon between its antlers. Mosaic tiles ornamented the pillars that framed the heavy double doors of carved oak. The house itself was faced with gray marble and exotic porphyry; the windows that faced onto the street were fitted with fine, expensive glass. Beside the door, a bell cord of red silk led away into the inner reaches of the house.

Gereint stood for a long moment, holding his horse's reins and gazing at the bell cord. But if he meant to stay in Breidechboden at all, he needed a place to stay. And he trusted Eben Amnachudran. And he was, he acknowledged to himself, curious about Tehre Amnachudran Tanshan. So at last he reached out, gave the cord a strong pull, and heard the distant clangor of the bell—iron, by the sound of it, but with a mellowness to the note that was unusual for iron.

Rapid steps sounded, and the shutter in the center of the door swung open. A sweet-faced older woman gazed out at him with some surprise.

"A letter from Eben Amnachudran for his daughter," Gereint said quickly, before the woman could say anything about tradesmen not being welcome. He gave the woman the letter through the shutter, expecting her to tell him to wait and take it away to give to her mistress.

Instead, the woman gave him a long, assessing look, nodded, slipped the letter out of its leather envelope, and read it herself. Then she looked up again, this time smiling a welcome. The shutter swung closed and latched, and there was the sound of the bar being drawn away. Then the doors swung open and the woman smiled at him. "Honored sir—please be welcome," she said warmly. "My name is Fareine Reinarechtan; I have the honor to manage Lady Tehre's household. Loop your horse's reins over that stag's antlers; that's right. I'll have someone come at once to take it around to the stable. It's quite convenient, not a quarter-mile down the street, and I promise you the animal will be well cared for; everyone keeps their horses there. Come in, honored sir, and be welcome."

Gereint stepped through the door, bowing slightly. It felt . . . very strange, coming into this house as a welcome guest, with a false name in that letter of introduction and the *geas* rings hidden by his boots. "Forgive me for intruding without warning. If a message had been sent ahead, it couldn't have come far before me. May I ask whether Lady Tehre Amnachudran Tanshan is at home?"

"She is, and I'm sure she'll welcome you, but if you will be good enough to wait, honored sir . . . I am afraid Lady Tehre does not like to be interrupted while she is working, but she will be down very soon, I am sure. Permit me to show you to the kitchen while I have a room prepared for you—Esmin! Such a long way you have come, all the way from the honored Eben Amnachudran's house?"

"I was very interested in Eben Amnachudran's description of his honored daughter's work, though he was not able to be very, ah, detailed. As I've business of my own in Breidechboden, the honored Eben Amnachudran was kind enough to provide me a letter of introduction."

"A fortunate moment for my lady, I am sure. Esmin! Where *is*—? Ah, Esmin, dear! Get a room ready for our honored guest, please, and mind you make certain there are plenty of towels by the water basin. Honored sir, Lady Tehre will be down very soon, I am sure . . ." Still producing a gentle flow of chatter, the woman led the way down the hall.

The reception hall was all red marble and porphyry, with fluted columns in the best southern style and mosaics on the walls. It gave way to massive vaulted rooms just as intimidating. Thankfully, the kitchen turned out to be much more approachable. It, too, was a vast room, but comfortable and friendly. Ovens lined one end and a huge table stood at the other, with a narrow stair leading down, Gereint surmised from the cold draft, to an ice cellar. There were two assistant cooks as well as the head cook, and a clutter of girls to do the scullery chores and run errands. To Gereint's faint surprise, the cook and both her assistants were women. Was all the household female?

The cook appeared to take Gereint's bony height as an amusing challenge. She was a placid, ample woman with small black eyes set in a broad moon-face. She jiggled when she laughed, which was often. The kitchen girls clearly adored her.

"I do like men who know how to eat," she remarked with approval, offering Gereint a second plate of sandwiches after he cleared the first with gratifying speed. "That'll put some bulk on those bones, so it will. And there are cakes to finish, plenty to have some now and leave some for the evening."

Gereint was pleased and a little surprised that the household staff did not seem to stand on ceremony: There must be a formal dining room somewhere but no one suggested eating there. He and the household staff alike sat around the big table to eat the sandwiches and stole slices of apple from the girl who was slicing fruit for pastries. The girl threatened to stab their hands, but laughed.

The second round of sandwiches vanished almost as quickly as the first, but there was still one untouched plate remaining when the kitchen door swung open once more. The household staff leaped up. Gereint got to his feet as well; the cook hissed sharply at one of the girls who was slower than he to take her cue. The girl flushed dark red and jumped up as well. Lady Tehre Amnachudran Tanshan swept in just as the girl made it up.

For a small woman, Lady Tehre managed to sweep very convincingly. On a first glance, she was very little like either of her parents. She was small breasted and narrow hipped, yet she did not look boyish, either. She had dark hair; not black like Sicheir, but dark like molasses, a rich brown with golden highlights. She wore it tucked up on her head in an untidy style that went beyond casual to thoughtless. It was lovely hair. Yet she was not actually pretty—or maybe she was, but she did not hold herself with the conscious awareness of a woman who knows she is pretty.

Tehre Amnachudran had nothing of her father's visible kindness or her mother's comfortable warmth. She looked . . . not precisely stern. But if she had been tall and stately, she might have possessed an intense, striking beauty that went beyond ordinary prettiness. Because she was small and delicate, she merely looked high-strung.

And, unlike her staff, she was not very welcoming of strangers. "A maker, do you say?" she said to Fareine, doubt clear in her tone. "I don't know—I haven't been—"

"Your honored father sent him," Fareine put in smoothly. "All the way from Meridanium." Gereint had given his name as Gereint Pecheran, which was one of the most common Meridanian names.

"Oh, did he?" Lady Tehre hesitated. "Well . . . well . . . let's go to my workroom, I suppose. Fareine—"

"I'll bring you something there," the older woman promised immediately.

"Good, good," Tehre said, but absently, very much as though she had not actually heard what Fareine said. She gave Gereint a mistrustful look, but waved for him to accompany her. "You're a maker? I'm working on this problem having to do with the elongation of cracks in large structures. Of course, when you're working with masonry, stone breaks when you subject it to remotely applied tension, I'm sure you know that, but what I can't see is how the cracks shift from slow, sporadic propagation to sudden catastrophic propagation. Do you work with masonry? Large structures?"

"I have." Not often, but Gereint did not say this. Women were often makers, but very seldom engineers, but Tehre Amnachudran certainly sounded more like an engineer than an ordinary maker.

The workroom proved to be a large, cluttered room on the main floor of the house, with wide windows that probably opened to the garden, though these were all tightly shuttered. Broad papers covered with delicate sketches in ink and charcoal were unrolled and pegged down on the tables—no wonder the windows were shuttered: Too strong a breeze would not be kind to those delicate papers. Expensive lamps shed an even, steady glow over the diagrams.

Edging closer to the table nearest the door, Gereint saw that one of the sketches was a detailed diagram, heavily notated, of some sort of mechanism with unfamiliar mathematical equations tucked around the edges. He frowned at the diagram, trying to make sense of it—it looked like someone had tried to design an extremely ornate bridge, a bridge with twin exterior galleries on either side, its galleries supported by pillars and connected to the bridge proper by high arches. The design might have made more sense to an engineer than it did to Gereint, who gave up on it after a moment and turned to studying Tehre Amnachudran instead of her mysterious diagram. Fareine edged past him and set plates of sandwiches and honey cakes carefully on the edge of one of the tables that was not entirely covered by sketches.

"You probably know that cracks don't usually run dangerously in bridges or walls or ships or things like that, until they suddenly do," Tehre said to Gereint, showing no sign of noticing the plates. She tapped one of the diagrams, where mathematical equations marched down the clear space of the margin. Gereint tilted his head, trying to read the equations, but they did not seem familiar.

Tehre said, "I think it's clear there's a critical length and once a crack reaches that length, it'll run catastrophically. You'd think that as the strength of a material increases, so the critical length would increase, but obviously that's not the way it happens, yes?" She spoke rapidly, her voice sharp and demanding—or not exactly demanding, but intense.

"Because anyone knows that some very strong materials like stone can tolerate hardly any kind of crack at all before they break under tension, which is why you can build with wrought iron under tension but you always put stone under compression, yes? So we really need to think of resistance to crack propagation as a property related not to strength exactly, but to the forcefulness of the blow it takes to fracture a piece of the material, do you see? What I think—" tapping the row of equations once more, she seemed suddenly to wonder whether Gereint was following this, and stopped, looking at him with doubt.

Gereint said, "I haven't worked extensively with bridges or walls, but I'd think that what you need most is proper definitions of qualities like 'strength' and 'forcefulness' and 'toughness' and 'brittleness' and 'flexibility.' And 'stretchability,' once you start thinking about metals, because once you start thinking about crack propagation through metal, it's probably 'stretchability' that allows for greater resistance to fracture, don't you think?"

Tehre gazed at Gereint as though actually seeing him for the first time. Her eyes, an unusual bronzy green, were large and striking in her delicate face.

Then she flipped open a large book on the nearest table, paged through it rapidly until she reached blank paper, and picked up a quill. "The length of a 'safe' crack in a structure must depend on the ratio of its 'brittleness' to the amount of tensile force applied to the material," she said, writing quickly. "No! Not the amount of tensile force *applied*, but the amount actually *absorbed* by the material. And so the critical length of a crack would actually be inversely proportional to the 'stretchability' of the material." She paused and blinked down at the book. "That seems counterintuitive. But isn't that right?"

Gereint said, "It follows, but it means you need a term for 'toughness' as well as one for 'stretchability.' One is more like resistance to fracture as a result of a blow, isn't it, and the other is more like resilience under tension. Or is that right?"

"I can see you two will do well," said Fareine. "But, Tehre, don't forget, you still need to eat one of these nice sandwiches."

"What?" Tehre turned to the old woman and stared at her for a moment before actually focusing on her. Then she laughed.

Gereint was surprised at that laugh. It was a nice laugh, filled with affection and genuine amusement—at herself, at her own intensity and distractibility. It occurred to him that Tehre might well borrow a word like "distractibility" to mean "ability to slip under friction" or something of the sort, and he smiled.

"We'll go out to the garden, I suppose," Tehre suggested. "Fareine, is everything"—she waved her hands vaguely, still holding the quill—"in order?"

"Your guest is properly settled," Fareine assured her mistress. "Thank you, honored sir; if you could take these plates, I'll go fetch jugs of wine and water, shall I?" She handed over the sandwiches and cakes and bustled out again.

Gereint raised his eyebrows at Lady Tehre, meaning *Which way?*

"Through here," the lady said, swinging back a small door. She immediately went on, walking backward through the doorway into brilliant sunlight and catching herself with the automatic skill of long practice when she tripped over the step. "You're a maker, did Fareine say? Or an engineer?"

"A maker, primarily. But I was wondering the same about you, since you seemed to be thinking about building large structures . . ."

"Neither the one nor the other," the woman said, a little bitterly. She looked around, seemed to spot a nearby shaded bench as though it was the first time she'd ever seen it, and sat down. Gereint followed, offering her the plate of sandwiches again, since she seemed to have forgotten about it.

"Or maybe both," added Tehre, taking a sandwich and gazing thoughtfully down at it. She was still thinking about Gereint's question, evidently. He hadn't meant it to be so complicated. But the woman said absently, "A maker and a builder and an engineer and a philosopher . . ." She looked suddenly up at Gereint. "I'm trying to understand how things work. But some important concepts are"—she made a frustrated gesture with the sandwich—"missing. I'm sure if I just define my terms properly . . . You're quite right, by the way, that's the first thing that has to be done, but you have to work with the concepts before you see what you need names for . . ."

"I have business of my own in the city, so your father was kind enough to suggest you might wish to offer me a guest room while I'm here," Gereint said after a moment, as the lady did not seem inclined to go on with her thought.

"Yes, of course, if you like," Tehre said, but Gereint had the impression she hadn't really heard him.

"Are you going to eat that, or just wave it around? Meat is expensive since the refugees from Melentser started arriving, you know," Fareine added, returning with the promised jugs and a pair of goblets.

"Oh," said Tehre, and took a bite. But her attention remained on Gereint. No wonder she was so small, if she never ate anything without being prompted.

"Wine, honored sir?" Fareine poured for her lady and Gereint and for herself, a little wine and a good deal of water, and then settled on the end of Tehre's bench.

"What do you make?" Tehre asked Gereint abruptly.

"Small things, mostly. But all kinds of things. Knives and lanterns, belts and boots, pots and plates . . ."

The woman laughed, unexpectedly. It was the same laugh as before, quick and genuinely amused. "Not a specialist! All right. I'm mostly working philosophically right now—with the philosophy of stone and iron and wood, with the building materials of the world." She sighed. "It's hard to actually *practice* building large structures just to see how they'll break if you apply different kinds of stresses. Have you read Wareierchen?"

"Yes," Gereint said promptly. "And Dachsechreier's *Making with Wood*, and Garaneirdich's *The Properties of Materials*. What do you think of Terichsekiun?"

Tehre's small face lit up, giving her, at last, the misleading appearance of uncomplicated prettiness. "Oh, his *Strength of Materials* is so fascinating! It's so interesting that cast iron acts so much like stone, isn't it, and so different from wrought iron?" She took another bite of her sandwich and chewed absently, lost in thought.

"You seem to have been thinking about bridges," Gereint commented, and was entertained to see how Lady Tehre was instantly distracted. She jumped to her feet, set her sandwich aside half finished, said, "I'll show you; come look!" and started back toward the work-room.

Fareine, looking resigned, gathered the half-sandwich up in a cloth and followed her mistress. Gereint picked up the platter, since it didn't seem proper to simply leave it sitting on the bench, and followed them both.

The diagrams were very interesting. There were large, detailed drawings of bridge after bridge—short, flat, beam-supported bridges across narrow gullies; high-rising arches across streams; rope-supported plank bridges that looked extremely precarious. Some of the bridges were made of many small arches, some supported merely at either end.

"Are these all after real bridges?" Gereint asked, leaning over a particularly unusual bridge made of open latticework in a single extremely long, flat arch. "This can't really be to scale?"

"Oh, it is, though! That one's from Linularinum—it crosses that river at Teramondian, you know, the Meralle? Terichsekiun referred to it and had a small drawing, but this one is more accurate and much more detailed. It cost a fortune, sending a man all the way to Linularinum to draw it for me, but it was worth it. See, this bridge has a span of a hundred fifty-nine feet, but a rise of only twenty-six feet. It's made of cast iron, so it's lighter than masonry would be, do you see? And that means it pushes sideways against its foundations much less than masonry would, which is why Terichsekiun says it works, but I'm not sure that's the whole answer." She bent intently over the diagram.

Gereint watched Tehre Amnachudran study one part of the diagram and then another and then absently pick up a quill and begin working out equations in the blank space along the edge of the paper, and wondered why she'd had such trouble finding other makers to work with her. She was obsessive, yes. But what she was trying to work out was very interesting. Surely any real maker would think so?

And, also . . . he clearly did not need to worry that this woman would prove very interested in who *he* was or where *he'd* come from. It hadn't even occurred to her to wonder. Ah. That might explain a great deal, after all. That lack of interest might well offend any man who believed all women ought to find him naturally fascinating.

Gereint merely found the lack of curiosity reassuring. Restful. He glanced at Fareine, who gave him a friendly smile and stayed in the background, possibly to run any errands her mistress thought of, but more likely as a guarantor of respectability.

Tehre brought out a new diagram and pinned it open across the others. This one also showed a bridge, but not like the others. This one had chains suspended from two high, parallel semi-circular arches and a roadway of beams suspended from the chains.

"That's unusual," Gereint observed, examining the diagram. "Where's this one from?"

Tehre gave him a glance that had gone suddenly shy. "Oh, well . . . I made this one up. When I was thinking about the differences between cast iron and wrought iron and steel, and about the bridges they'll need to build when they run that road through the mountains. It's supposed to be a real road, you know, the kind that will gladden the Arobern's ambitious heart—four wagons abreast and all the fretwork to match." Despite her acerbic tone, she sounded like she would enjoy a chance to test out some new ideas in the building of a really fine road.

"Steel wire is what I'd like to use for this," Tehre added. "Only that would be much too expensive, of course. So I worked it out for wrought-iron chains. Only you'd have to have *very* good makers to make those chains and bolt them to the decking of the road—I designed that like the deck of a ship, in a way. I'd like to show you the kind of bolts I have in mind and see what you think—have you worked with wrought iron?"

"I've worked with everything," Gereint assured the woman.

"Have you? That's good," Tehre said absently. She looked around vaguely. Fareine came forward and put her half-full mug of watered wine in her hand. Tehre gazed at the older woman for a moment; then down at the mug she held with much the same air of vague surprise and sipped.

"You should eat the rest of your sandwich, too," Fareine said, offering it.

"I suppose." Tehre allowed the woman to press it on her.

"Cakes, honored sir?" Fareine offered him the other platter.

"Don't get honey on the diagrams!" Tehre exclaimed, and then, with sudden pleasure, "Oh, are there cakes? Thank you, Fareine, but mind the honey."

The older woman smiled patiently and passed around damp cloths to take care of the honey.

"So," Tehre said to Gereint, and then paused as though unsure how to proceed. Then she asked cautiously, as though it was a potentially dangerous question, "So have you worked on bridges before? Or the ways structures fail?"

"Not specifically," Gereint admitted. "It sounds interesting, though."

"Everything's interesting," Tehre responded. She didn't say it as though she was making a joke; there was nothing arch or sidelong or humorous in her tone. She just said it. *Everything's interesting*, exactly as though she meant precisely that. Then she added, more wistfully, "But I do think I'm missing something: some fundamental concept that would let me see more clearly how bridges and walls and ships and little mechanisms like bows and clocks and dumbwaiters all work. I think I'm missing something that would help explain bridges and crack propagation and, and, I don't know. Why ropes break and stone shatters and metals bend." She ate a cake in two impatient bites, gazing moodily down at the diagram on the table.

"I've been mostly in the practical end of making," Gereint told her. "But I think you're asking good questions. You can tell me what you think about strength and cracks and resilience, and maybe I can help you come up with proper definitions of the qualities of materials. Why should Garaneirdich and Wareierchen and Terichsekiun have all the fun? Though maybe the first task is to clarify what all those great philosophers said and see how their terms match up to each other and the qualities you want to define."

Tehre gazed at Gereint with, possibly, the first real attention she'd paid him. "You've read all the philosophers? Yes, you have, haven't you? You'd understand what you read and summarize properly?"

She sounded doubtful on this last, as though, if put to the test, he'd possibly prove to be functionally illiterate. Gereint tried not to smile. He said gravely, "I think so, yes."

"Well, then. Well, then, if you could do that for me—exactly what you said—I have these equations I'm trying to work out—it would save me a great deal of time and then, you're right, maybe it would be easier to see what qualities are already defined and what Wareierchen and Terichsekiun might have missed—does that sound too arrogant?" she added, once again doubtful.

Gereint tried, again, not to smile. It was getting harder. "Not to me."

"All right. Good. Good! I'll show you my library, then. Or Fareine— Fareine! Would you show, ah . . ."

"Gereint Pecheran," Fareine reminded her.

Tehre blushed. "Of course!" she snapped. "Would you show our honored guest to the library? And get him anything he wants? Quills, paper, whatever? Thank you so much, Fareine; I don't know where I'd be without you. Honored Gereint, would you join me later, after I've had time to sort out these equations about cracks that run or stay? I think the thing to do after that, really, is set up the right kind of situation with masonry under tension and then see what we can get cracks to do . . ." She trailed off in thought.

"This way, honored sir, if you please," Fareine said to Gereint, and held a hand out to invite him to go before her.

"The honored lady doesn't mean to sound . . . That is to say . . ." the woman began, earnestly, as she guided him through the halls of the great house.

"Yes, that's plain." Gereint let himself smile at last, and then laugh. "She's not like anyone I have ever met. Not even like any maker I've ever met! She's working out *equations* about crack propagation? I don't recall even Terichsekiun explaining how to predict whether a particular crack will run instead of rest. That would be a very valuable contribution to the philosophy of materials and making, if she could do it."

"She'll do it. As you said, she might as well be an engineer as a maker: She thinks large-scale as often as small. And she really is a philosopher." Fareine, too, was smiling, as she registered Gereint's tone of amusement and approval. "Allow me to show you the library, honored sir, and then your suite. I hope you will be comfortable in this house. If you find any aspect of Amnachudran hospitality lacking, please bring the lack to my attention."

Not Tehre's, Gereint understood. He nodded.

The library was a good one, though very heavily biased toward natural philosophy and, to Gereint's mind, severely lacking in poetry. He laid out the books Eben Amnachudran had sent; then, after a moment's reflection, added the ones he'd stolen from Fellesteden to the library shelves. They went some little way toward remedying the basic lack of history and poetry—and they would be safe if anything happened to him. He tried not to imagine any of the things that phrase might encompass.

The household served the evening meal late, and more formally than Gereint had guessed from the sandwiches in the kitchen, though the dining room was at least not vastly oversized. Fareine attended with her mistress, of course, and so did one other young woman who Fareine introduced as Tehre's companion. Gereint gathered that she was a chaperone, meant to attend Tehre while Fareine saw to the business of running the household. From her shy manner, he guessed she'd just been elevated to her new position because of Gereint's arrival. Her name was Meierin. She was a little younger than Tehre, quiet voiced, pretty in an unassuming way. Gereint suspected that the girl was also stronger minded than she looked, if Fareine had chosen her for her mistress' protection.

The dinner was elaborate, the new cook showing her skills to her mistress' guest. Gereint made sure to comment on the dishes, which were all very good.

Tehre didn't seem to notice what she ate, except that when Gereint commented, she would blink, focus on the food for a moment, and say something like, "Oh, yes, very pretty," or "Why, this *is* a very nice way to have duck—do we have it this way often, Fareine?" Then she would go back to arguing with Gereint over the right way to define tensile strength. Gereint felt he was talking more during this one meal than he had in years, but neither Fareine nor Meierin could discuss makers' philosophy and Tehre was hard to redirect to more common topics.

"They say the griffin's desert is inimical to creatures of earth," Fareine commented at last, making a valiant effort to drag the conversation by main force to subjects other than tensile strength. "I gather you met the honored Amnachudran in the desert—what is it truly like?"

"Oh, yes, can you tell us about the desert?" Meierin asked eagerly, leaning forward.

"I wonder what is meant by 'inimical' in this context," Tehre said, diverted at last. "It would be interesting to visit the desert and examine its qualities." Then she blinked and asked, "But what was my father doing in the desert?"

"Collecting books from a private estate," Gereint explained.

"Oh, yes, that sounds like him."

"And Gereint met your father at the edge of the desert and helped your father when he met with an accident—it's all in the letter your honored father sent, Lady Tehre. The honored Gereint saved his life when your father met with an accident on his way home."

"Did you?" Tehre said, looking at Gereint in surprise. "Then we're all very much in your debt. What kind of accident?"

"A fall. Crossing the river. Anybody would have done the same." Gereint was uneasy at this close attention to his personal history.

Fareine shook his head. "That's not what the letter says." She turned to her mistress. "The honored Gereint dragged your father all the way home on a pole litter, collapsed as soon as the gates were opened, and raved in a delirium all that night and half the next day, for all Lady Emre could do."

A *delirium*. That was how Eben Amnachudran had explained the screaming to his household, of course. Gereint tried to keep his expression blank. Tehre was gazing at him with surprise and, for once, focused attention; Fareine with warm approval; Meierin with shy appreciation. Gereint said uncomfortably to Tehre, "Your honored father has been very kind to me."

"Apparently he had every reason to be," Tehre responded tartly. "But sending you to me wasn't kindness, I expect. Except maybe to me."

"I'm grateful for a comfortable place to stay in Breidechboden while I conduct my own business here." This was an open bid to change the subject, and Gereint expected an inquiry about what his business might be. He would then make something up or else evade answering, and with any luck they would be off this particular topic.

Instead, Tehre said, "Well, I shall certainly want to read that letter—but not now, if it makes you uncomfortable, Gereint. What have you found in the library? Sufficient?"

Gereint paused for a moment. Then he said, "Everything I could want, honored lady, except that I might like a copy of Teirenchoden's epic about the war between Ceirinium and Feresdechadren. Your honored father has a copy, but your library lacks one. And, come to that, a copy of Sichan Meiregen's epic about the later war between Meridanium and Casmantium. The one that describes the war in the fifth century, not the fourth. You have very little history in your library, and that *is* a lack because I'm sure the descriptions of the fortifications and the siege engines that breached them would interest you."

Tehre made a little *Hmm!* sound and looked at Fareine, who made a note. Then she said to Gereint, "I would like to hear more about the desert and how it differs from ordinary countryside—if you wish to describe it."

"That's an interesting question," Gereint answered at once. "The light, the air, even the dust is quite different in the desert."

"Oh?" There was no sign, now, that Tehre was in the least interested in how he had come to meet her father. She looked around vaguely. Gereint realized she was looking for a quill just as Fareine put one in her hand and laid out a little booklet of paper for her to write in.

Tehre took the quill without seeming to notice how it came to be in her hand and leaned forward intently. "Different how?"

Gereint easily discovered where the surgeon mage Reichteier Andlauban lived, and went to his house the day after he'd arrived in Breidechboden. But Andlauban was not at home.

"I fear the honored surgeon has gone to Weierachboden," his doorkeeper said, his apologetic manner professionally sincere. "We anticipate his return within three or four days, honored sir. Surely no more than five days. Shall I give the honored surgeon your name? Have you a token to leave?"

Gereint shook his head and assured the doorkeeper that he'd return in a few days. Then he went back to Tehre's house. He was disappointed, of course. It had never occurred to him that he would venture into Breidechboden and then find so trivial a problem in his way. What if Andlauban wasn't back in three or four or five days? What if whatever business had taken him to Weierachboden took longer than that? Just how long was Gereint going to have linger in Breidechboden? And what were the odds that he'd happen across some old acquaintance, one of his old masters—more likely a servant from one of his masters' houses—worst of all, a cousin? Someone, anyone, who would recognize him? He could just imagine turning around a corner and finding himself face to face with one of his cousins: Brachan or Feir or Gescheichan. Possibly Brachan or Feir might hesitate, might not believe they could actually have recognized him. But Gescheichan would not doubt himself for an instant.

This thought brought the sweat out on Gereint's forehead and stretched all his nerves tight; he felt now that every step he made outside the Amnachudran townhouse was dangerous, and looked over his shoulder until he was back within its protection. But, though he kept his head down in the city and tried to be as inconspicuous as possible, he also made himself detour into an open-air market long enough to buy the appropriate materials, and that evening he made Tehre a scale model of a bow-style catapult. He used cypress and tendon and wire, and he used his own money—or, at least, some of the money Amnachudran had given him.

He met, so far as he could tell, no one he'd ever known.

Gereint demonstrated the model for Tehre the next morning. "But if you scale it directly up, the dimensions might not be quite right," he cautioned her.

"Yes, I know," Tehre answered absently, examining the mechanism with delight. "Masonry's the only type of structure you can almost always scale up directly." She paused to think about this. "I think when you direct loads through a mechanism like this," she concluded, touching the model catapult, "it probably matters how strong the tensions are, because how the materials take the loads probably changes with the scale. With masonry, it matters less—as long as you keep everything in your building or bridge under compression. Because you never reach the compressive load that could actually break the stone."

"Stone breaks," Gereint objected.

"Buildings break," Tehre corrected absently. "But not because of too much compression on the stone. Generally somebody made the wall too thin or not heavy enough and the line of compression gets outside the wall and the wall tips up and falls over. Hmm. You've made a strong draw, here." She wound back the catapult string and loaded a stone ball in the cup. Then she touched the trigger. The stone flew true, striking with a satisfyingly solid *thud* the target Gereint had set up in the garden.

Tehre crowed with glee like a child. "Wonderful! *Wonderful!* Oh, I ought to have been looking at siege engines all along! Would you mind if I broke this? I'd like to fire it unloaded and see how it fails. Not today!" she added at once, suddenly realizing how this might sound. "It's a splendid mechanism and I want to play with it for a few days first, but later—"

"I know you're interested in how structures fail," Gereint assured her. "I can make you another one—as many as you like."

"Oh, could you? Please do start another one, would you? Just tell Fareine what materials you need, if you don't want to go out into the city to order them yourself." Tehre loaded another stone and asked shyly, "Would you like to fire this one?" as though she didn't think Gereint's reluctance to leave the house, or the fact that she'd noticed it, was worth the least comment.

It was typical, Gereint thought, that Tehre both noticed something odd about him, something he was in fact trying to conceal, and at the same time didn't notice that it was odd. He suspected she simply thought most people were odd and didn't notice when someone was odd in an unusual way.

He thought no one else had noticed his fear of going into the city. Well, possibly Fareine; she was an observant woman. But by the household as a whole, Gereint found himself accepted as a normal and valued man for the first time in nineteen years.

Perhaps for this reason, Gereint liked everything about the house and household. He enjoyed the liveliness of the primarily female staff, enjoyed the friendly warmth of the kitchen and the staff—and they

were friendly, right from the first, and only became more so. But Gereint didn't dare take any of the offers that came his way from several
of the young women. Even if he would risk insulting Lady Tehre, he
could hardly go to any woman while *geas* bound. But surely Andlauban would return soon . . . He touched the stiff leather envelope that
contained Amnachudran's letter to the surgeon, drawing assurance
from it.

The surgeon mage would soon return, and he'd agree to take out
the *geas* rings, and then at last Gereint would be truly free to find a different course for his life . . . though he found, to his own surprise, that
he would be sorry to leave Breidechboden if leaving meant losing the
chance to see what odd bridges and complex mathematical philosophy
Tehre Amnachudran might come up with.

But he *would* leave. The risk of being recognized by someone he'd
once known was just too great.

But in the morning, Tehre found him before the sun was even properly up. Gereint had risen early. He was in the kitchen, cadging pastries
stuffed with apples and golden raisins from the cook and letting the
kitchen girls tease him about his early morning and what did that imply
about his early nights and was he quite sure he was sleeping well? But
they scattered, startled, when the mistress of the house came in.

Tehre looked as though she'd been up for hours, or even all night—
but also as perfectly cheerful and rested as though she'd never missed a
long night's sleep in her life. "Oh, Gereint, good!" she said. "Are those
apple? Thank you," she added to the cook, accepting a fresh pastry.
"Gereint, an important lord is coming to see me this morning. Did I tell
you about that yesterday? Yes, I thought I forgot; Fareine must not have
thought it was important to mention it to you, but I've decided I want to
show off your catapult and then make it fail and explain about material
failures. I think that's exactly the sort of demonstration that will impress this man. He has lots of property and wealth and I want him as a
patron so he can represent me to the guilds. So do you mind? And I
thought I could explain that you're the one who made the catapult; that
ought to impress him and that would be good for you."

"Ah—" said Gereint, not very cogently. He found himself gripped
by a senseless but powerful conviction that the intended patron was one
of his cousins. Brachan or Feir or, worst of all, Gescheichan. But that
was foolish. His cousins were men of wealth and property, but not one
of them would be the least interested in bridges or material philosophy.
He would not know this man—whoever the man was, he was not likely
to know Gereint—especially after nineteen years.

"Good, then, come this way, I want to receive my new patron in my library." Tehre, nervous, seemed oblivious of Gereint's reluctance. "Cook, could you please provide some of these lovely pastries for my guest? That will surely make him decide to represent me." She said this last in a very matter-of-fact tone, clearly not realizing she was delivering a compliment. Catching Gereint's hand, she towed him out while the kitchen girls exploded with very quiet giggles behind them.

Gereint told himself, firmly, that the prospective patron would be someone he'd never met, someone who'd never heard of him. He even found that he looked forward to watching Tehre focus her formidable will on dragging this man into her plans. If the man was intelligent, he'd be delighted to represent her. If he was a fool, perhaps Gereint himself might help Tehre hook him, and thus repay something of the woman's kindness to him . . .

CHAPTER 4

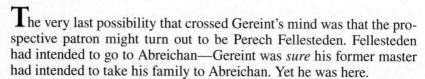

The very last possibility that crossed Gereint's mind was that the prospective patron might turn out to be Perech Fellesteden. Fellesteden had intended to go to Abreichan—Gereint was *sure* his former master had intended to take his family to Abreichan. Yet he was here.

For a long, long moment after Fellesteden came into Tehre's library, Gereint could not move at all. Not to speak, not to run, not at all. He felt he had been struck to stone by some inimical magic, as though he literally *could not* move.

Fellesteden, clearly, was just as astonished. "*This* is a surprise," he said, but his tone, smooth and pleasant, indicated that it was one that pleased him very much. But he always sounded like that when he was most dangerous—when he intended to indulge himself at someone else's expense.

"You know one another?" Tehre said, but then she picked up some quality in Fellesteden's tone or in Gereint's silence and stopped, her eyes narrowing.

"Harboring fugitives, are you, honored lady?" Fellesteden said to her, though his eyes did not move from Gereint's. "Was it you who removed his brand? Or had it removed? Of course it was." He began to smile. "Did you think to gain a loyal servant whose special qualities might go unnoticed? How very clever of you." His eyes moved at last to meet Tehre's. "But I had heard that about you. That you are clever."

Gereint said, "She knows nothing about it." He measured the door behind Fellesteden and the men he had brought with him—Perech Fellesteden always traveled with a retinue. He had today. There was no hope of getting past them that way. And there was no other door to the room.

"Of course she does," Fellesteden said mildly. He was still smiling. "Is it coincidence you are here? I think not."

Gereint shifted back a step.

"Derich," Fellesteden said, and one of his men-at-arms came smartly forward, his hand going to the hilt of his sword.

Gereint knew Derich. And there were far too many men behind him. He stopped. Derich smiled—not a smooth, polite smile like his master's: The man-at-arms had very little interest in smooth courtesy. His head was shaved in the manner of a soldier, but Derich was not a soldier—as Gereint knew very well.

Tehre knew neither Fellesteden nor Derich. She said sharply, "Fareine! Go for the patrol."

"Derich," Fellesteden said gently, before the old woman could take so much as a single step, "be so good as to ensure that no one leaves this household until I give permission. If anyone should happen to wish to enter, that's another matter, and they are certainly welcome to come in."

"My lord," said Derich, and lifted a hand, grinning. Men moved. One took Fareine by the arm. She looked, white faced and helpless in his grasp, to Tehre for help.

"This is entirely illegal!" cried Tehre, outraged. Not yet frightened.

Fellesteden looked thoughtful. "An interesting question. I think it will prove otherwise. I do think so. Gereint . . ." He stood for a long moment, studying Gereint. "Let me see your feet," Fellesteden said to him at last.

Gereint did not move. It felt very strange not to move in response to that smooth voice. Not to feel the bite of compulsion. It was not a freedom he was likely to enjoy for much longer.

And it was in a very real sense an illusory freedom, because Fellesteden sighed and shook his head, just a little. It was the exact gesture a tired father might use toward a recalcitrant small boy. "Shall I have my men compel you?"

Without a word, Gereint bent and removed his boots. The *geas* rings piercing through the flesh between bone and tendon glinted coldly silver. Gereint did not look at Tehre Amnachudran. He did not meet anyone's eyes.

"Not bound, after all," observed Fellesteden. "I am surprised."

"I told you," Gereint said, and was mildly pleased and considerably astonished to find his voice steady. "The lady knows nothing of me other than that I am a maker." He forced himself to look straight into Fellesteden's face. "You have no business here, except with me."

"Oh, well," Fellesteden murmured, and paused. "Do you know," he said then, "I imagine that may even be the truth, or why else would you be free? But who else would believe it?" His gaze moved from Gereint's face to Tehre's. "Theft of a *geas*-bound servant . . . honored lady, I am shocked. Shocked. Interference with the brand of such an infamous person . . . clearly to disguise his *geas* for your own benefit . . . Anyone would be profoundly shocked. I believe that we might well come to an understanding on this matter. If you are indeed clever." He paused again.

Tehre's face had gone blank. Her eyes were fixed on Fellesteden's face, but she did not speak.

"Derich . . ." Fellesteden murmured. "Derich—let us be certain this house is secure. The honored Fareine will be so kind as to assist us, I am sure. Please remain here, honored lady. You might well take these few moments to consider your situation. We may hope that you do indeed deserve your reputation for cleverness. A practical cleverness will serve you much better, at this moment, than defiance." He gestured to his men and withdrew, shutting the door gently behind him.

Tehre, her small fists clenched in silent fury, glared at the door for a long moment. Then she transferred the glare to Gereint. "That man," she said in a tight voice, "that man is going to accuse me of having stolen you from him. No. You came here from my father's house. He's going to accuse *my father* of having stolen you."

"I'll deny it," Gereint promised her.

But Tehre shook her head. "What good will that do? No one will listen to anything *you* say! Lord Fellesteden is a powerful man—he has powerful friends, friends at court, that's why I wanted his patronage! Somebody removed your brand, and then you turned up in my house? It doesn't matter what you say—it barely matters what I say: If Perech Fellesteden brings accusations against my family, everyone will believe him, not us!"

"I'm sorry—"

"That does very little good." Tehre stared at him for a brief moment, her eyes intense with thought and anger. She asked sharply, "Who *did* remove your brand?"

Gereint did not answer.

Tehre's lips compressed. She looked quickly around the room, thinking. There was still only one door, and Fellesteden's men would still be guarding it; outside, Tehre's female household would be thoroughly overmatched by his retinue. "This is absolutely illegal!" Tehre said furiously. And helplessly.

"Bind me," Gereint said suddenly, and when Tehre swung around to stare at him, "Bind me yourself! Don't wait for Fellesteden to do it! You can say—you can think of something to tell any judge." Gereint paused, trying to think what the woman might plausibly claim. "You can say you bought me legally. You can say I was unbranded when you bought me. You're too trusting of people: When the man who sold me told you that the judge ordered my face left unmarked, you believed him. I didn't contradict him because I didn't want the brand renewed. Anybody would believe *that*. Fellesteden will say I wasn't bound when he found me in your house, but it's his word against yours and I'll swear to any judge he's lying. I'll say anything you like; I'll *refrain* from saying anything you like. But you have to stop Fellesteden from claiming me. If he binds me—"

He didn't have to finish that thought. Tehre was already searching through the library for anything that would do for the binding. There were no fine silver chains handy, but she clearly knew that one did not actually need the chains. But nothing like a fine cord seemed to be available, either. She stopped and bit her lip. "Where's an embroidery kit when you need one?" she asked the air. Then she blinked, reached up to her head, and pulled the pins out of her hair. It tumbled around her shoulders, dark and thick, glinting with gold.

"That won't be very strong—" Gereint began.

Tehre cut him off. "It will be for me. Anyway, do you see anything else handy to use?"

Gereint didn't. He closed his mouth.

"I don't know what's to stop him forcing me to release you again," Tehre said, her small fingers darting along the strands of dark hair, braiding, braiding, faster and faster, pulling more hairs from her head to lengthen the cord. Her eyes were fixed on her work and at least part of her mind had to be, but she also said, "What will stop him?" as though it was a real question and she really expected Gereint to answer it.

Gereint opened his mouth and shut it again. He had no idea. Then he said, knowing it was impossible, "No matter what he does, you'll have to persuade him you won't."

Tehre made a scornful little sound, but she glanced up only for a second and her racing fingers did not slow. She finished the first cord and began on a second.

Gereint moved to the door and listened carefully. It was easy to imagine that he heard rapid, triumphant steps ringing down the hall, coming toward the library door. He couldn't tell if he really heard such sounds or not. "Hurry," he urged Tehre.

The woman didn't dignify this with even a glance, far less an answer. But she finished the second cord with flying haste and beckoned urgently to Gereint, who crossed the room in four long strides, swung a second chair around beside Tehre's, and put his right foot up so she could reach the *geas* ring.

Tehre threaded the first cord she had made through the ring and tied it off with a neat little knot. She had seemed far more outraged than frightened when Fellesteden had threatened her, but she was more frightened than she looked: Her fingers trembled against his ankle.

Steps sounded outside the room, loud and definite and not at all the product of imagination. Gereint gritted his teeth against a desperate need to urge Tehre to *Hurry, hurry, hurry* and forced himself to stand perfectly still while she completed the first knot. There were voices outside, loud but indistinguishable, and he put his right foot on the floor and his left on the chair.

Tehre completed the second knot, and the *geas* woke, twisted tightly around Gereint's self-determination and will, and bit deep. He caught his breath in something that was not quite pain and grabbed the back of the chair to steady himself against what seemed almost a physical dizziness, although it was not actually physical at all.

Just at that moment, Derich opened the library door. He stepped aside for Perech Fellesteden to enter. Derich entered at Fellesteden's back; another of Fellesteden's retainers held Fareine by one arm. The woman looked older and far more helpless than she had ever seemed before.

Tehre stood up, crossed her arms across her small breasts, tilted her chin up, and glared at Fellesteden.

Gereint moved a step out from her side. He was not at all certain now what could possibly prevent Fellesteden from forcing Tehre to cut the cords she had just made. He had wanted her to bind him for his own protection—to do it herself before Fellesteden could—but now Fellesteden could simply threaten Fareine; he could threaten one woman of her household after another, and he wouldn't stop at threats; Tehre could not possibly resist him—

"Gereint," Tehre commanded, staring straight at Fellesteden, "kill him."

Gereint couldn't believe she had said that. Perech Fellesteden couldn't believe it. In fact, *no one* could believe it. For that first instant, everyone in the room was frozen in astonishment. Except for Gereint. Because he did not have to believe it. It did not matter that *he* was shocked or that he had never in his life killed anyone and probably would not have been able to do it on his own; the *geas* could not be astonished and did not accommodate delay.

Gereint's body moved in automatic *geas*-driven response to Tehre's command. He yielded to it instantly, let the *geas* drive his lunge forward, put his own will behind it, and rode it for strength and force and, most of all, speed.

The man holding Fareine had a knife drawn; Gereint hit him hard in the throat, caught his knife as he staggered, spun, plunged the knife into Fellesteden's side and ripped forward and up, ignored the man's gasping cry as he jerked the knife out, and pivoted as Derich, shouting wordlessly, moved at last. Gereint caught Derich's wrist in his other hand and struck viciously at the other man's chest, but Derich twisted away and snatched out his sword, and the *geas* was already dragging Gereint back around to make sure of Fellesteden, whatever threat Derich presented at his back—

Tehre hurled herself bodily against Derich and the two went down together in a flailing tangle. Gereint had no attention to spare for that struggle, all his focus was on Perech Fellesteden. The man was down on the floor, on his knees, one hand braced against the floor, the other hand pressed tightly against the wound Gereint had dealt him. He stared up, his face white, his mouth open, unable to catch his breath to speak.

Gereint felt no pity at all. But it would not have mattered. Fellesteden was still alive, so the *geas* was still a goad, still a source of speed and violence. Gereint jerked Fellesteden's head back by the hair, whipped the knife across his throat, and felt the compulsion of the *geas* relax as the life went out of his old master's eyes. He did not watch, but whirled, looking for Derich.

Derich was just getting to his feet, and Tehre as well, though much more slowly. Gereint faced Derich, horribly aware that the knife he still held was not a match for the other man's sword, that even if he'd had a sword of his own, he would not have been a match for Fellesteden's man. Derich knew it too. He stalked Gereint, smiling tightly, as he always smiled when about to murder or torture or inflict any sort of brutality. Gereint wondered if Tehre might give him another *Kill him* command, and whether that might help—

Fareine, her face set and white, stepped forward, swung the long bronze statue of a flying swan up by its neck, and brought the heavy base of the statue swinging down toward Derich's head. The man jerked to the side and the swan hit his shoulder and arm a glancing blow. Not his sword arm. He shouted—the cry sounded more furious than hurt— and swept his sword around in a vicious low cut that would gut the old woman like a fish. Fareine cowered from the sword, lifting the bronze swan in a hopeless gesture of defense.

Gereint flung the knife he held, using all his maker's skill to encourage it to fly straight and hard and hit point first. But he knew even as he threw the knife that it would not strike Derich in time to stop him cutting Fareine in half.

But Tehre flung her hands out, making a twisting motion as though wringing the neck of a hen, and when Derich's sword struck the bronze statue, it did not batter past the statue and slash into Fareine's body. It wasn't that Fareine was holding the statue firmly enough to block the sword. But when the sword struck the statue, it *shattered*. Metal splinters exploded across the room.

Fareine dropped the swan statue, crying out as some of the steel splinters struck her—Derich shouted too, in surprise if not in pain—so did Tehre, in sympathy perhaps, she was too far away to have been injured—Gereint's knife snapped into Derich's lower back with all the force and precision he might have put into ordinary practice with a straw target when making throwing knives.

This time, when Derich cried out, it was definitely in pain.

Gereint was already on him. One big hand snatched the neck of the bronze swan from Fareine. But when Gereint swung the statue up like a club and brought it down, he put a lot more force behind the blow than the old woman ever could have. And his aim was better. It took only one blow.

Then he looked at last for Fellesteden's other retainer. He found the man at once, fallen where he'd stood when Gereint had struck him in the throat. He was not moving. So Gereint had hit him hard enough the first time. And no other enemy was in the room. And Fellesteden was— yes, Gereint confirmed, staring at his old master's body. Perech Fellesteden was dead.

They were safe.

For the first instant after that realization, Gereint could not believe what had happened, what he had done, what any of them had done. He braced his hands on his knees, lowered his head, and tried to catch his breath.

Tehre said faintly, "That was . . . We are . . ." and stopped. She closed her eyes, breathing deeply. The room stank of blood and terror, and her pallor only deepened. She opened her eyes again quickly.

Gereint went to her and put a hand under her elbow. "There's no time to faint, yet," he told her urgently. "Though, earth and iron, you deserve to!" He turned his head. "How many men did Fellesteden bring with him? Do you know, Fareine? There's no knowing what they'll do, now their lord is dead—"

Fareine straightened her shoulders. "They'll leave," she declared. "They'll get out! That's what they'll do. Their master illegally invaded the house of the honored Lady Tehre Amnachudran Tanshan and threatened the lady and her household! The honored lady has every right to bring charges, serious charges, against Lord Fellesteden! Or his—his heirs and estate, I suppose." She glanced quickly at the bodies and away again. But then she drew herself up and, although she was still trembling, glared haughtily at Gereint.

"That's . . . one possible view," Gereint allowed. He, also, still felt sick and shaken, but he couldn't help but grin at Fareine's prim tone. "Especially if the city patrol was here to see to it. Do you think—?"

"They can be brought," Tehre promised. "Fareine, you can—no. I don't know how you could get out of the house. The rest of Fellesteden's men must be watching the doors." She rubbed her forehead, trying to think.

"How many are there? Do we know?" Gereint asked Fareine.

"About . . . about ten," the old woman said, but uncertainly. She glanced involuntarily at the man with the crushed throat and winced, but did not let herself recoil. "Or nine, I suppose. There are men in the kitchens, in Tehre's workroom, in the garden . . . He sent men everywhere . . ."

"The servant's hall?"

"Yes. I told you, they're everywhere—"

Gereint closed a big hand on the woman's shoulder and shook her, very gently. "Nine men can't be everywhere. The bedrooms?"

Fareine thought about this. "No," she said at last in a surprised tone. "I don't think so. Tehre's suite is just down the hall, you know, and it looks out over the front walk. And those iron lanterns make a good step down . . . Tehre used to sneak out that way, when she was just a bit of a girl and her family stayed here."

"You knew about that?" Tehre asked, astonished, and Fareine gave her a wry look.

Gereint longed to ask why Tehre had, as a girl, snuck out of her father's house. But probably that was not the most urgent question to ask at this moment. He began instead, "Ah . . . Fareine . . ."

"Young man, I'm not so old I can't manage a little climb like that," Fareine said with some asperity. "If you will make certain none of Fellesteden's brigands are in the hall, please?"

Gereint flexed his hands and looked for the knife . . . remembered it was in Derich's back and swallowed. He rubbed his palms on his thighs and glanced unhappily at the body. But he needed a weapon before he opened that door.

Though Fellesteden's other retainer ought to have—yes. A sword, still in its sheath. Much better than trying to pull a bloody knife out of a dead man. Much better. Gereint didn't try to get the sheath off the retainer's belt, but gingerly drew the sword and straightened again. The

sword had decent balance, fit comfortably in his hand . . . ah. It was, he
realized at last, one he'd made himself, as he'd made many of the
swords and knives Fellesteden's men carried. The recognition carried a
strange kind of reassurance with it, as though Gereint had unexpectedly found a friend at his side in an uncertain situation.

He shifted the sword in his grip, glanced over at Tehre. He knew
very well that, sword or no, he was not a match for any of Fellesteden's
thugs. But if there was no more than one man . . . If he could at least
make the man hesitate . . . all he needed was to win enough time for
Fareine to get out of the house and the day was won . . . "Maybe we
should all go?" he said to Tehre.

The small woman lifted her head proudly. "I won't be chased out
of my own house by thugs! And anyway," she added more practically,
"if those men find their lord dead and want vengeance, I'm the only one
whom they might hesitate to attack. I won't leave my household at their
mercy. I can make them pause, at least, and all we need is for them to
hesitate."

Gereint hated for her to remain in danger, but he also knew she was
right. Taking a deep breath, he stepped past Fareine, flung open the library door, and stepped through with a bold, confident stride that
might deceive one of Fellesteden's men, if not himself.

The hallway was deserted. Gereint let his breath out, extremely
relieved.

"Tehre's bedroom is right down . . ." Fareine slipped past him and
hurried twenty feet down the hall, cautiously opened a door, glanced
into the room, looked back at Gereint, gave him an all's-well sign and a
shooing gesture that obviously meant, *Get back to Tehre.* Then she
slipped into the room and closed the door after her.

It seemed odd to let a woman, a matron who was no longer young,
climb down from that window, risking danger from Fellesteden's men
as well as simply from falling. But there was no other choice, and Fareine was right—he needed to get back to Tehre. If any of Fellesteden's
thugs discovered what had happened to their lord . . . Well, maybe
Tehre could make them pause and maybe she couldn't, but if not, he
would have to try to hold them himself until the patrol arrived.

In the library, Tehre was sitting in a chair she had pulled around to
face the door, carefully angling it so she could also more or less avoid
looking at the bodies. She was rubbing her face with both hands, but
she glanced up when Gereint came in. Her face was tight with strain
and weariness. When she saw he was alone, she nodded and pressed
her hands over her eyes.

Gereint laid the sword aside on a table and came forward.

"Fareine?" Tehre asked without looking up, in a small, tight voice, before Gereint could speak.

"Well away. There was no sign of any of Fellesteden's men. It shouldn't take the patrol long to arrive. With luck, before Fellesteden's thugs find out what's happened."

She nodded, lowered her hands, and glanced vaguely around the room. But her glance snagged on Fellesteden's body and stopped there. "He would have ruined us," she said after a moment, as though answering an accusation.

Gereint was not going to argue. "He would certainly have tried."

"Huh. Well, now he won't." But Tehre seemed to be unable to look away from the body. Gereint moved forward to lay a hand on her shoulder, and she flinched and jerked her gaze up at last, her breath coming sharp and quick. But after a moment she said, in a tone that only shook a little, "Lord Fellesteden threatened me, threatened my household—he intended theft and violence. He intended it from the first, in complete disregard of the king's law—he probably quarreled with my father in the north—thus he brought so many men." She glanced sharply up to meet Gereint's eyes. "Will the city patrol believe that? Will a judge?"

"When your enemy is dead, honored lady, you are free to offer any story that pleases you. It seems to me that one is somewhat plausible." Gereint paused. Then he said, "But here's a better story, if you will permit me. I've never encountered your father. I met your brother in Dachsichten. He suggested I come to you because he knew that you were looking for a maker to assist you in your work. He wrote you a letter representing me to you; your father never wrote a word to you about me. I came here for reasons of my own; you had no idea I was *geas* bound and can't imagine who might have removed my brand. Fellesteden recognized me. He never intended anything against your household; he merely recognized me and wished to reclaim his lost property. In a madness of rage and despair, I managed to kill him and both these other men. All the fault is mine. You and your household are merely witnesses. You summoned the patrol to protect yourself against me, not against Fellesteden's remaining men."

All of Tehre's formidable attention was now fixed on Gereint. She said nothing.

"It's a plausible tale. Fellesteden's remaining men will hardly object—they may even believe that tale *themselves*, if you tell it properly. You'd need to write immediately to your father and brother so neither of them contradicts this, um, adjusted version of events. And of course," he gestured awkwardly down toward his own feet, "you will need to cut those cords."

The woman began to speak, clearly a protest, from the rigid shake of her head.

Gereint interrupted her. "No, listen, Tehre. They can't do anything to me that hasn't already been done, do you see? But if I was bound under your control when I killed them, then *you* are responsible and I merely your weapon. If a judge finds against you—if he *does*, Tehre, and the precedent is all against you, believe me that I know—if you are found to have done murder, Tehre, *you* could be *geas* bound. Nothing would be worse, do you understand? And there is *no reason* for you to risk it!"

"My father removed your brand. Isn't that true?"

Gereint shook his head emphatically. "I will never say so. If anyone makes that suggestion, I will deny it. Tehre, the patrol will surely come very soon. Your cords—there's no time to hesitate—cut them, Tehre!"

"I can't leave you to take all the blame on yourself!"

"You can. Don't be foolish. Of course you can! You must! Do you want everyone asking about your father? They won't stop with you, Tehre! They'll ask why your father sent you a *geas*-bound slave with an unmarked face, and you won't like the answers they think of—"

A man's deep voice rang out somewhere in the house, barely audible. It might be one of Fellesteden's men. But Gereint thought it was probably the patrol.

Tehre's eyes widened with alarm. "I—" she began.

"Let me take the blame! It doesn't make any difference to me! I can't get away now anyway!" It occurred to Gereint that he might have earlier, if he'd managed to persuade Tehre to cut the binding cords quickly enough. Grab his boots and out the window right after Fareine—too late, too late, the opportunity had been fleeting and was gone. He tried not to think about it, but said urgently, "Cut me loose, Tehre! Hurry!"

Her eyes were wide and shocked, but her small mouth firmed with decision. She said quickly, "I'll petition—whom does one petition? Never mind: I'll find out and I'll buy your bond properly. I won't abandon you, Gereint, do you hear?"

"I would . . . I would be very grateful," Gereint admitted. He tried not to depend on the promise: Maybe Tehre would find herself or her family coming under too much suspicion if she tried to buy his bond. Maybe she would simply change her mind. He would have no recourse if she did. He gazed down at her for a moment. Those bronze-green eyes met his with utter conviction and he thought, surprising himself, *No, she will keep any promise she makes.*

He was surprised by his own confidence: no one was bound by a promise made to a *geas* slave. But even so, he thought *Tehre* would be.

And was even more deeply surprised at how important that seemed—that he should trust her, that even when he would not dare approach anyone he'd once known, neither family nor friend, there should still be someone he trusted in the world. And it had happened so quickly, and he had hardly even noticed—not really allowed himself to notice.

But everything he'd argued was still true. He stepped toward the woman, turning so she could reach the *geas* rings.

Tehre didn't need a knife to cut the cords she'd made herself. She'd woven strength and resilience into them, but when she touched them, the knots she'd tied in them came undone and all the braiding unraveled. The cords simply fell to pieces. Gereint stared down at the unidentifiable wisps of hair, feeling the *geas* once more release its grip and subside to the back of his awareness. This time, he had no hope that this freedom would last.

Boots rang authoritatively in the hall outside the library.

Gereint stepped quickly away from Tehre and tried to look like the sort of desperate criminal who might have killed three men in a wild fit of terror and rage. This was not very difficult. It was harder to imagine why he would still be here in this room—maybe he had been struck insensible in the struggle and had only just recovered—he caught up the sword, tossed it on the floor by a chair, went quickly to one knee and braced one hand on the chair's carved seat as though trying just this moment to haul himself to his feet.

Tehre stared at him, then sank back into her own chair. She looked tiny, young, feminine, fragile, and perfectly helpless. Putting a hand to her face as though dazed, she stared vaguely at the door.

The next moment a big man in the livery of the Breidechboden patrol flung the door wide. He stood a moment in the doorway, filling it: as broad in the shoulder as Gereint, though nothing like so tall. His eyes went quickly from Gereint to the sword discarded on the floor nearby, to Perech Fellesteden's body, and at last to Tehre Amnachudran. His mouth tightened. He stepped into the room, gesturing to his men.

Gereint flung himself to his feet, staggering, just in time for two more men of the city patrol to rush forward and grab his arms. Fareine, who had followed the men into the room, started to protest; Tehre said, cutting the older woman off before she could manage even one word, "Patrol captain! Please send your men to secure my house and ensure that my people are safe. I had better accompany them. I'm afraid there has been a great deal of confusion."

"Honored lady, I see there has," said the captain, shaking his head—not doubt, Gereint saw, but simply amazement. He gestured to his men, and they led Gereint toward the door. He did not fight them. Nor did he try to turn for a last glance at Tehre. He simply bowed his head and went where the men took him.

Six days in a windowless stone cell provided plenty of time to think of fifty better ways he might have handled a sudden confrontation with his previous *geas* master. The best of them involved avoiding the confrontation altogether. Gereint reviewed in painful detail his decision to come south at all, his decision to stay on the southern road from Dachsichten rather than turn west, his fatal acquiescence when Tehre had suggested he meet her new patron.

If he had chosen differently at any of those moments, he might have gone to Feierabiand as planned. He might even be in Feierabiand right this moment, rather than sitting here on the cold stone floor, watching occasional slivers of light creep across the floor as guards carried lanterns past in the hall.

Gereint spent some of his time chipping carefully at the stone of the door with the buckle of his belt. He thought about what Tehre had said about cracks and masonry, and he thought of how she had made Fellesteden's sword shatter—an astonishing act of unmaking, the very antithesis of making. If he could do that . . . he would do more than break the door: He would shatter this whole prison, pull all its walls down around him. But no matter how he tried, he could not find any way to coax the scratches he made to run through the stone and break it to pieces.

In moments of hope, Gereint thought he might eventually be brought out of the cell and led up into the light to find that Tehre Amnachudran had indeed purchased his bond. He remembered thinking, *She will keep any promise she makes*, and though the original conviction of that thought was lacking, he still hoped, sometimes, that it might prove true.

But in other moments, Gereint was certain Tehre would be furious that he had deceived her, furious with her father, too. Though she had not seemed angry. But she might find herself and her family endangered by too close interest—she would realize that she had to avoid, by whatever means, any suggestion that her father had sent Gereint to her house, or that her father might have been the one to interfere with the *geas* brand. Either way, she would not want to further any connection between herself and Gereint. She would not intervene for him.

He could learn nothing from his guards about any legal proceedings against Tehre—or any legal proceedings she might have initiated herself—or anything having to do with his own eventual disposition.

The door was heavy and always shut; the guards slid plates through a gap below the door twice a day. Gereint could hear them outside his cell. But they hardly spoke to one another; they never answered him when he called to them through the door. Anything might be happening. Tehre's family might be ruined; he would not know. His own auction might be underway and he would not know.

At first, Gereint expected to be brought before a judge and questioned about Fellesteden's death, about his own presence in Tehre's house, about his unmarked face and his reason for coming to Breidechboden. That might still happen. But it had not happened yet. He no longer knew whether to expect it. More than likely, some judge had already heard the evidence and made some decision without finding any need to question Gereint. He wondered what it might have been.

And at first he waited every day for men to come with the hot iron and restore his *geas* brand. He could imagine the iron vividly: He knew exactly the path it would trace across his face, the fiery agony of the branding. The angry scar it would leave, impossible to obscure, setting him aside once more from the world of free men.

This dread intensified over the first days and then ebbed as no iron appeared. In some ways, that surprised him more than the silence and the waiting.

On the afternoon of the sixth day, he heard the guards in the hall early—far too early for supper. So he was not surprised when he heard the bolts draw back and the door was hauled effortfully open.

He got to his feet and stood facing the door, thinking of the hot iron. He knew he would fight if they brought that in—though fighting could win him nothing, he would fight anyway—he knew exactly how it would be to be pinned down and held still while the iron came down against his face. Swallowing hard, he stared at the open door.

But no iron appeared, no pot of glowing coals. The guards brought only chains.

If he was chained, he would not be able to fight, whatever they did to him. He submitted to the chains anyway, seeing no immediate threat and, after all, no choice.

They brought him out of the cell and into a hall that, dim as it was, seemed bright after the more profound darkness of the cell. They brought him up a flight of stairs and along a hall, to a lantern-lit room with a basin of cold water and a bar of coarse soap. So his bond had been sold, Gereint surmised. Someone wealthy and important had bought him, and the director of the prison did not want to offend this person by handing over a filthy prisoner. The only question that concerned Gereint was—was that person Tehre Amnachudran? He set his teeth against the desire to ask; the guards probably did not know and certainly would not answer.

The guards took the chains off and waited while Gereint washed. They offered neither abuse nor even comment; they were utterly indifferent and did not even speak to each other. Gereint put on the new clothing they gave him. It was plain, but not as rough or cheap as he had expected. Gereint took the quality of the clothing as another sign, if he had needed one, that whoever had bought Gereint's bond was important or wealthy. Or most likely both. There were no boots, of course, but the guards gave him sandals. Gereint put them on and waited to see where the guards would bring him next.

The guards put the chains back on and led him again into the hallway, then up another flight of stairs to a better part of the prison. Here there were, at last, windows set in the walls. The golden light of late afternoon slanted through the windows and lay in long bars across the floors. Gereint's eyes watered in the brilliance. He blinked, bowing his head, and went without protest or question where the guards took him.

They took him to a richly appointed room that hardly seemed to belong in the same building as the windowless cell. Here there was at last a man wearing the heavy gold chain of a judge, and a clerk with a large book open before him and a quill in his hand, and a third man who was less easy to place. This was a small man. Small all through: not much taller than a child. But he was not young. It was hard to guess his age: He might have been fifty or sixty, or seventy, or older still. His hair was white as frost, worn long, caught back at the nape of his neck in a style almost aggressively nonmilitary. He had ice-gray eyes and fine, straight bones, elegant hands and an inscrutable smile.

It was easier to guess the small man's rank than his age, for he was well and expensively dressed; the workmanship of his sapphire rings was very fine. This was not merely a gentleman, Gereint thought, nor merely some petty lord. He was more than likely a court noble. He wondered if he'd ever known this man before . . . before, but certainly he was memorable, and Gereint could not remember ever having met a man like this one.

He looked at Gereint as a man might look at a horse he had purchased; as a captain might look at a man who had been transferred into his company; as an appointed judge might look at a prisoner. With that kind of deliberate detachment. Gereint met his eyes for just an instant and then, allowing sense to beat down pride, bowed his head. He watched the lord covertly through lowered lashes. So this man had purchased his bond—and where, then, was Tehre? The depth of his anger and sense of betrayal at her absence shook him. He discovered only at that moment how deeply he had depended on Tehre Amnachudran to keep her promise and buy his bond. He made himself stand quietly, with a slave's practiced passivity, showing nothing of the rage that shook him.

"Well, my lord?" said the judge. Expectantly, as though this was the end of a discussion and not the beginning.

"I think he may do," said the lord, cool and judicious. "I will take him, certainly, and we shall see." He turned his head toward the clerk, who offered him a small wooden box.

"I imagine my lord does not require instruction in the use of the *geas* chains," said the judge, in the tone of a man making a small jest.

"I believe not," agreed the small lord. His voice was smooth and light. It was impossible to read anything of his disposition from that voice. He took the box from the clerk, opened it, and spilled a pair of fine silver chains into his palm. Then he looked at Gereint and beckoned. The crook of one finger: *Come here*, as to a dog.

Gereint moved stiffly forward and stood still, his face blank, his shoulders aching from the awkward posture enforced by the manacles, and waited while the lord fixed the first chain in place and then the second. The *geas*, coiled patiently at the back of his mind, shifted with the first chain, then woke and sank sharp fangs into his will with the second. Gereint let his breath out. The rage that had shaken him a moment earlier died; fear leaped up in its place and immediately burned away, leaving nothing. He felt as though his heart had turned to ash. He looked into his new master's face as the lord straightened, but without much interest.

For a moment, the lord merely stared back at him. Then he said, "Gereint Enseichen. Kneel."

No hesitation was possible, but Gereint did not try to hesitate. Dropping to his knees, he bowed his head and said in his most passive slave's tone, "Master."

"So that's done, then, my lord," said the judge, satisfied. "Do you wish my staff to brand him for you?"

Fear was not entirely dead after all. Gereint tensed, but he did not look up. He knew at once he should have expected this: Of course they would wait until he was *geas* bound and could be ordered not to fight. So much easier for everyone. Except, of course, the man who must submit to the brand and could not even struggle against it . . .

"That will not be necessary," said the white-haired lord.

"As you wish, my lord. You are, of course, aware that by law a *geas*-bound man must be branded—"

"I am aware," repeated the lord, his smooth tone unreadable. "I will see to it myself. If you would be so good as to have your men remove the manacles. Thank you so much, honored Mereirnchan. You have been most helpful. Gereint"—as the chains fell away—"get up and come with me."

Gereint got obediently to his feet and walked behind his new master. Out of the room, out of the prison, to a very fine carriage, with two liveried servants waiting and four beautifully matched white horses to draw it. One of the servants placed a step in the street for the lord, who needed it to reach the high sill of the carriage door; Gereint ducked his head low as he followed.

The lord was already seated, looking perfectly relaxed, on the forward-facing seat. He gestured to Gereint to take the seat opposite.

Gereint might have said something—anything. He knew he should test his new master's patience, the limits of his temper. But he could not, at this moment, find the courage or resolve to do it. He said nothing.

The prison was hardly in the best part of the city. But they quickly left the area of narrow streets and shabby tenements, passed through neighborhoods where the roads were wider and lined with more substantial marble-faced apartments and small shops, and came to a district of private houses with small walled gardens—Seven Son Hill, Gereint realized, but they were on the city side of the hill now and not the lee side where the Amnachudran house lay.

They followed the curve of the road and the houses grew larger still, the gardens larger and more elaborate. The river, contained here between banks of white limestone and bridged with elaborate bridges of stone and iron, ran beside the road. The river should have been beautiful, but now the water was low, surprisingly low, lower than Gereint remembered ever seeing it. The water, unpleasantly thick and greenish, moved sluggishly between stone banks gritty with silt. In some places it seemed one might not need a bridge to cross the river, if one had not minded wading in the green water.

Public buildings with columns of porphyry or green-streaked white marble and statues of marble and gilded bronze appeared on the other side of the street, which widened until it resembled a parade ground more than a thoroughfare. They had come to the Hill of Iron and now took the main road that spiraled around it toward the king's palace. Porticoes and fountains, ornate columns and high-buttressed towers . . . They were approaching the palace itself. Gereint had guessed correctly: His new master was plainly a court noble.

The carriage drew up at last, and one of the servants leaped down from the driver's bench and hurried to place the step and open the door.

The white-haired lord motioned for Gereint to get out first. Gereint obeyed, glancing around as he emerged from the carriage. They had come to a wide courtyard bordered on two sides by gardens; behind them the graceful street wound back down the hill into the city. Before them, a colonnade of flying buttresses three times Gereint's height shaded great doors of gilded bronze that stood open in a wall of white marble and fluted columns.

The lord did not seem to notice this magnificence. He beckoned to Gereint and walked briskly toward the gilded doors.

From him, a gesture had the force of a spoken command. Gereint followed.

Once through the doors, there was a high-arched hallway with mosaics on the walls and priceless Linularinan rugs on the marble floor. Statues of gold and marble stood on plinths, and a pair of golden fishes leapt in a marble fountain, water cascading down their jeweled scales and splashing in the pool below.

They came to an antechamber paneled with carved and polished cedar, hung with sapphire curtains, and lit by round porcelain lamps. Men-at-arms in blue and white livery saluted the lord and stood aside, noticing Gereint only with flickering covert glances.

The antechamber opened into a graceful receiving hall graced with an intricate mosaic floor and a single huge painting. The painting was of a battle—immediately recognizable; Terechtekun's victory over General Lord Perestechen Enkiustich of Meridanium, at the White Cliffs. It must be Ferichtelun's famous painting; undoubtedly it was the original, but Gereint's new master did not slow, so Gereint could not pause to look at it.

The receiving hall gave onto a long hall with a polished marble floor and wide glass windows. The lord proceeded, without pausing, to the end of the hall and went through a carved door; Gereint, following as though leashed, found that they had come to a library or a study or an office, or perhaps all three. By contrast with the rest of the apartment, this room was almost plain. The rugs on the floor were of high quality, but they were simply blue, without pattern or decoration. The furniture was similarly good but plain, with a minimum of carving. The windows were paned with expensive glass and curtained with heavy sapphire draperies.

Between the windows, paintings on the walls showed different views of Breidechboden. The city was pictured in every season, but the perspective was always from high above, as though the artist had stood in the highest tower of the city in order to paint them. Gereint could see that the same skilled artist was responsible for all the paintings, but

Gereint did not recognize either the paintings or the hand. Underneath the paintings, the walls were lined with shelves of books and scrolls. Three tables stood in the room, each stacked with papers and more books.

Here the lord turned at last and stood, his hand resting lightly on the surface of one of the tables, regarding Gereint with impenetrable calm. He asked, "Do you know who I am?"

Gereint stared back at the lord, completely unable to guess what his new master might be thinking. "Forgive me, master; no. I have been gone from Breidechboden for a long time."

" 'My lord' will do. I know you have. Your bond has never been held by men of Breidechboden. Most recently, you belonged to Perech Fellesteden for eight years. For most of that time, Lord Fellesteden maintained his primary household in Melentser." The lord's smooth voice, like his calm face, gave nothing away: neither offense nor amusement nor satisfaction. He added without emphasis, "I am Beguchren Teshrichten."

Gereint blinked. He said after a moment, "The cold mage. The *king's* mage. I should have recognized—" He stopped.

The fine mouth crooked in wry humor. "You would be surprised how few men recognize me, despite the river of gossip that floods through this city. Men expect the Arobern's own mage to be taller, I suppose. But, yes. I am the king's mage. The last of his mages, now."

"What—?" Gereint began, then remembered he had no right to ask, collected himself, and stopped, reaching after the hard-won impassivity he'd learned, years ago, to wear as a mask.

But the white-haired mage did not seem offended. He was smiling, a small uninterpretable smile. "What do I want with you? Either nothing or a great deal. Let us find out which. Kneel, please, and look at me, Gereint."

Gereint obeyed immediately, of course; he did not have time to wonder about the command until he was already down. But when he looked up, he found his gaze unexpectedly caught and held by the compelling ice-pale eyes of the mage. Beguchren Teshrichten stepped forward, rested one hand on Gereint's face, and sent his mind probing suddenly past the slave's blankness that Gereint showed him, through the surprise and anger and fear beneath, slicing into memory and laying bare the privacy of mind that was the only privacy a slave could own.

At first, Gereint was too shocked to resist this intrusion. Images rose through his mind, memories that he had not called up for years, the past washing across his awareness like a tide: Memories he had learned to put away when he had become a slave, recalled now by an inquisitive awareness that was not his own. His mother's face came before his eye; his sister's. His cousin Gescheichan's, first as a smiling narrow-faced boy and then, for a flashing moment, as a man, his expression closed and hostile.

Gereint remembered the thin, bony hands of his first tutor, setting before him a massive leather-bound volume of poetry . . . It had been one of Teirenchoden's epics, the words marching across the fine vellum in a fine, strong hand, the pages illuminated with gold leaf and delicate washes of color from the illustrator's brush. He had loved the dusty smell of it, the heavy feel of the pages . . . History and poetry had opened up before him in that volume, though he had not been able to read it, not then. Nor had he known how desperately important such books would be in maintaining his sanity, later in his life. He had been seven . . . He stirred, trying clumsily to close his mind's eye to that memory, fighting the intrusion that opened his mind to that foreign, knife-edged awareness.

The mage's mind shifted, eased away, turned, sliced inward once more. Gereint remembered running through the rain on a summer night, running to reach the shelter of an open door. Lightning had flared around him; thunder had rolled down deserted streets, no one else being fool enough to brave the storm. He had been young and strong and innocent of any knowledge that life might hold storms worse than those loosed from a dark summer sky. There had been a girl waiting in the doorway, laughing at him because he had run through the rain to come to her. He had reached out to seize her hands and lightning blazed behind him, lit the whole city with dazzling light, and he met her beautiful eyes and laughed with joy.

That memory tried to shift and turn, tried to become another memory. *"No!"* Gereint said, but he could not tell whether he cried the word aloud or only in the silence of his mind. He fought the intrusion determinedly, blindly. But the mage's mind was too powerful to fight; it cut into his with a relentless skill he could not resist; he could not stop the probing curiosity. But he found a way to let his memories become fluid instead. When the mage tried to reach after them, he let the past flow away like water, impossible to grasp or hold.

Then the mage lifted his hand and Gereint found himself, dizzyingly, back in the study, kneeling on the thick blue rug. The frost-haired mage was gazing down at him with sympathy, but without apology. Gereint panted as though he'd been running or fighting. He supposed he had been, in a way. He did not know what to say, what to do. He was shaking. His expression was probably far too easy to read. He dropped his eyes, though it was a wrenching effort to look away from the mage, as it would have been hard to look away from an unpredictable coiled serpent or crouching wolf.

The king's mage said, his tone perfectly matter-of-fact, "As it happens, I have need of a gifted maker, a maker with certain predispositions and skills. I am prepared to be generous to such a man, if he offers me loyal service."

Gereint, still trembling with reaction, had to suppress a startling and extremely unwise desire to laugh or curse or weep, or perhaps all three. He had no right to demand, or even request, any answer or justification from his master. So he set his teeth hard against any question, bowing his head.

"The *geas* compels obedience," the Arobern's mage murmured. "Dedicated skill, however, is more difficult to compel. As you know better than most, I imagine, Gereint Enseichen." He paused, then said gently, "Look at me."

Gereint had no choice but to meet his eyes, though he looked up with trepidation. But this time the mage's ice-pale eyes met his without effect. The mage's expression, he found, was utterly unreadable. "If you give me such service, I am prepared to be generous," he said.

"Of course I will serve my lord to the best of my ability," Gereint said smoothly, managing the smoothness only because he'd had years of practice keeping everything out of his voice.

"If you do, I am prepared to free you." The mage made a small gesture, indicating the rings that pierced Gereint's ankles. "You seem to have found yourself unable to remove those. I could remove them easily. Legality is not a concern. The Arobern would grant me your freedom, if I asked." He paused to study Gereint's expression, and once more smiled his small, inscrutable smile at what he saw.

Of everything the king's mage might have said, this was perhaps the least expected. Gereint felt as though he had been struck through by a spear, save that there was no pain. But he felt, oddly, as though he was waiting for pain to strike suddenly outward from an unfelt wound.

"Well?" Beguchren Teshrichten asked at last. "Is this a reward that would interest you?"

"You know it is," Gereint whispered. He did not know whether to believe the mage. But he knew he wanted to believe him. "For the hope of that reward . . . I will serve you, my lord, as well as I can."

The small, fine mouth quirked with unexpected humor. "Better than you served your previous master, I hope. Tell me . . . who removed the brand from your face? Or conspired to have it removed? One of your cousins? A friend? Tehre Amnachudran? That's been suggested, though the proposed motive seems thin to me."

Caught by surprise, Gereint hesitated. Then he said with practiced conviction, "A man in Dachsichten. A surgeon who dislikes *geas* magic on principle and for whom I did a small service. I could give you the name he told me, but I doubt it was his right one."

There was a brief pause. Then the king's mage said, "Gereint, you are lying to me. What surprises me is that you would believe you might do so successfully."

Gereint had not actually expected the mage to be deceived. But he had hoped a smooth, fairly plausible tale might serve—at least that the lord mage might not care to pursue the question. Seeing this hope fail, he bowed his head and said nothing.

"Gereint?" Beguchren asked, with deliberate patience. "Do you not wish to earn your freedom? You will not do so with lies. Tell me the truth."

"I . . . it was . . ." Gereint took a breath. He began again, "My lord, the truth is, I cannot answer that question. I am willing to serve you, my lord, very willing, but I beg you will not ask me."

The king's mage regarded him steadily. "But I do ask you, Gereint."

"My lord . . ." Gereint tried to catch his breath and balance against what seemed suddenly treacherous footing. "My lord, you ask for my loyalty. What would it be worth if I betrayed so easily the loyalty I owe elsewhere?"

The mage crossed his arms across his chest, tilted his head to the side, and answered quietly, "But *I* will have your service. It is not acceptable to me that you should owe loyalty elsewhere. Did one of your cousins help you? Brachan? Gescheichan?"

Gereint laughed bitterly at the suggestion, then realized if he'd only thought more quickly, he might have cast suspicion toward his cousins and away from Tehre and her father—then was at once disturbed that the idea of doing so even occurred to him. And twice disturbed to know he'd have done just that if he'd thought it might work.

He found his hands closed into fists and forced them open. He tried to think. It occurred to him that the entire offer the king's mage had made him might be false; that the offer of freedom might be merely a ploy to find out the answer to the question he had asked. This immediately seemed likely—and then, after another instant, extremely unlikely: Why should the *king's own mage* stoop to trickery when he could open a man's mind like a book and read the memories hidden there, never mind drawing upon the compulsion of the *geas*? But the next moment, the possibility again seemed very real. He could not decide.

Gereint looked at his master's face, found the calm impassivity completely impenetrable, and took a hard breath. "If you want my dedicated service, you will have to accept my silence on this one question," he said at last. "Maybe you can take it from my mind; I don't know. But I'll try to prevent you. I will not answer willingly."

Their eyes met and held. Gereint waited for the mage's mind to slice into his, but it did not happen. "While I would prefer your willing service," Beguchren Teshrichten said at last, "your absolute submission will be adequate. Punishment as well as reward is within my authority. Do you understand?"

Gereint understood *that* very well. He said nothing.

"Do you believe you can withhold any answer I would demand? You have no protection whatsoever against anything I might choose to do to you," Beguchren reminded Gereint, unnecessarily.

Gereint stared silently back at him, taking refuge in a slave's practiced impassivity. It was the only refuge available to him.

"Strip," the mage commanded him. "And wait here for me." He turned his back and left the room.

Gereint had never imagined he would have reason to be grateful to Perech Fellesteden for anything. But he found he was grateful now for the hard lessons in endurance he had learned at Fellesteden's hands. He knew how to accept humiliation, how to believe that all things pass, how to flatten his awareness so that he did not think even a moment ahead—so that he barely thought even of the moment as it actually passed.

What he could not believe was that the king's mage had first lifted him so high and then cast him so far down—no. No. He had done it to himself. Nothing the mage had said had ever been real, and an experienced slave should have known it was not real. Beguchren Teshrichten had never intended to free him. Only to hold out the hope of freedom . . . Gereint folded his clothing neatly across a nearby chair and turned to face the mage as the mage returned.

Beguchren carried a branding iron in one hand and a riding whip in the other. Next to the iron, the whip seemed almost innocent. Gereint tried not to stare at the iron. He fixed his gaze instead on one of the paintings: a scene that showed the south side of the Hill of Iron in the afternoon of a mellow autumn day. The white marble of the king's palace seemed, in that golden light, to have been poured out of honey; the gilded rooftops on the towers seemed to be made out of flame. It was a beautiful painting, full of warmth and peace; a surprising piece, perhaps, to find in the dwelling of a cold mage.

"Gereint," Beguchren said softly. His voice was still soft, but it carried all the implacable cold the painting denied.

Gereint looked at him, he hoped, steadily. Everything depended on the next moments: If he yielded now to the mage's demands, then they would both know he would always yield before any threat. But if he held fast, he might persuade the mage that he could not be broken. That belief might set the terms of this new servitude into a more tolerable path. If anything could. Gereint stared at the mage with flat defiance and said nothing at all.

But the white-haired mage's air of calm assurance was chilling. Beguchren laid both iron and whip on a table and faced Gereint. "I will set the brand back on your face, give you this whip, and send you, naked, to the bottom of Wide Hill. I will command you to tell any passersby that you are being punished for impudence and defiance and that your master invites them to punish you as they choose." The mage paused. He touched the iron with a fingertip, and its circular head first frosted and then smoked with a cold as frightening as any coal-red glow.

"Or you may simply obey me," added Beguchren, after a silence long enough to allow Gereint to contemplate the threatened punishment. "Do as I command and I will forget your defiance. Serve me well, and I will restore your freedom." Another pause. "Well?" he asked at last.

Wide Hill encompassed the worst areas of Breidechboden. Gereint could well imagine the reaction of the rough denizens of that area to such an invitation. He knew he had probably paled. But he did not let his expression change. In a way, he was even glad of the brutal threat, because he was far too angry now to capitulate. He said harshly, "You had better send retainers of yours to be sure I survive your punishment, *master*. We can both imagine, I'm sure, the creativity of the men who will find your invitation amusing."

Beguchren began, sounding mildly exasperated, "Gereint—"

Gereint stepped forward, picked up the iron by its wooden handle, and held it out to his master. "You had better phrase your command carefully when you send me down to Wide Hill. Or I swear I will kill the first baseborn dog-livered coward who touches me."

There was a silence. The mage did not move to take the iron.

"Perech Fellesteden owned me for *eight years*," Gereint said with contained fury. "Do you think there is anything of degradation I do not know? Do what you will: I have been trained to endure and I will yield *nothing*."

Beguchren Teshrichten took the iron from Gereint and laid it once again aside on the table, where the vicious cold of its head scored the polished wood as a flame might. The mage smoothed the mark out of the wood with the tip of a finger, studied Gereint for a moment longer, and then said, his tone absolutely uninflected, "Come with me. You will not need to dress."

It would have taken Gereint an instant to recover from the surprise of this apparent admission of defeat and follow the mage, except for the compulsion of the *geas*, which did not allow hesitation.

This time, his master led Gereint to a starkly plain, windowless room that contained only a table cluttered with the obscure paraphernalia of a mage and a narrow thin-mattressed cot. Beguchren picked up and contemplated an iron flask. He appeared utterly unconcerned about Gereint. Gereint, for his part, stood in the doorway and tried not to speculate about the things on the table or wonder why there was a cot in this room.

Beguchren poured a generous measure of pale green liquid from the flask into a earthenware cup, turned, and held the cup out to Gereint. "Drink this," he commanded. "And sit down there." He indicated the cot.

Gereint took the cup and tossed the green liquid back like cheap ale. It tasted like herbs and winter ice, like new-mown hay and hoarfrost. The taste was not unpleasant, but nothing in the taste was familiar or identifiable, and the liquid chilled his tongue and throat unpleasantly. Gereint gave the cup back to the mage and sat down on the cot. He waited to see what would happen. He wanted to ask, but would not give his new master the satisfaction of knowing he was frightened.

Dizziness rose up through Gereint like a mist, spreading from his belly outward along all his limbs, rising last to his head. He seemed to taste the drink again and swallowed heavily against a sudden nausea, which at least did not grow worse. The dizziness did, however. He closed his eyes against it. He knew he should lie down, but he was no longer certain exactly where the cot was. He felt around uncertainly, searching for its edges. But his fingers felt distant and . . . strange, like they belonged to someone else very far away . . . A small, strong hand closed on his arm, and he let himself be led downward, though in a way it seemed he was rising and not falling. Cold green mist poured through Gereint, carrying his mind upward as it rose to the clouds . . . He was very cold . . . and then nothing was left but green mist.

CHAPTER 5

Gereint woke in a large, heavy bed hung with sky-blue curtains. The mattress was soft. That was what he knew first. The mattress was soft and there were plenty of down-stuffed pillows. The curtains that surrounded the bed turned the light to a softly luminous blue. The ceiling was white plaster. Gereint gazed at it, trying to think. The sounds of birds singing came to him, muffled by the curtains. The delicate liquid songs of finches and sparrows . . . So it was morning.

He felt . . . very strange. Light, in a way that had nothing to do with his actual weight. As though he had laid down some great burden in the night. But he could not remember anything of the night that had led him to this room and this bed. He tried to think back further but could not remember the previous evening either. Yet he did not think he had been ill, certainly not so ill that he should not remember the past day. He frowned at the ceiling, pushed himself slowly to sit up, and put aside the bed curtains.

The room beyond the bed was all ivory and rose and blue, gentle in the soft morning light. There was a painting on the far wall: The artist had painted Seven Son Hill at dawn in the springtime, from above, as though he had captured the view of a finch or a sparrow.

Memory rose through Gereint like mist. His breath caught. He shut his eyes and pressed a hand across his face, at once terrified and violently furious. All the horror of the previous days flooded through him, utterly unexpected. He thought he might shout; he thought he might weep. He held perfectly still, pressing his hands across his eyes, and waited, shaking, for the storm to pass.

It did pass, eventually. The room was quiet except for the songs of the birds. He might have been the only one awake in all the house, in all the court entire, except for the birds.

The shaking eased at last. Gereint took hold of the bedpost and got to his feet. He was naked. But if the king's mage had done anything to him while he was unconscious, he could not tell it. He felt normal. Except for that odd lightness, so that he wondered whether, if he leaped down from the window of this room, he might float down to the gardens below as gently as a down feather from his pillow. This was not an unpleasant feeling. But it was unusual and uncomfortable because he almost thought he should recognize the feeling, only he did not.

There was a jug of water, a wide brass basin, and a small pile of folded clothing on a table next to the bed. The room was not large. It contained little save for the bed and the table and a small writing desk. There was paper on the desk and a quill and a bottle of ink. The ink was sapphire blue.

Gereint poured water into the basin and washed his face. He put on the clothing. It was not blue and white nor any other livery, but plain brown and tan. But the material was good, and the clothing fit.

There were no boots, but house sandals sat under the table. Gereint picked them up and sat down at the desk to put them on. And stopped. He sat still for a long time, staring down.

The silver *geas* rings were gone. Not merely the little chains Beguchren Teshrichten had threaded through them: the rings themselves. Gone entirely. Nothing but small scarred holes interrupted the smooth skin between tendon and bone. When Gereint tentatively reached down to touch his ankles where the rings had been, he felt the holes. But the rings themselves were *gone*.

Gereint had felt only joy and gratitude when Eben Amnachudran had removed the brand from his face. He did not know what he felt now.

There were servants outside the blue room: a broom-wielding woman in servant's drab brown and, more to the point, a man in livery waiting outside the door. The man, who addressed Gereint as "honored sir," guided him through halls and up stairs and along a pillared gallery open to the weather, and at last through an intricately carved portico into an antechamber hung with blue and violet and decorated with mosaics of birds and trees. All of this was clearly part of the palace; all of it was clearly designed to impress and overwhelm.

It made Gereint angry—he was ready to be angry, he found. To be *furious*. Everything in this place was meant to manipulate, to make a man feel small and subservient—and that meant everything was of a piece, because everything here had been a manipulation, right from the beginning—and for what unguessable purpose? Beguchren Teshrichten needed Gereint, clearly. And had deliberately put him through all that farce of bait and threat, and for what? For what?

The liveried man gestured respectfully that Gereint should wait in the antechamber and himself went through a curtained doorway. Gereint did not wait, but followed on his heels.

"My lord—" the man was saying to the frost-haired mage.

The mage himself was sitting on the edge of an enormous desk, looking rather like a child who had made himself at home in his father's study. A man sized to fit the desk was lounging in a chair to one side of the room, but Gereint barely looked at him. He had no attention to spare for anyone but the mage.

Beguchren Teshrichten had been running the long feather of a quill pen absently through his fingers. He did not seem to be paying very much attention to the liveried man, but he looked up sharply when Gereint came in, waved the man silent, and hopped down off the desk to face Gereint. He was not smiling, but his calm seriousness was just as inscrutable as his smile. He said to the man, in a tone of polite dismissal, "Thank you, Terechen," and the man darted an unsettled look at Gereint and went away.

Gereint had just enough self-command to wait for the liveried man to leave. Then he took two steps forward and said through his teeth, "The man who took away the scar of the brand did it for kindness. And why did you do *this*?" He gestured sharply downward. "Not for kindness, is it? What is this but payment for service—and for *what* service? What was that game with the threats and the iron? What do you *want* from me?—Not that it matters: if you think I'm interested in playing your game, you're badly mistaken, *my lord*."

The mage did not answer, but impassively looked aside from Gereint's angry stare, laying the feather quill carefully down on the desk.

The other man, however, stood up and set his fists on his hips. "What?" he demanded. He was not quite as tall as Gereint, but broader all through, and his voice matched his big frame: deep and guttural. That deep voice was especially harsh now, with annoyance and also with an odd kind of disdain. "You object to payment, do you?" he went on, glowering at Gereint. "What, do you find the payment is not sufficient? Is it base coin? What service would you have refused for this coin? Would you wish to specify? Well?"

Taken aback by this unexpected rebuke, Gereint stared at the big man. He had assumed Beguchren Teshrichten was master in this place; now he did not know. This man was heavyset and powerful, but his air of authority went beyond his size. He looked like a soldier: black hair cropped short on his head, thick beard close-trimmed to outline an aggressive jaw. His features were strong, even heavy, but his eyes snapped with energy and outrage.

It was the outrage that finally prompted Gereint's belated recognition: There was authority in that guttural voice, but the anger was also clearly the ire of an offended friend. Beguchren Teshrichten, as everyone knew, was the *king's* mage. This . . . this was the king. Brechen Glansent Arobern. *The* Arobern, himself. As soon as the possibility occurred to Gereint, he was sure it was true.

"Well?" repeated the king, still scowling.

Gereint, appalled, took a breath and tried to think what response he could make.

"Forgive him, my king: He is justifiably both angry and frightened," Beguchren Teshrichten cut in. His light voice was as smooth and unreadable as ever. "Under the circumstances, I would be amazed at equanimity. If I'm not offended, why should you be?" The mage came a step toward Gereint and added to him, "My actions were unpardonable, but may I ask you nevertheless to pardon them?"

Gereint stared at him, still unable to respond.

The king shook his head, looking only slightly mollified. "What Beguchren does not say is that he was following my orders." He pointed a heavy finger at a chair near Gereint. "Sit down and listen."

Gereint sank into the indicated chair.

"You were to be returned to Perech Fellesteden's heirs," the king told him grimly. "Only Lady Tehre Amnachudran came to me and told me a story that interested me. Beguchren has an urgent need for a strong maker. I told Beguchren he could have you. I said: How useful, the man is already *geas* bound! But Beguchren said if he could have free loyalty instead of bound obedience, that would suit him better. So I told him to try your loyalty and courage. I said, prove both or be satisfied with the *geas*. That was my order, do you understand?" He paused.

Evidently satisfied by the quality of Gereint's silence, the king then went on: "So you are here, free. And I have no use for these, unless I think of another use, do you understand?" He picked up a pair of small silver rings from a side table and threw them down on the polished desk so that they rang like bells.

Gereint had not noticed the rings until the king picked them up, and flinched involuntarily as they rolled and chimed on the desk. He knew what threat the king was making with that gesture—then he realized, belatedly, what threat the king might *actually* be making and could not stop himself from flinching a second time.

"So," the king said, giving him a hard stare, "you serve my friend

Beguchren as he requires, and I will let *you* choose how to dispose of those, do you understand me, Gereint Enseichen? You may melt them down or throw them in the river, what you wish. That is the coin *I* offer—but if you will not serve my mage, I will think of something else to do with them. Do you understand?"

Gereint began to say "yes," found his mouth too dry to speak, and swallowed. At last he managed to whisper, "I understand."

"I think you do," the king said. "Beguchren, tell me later what you decide. But soon. Yes?"

The mage inclined his head a minute degree. "Of course."

"Hah. Of course you will," said the king. He gave his mage a short nod, and Gereint one last scowl, and went out.

"He is not so harsh as he pretends," Beguchren said, wryly apologetic. "Gereint Enseichen, I did not wish to, as you say, play a game of threats and the iron with you, and I ask your pardon."

Gereint did not answer. He was not sure he *could* answer. He felt as though he'd battered down a door and stormed through, only to find he had stepped over a cliff. As though he were still falling, even now.

"You're very angry," the mage observed. "And—understandably— very frightened." He turned and went to a sideboard, poured wine from a carafe into a silver cup, topped the cup up with water, came back, and held the cup out to Gereint.

Gereint took it silently and held it, not drinking.

"I have no doubt you've swallowed a great deal of anger and fear in your life," said the mage. He leaned his hip against the edge of the desk, barely tall enough to do so, and tilted his head, meeting Gereint's eyes. His manner was more assured than many a court noble's; indeed, his manner was entirely unlike the usual arrogance of an ordinary court noble; the white-haired mage seemed to combine assurance with an unusual, wry matter-offactness. He added softly, "I'm glad you trust me enough to show your anger to me. The Arobern was wrong to admonish you for it."

Gereint put his cup down on the arm of his chair hard enough that the watered wine nearly sloshed over the rim and started to get to his feet, then changed his mind and sank back. He demanded harshly, "What do you want from me? What did you *do* to me?"

"I did nothing, or nearly nothing," the mage said gently. "Truly, Gereint. I went into your mind, but you know what I saw there. You have a specific sort of gift: not merely strong, but peculiarly, mmm, flexible, and flexible in particular ways. Did you know?" He paused, but when Gereint did not answer, he went on. "Your gift is suitable, I believe, for my need. I needed to know whether that was so. So I went into your mind, into the private memories you hold. That is why you are so angry. But I had no choice. Gereint Enseichen, I ask your pardon."

For the third time. Gereint was beginning to feel that continued refusal might merely be churlish. He managed a curt nod.

Beguchren bowed his head a little, despite the ill grace of that nod. "Good. Thank you. You say the man who removed your brand did it for kindness; you claimed a man in Dachsichten did it for principle. Will you believe, at least, that if I did not act from kindness, I might have done so from principle?"

"Cold magecraft is what fashions the *geas* rings!"

"My principles are not entirely consistent, I admit." The mage paused, then added softly, "But I was glad to free you, Gereint."

Gereint stared at him wordlessly. If he had spoken, he knew he would say too much, so he said nothing.

"It's true I act from my need. But what I need from you, you must give willingly. Perhaps time will lay a foundation for trust to grow. There will be at least a little time. I will be going north tomorrow. You will go with me. I will expect you at the Emnerechke Gates at dawn."

It did not escape Gereint that the mage still had not said what it actually *was* he needed from him. Clearly, he was not going to. He did not ask again, but said instead, "You'll expect me, will you?"

The pale-eyed mage tilted his head. "Shall I not? I know you are capable of gratitude. You might belong now to Lord Fellesteden's heirs; what do you owe me that you are here"—a slight downward gesture with two fingers—"and free?"

Gereint set his jaw.

"And beyond any consideration of debt and gratitude . . . I need your help," the mage added softly. "I do not wish to sound overly dramatic, Gereint Enseichen, but as it happens, we have encountered some difficulty in the north. There are no more mages now, you know. Only I. I am in need of a maker with a strong gift, a certain kind of gift; the kind I believe you possess. A man possessed of both courage and integrity; a man"—and this time the slight, wry gesture compared his own height to Gereint's—"who is physically strong. So . . . I shall expect you at the Emnerechke Gates at dawn. Shall I?"

Gereint wanted, for no reason he understood, to say "Yes." He wanted to bow his head dutifully and agree. He set himself hard against any such acquiescence and said nothing.

"Then, though you may wish to take your leave elsewhere in the city, I shall expect you at the gates at dawn," concluded the mage imperturbably, exactly as though he had agreed.

It was a dismissal as well as a command. Gereint got to his feet, turned his back on the king's mage, and walked out.

Fareine opened the door of Tehre Amnachudran's house when Gereint knocked. Her smile held surprise and delight; her glance downward toward Gereint's feet seemed perfectly involuntary.

Gereint was still wearing the sandals he had been given. He obligingly turned one foot so the woman could see his ankle. "Legally," he added. As he said it, it came home to him, almost for the first time, that this was true. Legally free, as he had never truly expected to be again in his life. It should have been a realization of powerful joy. Perhaps it would be, eventually. But he remembered the Arobern throwing the silver *geas* rings down on the desk and declaring, *I have no use for these, unless I think of another use.* He said, "I need to speak to Tehre."

"Of course. The honored lady's in the library. You are most welcome! She has been very worried for you." Fareine stepped back and swung the door wide.

Tehre Amnachudran was sitting at the library's largest table, surrounded by heavy books and scrolls, most of them open. A sheaf of blank papers lay at her elbow and she was holding a long quill in one fine-boned hand. Gereint did not expect her to notice any intrusion, but she looked up sharply when the door opened. Then her small face lit with an unconsidered smile and she jumped to her feet. "Gereint!"

Gereint turned his foot to show her, too, his ankle. "They tell me I have you to thank for this," he said. Not directly, but Tehre had clearly forged the first link of that chain and hammered it into shape. "You went to the *king*?"

"Well, I had to," Tehre said simply. "They said you would go to Lord Fellesteden's heirs; they said I couldn't even petition to buy you. So I had to go to the Arobern. No one else can overrule a judge, you know." Then she stood still for a moment, her formidable attention focused on him. "He said he would give you to Beguchren Teshrichten. Did he?" And, deeply suspicious, "Are you all right?"

"He did," Gereint answered. "And I don't know. But I'm free of the *geas*, and that's not something I ever expected. What did you tell the Arobern? You told him the truth? That was foolish—"

"I had to," Tehre repeated, surprised. "Not quite *all* the truth—not the part I've only guessed at myself." She meant she had carefully left out any speculations about just who might have removed Gereint's brand. "But most of the truth, yes. How else could I persuade him to listen to me? It worked: He believed me about Fellesteden, you know.

He said he needed a man who could be loyal. I told him you would do very well."

"He might have put *you* under the *geas*—"

"But he didn't."

Gereint didn't say, *He still might.* He thought again of the Arobern's heavy voice declaring, *I have no use for these, unless I think of another use.* He said harshly, "You should never have gone to him!"

"But I did," Tehre said reasonably, "and it's done. And the Arobern freed you, so everything is fine. I didn't tell him my father interfered with your brand, you know. Only that you didn't have it when you came to my door." She gave a little nod, as though to add, *So that's all right,* and turned back toward the table. "As you suggested, I've been working on synthesizing our current understanding of the philosophy of materials—"

Gereint was sure she had been.

"It's slow work," Tehre added, staring down at the piled and scattered books with a dissatisfied expression. "It takes me away from actually working on the mathematics—I think I'm close to formulating a useful equation about the velocity of propagation in a crack once it actually starts to run, and here I am looking up what other makers and philosophers have said about things that are only obliquely related." The woman began idly sketching parabolas down the margin of a book, fitting tangent lines to them as she went. She added, "I would greatly prefer to have you do this for me," and turned her head to give Gereint an intent look.

"I am to go north in the morning," Gereint told her. "With Beguchren Teshrichten." He was surprised at the regret this statement caused him: He had not realized that he did, in fact, want simply to say "yes," and take the quill out of Tehre's hand.

"Oh!" said Tehre. She paused, her eyes narrowing. "How far north? Tashen?"

She meant, *Anywhere near my family's house?* Gereint opened a hand in a gesture of uncertainty. "I don't know. So you had better write your father, if you haven't already."

"Oh, I have. I will again. You came to tell me that? Thank you, Gereint. That may be important, if you—and the lord mage—should go so far." Tehre paused. Then asked, "Why north? What does the king's mage want with you?"

Gereint shrugged ignorance. "I would tell you if I knew. There's evidently some trouble in the north. With the new desert, I suppose. I don't know what or why the lord mage thinks I'd be useful to his hand in dealing with it."

"Trouble. Huh. In the north, but you don't know what it comprises." Tehre glanced down at her sketches, then back up at Gereint. "I wonder what this 'trouble' is, and how close it's come to my parents' house. Maybe . . . hmm. Maybe . . . there are all those refugees, and Fereine says they say the desert pursued them south. I wonder how large the new desert actually is?"

"Larger than one would think necessary to encompass Melentser," Gereint said, a little too quickly for a man who was supposed to be from some town in Meridanium and not from Melentser at all. He added, "Or so I've heard."

Tehre nodded, looking thoughtful. "I wonder if it's still growing? Beyond the agreed bounds? It could be very hard on the north if the desert presses too close to the towns. And on the south if any more people have to leave the north. The prices of everything are already high, even with only the people of Melentser forced to leave their homes." Her eyes were dark with worry. "My family . . . Well, but Beguchren Teshrichten is very powerful. I suppose he will be able to settle this 'trouble,' whatever it is."

Gereint, remembering the mage's hooded eyes and inscrutable smile, thought this was probably true. "But in any case, I wished to see you, honored lady, to thank you for interceding for me. And, yes, to ask whether you'd sent a letter to your father, and urge you to send another. And . . . that is, if you don't find it an imposition, I find I would rather leave Breidechboden from the house of a friend."

"Of course." Tehre sounded faintly surprised, but she looked pleased. "If you're not leaving until tomorrow morning, you can help me break your catapult. I thought you would miss that; I'm glad you'll be here for it. I want to see if I can slow the fracturing process enough to let me really study how the materials break. Do you think you can help me with that? You've probably tried to slow down something that was in the process of breaking, haven't you?"

"Carriage wheels, and an axle once."

"Perfect!" Tehre declared, and headed for the garden, abandoning the books without a backward look.

Gereint gazed after her for a moment, smiling. The woman's focus on work was . . . soothing. Comfortable, in a way he couldn't really put into words. He could feel knots of tension in his neck and back relaxing. He didn't know what he thought about Beguchren; he barely knew what he thought of his freedom, such as it was—but he knew he was glad to find Tehre Amnachudran absolutely unchanged. He knew that whatever lay to the north, he would be glad to think of her in this house, breaking mechanisms and developing equations to describe how they fractured.

CHAPTER 6

Tehre did not know what she thought of Gereint's going north with Beguchren Teshrichten, but she knew she was glad he was going north as a free man. Or, if not free, at least no more bound than anyone subject to circumstance and the ordinary pressure a powerful man could bring to bear. On the other hand, that was surely compulsion enough. But it was much better than being *geas* bound to whatever brute was the heir of Perech Fellesteden. She was quite sure that, whoever the heir might be, he was a brute. What other sort of heir could a man such as Lord Fellesteden possibly have engendered?

Gereint left her house well before dawn. Fareine woke Tehre, as she had asked, and Tehre flung on the simple dress she'd laid out ready, pinned her hair up, and ran down to the main door to bid him a proper farewell. He had said, *I would rather leave Breidechboden from the house of a friend.* It had been important to him. So he had come here. To tell her about the king's mage and urge her to write her father—of course. But also because it had been important to him to have the house of a *friend* behind him when he left the city. He evidently had no family—or no family to whom he could go. Tehre had found herself shaken by pity at the idea that Gereint had been abandoned by his family. Whatever he had done. No matter what *she* might do, she knew *her* family would never close their house to her.

So she met Gereint at her door to bid him farewell, as a friend would do. He was surprised and, she thought, touched. Tehre wished him luck and fair weather, as she might have wished any friend going out on the road from under her roof.

The tall man tilted his head and quirked an eyebrow at her. "I'm sorry I didn't have the chance to build you a whole series of catapults."

So was Tehre. She nodded wistfully. "I'll break other things, I suppose," she said, and he chuckled, though she hadn't meant to say anything funny. But she didn't mind. Gereint laughed at her in a way that made it seem that he was inviting her to share the joke.

"You do that," he told her. "Thank you, Tehre. Fareine." He nodded to them in a way that made it plain he was sorry to leave. Then he left.

"Beguchren Teshrichten," Tehre said thoughtfully, looking out at the dim street after he was gone. "And 'trouble' in the north."

"Tehre?"

"Nothing. I just wonder . . . nothing, Fareine." Tehre shut the door on the faint pearly light of the false dawn and went back to her room to dress properly.

The Arobern's palace was an exercise in the builders' craft: ornamented nearly, but not quite, to the point of absurdity. As a child, Tehre had loved the sheer extravagant excess of it; even now, she loved the pinnacles and great statues that lined the tops of the walls—especially the shorter walls, of course. She understood now, as she had not as a child, that the higher walls had enough extra weight of their own that they did not need the weight of statues to stabilize them against the sideways thrust of the slanted roofs. But the statues were nice in their own right, and the stonecarvers had no doubt enjoyed making them.

Tehre's carriage passed a long colonnade where the columns, otherwise simple, had been painted purple and crimson—except where they had been gilded—and through a marble gate topped by a short, thick architrave. A straight stone lintel such as an architrave was not, of course, structurally stable. This one had cracked exactly as one might have expected: twice symmetrically on the upper surface and once, in the middle, on the lower, thus turning itself into a much more stable three-hinged arch.

Tehre would simply have suggested constructing an arch in the first place, but it was interesting to think about the way the stone had responded to the stresses it had found unacceptable. An interesting example of why one needed to consider the tensile stresses and thrust lines that bore on any given point within a structure; it was hardly coincidence that the straight lintel had cracked at those precise three points; those were the hinge points of the "arch" ring, of course. There should be a way to represent the relationship of the tensile stresses and the resulting thrust lines to the thickness of the stones used in the construction . . . One might let thrust t represent the ratio between the strength of the thrust at a given location within the structure and the cross-sectional area of that location, and that might let one calculate . . . Oh, had they arrived?

Tehre blinked and gazed out the window; it seemed the trip had gone rather quickly. She wished she had paper and a quill to note down her thoughts about architraves and thrust lines and the forces at work on the stone. She even glanced around the carriage vaguely, as though she might find such supplies on the seat beside her. Of course, there was nothing so useful in the carriage, on the seat, or elsewhere. She ought to put a box of writing things in all her carriages . . . She had thought of that before, but she never remembered.

The carriage had drawn up before a massive set of gilded brass doors and her driver hopped off his seat and came around to place a step for Tehre. "Will the honored lady wish me to wait?" he asked.

"No," Tehre said absently, studying the doors. "No, I don't know how long I'll be. I'll get a public carriage home." She wondered if anyone would mind if she examined the door hinges. Hinges on doors that size must be under a great deal of tension. Stresses in metal were very interesting. They would probably fail by shearing, if they failed . . . She decided reluctantly that she probably should not take time to look at door hinges, no matter how interesting, and simply walked through the doors.

There were men-at-arms in the Arobern's livery, and a quite exalted chamberlain. Tehre had met the chamberlain previously; he nodded to her and smiled and said a lot of polite things that all meant, *You'll have to wait while I see if the king wants to disarrange his complicated schedule for you.* Tehre allowed him to guide her to an antechamber to wait. It was, at least, a particularly nice antechamber, with chairs that were comfortable as well as expensive and windows that let in plenty of light and air. The chamberlain hadn't forgotten that, on her previous visit, the Arobern had indeed been pleased to see her.

Only one other person was in the antechamber: a man Tehre didn't know at all. He didn't seem to have any attendants or servants . . . Well, Tehre hadn't brought even Fareine with her, so neither did she, and what did that prove? The man was tall, though not anything like as tall as Gereint. But there was something else about him she was not quite able to identify.

Then the man rose politely to nod to her and murmur a courteous acknowledgment, and Tehre realized that he was not Casmantian.

How interesting. Probably he was Feierabianden; at least, there were very good reasons a Feierabianden lord might be here in the Arobern's palace, and Tehre did not know of any reason a lord from Linularinum would be.

Tehre wished now she had let Fareine accompany her; she did not know how to speak to a foreign lord. Tehre never really knew what to say to anyone. She always seemed to make some perfectly obvious comment that nevertheless offended somebody. Fareine always knew what to say to everybody. Only Fareine was sometimes not willing to be very direct, and this morning Tehre had wanted nothing else but to get at once to the point, or why else bother coming back to the palace?

Well, but surely it was not polite to sit and pretend she was the only person in the room. Tehre said carefully, in the Terheien she had learned as a girl and had not spoken since, "My name is Tehre Amnachudran Tanshan." Exactly like a schoolroom lesson. "Be welcome to Casmantium and to Breidechboden. What is your name, lord?"

The lord of Feierabiand smiled, no doubt recognizing the careful, rote statements and question. He answered in strongly accented Prechen, "Lady Tehre Amnachudran Tanshan, I am Bertaud son of Boudan, Lord of the Delta and servant of Iaor Daveien Behanad Safiad."

He was careful and slow with her name, which lilted strangely across his tongue. On the other hand, the unfamiliar Feierabianden names sounded like they belonged in his mouth; Tehre could never have pronounced them as he did. It occurred to her that language was a making; words were like the bricks in a wall and syntax the mortar that joined them together. Pronunciation was like style; the maker's signature. She smiled.

"You are a court lady?" the foreign lord asked her. "Forgive me that I do not know your name . . ."

"No," Tehre said, surprised. "I am . . ." What was the word in Terheien? "A maker," she said in Prechen, because she could not remember the Terheien.

"A maker," said Lord Bertaud, and obligingly repeated the term in Terheien. "The makers and builders of Casmantium are famous even in Feierabiand."

"Yes," Tehre said, happy to strike familiar ground. "Andreikan Warichteier says in his *Principia*, 'Casmantium for making, Feierabiand for calling, Linularinum for law.'" Only she could not recall the Terheien for "law" and had to use the Prechen. She gazed at the foreign lord curiously. "Do you call? What is it like, to call?"

"Call?" he repeated, shaking his head to show he did not understand her. He repeated the word in Prechen: "Call? To call out, is this the term?"

"Oh—yes. But I mean 'calling.' Those who call, mmm." Tehre searched for the word for "animal," could not find it, and said carefully, "Dogs, horses, mice. So?" She was amused that she remembered the Terheien for "mice."

But the Feierabianden lord frowned and gave a terse shake of his head. "No. I do not call."

And she had angered him by asking. Maybe he was ashamed he

could not call, if, as Warichteier had implied, almost everyone in Feierabiand could. Tehre did not know whether she should apologize. She
had been pleased to meet a man who might call; she had never met
anyone who could tell her about that sort of magic, so different from
making. At least, she assumed it was very different. An interesting
question: Maybe the experience was similar, though the expression of
the gift was dissimilar? But she was sorry to have offended the foreign
lord. She did not know exactly what she should apologize for, so it
seemed safer to say nothing. Probably she should not have spoken to
the Feierabianden lord at all . . .

But he said, seeming sorry to have frowned at her, "What do you . . .
ah, make?"

"Oh . . ." Tehre was pleased the lord was not irretrievably offended
after all. She wondered how to explain the philosophy of making in a
language she barely spoke well enough to say, *My name is Tehre, what
is your name?* But she tried to explain. "I think about making.You understand? I study . . . how to make. How, ah, how things . . ." She did
not know the words for "break" or "fail."

But Lord Bertaud was nodding. "You study. Like a mage."

"A little like a mage," Tehre agreed, though she was doubtful about
the comparison. Perhaps in Feierabiand the mages were all also scholars. Mages did study things, she supposed. Magical things. She wondered whether there was a philosophy of magic passed along among
mages, as there were philosophies of natural materials, and if so what
it might comprise.

"And you—"

But the lord's question was cut off because the chamberlain came
back just then. Tehre was almost sorry for that; the Feierabianden lord
was interesting, even if he did not have the gift of calling.

"My lord, the Arobern will see you at once," the chamberlain said
to Lord Bertaud, in Terheien much better than Tehre's. "But," he added
to Tehre in Prechen, "I am sorry, Lady Tehre, the Arobern does not
have time to see you now and asks that you make an appointment for
an audience at a later time. Perhaps in ten days?"

"But—" Tehre protested. It had not occurred to her that the Arobern
would refuse to see her. She might have gone to see Beguchren Teshrichten himself, if she had gone the previous day. She saw now that
she should have done it that way, although it was the Arobern and not
his mage she wanted most to see. But the mage might have made time
to see her. But now it was too late. She said unhappily, "But . . ." But
then did not know what to say after that. If the king would not see
her . . . She looked doubtfully at the chamberlain.

"I did give him your name, Lady Tehre," the chamberlain said gently.

Lord Bertaud had been watching her face. "Perhaps the lady will walk with me," he said suddenly. "I am not . . ." He hunted for a word and guessed, "hurry?"

"My lord," began the chamberlain.

The Feierabianden lord looked sternly at the chamberlain. "I would, ah. Glad. Ah, I would *be* glad, if the lady would walk with me. I do not mind to wait. The king will not . . ." He hesitated and used the Terheien word, "Protest."

He sounded very certain of that last. Tehre realized—she should have realized it at once—that Lord Bertaud was very probably a representative and agent of the king of Feierabiand. Yes, of course, he'd said, *a servant of Iaor Something Something Safiad*. Iaor Safiad was the Feierabianden king, Tehre was almost sure. Certainly it was some Safiad or other.

And after the summer just past, no doubt the Safiad's trusted representative could say, *The king will not protest*, and be quite confident. Everyone knew, though no one said in so many words, that the Safiad king had comprehensively defeated the Arobern's plan to annex part of Feierabiand—that the improvements to the western road across the mountains were a gesture of magnanimity from the victor toward his defeated opponent. That the Arobern had been required to send his little son as hostage to the Safiad court. Tehre wondered suddenly whether this Lord Bertaud had been responsible for arranging that as well. It seemed very likely.

She said, not glancing at the chamberlain, "I am grateful for your kindness, Lord Bertaud," and smiled at the dutiful schoolroom phrase. But she *was* grateful, even if it was merely a whim born of the foreigner's wish to show a glint of steel beneath his polite court manners.

"I am glad to help," the lord answered graciously, and offered her his arm in a gesture just short of flirtatious. Perhaps that was the ordinary court manner in Feierabiand.

Tehre smiled again, took the lord's arm, and allowed him to guide her out of the antechamber just as though he knew where in the Arobern's palace he was going. The chamberlain, suppressing a just-audible sigh, hurried to get round in front of them so he could actually show them where to go.

Brechen Glansent Arobern was a big, aggressive man; black bearded, his hair cropped very short in the manner of a soldier. He affected a soldier's style, but if it was an affectation, everyone nevertheless agreed that he was a dangerous man to meet on the field of battle. It was a matter of common astonishment that the Feierabianden king had defeated him—but then, everyone knew the Arobern's defeat had not exactly come about on any ordinary field of battle. It was said that the Feierabianden king had allied with the griffins, and generally agreed that he would come to regret that dangerous alliance.

But the heavy gold chain the Arobern wore around his throat was not a soldier's ornament, and the contained restless power of his presence went well past the simple physical charisma of even the most impressive of soldiers. When he scowled at the Feierabianden lord, the whole room seemed to hum with the power of his displeasure; when he transferred that scowl to Tehre, she felt that disapproval as almost a physical force. She tipped her chin up and tried not to blink in dismay. The king had not been like this before; but then, when she had previously come to see him, she had not come in defiance of his command or in the company of a representative of the Feierabianden king. She tried not to look nervous.

"Forgive the lady," Lord Bertaud said, fairly smoothly, considering his awkward Prechen. "She said she wished to see you. I said I did not mind to wait." He offered a small, deferential bow.

The Arobern turned his thunderous scowl back to the foreign lord . . . Then surprised Tehre with a deep, amused chuckle. The humor might have had a hard edge to it, but it did not seem forced. "Well," he said to Tehre. "If you wish so strongly to see me, perhaps I should make time, hah? As my guest promises that he is patient." He beckoned to her and turned aside, leading her to the other end of the room where they could speak in semi-privacy.

It was a large room, but thankfully not one of the great halls with porphyry pillars and marble floors and high, vaulted, echoing ceilings. This was a quieter room, one with thick rugs and comfortable furniture, the sort of room where the Arobern might well prefer to conduct actual business rather than stylized audiences. He waved her to a chair, dropping heavily into another.

Tehre perched on the edge of the indicated chair and tried nervously to decide whether the king was actually annoyed with her or not. She could not tell.

"Well?" the Arobern said. "I am grateful you led my attention to Gereint Enseichen, and so I am willing to be patient. But if you have encountered difficulties with Lord Fellesteden's heirs, that is a matter for the city patrol or for any of my judges, not for me. Or you wish to sue his estate for damages? That, too, is a matter for a judge and not for me."

"Of course," Tehre said, surprised. "That is, Lord King, I didn't come about Lord Fellesteden at all. I wanted to ask about Beguchren Teshrichten, and whom would I ask except you, since he left the city at dawn? I wondered what the trouble in the north is, and what the lord mage wanted of my friend Gereint. He freed him, I know. But I don't understand why, and I wonder if he imposed a different kind of bond when he took away the *geas*?" She paused and looked carefully at the Arobern. Tehre knew she sometimes mistook the effect of something she said, but if the king was angry, she couldn't see it. He only gazed at her, patiently neutral.

Tehre went on, "If your honored mage wanted a maker, well, there are many fine makers in Breidechboden. I'm a maker myself, and not the least skilled of all makers, though I know it's not modest to say so, but it's true. But I don't remember hearing that the Lord Mage Beguchren Teshrichten was seeking a maker, so he didn't just say so and ask for makers to apply to him, did he?

"And you told me you needed a man who was—who had a great capacity for loyalty. That was what you said. But what you meant was that *Beguchren Teshrichten* needed a maker who had that capacity, and for some reason he preferred a maker who was *geas* bound even though the first thing he did was take away the *geas*. I think that's odd. I've tried and tried to think what the lord mage might have had in mind when he chose Gereint, only I can't.

"And then they went north. So there's something important to do in the north, something to do with the griffins and the new desert because why else would you send your mage? And it's a problem, or there's a problem associated with it, or the lord mage expects to have problems when he tries to do it or solve it or handle it. And Gereint's a good maker, but I don't know if I would look for a maker on the grounds of *a great capacity for loyalty* if I had a problem with *making* in mind: I would look for the *best and strongest* maker, whoever that might be. But Gereint came from the north, didn't he? He said Meridanium, but I wonder if maybe it wasn't really Melentser? So I'm worried that *making* isn't exactly what the lord mage had in mind when he specifically wanted *Gereint* to go north with him—"

The Arobern lifted a hand, stopping Tehre. He said, sounding a little amused, "You are very direct, Lady Tehre."

"People say that," Tehre admitted. "Sometimes people get angry. If I've made you angry, I'm sorry. I didn't mean to. I don't understand how anybody ever gets anything said or done if they aren't willing to say what they mean. My family is in the north, you know, and if there's trouble there, I'm worried for them." She added belatedly, "Lord King."

"Lady Tehre, I am not angry with you," the Arobern said mildly.

"You are right in this respect: There is a problem in the north." He watched Tehre narrowly. "It is not your concern, however. It is not a matter for makers or builders, you understand? It is a matter for mages. And as you say, I have only one mage, now."

"But Gereint—"

"The man is your friend, you say? Yet you have known him only for days, and not even by his right name, is that not true?"

"Even so," Tehre said, she hoped with dignity. She knew she had flushed. It was true she had not known Gereint's right name until the king had used it himself, but she hoped she had not given this away somehow. She said firmly, "I don't have many friends, Lord King. But when Gereint *Enseichen* needed the house of a friend to go to, he came to my house."

"I understand what you say." The king leaned back in his chair, looking at Tehre. "Lady Tehre, I understand your concerns. I promise you, so far as I am aware, your family, however far north they may be, is not in immediate danger. If danger arrives at the doorstep of your family's house, I think it will not come so swiftly that they and all their household cannot retreat before it."

"But . . ." said Tehre, but then did not know what to say. She blinked, trying to rid herself of the image of her father's house surrounded by sand and red stone.

"I have considered carefully," the Arobern said firmly, "and I am satisfied to leave matters as they stand."

"Oh." Tehre tried to think. She began uncertainly, "But—"

"No," said the Arobern, holding up a hand to stop her. "Let your friend go north. Let my mage see to this problem, as I have sent him to do. Attend to your own house, Lady Tehre." He got to his feet and stood looking down at her.

After a moment, Tehre realized that this was actually a command. She rose quickly. "Lord King—"

"No," said the Arobern. Patiently. But with enough firmness that she knew she could not protest again. He added, "Lady Tehre, I see that you, too, have a great capacity for loyalty. I admire this. But, no. Go home. When there is news of practical importance from the north, you will hear it, I promise you."

Tehre hesitated. Then, as there was nothing else she could do, she bowed. "Lord King."

"And another time," the king said, showing a glint of iron under the patience, "I hope you will be content to wait for a proper appointment, Lady Tehre."

Tehre caught back several things that occurred to her to say. Her mother would have been amazed. Instead of saying anything at all, she bowed again, lower, in apology, backed away three steps, bowed once more, and retreated. Not in very good order, she knew.

Go home. Like she was a child. Or, she admitted to herself, perhaps merely like she was subject to the commands of her king. That was harder to protest. If the Arobern had ordered her to go home without talking to her at all, that would not actually have been surprising. He *had* been patient.

She was angry anyway. She was both angry and frustrated when she left the palace and told a servant to hail a public carriage for her. But the anger faded as the carriage rattled through the streets of the city, and by the time she stepped down and waved at the driver to go around to the kitchen door for payment, she was no longer angry at all. But she was still intensely frustrated.

"Tehre . . ." Fareine brought her a plate of apple pastries in the library, since she had not eaten breakfast.

Tehre picked one up, put it down, and asked, "Fareine, do we have a map of the north somewhere?"

Fareine regarded Tehre uneasily. "Several, I should think. But—"

"Would you get one for me, please?"

"What did you find out about Gereint? Or the lord mage? Isn't that what you went to find out?"

"Yes. Nothing." Tehre tapped her fingers on the polished surface of the table. "I saw the Arobern—"

"You went to the king? Again? Tehre, you're going to offend him, doing that!"

"Yes, maybe. Anyway, it didn't help."

"You couldn't speak to him?" Fareine sounded as though she suspected such a failure might have been a good thing.

"I talked to him," Tehre corrected. "He wouldn't talk to me." She was silent for a moment, contemplating the pattern of that encounter. "I might have said too much, too openly," she concluded. "But he said far too little. Fareine, would you please get me a map?"

"If I won't, I suppose you'll get one yourself. So I suppose I will. If you'll eat a pastry for me."

"Oh . . ." Tehre picked the pastry up again and bit into it. The apples were nothing like as good as the ones from her mother's orchards. She ate the pastry anyway, brushing crumbs absently off the table onto the floor, ignoring Fareine's little sound of protest. "What?" she said impatiently. "Do you want me to get grease spots on the scroll?"

"No," sighed Fareine. "I'll get a girl to come sweep."

"Yes, please," Tehre agreed absently, and set the plate with the

remaining pastries on one edge of the map to hold it open. Then she studied it. It was really more a map of the northeastern province of Meridanium. The Terintsan River formed the western border of Meridanium,
small towns scattered along its length until it joined the Teschanken in the
confluence at Pamnarichtan. Well to the north and west, at the edge of the
map, lay Melentser.

Or that was where Melentser *had* lain. Tehre supposed it had all
gone to desert now. She wondered how long the city would last under the
pressure of sun and scouring sand-laden winds. Would all the tall buildings, so proudly raised over the years by builders and engineers, merely
wear away? That might take a long time. Or would the desert somehow
destroy the remnants of the human city quickly? And if so, how?

And why did Beguchren Teshrichten want to go north toward that
desert? And why did he need a maker to go with him? Not just a maker,
but one from the north, maybe from Melentser, a man who might have
actually seen the desert come to the city. Yes, Gereint had probably
used the coming of the desert to get away from Lord Fellesteden; that
seemed logical. But did the cold mage specifically want a man who had
been in Melentser, or a man who had been *geas* bound? Or both?

Too many questions, and no way to answer any of them. Tehre
sighed.

"You—" Fareine began, but stopped.

"I think . . ." Tehre began. "I think—"

But one of her other women interrupted her. She came quietly to
the door, waiting for attention.

"Yes?" Tehre asked the woman.

"A visitor, my lady," murmured the woman apologetically. All the
household knew Tehre did not like visitors.

Tehre nodded, developing and discarding half a dozen quick
guesses about who might have come—Gereint again, not likely; a servant from the king, more possible but still unlikely; her brother? A
messenger from her parents? Oh, probably a representative from Lord
Fellesteden's heir; now *that* seemed likely. If unwelcome. Tehre tried to
think of a highly regarded judge in Breidechboden to whom she might
appeal, if there was going to be trouble from that direction after all . . .

But the woman said instead, "A foreign lord, honored lady: a Lord
Bertaud. He didn't give his other name . . ."

"They don't," Tehre agreed, blinking in surprise. "In Feierabiand,
they say Somebody son of Somebody. Or daughter, I suppose." But she
was not thinking about this interesting difference in customs. She was
thinking about the Feierabianden lord she had met in the Arobern's
palace. He had been kind to her . . . or interested in her, or more likely

her business with the king . . . She said, "I will see him, of course. In, well . . ." She looked questioningly at Fareine.

"Your reception room has half a disassembled catapult in it," Fareine murmured.

"My workroom?"

"Not suitable. It had better be here, I suppose. Let me get this plate—is the floor clean? Honored lady, you need to go put your hair up."

"It is up . . ."

"It's coming down," Fareine said inflexibly. "Go put it up properly. I'll go myself to welcome our guest. Does he speak Prechen? Well, at least that's in his favor . . ." She went out.

Tehre ran up to her room, took one surprised look in her mirror, tried to tuck recalcitrant strands of her hair back where they belonged, gave up, took down the whole mass, and began impatiently to put it up again. Luckily Meierin arrived to help.

"Fareine says your green dress is fine," the girl told Tehre. "But she said to remind you that you can't wear gold in your own house; where are your copper earrings? Oh, never mind, here we go," and she collected earrings and bangles of fine twisted copper wire and helped Tehre put them on. "I've never seen a Feierabianden lord," she remarked wistfully, stepping back to look Tehre quickly up and down and add one last copper pin to help hold her hair in place.

Tehre laughed. "Bring a plate of cakes in a few minutes."

"Thank you!" said Meierin, smiling back, and ducked out to run down to the kitchen.

Tehre left her room with a good deal of stately care to avoid losing any pins, descended the stairs, and entered the library once more.

Lord Bertaud . . . son of Boudan, was that right? Such strange names, so soft in the mouth. Tehre smiled and inclined her head and limited herself to, "Lord Bertaud. Welcome." That should be safe . . .

The Feierabianden lord had been standing by the table, gazing thoughtfully down at the map that was still laid out there. But he looked up when Tehre came in, took a step forward, and bowed very correctly. "Lady Tehre Amnachudran Tanshan," he said, careful on the rolling syllables of her name. It sounded very exotic on his tongue. He went on in Prechen: "I, ah . . . intrude, not?"

"No, no," Tehre assured him in Terheien. "Welcome. I, mmm, I am glad you visit." She did not remember the Terheien for "visit," but he seemed to understand the Prechen. "Do you sit, honored lord? I mean, mmm . . ."

"*Will* you," the lord reminded her. "*Will* you sit. Yes. I thank you."

Tehre nodded, grateful for the prompt. She said ruefully, "*Will* you.

Yes. Thank you. I should have study harder with my, my . . . teacher, when I am a girl. *Was* a girl."

"Yes," Lord Bertaud agreed, smiling. "I, the same. I speak Prechen for day, for week, but still not good."

"Well. Not *well*. Good is . . . the cakes." She gestured to the plate Meierin brought in and silently offered around. "The cakes are *good*. You speak Prechen *well*. You see?"

"Yes. Though I think I do not speak well," added the Feierabianden lord. He smiled at Meierin and took a cake. Meierin blushed, returned his smile, and backed away, bumping into one of the chairs as she retreated.

"Just leave the plate," Fareine said, casting a tolerant glance at the girl and waving a brisk dismissal. "Go on, go on, my dear, before you drop those." She took the plate herself and set it on a small table where their guest could reach it.

"You come, why?" Tehre asked, and gave Fareine a puzzled glance when the older woman rolled her eyes.

Whatever objection Fareine found in the simple question, Lord Bertaud seemed not to mind it. He glanced down, frowning, but Tehre could see he was only trying to find the words he wanted.

Lord Bertaud said at last, "I hear a little of what you say to, ah, the Arobern. I hear a little of what he say to you. 'Trouble in the north,' you say. 'Griffins, desert,' you say. The mage, the king's mage, Beguchren Teshrichten, he goes north, is that so? There is a problem there, where the desert is. Melentser. I ask the Arobern." He made a small, frustrated gesture. "He say, 'Do not worry, not your problem.' But I think of the griffins in Feierabiand this summer, and I do worry. I wonder, what problem? I wonder, what does the king's mage do in the north? I think maybe you know because your friend go with the mage, is that not so? So I come here to ask. Do you understand?"

Tehre thought she did. "The griffins brought their desert into Feierabiand, is that not so? But they were on your side, everyone knows that; in the end, they came in on your side against us and that's why your people could defeat our king—" She realized suddenly, partly from Fareine's expression, both that she was speaking rapidly in Prechen and that this last statement might be taken as an insult to Feierabiand. She stopped.

But Lord Bertaud only nodded and said, "Yes. That is true."

Well, no wonder he was worried. And if this Feierabianden lord had been involved in all those events during the summer, no wonder the king did not want to tell him anything important. The memory of that defeat must burn like fire to a proud king such as the Arobern.

It occurred to Tehre, belatedly, that perhaps she should not say more to Lord Bertaud when her own king had already rebuffed him. But, then, she really could not tell him anything; she did not *know* anything. She explained, this time careful to speak Terheien, "I wonder also. I ask many question also. I do not know. My lord king the Arobern, he says, yes, there is a problem. But he does not tell me what." She echoed the lord's earlier gesture of frustration. "I do not know."

"Ah." Lord Bertaud looked down for a moment. Then he looked over at the map on the table. "That?"

"Oh . . ." Tehre did not know quite what to say.

The lord got to his feet, went to the table, bent his head over the map for a long moment. He traced the crooked line of the Teschanken River with the tip of his finger. Tapped a spot in the far north, hard against the mountains. "Here," he said. "Melentser. Is that so?"

"Yes . . ."

"Yes." The lord turned from the map, crossed his arms over his chest, and regarded Tehre for a long moment. "You go north?"

Tehre, startled, began to say "no." But then, returning that earnest gaze, she did not deny it after all.

"You must be joking," said Fareine, gazing at her in total exasperation. "Except you never joke. *Tehre* . . ."

"I think," Tehre said slowly, in Terheien, not looking away from Lord Bertaud. "I think . . . maybe I go north." And, to Fareine, "Hush, Fareine! I can certainly go visit my parents, can't I? That's perfectly respectable, and I want to *know* what's happening in the north, not just sit here and worry! Don't you? And I'm a very broadly skilled maker, you know, much more so than Gereint. Maybe the king believes he has to have a man to deal with whatever is wrong; maybe Beguchren Teshrichten, for whatever reason, believes Gereint is just the right man, but maybe they both ought to consider their options a little more widely, do you think?"

Fareine, who had opened her mouth, looked faintly nonplussed and shut it again.

"Surely you wouldn't think I just wanted to chase north after a . . . a . . ." Tehre glanced quickly at the foreign lord and instead of *lover* finished with a far more obscure word: "Swain." She let the tartness of her tone suggest what she thought of this suggestion.

Fareine blushed, but she said stubbornly, "Tehre, dear, traveling with a foreigner? Meaning no offense to the honored lord, but your reputation isn't something to toss aside into the street—think of your honored father and lady mother!"

"There's no reason for anyone to think anything of my reputation one way or the other," Tehre said crisply. "As you know perfectly well. If anyone even notices anything I do, and why would they? But if I decide to visit my parents and then choose to travel in company with a respectable and honorable foreign lord who also happens to be going north, that's just good sense and why ever would anybody think twice about it?"

From Fareine's expression, she would have liked to argue with this, but she couldn't quite manage it. But she said, "Aside from 'everybody,' you might give a thought to what the *Arobern* might think! You're used to being cleverer than most people, but he's not a fool, Tehre."

Tehre paused. This was harder to answer. At last she merely shrugged. To the foreigner, she said again, "I think maybe I go north. My . . ." She could not remember the Terheien for "parents." "My father and mother live here." She touched the map. "I think maybe I go, ah, see my mother. One day, two, maybe. Then I go. But the . . ." "path," "street," "trail," what was the word for "road"? "The way is, ah, it is not safe. I find other person to go with. Yes?"

Lord Bertaud nodded. The swift exchange with Fareine had been too fast for him, but he understood her slow Terheien well enough, however clumsy. It was the satisfied sort of nod that said, *I knew I was right.* He said, "I go north. You, me, is that so?"

"Yes," Tehre said, satisfied. "You are kind to offer."

"The Arobern—" Fareine began, herself far from satisfied.

But Lord Bertaud only shook his head and held up a hand, smiling at the old woman. He said to Tehre, but also to Fareine, "I do not ask leave to come and go." He smiled at Tehre, not a cheerful smile, but somehow confident and grim and sad all at once. "But I do not, ah. Speak well. I do not . . . I am from Feierabiand, anyone can see. It would be good to go with a person from Casmantium. You go north, I go north, is better, yes?"

Tehre met the foreign lord's eyes. She tapped the map again, north of Tashen, where her father's house lay. "You, mmm . . . You might come and will be, mmm, my mother's guest?"

Lord Bertaud looked at the map, and then carefully at Tehre. "Generous, you. Yes. I come."

Tehre remembered very clearly the Arobern telling her, *Go home.* "I," she said firmly, "also do not ask leave to come and go."

CHAPTER 7

When Gereint left Tehre's house, in the dark before dawn, he headed down the street with a long stride as though he knew exactly where he was going. But, though he had not admitted it to Tehre, he was actually struggling with a dilemma. Because the Emnerechke Gates were not the only gates that led out of the city. There was still the other road, the one that ran west toward Feierabiand.

Trouble in the north; yes, that was interesting. But then, an intelligent man would not necessarily rush *toward* trouble. If the *king's own mage* was heading north, how crucial could Gereint's presence be? All this *I need a maker* aside . . . there were no few strongly gifted, highly skilled makers in Breidechboden. Some of them must surely suit Beguchren's need, whatever that might be. If Gereint did not appear at the Emnerechke Gates at dawn, Beguchren Teshrichten could invite or compel one of them. Or a dozen. Earth and iron, the king's mage could probably march every maker from the city into the far north in one long *parade* if he chose. They'd probably feel it an *honor*. Gereint did not even want to know why the king's mage had found *him* so uniquely suitable for whatever purpose he had in mind. Though probably he was going to find out.

But when he came to the cross street, he paused. He looked for a while down one cobbled avenue, where chilly wisps of morning mist drifted pearl white in the lamp light of the streets, hiding the farther reaches of the city from view. Then down the other way, equally veiled in dim light and mist. North? Or west? If he went west, how far would he get before he found Beguchren Teshrichten waiting for him? The man was, after all, a mage. Gereint could easily visualize his inscrutable smile as Gereint came around some bend in the road and found him standing there, waiting.

Though he would more likely be sitting in the courtyard of some pleasant inn, sipping ale while he waited. Or an expensive vintage of wine, more likely. And he might not be smiling, if Gereint tried to run for Feierabiand.

Gereint also thought of the *geas* rings chiming down out of the Arobern's hand: *I shall find something else to do with these, do you understand?* The threat frightened and angered him in nearly equal measure. He might challenge the king's mage. But he was afraid to try the king's own temper.

And he had told Eben Amnachudran, *You will not regret this by anything I do.* He had promised him, promised Tehre. *No harm will come to you because of me.* Had he not said that to each of them? Promises like that were meant to be like stone, like earth: solid and enduring. Had he made his to be merely like the morning mist, dissolving at the first glint of sunlight? He stood for a moment longer, staring away to the west.

But then he turned, reluctantly, to the north.

The streets in this part of Breidechboden were wide, well cobbled, lit by glimmering lamps whose silvery light echoed the moon. The lamps shed their light across the facades of beautifully appointed houses and across the wrought-iron gates that guarded them. Many of the gate posts were topped with figures that rose out of the drifting mist, startling and vivid—grotesques with badger bodies and bat faces, or mastiff dogs, or slim falcons. The figures announced family and affiliation to any knowledgeable visitor. Gereint knew some of them: The bat-faced grotesques marked the house of some scion of the Pamnarech family, and the mastiff dogs indicated an affiliation with the noble Wachsen house . . . Gereint passed them by, feeling oddly homesick for the leaping deer that marked the Amnachudran townhouse.

No one else was out upon the streets. Gentlefolk were all abed, even their servants not yet stirring. Bakers might be already sliding loaves into their ovens and carters were certainly bringing produce to the market stalls, but there were no shops here. Yet somehow Gereint did not feel either obtrusive or out of place in this solitude. He walked quickly through the dim streets, his head up, listening to the sound of his own sandals on the cobbles. His own footsteps seemed very nearly the only sound in all the city.

The great houses of the nobility and the wealthy eased imperceptibly into the apartment blocks of the moderately well-to-do. Late carts and wagons were audible in the near distance; several wagons passed

Gereint as he came to the part of the city that held shops and markets as well as apartments.

The first shutters clattered open in one of the apartments near at hand and a woman leaned out, peering at the morning with an expression of weary surprise, as though she'd never seen the gray predawn streets before in her life. Her eyebrows went up when she saw Gereint. She gave him an unenthusiastic but companionable nod, one person up too early to someone else up even earlier, but withdrew back into her apartment without waiting for him to return her nod.

The Twin Daughters glimmered near one horn of the crescent moon, almost lost in the pearl-and-lavender dawn, and then the sun rose behind Gereint and both the moon and the late stars were lost in its strengthening light. The sunlight struck off the east-facing walls of apartments and tenements and shops, turned plaster to ivory and brick to amber, gilded the damp cobbles, and outlined the heavy stone pillars of the Emnerechke Gates in fire.

Breidechboden rose up the hills behind him. High cirrus clouds stretched out in feathery peach and pink above the hills. The distant city, clean and silent in this moment between night and day, was all rose-washed ivory where the early light fell across it, or lavender and slate and pearl gray where the shadows of the hills still lingered. To his right, the open road led north through fields gone late-summer gold with ripening grain.

A fancy carriage with gold-scrolled doors and high narrow wheels, matching coppery chestnuts with braided manes standing before it, waited just inside the Emnerechke Gates, catching the eye with its stillness as well as its ornate decoration. The common carts and wagons made their way around the carriage, its fineness preventing their drivers from any display of annoyance more overt than a roll of their eyes.

Did Beguchren Teshrichten reject simplicity and plainness on principle? Though Gereint supposed it was at least possible the carriage belonged to some other lord . . . but he knew it belonged to the king's mage. He walked slowly toward it.

Not at all to his surprise, the driver set the brake, twisted the reins of the horse around the post, and jumped down to open the door for him as he came up. From within the carriage, Beguchren Teshrichten, his expression blandly uncommunicative, turned to give Gereint a little nod and gestured toward the bench beside him.

Gereint stepped up into the carriage, ducking his head under the low roof, and somewhat uneasily took the indicated seat. He would have preferred to sit farther away from the mage, but the carriage was a small one. Even so, Gereint felt the presumption of sharing the lord mage's bench. He sat as far toward the window as he could and said nothing. The driver picked up the reins and started the horses moving at an easy trot, weaving among the farmer's wagons and easily outpacing the common outbound traffic as they left the crowds behind.

"Good morning," Beguchren said, in exactly the polite tone he might have used to an honored guest in his own house. The little mage was as finely dressed as he had been the previous day: lace at his wrists and gold thread on his shirt, tiny pearls beading the cuffs of his highheeled boots, and, on three fingers of his left hand, those delicate sapphire rings. He might have been heading across the city to attend a court function rather than departing Breidechboden for a long journey north.

Gereint asked, after a moment, "Do you always travel in such little state, lord mage? Just a driver, and no other servants or men-at-arms? You don't precisely fear brigands, I gather. No doubt for any number of excellent reasons."

"Just so," agreed Beguchren, smiling slightly. "But, Gereint, please call me by my name."

Gereint looked away, out the window of the carriage. Watched the scattered buildings on the outskirts of Breidechboden give way to low golden hills, the last of the morning mist burning off in the sunlight. At last he turned back at the mage, "Lord mage, why are we going north? And how far north, and where precisely? Melentser? Why did you go to such trouble to bring me—me, especially, with you? What are you doing, and what is my part in it?"

There was a long, thoughtful silence. Beguchren said eventually, "I need a maker. Not merely any maker with a reasonably strong gift. A man who has been *geas* bound for many years . . . I expect such a man to have gained, shall we say, certain predispositions and inclinations. Qualities that matter more than mere strength."

Gereint said drily, "Oh, yes: a capacity for loyalty?"

To his surprise, the mage laughed. "Hardly. No. That's a quality any man may either develop or not, I imagine, but I would hardly expect servitude to enhance it. No," Beguchren said, seriously now, "I mean, among other qualities, endurance. An ability to smother strong emotion. I might say, self-abrogation."

It was Gereint's turn for silence. A slave might certainly develop all those qualities. But he was not at all certain he wished to know why the mage valued them. He asked at last, abandoning for the moment that line of inquiry, "How far north are you going?"

"We," Beguchren said gently. "How far north are *we* going? And we are going all the way, Gereint. To the place where the country of earth gives way to the country of fire."

"Melentser?"

"Perhaps."

"What if I refuse? What if I get down out of your fine carriage and walk away?"

"Walk away," suggested the mage, still gently, "and find out."

Gereint did not move. He said, testing carefully, "I'd find you in my mind, would I, compelling my direction?"

The mage's silver eyes glinted. "No. No, Gereint. That's one promise I believe I may safely offer you: I won't go into your mind again."

Gereint considered this. As promises went, that one seemed less solidly based than some. He allowed his tone to take on more of an edge, "Do you think I should trust you, lord mage? You asked me what I owe you, but I hardly know why you asked. It's clear enough what answer you think I should make. You believe I should do your bidding and walk at your heel like a dog."

Beguchren, refusing to be drawn, answered only, "Do you trust me, Gereint?"

Gereint was uneasily aware that, though there was no honest reason it should be true, the answer might be "yes." He said, "No, my lord."

"Perhaps you will learn to."

They had passed out of the immediate vicinity of Breidechboden. This far south, there were few woodlands, and those were cultivated as carefully as wheat fields, but for wood and game. The polite, civilized countryside rolled out endlessly green and fertile, blocked into neat fields and pastures and orchards. Sometimes beside the road and sometimes well away to the east flowed the Teschanken, riverboats running with the current down toward Breidechboden or hauled by teams of oxen back up toward Dachsichten.

More traffic passed north and south on the road: fancy high-wheeled carriages of men of property; plain coaches for ordinary travelers; riders in company or alone— everyone knew there was no risk of brigands between Breidechboden and Dachsichten. Gereint suspected there were more travelers than usual, northern folk uneasy at the new desert, trickling south in families or small groups. He remembered the patrol officer at the gates saying, *Wanenboden might be better*, and wondered if any southern city was actually going to welcome displaced or nervous northerners.

"The river runs low this year," Beguchren murmured. "You see how all the boats are small, with short keels and shallow drafts."

Gereint glanced at him, surprised. But the mage did not seem inclined toward further comment. When Gereint did not answer, silence fell once more.

They changed horses at a posting house along the river, trading the chestnuts for a pair of flashy bays with white feet and white faces. Beguchren permitted a short rest in the courtyard of the posting house while his driver assisted in leading the chestnuts away and then bringing up the bays to harness in their places. Beef pies appeared from the posting house, and good wine. Gereint, studying the horses, asked, "Do you *own* any plain horses, my lord?"

Beguchren appeared honestly surprised. "Why should one not enjoy beauty in everything, if possible?" he asked reasonably. "And they are fast, sturdy animals. We will trade horses once more today; I don't intend to stop for the night until we are well on the other side of Dachsichten. I hope to reach Pamnarichtan by tomorrow night—though I realize that requires an optimistic estimate of our pace. We will see what we can do to press on a little."

Gereint debated inwardly another moment, but finally asked, "My lord . . . why such haste? And why now? If the . . . the trouble earlier this summer created this problem, then why delay in Breidechboden while the days stretched out toward autumn?"

"We did not realize at once what we . . . that a problem had arisen. Then we took some time to consider what we might do."

"We?"

"The Arobern and his brothers and I, and others. We moved swiftly enough, Gereint, once we decided what direction to take. But whether it was fortune or fate that set you in my hand at the moment I needed you, even I cannot say."

Gereint guessed that whoever might have been involved in considering what they might do, the king and his mage had been the ones who had decided. He asked, "What do you want from me? What part do you mean for me to play?"

Beguchren gazed down at the table between his hands, so that it seemed he did not intend to answer at all. But at last he looked up, meeting Gereint's eyes. "When we reach the country of fire, I will answer all your questions."

Gereint stood up from the table, turned his back, and walked away.

The bays were harnessed, the remnants of the pies cleared away, the driver back on his high perch . . . and Beguchren had entered the carriage. Which did not move. The horses shifted restively, tossing their heads, impatient to go now that they were harnessed and ready. The driver held them. He did not look toward Gereint, who had stopped in the shade of the courtyard wall and now waited, arms crossed and jaw set, to see what Beguchren would do.

The answer appeared to be: nothing. The carriage waited. The posting house gate stayed open. The driver held the horses in place, though they mouthed the bits and showed something of a desire to jig sideways. Beguchren did not even look out the carriage window.

Not letting himself think about what he was doing, not letting himself consider whether he was making a decision or merely a test, Gereint swung about and walked away from the posting house, heading west. He clambered straight over a rail fence and strode across the pasture that bordered the road, ignoring the cattle that grazed in the distance. It didn't occur to him that there might be a bull until he was across the fence and then he would have looked foolish if he'd turned back. So he went on. The bright sunlit day seemed to close around him like walls, for all he could see the wide spaces of the pasture.

He needed to understand the king's mage. Just as Tehre tested the limits of structures in order to understand them, Gereint thought, a sharp defiance of Beguchren's intentions might reveal far more than quiet compliance ever could.

Even so, Gereint felt a strangely powerful sense of guilt as he lengthened his stride. *What do you owe me?* the silver-eyed mage had asked him, but neither of them had answered that question. Gereint was answering it now: nothing. But he knew that answer was false—

—the rough ground under his feet slid sideways. He staggered, took a quick step to catch his balance; his foot came down on the packed earth of the road rather than on the pasture grasses. The sun had abruptly shifted its place in the sky, shadows lay out at an odd angle; his head swam with the confusion of direction and place. The gates of the posting house stood near at hand, and by the gates, the fancy carriage with its matched bays. The driver was staring at him. The posting house staff had left their tasks and clustered by the gate, also staring.

But there was no movement at the carriage window. Having brought Gereint back to the posting house, Beguchren seemed perfectly content to wait all day for him to come back to the carriage.

If Beguchren wanted to compel obedience, why take away the *geas*? And if there was all this need for haste, why was he so patient now? Why not twist the world about and drop Gereint directly into his carriage? Or the both of them straight into place at the edge of the desert?

"Earth and ice," Gereint muttered. The philosopher Beremnan Anweierchen had written, *Obedience is a quality a man imposes on himself; if it is imposed from without, it is not obedience, but compulsion.* Anweierchen, Gereint concluded, hadn't known what he was talking about. All this pressing to get on, fresh horses waiting at posting houses and this *Pamnarichtan by tomorrow night* haste. And now Beguchren was willing to simply sit all afternoon in that quiet carriage?

Finally, Gereint crossed to the carriage with long, impatient strides, jerked the door open, stepped up to the bench, and flung himself onto the seat. But when Beguchren looked at him, he glanced down with a slave's bland, submissive deference and murmured, "I beg you will forgive the delay, my lord."

A trace of color actually rose in Beguchren's face. "Gereint . . ." the mage began, then stopped and instead leaned forward to tap the back of the driver's seat. The driver eased the reins, and the horses, glad to be moving at last, leaped forward in a canter rather than the customary collected trot.

Beguchren tried to catch himself against the jolt, but he was flung first hard backward and then forward by the lunging start of the horses. Gereint had no such difficulty; he put a foot against the opposite wall, closed a hand on the edge of the window, and, without thinking, put out his other arm and first caught the smaller man and then braced him until the motion of the carriage steadied. Then, embarrassed at both the familiarity and the very automaticity of the response, he let go and drew away to the farthest extent of the carriage.

The mage might also have been embarrassed. He straightened his sleeve fussily, concentrating on that. He said, not quite glancing up, "Thank you, Gereint."

Gereint barely looked at him, but answered in his most colorless tone, "Of course, lord mage."

Beguchren hesitated, began to speak, stopped, and finally said nothing. Silence stretched uncomfortably between them. Gereint could not decide whether he was satisfied or ashamed to have achieved this silence. He hoped the mage felt as uncomfortable with it as he did.

And perhaps he did, for he began at last, "Gereint . . ."

Gereint refused to look at him.

Beguchren sighed. He asked, "Should I have left you bound? Would you have been more comfortable under the compulsion of the *geas*? I might have left you bound right to the last. But I wished you to choose freely to come with me."

"As long as I don't choose freely to go my own way?"

"Just so."

Gereint shook his head, baffled. He should have been angry as well as baffled, but anger seemed to run out of him like water from a cracked fountain; he could not hold to it. "When you won't permit me to use the freedom you gave me, you can't expect an avowal of gratitude!"

"I don't."

"What do you *want* from me?" Gereint demanded.

Beguchren sighed. Nodded out the window. "At the moment, only your company on a pleasant, if long, day's journey."

Gereint set his jaw . . . then laughed suddenly. The argument seemed too ridiculous to keep up, when the mage continually slid sideways and left Gereint arguing alone. He said, "One day's journey and another, and soon enough we *will* be looking out into the country of fire. And you'll tell me then."

"I will."

Gereint only shook his head.

They traded the bays for young, energetic dappled grays at the next posting house, this time with less of a pause. As promised, they reached Dachsichten before dark and passed through the bustling town without stopping. Even the grays were long past any desire to run; the driver let them fall into a steady walk. Gereint asked no questions about when they might stop.

An hour north of Dachsichten, as dusk silvered the sky and the earliest stars glimmered into view, the carriage slowed, turned off the road, bumped gently across a grassy verge, and came to a halt beside a large pavilion of blue and ivory cloth, with orange and gold ribbons braided down its front, and more ribbons, bound to its roof, rippling in the breeze that came off the river. A fire leaped cheerfully before the pavilion; round white lanterns hung from poles on either side of its door. By their light, Gereint could make out half a dozen smaller tents around and behind the pavilion, blue and pink and flame yellow.

Men in the royal livery came to take the tired horses; another man, this one in the mage's own blue and ivory, appeared at the doorway of the carriage, placing a step and murmuring deferential welcome. Beguchren allowed the man to take his arm and assist him in stepping down. The mage, now that Gereint came to look at him carefully, looked drawn and weary. He turned at once toward the fire and pavilion.

Gereint stepped down from the carriage without assistance and walked aside, working off the stiffness of travel while watching the servants whisk around. He'd been surprised the lord mage had been content to rest overnight out in the open rather than in a proper inn. Now he wondered why he hadn't guessed what sort of arrangements had been made. Little effort had been spared; he could glimpse a low table within the pavilion and the silver glint of warming dishes.

Beguchren went into the pavilion and settled at the table; almost immediately one of the servants came over to Gereint with a formal invitation to dine with the lord mage. He followed the man to the pavilion without a word, ducked under the graceful awning, and settled on a cushion laid on the floor in lieu of a chair. There were other cushions and bolsters laid out and screens of fine cloth to block the rear of the pavilion into private rooms.

Gereint glanced around at the pavilion and the crowded table. "Luxurious."

Beguchren smiled. He took the cover off one warming dish and another, revealing plates of venison in gravy and quail in cream. Passing the quail toward Gereint, he said, "I didn't expect this, in fact. I asked for a simple tent and a change of horses. But the Arobern knew where I intended to stop, and it pleases him to make generous gestures toward his servants."

Gereint could not think of anything to say to this. His only experience of the king had not led him to expect generosity. Though, then, he was not precisely one of the king's servants. Or certainly not the way Beguchren Teshrichten was. He said at last, trying to mend his tone, "You have served the king . . . for a long time, I think?"

Beguchren inclined his head. "All his life. Though . . . at times less well than I might have wished."

Gereint guessed that the cold mage was thinking now of the summer, of the griffins and the disastrous foray into Feierabiand that had surely led now to this second foray. Whatever its purpose. He might have asked again, but he knew Beguchren would not answer. He might have asked anyway, offered one little cut and another against the man's temper . . . but he found, strangely, that he had no heart for that game. He asked instead, simply, "How far do you intend to go tomorrow? You're still thinking of traveling all the way to the confluence of the two rivers, staying the night in Pamnarichtan? That must be fifty miles from here, surely, for all we pressed hard today: another long, hard day. Have you arranged for fresh horses all along the river road, then?"

Beguchren glanced up thoughtfully, meeting Gereint's eyes with a strange kind of appreciation that suggested he had noticed Gereint's restraint. "I would like to get all the way to Pamnarichtan, yes. But we will not be changing horses, so I think we will likely not make it quite so far." Also because of the earlier delay Gereint had caused, he did not say. "Likely we will stop at Raichboden."

They would not actually stop at Raichboden itself. The town was fifteen miles south of Pamnarichtan, but east of the river; it was the southernmost town in the province of Meridanium, for which the river was the border. But there were a few amenities surrounding the ferry landing on this side of the Teschanken, including a decent inn to serve all the overoptimistic travelers who found the road north stretching out longer than they'd hoped.

"We should reach Pamnarichtan by midmorning the next day, I imagine," Beguchren added. "Then I think we will go up toward Metichteran, cross the river on that impressive bridge Metichteran boasts, and then simply continue north toward Tashen. We can stop in Tashen. And from Tashen, we will simply ride north and west until we strike the edge of the desert."

Gereint nodded, keeping his expression bland with a slave's hard-earned skill. Eben Amnachudran's house was north of Tashen and east of the river. How likely were they, realistically, to stop there? Likely enough, he concluded. And if Lord Mage Beguchren Teshrichten found that Amnachudran knew Gereint and heard that story about Gereint bringing the master of the house back on a litter, how long would it take him to guess just who must have removed the *geas* brand? Not long, was the obvious answer. Gereint wondered whether Tehre's letter had yet arrived at her father's house, and what Eben Amnachudran might have made of it. He said nothing.

"I will ask you to be patient," the mage said quietly, mistaking Gereint's silence. "I know you are still angry with me. But we will come to the country of fire soon. So I ask you to be patient and bear with my reticence only a little longer."

Gereint met his eyes and, after a calculated pause, nodded a second time. But when he went aside to his private tent, he lay awake for a long time, thinking about the road north.

In the morning, Gereint half expected the Arobern's servants to pack up all the finery and ride along with Beguchren's carriage. But they only served an elaborate, if swift, breakfast while fresh horses were brought out. The horses were black mares with white feet and white stars on their foreheads and dark blue ribbons braided into their manes and tails. And, to Gereint's surprise, this time the horses were saddled and bridled rather than harnessed to the carriage. He looked at Beguchren, raising his eyebrows as he noticed that the mage was dressed this morning in clothing that, while still expensive and fine, was much more practical for traveling. Though there was still a little lace here and there, and he still wore those sapphire rings.

"As you said," the mage answered that look, "the roads in the north are not as good." He gave the carriage a look of regret and took another cheese-filled roll from the generous basket provided.

The roads were perfectly all right until north of Pamnarichtan, but Gereint did not challenge this putative explanation. He was not surprised when Beguchren took the reins of the first horse and gestured for the man to give the other horse's reins to Gereint; he was not surprised when not a single servant or man-at-arms mounted a horse to accompany them. He didn't *understand* it, but he wasn't surprised.

Beguchren, Gereint noticed, rode as though he'd been suckled on mare's milk, as the saying went. Well, perhaps that wasn't surprising. Any nobly born boy would be taught to ride young, and this was something a small and delicate boy might do as well as his larger brothers and cousins. If he'd had brothers and cousins. It seemed likely; most noble families were large.

He found he could, surprisingly easily, imagine the little lord as a boy. He'd learned that bland, inscrutable smile in boyhood, Gereint guessed, to hide what he felt when every other boy was bigger and stronger and, probably, treated their little cousin with contempt. Or worse, with casual disregard. Gereint was surprised by the strength of the sympathy he felt for that long-vanished boy.

They rode beside the river most of the day. They seldom spoke— Gereint had nothing to say if he couldn't ask questions, and Beguchren seemed content with the silence. The river spoke, filling what might have been an uncomfortable quiet with continuous rippling babble as it ran through reeds and across its pebbly bed. It ran low, revealing shelves of gravel and sand abandoned by the retreat of the water. Dragonflies perched on the reeds and darted like jeweled needles over the brown water; a kingfisher dove from the overhanging branch of a tree in a dash of sapphire no less pure than the stones on the mage's rings, and broke the water into glittering spray where it struck after a minnow. The flatboats stayed far out from the banks, keeping to the middle of the channel. There were no keelboats; the water had drawn too far from the bank where the oxen would have leaned into their collars to haul the boats upriver.

There were few other travelers on the road. Those that they passed were mostly going south, and mostly traveling in large parties. These met Beguchren and Gereint with curious stares, but drew aside to yield a respectful right-of-way; Beguchren was, despite his lack of a proper entourage, still very obviously an important lord. It occurred to Gereint that the small mage was deliberately substituting a blatant display of wealth for the physical size and strength he lacked. Once he thought of this, it seemed obvious, even inevitable. But then he caught a sardonic glint in the mage's eyes and was no longer sure the explanation was anything so obvious, after all.

"Pamnarichtan and Raichboden, Manich and Streitgan have all sent men to patrol the road," one man-at-arms told them, turning away from his own company to ride beside them for a few minutes. "In fact, all the northern towns are contributing; well, except for Tashen. You know how Tashen is: They're not personally having trouble, so what do they care? All the towns of Meridanium province, I should say, plus Pamnarichtan. We're all agreed we're tired of the brigands." He shook his head. "I don't know what's been worse, the dregs of Melentser who saw opportunity in their own city's misfortune, or the straggling refugees who put off the southward journey and made themselves into prey. Well, we're clearing them out—pushing the stragglers on south and hanging the scum who've turned to brigandage—but I wouldn't say it's exactly safe to ride along here just yet with only one retainer." He gave Beguchren a respectful nod. "Begging your pardon for my forwardness to say so, lord."

Gereint didn't comment on the man's taking him for Beguchren's retainer; in too many ways it was an uncomfortably accurate assessment. He gave the mage a sidelong glance, waiting to see how he would respond.

"I thank you for your concern," Beguchren answered in a mild, assured tone. "I have carefully considered this risk, and I am satisfied with my decision to proceed as I am. But I am glad to know that the northern towns are undertaking a permanent solution to the problem. Tell me, if you will, has the Arobern sent assistance from the south?"

The man-at-arms eyed the mage with sharp interest and deepening respect. "Lord, not so as I know."

"An oversight, I believe," Beguchren murmured. "In these unsettled times, perhaps unsurprising. Still, the cost of dealing with these brigands clearly arises from the resettlement of the people of Melentser, and as such the governors of the northern towns are entitled to reimbursement for some portion of their expenses incurred in the effort. Whose man are you? Geiestich? Warach?"

"Lord . . . my name is Gentrich Feiranlach, and I ordinarily command the southern cohort of the Raichboden patrol."

"Geiestich's man, then," said Beguchren, naming the governor of Raichboden. He produced—from the air, as far as Gereint could see—one of the intricately carved purple-dyed bone tokens that marked the authority of a king's man. He gave this to the man-at-arms. "Take this to Geiestich and tell him I suggested he apply for proper reimbursement. If he sends this token with his request, I think it will be met with favor."

The man-at-arms clearly thought so too, from the depth of his bow as he accepted the token. "Lord. Thank you, lord, and I know my lord the governor will be grateful. I beg you will permit me to lend you a reasonable number of men for the remainder of your journey, lord. The north would be ashamed if harm came to a servant of the king in our lands—"

"Thank you," Beguchren said patiently. "But I assure you, I have considered the risk, and I am satisfied with my decision to proceed."

The man-at-arms hesitated for a long moment. Then he bowed once more, accepting this dismissal, and reined his horse around, lifting it into a canter to catch up with his company.

"He thinks you're one of the Arobern's personal agents," Gereint commented watching the man go.

Beguchren gave Gereint one of his most inscrutable looks. "I am. Why else would I have that token?"

Gereint had no answer for this. He asked instead, "Why not accept the offered escort, at least? Surely brigands would at least slow you down a little."

"Us," the little mage said patiently. "Slow *us* down, Gereint. No, that possibility doesn't unduly concern me. If brigands are drawn toward convenient prey, why not let them come to us? It's easier than tracking them down, and a good deal better than letting them find truly vulnerable travelers to attack, don't you think?"

Gereint stared at the mage in surprise. "You're using yourself as *bait*?" This hadn't occurred to him.

"It's perfectly safe," Beguchren said, nevertheless sounding a little apologetic. "Or, at least, nearly."

"I don't doubt it." Gereint stared at him for a moment longer. The mage looked exactly the same: small and neat handed, fastidious and vain, weary with the day's travel. But he had changed shape yet again in Gereint's eyes.

They did not make it within sight of Pamnarichtan before dusk. They had not even made it within sight of the Raichboden ferry landing, though Gereint thought they must be getting close at least to that. He thought Beguchren might turn off the road to find a campsite, but the mage did not even seem to notice the dwindling light. They rode between the river on one side and, on the other, a dense scrubby woodland that seemed to Gereint to make excellent cover for brigands. Beguchren did not, of course, seem concerned about the possibility. For all Gereint knew, the mage agreed with him about the possibility of brigands, but thought it an advantage rather than a drawback.

The sun slid lower and lower in the sky, sinking behind the woods that crowded the riverbank. Narrow fingers of golden light pierced through the tangled branches and stretched themselves across the road. The river turned from green to opaque gold as the angle of the sun shifted, and then to dusky blue. Yet, though he allowed his horse to fall into a gentle amble, Beguchren still did not suggest they halt.

Gereint hesitated. Then nudged his mare up beside Beguchren's and asked at last, "We're not stopping?"

Beguchren didn't even turn his head. "I do think we can at least come up to Raichboden before full dark, don't you?"

Indeed, no. Gereint shrugged and said instead, "All right. We'll press on to the inn at the ferry landing: fine. Then we'll go through Pamnarichtan by midmorning tomorrow, I suppose; reach Metichteran sometime in the afternoon, be in Tashen by supper time. Unless I decide to settle on the riverbank at Raichboden and fish instead."

There was a pause. Then Beguchren, turning his head at last, asked softly, "Do you think you're likely to do that?"

Gereint gazed at the ears of his mare. He did not look up. He didn't want to see Beguchren's unbreakable composure—but, if he had managed to disturb that composure, he didn't want to see that either. "You won't tell me what you want me to do for you until we reach the desert. But will you tell me *why* you won't tell me now?"

There was no response.

"You won't. You think if you tell me now, I'd turn this pretty black mare and ride back down the river road as fast as she can take me, though after a day as long as this, I don't suppose that's all that fast. I don't know why the possibility concerns you, since you can use magecraft to hold me. Do you simply not want to put yourself to the trouble?"

"Gereint—"

Gereint looked over at the mage at last, a hard stare. "What will you do, my lord mage, if I fight you? You can turn the road about on me, but what if I simply sit on the riverbank and refuse to take a step? What then? Wait patiently until the season turns and the snow comes down? I hardly think so. So what would you do?"

Begurchren checked his mare, twisted in the saddle to give Gereint his full attention, and leaned on the pommel, frowning. "Gereint . . . please don't fight me."

"You put that as a request, but it's a threat." Gereint, perforce, had brought his horse to a halt as well. It mouthed the bit uncomfortably, and he found he was gripping the reins too tightly. He made his hands relax, with an effort.

"Not at all," Beguchren said mildly.

"A warning, then. Or will you tell me it's an appeal?"

"That's closer."

"Which?" But there was no response to that. Gereint shook his head. "You wanted a man 'with a great capacity for loyalty.' But why? It isn't loyalty you're after from me. You said you don't want the forced obedience of the *geas*. But that's exactly what you do want—only without the *geas*."

"No. It's true that that's what I have now. But it's not what I want."

The urge to say *Yes, all right, I'm sure it will be fine. Don't bother yourself about it* was amazingly strong. Gereint shuddered with the effort to control that urge. For half a shaved copper coin, he would have whirled his horse around and ridden away—heading anywhere. Except such an attempt would not work. And he could not even bring himself to wish it would. "Are you doing this to me? Stop it!"

"I can't. I'm not precisely doing it." Beguchren paused, stroking his mare's neck as it fidgeted. He went on after a moment: "You're feeling the pull of a natural affinity. In a way, it's similar to the *geas*. I'm sure you feel the likeness. That's one reason it disturbs you. But this, unlike the *geas*, you can overrule, if you wish. You're overruling it now."

Gereint shook his head, trying not only to understand what the mage was saying but also to clear his mind. This wasn't at all like the *geas*; Beguchren was wrong about that. It was more like an inexplicable impulse, despite everything, toward trust. "Is this why you wanted this slow journey together, just you and me? To let this 'affinity' develop?"

"What does Andreikan Warichteier say in his *Principia* about the relationship between mages and their students? About how men become mages?"

Faced with these academic questions, Gereint found himself steadying—and knew Beguchren had asked them for that purpose— and couldn't even resent him for it, though he wanted to. Or felt that he ought to want to. He said, "Less than I wish he had, now. I'm not any kind of mage or potential mage—"

"How do you know?"

Gereint said, as quietly as the mage but with so much intensity that he might have shouted, "If you're so powerful, then whatever I am, skilled maker or poor excuse for a mage, *what do you need me for?*"

"I'll tell you once we reach—"

"The country of fire! Yes, so you say! You'll tell me, it will be something terrible, I'll refuse, and you'll force me to do it anyway—"

Beguchren held up a hand, shaking his head. "No, Gereint, there you are wrong, I promise you. What I will need you to do for me is nothing I or anyone else can force you to do. Or the *geas* would have sufficed."

Gereint controlled, barely, an impulse to fling himself down from the saddle and stride away into the woods. His hands were shaking, he found, and he closed them hard around the reins to hide the fact. He said tightly, "Why did you free me? To coax me to trust you? Did you think that likely to work?"

"Under these circumstances? No."

Gereint waited. But Beguchren did not explain, only started his horse moving again, gently, upriver. Gereint's mare followed without any signal from him.

Gereint shook his head. He said grimly, "Warichteier says that like calls to like, and that there's a natural affinity between mages and natural creatures of earth. You seem to believe I might be some sort of mage. I hope you haven't set all your hopes on that. I'm only a maker. But I'll stop fighting you. All right? I won't fight you, my lord mage. I'll go north as far as you wish, as fast as you wish. But I don't believe for a moment you don't intend to force me to fit your need. Whatever that may be."

Beguchren hesitated, his eyes on his mare's neck. He began to speak, then stopped, hunting for words. At last he lifted his gaze and began, "Gereint, necessity can bind a man more tightly than any *geas*. Magecraft," said Beguchren, "like any magic, is a natural quality. Warichteier was half right, but only half. A mage is . . . a point of focus in the world. A point where forces balance and pivot. Any mage is like that, though earth and fire mages balance different and opposing forces. When we study, what we learn is to notice what we're doing to the world and, hmm, how to bend in the right direction the pull we always exert, do you see? For all his learning, Warichteier was not a mage and he did not really understand magecraft. That is why his commentary on the subject is so opaque and not altogether accurate."

"A cold mage—"

"We say 'cold mage' when in a sense we mean merely 'a mage trained to oppose fire.' But if an earth mage develops his . . . inclination . . . to oppose fire, he gives up certain kinds of power in order to emphasize certain other kinds. Do you understand?"

Gereint didn't, but didn't like to say so, lest Beguchren realize he was speaking almost freely and stop.

"To be sure," Beguchren added, "an ordinary earth mage must give up certain kinds of, hmm, power as well. Whereas a gifted maker such as yourself is not any sort of mage: A gift is different in kind from magecraft. However—" He lifted a hand—to gesture, to demonstrate something, it was not clear. Because a short little hunting arrow flicked through the air not a hair's width from the mage's fingers and disappeared with a wicked little hiss into the dark river, and two more sank, humming, into the earth at their horses' feet.

Gereint would not have thought there was enough light left for shooting. Clearly there was. Mouth dry and heart pounding, he checked his horse. Beguchren had drawn up as well, peering into the dusky woods with no great alarm so far as Gereint could see. Another arrow whipped past in front of them. Gereint lifted his hands to show they were empty and muttered under his breath, "I thought this was *perfectly safe?*"

"It is," Beguchren replied seriously. "Or nearly. Shh. Don't frighten them away." As Gereint wondered how exactly either of them could possibly frighten away a troop of brigands—frown sternly at them?—the smaller man also held his empty hands out in token of surrender.

Gereint said grimly, "If that first one was a warning shot, it came remarkably close to hitting you—and if they just want to stay under cover and shoot us both, I don't know what's stopping them—"

"They might intend to take me as a hostage," suggested Beguchren. He didn't sound overly concerned about the prospect. "Perhaps someone among them has realized that they might send to my family to demand a rich ransom."

Gereint stared at him. "You believe they'll think that far ahead, with the men-at-arms of all the northern towns beating through the woods for them? I hope you have some way to protect us besides depending on the reluctance of murderous dog-livered cutthroat brigands to shoot us out of hand."

Beguchren gave him a look.

"Well, you haven't been very quick to show it, if you do!"

"Gereint, I should think you, of all men, had learned patience?"

"You might think so," Gereint muttered, and saw Beguchren's mouth twitch toward a smile. If the brigands hidden in the woods saw that smile, he thought, then if they had a thimbleful of sense among them, they'd sneak away from this camp as quietly as they'd come and not stop running till they hit the edge of the desert . . . Maybe they had. There was certainly no sound from the woods, and no more arrows. "Where *are* they?" he asked again.

"I think . . ." murmured Beguchren. "Yes, I rather think they are coming out now."

This was true. The brigands had finally decided that their quarry were truly at bay, and were slowly coming out into the moonlight. One, and then another, and then a third—all with bows—another, armed more simply with a club. A fifth man, and a sixth. "Not eager to close in, though," observed Gereint.

"You probably frighten them."

Gereint almost laughed. "Bows?" he reminded the smaller man.

"I don't suppose they'd have turned to brigandage if they were brave men—" But Beguchren fell silent as the men finally began to approach. There were eight altogether. Only three had bows—though three were certainly enough. The rest carried clubs. To Gereint, they looked alarmingly ready to use those clubs. Even eager. They looked warily at Gereint, but their glowers were directed toward Beguchren.

"It's my size," the mage murmured. "A certain sort of man resents wealth in a man smaller than he is. If you were the one wearing the rings, they'd still be planning to kill you, but they wouldn't feel they had to break all your bones first."

Gereint gave the smaller man an incredulous glance. "Of course they would. They resent me just for being bigger than they are, whether or not I'm wearing a lot of sapphires. I hope you have something in mind other than appealing to their generous natures."

"Do you think that's all of them?"

"All who are going to come out, at least."

Beguchren nodded. "I think so, too."

The leader of the brigands, a man nearly as broad across the shoulders as Gereint, hefted his club. He had a mean look to him, like a scared dog that nevertheless meant to bite. If he intended to take Beguchren as a hostage and let Gereint go in order to collect a ransom, it wasn't apparent at the moment. He looked a lot more like he meant to beat them both to death himself. He looked them over, then said, in a growling, contemptuous tone, "Where'd you hide the rest of it?"

Beguchren shook his head in gentle puzzlement. "The rest of—?"

The man gestured again with his club. "Those rings can't be all you've got. You're stupid, but you can't be *that* stupid. Everybody knows to hide their money." He flicked the club back and forth mockingly. "Get down off that horse, little dog-lord, and tell me where you put it. In the saddle cloth? The saddle? Huh?"

"I guess they're not thinking about hostages," Gereint murmured, glancing down at the mage. "If you're going to do something, now might be a good—" He stopped.

Beguchren had reached out across the distance that separated his horse from Gereint's and taken hold of Gereint's arm. He gripped hard, not as though he sought support, but more as though he needed to mark Gereint's position. He was gazing at nothing, his expression abstracted. After a moment, both the packed earth of the road and the black river that had been all but hidden in the dusk began to shimmer with a pale, cold radiance like moonlight through winter fog. The air chilled, as though the seasons had suddenly shifted forward straight to winter, passing through the rest of summer and all of autumn in an eye-blink. The pale light grew steadily brighter, though no warmer.

Most of the brigands simply gaped. Two of them started to edge back toward the woods, but they stopped before they had retreated more than a few steps.

Like moonlight, the cold light of the stones was gentle to the eyes. Though it was bright enough to cast shadows, Gereint did not need to squint through the light to glance at Beguchren's face. The mage looked perfectly calm and quite unmoved. The pearly radiance filled the whole road between river and woods. Like moonlight, the cold magelight stripped color from the world it revealed. The white feet of the horses gleamed like lanterns in the cool light; they sidled and backed, but did not panic. Gereint would have liked to panic himself, but did not dare. He reached out quickly to catch Beguchren's reins, afraid of what might happen if the two horses moved apart and the mage lost his hold on Gereint's arm. The tangled branches and leaves of the woods were black and dense; the river, rimed with ice at its near edge, glinted an almost metallic silver.

The brigands did not fall. They were dead where they stood. Frost sparkled on their faces and hair; their eyes were wide open and un-blinking. Their skin was white as ice; their clothing stiff and glittering. The cold shattered their clubs and bows; the wood broke with clean, crisp snaps. The dangling bowstrings cast back the light as though they had been made of silver wire.

Gereint sat very still. Beguchren still gripped his arm; he did not want to find out what would happen to him or to his horse if the mage let go. The pale light was ebbing at last, washing slowly down out of the air like fog, sinking into the earth and water. It left frost behind, spangling the ground like a fine diamond net. The cold eased as the world remembered summer warmth; the natural moonlight, now alone, seemed pallid and weak.

Beguchren drew a deep, slow breath and let go of Gereint's arm.

Gereint immediately backed his mare half a dozen steps. He was shuddering, not entirely with the lingering cold.

Beguchren blinked, shook his head, breathed sharply, and straight-ened his shoulders. Then he gave Gereint a sharp look, seeming for the first time to realize Gereint's horror. "What I did was swifter and kinder than hanging."

Gereint took a breath, but stopped without speaking. Took another breath and let it out again, still without saying a word. He looked around at the eight dead brigands. As he stared, the first one fell at last—stiffly, as a rigid board might fall, not limply like a shot deer. Then the sec-ond. Gereint tried not to flinch at the heavy thudding sounds as first one man and then the other hit the ground. The horses pricked their ears forward in nervous curiosity at this strange human behavior. When they shifted and stepped, their hooves left dark prints in the frost.

Gereint made himself meet the mage's eyes once more. He said at last, "You're one of the king's agents. So you had the right."

Beguchren inclined his head. "Anyone has both the right and the duty to clear the road of brigandage if he can. But, yes, the Arobern specifically asked me to assist local efforts as I found the chance." He paused. Then he said gently, "I think we can get to Raichboden yet this evening. I don't think we would be comfortable camping along the river in the dark."

"No," Gereint agreed grimly, and put his horse into a trot, slightly too fast a pace for the dim light, but it seemed as glad as he to leave the icy brigands to thaw behind them. He did not even want to think about the dreams he might have this night—if he dreamed; he doubted he would sleep at all and probably that was just as well. He glanced involuntarily over his shoulder as a third brigand fell, with a ringing, crystalline crash, behind them.

They found the inn at the Raichboden ferry no more than a mile farther north. The ferry was not at the landing but tied up at the dock on the town side of the river. Or not actually *at* the dock; the water level was so low that the ferry had simply been run up on exposed mud flats near the dock and tied up there. Fortunately, the inn on their side of the river was a good one, and well accustomed to late-arriving travelers. It had a small but decent private room, with two clean beds and, best of all, a bath basin already filled with steaming water. Beguchren provided the soap. The soap was smooth textured and rose scented, exactly the sort of soap Gereint would have expected the mage to carry if he'd thought about it. He almost wanted to laugh. He would have laughed if he'd been trying to use this fine soap to scrub grease off pots, rather than the memory of death off his body. He was glad to use the bath first, while the king's mage arranged for men to go back down the road in the morning to collect the bodies for a proper, if symbolic, hanging. Beguchren also arranged for broth and bread, neither of which Gereint thought he could stomach.

"A little broth, at least," Beguchren said quietly. "You need something."

Gereint accepted a mug, though he merely turned it around in his hands rather than sipping. He couldn't decide whether the rich, meaty smell was appetizing or nauseating.

Beguchren said softly, "It's not precisely honorable, I know—"

"It's not a sport," Gereint said grimly. "Or a hunt. Do you think I don't know that?"

"Of course you do."

"I'm surprised you couldn't just whistle for them to come crouching trustingly to your feet like dogs, and then freeze them solid with your magelight—"

"Gereint!" Beguchren set down his own mug so sharply the broth spilled onto the table. "Please don't mistake brigands like that for men like yourself. There's not one of them, gifted or not, who hadn't turned his back on *any* kind of trust. You know that is true."

Gereint made no answer.

The mage went on more gently, "Nothing could have saved them, even any among them who might somehow have retained some trace of decent human sensibility. If taken by men-at-arms, they would all have been held for hanging. Would that have been kinder?"

Gereint bowed his head a little.

"Can you eat something? Will you let me—" Beguchren paused. Then he went on, but with an odd note of constraint in his light, smooth voice: "Will you permit me to ease your rest tonight? If you wish, I can ensure that you do not dream. Will you take my word that I would do nothing but give you dreamless sleep?"

Gereint looked over at the mage. He could see that Beguchren expected him to refuse and guessed as well that, surprisingly, he might be hurt by the refusal. He said finally, "I'd take your word. But I think even men such as those are worth one or two bad dreams."

Beguchren gazed at him for a moment. Then he nodded. "So long as you can rest a little. It will be a long day tomorrow; almost as long as today. I'd like to get at least to Tashen tomorrow, if we can. Past Tashen, if possible."

"Past Tashen" was very likely to mean right into Amnachudran's lands, if Beguchren insisted on going upriver on the east side of the Teschanken. One more worry to run through Gereint's dreams. He didn't let his expression change, but merely nodded and said, "And then the day after, the desert." He didn't say, *And then you can end all this mystery and tell me at last what you mean to do in the griffin's country.* But he didn't need to. Beguchren bowed his head in agreement.

Gereint stood up and glanced inquiringly from one small narrow bed to the other.

"Whichever you like," said Beguchren.

Gereint nodded. He didn't, under the circumstances, wish the mage a pleasant night.

CHAPTER 8

Immediately outside Breidechboden, the road that led west toward the ornate and wealthy city of Abreichan widened enough for four carriages to travel abreast. Indeed, for the entire distance between Breidechboden and Abreichan, the road was that wide. And for that whole distance, it was paved with great flat stones quarried from the local hills and lined with tall plinths topped with grim-faced stone soldiers chiseled roughly out of granite. This road was always guarded, those carved soldiers proclaimed. Travelers journeyed under the protection of the Arobern kings. Brigandage might from time to time be a concern in the wilder north, but here in the broad, rich lands of the south, that protection was constant and powerful. Only after a traveler passed west of Abreichan and pressed on toward the little mountain towns of the far west did that protection become less reliable. After the Arobern completed the planned improvements to the mountain road, that might well change: the king would not want brigandage to soil his new road.

Tehre wished they were actually traveling west. She had never even been so far as Weierachboden, far less Abreichan, which everyone knew rivaled Breidechboden in splendor and ostentation. But even more than she wished to see the cities of the western plains, she longed to go all the way to Ehre and watch the builders and engineers of Casmantium go about the business of flinging their great road through the mountain passes to Feierabiand. The engineers would be carving their new road out of the sides of the mountains, bracing narrow paths that overhung desperate precipices, building buttresses to make a level road where nothing level had ever existed, bridging steep-sided chasms with arches and architraves and, possibly, hanging bridges with wrought-iron chains . . . Tehre had not even realized, until she turned her face to the west and put Breidechboden at her back, how much she would have loved to take this road *all* the way.

But they were only taking the western road to encourage casual observers to think that Lord Bertaud was heading back to Ehre; he might not ask the Arobern for leave to come and go, but then neither was he inclined to throw open defiance in the king's face. Nor, once she thought about it, was Tehre.

Lord Bertaud had brought a small entourage, as Tehre ought to have guessed he would. A foreign lord was hardly likely to travel anywhere in Casmantium alone. He'd brought a couple of men-at-arms and a driver and a servant. They were his own people, Feierabianden. Not one of them had more than a word or two of Prechen; no wonder Lord Bertaud had wanted Tehre's company for this journey.

Nor, of course, could Tehre travel alone amid strangers. She hadn't initially thought of this, a failure of sensibility about which Fareine had found a great deal to say. Fareine herself had not come; someone needed to supervise the household, and she was too frail in these years to travel quickly or easily, and after all this was not *really* a leisurely journey home. Or at least, in the event, it might prove to be something other than a leisurely journey home.

So Meierin had come. The girl had never been out of Breidechboden and was eager to travel, and Tehre liked her—and, more important, Fareine approved of her.

"She is a responsible child, and she has some sense," Fareine had told Tehre. "And she's young enough to think long days of travel are an *adventure*." The old woman had shaken her head in wistful regret for her own past youth, when she, too, had longed for travel and perhaps even for adventure.

Lord Bertaud's carriage was a good one, well built, but plain . . . He probably had a fancy one to show off his consequence. This one was much better for quiet travel. And comfortable. The seats were broad and well cushioned, and leather cushioned the windowsills below sheer curtains that let in light while keeping out dust. There was enough room on both the front and rear benches to allow three people to sit together—even four, if they were slender or friendly. Certainly there was ample room for Tehre and Meierin to sit facing forward, Lord Bertaud having courteously taken the backward-facing bench. Tehre gazed out to the west. The early sun struck the distant stones of the road to gold; it unrolled, gleaming, through all that gentle country toward Weierachboden, and she wished again they were going west.

Meierin touched Tehre's sleeve, and she became aware that Lord

Bertaud had said something to her. She blushed with embarrassment, having no idea what he had said. Meierin could only shrug helplessly; the girl did not speak Terhcien, of course, and probably also had some difficulty understanding the foreigner's accented Prechen.

"I beg your pardon?" Tehre said—then realized she'd spoken in Prechen and paused, searching for a similar phrase in Terheien.

But, "No," said Lord Bertaud, and borrowed her own phrase: "I beg your pardon, Lady Tehre; I did not mean to, ah." Looking frustrated, he said something in Terheien, then added in Prechen, "You were thinking. I did not mean to bother."

"It doesn't matter at all," Tehre answered quickly, then groped for the proper phrase in Terheien. But Lord Bertaud was nodding politely, so apparently he had understood. Tehre wondered how to explain that she was always drifting into abstraction and that if Lord Bertaud worried about interrupting her thoughts he would never be able to speak to her at all. Though she had to concentrate, to speak Terheien. If one took language as a *made* thing, words and syntax and the thought behind both, then did that imply that makers ought to be able to work with language somehow? Well, Linularinan legists did, in a way, though as a tool rather than as a product.

Gereint would have been the perfect person with whom to discuss this idea: He'd know if one or another of the great philosophers had already considered it. In fact, he'd probably know if a minor, obscure philosopher had. Or a poet. Maybe especially a poet . . . She wondered where he was at this moment, and whether he might be discussing some peculiar philosophical idea with Beguchren Teshrichten. She blinked and sighed, gazing out the window through the sheer curtain, finding that they were passing now through the villages and sprawling farms that lined the western road. Soon they would find some little country road that would lead them around to the north . . .

"Lady Tehre," Meierin said, in that patient tone that meant Tehre had forgotten something. Tehre blinked at her. The girl said, "Lord Bertaud wanted to show you . . ." and her voice trailed off as Tehre exclaimed in dismay.

She turned to the Feierabianden lord. "I always distract," she said apologetically. "Please forgive." She concentrated on her Terheien and asked carefully, "What do you have?"

Lord Bertaud showed her the small map he had brought, turning it so Tehre could see it. "Where?" he wondered.

Tehre leaned forward, studying the map with interest. It wasn't detailed enough to show the little roads around Breidechboden; it showed only the great cities and largest towns. And the river, of course, for it was the Teschanken that gave life and prosperity to southern Casmantium.

Tehre braced a hand on the seat against the mild jolting of the carriage. "Here," she explained, showing the foreign lord their approximate location. "We go here. This way. Around to the north, to the river road. Then to Dachsichten."

"Dachsichten," repeated Lord Bertaud, trying out the name. His tongue gave it a strange, soft pronunciation, more like "Dashenten." He looked at Tehre, eyebrows rising, half smiling at his own incorrect pronunciation.

"Dachsichten," Tehre told him, enunciating the name slowly and carefully, emphasizing the breaks in the word. "Dachsichten." Impatient with leaning awkwardly forward, she moved to sit next to the foreigner, bending to avoid knocking her head into the low roof of the carriage and catching awkwardly at the window as the vehicle jolted.

Lord Bertaud, eyebrows lifting with surprise, nevertheless caught her hand to steady her as she changed seats.

She dropped onto the seat next to him and began to point out the towns on the map, starting in the southwest of Casmantium and working her way east and north. She pronounced each one carefully and slowly, pausing to let Lord Bertaud try each word before she went on to the next. "Ruchen. Abreichan. Weierachboden. Wanenboden. Breidechboden. Dachsichten. Geierand—that is, mmm, close? Close to Terheien, yes?"

"Yes," Lord Bertaud agreed, looking grateful that one of the names, at least, came easily to his tongue. "The rest, no." He shook his head in rueful dismay over the other names. "So hard to say! There should be a way to learn easy. More easy?"

"More easily," Tehre told him, and wondered whether, if one treated words as materials and languages as mechanisms . . . and syntax as joints . . . hmm. When constructing a mechanism, the trick was to see it, hold it whole in the mind while one's hands worked with the materials. The maker's clear and focused intention was what set quality into a made thing. What would the equivalent of that focused intention be if one was working with something intangible like language? She asked suddenly, "Feierabianden places? Names?"

Lord Bertaud gave her a puzzled look.

"Give—say—Feierabianden names?" Tehre wondered how she could put her request more clearly, but after a moment, he seemed to decipher her meaning.

"Terabiand," he said obediently. "Bered, Talend, Nejeied, Sepes, Niambe, Sierhanan, Sihannas, Annand, Tamiaon—"

Tehre held up her hand, stopping his recital so she could think. Words and syntax, yes, but also something else. She didn't quite mean "pronunciation." Style, one might say. Like the style of the palace in Breidechboden, all massive stonework and flying buttresses and archi-traves, those last built stubbornly straight although anyone could see they would crack; that aggressive, heavy style was entirely different from the graceful and modest wooden buildings of the forested north. Hmm. Words and syntax and style . . . One would not express these abstractions with mathematical equations, but perhaps one might find a way to express the components of a language in some relatively precise way. Hmm . . .

Tehre blinked back to awareness of the carriage with Meierin touching her hand, and realized they were no longer moving. They had stopped. She gave the girl a raised-eyebrow look of inquiry.

"There is a farmhouse here," Meierin explained, not quite hiding a smile. "It is after noon? You must want something to eat?" It was plain Meierin had received firm instructions from Fareine about feeding Tehre.

"There is a house here where they sell food," added Lord Bertaud, sounding a little apologetic about it. "If you wish, we stop here for a little while?"

His inflection suggested that this halt was up to Tehre, that they might simply go on if she preferred, but after all, it was his carriage. Besides, now that she thought of it, Tehre *was* hungry. She allowed Lord Bertaud to help her and then Meierin out of the carriage, turning to gaze curiously at the farmhouse with its trestle tables and long benches. Clearly a lot of travelers passed this way, and the farmer—or his wife—had decided to make the most of the convenient road that ran so close to their house. Theirs was not the only carriage that had stopped here for a midday break. The tables were already loaded with dishes, drawing in travelers with enticing smells of roasting meat and baking bread.

"Did you pay the women here?" she asked Lord Bertaud.

"You are my, ah, my . . ."

Guests, Tehre presumed he meant. "Not at all," she corrected him. "I am glad to travel in, ah, in your protect, Lord Bertaud, but you are *my* guest." She shifted gratefully back to Prechen. "Meierin, pay the woman. Remember the honor of my family and be generous." There *had* to be a better way to learn a language than all that fumbling for half-known words . . . She wandered toward the table, wondering if there was roasted chicken.

There was roasted chicken. And beef pies. And eggs baked in pastry. No wonder so many people stopped here. Tehre nibbled thoughtfully at a bit of chicken, set her plate aside, and said to Lord Bertaud, "Say for me a, mmm, a story. Yes?"

The foreigner smiled uncertainly. "A story?"

"Of your travel? Or a story for children? Any story. Say first in Prechen and then in Terheien. Yes? Please?"

Lord Bertaud tilted his head, still uncertain and also curious. "Same story? In Prechen and Terheien?" Smiling, he made a comment in Terheien that was too quick for Tehre to catch but was probably something like, "*Well, I suppose we both need the practice, don't we?*"

He told a children's story about three foxes and a rabbit. He told each bit of it first in flowing, graceful Terheien and then in halting Prechen. The story took the rest of the midday break and a little longer than they had probably meant to stop, but Lord Bertaud was too easynatured to break off once the farmwife's children and several of the travelers drifted over to listen.

"But the third fox wasn't clever, really," protested one of the children after the story ended. "He was just lucky. The rabbit was the clever one, really."

"The rabbit was a little too clever for her own good, don't you think? Like quite a number of little rabbits," said her father, a carter, smiling. He gave Lord Bertaud a little bow, swinging his daughter up to his broad shoulder to carry her back to his cart. "Thank you, honored sir. Well told, may I say so?"

Tehre barely heard the other travelers murmur similar comments. She was trying to frame words in her mind, as she might have placed bricks in a wall or stitches in a tapestry. They were harder to work with than bricks or thread. Or perhaps it was the nebulous nature of the framework into which she was attempting to set them.

She was not really aware of re-entering the carriage or of the jolt and sway as they turned back onto the road. After a time, Meierin said something she didn't pay any attention to. Finally Lord Bertaud leaned forward and said questioningly, "Lady Tehre?"

Him, Tehre noticed. He had all of Terheien ready on his tongue and in his mind: a river of words, an *ocean* of language. She could feel it in him, almost as though it had physical weight and was drawn by powerful tides. Tehre offered him her hand.

He took it, a little hesitantly. Tehre closed both her own small hands firmly around his broad one, and built a great wall between them. She built it of words, Terheien on his side and Prechen on hers. She defined the wall as a dam between one language and the other. Then she opened a sluice gate in the dam and locked it in place. Then she opened her eyes—realizing for the first time that she'd closed them—let her breath out, and said ruefully, "The hard part is that you have to get the whole thing in place at once, don't you, or it won't hold at all, and you have to put in the sluice at the same exact time you're building the dam or you won't get it in right. I think I got it right. *Did* I get it right?" She looked inquiringly at Lord Bertaud.

He was staring at her, astonished. "You—what did you do?"

"Am I speaking Terheien?"

"Yes!"

"Then I did get it right." Satisfied, Tehre glanced around for writing materials. Then, frustrated, she sighed and cast her hands upward. "Meierin, this is so provoking! Will you remember to find some quills and paper? I know I won't remember. Oh, I beg your pardon, am I still speaking in Terheien? Here, let me . . ." She built a language sluice for the girl as well. It was easier this time because she could use the wall she'd already made, but she longed for a quill and paper to help organize her ideas about the building of insubstantial structures. Hadn't Brugent Wareierchen said something about mathematics being a kind of making? Was that at all the same as language being a making?

Gereint would know—she wished Gereint was here; she wished she could show him what she'd made and find out what he thought about it—maybe he could think of a way to make it more generalizable . . . or get around the problem of needing somebody to hold each language in place on either side of the wall . . . It would be nice if you didn't actually have to have someone who knew Terheien at hand in order to build this sort of structure, but at the moment she couldn't see any way around that . . . She said, "Make a note, Meierin, would you? I want to look up what Wareierchen said about law and magic, and whether he said anything about language as an abstract making when he was writing about law. I can look that up in my father's library. Don't let me forget about that."

Meierin nodded, her eyes still wide and stunned. "Are you—are you speaking in Terheien?" She turned to Lord Bertaud. "Honored lord, is she—*is* my lady speaking in, in Terheien?"

"You are both speaking Terheien," the lord said, shaking his head. He didn't glare at Tehre, exactly, but clearly he wanted to. "Am I speaking Prechen?"

Tehre was embarrassed. "If we all keep forgetting which language we're speaking, I'll try to think of a way to make it easier, but I think an ability to keep track will come with practice."

"Lady Tehre—" The Feierabianden stopped, shook his head again, and said, "I believed you to be a maker. But I think, esteemed lady, you must instead be a mage? I did not realize—"

"I'm not precisely a mage," Tehre said, surprised. "It's just as well: Mages are so impractical, you know." Then she wondered which language she was speaking and concentrated on listening to the sound of her own words. She went on slowly, barely paying attention to what she was actually saying: "And they sacrifice so much of their natural character as they develop their magecraft, don't they?" She was still speaking Terheien. She repeated the sentence in Prechen, carefully. She tried, experimentally, to mentally order a lecture on the sort of stresses that fracture wood as opposed to steel, concentrating on the shape of her sentences . . . In fact, the way she framed ideas seemed to shift a little depending on which language she let come to her tongue. That was unexpected. She should try poetry. That should offer interesting insights about the nature of language. "Lord Bertaud, do you know any poetry?"

"I'm frightened to admit to any knowledge of anything whatsoever," murmured the foreigner, his eyebrows rising. "Esteemed mage, I don't understand how you did this, but I—"

Tehre shook her head quickly. "I'm not a mage, truly. Haven't you been listening? A mage is a . . . a focal point for power, you know? Or so Warichteier says, and I suppose he's right, he is about most things, I believe. I'm not like that."

Lord Bertaud raised his eyebrows. "Aren't you? I suppose a Casmantian maker understands the difference between making and magecraft . . ." But his tone was faintly doubtful.

Tehre shrugged impatiently. "I just think about things. Though I didn't know I . . . I've never actually thought about language before. It's interesting what you can do, isn't it, if you think about language the right way?" She considered pronunciation. "I suppose . . . No, that doesn't make sense. Or maybe . . . no. Hmm." Perhaps pronunciation had to do with capturing the style of a language . . . "I *do* wish I had a proper quill and some paper," she said, with sudden, intense impatience. "I can't think properly without a decent quill in my hand."

"I will find for you the very best paper and quills available in Dachsichten," Lord Bertaud promised her. "If you wish me to tell you another story, lady, believe me, you have only to ask."

Tehre laughed. But she hoped he remembered his promise to find writing materials. Or that Meierin did. She already knew she would probably be distracted somehow and forget.

In the event, Tehre was indeed distracted from any possible concerns about feather quills and good paper long before they arrived at Dachsichten. Because that very evening, they saw their first griffin.

The griffin was flying fast, low above the river, heading south. They saw it shortly before dusk, after they had stopped for the evening. No inn being convenient, they had simply camped beside the river, though with the supplies Lord Bertaud's retainers carried, this did not present much hardship. The campsite was a pretty one; three other parties had stopped in it as well, so there were tents scattered like a field of red and blue flowers all across the campsite. Lord Bertaud had set up his tents so they overlooked the river.

Tonight the sunset had piled up in rich purple and gold in the west; heavy golden light lanced through breaks in the towering clouds and set the river alight with reflected glory, poured across the rolling fields on the other side of the river, and turned every stalk of ripening grain to rich gold.

In this light, the griffin, too, looked like it had been fashioned by some tremendously skilled craftsmaster. The long feathers of its wings might have been made of black iron and red copper, its lion pelt of the smoldering coals that glow at the heart of a fire. Its savage beak and talons flashed like metal. The sun threw its shadow out across the river, but its shadow was made of light, of fire, and was not a real shadow at all. Tehre thought it looked altogether beautiful, but almost more like a clockwork mechanism than a living creature; she was half inclined to look for the cords that suspended it from the sky.

The griffin was soaring like a great eagle, wings stretched out wide and still, seeming to rest suspended in the air. Its motionlessness added to the illusion that it was not really alive. It looked a little, Tehre thought, like a butterfly in amber, for the light that surrounded it seemed richer and heavier and somehow more concentrated than the sunlight that fell across fields and road and river. It did not seem to notice them; it did not seem to notice anything. It was moving fast, its fierce eagle's glare fixed on the river before it. But then, as the griffin whipped past the campsite, it suddenly turned its head and looked with swift intensity at the travelers who, frozen with astonishment, stared back at it. Its eyes were black and fierce and utterly unreadable. Tehre wondered what it saw and whether to it they looked like they were not quite like living creatures.

Then it was past, gone. The sun dipped below the distant horizon. It was suddenly, comprehensively, dark. For a long moment, despite the light of the half-dozen campfires various travelers had lit, it seemed that the griffin had carried all the light of the world away with it.

There was a long, fraught silence. Then a sudden babble of voices, everyone in the campsite speaking at once, asking one another what they'd seen and what it meant and had it really been a griffin and what did that mean and would it come back and what would it do if it did return? Everyone in Lord Bertaud's camp was asking the same questions, too. Except, Tehre saw, for the lord himself. The foreigner was not paying any attention to anyone else. His expression was set and blank, as unreadable as the griffin's. He was standing perfectly still, staring steadily downriver after the griffin.

CHAPTER 9

Just at dawn, Beguchren led Gereint out to the inn's small, empty courtyard and stood watching with bland patience as their horses were saddled and brought out. None of the inn's few other guests was up quite yet, though the inn staff were stirring about their morning tasks. A girl, bringing fresh loaves back to the inn from some local baker, timidly came over to offer them a loaf. She didn't dare speak to Beguchren, but gave the warm bread to Gereint, along with a shy smile. And the innkeeper himself came out of the stable along with the boys who led Beguchren's black mares, having personally assured that the horses would be ready no matter the early hour. Probably that story about the dead brigands they'd left a few miles south had assured attentive service. Though, at that, Beguchren's imperturbable calm and expensive rings might have been enough.

So they left the ferry landing almost as they had entered it, in pale, shadowy light. The river was still all but invisible in the dimness, just perceptible as a black smooth ribbon and a ripple of sound. The fat crescent of the moon still stood overhead, with the Twin Daughters glimmering by one of its sharp tips.

That was the moment when they saw their first griffins. It had never occurred to Gereint that the griffins would leave their desert to venture this far into the country of men. But he saw at once that Beguchren was not surprised.

There were five griffins. They were flying high, so high they might almost have looked like eagles, except somehow they didn't look anything like eagles. Even at this distance, the sunlight struck off them as though they were made of gold and copper and bronze, but that wasn't why they caught the eye. There was something else, something about the way the sky glinted and changed above them, something about the way the wind itself almost seemed to glitter as it tangled in the feathers of their wings. They flew as geese fly in the fall: in a narrow spearhead formation. They traveled in a long curving arc that carried them from the southwest away to the east and north. They could not be coming from their desert, not from the southwest. But if they were returning to it, then they were strangely far east, and heading more easterly still.

Gereint stared after the griffins until they vanished into the far reaches of the distance and then pulled his gaze, with some effort, from the sky and turned to Beguchren.

The mage was not looking at him. He was gazing steadily into the sky after the griffins. His expression was as blandly inscrutable as ever, but his mouth was set and there was a tightness around his eyes that suggested he was not quite as calm as he appeared. His grip on his mare's reins was so tight his knuckles were white. As Gereint watched, he loosened his hold on the reins and set one hand on the pommel of his saddle instead, seemingly for balance, or possibly support, for then he leaned forward and bowed his head over the mare's neck as though suddenly gripped by weakness.

"Are you well?" Gereint asked tentatively.

Beguchren did not look up. "Of course."

Gereint paused. Then he said tentatively, "I'm surprised to see them this far south. Or this far east."

The mage straightened in his saddle, put his shoulders back, lifted his head, and said, "Yes." His tone was perfectly neutral. He did not glance at Gereint, but stared straight down the road between the ears of his horse.

Gereint had thought he might ask again, given the sighting, whether the mage might tell him why they were going north. Perhaps seeing griffins would count as coming to the desert? But something in Beguchren's blank neutrality made him hesitate, and the moment passed. He said instead, "It should be possible, as you suggested, to reach Pamnarichtan this morning and Metichteran sometime this afternoon."

Beguchren took a breath. Then another. He managed a slight smile, giving Gereint a sideways look. "You don't wish to go fishing?"

"No," Gereint said slowly. "Or even if I had, not after seeing the griffins. Somehow this doesn't seem like a morning for fishing." He concentrated, in fact, on keeping his own tone as neutral as Beguchren's. It wasn't as easy as the mage made it seem.

Yet somehow Gereint felt, for the first time, truly easy about his decision to continue north, as though it was truly *his* decision, unconstrained by the mage's subtle—and not-so-subtle—compulsion. But was it the griffin sighting that had made the difference? Or some indefinable alteration in the mage's manner? Something else entirely?

But Beguchren said only, "Good," turned his mare's head to the north, and nudged her into a trot.

Gereint followed, wondering whether he was right to hear more than one meaning in that simple word. He tried not to look away into the woods beside the road or imagine that the occasional snap of a branch in the woods along the road revealed the approach of more brigands. He knew Beguchren had been right, that every decent traveler did have the duty to put down brigands if he could—but he did not want to see the king's mage bring that frozen light glimmering out of earth and water a second time.

But the woods were quiet.

Gereint tried not to think about riding along this road in the other direction, with Sicheir and the rest, on the way to Breidechboden and freedom. That ride had been wound about with uncertainty and worries. Despite remembering all of them perfectly clearly, that journey seemed, in memory, one of the more pleasant interludes in his life, and Tehre's house at the end of it a haven of peace.

What would Tehre be doing this morning? Breaking something, undoubtedly. Some small ordinary household object, or a catapult somebody had made for her—somebody else, and how foolish to be jealous of that unknown and hypothetical maker—or a wagon or carriage or who knew what. Maybe a model bridge. Maybe she'd persuaded the Arobern to let her have a large building to tear down. Gereint thought of the way Tehre had made Derich's sword shatter upon striking the bronze swan and wished he could watch her bring down a building. What kind of minor stress might she use to make stone shear and shatter? It would be fascinating, he was sure. And impressive.

The road was very quiet. Only birds sang, not with the urgency of spring, but with a desultory chirp here and there. Other than the sluggish river to their right, only squirrels moved, running along the occasional branch or darting across the road. Probably the odd rustle back in the woods was a squirrel. Or a deer. Almost certainly none of the rustles signaled the presence of brigands or wolves or anything in the least alarming. Gereint wondered what Beguchren would do if a brigand in the woods tried to shoot them from hiding, then tried hard not to wonder about any such question. He did not really want to know.

For all his comments about pressing the pace, the mage had let his mare fall into a gentle walk. He rode with the reins loose and his head bowed. Maybe he, also, was concentrating on the sounds from the woods?

They rode into Pamnarichtan about four hours after leaving Raichboden. The horses, sensible creatures, pricked up their ears and tried determinedly to head for the hay and grain scents of the stable at the southernmost inn, which overlooked the confluence where the Nerintsan ran into the Teschanken.

Gereint reluctantly held his mare and the packhorse from leaving the road. He looked at Beguchren. "We don't *have* to stop here you think it's urgent to get on."

"No, we'll rest here. And get something to eat. If we don't, I imagine we'll wish we had long before we reach Metichteran." Beguchren let his horse turn toward the stable.

Beguchren sounded as calm and unruffled as ever, but Gereint saw that the mage was holding the reins with one hand and bracing himself unobtrusively against the pommel of his saddle with his other, much as he had immediately after the griffins had passed. He watched him narrowly, surprised. Just how hard had it been on him to do what he had done to those brigands? But Beguchren had seemed all right afterward . . .

Gereint let his horse follow the mage's mare, then nudged it into a slightly faster pace so he would reach the inn's stableyard first. Swinging quickly down from his saddle, he came around into position to offer Beguchren a steadying hand and his bent knee as a stepping block.

Beguchren looked slightly taken aback, which for him was like an exclamation of surprise. For a moment he only looked down at Gereint. But he did not order him out of the way or make a point of dismounting without help. He merely said at last, "Thank you, Gereint," and accepted the offered assistance.

Gereint kept his arm under Beguchren's hand for a long moment, until he felt that the smaller man was steady on his feet. The inn's stable boys came out to get the horses. Gereint told them, "Go ahead and untack them and rub them down. Give them some grain. My lord will be here an hour or more and he'll want them rested."

"Honored sir," murmured the boys, with covert, fascinated glances that measured the difference in size between Gereint and Beguchren. But the white-haired man was so obviously a lord that they were respectful and quick and didn't whisper to each other until they were out of sight.

"There's a table in the shade," Gereint said, nodding to it. It was also the closest table. "I'll tell them to bring something to eat as well as tea, shall I?"

"Yes." Beguchren lifted his hand deliberately from Gereint's arm. "Thank you," he repeated calmly, and walked quite steadily to the table.

But he gripped both the edge of the table and the arm of the chair to brace himself before he sat down.

"Tea," Gereint told the inn staff. He spoke briskly and casually, as though he had no doubt whatsoever that service would be instant and respectful—exactly the way an important lord's retainer would speak. "With honey and milk. Wine, whatever you have that's good. Sweet rolls—you have sweet rolls? Good. Sliced beef and eggs. Quickly, now, you understand?"

"Honored sir," murmured the women, and vanished to see to it.

Gereint went back to the table and leaned against the shading oak, his arms crossed. He found he was frowning and tried to smooth out his expression.

"You needn't look quite so worried," Beguchren murmured. He'd tilted his head back against the headboard of his chair and closed his eyes, so how he could know whether Gereint looked worried or impatient or irritated or anything was a question. His face was tight-drawn, the bones sharply prominent under the skin. He looked much older than he had in Breidechboden: Gereint would now have believed him to be in his sixties or even his seventies, and he wondered again how old the mage actually was.

"Is it what happened last night?" Gereint asked him. "I thought you seemed well enough after—after. But I was, um, I don't know if I would have noticed anything, ah, subtle."

Beguchren did not answer. Gereint found himself frowning once more and tried again to make his expression bland. The women brought tea, glazed rolls still warm from the ovens, and assurances that beef and eggs and bread were on the way. Beguchren opened his eyes and lifted his head when the women came up to the table, but he made no move to serve himself. It might have been a lord's arrogance, but Gereint, suspecting that the mage's hands might shake if he tried anything as demanding as pouring out tea, poured it himself without comment. He added two spoonfuls of honey and a little milk and handed the cup across the table. Beguchren, looking mildly amused, took the cup—in both hands, Gereint noted—and drank half of it at once, like medicine. The cup rattled in its saucer as he put it down.

"Why didn't you say something?" Gereint asked him. "Too stubborn?"

Beguchren shrugged, a minimal gesture. "By the time I realized the difficulty, we'd come so close to Pamnarichtan it seemed foolish to stop short." He'd folded his hands in his lap, waiting perhaps to regain enough strength to drink the rest of the tea.

"Was it the magecraft last night?" Gereint asked again. "Or is it just"—he did not want to say *a weakness*—"something that happens?" he finished.

A slight pause. Then Beguchren shook his head. "Not the mage-craft. The proximity of the griffins this morning."

Gereint thought about this. Then he stood up to help the women from the inn lay out platters of beef and bread, eggs, sausages, and fried apples. Beguchren ignored this activity with a lordly disdain for noticing servants, which was, Gereint suspected, actually a way of disguising that he could not lift a platter himself. Once the women had gone, he filled a plate for Beguchren first and set it across the table in easy reach, then one for himself.

Beguchren took a sweet roll and ate it slowly. Then a bit of beef and an egg. He lifted his eyebrows at Gereint. "Did you order everything in the kitchens? There's far too much."

"For you, maybe." Gereint filled his own plate a second time. "The griffins did this to you. Just flying past, a quarter-mile away? And you want to go up to their desert, do you, and find them in it?"

"Gereint . . ." Beguchren began, then shook his head, smiling with rueful humor. His hands had steadied at last. He said, "It's a consequence of the events in Feierabiand, I believe. The griffins expended a great deal of power there. I was . . . overpowered, I suppose."

And the rest of Casmantium's cold mages had been killed. Gereint had heard that. Because they had been less powerful than Beguchren Teshrichten? Because Beguchren had been with the king? Or because Beguchren had simply been lucky? Or for some other reason entirely?

Gereint wondered just what the battle between the griffins and the cold mages had entailed, and exactly how thoroughly the griffins had won it. Then he wondered whether he really wanted to know.

"The effects seem both more wide ranging and more lingering than I might have wished," Beguchren added, a touch of apology in his tone.

And might get worse if they encountered more griffins? Or encountered them more closely? Gereint remembered how profoundly inimical he had found the desert. And Beguchren was a cold mage: far more opposed to the desert than any man with a mere gift for making. The two philosophers Gereint respected most, Andrieikan Warichteier and Beremnan Anweierchen, both agreed that opposition to the griffin's fire was the entire purpose and character of cold magecraft.

Beguchren had said they would go north *all the way*. But if a handful of griffins passing a quarter-mile away had strained him to the end of his strength, what would stepping into their desert do to him? Gereint said, "You should have a carriage. Why did you leave yours behind in the south?"

Beguchren shook his head, a small, surprisingly gentle gesture. "I did not wish to risk a servant of mine. Irechen has been my driver for many years."

Gereint thought of and dismissed several obvious rejoinders. In the end, he said merely, "You might have asked me to drive. I wouldn't want to try six-in-hand, but I could certainly have managed a little rig like that."

Beguchren's eyebrows rose. He said after a moment, "I suppose I could have done. I didn't think of it."

Gereint leaned back in his chair, trying not to laugh. He kept his expression sober with an effort.

"Well," Beguchren said, a little nettled, "the roads north of Metichteran, as you have said, are not so good. And you know we will not be able to take horses into the desert. We will leave them, at the end, and go up on foot."

"Well, I suppose I can carry you, if necessary."

A flicker of offense in the pale eyes was followed almost at once by a glint of wry humor. "I suppose you could. If it became necessary. I don't believe that's likely."

Gereint didn't comment on this optimism. Beguchren *had* said he'd wanted a maker who was physically strong. Gereint had not asked why. He did not press the mage now, only split a sausage and laid it across a slice of bread. Then he asked instead, "You still wish to try to ride on to Metichteran today? It's, what, twenty miles, a little more?" By himself, and given Beguchren's tall black mare, Gereint was confident he could ride that far in five or six hours. He could *walk* it almost that fast, if he needed to. But Beguchren? He did not want to force the mage to admit to an incapacity he likely found shameful. But neither did he want to see him collapse halfway to Metichteran.

"I'll be well enough in an hour," Beguchren answered, mildly enough.

Gereint tried not to look doubtful.

Beguchren peeled and sliced an egg, layering the slices fastidiously across a piece of bread. He murmured, not looking up from this task, "I might ask the inn to wrap up some of this excellent breakfast."

"Including plenty of sweet rolls," Gereint surmised. "And cakes of sugar. Yes. I'll arrange it, lord mage."

The mage looked up at that, frowning. Not about the sugar. "Gereint—"

Gereint held up a hand. "Nobody here would understand it if I called you by name, lord mage." Nor would he regardless, but he did not say so.

"Nor will you," Beguchren said, echoing this unspoken thought. But he made a small, dismissive gesture with two fingers. "Never mind. Yes, Gereint, please acquire some more sugar. As I am sure you recall, I would like to reach not merely Metichteran by this afternoon, but Tashen by this evening."

This seemed wildly optimistic to Gereint. He didn't say this, either, but merely stood up and went to see about wrapping up a packet of food. With plenty of sugar.

The horses, happy with their rest and the sweetened grain the stable boys had given them, were inclined to stride out briskly. Gereint kept a wary eye on Beguchren, but the little mage showed no sign, now, of exhaustion or collapse. He was quiet, but then he was constitutionally quiet, so Gereint had long since concluded. Even if he had been surrounded by his own retainers or friends . . . did he *have* friends? Other than the Arobern, who could not be precisely a *friend* . . . It occurred to Gereint for the first time that he knew nothing at all about the mage: earth and iron, the man might even be married, though it was hard to imagine so reserved and inscrutable a man with a wife, or children or even parents or brothers of his own blood. Nor could he imagine invading that impenetrable reserve with questions.

But even if surrounded by friends, Gereint could not believe that Beguchren Teshrichten was ever precisely demonstrative. And Gereint himself, if not precisely an enemy—nor precisely a servant, nor precisely a prisoner—was certainly not a friend.

The country between Pamnarichtan and Metichteran was rougher than Gereint had remembered. Nor had he made sufficient allowance for the way the road climbed far more often than it ran level. Coming the other way, they had gone mostly downhill. Now, riding constantly uphill, they could not press the horses faster than an easy walk. There were more stones and snags, too. A fine carriage would have had a slow and difficult passage; even a farmer's wagon would be prone to broken wheels and axles. Gereint guessed that most carters and such who regularly used this road were probably makers, the sort sufficiently gifted that they could coax a breaking wagon to last from one town to the next. Perhaps Beguchren's leaving his carriage behind had been more reasonable than he'd first thought.

Gereint's own mare began to cast a shoe; he felt two of the nails start to shear and the rest to bend, and caught the metal with his wish that it hold, hold, hold. The nails held. Gereint didn't mention the problem. If he could coax the shoe to last to Metichteran, any smith could replace it; if it didn't, there wouldn't be anything to do but lead the mare and walk himself. He wondered what Tehre Amnachudran would think of shearing nails. Probably she would rather let them shear and watch how they broke. But probably she could brush a thumb over them and set them back into place without benefit of a smith, if it occurred to her to bother. He smiled, imagining the casual, distracted manner in which she would do such a small, difficult task.

The woods crowded close to the road here, and on their other side the river was narrower and swifter than below the confluence, and beyond the river the woods stretched out again, impenetrably dense and green. The woods might have hidden any number of brigands or wolves or mountain cats or dragons, but Gereint did not glimpse anything more dangerous than a squirrel. Occasionally a large animal thudded away into the woods, unseen. Each time, Gereint glanced at Beguchren. Each time, the mage, his expression unvaryingly bland, shook his head.

"How do you know?" Gereint asked him, the third time this happened.

Beguchren shrugged, a minimal gesture that barely lifted his shoulders. "I know."

Gereint shook his head, not in disbelief, but in surprise. "We look so harmless. I'd accost us, if I were a brigand. They can't all have been cleared out."

"The cleverer ones may have headed west, as Meridanium has begun clearing these roads near its border. Or even south, to see if they can get honest work now that robbing travelers has become more dangerous. Or—" But Beguchren paused and then finished, "Or simple luck may be keeping them out of our way."

Gereint wondered how he'd meant to finish that sentence. But he said only, "Luck for them."

Beguchren only shrugged a second time, dismissing any possible concern about brigands. Or wolves or mountain cats, probably. Even he might have paused if a dragon had come out of the woods, though. Not that one would this close to the towns of men.

There were no boats at all on the river now. Even in the spring floods, the channel here was dangerous: changeable and filled with snags. Now, in late summer, the river had narrowed to a swift slender ribbon, barely more than a creek, that raced down only the deep center of its exposed, rocky bed. Gereint guessed, as the morning passed and the road grew rougher, that it would take a good deal longer than five or six hours to reach Metichteran.

They saw no more griffins. Though the way the woods closed off any decent view of the sky, fifty griffins might have flown past half a mile away and been completely invisible to travelers on the road. But then, probably, Beguchren would know they were there. Probably he *would* collapse if griffins came near. Gereint watched him warily. But the mage showed no sign of difficulty. During the occasional break for sweet wine or a bite of bread or a cup of hot tea, he dismounted and moved with only a little more than ordinary stiffness. So far as Gereint could tell.

They passed the occasional party heading south. No one was traveling in a really large company, but no one was traveling in a group of less than half a dozen, either, and everyone was armed at least with crossbows. None of them were men of rank, and no one ventured more than a respectful nod to Beguchren. Gereint might have stopped one or another to ask for news, but he kept an eye toward Beguchren, and when the mage did not pause, neither did he.

They rode into Metichteran in late afternoon, seven hours after leaving Pamnarichtan. It had been a market day, clearly: The streets were busy with farmers packing up their surplus to cart back to their farms, or bargaining with the most frugal of the townsfolk for the last bushels of bruised apples or spotty turnips. The famous bridge across the Teschanken was busy, too, though the water level was low enough that children were picking their way right across the river's bed. Gereint gazed down at the fitted stones of the bridge's arch as they crossed. It seemed to him that the hooves of the horses rang against history as much as against stone. Blood and battle and years mortared the stones. He wondered suddenly whether they might be riding into a tale themselves; perhaps some traveler in some distant year would look down at this bridge and think, *Beguchren Teshrichten crossed the river here to do battle against the country of fire* . . . He hoped not. He hoped, fervently, that nothing that happened would be exciting enough to remember in tale or poem.

The yard of the inn in East Metichteran was even busier than the streets had been. Surprisingly busy, indeed, as it could not yet be time for the supper crowd . . . Indeed, no one was yet ordering supper. The townsfolk and the lingering farmers were instead gathered around the inn's tables, drinking ale and talking animatedly.

Gereint swung down from his mare and wordlessly moved to assist Beguchren down from his: abnormally weakened or not, that was a tall horse for a small man to ride, and mounting blocks were not really high enough for him.

Beguchren accepted his assistance equally wordlessly, allowed

Gereint to take his reins, and stood for a moment, gazing with narrow interest at the gathering around the tables.

"The inn staff must be over there, too," Gereint commented. He considered, briefly, taking the horses into the stables himself. Then, looking thoughtfully at the tables and the chairs and the jugs of ale, he reconsidered. He whistled instead, loud and sharp.

A startled silence fell across the inn yard. Beguchren gave him a dry look. Gereint only shrugged. "What's the point of traveling with a court noble if one doesn't put rank to use?" he murmured, and lifted an eyebrow pointedly at the cluster of youngsters he guessed were the stable boys. He'd guessed correctly, from the way they jumped up and hurried forward.

"Sorry, sorry, honored lord," muttered a fat, balding man, clearly the innkeeper, assessing Lord Mage Beguchren Teshrichten's horse and clothing and manner with an expert eye. "We're all distracted just now, honored lord, but just let me show you and your man to our best table—we *do* set the best table in Metichteran, I promise you—just this way, if you will permit me—"

"Distracted?" Beguchren inquired, in his most neutral tone.

"From the sightings! Griffins, honored lord, all this afternoon!" The fat man's broad gesture sketched their path, from west and south to the northeast. "Four or five at a time, honored lord, and we've never seen griffins down this far south before, not even before, well, I mean to say, not even when there were a gracious plenty over yonder." This time his vague gesture toward the northwest indicated, by implication, the original sweep of the griffins' desert prior to their claiming of Melentser.

"I see," said Beguchren, still at his most neutral. He allowed the innkeeper to evict a crowd from a table under a big oak near the inn's door and pull the chair at its head out for him. "How many altogether, would you say?"

"Forty, fifty all told! Not that we could say whether they were forty different griffins, you know, honored lord, or the same ones circling about. Penach, he's my oldest boy, he said he thought it was the same ones each time, but how even young eyes could see so clearly I don't know. You won't want ale, honored lord: let me send for wine—our best—local, of course, but it's accounted fair enough by our guests—" He turned and waved sharply to a hovering girl, who darted away into the inn.

"And tea," Gereint said firmly. He pulled a chair out for himself and sank into it with a sigh. It wasn't a particularly well-made chair, unfortunately. Not very comfortable for a man who'd been in a saddle all day. Maybe Beguchren's chair was better. He glanced at the mage, trying to assess his general condition.

"I'm quite well," Beguchren assured him, in a mild tone that Gereint did not trust at all.

Gereint raised his eyebrows at the mage. He said to the innkeeper, "And something to eat. Bread with butter and honey. Or berry preserves."

"Of course, of course, honored sir," said the innkeeper hurriedly, and waved again to the girl, who'd hurried back with the wine, a pitcher of water, and—no doubt—the inn's best silver goblets. The man himself, perspiring in the late-summer heat, seemed disinclined to dash back and forth himself. He glanced nervously at Beguchren, who poured a little wine into his goblet, topped it up with water, and sipped. There was no way to tell from the mage's manner or expression what he thought of the inn's best local wine.

It actually wasn't bad, was Gereint's own estimation, when he tried it. For a locally produced northern wine. Not up to the quality one expected in the south, of course. Perech Fellesteden would probably have dumped it out of his goblet onto the inn's yard and might have made the innkeeper lick it up from the dirt, but Fellesteden had been much inclined to dramatic gestures, and why was Gereint thinking of his old master at all? Ah. Because he was thinking of Melentser, and the griffins flying among the red sharp-edged spires they had raised among the ruined buildings of the town. He closed his eyes for a breath, opened them, and looked deliberately at Beguchren.

"Perfectly acceptable," the lord mage told the innkeeper gravely. And to Gereint, "There is no need to hover. I have taken precautions."

"Precautions, is it? Here comes the bread. I trust you'll do me the favor of eating a slice or two, with plenty of honey. My lord."

"Yes, an additional precaution is perhaps not out of order," Beguchren said, with a barely perceptible glint of humor. He added to the innkeeper, who was looking baffled and worried, "When did the griffins last pass over the town? Can you estimate?"

"Yes, well, yes, that is to say, I suppose it was an hour or so ago, honored lord. Doesn't that seem right to you?" the innkeeper appealed to the girl, who was laying out plates of sliced bread and crocks of honey and blackberry preserves. The girl looked startled at being addressed, but agreed that this was about right.

"I do believe," Beguchren said to Gereint, "that it would be wisest to go on to Tashen today."

Gereint made no comment until the innkeeper and the girl had both bustled away. Then he said, "That wasn't an easy ride we've already had today. It's so important to travel another fifteen miles or so?"

"The road from East Metichteran to Tashen is better, I believe."

"It is. Even so . . . What does it mean, my lord mage, that the griffins are flying over Metichteran? Does it matter whether it's the same ones over and over, or different ones each time?"

"Gereint—"

"Don't trouble yourself, my lord. Pretend I never asked." But Gereint kept his tone mild. He spread a piece of bread with the berry preserves and ate it thoughtfully. "Fifteen miles. However good the road, the horses are tired. That's four, five, six hours? We won't manage it before nightfall."

"I can make a light."

"Ah. Will it continue to light our way after you've collapsed?"

Beguchren put down the slice of bread he'd been holding and regarded Gereint for a moment. "You know, you used to be afraid of me."

"I've given up reminding myself I ought to be afraid of you. My lord."

Beguchren gave him an unreadable smile. "Good."

"I suppose I can tie you to your horse, if you fall off."

"I suppose you can. I think we will arrange for fresh horses here. And perhaps we will leave the packs here. We will not need them in Tashen."

"I think we should take them. In case we stop a mile short of Tashen. You should eat that, my lord. And you should rest while I arrange for a change of horses."

Beguchren gave a little wave of his hand, conceding all these points with a casual air Gereint did not trust at all. But the mage only smiled blandly even when Gereint gave him a look of pointed suspicion. Giving up, Gereint, got to his feet and looked around to find the innkeeper. He would inquire about horses that might be for sale, and about the cost to board the black mares . . . Maybe he should ask Beguchren to let him show the token; that should guarantee the horses would be well cared for . . . He turned back to ask about the token. Thus, he was looking straight at Beguchren when the little mage suddenly folded bonelessly forward across the table.

Gereint took one long stride back toward the table. Then a horse, not one of Beguchren's, suddenly reared, screaming. Gereint spun on his heel, startled, as boys flung themselves at its head. They grabbed for its bridle, but the horse reared again, tore itself loose, and raced out of the inn's yard, hooves thudding dully on the packed earth. Gereint stared after it. But a flurry of exclamations all across the inn's yard made him look sharply around, and then at last, following the direction of others' gazes, up. He stopped, transfixed.

Three griffins cut across the cloud-streaked sky, glittering like bronze spear points in the late afternoon sun. They flew barely high enough to clear the trees and the taller buildings of the town. A great silence had fallen. Gereint could actually hear the rustle of the wind through the griffins' wings. The sound was more like stiff cloth flapping in a hard wind than like the gentler rustling he would have imagined.

He could see every long feather of those wings, even pick out the smaller individual feathers of the griffins' chests and forelegs. Each feather looked like it had been beaten out by a metalsmith and then separately traced with gold by a jeweler; the griffin's lion pelts blazed like pure gold. The light flashed across their beaks and talons as across metal. Gereint guessed those talons were nearly as long as a man's fingers, curved and wickedly sharp; he was struck by a distressingly vivid image of what talons like those might do to a man if a griffin struck him.

Something about the afternoon light had become strange. It took a moment for Gereint's mind to catch up to his eyes, but at last he understood that the light seemed fiercer and more brilliant around the griffins; each one was limned with it, every feather outlined by it. The sunlight itself seemed to radiate from the griffins as much as from the low sun. And the light that fell across Metichteran was suddenly heavier, deeper, hotter than any light should be, even in late summer. Not quite like the brutal sunlight of the desert, but close, closer than anything Gereint had ever wanted to experience again. The sky beyond the griffins had gone strange, pale, harsh . . . The very sky seemed to glint like metal. The wind carried the scents of dry stone and hot brass.

The griffins did not look to either side; their flight was arrow straight. They flew from the southwest toward the northeast. Though it seemed to take a long time for them to pass over the town, it could not have taken more than a moment. Then they were gone. The light that lay across the inn's yard eased once more into normal afternoon sunlight, and the breeze that came across the town from the hills was cool and scented with pine, as well as the normal horse-and-cooking smells of the town.

The silent stillness that had gripped the town ended suddenly, and exclamations and shouts and questions once again filled the air. Men scattered in all directions, or clustered in groups and leaned forward in furious debate about what had just happened and what they should do about it. Stable boys went after the frightened horse, and the fat innkeeper sank, trembling visibly, into a broad chair and mopped his forehead with his apron.

Gereint stared at the innkeeper for an instant, then abruptly, with a shock, remembered Beguchren. Cursing under his breath, he spun back toward the table. The little mage was lying half across the table and half across the bench. His hands were limp, his eyes closed, his breathing shallow and quick, his face very pale.

Gereint reached Beguchren's side in two hurried steps and caught him, barely in time, from sliding off the bench onto the ground. He had commented, not very seriously, about being able to carry the smaller man. He had not expected to need to. But now he picked him up in his arms, finding his weight a negligible burden. But then he only stood for a moment, uncertain. But, however urgently Beguchren had wanted to press on, Gereint could see only one option now. He went over to the innkeeper, who was still sitting limply on his wide chair, staring up with wide, worried eyes into the empty sky. Gereint had to clear his throat loudly to get his attention. But then the fat man brought his wide stare down at last to ground level, took in Gereint and his burden, flinched, and clambered hastily and clumsily to his feet.

"My lord is ill," Gereint stated, as though this was not abundantly obvious. "He will need your best room. A good room, at least, if your best is taken. Whatever is quickest." He emphasized the last word with a flattening of his tone and a direct stare.

"Of course, of course, yes, honored sir, we've plenty of room, all our rooms are good, if you could just bring the honored lord this way—" the innkeeper said, all in one breath. He gave Gereint a beseeching look, perhaps imagining that his staff would be expected to nurse an important but delicate lordling and be blamed if anything went wrong—or perhaps imagining the lord might actually *die* in his inn, and envisioning the recriminations that might follow. Gereint fancied he could see those exact thoughts arise, full formed, in the fat innkeeper's mind. The man asked with clear trepidation, leading Gereint up a flight of stairs, "Is the honored lord *very* ill, do you know, honored sir?"

"I think not," Gereint assured him. "I will care for him myself, honored innkeeper." He glanced at the room the innkeeper showed him, approved it with a brief nod, and added, with conscious hauteur, "Have someone bring broth and tea. And a crock of honey. And soft bread, with something off the spit for me, when you have it ready. Have my lord's horses carefully tended. One of them has a loose shoe. Get a smith to check them all. And don't let the saddlebags sit out in the stable, have them brought here! Is that all clear?"

"Absolutely clear, honored sir," muttered the innkeeper, and hastily backed out of the room before Gereint could make any further, possibly more difficult, demands.

Gereint laid Beguchren down on the bed—the linens appeared clean, at least, and he saw no immediate sign of bugs. Then he stood back and just looked at him for a moment. Then laid the back of his hand against the mage's forehead. Limp and pale and cool, and Gereint was no healer. He could hardly coax the man toward strength and health as he would coax nails to hold or wood to resist splintering. Though Tehre might have managed something. Tehre would probably treat healing magic as a kind of making. In fact, if she treated *everything* as a kind of making, that might go a long way toward explaining why she was so *broadly* gifted.

But he still had no idea how to handle any kind of healing himself. But then, if his guess was good, Beguchren might need nothing but rest and food. Until the next time a griffin flew overhead, to be sure.

Gereint pulled off Beguchren's boots and, as it seemed far too great a liberty to do more, settled for tucking a blanket around his slight form. The blanket was a light, soft wool, better than anyone had a right to expect in a common inn. Perhaps the innkeeper hadn't exaggerated so terribly when he claimed his rooms were good. A boy brought the saddlebags, and then the girl arrived in a flurry, too shy to look at Gereint. She blushed and stammered as she told Gereint, in a whisper, that supper would be served beginning in an hour, but she would bring him the first meat that was ready. She was obviously trying not to even glance at Beguchren as she laid out an earthenware pot of broth, a plate of bread, a crock of honey, and the tea things.

Gereint thanked her gravely and let her escape. The room was close and hot in the summer evening, but it was a comfortable, natural warmth, nothing like the inimical heat carried on the wind from the griffins' wings. Was Beguchren already looking a little less pale? Might there be a little tension in the small hands that lay so quietly on the blanket? Gereint fancied there might be—unless he was simply imagining what he wanted to see. He studied the man's breathing and was sure his breaths were deeper and more relaxed, no longer the rapid shallow breaths of shock and weakness.

Beguchren opened his eyes. Blinked. A faint, puzzled crease appeared between his eyebrows.

"Easy," Gereint murmured. "We're at the inn at Metichteran. We're staying here overnight after all. We'll hire a carriage or something in the morning."

A faint smile curved Beguchren's mouth. "Is that the plan?"

"It is now. Have some tea." He let Beguchren hold the cup himself, but kept his own hand ready to steady it if necessary. The mage managed to raise the cup successfully, but his hand shook badly as he tried to lower it again; Gereint closed his fingers around the cup and Beguchren's smaller hand and guided the cup down to the tray on the bed table. Beguchren seemed not to notice this assistance. Gereint certainly made no comment about it.

"I'll be well enough in the morning," the mage murmured.

"Unless the griffins fly over again."

"Yes," Beguchren said, in an absent tone. "I shall have to do something about that."

Gereint waited, but the mage did not seem inclined to unfold any specifics about this "something" he might do. Gereint said after a moment, "There's broth and bread. With honey."

Again, a slight smile. Not inscrutable at all, Gereint found: that smile contained a rueful, self-deprecating humor; a strict, bitter pride as well as an awareness of the foolishness of pride; a faint, barely visible echo of the effort necessary to put it down. When had he become able to read the little lord's smile?

"I'm not actually ill," Beguchren said mildly. "I believe I will be able to handle something more fortifying than broth."

Gereint didn't argue. He only handed Beguchren a mug of broth, watching to see that he could hold it steady. He wanted to ask what the mage meant to do about the griffins, or about his own weakness. Instead, he drew the room's only chair around so he could both see out the window and keep an eye on the resting mage. There was a good deal of movement through the inn yard, and voices, raised in worried argument, came clearly through the window—too clearly, but though Gereint did not want Beguchren disturbed, he did not want to shut out the light and air, either.

The low sunlight slanted through the window and lay across the floor and the foot of the bed. It was perfectly ordinary sunlight. Gereint found it hard to recall, now, exactly how the light that had blazed around the griffins had differed from this homey light. He frowned out the window, watching the sinking sun layer the sky with carmine and gold . . . There was no sign of any griffin in the air. A hawk turned far above, but the sky above it was an ordinary sky, and the light that surrounded it ordinary light.

If Beguchren was awake, he was doing a very good imitation of a man asleep. Gereint left him alone. The voices rising from the inn's yard faded as—if Gereint's nose did not deceive him—supper began to be served and folk retired to the common room and to the tables at the edge of the yard to eat. The girl, true to her word, brought meat up to Beguchren's room—beef, of course, in this hilly country, and more bread, and sweet roasted turnips and onions. With a small stack of the wide, rimmed plates used to serve someone in bed. Gereint nodded in appreciation of her thoughtfulness and, to encourage more of the same, found a coin for her in Beguchren's belt pouch.

Beguchren did not move through any of the coming and going. Gereint did not disturb him. He ate most of the food himself, setting a little aside under an upended plate to keep warm in case the mage might actually want it later. The broth had cooled. Despite the close warmth of the room, he asked the girl to bring a brazier and to put the pot of broth and the covered plate over the coals to keep warm.

Outside, the sun sank slowly behind the hills. Its last light came scattering through the branches of nearby trees and across the rooftops of the town. The moon, fatly gibbous, stood above the highest rooftop. Above Metichteran, the wide sky was empty of everything but high, delicate clouds; the hawk had gone to its roost. The first stars came glimmering into the violet-streaked sky, and dusk closed across the world as the sun set at last. Gereint got up to close the shutters and light the oil lamp that hung in a corner of the room.

Across the room, Beguchren stirred, opened his eyes, and sat up.

Gereint was so startled he nearly knocked the lamp off its chain. The mage looked far better now than he had earlier; Gereint didn't think it was merely the ruddy light of the lamp that lent him color. He glanced around with something that, if not energy, seemed at least alertness. "Is there food?"

"Broth? Beef?"

"Both, if you please. Is there more honey?"

"Nearly a full crock." Gereint poured broth into one of the clean cups and carried it to the bedside. This time, the mage seemed to have no difficulty lifting or steadying the cup. Gereint said, not quite a question, "You seem much improved."

Beguchren glanced up at him. "There won't be griffins over Metichteran at night."

"Ah. Yes, I recall some minor philosopher . . . Who was it? Lachkeir Anteirch? Anyway, one philosopher or another said something about 'the absence of fire between dusk and dawn.' Does that mean you are less pressed by the griffins' presence now? Or that you are less, ah . . ." He hesitated, trying to frame his question.

"Less pressed by the effort to keep them away from the country of men? Both." Beguchren finished the cup of broth and looked inquiringly at the covered plate on the brazier.

"A moment . . ." Gereint tried, not altogether successfully, not to burn his fingers transferring the beef and turnips onto a plate cool enough to touch. He brought this plate to the mage, watched for a moment to be sure Beguchren could handle it, then went to spread honey on slices of bread and arrange these on a second plate. He asked, "*Were* you keeping them away from Metichteran?"

There was a short pause as Beguchren visibly searched for words. "I was reinforcing the . . . earthiness of this country. You recall how a mage focuses power. Hmm. Or bends and balances the forces that exist in the world; that might be more a more accurate way to put it."

Gereint nodded, not mentioning that this did not seem an overwhelmingly clear description of magecraft to him.

"The nature of earth is antithetical to the nature of fire. I, hmm. Brought out that quality a little more strongly in all the countryside around Metichteran. This should have made any griffins currently in the vicinity very uncomfortable indeed. You didn't see any after those this afternoon." The mage sounded very certain.

"No," Gereint agreed.

"No. They retreated to their own country."

"Huh." Gereint thought about this. "All of them?"

"They aren't mages. I believe—I hope—there is only one true mage left among the griffins, and he is not here."

Or Beguchren would know, presumably. Gereint lifted his eyebrows. "If he should come here?"

"I do not believe the griffin mage will challenge me here. In the country of earth, I am generally stronger than any mage of fire, whatever his provenance."

There were too many qualifiers in this statement to give Gereint much confidence. He asked, "Is it not difficult, doing, ah, this? You were already weary, surely?"

A wry smile. "The brief answer is that it is much easier to make earth more itself than to press against an intrusion of fire into earth. I will rest tonight, in this comfortable bed you insisted on procuring for me, and in the morning, I promise you, I will be strong enough to travel."

"Then you are still determined to go north." Gereint tried to keep his deep skepticism about this course out of his voice.

"Gereint . . . someone must."

Gereint thought about the griffins spending all the previous day flying in a vast circle, passing over Metichteran over and over. And over other nearby towns and villages? That northeast course of theirs might well take them over Tashen. He thought about the way the sky and sunlight had changed as the griffins crossed the sky, how the wind from their wings had smelled of hot stone and metal. He thought of the twisted, sharp-edged towers of red stone that had cut through the earth in Melentser, shattering streets and buildings; of the sand that had drifted through the streets and into the empty houses.

The mages of Casmantium . . . especially the cold mages . . . had dedicated their strength for hundreds of years to keeping the griffins and their desert out of Casmantium proper. And Beguchren was the last of the cold mages. The picture that came to mind, now, given those two statements, was . . . decidedly troubling. Gereint said abruptly, "What does the Arobern expect you to do here? Alone?"

Beguchren met his eyes. The small mage was no longer smiling. "I'm not alone, Gereint. You're here with me."

Gereint wanted to snarl in frustration and stomp in circles. He suppressed this immediate reaction, paused. Asked at last, "What *is* it you expect from me?"

For a beat and a second beat, Beguchren regarded him in silence. But he did not look away. And rather than putting Gereint off with the customary promise or threat—*I'll tell you when we reach the edge of the desert*—he said at last, "One creates . . . or I believe it is possible that one might create . . . a new mage, full-formed, from a sufficiently gifted maker. If the maker is willing to, hmm, reshape himself according to a new pattern."

Gereint didn't move.

"The process would inevitably involve a remaking of, as it were, the self," Beguchren added, his tone becoming . . . not precisely apologetic. Nor precisely defensive. But perhaps . . . almost diffident.

"That's the part you can't compel," Gereint observed, after a moment to consider the idea. "Not to say, the part that made you think of, what was the term? Self-abnegation?" He paused again, then added, "I thought gifts such as making were thoroughly distinct from the true power of magecraft?"

"They are. That's why the self of the maker requires to be remade. I did say Warichteier was, shall we say, not entirely correct in his conclusions regarding magecraft. Or correct in not entirely the right ways." It was the mage's turn to pause. This time the pause lengthened uncomfortably. He asked at last, "Gereint, should I have told you at once? Or, indeed, now? I hoped you might come to trust me a little on the road. But I know it's a kind of little death I ask of you."

Gereint moved his shoulders uncomfortably, a small motion that was not quite a shrug. "Are you asking for an analysis of the quality of your . . . building materials? Or your tactics?"

Despite the deliberate lightness of his tone, Beguchren didn't smile. "Both, I suppose."

"If you'd put me off again, I would have been angry. I'm glad you told me at last. And I'm glad to know. The other . . . how should I possibly estimate? I'm not a mage; I have only the faintest notion of what magecraft entails; I've never studied any of—whatever mages study."

"I have," Beguchren said mildly. "You're a strongly gifted maker, but there are other makers with strong gifts. But it's not your ability that concerns me. It's your willingness, which I can and must estimate. So. Will you come with me now to the edge of the desert?"

Gereint could see that the mage expected him to say "yes." He asked instead, deliberately, "Will you permit me a choice?"

Beguchren did not look away. His ice-pale eyes were steady on Gereint's. "Certainly. As long as you make the correct choice."

Gereint didn't quite laugh, but wry humor crooked his mouth. "Oh, indeed. And what is it you intend to do, there at the boundary between fire and earth, once I make your correct choice? No, don't tell me: It depends on what I do."

"Of course."

"I'm only one man. I don't understand why you didn't require half the makers in Casmantium to accompany you. I don't believe one man can make so great a difference as you imply. Certainly not, well, me. What possible difference can I make, even if I do everything exactly as you ask?"

Beguchren hesitated, then answered, "I did say that your power, as such, is not my concern. I must ask you to trust me that it will suffice. If I had brought half the makers in Casmantium with me, they would only have tangled their intentions and strength with one another and with mine."

"Um," Gereint said noncommittally. He half wanted to challenge this as an evasion, but he feared he understood the mage all too well. But he also feared Beguchren was simply wrong about what was and was not possible to make. Or remake. The idea of recasting a maker into a mage seemed perfectly demented. He lifted his own hands, studied them as he opened and closed his fingers. He could feel his own gift in his hands, solid and familiar. He had no idea what it would feel like to *pull on the world* or *balance opposing forces* or whatever Beguchren had said mages did.

Even if Gereint was willing to try, and found this "remaking of the self " possible, it was hard to believe it would make any substantial difference to any contest between Beguchren and the griffins' mage—and if he understood what Beguchren was not quite saying, that was what the cold mage expected. Or what he was aiming to provoke.

But he also felt, obscurely but with conviction, that it would be wrong to turn aside before he and Beguchren reached the edge of the griffins' desert and at least looked out upon that country of fire. After coming so far, after the cold mage had expended such effort, arguing over this last step of the journey seemed simply wrong. Whether the mage offered compulsion or merely asked for Gereint's cooperation.

He said, in a deliberately casual tone, "You'd never reach the desert alone, would you? So I suppose I must go at least so far."

Beguchren inclined his head in quiet thanks, exactly as though he had merely asked for cooperation and never thought of compelling anything at all.

Metichteran and Tashen had grown up from simple villages at nearly the same time, once the constant warfare between Casmantium and Meridanium had finally given way to the peace created by the decisive victory of Casmantium. Tashen had grown into the largest city of the north: a small bastion of, to Gereint's mind, rather self-conscious culture. Metichteran, Tashen's gateway to the south, had cheerfully settled for becoming a comfortable town of farmers and tradesmen. Gereint much preferred Metichteran, though Perech Fellesteden had generally lingered only in Tashen during his occasional journeys from Melentser to the southern cities or back.

The road between the two towns was quite good, if worn and weather beaten. The edges of the stones had been rounded by time. Some of them had cracked right across during the long northern winters; mosses grew in those cracks and along the edges of the road. But not a single stone was so broken it needed to be replaced, nor did the mosses grow far enough out from the cracks to make the road slippery. The builder's magic that had been set deeply into this road did more than cause the stones to resist weathering. The horses' hooves sounded just a little muffled on the close-fitted stones, for the builders had set sure-footedness upon their road to protect horses from slips and falls.

North of Metichteran, the forest thinned out to pretty woodlands, and then to fields and pastures that spread off to the east and north. The land gradually shifted from gently rolling to frankly hilly, with scrub woodland left to occupy the steeper slopes. Enormous trees spread out their broad branches to shade old farmhouses that had probably been built before the conquest of Meridanium. Here and there, a small apple orchard was tucked close to a house. The scent of apples was sweet on the breeze.

Low stone walls delineated the edges of the farms and pastures. The hardy little northern cattle grazed in the pastures; in the fields, wheat and barley, already going golden with autumn, glowed with a color that would have looked rich if Gereint had not compared it to the colors of griffins. He looked for griffins now, keeping a wary eye on the sky. But he saw nothing besides a single vulture, its wings slanted upward in the characteristic angle, gliding in its slow circle on the high thermals.

"Are you doing something to keep the griffins away?" he asked Beguchren, breaking the silence that had grown up between them. It was not a tense silence, more a sign of a mutual abstraction. They both had a good many things to think about, Gereint supposed. He wondered if the mage's thoughts were as circular and uncomfortable as his own.

Beguchren glanced up. He had seemed much stronger this morning, much more himself, but now his gaze was blank and unfocused. Gereint was momentarily alarmed; he had not realized the mage was so weak—he leaned forward, ready to try to catch the small man if he slumped out of the saddle—but then Beguchren blinked and Gereint settled again, warily, as awareness seeped back into the mage's expression.

Beguchren moved his shoulders, not quite a shrug, answering the question Gereint had, in that moment of alarm, almost forgotten he'd asked. "Not precisely. Not now. I'm drawing the deep magic of earth after us as we ride; it is set so deeply in this road, it takes only a touch to wake it. Roads *are* boundaries; they can easily be persuaded to, ah, bound. That hardly counts as 'doing' anything."

"Ah."

"Mostly I'm simply . . . listening. But I hear nothing. There are no incursions out of the desert, not this morning. I think the griffins are become cautious, now they know I am here."

"Um."

Beguchren smiled. "They do know, I assure you. And they know I am coming to them. I think they will wait. They will not wish to challenge me while I am in the country of earth. Certainly not while I have such an old and powerful road under me."

"They're afraid of you." Gereint didn't quite let this turn into a question.

"I hope they are."

"Um." Gereint hoped that, too.

The silence fell again, but now Beguchren seemed more inclined to remain aware of the road and the countryside. He glanced after the

flash of a redbird in the woodlands, gazed admiringly at a huge chest-
nut tree standing by the road, raised an eyebrow at a stocky black
dog that stood alertly near a small herd of tawny cattle to watch them
pass. The mage was, Gereint realized, enjoying the ride. Only it was
more than that. Beguchren looked about himself with exactly the air of
an elderly man who, traveling, suspects that he is on the last journey of
his life: as though he had set himself to enjoy the countryside as much as
possible. As though he were making his farewells to the world through
which he traveled.

Or so it seemed to Gereint. He didn't like it. But neither could he
think of a way to comment. At last, simply to break a silence he, if not the
mage, now found a little too fraught, he asked, "Will we stop in Tashen?"

Beguchren glanced up, mildly surprised. "No, no. No, we'll go
straight through and continue on north. We may yet find the desert's
edge today."

The mage sounded neither dismayed nor enthused about the prospect. Gereint knew which reaction seemed more natural to *him*. He
half wanted to ask about magecraft and the maker's gift and what it
meant to *remake the self.* But he also wanted, much more strongly, to
ignore the whole question. He said nothing. Beguchren ran his hand
absently over his mare's neck and watched a covey of quail dart along
the edge of a pasture where a dozen ponies grazed.

They reached Tashen midmorning and, as Beguchren had said, barely
halted. The streets seemed abnormally quiet, the courtyard of the governor's mansion abnormally crowded. Gereint suspected, uneasily, that he
knew the reason for both aberrations. No matter how the people of Tashen
prided themselves on their refined sophistication, he was afraid they had
seen things over the past days that had pressed them beyond their ability
to pretend nonchalance.

They paused only long enough to buy half a dozen meat pastries
from an ornate stall in the beautifully laid out open market near the
northern edge of the city. Gereint asked the pastry vendor about griffins, and then found it hard to get away again because the woman was
so eager to talk. Griffins thick as sparrows, to hear her tell it; and the
past three dawns with a sun that came up huge and hot-gold, and dusks
where it only sank late and with seeming reluctance behind blood-red
hills. "And there's a nasty red dust in the air, gets into everything," she
told Gereint earnestly. "Hard to roll out pastry with dust mixed right in
with the flour on the board! You're all right, though, honored sir: Today
is better than yesterday or the day before. Those should be good pastries. Everyone knows I make the best ones in Tashen."

Gereint nodded gravely. "Then we'll take a couple extra." He added a bag of apples to his purchase for good measure.

"You watch yourselves!" the vendor called after them. "Stands to reason it's worse the farther north you go, and besides, my cousin brings me these apples from a northern estate out that way and he says there's worse than dust out that way. The governor should do something about it, that's what I say!"

She did not suggest anything the governor might do, but perhaps, Gereint reflected, it was comforting just to tell herself that someone might be able to "do something" if he only decided to trouble himself.

It still lacked an hour or more to noon when they left Tashen behind and headed out on the much more narrow road that ran north, parallel to the river but far to the east of it, into the hills. Gereint passed a share of the apples to Beguchren. They ate them as they rode and fed the cores to the horses. Neither of them mentioned red dust or crimson sunsets.

Barely two hours after noon, they came around a slow curve in the road and found themselves riding toward a large sprawling house at the base of low hills, with wheat tawny in the fields and apples ripening in the orchards.

Gereint took a long breath and let it out again. He only hoped, fervently, that at least one of Tehre's letters had made it to this house far in advance of his own arrival in company with the king's mage.

CHAPTER 10

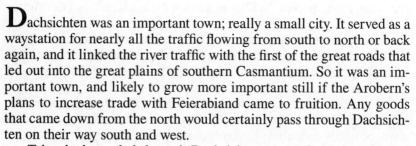

Dachsichten was an important town; really a small city. It served as a waystation for nearly all the traffic flowing from south to north or back again, and it linked the river traffic with the first of the great roads that led out into the great plains of southern Casmantium. So it was an important town, and likely to grow more important still if the Arobern's plans to increase trade with Feierabiand came to fruition. Any goods that came down from the north would certainly pass through Dachsichten on their way south and west.

Tehre had traveled through Dachsichten many times, but she had never liked the town. It seemed too conscious of its own mercantile importance, too inclined toward bustle and business at the expense of grace and artistry. Its buildings were mostly of brick, because bricks could be made cheaply from the lowland clay deposited over the ages all along the wandering path of the river. Perhaps using bricks rather than stone or timber made sense. But the color of the clay was an unpleasant harsh yellow. And the buildings were steep roofed and sharp cornered, a style Tehre had never liked; and they were too tall and too crowded along the streets even in the wealthiest part of the city. Dachsichten was simply, inarguably, ugly.

"It is very different from Breidechboden, is it not?" said Lord Bertaud.

"'Haste in building always leads to regrets,'" Tehre quoted, and added, "Aesthetic regrets, if not regrets because of unsound construction. There was no *need* to crowd Dachsichten like this, and I'm sure even this brick could be made more attractive with better design. The northern towns are far more beautiful, Lord Bertaud. Especially Tashen."

"Your family lives there?"

"Near there. I shall be pleased to show my home to you, Lord Bertaud."

"Honored lady, I shall look forward to it," the lord answered with automatic grace, but the smile had faded. He still gazed out at Dachsichten, but Tehre supposed his thoughts had gone back to something else, something difficult.

"But we'll stay the night here?" Meierin asked hopefully. She leaned forward, peering out at the narrow streets and ugly yellow buildings. "Can't we, honored lady? It's almost late enough we ought to stop, and wouldn't you like to sit in the inn's common room and watch the people? Look, those ladies have such interesting embroidery on their bodices—"

Tehre was not very interested in embroidery, but suspected from the abbreviation of the bodices in question that the ladies in question might not be, well, ladies. Though obviously they were wealthy. But she smiled at Meierin. "We do, usually. There's an inn at the northern edge of town where we normally stop. As you say, it's almost late enough we ought to stop, anyway."

The inn was large, clean, and well appointed. Tehre had stayed in it several times and expected all this. Its common room was pleasant enough, she supposed. Its ceiling had interesting beam architecture.

But what she had not expected was to find her brother in that common room when she came down for supper.

Lord Bertaud was not yet in evidence. But her brother, Sicheir, had already laid claim to a long table to one side. He did not look surprised in the least to see his sister, but only stood up and politely drew her chair out for her.

Tehre cast her gaze upward. "Fareine wrote more letters than just to my father, I surmise. Sicheir—"

"Tehre." Her brother came to take her hands, giving her an anxious up-and-down glance. "Fareine wrote, yes. You should have sent me word yourself. Are you well? Are you sure? I think I got a tolerably complete account—is it true the Arobern didn't seem inclined to blame you, us? It *is* still true that Lord Fellesteden's heirs aren't trying to charge you legally somehow? Did you leave someone looking out for our interests in Breidechboden, besides the estimable Fareine?"

"Fareine will contact a good legist if there's difficulty," Tehre assured him. "The Arobern already ruled against Lord Fellesteden's estate when he gave Gereint to his mage, so the precedent is set our way. Maybe the heirs are glad he's gone: He was a terrible man. Fareine must have told you what he tried to do."

"And I'm very glad she did," Sicheir said firmly, drawing her toward the table. "Come sit down, do, and give me a more complete account. I think perhaps you were wise to leave the city, though I don't want anyone thinking our family would run from a threat or entanglement. I thought of going to Breidechboden myself, taking up residence, being a visible presence." A solid, aggressive, male presence, he did not say. But that's what he meant.

Tehre glared at him. "*I* could have stayed just as well. I didn't leave Breidechboden because I was afraid of Fellesteden's heirs!"

"Of course not," said her brother, meaning that maybe she should have. "Though you should have sent for me. Tell me everything, will you? And about this foreign lord—especially about the foreign lord. What's he want in the north, do you even know? Or at least, what reason did he give you? You've no reason to trust a word he said, you know, foreign as he is! You know, the Arobern may not be very happy with you agreeing to escort this Feierabianden lord into the north— likely he's a spy, did you think of that?"

Tehre blinked. "He can't be. Spies sneak, don't they? They're unobtrusive, you know, they get into things and you never know it. Lord Bertaud is about as conspicuous as anybody could be. He can't sneak about, how could he? Anybody can see he's foreign!"

"Tehre, sometimes a spy doesn't have to tiptoe. This man—"

"He belongs to the Safiad. It's no secret; everybody knows it. Anyway, it doesn't make any sense, him leaving Breidechboden for the north, except just for the reason he said, because he wants to see what problem there is with the griffins. It's only natural he'd want to know about that, don't you think?"

"And only natural the Arobern wouldn't care to have him strolling up north to look, especially if there's something to see—"

"He said plainly the Arobern can't tell him where to come or go—"

"All the more reason not to be seen in his company, when he waves his untouchable defiance at the Arobern! Tehre, you've got to leave him. I'm here now. I brought a few men with me, we don't need the foreigner's men, least of all do we need *them*! We'll go back to Breidechboden, or if you insist we can go on north, but just you and I and our people, decidedly not in some foreign lord's dubious company!"

Tehre hesitated. In a way, this even made sense. But she said slowly, "It's obvious why he wanted to travel with me. He made no secret of that, you know. The company of a Casmantian, especially a Casmantian lady, eases his way through our country. I told him I would travel with him, Sicheir. I told him he could visit our father's house. I can't now say I changed my mind—"

"Of course you can!"

"—and just leave him on the road. It wouldn't be right!"

"Tehre . . ."

"And it's *not necessary*. You're far too concerned about appearances, but I don't think anything looks as bad as you think. Sicheir, maybe you'd better tell me now what you've heard. Just what did Fareine put in that letter?"

The problem, as Tehre knew perfectly well, was that if she stamped her foot and cried, *I can take care of myself*, she would look like a child. If she went cold and angry, she would look like a wicked-tempered harridan, and moreover would seem to distrust her brother. Yet, though she could not shout or even complain, if she was sweet and reasonable and said anything like *Well, I'm glad you're here* to her brother, that would make it seem that she agreed Fareine had been right to send for Sicheir, which she did *not*.

She rubbed her forehead, wondering if there might still be time to turn away the headache she felt coming on if she asked the inn staff for willowbark tea immediately. "Fareine pulled you away from your work—the work of a lifetime, and what if the Arobern's administrators won't permit you to come back? Sicheir, you walked away from the Arobern's new road; are you going to be able to go back to it? Tell me you haven't lost your chance to work on it—"

"I told the court administrator overseeing the work that I needed to see to urgent family business. He understood. Tehre—"

But Sicheir did not have an opportunity to finish his thought. At that moment, Lord Bertaud himself came down the stairs into the common room, paused for a moment, located Tehre, and noted Sicheir's presence. The expression fell off his face instantly, replaced by the courteous, empty smile of an experienced courtier suddenly dropped into uncertain circumstances. He made his way across the room, weaving between the tables, nodded to Tehre, and turned that blank smile to Sicheir.

Tehre said, "Lord Bertaud, may I present to you my brother, Sicheir Amnachudran? Sicheir is an engineer and a builder; if you have any questions about the new road, you should ask him. Sicheir, this is Lord Bertaud—" She should say, *son of Somebody*, but what was the name he'd given her? Some soft-sounding Feierabianden name; she couldn't remember. She said instead, "Of Feierabiand, one of the Safiad's close advisors." Well, he hadn't said so, but he must be, for the king of Feierabiand to send him here. She finished, "The Safiad sent him to oversee the construction of the new road, so if you have any thoughts about that, I'm sure he'd be glad to hear them."

"To be sure," the foreign lord said smoothly. He answered Sicheir's respectful bow with a little nod of his own and added, "The road is a great undertaking. I have studied the plans carefully. Only the engineers of Casmantium could build such a structure. But perhaps you could explain to me the difference between an engineer and a builder?"

Sicheir blinked, startled and disarmed by this interest. "Well, lord, the distinction is clear enough. An engineer understands the theory of building, but a builder has the gift of making. Engineers might direct the new construction, but it's builders you want to actually lay their hands on the stone and iron. You have makers in Feierabiand, of course. Some, surely, must become builders?"

"But not like yours. It seems to me the new road will come to rival any structure ever built by the hands of men. The plans for the bridges and the buttressed roads are quite extraordinary."

"You're kind to say so, lord. If I may observe, you speak Prechen very well."

"Ah—" Lord Bertaud glanced at Tehre, who did not want to try to describe her insight about language as a made structure and therefore merely gazed back with bland, innocent eyes. "Ah," murmured the foreign lord again. "Thank you. Ah, forgive me—"

"One would say, 'honored sir,'" Sicheir explained, apparently understanding the dilemma, which Tehre had not. "My sister has her title from our mother and her family—the title of nobility passes only from mother to daughter in a morganatic marriage such as our parents'. It's different in Feierabiand, I believe."

Lord Bertaud gave an ambiguous little tip of the head and made a polite little gesture of invitation, meaning they should all sit. "You are my guests," he declared. "No, please permit me the indulgence. Tell me about the road and the experience of building, honored Sicheir. What is your part in this great project? Have you been involved with anything comparable in the past?"

Tehre sat back and watched as her brother was, despite his concerns and suspicions and more than half against his will, drawn out into a companionable discussion of the Arobern's road. She had not precisely seen Lord Bertaud as a real court noble; he seemed too direct, too little pretentious. Now she saw that he was indeed an experienced courtier. Was charm, too, possibly a sort of making? Not even as structured as language, far less than a proper structure of stone or wood. What would the components of a courtier's charm be? Come to that, what exactly would the finished structure be? Maybe the analogy would not stretch quite so far . . . Then, as Sicheir began to sketch the first of the great bridges that would span a wide chasm, she dismissed the question and leaned forward.

"Is that to scale? Then it's all wrong. Masonry's too heavy for that width," she commented. "You have to have too much rise for that run. It could be done if you had a series of arches, but you can't put in a series if there's too much fall under the bridge, and I'm sure there is. No, Sicheir, not only will this design be very difficult to build, it'll be thoroughly unsound. Who designed this?"

"Tirechkeir."

"Yes, it's just like Emnon Tirechkeir to design something that looks like a radical departure but that really draws on a long tradition of design that doesn't actually apply to the situation at hand. The first problem is a wrong choice of materials. I really don't think masonry is the proper material to span such a long distance."

"It's available. We can get any quantity of good stone out of those mountains. That's a big asset, Tehre."

"However easy it is to get, it's far too heavy for this use. You'll never get it anchored properly, or if you do, it'll be because it's too steep to be practical." Tehre looked around absently for paper. Someone pushed a whole stack of good-quality draftsman's paper across the table to her—oh, Lord Bertaud, how clever of him to see what she wanted—she took the quill out of her brother's hand and began to sketch. "Now something like this would be much lighter and far easier to build. See, you can make *very* steep arches, as long as you hang the bridge *from* the arches rather than making the arches the footing of the actual bridge itself. You'd cast these arches of iron, you can do that in Ehre, there's no need to try to do it in place. Then just lift them into place from either side. Then use wrought-iron chains and suspend a timber bridge from the arches—"

Sicheir picked up the sketch and stared at it.

"It will work," Tehre insisted. "The theory is perfectly sound. Just because no one's used this kind of structure before doesn't mean it's not sound. Here, look, let me show you how the mathematics work out. I know the mathematics can be misleading, there's something missing from our understanding of the equations . . ." She tapped the quill absently against her lips, thinking about missing quantities and concepts.

Sicheir interrupted her abstraction with practiced emphasis. "Oh, I believe you. It's not that I don't believe you. Tehre, you ought to come back to Ehre with me; you should help me present this to Prince Bestreieten himself." He saw her baffled expression and said patiently, "The Arobern's brother is overseeing the whole project, Tehre, you knew that, surely! He'd be interested in this—and if no one else has ever built a bridge this way, he'll only be more interested: He knows very well his brother would love to have special, unique bridges for his road. If you come—"

"I can't," Tehre said, surprised. "You know I'm going north." She paused, her eyes narrowing. "You *do* know I'm going north. Sicheir, that isn't kind, pretending you want me to come to Ehre when really you simply don't want me going north with Lord Bertaud."

Everyone stopped, looking at the foreign lord.

Lord Bertaud leaned back in his chair, tilted his head quizzically to one side, and regarded Sicheir with raised-eyebrow curiosity.

Sicheir flushed. So did Tehre, realizing for the first time that she had, once again, managed to say something desperately tactless. She should have let Fareine come after all; Fareine would have known how to interrupt her, or what to say now to smooth the moment . . .

"Honored lady, your honored brother undoubtedly *did* come find you to ask your advice about the bridges," Meierin said in her quiet little voice. "It will be much harder for him to ask you about things like this," she tapped the sketches they'd been drawing, "once you are so far away in your father's house."

Then the girl turned gracefully to Lord Bertaud and went on, sweetly reasonable, "Of course the honored Sicheir Amnachudran is grateful for your offer to escort Lady Tehre to her father's house, Lord Bertaud. It was so kind of you. You've seen how skilled a maker the honored lady is; perhaps you will be kind again and forgive the honored Sicheir his attempt to persuade his honored sister to go west with him now? Of course"—with an understanding nod for Tehre—"she will not go. You should know"—with a reproving look at Sicheir—"that when Lady Tehre says she means to visit your honored parents, she will not change her mind for anything."

Tehre stared at the girl. "You sound just like Fareine!"

Meierin lowered her eyes modestly. "Thank you, honored lady. I hope I have profited from the honored Fareine's instruction."

"I thought—" Tehre began, then stopped. She said instead, warmly, "Fareine did tell me you were sensible." Then she turned to glare at her brother. "And I thought *you* were sensible, too! I want to know what's going on in the north. Don't *you* want to know?" She flung up her hands at Sicheir's blank look. "*What* did Fareine write in that letter?"

Sicheir hesitated, his gaze sliding sideways toward the foreign lord.

"Never mind," Meierin said before the pause could grow awkward. She patted Tehre's hand urgently. "You can discuss the letters with your honored brother *later*, honored lady."

"There's no need for haste," Sicheir seconded. He rapped the table firmly to summon the inn's staff. "We'll have supper—Lord Bertaud, won't you permit me the privilege?"

Tehre rested her elbow on the table, set her chin on her palm, and stopped listening to the polite argument about who was whose guest. She thought instead about time and travel and uncertainty, and who knew what about everything. Or anything.

After some time, she put her spoon down, only then realizing that supper had been served and that she had been eating it. It was a thick barley soup with beef and carrots, a very northern dish that reminded Tehre, once she noticed it, of her home. She suddenly longed for home, for her mother's voice calling cheerfully down the polished halls, for her father's quick interest in building and materials and making and, really, everything . . . She thought of the griffin they had seen, the way the late sunlight had struck across the metallic feathers of its wings and turned its lion pelt to ruddy gold. The fierce unhuman stare it had turned their way.

Then she thought of that griffin flying above her father's lands and house. For some reason she did not understand, the image made her shudder with dread. Looking up at her brother, she said, "You need to come north with us, Sicheir."

A startled silence fell. Tehre looked from Sicheir to Lord Bertaud. They both looked equally baffled.

"Yes, Tehre," Sicheir said at last. "We were just agreeing that might be as well."

Tehre flushed. "Oh, were you?" She had missed this. "But your work?"

Sicheir only shrugged. "Family comes first. I'll send some of your drawings back to Prince Bestreieten with a suggestion that he consider something like it."

"Oh." Tehre thought about this. "Tell him, tell them all, that the drawings are yours. The administrators are much more likely to try the design if all their pet builders think it's yours and not mine."

"Tehre—"

"Later, after the bridges are built, you can tell them the design is mine. There's nothing they can do about it then. I want to see this," she tapped her rough sketch with the tips of two fingers, "built and raised and carrying proper loads. Don't you?"

Sicheir gave a conceding little flip of his hand, frowning. "Maybe you'll agree to go west with me later."

Lord Bertaud slid the sketch across the table and studied it with interest. "Most unusual."

"I got the idea from a Linularinan bridge," Tehre explained. "And from thinking about ways to actually *use* really steep arches."

"I wish to see this design put to a practical test," the foreign lord declared, and raised his eyebrows at Sicheir.

"Huh." Sicheir sat back in his chair, looking extremely thoughtful. "Yes. That might do."

Baffled, Tehre looked from one of them to the other. If Fareine had been here, she would have asked her later what they meant. But Fareine was not here. She glanced at Meierin. To her surprise, the girl was nodding and looking pleased. She leaned toward Tehre and whispered, "It's how Lord Bertaud will explain why you agreed to guide him into the north: He promised you patronage and you knew he would be a very powerful patron, at least for a little while, until everyone can see your bridges are the best. Everyone will understand this explanation. It'll prevent all sorts of, you know. Other questions."

"Oh." Tehre tried to decide whether this actually made sense but gave up almost at once. Materials and mathematics were far more straightforward than deciphering what people thought. They so seldom seemed to think at all, really, which was probably part of the problem. "Well, if you think so," she added, and, as everyone now seemed contented to go north, went back to sketching bridges. But even while structures of iron and stone flowed out of her quill, griffins continued to fly through the back of her mind.

But they did not go north in the morning. Tehre stayed up for a long time, sketching by candlelight. She found griffins creeping into her sketches, flying above and through and below the cliffs and chasms and bridges that flowed out of her quill. The fierceness of the mountains she drew and the fierceness of the griffins informed each other, so that sometimes when she meant to draw a jagged cliff edge she instead found herself tracing the savage line of a beak or the clean-edged sweep of wing or the taut curve of muscle beneath a lion's pelt.

When she blew out the candles and made her way through the darkness to the bed she was sharing with Meierin, the glint of fire seemed to linger just out of sight, caught in a griffin's fierce eye. When she finally slept, she dreamed of griffins soaring in high spirals over Breidechboden, fire falling from the wind from their wings . . . She murmured in her sleep, half waking in the dark.

"Lady . . . you're dreaming," Meierin whispered back, sleepily, reaching to pat her arm. "Go back to sleep."

"Where are we?" Tehre asked her, her eyes still filled with dreams of fire, glad to have the practical, sensible girl to ask.

"Dachsichten. Remember? The inn in Dachsichten."

"Oh," Tehre said vaguely, not really remembering but willing to trust Meierin's word for it. She closed her eyes again and dropped her head back to the pillow, and if she dreamed again after that, she did not remember.

In the morning, Tehre felt exactly as though she'd stayed up too late and had too many strange dreams. Her eyes felt gritty, and the incipient headache she'd ignored the previous night had shifted to the back of her skull and settled in to stay. She wanted a long bath, several cups of hot astringent tea, and to go back to bed in her own room. What she had was a cold basin to wash her face in, a wrinkled travel dress, and a long, rough carriage ride to occupy the whole day. She sighed. There should at least be tea.

She and Meierin washed their faces in the cold water, helped one another dress, came out into the hall, and found the doors of Sicheir's room already standing open. Sicheir was sitting on the bed in his room, studying the sketch of the suspended bridge Tehre had drawn for him and frowning. He jumped up when Tehre peered around the edge of his door.

"You're up! Good!" he said, impatiently, as though she had slept very late.

"It's hardly past dawn," Tehre protested. "If you'd wanted a very early start, you might have said so. Who knows if Lord Bertaud is even awake yet?"

Meierin slipped past Sicheir's room to rap gently on Lord Bertaud's door. The lord opened it after a moment. He looked, Tehre thought, exactly like she felt: tired and headachy and like his rest had been troubled by unusual dreams. His smile was really more a grimace. "Lady Tehre," he said. His eyes went to Sicheir and he hesitated for a moment, then looked back at her. "I am concerned about the griffin we saw; I am concerned about what may be happening in the north of your country," he said baldly. "We must talk."

"Yes," said Tehre, more certain than ever that he, too, had dreamed of griffins and fire. "But, please, over *tea*."

But when they came down to the common room, they found the innkeeper, harried and sweating lightly, coming to meet them. With a worried jerk of his head, he indicated the finest of his tables, the one set back away from the heat of the kitchens and closest to the wide east window. The pale dawn light lay across that table and the tea things and sliced bread it held, and across the bony face and deep-set eyes of a man who sat there, waiting for them.

The man rose as they stared at him. He was clad in good-quality traveling clothes of leather and undyed linen, much too plain for a merchant but much too good for any simple tradesman or farmer. He was tall, lanky, his hands bare of rings, his face lined with weather and experience. He looked tired, as though he'd ridden through the night and only just arrived at the inn. Tehre had never seen him before in her life. She looked questioningly at her brother, at Lord Bertaud. Both men looked as puzzled as she felt.

Then the man reached into the collar of his plain shirt and took out a fine gold chain, on which hung, pendent, a carved bone disk that had been dyed purple.

Tehre stood frozen, and felt Meierin and her brother go as suddenly still beside her. Lord Bertaud, puzzled, glanced from each of them to the others. A wariness came into his eyes, and the politely neutral courtier's expression came down across his face. He drew a breath, but he did not speak, waiting instead for Tehre or Sicheir to give him a lead he could follow. Tehre would have been happy if she'd had an idea about what lead to give.

The man let the token fall against his shirt in plain sight and came forward a step. "Tehre Amnachudran Tanshan?" he asked her. His eyes moved to Lord Bertaud. "Lord Bertaud, son of Boudan?"

"Yes," Tehre admitted, her mouth dry. Lord Bertaud lifted an eyebrow and inclined his head. If he felt in the least nervous, his courtier's mask hid it so well Tehre could not tell.

The man bowed his head a little and then asked Sicheir, "And you, honored sir?"

"I—" Sicheir cleared her throat. "Sicheir Amnachudran, my lord. This lady's brother."

"Of course," the man murmured, neither surprised nor, apparently, curious about Sicheir's presence. He turned back to Tehre. "Lady Tehre, I am Detreir Enteirich. My master, Brechen Glansent Arobern, sends me to you to proclaim his desire that you attend him at once in Breidechboden. Will you come?"

It had never crossed Tehre's mind that the king would actually care that she had ignored his wishes and instead headed north; it was so small a defiance, and she so unimportant, it seemed incredible he had even noticed. And instead he had not only noticed but cared enough to send one of his own agents after her . . . She wondered whether the agent had tracked them through the back roads around the capital, or whether he'd simply come straight to Dachsichten . . . Her family always did stay at this inn when they traveled either north or south. It had not occurred to her to stay anywhere else. She could only say, helplessly, "Of course."

Detreir Enteirich bowed acknowledgment. Then, straightening, he turned to Lord Bertaud. "My lord," he said gravely, "my royal master acknowledges that he cannot require your attendance. However, he requests your presence at his court. He bids me say to you: As you were so kind as to escort Lady Tehre north, he hopes your kindness will not permit you to abandon her as she returns south."

Lord Bertaud flushed, slowly. His jaw set, the neutral courier's manner falling away like the mask it was. "Does he say that?" He paused, clearly on the edge of continuing: *Well, you can tell your royal master.* But he didn't say it. He glanced at Tehre, hesitated, and said to her instead of addressing the king's agent, "Lady Tehre, I would be honored if you would permit me to escort you wherever you wish to go."

Tehre nodded gratefully. If the king was angry enough to send one of his agents after her, she thought she might be very happy to have the Feierabianden lord ready to speak for her before the throne.

"I'm coming, too," Sicheir said sharply, just a little too quickly.

The agent turned his head to gaze at Sicheir. "Yes," he said, and paused, studying the other man. Then he continued, "I believe that would be wise. I am permitted, if not required, to inform you that Casnerach Fellesteden has brought a legal action against Lady Tehre and against your family, in regard to the death of his uncle, Perech Fellesteden."

There was a small, frozen pause. Sicheir drew a breath, looked once at Tehre, and let it out without speaking. Then he said, "We'll want to begin legal proceedings against Casnerach Fellesteden and against the Fellesteden estate."

"Of course," agreed the agent. "That is why I suggested you return to the capital. I think—personally, you understand—that you would be very wise to return to Breidechboden and address your legal affairs." He glanced at each of them in turn and added to Tehre, "I am instructed to make all reasonable haste. A brief delay for tea and breakfast seems reasonable. But, Lady Tehre, I must ask you to accommodate my necessity."

"Yes," she said numbly.

The agent bowed again, politely, and strolled out to the courtyard to wait for them.

Tehre blinked, swallowed, and said at last, "Meierin—tell the innkeeper we will want plenty of tea, will you?" and walked over to the table where the Arobern's agent had been sitting.

"How can you be so calm?" Sicheir demanded, taking a long stride to get in front of her, gripping her arm to make her stop and face him. "Tehre—"

"You're shouting," Tehre observed. "People will look." It wasn't quite true, and the common room was still nearly empty, but it made her brother stop and think, and it got him to let her go. Tehre pulled out a chair and dropped into it, feeling that she might still be dreaming—she would have preferred to dream of griffins and a fiery wind rather than think about what had just happened. She thought she might never have woken into a less welcoming morning. She would have gladly pulled the inn down on itself, brick by ugly yellow brick, if it would have hurried the staff with the tea. Instead, she rested her elbows on the table and laced her fingers over her eyes. The headache reverberated at the back of her skull.

"Tehre—" her brother began again.

Tehre interrupted without looking up. "Do you think the stable boys have our horses ready? And Lord Bertaud's carriage? Are all our people up?"

Sicheir paused. "I'll go see to it," he said tightly, and strode out.

Lord Bertaud put a cup of tea in front of Tehre—hot and bitterly astringent; he must have watched to see how she liked it. He pulled out a chair of his own. The echoes of hurried men drifted through the inn, so Tehre assumed Sicheir must have roused out all the retainers and guards and servants. She wanted to run in circles, shrieking. She slid her hands back over her eyes instead.

"If I may ask," Lord Bertaud said quietly beside her. "Who is this man? Not a court lord, surely?"

Tehre dropped her hands to the rough surface of the table, looked at her tea for a moment, then picked up the cup at last and sipped. The astringent liquid seemed both to clear her mouth of the cottony feel of too restless a night and her mind of the shock that had met them along with the dawn. She put the cup back down, looked at the Feierabianden lord, and sighed. "A king's agent," she explained. "He speaks with the king's voice; orders from him are as binding as commands from the king himself. I think—I think the Arobern must *really* have meant it when he told me to go home. But who ever would have expected—?"

"I think perhaps your king is angry with me, not with you," Lord Bertaud said. He gave her an inquiring glance. "Do you think? He can't command me to return, so he commands you and offers a slight against my honor if I refuse to accompany you. Well, we shall see." His eyes, over the rim of his own cup, were shadowed and grim. "You might have done better to go north on your own, Lady Tehre. I am sorry—"

Tehre shook her head. "If Fellesteden's heirs are moving against me, against my family, somebody had better be there to counter them. Though Sicheir—if the Arobern is angry with me, though I hope you are right about that, but if he is, then *Sicheir* is the one who should answer whatever charges have been made." She was silent for a moment, thinking about that. Then she added, "I'm sorry the Arobern is using me to compel you to return." And angry, she found. She was even more angry than frightened. The king's sending an agent after her somehow solidified her conviction that whatever was wrong in the north was *terribly* wrong. The king ought to have told her what it was, he ought to have *sent* her north, did he really think she would only stumble over her skirts and get in the way of his mage?

"Ah," Lord Bertaud said softly. After a moment, he added, "Lady Tehre . . . I confess I feel a great urgency to go north."

Tehre began to say, *Oh, you, too?* But then she put one puzzling observation together with another and said instead, "Oh, because of the griffin we saw flying over the river?"

An unconsidered gesture from the Feierabianden lord nearly tipped over his cup; he steadied it hastily and gave Tehre an unsettled look.

Tehre had no idea whether she should apologize, or, if so, for what. It seemed obvious that Lord Bertaud had, or felt he had, some connection or understanding with the griffins. Probably he did. The Feierabianden king had reached his accommodation with the griffins *somehow*. She slanted a curious look at the foreign lord. His manner was bland, his expression neutral, his eyes hiding . . . what, she wondered. What had Lord Bertaud's role actually *been* in the brief, ferocious struggle in Feierabianden in the early summer?

She did not ask that. She asked instead, "What does it mean that we saw a griffin so far south? Why do you need to go north?"

Lord Bertaud's mouth tightened. He did not answer.

Tehre tapped the table restlessly with the tips of her fingers. "You said you would escort me south. I could free you from that promise—"

"Lady—"

"But if you could tell me why you need to go north, maybe I could see whether I, too, should go north. Even in despite of my king's command." She tilted her head back, meeting the foreigner's eyes with direct inquiry. "Do *you* know what the trouble *is* in the north?"

"No," the Feierabianden lord admitted in a low voice. "But I think it may be worse than even your king suspects. I have—" He paused, then shrugged and said simply, "I have a suspicion about this."

"A suspicion," Tehre repeated. She eyed the foreigner. "A suspicion, is it?"

But then Sicheir came back in, and after him the king's agent, and there was no more chance to speak privately.

CHAPTER 11

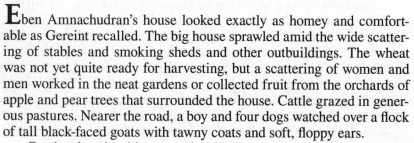

Eben Amnachudran's house looked exactly as homey and comfortable as Gereint recalled. The big house sprawled amid the wide scattering of stables and smoking sheds and other outbuildings. The wheat was not yet quite ready for harvesting, but a scattering of women and men worked in the neat gardens or collected fruit from the orchards of apple and pear trees that surrounded the house. Cattle grazed in generous pastures. Nearer the road, a boy and four dogs watched over a flock of tall black-faced goats with tawny coats and soft, floppy ears.

Gereint, keeping his expression blank, glanced sideways at Beguchren. The mage was studying the estate and frowning. "What?" Gereint asked, just a little too sharply.

"That pond is empty," Beguchren answered, not appearing to notice the sharpness.

Gereint frowned, too, and followed the direction of the other man's gaze. It was true. He had not noticed at once, but the new pond Eben Amnachudran had recently constructed, nearly filled with water when Gereint had first seen it, now contained only a glaze of dry, cracked mud across the bottom. He looked farther, up the hills, and found that the stream that should have fed the pond was dry as well. "It's late in the summer, now," he said uncertainly. But in his mind, he heard Amnachudran's voice: *My house is at the base of some low hills, where a stream comes down year-round.*

Beguchren shook his head. "Not that late. And there should be plenty of rain here and in those mountains"—he nodded toward the gray-lavender shapes of the far mountains—"no matter how late the season."

"The griffins are interfering with the rain?" Gereint asked him.

Beguchren only shook his head again and nudged his mare forward at a gentle walk.

Gereint followed reluctantly. He imagined riding into the courtyard and one of the hostlers coming forward to take their horses; he could all but hear the man's friendly *Ah, Gereint, back for a visit?* and Beguchren's raised eyebrows. The mage might be distracted by thoughts of griffins and dry streams and lack of proper rainfall, but he could hardly be so distracted as to miss anything of the sort.

It wouldn't have to be a hostler. One of the maids could say something, one of the men-at-arms who had come south with Sicheir and returned. Eben Amnachudran himself, if Tehre's letters had gone astray: *Why, Gereint, back from Breidechboden! Didn't you get on with Tehre after all, then? And who is your friend?*

He should have sent a letter himself—he should have hired a fast courier to carry it. He and the king's mage might have outridden Tehre's letter if she'd sent hers with some slow, heavy-laden merchant or tradesman. Why hadn't he *asked* how she'd sent the letters?

But the man-at-arms at the gate was not one Gereint recognized, and the hostlers who came to take their horses were equally unfamiliar. The man-at-arms took their names with a kind of grim satisfaction that suggested the recent presence of griffins even before he spoke. "We are very glad to bid you welcome, lord mage!" he said to Beguchren. "We have been much troubled of late. Please allow me to guide you—I will send at once to the honored Eben Amnachudran, master of this house—I assure you, lord mage, he will be very glad to welcome you."

The man-at-arms sent servants running, himself leading them to a library, a warm, comfortable, crowded room lit by round porcelain lamps and heavy with the dusty smell of old books. Half a dozen chairs were arranged in a small group near the room's one window. They had elaborately carved legs and backs, but their cushions were thick and soft and the rug beneath them was large and likewise soft. Gereint was too nervous to sit down, but he pointedly shifted a chair a little out from the others for Beguchren. The mage gave Gereint an ironic look, but settled into the chair without comment.

Eben Amnachudran came to them there, a very few minutes later. Gereint stared urgently into his face, trying to ask without words, *Did you get the letters, do you know what happened?* Trying to command soundlessly, *Don't know me, don't recognize me.*

Amnachudran did not even glance at Gereint. His smile was welcoming and appeared perfectly guileless, but he focused entirely on Beguchren. Gereint felt the knots of tension in his neck and back begin, very slowly, to relax.

"Lord mage!" Eben Amnachudran said to Beguchren, bowing swiftly. "Welcome, my lord, to my house and to the northern mountains, and may I be so bold as to say you're very welcome indeed? We have had a challenging few days. I hope that is why you have come?"

"Yes," Beguchren began, but paused as Lady Emre came in. She was carrying a large platter with tea things and cakes. She nodded, smiling, and said warmly, "My lord mage."

To Gereint's well-concealed—he hoped—surprise, Beguchren rose, walked forward, and took her hands. He was almost exactly her height. He said, "Emre. How long has it been?"

"Too long, truly. Please, sit. May I offer you tea? I believe you take honey and milk in your tea? Have a cake, do. Our cook would be the envy of many a great house in Breidechboden, so perhaps it's as well we dwell so far removed, though it means we see our friends too seldom."

Eben Amnachudran watched this cordial meeting between his wife and the king's mage with no sign of surprise. He had known, Gereint surmised, that they were friends. Or at least warm acquaintances. Well, his wife was one of *those* Tanshans; small surprise she should have at least some acquaintance with a court mage. And, being herself, any acquaintance would naturally be a warm one. That was good, surely.

And, better still, Emre Tanshan, like her husband, glanced at Gereint with not even the smallest flicker of recognition. "And your associate?" she said to Beguchren. She turned to Gereint with the exact polite smile she would, no doubt, have given any stranger arriving in a friend's company. "Would you care for tea, honored sir?"

There was tea all around, and cakes. The cakes were made with chopped apples and coarsely ground walnuts and had been generously glazed with honey. Eben Amnachudran took a chair near his wife and let her carry the conversation, which she did effortlessly, staying to safe subjects: painting and poetry and court gossip, but nothing unkind or even ungenerous. Neither Emre nor Beguchren mentioned griffins.

Amnachudran sipped tea and said very little, but his gaze was shrewd and knowing. He glanced once, unobtrusively but not quite covertly, at Gereint. Then he offered him a plate of cakes and a smile. "You are a mage yourself, honored sir?" he asked courteously.

"An associate," Beguchren answered for Gereint, smoothly, while Gereint was still wondering how to answer. "Honored sir, perhaps you and your lady wife will describe for me now the events of, as you say, your 'challenging' days? You have, perhaps, seen griffins flying overhead? Perhaps repeatedly crossing your sky?"

Eben Amnachudran and his wife shared a wordless glance. Then Amnachudran turned back to Beguchren. "My lord, as you say. Not today, as happens, but I set one of the boys to counting: We have had griffins pass overhead thirty-seven times, beginning nine days ago and continuing through the day before yesterday, at intervals from three to fourteen hours, averaging nine hours. We have seen three to seven griffins at a time, with the modal number of griffins being three."

Gereint was mildly amused. How like a scholar to calculate intervals between flights and numbers of griffins. He glanced at Beguchren, wondering if the mage found these numbers useful. Beguchren showed nothing but impenetrably polite attention.

"The track of their flight," Amnachudran was continuing, "has shown a steady trend . . . If you would be so kind, my dear . . ." His wife brought a scroll from a rack and helped her husband unroll a map across the widest table in the room. Everyone leaned forward to look.

"You see, the first flight we saw curved along here, above the hills." Amnachudran traced a curving line north of his home with the tip of a finger. "I did not begin to chart as early as I should have, but by noon of the second day, the line was here, parallel to the original line, you see, but almost directly above the house. And by that evening, here." They could all see the progression of that line from north to south. The last flight Amnachudran drew for them had been along a line well south of the estate.

"Extrapolating from this trend . . . and in the clear understanding that trends usually do not continue indefinitely . . . nevertheless, I calculate that these overflights probably began to cross over Tashen four or five days ago."

"Yes," murmured Beguchren.

"That is a concern, my lord, because . . ." Amnachudran hesitated. "It might be better to show you . . ."

"Please tell me," Beguchren said quietly.

Amnachudran opened his hands, a gesture of concession. "At first it was only red dust," he said. "And sand, and a hot wind. That wind still blows every morning. Or not this morning, did it?" He glanced at his wife for confirmation, and she nodded. He went on. "But for the past several days. It comes off the mountains, so it should be a cool wind, but . . . and it's not merely a hot wind, it's a wind allied to fire, as Beremnan Anweierchen describes in his *Countries Near and Far*. Are you familiar—?"

"Yes, I understand. And after the dust?"

Emre Tanshan leaned forward anxiously, her hands clasped in her lap. "We sent word south, Lord Beguchren. So they would have warning.

First came the red dust, carried on a hot wind. And the sun began to come up . . . different. Fiercer. Then . . ." her voice trailed off.

"We sent men upriver and down," Amnachudran said, picking up the tale once more. "After our stream failed. It's not only our stream and our pond. The river, the upper Teschanken, where it comes down out of the mountains, it's run dry. Not merely low. The men who went upriver tell me that the desert has cut across the river's channel and claimed all the mountains along there—" His wave indicated the general extent of the desert, north and much too far to the east. "Now, you may know, my lord, that Gestcchan Wanastich describes finding, in his history of Meridanium, an immense lake high in the mountains. A lake that feeds the Teschanken and, so Wanastich had it, the Nerintsan River as well. I always wanted to follow the river north and find that lake," he added tangentially, his didactic tone going wistful on this thought. "It must be a splendid sight: a lake as great as a sea, cupped in the mountains between earth and sky . . . Well." He recollected himself. "But whether the lake itself has been encompassed by the desert and has actually gone dry, and what an immense undertaking it must be to destroy so great a lake—but, that is to say, whether the griffins have destroyed the lake or merely cut across the Teschanken south of the lake, we've no way of knowing."

There was a little silence. Gereint thought about the Teschanken and Nerintsan Rivers, which not only linked north to south but also watered all of Meridanium and the whole eastern half of Casmantium. If the whole lower Teschanken ran dry—not merely low, but dry, as Amnachudran said—he said in a low voice, "Casmantium can't exist without the river."

"Not as it is presently constituted, no," agreed Emre Tanshan.

"Without the rivers, a good part of the north will turn to desert," put in her husband. "Not necessarily to a country of fire, but to a country where men cannot easily live. Our rain rides the cool winds off the mountains: If the griffin's lay their desert across those mountains, none of our northern towns will survive. Tashen, Metichteran, Pamnarichtan— and over in Meridanium, Alend and Taub, Manich and Streitgan and Raichboden—everyone will have to flee south, as the people of Melentser did."

"Dislocation enough to have the folk of Melentser displaced. But if the whole north empties, we will have nowhere to go," Lady Emre said in a low voice.

"The river sustains Dachsichten as well," murmured Gereint, not really speaking *to* anyone, but merely speaking aloud because his mind had leaped ahead and presented him with images too grim to contain in silence. "And Breidechboden. Geierand will do well enough, and Wanenboden, and Abreichan. Or they would, if not for northern refugees. But there will be so many refugees." He could imagine, far too vividly, the flood of desperate folk from north to south, hopelessly in excess of the numbers the south could sustain.

Peaceful towns like Geierand would simply be overrun and destroyed, as surely as though a plague of locusts had come down on the land, and far more thoroughly. But Breidechboden and Abreichan—he knew that the great cities of the south would arm against the mass of northern refugees—they would have no choice—he tried not to imagine soldiers in their shining ranks drawn up against the ragged multitude of refugees, but the images were vividly compelling and he could not put them out of his mind. He said, his tone hushed with horror, "Casmantium will be destroyed. It can't sustain this blow. Something will survive, but . . . I think it won't be a country any of us will recognize. It will be something small and poor and weak and well practiced in brutality . . ."

Beguchren settled back in his chair, tented his hands, and gazed at Gereint over the tips of his fingers. "Destroying Casmantium is, I believe, the griffins' whole intention," he agreed.

"How can they dare? However strong they are—however few cold mages we have—how many griffins can there *be*? A few thousand? They must know we will spend however many men and mages we have to stop this—"

"Due to a slight miscalculation on our part, and a tremendous stroke of good fortune on theirs, the griffins at this time possess an immense advantage that we may not, in fact, be able to overcome." Beguchren's quiet, uninflected voice concealed, barely, a horror that, Gereint was beginning to suspect, equaled his own.

Everyone gazed at the frost-haired mage, waiting. For a moment, Gereint thought he was not going to answer their unspoken question. But he said eventually, "I should think you had word of the, ah, the broad outline of events in Feierabiand."

"Well, yes, an outline, at least," Lady Emre said sympathetically. "I was very sorry to hear of your loss, Beguchren."

"Yes," the mage said, and paused. For the first time, Gereint wondered exactly how many cold mages had died in Feierabiand: all of them, he knew, except Beguchren. Half a dozen? A dozen? And how many of those mages had been Beguchren's personal friends? He had understood the tactical problems that arose from the lack of cold mages—or at least, he had understood that tactical problems did arise from that lack—but now, for the first time, he flinched from the question of how it would feel to be the only surviving mage.

"But you—" began Amnachudran, but stopped.

"But, Beguchren," protested Lady Emre, bolder than her husband, "you're only one man, after all, however powerful—"

"I can effectively oppose fire. I am alone, but so is the remaining griffin mage, I believe." Beguchren's voice had gone taut. "He is very powerful, but I can challenge him. If it were only he and I, I would challenge him and win. But there is now a fire mage in the high desert who was born human, whose nature is not quite the nature of a griffin. Had you heard so? Well, it is true. She lends the griffins an advantage I—we—cannot well answer.

"We hadn't thought the griffins bent on our destruction. They seemed otherwise inclined, and we didn't understand that they might use Melentser as a bridgehead to support an attack on all of Casmantium. Or, as you might guess, we would have tried much harder to prevent them taking Melentser. But we failed of imagination, to our great cost. Now, with that human fire mage to support them, a few thousand griffins may well match all the men and mages we can possibly bring to this . . . conflict." He did not quite say "war."

"But . . ." Gereint protested, but then, under Beguchren's level gaze, did not know what to say and fell silent once more.

"I have one method in mind that may hold some promise." Beguchren turned his gaze toward Eben Amnachudran. "I will wish to see the desert. I also wish my associate Gereint Enseichen to see the desert."

Gereint kept his expression placid, refusing to be drawn.

Beguchren finished quietly, "Then I will need a day or two to arrange . . . certain matters. I will have instructions for you, I believe. And then . . . we shall see what can be done."

"If you believe anything can be done, my lord," Eben Amnachudran said fervently, "I assure you, my household and all my resources are entirely at your service."

Beguchren inclined his head in courteous, unsurprised acceptance of this offer. But his glance at Gereint questioned whether Gereint too might be willing to place everything he owned and all his resources at his service.

"I understand why you want me to see this," Gereint said to him a little later, as they made ready to ride up into the hills and look at the desert that, they were assured, lay hardly any distance from the estate. "But I've seen it before. It hardly seems necessary to ride out to the desert on my account. What if there are griffins there? Their mage, the one you say opposes you, what if he is there now, today, waiting for you?"

"He is not. He is the last of the great griffin mages; he will be too wise to risk himself against me when he has no need. He will not face me directly unless I can manage to force a confrontation."

"Can you?"

Beguchren lifted an ironic eyebrow. "The griffin mage thinks not, I suspect. He is mistaken. I will force him to face me, Gereint, but not today, and not until I have arranged circumstances to my liking."

Gereint shrugged noncommittal acceptance of this assurance, took the reins of both the horses a hostler had led out for them—not the black mares, which had been turned out to rest, but a pair of Amnachudran's horses that he had loaned them for the afternoon—and without comment turned to assist Beguchren to mount. Equally without comment, the small mage set his foot in the cupped hands Gereint offered. Straightening, Gereint tossed him up into his saddle without effort. He said, "An easy ride up into the hills, an easy ride back in time for supper: That's the idea, is it?"

Beguchren gathered up his reins, gazing down at Gereint with a wry look in his pale eyes. "Just so."

"We don't intend to do anything more than look at the desert this afternoon."

"Just so," Beguchren repeated.

Gereint shook his head, asked rhetorically, "Why do I doubt that assurance?"

"You needn't. It's quite true."

"I've seen the griffin's desert before," Gereint repeated.

"Then this afternoon you can see it again. Or will you balk?"

"Now? No. Maybe later. Now, it's either too late to shy away, or too early." Gereint swung up into the saddle of the other horse, a sturdy bay gelding with the height to carry a man his size, and gave Beguchren an ironic little nod.

The mage didn't flinch from that irony, but only led the way out of the courtyard and through the near orchard without hesitation, heading straight north as though he knew exactly where he was going.

He probably did, Gereint reflected. Probably he could feel the precise border where the country of earth gave way to the country of fire; probably it was like an ordinary man watching a storm approach across the southern plains, or the line of a swift brush fire pass through a woodland. Something obvious, powerful, and potentially dangerous.

There was no red dust riding a hot wind today; Beguchren's doing, Gereint suspected. But the orchards showed the effects of the past few days: The leaves of the apple trees had gone dry and brown around the edges, and the green was leaching away to browns and yellows as though the season had already turned. Ripe and near-ripe fruit had been picked, but the unripe apples still on the trees were shriveling on the branches.

They passed the empty pond and rode up along the dry bed of the stream that should have fed it, topped the hill and headed up again at an angle along the slope of the next hill. Then they crested that hill and looked down across the slope that fell away from them toward the next, higher, rank of hills, leading to the mountains beyond.

The edge of the desert lay directly over the crest of the hill less than a mile to the west from Eben Amnachudran's estate. Gereint had expected to find the border close at hand, but never so close as this. He drew his horse to a halt, staring, appalled, at that boundary. "How can it have come this far?" he whispered. "They've brought their desert all the way across the river. How can they have done this?"

"When we gave them Melentser, we gave them a hold they have used to claw their way across all this country," Beguchren answered. "Let us go down to it." Gereint could read no expression in the mage's fine-boned face.

Gereint had forgotten the strange, terrible, profoundly foreign power of the griffins' desert. He had forgotten the ferocity of its sun, the hard metallic glint of its sky, the savage knife-edged red cliffs that sliced the hot wind into ribbons. Flames flickered among the red sands, dying away again like water ebbing on a beach, leaping up without tinder and burning without fuel. No griffins were in sight; not riding the fiery wind nor lounging upon the red cliffs. But near at hand, two of the scimitar-horned fire deer flung up their heads in alarm at the glimpse of men and horses and fled across the desert in long low bounds, flames leaping up where they disturbed the sand.

Gereint feared that Beguchren might cross the intangible boundary between earth and fire and set foot on the red sand, under that fierce sun. He did not know what he expected might happen then—a hundred griffin's coming down, outraged, out of that empty sky? The griffin's own mage pouring himself out of the burning wind? Or that other mage who had once been human flickering out of the hot wind to meet the cold mage, perhaps. But Beguchren drew his horse to a halt a little on the earth side of the border and merely gazed into the country of fire, his gray eyes impenetrably remote.

Gereint nudged his own horse up beside the other and asked in a hushed tone, "You mean to challenge . . . all this? Alone?"

"Not alone," Beguchren murmured.

Gereint stared at him, incredulous. "You should have brought every mage in Casmantium with you. Some must remain. If not cold mages, at least ordinary earth mages." He tried not to allow his voice to rise to a shout, but found he could not match Beguchren's composure. "What does the Arobern think he's about, sending you alone? If you need makers—if you need makers who can leap right through vocation and gift and power and remake themselves into mages to serve you, then you should have brought every maker in Breidechboden here! And you only brought me?"

Beguchren returned a calm gaze. "The Arobern wanted to give me an army. I persuaded him to give me a free hand, instead. Ordinary mages would not understand what they saw here: They would see"—he nodded toward the desert ahead of them—"*all this*, as you say, and they would lose all capacity for balanced thought. They would only wish to argue with me. Nor do I need every maker in Breidechboden—or if I do, then nothing will suffice. If I am right, I will in fact need only one maker."

"You can't . . . How can I possibly . . . What is it you intend to do?"

"Let us go back a little way." Beguchren reined his horse away from the desert's edge and toward a tumble of flat gray stones set amid a patch of tough, wiry-stemmed bindweed, its graceful heart-shaped leaves and perfumed white flowers as yet untroubled by the encroaching desert. Beguchren slid down from his horse and waded through the tangled vines to sit on one of the stones, gesturing to Gereint to join him. "Let it go," he said, of Gereint's bay gelding. "They won't wander far."

"Unless a griffin comes."

"None will, today. Sit down. I'll tell you a story."

"Will you? About this past summer?" Gereint slipped his horse's bit, twisted the reins around the pommel, and picked his way through the weeds to join Beguchren. His horse dropped its head, untroubled by the burning desert not a hundred feet away, and began nipping leaves off the bindweed.

"Yes. But my story begins earlier than that." The white-haired mage tucked one foot up, laced his fingers around his knee, and watched the horses. His expression was closed and ironic; Gereint suspected that he was not seeing the horses or the bindweed or the stones or even, perhaps, the desert beyond. Beguchren said, his tone perfectly level, "This was my fault, you know. Or the fault of all the cold mages, if you like, but only I remain to take the blame for our mistake. That is only just. It was my mistake as much as anyone's. How shall I put this? We saw an opportunity to use the king's ambition to destroy the griffins once and for all, and we took it."

Gereint didn't think that he made any sound or movement, but the mage's fine-boned face turned to him as though he had exclaimed aloud. Ice-pale eyes met his, remote as winter.

"We didn't think of it in quite that way, of course," said the mage. "The king was ambitious for a new conquest, and we, well, we longed to rid Casmantium of the threat of fire. Someone thought of a plan. I hardly know, now, whose idea it was, in the beginning. But I favored it as strongly as anyone." He was silent for a moment.

Gereint did not speak; he hardly breathed.

"We thought we would drive the griffins out of their desert and across the mountains into Feierabiand," Beguchren went on at last. "We thought we would send them before us, a storm of fire and wind, and that, coming behind them, we would find Feierabiand distracted and weakened. Then the king could have his new province—or if he failed of that ambition, we did not care. We thought we and the mages of Feierabiand would, in the end, join against any few remaining griffins and destroy them utterly. Then the country of earth would in time overwhelm the country of fire." He paused again.

After a moment, when the mage did not continue, Gereint said quietly, "Everyone knows something went wrong. But I never heard anything but guesses as to exactly what happened."

Beguchren's mouth crooked; his smile held irony rather than humor. He said, "Nothing went wrong, at first. We came into the desert swiftly and quietly and came upon the griffins in the dark. We drew upon the long, slow memories of the sleeping earth. We smothered fire with the weight of earth and laid a killing cold down before us and around us, and they could not withstand us. In those first moments, we destroyed almost all of the griffin mages: all but one. Anasakuse Sipiike Kairaithin, greatest of the griffin mages. But even he could not hold against our concerted effort. The griffins fled west and south, just as we had intended, and we spun a net of frost across the sand behind them to hold their fire from rising again . . .

"It was not an effortless victory. We lost Leide. She had hair like a drift of snow, eyes black as a midwinter night, and a cold, clean power like the heart of winter. We lost Ambreigan, who was eldest of us all: He was too proud, and tried to stand alone against three griffin mages. But there were seven of us who lived to see the dawn, and likely it was a gentler dawn than that country had ever seen. Though we grieved, we counted our battle a victory and we declared our war as good as won." He stopped.

This time Gereint did not prompt him. But after a moment, the mage went on, starkly. "Then the griffins found in Feierabiand a weapon none of us had expected. A human girl, a girl right on the edge of waking into her power as a mage. Kes, daughter of . . . some Feierabianden peasant, I suppose. We don't know her birth, but it doesn't matter. Sipiike Kairaithin found her and took her and poured fire into her. He corrupted the magecraft in her before it could wake."

Gereint exclaimed, "He made her into a *griffin?*" and then, afraid Beguchren might stop, leaned back and pressed his lips together, trying to pretend he had not spoken.

But the mage barely seemed to have heard him. Though he glanced at Gereint, he did not really seem to see him. He spoke quietly, almost as though to himself: "He made a fire mage of her. He made a weapon of her. Or, not exactly a weapon. He made her into, not a sword, but a shield. He made her into something no griffin could be: a healer of fire. We did not realize at once what he had done. He made it impossible for men to do battle with griffins, for that girl would heal them as swiftly as they were struck down. We did not understand this quickly enough. By the time we discovered it, we had already lost everything. We were too confident."

Beguchren meant himself and his fellows, Gereint realized: He meant the cold mages. He was not thinking of the Arobern or the ordinary soldiers at all. He spoke with a kind of calm desolation that was very hard to listen to.

"While soldiers battled, Sipiike Kairaithin hunted us down and killed us," Beguchren said, still with that terrible calmness. "We did not understand quickly enough . . . and then we found the King of Feierabiand had made a terrible bargain with the griffins and allied his country with fire. And so we were defeated. And at first we"—now he meant himself and the Arobern, Gereint guessed—"at first we thought that was the end of it." He bowed his head for a moment, then seemed to recollect himself out of memory. He turned back to Gereint, smiling his wry, imperturbable smile. Gereint found he had preferred it when he had not known what depths of loss and grief lay behind that smile.

"We expected a little political maneuvering, a temporary embarrassment, shall we say? But it is clear now that the griffins intend to force their way to a stronger, more decisive victory than we imagined. I think, now, that they intended this from the first." The mage nodded toward the desert, where golden flames flickered across red sand and the fierce sun glared down out of a metallic sky. "We gave them Melentser and the surrounding country. The griffins said they did not desire vengeance, that they would be content to have Melentser as their indemnity. But they are treacherous creatures. We did not expect—how could we?—that the griffins would drive their desert so far east, or use their new foothold in our country to strike against Casmantium's very life. It did not occur to us that they could, or perhaps it did not occur to us—even to me, though *I*, of us all, should have suspected it—that they would realize their own advantage and press it home."

"So you came here," Gereint said quietly. "You alone. Except for me."

Beguchren moved his shoulders, not quite a shrug. "I would do anything to redeem our mistake." He glanced up, meeting Gereint's eyes. "I would certainly sacrifice one maker. One skilled, strongly gifted maker; the sort of maker who already has a thread of magecraft running unrecognized through his mind and soul and gift. That sort of maker might do for me what must be done." He paused. Then he went on, deliberately, "It was not your mistake, Gereint. But I am compelled to ask you to help me repair it."

Gereint met his eyes. "But you can't force me to help you," he said. It was not quite a question.

Beguchren bowed his head again. "If the *geas*, if any part of magecraft, could force you to answer my need, I would use it. As it happens, nothing I know can compel you to the . . . immolation and remaking of the self that is necessary."

"Save voluntary self-abnegation." Gereint tried to keep to the same deliberate tone, with how much success he could not tell.

Beguchren inclined his head. "Just so. But not today." He rose, glanced once more across the hillside to the burning sands of the desert, and then stepped instead toward his horse.

Gereint also got to his feet, took one step across the mat of tangled flowers, and called after him, "Why not today?"

The mage stopped and swung around. For nearly the first time in Gereint's experience, he seemed surprised. He began to speak, hesitated, and said at last, visibly choosing his words, "The, ah, appropriate circumstances are not yet properly arranged. I dare not act until I have done everything possible to ensure success. But hold to this image"—he nodded toward the desert, beautiful and terrible and utterly foreign to the country of men—"and when the day comes at last down to the hour, I hope you will ask that question again."

The ride back to Eben Amnachudran's house was very silent and not nearly long enough to suit Gereint, who would have liked a good deal more time to think through everything Beguchren had told him. They had seemed to Gereint to stay a long time looking at the desert, to sit a long time on the gray rocks. But the sun was still high above the western horizon when they came back through the orchard and into the courtyard. Here in the country of men, the sun seemed only a little too large and too fierce as it dropped slowly toward the western horizon.

Clouds stretched in crimson bands across a deep azure sky; the tawny hills rolled out below, with the distant mountains a ruddy gold above. It was beautiful. But both hills and mountains should have been green with late summer, not tawny and gold with autumn.

Hostlers came to take the horses, darting anxious glances up at Beguchren and only slightly less anxious ones toward Gereint. He thought he recognized one of the men. But the hostler gave no sign that the recognition was mutual. He only gave a respectful little nod and wordlessly took the bay gelding away to the stables.

They found Eben Amnachudran in the room that was both his office and his wife's music room; or Beguchren found him there. Gereint only followed, silent and self-effacing.

The spinet was the same, the floor harp, the racks of scrolls. But the books were all neatly put away on the shelves. Gereint recognized some of the ones Amnachudran had brought from his friend's house, set now in their own places on those shelves; gold lettering embossed on rich brown cloth, or silver on red silk, or powdered opal on black leather: Maskeirien's eclogues, Deigantich's allegory about the white eagle and the black wolf, Hrelern's four great epics, Fenesheiren's *Analects* . . . They made Gereint think of the quiet days he'd spent cataloging philosophers' theories of materials for Tehre in the Breidechboden townhouse. He wished, with a sense as of something long ago and now forever unobtainable, that he might someday finish that work and see what use she might make of it.

"A beautiful library," Beguchren said to Eben Amnachudran, and with a slight shock Gereint recognized the faint wistfulness of his tone. The mage went to the shelves, touched one embossed leather binding and another. He turned to give Amnachudran a nod of wry self-deprecation. "One does not expect to find a collection of this quality outside the capital—or I had not. It's a lesson for me. You must have gone to great trouble to build this collection."

"Some of the choicest volumes I inherited after the loss of Melentser," Amnachudran said. "Unfortunately." He had risen respectfully to greet the lord mage, and now paused. Then he added, with a glance that took in the contents of the room, "Perhaps I had better send these south, lest some scholar inherit them from me a little sooner than I'd anticipated." His glance, sharpening, returned to Beguchren. "Perhaps you might advise me in that regard, my lord."

"The precaution might not go amiss," Beguchren said softly. He lifted a hand toward a set of chairs near the desk. "You will have a day or two to do so, if you wish. Let us sit and discuss what we shall do."

"You have instructions for me?" Amnachudran moved toward the chairs but waited for the mage to sit first. "I had hoped for that, but I did not know whether to expect it. If you have something useful for me to do, my lord mage, I would be delighted, I promise you."

Beguchren took the largest and most luxurious of the chairs and then, to Gereint's surprise, produced the purple-dyed token of a king's agent. He turned this token over in his slim fingers. It multiplied in his hand, bone clicking softly against bone, one elaborately carved token becoming two, and then four, and then eight . . . The mage cast the handful of tokens across Amnachudran's desk, where they rattled like dice: half came up with the Arobern spear-and-shield uppermost and the rest with the tree-and-falcon.

Beguchren said in his coolest, most precise tone, "Send to Tashen, to Metichteran, Pamnarichtan, Raichboden, Streitgan, Manich, Taub, and Alend. All towns of any size where fewer than three days' fast travel will allow your messengers to reach the town and for men, returning, to reach this house. I will require men-at-arms from each of those towns. Each governor must send me no fewer than fifty men, even if he must arm tradesmen and farmers to fill out the numbers." He added, at Amnachudran's slightly stunned look, "They will bring their own supplies. Their own weapons, rations . . . tents. They do not need horses; we will not take horses up to the country of fire. You will write the orders; put in what you like. You will not be required to furnish anything but space to keep them."

"But, my lord—" Amnachudran began, then stopped.

Gereint, not so inhibited after days on the road with the mage, asked bluntly, "If you wanted an army, why strip these little northern towns of their half-practiced men? Why not take the professional army the Arobern tried to give you?"

"But I don't want an army," Beguchren said softly. He did not look directly at either of them, but only gazed with remote and rather terrible detachment into the air. The lines of his fine, ascetic face seemed to shift before Gereint: now familiar, now cold and strange. "I don't want officers who will insist on describing military options. There are no sound military options, now. I don't need soldiers who will march into the desert and die bravely. No, I don't want an army. I want a diversion."

"A . . ." Amnachudran began, but once again stopped. He glanced at Gereint, took a breath. Let it out. Looked back at the mage. "My lord mage . . . I will send to the towns, just as you command. But may I ask: a diversion for what? It will make a difference, perhaps"—he added apologetically—"for what the men are to bring, and for what, ah, other arrangements must be made."

"You are asking whether I mean to send these men to their deaths?

There is some risk. But, I hope, not a dire hazard. If the diversion does not work swiftly, it will not work at all."

"But you'll sacrifice them if you must," Gereint said. Not a question.

"Oh, yes." Beguchren turned his ice-pale gaze to Gereint, no less remote for that sudden, intense focus. "I will draw Sipiike Kairaithin and his human fire mage to this place; I will compel them to face me . . . in the country of earth, if I can. In the country of fire, if I must. If I am able to destroy Kairaithin, that would be as well. But it is utterly crucial that the human fire mage be destroyed. Only that is vital. Her death can and will shift the balance from deep defeat to decisive victory. If this one objective is achieved, it matters little what happens to the griffin mage or to me. I will certainly sacrifice all those men to achieve that aim if I must. But I think that particular sacrifice need not be made."

There was a small, profound silence.

Then Beguchren said to Amnachudran, in a perfectly matter-of-fact tone, "Three days to gather, shall we say? But once the men are here, I believe events will move very swiftly." His glance moved, opaque, unreadable, to catch and hold Gereint's eyes. He moved his hand, a tiny gesture toward the north, indicating the desert. "And if we do not achieve victory swiftly, we will surely be defeated."

"Yes," Gereint said, a touch impatiently. "You needn't keep on. I understand."

Beguchren did not quite smile. "Yes. Very well." He glanced at Amnachudran. "You are clear on what you will do?"

Eben Amnachudran hesitated, his round face creased with worry, but he nodded.

"Within reasonable bounds, Gereint Enseichen will be able to answer any concerns you may have," the mage stated, optimistically, in Gereint's opinion. He gripped the arms of his chair, rose, and sent a remote glance from one of them to the other. "It is early, I know. However, I believe I shall retire. Gereint—"

Gereint's now-practiced eye found the subtle evidence of incipient exhaustion in Beguchren's very stillness, a stillness that was meant to conceal the tremors of sudden weakness. "Shall we—are there griffins near at hand?"

"I am holding clear the boundaries of earth," the mage murmured in absent assurance. "They do try me. But I hold the boundaries." His glance sharpened, moved to catch Amnachudran's eyes. He added, "They will wait to see what I mean to do before they set their strength against me, and what they think they see will please them—but in the end dismay them utterly. If all men play their parts with passionate sincerity."

Amnachudran's eyebrows drew together in a kind of bewildered resolution. "We'll see that all men do, then."

And if Beguchren did not lie down soon, his part would be a collapse that would dismay him and frighten everyone who wanted to depend on him, was Gereint's opinion. He confined this thought to a sharp-toned, "I'll bring up your things myself. Permit me to escort you." He took the long stride necessary to bring him to the mage's side, ready to offer covert support if necessary.

"I'll have someone show you," murmured Amnachudran, his eyes narrowed with concern. Yes, Gereint well remembered the scholar's perceptiveness; Amnachudran had missed nothing. But he only went to the door and called for servants. "Tehre's room, for the lord mage," he told the women who came in answer to his call. "And the brown room for the honored Gereint Enseichen."

"You're very kind, honored sir," murmured Gereint, with a wry, ironic inflection that he trusted only Amnachudran caught.

The scholar moved his shoulders in a minimal shrug. "If you have a moment later, honored Gereint, perhaps you might indeed answer the concerns I do have? Within, to be sure, reasonable bounds?"

"In only a moment," Gereint assured him, and accompanied the frost-haired mage down the hall, ready to catch him if he went down. For the moment, Beguchren was concealing his weakness well enough . . . If it was not too far . . .

The room was not far. "You'll be well enough?" Gereint asked, watching the mage all but vanish into the embrace of a large and well-cushioned chair. The line between reasonable concern and hovering seemed difficult to tread, at the moment. "I'll send for tea—"

"Of course you will." Beguchren's tone was reassuringly dry. "I am quite well, Gereint. You do not need to stay so close. Go, if you wish."

Gereint gave a noncommittal shrug. "If you say so. I don't understand. You say no griffins are overhead. It's nearly dusk. If you're"—*so weak*—"experiencing such difficulty now, how can you possibly face this powerful griffin mage you say is your enemy, not to mention the human fire mage he made?"

Beguchren half smiled, leaning his head back against the headboard of his chair. "Physical strength matters less than you might think in a challenge of this sort. Besides, Gereint, when it comes at last to that challenge, I won't be alone."

Gereint looked at him for a moment. Then he said merely, "All right." He rose, turned to go out.

"Gereint," Beguchren called after him, and he turned back, surprised.

But the mage did not speak again, only looked at him with uncharacteristic irresolution.

After a moment, Gereint shook his head. "It will be well enough," he said quietly. "In three days, and certainly tonight. Rest. The servant will be along soon with tea. And anything else you need, I'm sure. I'll see you in the morning. I assure you I will." He went to the door, glanced back at the mage. Beguchren was sitting quietly, watching him, his expression unreadable, his fine features shadowed by the winged headboard of the chair. Gereint hesitated another moment. Then he left him there like that, sitting alone in the dark.

Eben Amnachudran was still waiting in the library-study-music room when Gereint made his way back to it. He was alone, absently turning the pages of a book so large it barely fit on the desk. The book was bound in black leather . . . Erichstreibarn's *Law of Stone and Fire*, he saw.

"Topical," he commented.

"Hah." Amnachudran rose quickly and came to take his hands, looking searchingly into his face. "I have received the most incredible series of letters, fortunately in time to expect you and the lord mage. Are you well? How was Tehre when you left her? Did you know she is coming here? In company with a lord of Feierabiand, apparently."

"She's coming here?" Gereint repeated. And, "With *whom*?"

"I've sent men by every conceivable path she might take, to stop her on the way and warn her not to come. Half the folk on the road must be mine: I sent nearly all my people south days ago, after I understood the progression of the desert's edge. Including nearly everyone who would know you by sight, by the way. Someone will find her, I'm sure. I don't want her to come around the last curve of the road and find sand and fire where her home used to be . . . She's worried about her mother and me. And you, I believe, though she didn't quite say so. You must have suited one another rather well, or so I gather, reading between the words." He moved to sit down, waving Gereint toward a second chair. "Tell me everything."

This was difficult to do without terrifying Amnachudran over things that might have happened, but Gereint tried. The scholar listened without questions or interruptions, but his mouth tightened twice as he caught back an exclamation only with an effort. At the end, his face was pale and set. When Gereint had done, he asked only, "Do you truly think the king meant what he said to you as a threat against my daughter?" and, when Gereint had no answer, "He can't blame her for Lord Fellesteden's death. At least, he'll find little sympathy for that judgment if he tries: a young noblewoman defending herself and her household against attack the only way she could, with the only weapon to her hand?"

"You know people, I'm sure. If he tries, you must make sure the tale that whips around Breidechboden blames me, not her."

"Yes, Tehre told me what tale you suggested for her. Though she left out . . . never mind. It was clever of you to recast, ah, events as you did. And generous." Amnachudran moved restlessly, rising to light a lamp that hung over his desk; the dusk had crept down from the hills and across the house and Gereint had not noticed. The flickering light of the lamp sent shadows wavering through the room, made it into a small haven of human warmth beneath the crouching darkness.

The scholar went on, coming back to resume his seat: "But the king himself knows the truth about what happened at my daughter's house, does he not? Nearly all the truth. So no false tale can be put about now. Perhaps it's just as well. I do know various people, and my lady wife has a great many friends, and the Tanshans would hardly want a daughter of Emre's dragged down into the mud. No . . . no. The king won't make good that threat. He has no reason to move against Tehre anyway. You are here, after all."

Gereint opened his hands in a gesture like a shrug. "I think you needn't concern yourself. Either the lord mage will succeed and the Arobern will be happy, or he will fail, and the Arobern will have much more important concerns than how Perech Fellesteden died, and by whose hand or will. Though, unfortunately, so will everyone else."

Amnachudran gave Gereint a sharp look. "*Will* he succeed? What is this weakness? Or did I mistake what I thought I saw?"

That took a moment. At last Gereint said carefully, "It's an intrinsic weakness, I believe, but exacerbated by the close presence of griffins. And possibly by the desert itself. I don't quite . . . I expect going out to look at the desert might have brought it on, or maybe working to keep the edge where it is and the griffins from pressing into our country . . . He doesn't like people to notice it."

Amnachudran nodded. "I could see that, too. He hid it . . . fairly well, I suppose."

"He does, usually. He says physical strength will matter little in the conflict he means to provoke."

"Really."

"And he reminds me that he will not face the fire mages alone."

Amnachudran looked down at his clasped hands. Then he said, "Ensemarichtan Temand disagrees with Warichteier and Anweierchen about the fundamental distinction between magecraft and ordinary magic. I gather that Beguchren Teshrichten agrees with Temand."

"He went into my mind," Gereint said slowly. "Right after he . . . after the Arobern gave me to him. And then he said I would suit his purposes and . . . began to set me tests, though I don't . . . I didn't understand at once what he was doing. I suppose I must have passed them. Enough of them. I haven't read Temand. But I know Beguchren means to make me into a mage. Or, no. He means me to do that to myself."

"Yes." Amnachudran tapped his fingers restlessly on the arms of his chair. He rose again, went to his shelves, and came back with a heavy volume bound in plain leather. He brought this back to his chair, absently propped a foot on the upholstered seat, rested the volume on his knee, and flipped it open, not quite at random. "Magecraft . . . mages . . . magic and the gift. Yes. Temand says, *The making of a mage thus depends on a definition of the self and on the power to bend that definition; magecraft does not blend with the ordinary gift, but in that definition can lie the link between mage and ordinary man, for every man defines himself* . . . And then he goes on about, hmm, this and that." The scholar closed the book, his shrewd eyes meeting Gereint's.

"Yes. The lord mage said that about definition of the self. Or the making of the self, which I gather is the same thing."

"Yes, did he? Gereint, he will make you into a mage, but for what? What help can a brand-new, utterly inexperienced, entirely untrained mage possibly *be* to the king's own mage? He means to betray you: bring you into power and then rob you of that power. That is how he will find the strength to overcome this weakness of his, defeat the griffin mage who is his enemy, and destroy this human fire mage he so greatly fears."

Gereint was silent for a moment. Then he asked, "Is it betrayal if you see it coming?"

Amnachudran's eyebrows rose.

"He told me, *I will do anything.* Before you made your guess, I made mine, and with a good deal more evidence. He told me flatly he means to sacrifice me in this. But what am I to do, knowing that?" Gereint went to the window, looked out into the dark. Nodded toward the north where the desert lay hardly a spear throw from the house. He said, "He will sacrifice me, and those men you'll call up, and himself. Well, what else is he to do?"

Amnachudran began to speak.

Gereint shook his head, stopping him. "I could let him drag me to the edge of the desert, but clench my eyes shut and refuse to look at it, like a child refusing to look at something that frightens him. Let the griffins' fire burn the rivers dry and plunge Casmantium into disaster: Beguchren would try to stop them by himself, I expect. He would die. Then I would be truly free." He stopped, lifted an eyebrow at Amnachudran.

The scholar looked very sober. "You won't do that."

"No. How could I?"

The pause spun out in the room to meet the greater silence waiting outside the house.

"Three days," Amnachudran said softly.

"They say waiting's the hardest part."

"They do say that. I'm sure it's sometimes true."

Gereint smiled, a touch grimly.

"Well." Amnachudran smiled in return, with some evident effort. "I'm sure supper is waiting for us, and Emre hates waiting supper. Come down with me. You can tell us about Breidechboden, and about the things Tehre's been working on, if you understood them." *And not about fire or the desert or anything to do with griffins*, he did not say. But Gereint understood that, too.

CHAPTER 12

The three days swept by in a hurried blur, which was strange because every separate moment seemed to linger as it passed. Messengers arrived; the swift little Nerintsan River had gone dry as old bone, and in Meridanium Province the desert had come down the mountains almost to the northernmost town of Alend. All the people had fled the threatened town, pressing south to Manich or Raichboden. None of the refugees had gone west from Alend to Tashen, not merely because Tashen was not a Meridanian town but also because, the messengers said, everyone thought Tashen was too far north.

"And what does that say about us?" Eben Amnachudran said wryly, meaning that they were well north of Tashen themselves. He had sent almost all the rest of his household south as well—not merely to Pamnarichtan or Raichboden, but all the way south to Breidechboden. "And lucky we have a house there to receive them," Lady Emre said, no doubt thinking of the thousands of displaced northerners who did not have southern property or relatives.

But the estate was far from deserted. Men gathered at Amnachudran's home. A town of tents bloomed amid the orchards and pastures, red and blue, or orange and gold for the men from the Meridanian towns. Every governor had sent the required contingent, or near enough. They were not, in general, soldiers. Virtually all of the men carried spears and many had bows slung over their backs, but only about one in five had at their sides, in plain, worn scabbards, swords that had belonged to their fathers or grandfathers.

Steel flashed in the sunlight as their officers tried, cursing, to shape men-at-arms from a dozen towns, mixed with a generous number of unpracticed tradesmen and farmers, into coherent companies. But

Beguchren, looking down at them from a wide window, did not seem dismayed by their disorder.

"Tashen is short," Amnachudran commented. It was the morning of the third day. He had brought a wide map and pinned it open on the largest table in the house, which was in the library. There was plenty of room for it there, as nearly all the books had been sent to the greater safety of the Breidechboden townhouse.

Amnachudran stood deferentially by Beguchren's chair as the mage settled into it and leaned forward to examine the map. Gereint wondered whether the mage had guessed that the chair, the tallest in the house, was not a normal accoutrement of the library but had been provided especially so he would not have to stand. Lady Emre was, he suspected, the subtle force behind the tall chairs that always happened to be in any room frequented by the mage and the frequency with which girls came around to offer tea with honey and milk, or bread with sharp golden cheese and apple butter, or tarts made with tart apples or buttery pears. Eben Amnachudran had tried to send his wife south along with his library and the household. But she had refused to go.

If Beguchren realized he was being cosseted, he did not object. Nor had his strength failed again during these days . . . so far as Gereint could tell. Now the mage turned a cool, neutral expression toward Amnachudran.

"You can't actually blame Tashen for sending a short count," the scholar went on. "I'd be amazed if they had fifty sound men left in the whole city. Everyone with sense must have headed south days ago."

"One might say the same for Metichteran," murmured Beguchren. "It's half the size, if that, and yet the governor of Metichteran managed to find fifty. All men-at-arms, too, and I think a quarter or more of the men from Tashen are shopkeepers and farmers. I rather believe the governor of Tashen has kept his own personal men-at-arms for his own personal protection."

"Is this of practical importance?" asked Lady Emre, her eyes dark with thought and worry. "There is still time to send a firmer command to Warach if we must." Warach Beichtan was the governor of Tashen. "But it would be faster to fill out the count ourselves. We could do it, if we call up every man remaining to our household. As long as you don't need them to do more than wave a spear right-end up. We, too, have few men left save the odd farmer and orchardist."

Beguchren slanted a warm look up at the woman. "Thank you, Emre, but I think that will not be necessary. But when Warach Beichtan disregards my command, he disregards the command of the king. And when he reserves his men for his own protection, he offends against the responsibility he holds to guard his people." He paused, his gray eyes now cool and thoughtful. "Make a note of this," he said to Amnachudran. "You are one of the Arobern's judges, yes? If appropriate, later, you will send word in that capacity to the king of Beichtan's dereliction."

He meant, *If we win the victory but I am dead.* And he meant it for an order. Eben Amnachudran bent his head obediently, acknowledging the command.

"No," Beguchren continued, now speaking to them all. "We have nearly four hundred men in all. That will suffice. So long as, as you say, they all wave their spears right-end up." He glanced up at Gereint. "We will go up toward the desert at . . . shall we say, at the fifth hour past noon? Our little army will brandish their spears and put on a show, but we shall hope they need not be put to the test of battle."

"If they are?" Amnachudran asked him. "We have no real general to lead them; they have barely had a chance to train; they are unfamiliar to one another and under officers they do not know. They will be slaughtered to a man . . ."

"If it comes to battle," Beguchren said softly, "then it will not matter whether they are slaughtered in these hills or die later in their own homes or on the road south or at the gates of a southern city that will not let them in."

There was a moment of silence. Then Amnachudran said steadily, "If you permit me, my lord, I will lead those men myself. I do not claim to be any kind of general. But at least I have studied military history, and most of those men know me."

Gereint, standing behind Beguchren, swallowed a sharp protest and watched Emre Tanshan do the same. Beguchren leaned back in his chair and regarded Amnachudran with close attention. He said at last, "Honored Amnachudran . . . I am willing to leave these men in your hands. You are clear on the role I mean for them to play?"

"We must make a show. You intend the griffins to come down to do battle, so we must seem to offer them one. Then they will bring this fire-healer of theirs into your reach. Then you will do . . . what you will do, and all will fall out as it will."

"Just so." Beguchren paused. Then he said decisively, "It would indeed be well to have those men led by a commander who understands clearly what I require. You may arrange matters in that regard as you see fit." He tapped his hand gently on the widespread map. "I had hoped to avoid it, but I think we will need to enter the desert. We will go up here or here. Those are sensible lines of attack that suggest a reasonable objective. We will appear to wish to press the griffins away from the northern reaches of the river, perhaps freeing the waters to come down, if indeed Wanastich's lake is still there and only the rivers dry."

"They will believe we might attempt such an ambitious objective?"

"Desperation might reasonably drive us to this strategy. And then . . . I will be with you."

"Ah." Amnachudran gazed down at the map, his expression thoughtful. Then he looked at the mage. "But we will not be able to depend on you. Yes?"

"When fighting begins, if it begins, I will not be able to help you. Save by procuring a swift victory through, as it were, a back door. That will be my intention. Once their human fire mage has been destroyed, the griffins will—must—reconsider their aggressive intent."

The scholar nodded. He looked at his wife. Emre Tanshan gazed back at him, her face set and pale. She said, answering the question he had not asked aloud, "I will wait here. If you are victorious, you will probably need a place to bring the wounded, and people to care for them, and a strongly gifted healer. And . . . and if the day goes otherwise, you will need someone to organize a retreat."

Amnachudran looked as though he wanted to object, as though he longed to command his wife to flee for the south now, this moment. He also looked like a man who knows he can't give any such order, or that if he does, it won't be obeyed. He said nothing, but went to her and touched her face. She lifted her hand, covered his hand with her own. Neither of them spoke.

Beguchren said merely, "Good." And then, "The fifth hour past noon. So we must prepare for that." It was a dismissal, and Amnachudran and his wife took it so. They went out together, her hand tucked in the crook of his arm.

Gereint crossed his arms over his chest, leaned his hip against the edge of the table, glanced down at the map, and then looked up deliberately to meet the mage's pale eyes. He said nothing.

"You will stay close to me," Beguchren told him. "We dare not act too quickly, and yet when we come to act, we must do so decisively. Sipiike Kairaithin must not be allowed to guess what we intend."

Gereint appreciated that "we," delivered without a trace of irony. He nodded.

"Gereint—"

Gereint held up a hand. "Don't say it. It's not necessary, and I would take it as a slur."

Frost-pale eyebrows rose over eyes the color of a winter dawn. But the mage only bowed his head a little, accepting this.

"And you?" Gereint saw the faint puzzlement in the mage's eyes and elaborated, "*You* are well enough?"

"I shall do very well," Beguchren said, blandly unemphatic. He rose. If he was suffering now from any weakness, he concealed it with admirable thoroughness.

The hills seemed steeper when one walked up them instead of rode. The mountains were not so far away; they rode through the foothills even now, close beside the Teschanken River. Or, more precisely, beside the bed where the Teschanken ought to have run. The riverbed was dust-dry now, the rounded stones exposed to view. Before them rose the sharp teeth of the mountains. Close at hand, three peaks rose hard against the sky, high granite faces shining in the late afternoon sun, dark forest cloaking their lower slopes. Two more mountains loomed to their left, on the other side of the river, seeming so close the company might walk between them by dusk.

Only Beguchren and Eben Amnachudran rode: Amnachudran because he needed to ride from one end of the marching column to the other, and the cold mage putatively because of his rank but really, Gereint suspected, to spare his strength. But also, quite deliberately, to make a show.

Beguchren was riding one of Amnachudran's horses, a gray gelding with powerful quarters and an amenable nature. The cold mage did not carry bow or spear or any weapon more dangerous than a small belt knife, but, not much to Gereint's surprise, he had somewhere found blue ribbons to braid into his horse's mane and tail. He was sitting up very straight in the saddle, with his shoulders back and his head high. He wore fine white clothing that he must have brought all the way from Breidechboden for this exact purpose: Tiny white pearls gleamed on his belt and on the cuffs of his low boots, and there was a single blue ribbon braided into his white hair. With his pale coloring and silver eyes, he looked very much as though he had been sculpted out of ice. The whole intention was to make a show, and so he did: he might have been a parade all by himself.

There were reasons to limit the number of horses. No one, not even Beguchren, would actually take a horse into the desert. This was not Feierabiand, where horse-callers might have held the animals docile and obedient even under a rain of fire. Horses would be nothing but a liability when—if—the griffins came down, and everyone knew it.

The afternoon was a fine one, though unseasonably warm. But it seemed far grimmer when one walked in company with four hundred men who all thought they were marching to battle. The men trusted Eben Amnachudran: Gereint saw how they looked to the scholar and saw that they all knew him, or knew of him, and that they were glad to have them lead them. He had not guessed that Amnachudran was so well known. He remembered him saying, *Having to run down to Tashen every time we wanted a judge was so inconvenient. Everyone seems to prefer to simply come to me.* Gereint had not, at the time, quite understood how broadly that "everyone" applied.

And they trusted Beguchren. Not as they trusted Amnachudran, but they trusted his power and skill. The officers, Gereint suspected, probably mostly guessed that Beguchren meant to sacrifice their company— any who were not fools must at least wonder. But Amnachudran had at least persuaded them that the mage meant to do it to some purpose. Thus they went forward with purpose and faith.

A sweet breeze came from the south, across the hills, smelling pleasantly of autumn grasses. The sun lay low in the west, but its light was an ordinary light and its warmth no more than pleasant in the afternoon. The hills might lie dry and golden with the too early autumn forced on them by the pressure of the griffins' approaching desert, but they were beautiful and peaceful in the quiet, and there was not a trace of red dust in the air.

Then they came over the crest of the hills and looked down upon the country of fire. To either side, the hills were sweet with autumnal gold; to either side, the mountains were still green with forest just beginning to turn red and gold; their high, wind-polished faces glittered with ice. But straight before them, running north and west, the desert shimmered with fire all the way out to the far horizon.

All the men stopped, as though by shouted command. They halted high on the summit of the hills and gazed down at the burning sands. There were no griffins in sight, but the desert itself seemed threat enough, and there cannot have been a single man of their number who did not think of simply dropping his spear and walking away, south. They were not, after all, soldiers.

Then Eben Amnachudran rode his horse out in front of the little company, turned to face the men, and declared in a clear, loud voice, "Beguchren Teshrichten, the king's own mage, is here to stop that country of sand and fire from coming down across all our homes. He did not bring an army from the south, because he does not need one. What he needs is the honest courage and resolution of ordinary men of the north, and he knew he would find that waiting here for him. And so he has." Then, in the great silence he had created, he turned, deliberately, toward the silver-eyed mage. "My lord, what will you have of us?"

"Courage and resolution," Beguchren answered, just as loudly and clearly. "We will go down into the desert, and when we are finished here, it will be once again a country of earth."

"As you command, my lord," Amnachudran said formally. He was not carrying a spear, but he lifted his arm and pointed forward, and the officers took up the command in their sharp, carrying voices, and they all went down the hill, along the ripple in the red sand that marked the bed of the dry Teschanken, and into the griffins' desert. At the edge of the desert, Amnachudran swung off his horse and stripped the saddle and bridle from it and let it go, and Beguchren did the same. And then they went down into the country of fire.

Little flames flickered amid the sands, and the towering sharp-edged cliffs stood hard against the fierce, brazen light that lay heavily across the desert, nothing like the ordinary sunlight in even the hottest southern summer. Gereint vividly remembered the brutal hammering power of the desert sun. He closed his eyes, swallowing, as he walked beside Beguchren, across the boundary, and out of the country of earth. But though he could tell when he crossed the boundary, the heat did not come down from the molten sky nor strike up from the fiery sands with anything of the ferocity he recalled, and he opened his eyes again in astonishment.

The fires died away as Beguchren walked across the desert, and the red sand somehow took on a softer look, as though it might lie thinly over ordinary soil. As all the men followed him, the desert itself gave way beneath them and around them, yielding to his power, and although the light pounded down upon the surrounding desert, it lay on them gently, and a sharp wind followed them from the south, bringing the scents of earth and water and growing things into the country of fire.

Gereint looked sharply at Beguchren. The mage's face was calm, but his eyes were narrowed and his mouth set hard with strain. Gereint wanted to ask, *How long can you keep earth under our feet and a natural light over our heads?* But if he asked, everyone who heard would know there was a question about it. So he did not ask.

"We will go this way," Beguchren said quietly, and walked straight forward into the stark desert, between the high mountains, which now seemed much farther away, half hidden by—well, not by dust nor by haze but seemingly by some quality of the air itself. Amnachudran nodded in return and waved to his captains, and the company strode straight ahead almost without hesitation.

Before them, the fire died down under the sand; above them, the sky softened from its terrible metallic ferocity; to either side of their line of march, the sunlight lay gently on the desert. Gereint understood, now, why Beguchren had been so certain that the griffins would come down to meet them. This was not a challenge that could be let pass.

And on that thought, the griffins came. They came from the west, out of the blaze of the lowering sun, slicing across the face of the mountains alone or in small groups, cutting paths of stark beauty through the empty sky. Gereint first thought there might be about a hundred of them all together, but more came, and more after those, and he saw, appalled, that there actually were many more griffins than they had brought men.

Even in those first moments, when they were still distant, no one could have mistaken the griffins for hawks or eagles or any bird; the light that struck off their wings was too harsh and their beaks flashed like metal. They cried out in high, fierce shrieks like hunting eagles, and the sky behind them turned red with the violence of wind-driven sand; fire scattered down across the sand from the wind of their wings.

"We will hold them here," Beguchren declared, in a sharp, loud voice meant to carry. "As long as we hold firm, they will not be able to come down as they wish. Remember what we are about, do you hear? Hold, hold, and I shall protect you. Do you understand?"

They had discussed this, but it was not the same when one actually watched the griffins come sweeping across the wind. Eben Amnachu-dran had gone dead pale, but he nodded and turned to the men. Begu-chren did not watch him, but gripped Gereint's arm and nodded aside, to where the red desert mounted up a rugged hill. Gereint thought he merely meant to take a place up on that hill where he could be seen, like a talisman. Then he saw the frost that spangled the sand where the mage set each foot, spreading outward from where he walked, and re-alized that a cold wind had risen and was blowing with increasing force past them from the south. After that, it occurred to him that Beguchren meant to teach him this power, and then he was truly frightened, be-cause the glittering ice that challenged this desert was nothing he un-derstood at all.

They did not go far, but when they turned, the griffins were almost upon them. They looked enormous; he had not realized they were so large: the size of lions, he thought first, but they had not even yet ar-rived and grew still larger in the vast sky; the size of ponies, and then heavy cart horses, and then at last they came down, with appalling speed: splendid and terrible creatures of bronze and copper and gold and jet, with ferocious talons and brilliant inhuman eyes. But the fire they brought with them only spattered harmlessly against Beguchren's cold wind, and the men held firm, their spear points glittering like chips of ice in the sunlight; arrows whistled into the sky, very few at first and then more: Most of the men had been too stunned to shoot at once. Watching the arrows rise, Gereint said, without thinking, "I should have made those arrows—or some of them—"

"There wasn't time," Beguchren answered. "I put my name and intent into them. That isn't quite the same as making them for this exact purpose, but it will serve."

Rather than striking down through the arrows and into the waiting spears, the griffins spun away to every side and climbed swiftly back into the heights of the air. They were not shrieking now: They were silent. But Gereint could hear the wind rushing through their great wings, with a sound like stiff cloth in a high wind or, to a sufficiently attuned imagination, like the roaring of a fire. The arrows did not reach them but began to fall back to the ground. Every one of them burst into flames before it struck the sand.

"We turned them," Gereint said to Beguchren, and he found that his voice was shaking, and he was not even ashamed of that. And then, with perhaps more accuracy: "You turned them."

The cold mage barely seemed to hear him. His head was back at a sharp angle: He stared upward with an almost frightening intensity. "He is not here," he said, not so much to Gereint as to himself. "*She* is not here; that is why they turn aside. Where are they? Do they think I am not serious in my challenge?"

Gereint did not know how to answer.

"They *will* answer me, if I must turn every grain of sand to good earth and every rising flame to a chip of ice," the mage declared. He waved sharply at Amnachudran, and the scholar called out to his captains, and the little company began to make its way along the dry path of the river, west and north, up the rising slope of the foothills. Their spear points dipped and rose as they marched, in series, like flashing ripples rolling across a lake. They did not call out or shout; even the commands of the officers seemed muted. As though commanded to review before their lord, every row of men turned to look up at the cold mage as they passed his position. For reassurance, Gereint knew. From his deliberate hauteur, Beguchren knew it too.

The griffins wheeled in a great circle, now very high aloft, now so low the long feathers of their wing tips brushed the sand. But they did not come within bowshot of the company. They were glorious and terrible. Their feathers might have been beaten out of bronze and then traced with copper or gold; powerful muscles rippled under lion haunches as golden as the purest metal. Their beaks and talons flashed like knives and their fierce eyes were flaming gold or coal black or brilliant copper. One griffin was pure white, the white of the hottest flame at the fiercest forge; another nearly as pure a black, but with gold barring the long feathers of its wings and dappling its haunches; a third, black flecked with crimson and copper. But they did not close against the men, but only swept up and around and down again in their great circling path.

"They're waiting," Gereint said suddenly, realizing this must be true.

"Yes," Beguchren answered, but absently, as though he barely heard. "For their human fire mage who can keep them whole. They will not come down against our arrows and spears until she is here. She *must* come. They cannot possibly mean to permit our incursion, and they will not attack without her. Maybe they are waiting for Kairaithin— maybe *she* is waiting for Kairaithin. Ah!"

This last exclamation marked the appearance of another griffin. It did not soar in from the deep desert as the others had; it did not come down from the heights or out of the crimson sunset in the west as the sun slid down on its slow path beyond the mountains. The griffin was simply there, balancing on the fiery wind, out of bowshot but close enough to make out clearly.

The new griffin was slim and graceful; large, to be sure, yet smaller than most of the other griffins. It was a rich dark brown, the feathers of its wings barred with gold. On its back, as on a horse, perched a small human form.

The pair spiraled around and slid down across the wind, and as they approached, Gereint saw that the rider was a girl. Only she wasn't really a girl. Gereint stared, trying to understand where the difference lay. It was a little like looking at a very fine statue of a woman: It might mimic the form of a woman very, very well . . . but no one could possibly mistake the carved stone for a living woman. This girl was living, but it was immediately obvious that she was somehow not human. Her fine hair blew around her face like gossamer thread spun out of white-gold flame; her skin seemed translucent, as though almost-visible light burned through it; her face was alight with a terrifying inhuman exultation. Her hands were buried in the feathers of the brown griffin's neck. She was laughing. Gereint flinched from the sound of her laughter; he could not understand where the difference lay, but it was not the laughter of a human woman.

"There," said Beguchren, his voice urgent and tense. He swung to face Gereint, his fine face set hard, his ice-pale eyes intent. His small hands locked around Gereint's broad wrists. "And their mage is not even here. There will never be a better time! Do it now!"

Beguchren had refused to explain in detail how Gereint was to remake himself into a mage, saying that a maker had to find his own way to any making. Gereint had accepted this vague instruction at the time, turning over in his mind possible methods by which the "self" might be "remade." He'd thought he understood, in principle, how it might be done. But all this vague advice and subsequent thought seemed a good deal less helpful now. He had intended to make himself into a mage for Beguchren; he had come into the country of burning sands to do precisely that; he knew perfectly well that the lives of everyone in the company depended on his ability to do it. But now it came to the moment, he had no idea how it might be done.

Beguchren saw his helplessness, but the cold mage only shook his head. "I cannot help you. If you do not find the way, it was all for nothing and we will all die here: Our bones will burn to ash and blow away in the wind and the desert will lie across our rivers forever—"

"I know!" Gereint exclaimed.

Beguchren gave him a tense nod, let him go, and turned to stare down at the company of men. It was not yet quite besieged; the griffins, welcoming their human fire mage, had raised their burning wind and come at last down upon the men. But arrows flickered out into that savage wind, and spears tilted and rose, and Beguchren drove up, from the now-distant country of earth, a stinging wind that glittered with ice crystals, and so the griffins did not, as yet, close to battle.

If we do not achieve victory swiftly, we will surely be defeated, Beguchren had said, and Gereint had understood exactly how he was expected to contribute to that victory. Now, staring instead down the sweep of the desert straight into defeat, it occurred to him for the first time that Beguchren might have meant the little company of men not only serve as a feint against the griffins, but also to drive *him* forward: *We will all die here, our bones will burn to ash and blow away in the wind* . . . Yes, the cold mage had brought them deliberately into peril and set all their lives in Gereint's hands. Anger drove him, and despair. He dropped to his knees on the sand, burying his hands in it.

The sand was, in a strange way, living—not as good garden soil was living, but alive with fire. It was unalterably opposed to everything he loved; it would destroy anything of earth that it touched . . . The magic of earth ran through him: He knew it, tried to feel it; the effort was like trying to feel the flow of blood in his veins. It was impossible to truly feel something so integral to his body and to life.

Except that the power of earth was at such odds with the power of fire, and in the conflict that blazed between the two he almost thought he could perceive both . . . Rising, acting on nothing like a thought, merely on impulse borne out of terror and desperation, he reached out, jerked the knife off Beguchren's belt, tossed the sheath aside, caught the mage's wrist in a hard grip, gave Beguchren one instant to see his intention, and flicked the tip of the knife sharply against the palm of the mage's hand. Then his own, and he closed his hand hard around Beguchren's small hand, palm against palm.

It was not any kind of technique he'd ever read about or thought of, nothing that would have been useful when working with wood or stone or metal or any normal material. But he shut his eyes and defined blood as symbolic of self; Beguchren's a cold mage's self and his a maker's, and he did something with their mingled blood he could never have described but more or less seemed to recognize. And then he followed the pattern he had made, or completed, or perceived. It was not a pattern he understood, but he followed it anyway, and felt his blood, or mind, or self, slide with surprising ease into that shared pattern and then follow a half-forgotten intention at last into the pattern of magecraft.

Doing so, he died. It was like death. He had not understood what it would be like: like a shattering of memory and identity, like the flowing out of his heart's blood. He would have fought this loss if he had understood how to fight it, but it was already too late to undo it. He struggled, but it was like the struggle of a drowning man against the ripping current of a river; there was no firm ground beneath him and the air was closed away from him, unreachable . . . He was drowning, not in water but in a wild tide that he recognized, dimly, as magecraft. Something integral to everything he had been cracked across, and something else rose in its place, as though one building had been torn down to make room for another.

Gereint drew a hard, shuddering breath and . . . opened his eyes. He had not been aware of closing them.

The desert had changed. It was still starkly beautiful, stretched out under the bloody sky, reflecting the last fire of the setting sun. But it had become not merely terrible but dreadful. He shuddered uncontrollably, looking out at it: It *pressed* at him with suffocating force. It would kill him if it could, and burn his bones to ash that would blow away on the wind. It *wanted* him to die. He had felt this before, but now the sense was a hundred times stronger and somehow more personal, as though the desert almost had an actual *self* of its own that was utterly opposed to everything natural and human.

Like the desert, the griffins had become dreadful. He remembered clearly that he had found them beautiful. But now he saw that they were profoundly inimical, in a way he'd previously completely failed to understand. And the brown griffin and the once-human girl were far the worst. They appalled him. He choked on revulsion against them . . .

A strong, small hand closed on his shoulder and he looked up, swaying because the desert underfoot seemed to shift with anger; he thought it would burst into flame beneath him and spun a web of frozen quiet across the sand to hold it quiescent.

Then Beguchren moved to face him, set a hand on his other shoulder as well, and met Gereint's eyes. His silver eyes were filled with ice and intensity. Without hesitation, with a skill and power that Gereint could not understand, could barely recognize, Beguchren stripped the new power from his blood and mind and self, turned, and sent a glittering net of ice and power flashing through the hot wind toward the girl and her griffin companion.

Gereint folded down to the sand, unable to brace himself up even on hands and knees. He felt not merely weakened but half blinded and deafened and all but disembodied by the loss of power; worse, he felt somehow that the world itself had been stripped of presence and reality, that what remained was nothing but an attenuated echo of the world that had surrounded him a moment earlier.

But the brown griffin staggered in the air, crying out in a high harsh voice as the icy net closed around it. The girl cried out as well, her voice high and sweet and not at all human.

And a massive griffin, black as charcoal, touched with red the color of smoldering embers, blazed out of the wind between Beguchren and the brown griffin, and Beguchren's net shattered into shards of ice that dissolved into the fiery light of the desert sunset.

Gereint thought he shouted, but his voice was only a thin gasp.

Beside him, Beguchren made no sound at all, but turned to face the dark griffin, his expression strained and tense, his eyes filled with a pure and frozen blaze of power that had nothing to do with desert fire.

In the west, the sky burned with a crimson light as the sun sank at last beyond the fiery horizon. Then the light died, and the hard desert night crashed down around them. Yet the darkness was broken by a bloody light that seemed to emanate from the fiery wind or from the griffins themselves, and from a frosted silvery radiance that surrounded the cold mage. By that light, Gereint could see the great black griffin stoop down across the sky toward Beguchren, and he saw Beguchren take a small step backward, and it occurred to him, for the first time as a serious possibility, that the cold mage might, despite everything, simply find himself overmatched in this challenge. But Gereint did not have enough strength remaining to be afraid. The darkness closed in upon him, a greater darkness than even the desert night could impose, and his awareness spiraled down into the dark, and dissolved in it, and was gone.

CHAPTER 13

The road between Dachsichten and Breidechboden was much too good, Tehre decided. Even if you weren't in a great hurry, your carriage would travel smoothly and swiftly, and if you *were* in a hurry, well, you could travel very quickly indeed. Even with the very best roads, however, no one but a courier or a king's agent could cover the whole distance from Dachsichten to Breidechboden in one day. Which was just as well, Tehre thought.

Sicheir rode his own horse, not too near Detreir Enteirich. Though Meierin rode with Tehre in the carriage, the girl was silent and pale. She sat with her hands folded primly in her lap like a child, and her gaze fixed on her hands. She evaded Tehre's eye and said very little. Tehre was aware she should reassure the girl, but did not know what she might say. She would have liked to send her out to ride with Sicheir so that she could speak privately with Lord Bertaud, but of course that was impossible. Lord Bertaud had turned his carriage south without apparent hesitation, but his eyes were secretive and bleak, and Tehre knew his grim mood had nothing to do with fears of the Arobern's anger.

She said at last, speaking straight across Meierin since there was no choice, "Will you go all the way back to Breidechboden?"

Lord Bertaud lifted his eyes to meet hers, but he did not answer.

"You needn't," Tehre said firmly. "Did I make that clear? But you need to tell me what *I* should do."

"Lady—" Meierin said tentatively.

"Hush," Tehre told her. She hadn't looked away from Lord Bertaud. "You know, if you simply turned about and headed north again, there wouldn't be anything at all the Arobern's agent could do to prevent you."

"He could prevent you, however," Lord Bertaud said, frowning.

"Not necessarily, if I were with you. If he had to set himself against you, honored lord, I don't know what he'd do. The Arobern's agents have wide authority. But they have to use it with discretion. It would even be an act of war to raise a hand against you. Wouldn't it?"

"And an act of treason for you to defy him. Isn't that so?"

"Lady!" Meierin exclaimed.

"Hush!" Tehre said, more firmly this time. "Meierin, hush. Not even Fereine will blame you for anything I do, you know."

"Yes, she will—"

"Well, tell her I said she mustn't." Tehre turned once more to Lord Bertaud. "Well?"

The Feierabianden lord said nothing for a long moment. His expression had become abstracted, but some of the bleakness had gone from it. Tehre said nothing, did not move, tried not even to breathe obtrusively. She heard his voice in her memory: *I think it may be worse than even your king suspects. I have a suspicion about this.*

At last Lord Bertaud lifted his gaze to meet Tehre's. He said, "What you did with language . . . I said you must be a mage. You said you are not. Tell me, lady, are you in truth a mage as well as a maker?"

"No," Tehre said, surprised. "No, I'm a maker, and maybe something of an engineer, but not a mage. I'm sorry—if you need a mage, I'm afraid there aren't any more—"

Lord Bertaud dismissed this concern with a wave of his hand. "The one remains. The king's mage. The cold mage. Beguchren."

"Beguchren Teshrichten," Tehre agreed, mystified. "Yes."

"He went north."

"Yes?" Tehre couldn't see where the foreign lord was heading with this. She tried to wait patiently for him to explain.

"Mages of earth and fire . . ." Lord Bertaud began, and stopped.

"There is an antipathy," Tehre said cautiously. "All the philosophers agree there is an antipathy."

"Yes." Lord Bertaud's mouth tightened. His gaze had turned inward. Whatever he was seeing, Tehre thought, it was not the interior of the carriage or the neat fields that lined the road. He turned to her with sudden decision. "You're very powerful. But you are not a mage."

Tehre nodded to each statement, baffled.

"Your king should have sent you north. Not his mage, but you. And me, perhaps. Well, we shall see what this Detreir Enteirich does with his authority and his discretion," Lord Bertaud declared, and leaned forward to speak to his driver.

Detreir Enteirich appeared beside the carriage almost before it had completed its turn. "Stop!" he ordered the driver. But the driver was one of Lord Bertaud's retainers and not Casmantian at all, and he did not stop, but instead clucked to the horses and made them trot more briskly than ever. Northward.

"Lord Bertaud!" the king's agent said, falling back to ride alongside the carriage so he could speak to them through the window.

"I said I would escort the lady wherever she might wish to go," Lord Bertaud said blandly. "It appears she wishes to go north."

The agent digested this for a moment. Then he leaned down a little in the saddle, peering past Lord Bertaud to Tehre. "Lady Tehre—"

"Yes, I know," said Tehre.

"This defiance is treason, lady—"

Yes, Tehre began to repeat. But agreeing made it seem more real, and she found herself flinching from the word. She said instead, almost pleadingly, "But the Arobern gave me the wrong command. He's given me the wrong command twice! I don't *want* to defy the king, truly, but he should have told me to go north. We have in Lord Bertaud someone who's even allied to the griffins, and the Arobern won't listen to him, either!"

Detreir Enteirich's mouth tightened. "Lady Tehre Amnachudran Tanshan, is that what you will tell the king?"

"No!" cried Sicheir, from the agent's other side. "Tehre—"

"*You'd* better go to Breidechboden," Tehre said sharply. "One of us needs to, if that Fellesteden heir is going to make trouble."

"Tehre—"

"I can't!" Tehre said. "Sicheir, I can't! I have to know what's happening in the north! Don't you see I have to?" Before her brother could answer, she closed her eyes, clenched her hands into fists, and broke the solid roadway behind and to either side of the carriage. She didn't understand exactly what she did. It was a little like getting that sword to shatter, when Fellesteden's thug had tried to cut Fareine; it was a little like exploiting a weakness in a mechanism such as a catapult so that it would break. But it was not exactly like either of those things. There was a deep-set maker's virtue in the road, so that no matter the weather, it would not erode or crack or grow muddy. But Tehre broke it anyway. Beside them and behind them, all the mounted riders fell away, shouting.

"But you are not a mage," Lord Bertaud said seriously, peering out the window of the carriage.

Tehre didn't know whether to laugh or cry. "No! I didn't know I could do that. But it wasn't magecraft, anyway. More like making, only backward. Can you stop the carriage?"

Lord Bertaud's expression grew even more serious. "You have

changed your mind? You wish to go back?" He hesitated. "It is a grave matter to defy your king."

"No!" repeated Tehre. "I mean, yes, it is, but no, I haven't changed my mind! Only we need to let Meierin out." She looked at the girl, sitting stiff and horrified beside her. "Meierin, tell them . . . I don't know. Anything you like. Tell them I'm sorry, but I know there's something terribly wrong in the north and I'm going, and Lord Bertaud is, and you tried to stop me but I wouldn't listen. That's all true, so you ought to be able to sound very sincere."

"Lady Tehre—honored lady—"

"Go on," Tehre said inexorably, and reached past the girl to open the carriage door. "And tell them not to bother coming after us! Not even the Arobern's agent has any right to stop Lord Bertaud, and they should think carefully about whether they want to offend him by trying to make me go back. And I won't, anyway. Remind them about the road!"

"I think I won't need to," Meierin said shakily. "I think you're right; I think the lord mage should have asked *you* to go with him, maybe the honored Gereint too, but he should have asked *you*. If you think you should go now, then I think so, too. Honored lady—good fortune go before you and beside you! I'll tell them just what you said. Only, if something is so terribly wrong in the north, fix it; please fix it! *My* family's in the north, too, you know!"

Tehre did know this once Meierin reminded her, and blushed because she had needed the reminder. She nodded wordlessly, and the girl stepped back—carefully, because the road was rough and broken where she stepped. And Lord Bertaud leaned forward and rapped hard on the back of the driver's high seat, and the driver lifted the reins again, and the horses strode forward. Not running. Merely at a collected trot. Because they were not running from anybody, because if they had to run they had already lost their ability to assert their own independent action.

But they did not have to run. No one, not even Lord Bertaud's other retainers and servants, came after them.

It was nearly dusk when they stopped, neither at a farmhouse nor at a campsite, but simply drawing off the road behind a small copse of oaks and hickories. Not out of fear of pursuit, Tehre knew. Merely because Lord Bertaud had no inclination to seek out any kind of company. Neither did she.

Tehre had barely noticed the change in the light. She had been thinking about making, and magecraft, and risk, and treason, and had not really noticed time passing at all. She walked the stiffness out of her bones while the driver saw to the horses and Lord Bertaud made up a fire. None of them spoke much. The driver modestly produced bread and hard sausage from his personal supplies, and they toasted these rough provisions over the fire.

"I can rest in the carriage, I suppose," Tehre said, a little doubtfully, as the last glimmering glow of the sun sank low in the west. She had not had to think about such practicalities herself for a long time. Ever, really. "But I don't know . . . maybe we should have found a house to stop at, after all—"

"We won't need a house," Lord Bertaud said abruptly, and stood up.

The fire had burned down to low embers; the flames now were sparse, flickering low amid ashen coals. Lord Bertaud stood close by the fire, a featureless black shape against its ruddy light. Tehre couldn't see his expression. But his voice was grim.

A man flickered into existence by the fire, shaping himself out of the rising night wind and the glow of the fire, and Tehre stared. So did the driver. So did Lord Bertaud, but there was something different in his startlement, as though he *was* surprised, but not at the same thing that had startled Tehre or the driver. Tehre rather thought he had been startled by the man's sudden appearance, but only by the suddenness, not by the appearance itself.

The newcomer was cloaked in black, but the firelight picked out a crimson gleam at his throat and wrist—the shimmer of fine cloth. His hair was black as the night; blacker, for the silvery moonlight could have relieved any ordinary darkness, but it barely seemed to touch this man. The firelight showed a face that was spare, strong boned, haughty; deep-set eyes; an arrogant tilt of the head. And the man's shadow, Tehre saw with a dawning sense of amazement and dismay—his shadow, pulled into shape by the light of fire and moon, billowed out huge and strange, not dark at all, but fiery in the dimness. It was not at all the shadow of a man. Feathers of flame lifted and fluttered around the shadow's head and its long graceful neck; its eyes were black as the coals at the heart of a fire.

But then, she realized, nothing about the man, save the shape he wore like a cloak, was actually human.

Lord Bertaud stepped forward to greet the stranger, and Tehre was bewildered by what she saw in his face: gladness and relief and anger and an odd kind of dread—a strange and complex blend of emotions that should have been contradictory and yet seemed all of a piece. But amazement, she thought, was notably lacking. He said sharply, heatedly, as though answering a challenge or continuing an argument, "I did *not* call you!"

"You called me in your dreams," the man answered. "I heard my name in your dreams. You called me with your intentions." His voice was exactly as Tehre might have expected: harsh, angry, edged with challenge. "I came so that you would not need to call me aloud. Why are you here so far from your own country, man, if not to stand between men and the People of Fire and Wind?"

The Feierabianden lord did not answer.

The griffin mage—clearly he was a griffin, and if he wore the shape of a man and pulled himself out of the wind he must surely be a mage—this man who was nothing like a man waited a long, stretched moment. Then he said, "Why else are you on this road but to come up to the new desert we have made? And what do you mean to do there? What has the Casmantian king offered you to persuade you to ally with him against us despite all your oaths?"

"I am *not*—" Lord Bertaud began, sounding outraged, but then stopped himself, his breath coming hard. He said instead, "What are your people *doing* in the north?"

"We are breaking Casmantium's power," the griffin mage said harshly. "Should we wait for another cohort of cold mages to be raised up? For Casmantium to strike again into our desert and kill us as it pleases? Should we yield all the country of fire to the soft wind, to the dim, pale sun, to the steel plow and the growing grain, the stone walls and roads of men? I think not.

"Our fiery wind will sing through the northern hills; we are bringing our country east below the high lake. We will turn Casmantium's great rivers to dry dust; its tame fields will crack and wither. The Arobern flung ice and earth against us; we will return wind and fire. Let him send ten thousand soldiers against us: He will discover we have become impervious to even the coldest steel. Thus all men will see the people of fire are strong and dangerous to offend."

Tehre could see at once what would happen to Casmantium if the Teschanken River went dry; withered fields were only the beginning of it. Light-headed with horror, she swayed and put a hand out, but there was nothing to support herself with but air. The griffin mage turned his head, a sharp birdlike movement. His fierce eyes caught her out of the darkness, and she stood frozen under that black, contemptuous stare, as a mouse frozen under the fierce gaze of a hunting falcon, unable to look away or move.

"No!" Lord Bertaud said sharply. He came swiftly to her side and put a protective hand on her arm, turning to stand beside her.

Tehre, somehow freed by his touch or voice, blinked and shuddered. The Feierabianden lord seemed nearly as horrified by the griffin mage's words as she had been, but *he* was not shaking. His grip on her arm was almost painful—she would be bruised, later—but she put her hands over his and clung.

Despite the griffin's brutal speech, there was a strange edge to his ruthlessness and arrogance, as though he were waiting. As though he expected . . . something . . . Tehre could not imagine what. His stare, when his eyes met hers, was indifferent. Pitiless. But there was something else in his face when he met Lord Bertaud's eyes. But Tehre could neither recognize nor understand what she saw, just as she could not recognize or understand what she saw in the face of the Feierabianden lord.

"You agreed with this plan?" Lord Bertaud asked in a low voice. "I thought your people were content simply to take back the city of Melentser. And instead, you do *this*? Without even telling me? This is a wind you agreed to ride? Or was this Tastairiane and Esterikiu Anahaikuuanse?" The flowing griffin names came to his tongue much more easily than Casmantian names had, which seemed ironic. He went on: "You've shown before, if you have to, you can bring your king around to your opinion—"

The griffin mage held up a hand, a sharp gesture that cut Lord Bertaud off nearly in midword. "Eskainiane Escaile Sehaikiu was sometimes my ally and yours, man. Now that he is gone, the Lord of Fire and Air has little patience with moderation. Taking Melentser might have pleased some of us. But once we claimed Melentser and perceived the strength its return brought us, then we saw what other wind had risen up to call us to fly. Then we discovered what more we might do. I will admit," he added harshly, "I did not expect *you* to present any opposing argument. Certainly not personally. This is nothing to do with Feierabiand. A weakened Casmantium is even to your benefit. Is it not?"

Tehre didn't understand why the griffins cared what argument Lord Bertaud might make—it must have to do with his role in the summer's war, and earth and iron, what *had* his role *been*? But to her dismay, Lord Bertaud did not immediately refute the griffin mage's suggestion. She said urgently, "If the lower Teschanken goes dry, Casmantium won't only be weakened. We'll be destroyed! They can't do this, can they? Can they? If we send ten thousand men, surely they couldn't really defeat us?"

But Lord Bertaud looked as though he thought they could, and Tehre stopped, horrified. She cried, "If the griffins will listen to you—if this Lord of Fire and Air will listen to you—you mustn't let them do what he says they mean to do!"

"Woman, do you think any man of earth may instruct the people of fire as to which wind to ride, or whether to call up fire or let it die?"

demanded the griffin mage, directing the hot force of his attention on Tehre for the first time.

Flinching under that stare, she nevertheless made herself meet his eyes; she even managed to speak. "No, but you said—you implied—" But she could not manage any sort of coherence, stuttered to a halt, tried to collect her wits, and appealed instead to Lord Bertaud. "Your country is allied with the griffins now, isn't it? Your king is an ally of their king, isn't that right? You're an agent of the Safiad. Don't you speak with his voice? Isn't there something you can do? Are you certain there's nothing you can do?"

Lord Bertaud gently freed his wrists from her grasp, but then he took and pressed her hand in reassurance. He said to the griffin mage, "Kairaithin . . ."

"Hush!" said the griffin mage, lifting his head suddenly, as though he had heard a shout. Tehre listened, but she heard nothing at all— nothing save the breeze in the oaks. But the griffin mage took a swift step back away from the fire. He said, his eyes on Lord Bertaud, "I must go."

The Feierabianden lord hesitated, glancing at Tehre. Then his mouth firmed as he made a decision and he let go of Tehre's hand, took a step forward, and said to Kairaithin, "Take me with you." His tone was midway between a command and a plea. "Take me with you. Us. Take us with you."

"There will be nothing you can do," the griffin mage said harshly. "Except one thing. And will you do that, man?"

Lord Bertaud hesitated and then shook his head. He answered in a low voice, "No. I won't. I don't want to." He lifted his head, then, and stared into Kairaithin's black, unhuman eyes. "If you were presented now with the same choice you were given at Minas Ford, how would you choose?"

The griffin mage did not answer.

Tehre stared from one of them to the other, aware that she did not understand everything that either of them meant. She hardly understood anything, and that was a dangerous ignorance if the griffins truly meant to destroy Casmantium and had the power to do it. As both Lord Bertaud and Kairaithin seemed to believe.

"I *must* go," Kairaithin said suddenly, sharply. "Beguchren Teshrichten has struck into our desert. Man, I must go."

"Beguchren?" Tehre said, startled and intensely relieved. "Oh, maybe it will be all right, then—he's not *alone*, is he?" She thought of Gereint. And of her father. Maybe her mother had fled south? Maybe everyone had; except what if Beguchren Teshrichten had needed help of some kind, any kind? Her father would have stayed to help the king's mage if he thought he could be any use. And Gereint had gone north *with* Beguchren, which was all very well. He was a strongly gifted maker, but she knew without any need for false modesty that he wasn't as broadly gifted as she was—she said, "I *have* to be there!" and stared in appeal at Lord Bertaud, who clearly had some strange influence with the griffin mage.

"We shall all go," Lord Bertaud agreed. He put his arm around Tehre's shoulders and said to Kairaithin, "We'll all go."

The griffin mage did not argue; he did not, Tehre supposed, much care whether a couple of human folk trailed after him or not. Probably he was sure there was nothing they could do to interfere with the griffins' plans; probably he was right. But she knew she had to go if she could. Though she did not know exactly why Lord Bertaud felt *he* had to go into danger and terror in the north, when Casmantium wasn't even his country. But she wasn't going to argue. She put her hand over his where he gripped her shoulder, lest he try at the last moment to leave her behind.

Before them, Kairaithin stretched out, expanding, his shadow seemed somehow to close around him and then open violently outward. Great black wings narrowly barred with ember red stretched and opened; black feathers ran down from his fierce eagle's head and neck, ruffled like a mane around his shoulders and chest, and melded to a powerfully muscled lion rear. His eyes were the same: black and pitiless.

Tehre had seen illustrations of griffins, of course she had, but the sheer ferocious power that radiated from the griffin mage was nothing she had ever imagined. She tried, quite involuntarily, to back away; only Lord Bertaud's arm stopped her. She realized she had stopped breathing; it was a surprising shock to start again. She did not look at Lord Bertaud; she could not look away from the griffin.

Then the black wings came down, and either the red barring across the feathers caught light from the glowing embers of the fires or else flames actually flickered to life amid those feathers—Tehre couldn't tell which—and the griffin lunged forward and up. The wind from the downbeat of his great wings struck across them, furnace hot and dry, and Tehre, staggering, realized they were now standing within a night that was utterly different from the gentler night they had left behind.

The stars overhead were diamond bright and hard, very different from the delicate flickering stars of the country of earth. The lay of the land here was much steeper than the farmland between Dachsichten and Breidechboden, tall mountains rearing hard against sky, visible by the stars they blocked from sight. Sand shifted dangerously underfoot, heat rising from it almost as though they stood on banked coals. They did, in a way, Tehre understood suddenly: She could feel, with her maker's sense of materials, the slow shifting heave of molten rock below the sand—not so far below.

A wind netted with fire came down upon them, so that she cried out, brushing futilely at sparks that came down across her hair and shoulders. Lord Bertaud patted out tiny smoldering fires on her back and in her hair, and Tehre quickly did the same for him, standing on her toes to brush urgently at a small blaze eating its way across his shoulder toward his neck.

Then a different wind rose, utterly foreign to this burning country, stinging with ice, and all the fire above and below them died.

Somewhere close at hand, a griffin shrieked like a hunting falcon. Tehre flinched and stared toward the sound. She could not find the griffin that had cried out above them, but for the first time she realized she *could* see, a little. Not by the light of the stars, though each seemed to shed a tiny trace of heat and light, but by a burning glow that seemed to emanate from the griffins that slipped past high overhead and from the wind that they rode, and by the cold light that flung itself out in defiance from a nearby hillside. The source of that light was Beguchren Teshrichten, of course, who shone with silvery radiance. Near the cold mage crouched another, much larger man: Gereint, Tehre assumed. Above them, between them and the high, deadly forms of the soaring griffins, soared the dark shape of Kairaithin; the fiery wind from his wings met Beguchren's cold wind and matched it, and drove it back toward the mage.

And below them, far down the hill, below Tehre and Lord Bertaud, was clustered a small number of soldiers in leather and bits of mail, bright spear points rising above them, griffins spiraling through the air above them like so many falcons circling above mice, waiting only for Kairaithin's strength to overmatch Beguchren's before they came down to kill as they chose.

"He'll hold them," Tehre said, to herself more than to Lord Bertaud; she only realized she'd spoken aloud when she heard her own voice, fragile in the vastness of the desert.

"I don't think so," the foreigner answered grimly. He took a step up the hill, toward the cold mage, then hesitated and looked instead down the slope toward the threatened company.

"No, this way," Tehre said. She caught his hand and tugged him uphill. When he still hesitated, she added urgently, "If Beguchren falls, everyone will fall! Everything turns on him: If we can help him, that's where we should be!"

This was logical and obvious, and Lord Bertaud yielded. They ran up the hill together, hand-in-hand like lovers, steadying each other when the fire-laced desert wind gusted down upon them from one direction or the ice-laden cold wind came battering from the other. Neither Kairaithin nor Beguchren seemed to notice them, either to help or hinder. They struggled at last to Beguchren's position. The cold mage still did not notice them, and Lord Bertaud hesitated, staring first at the mage and then upward toward the dark griffin he fought.

Tehre, crouching low to keep her balance under the violent winds, went instead to Gereint. She had known it had to be him, here on this hillside with Beguchren Teshrichten. Who else would it be? And it was. But he seemed barely conscious. He was not injured. When she looked as a maker, Tehre could find no weak or broken place in the structure of his body. But he seemed dazed with horror or exhaustion. He was kneeling, sitting back on his heels, his head bowed and his hands pressed over his eyes as though in denial of the desert and the fiery wind and the griffins and everything to do with any of them. That didn't seem like him at all. She patted his shoulder and then his face, but though he lowered his hands, he did not seem to recognize her. Indeed, there was barely even a flicker of awareness in his eyes. And he moved as though he had to shift the weight of the world to move even a finger.

Baffled, Tehre twisted about and tucked herself down on the ground beside him, watching Beguchren instead. The king's mage was battling Kairaithin, that was obvious. The griffin mage had come down to the desert and now stood facing Beguchren, his massive wings half spread amid blowing sand and leaping flames. Hardly anything farther away than the griffin mage remained visible: Though she tried to see the company of men, the night and the desert wind hid them from view.

Kairaithin lifted a feathered forelimb as though to stride forward, but then he replaced his taloned foot in precisely the same location from which he'd lifted it. Tehre thought the griffin mage had tried to move toward them and that Beguchren had stopped him. The cold mage was leaning slightly forward, frowning, his face masklike in the strange light, his eyes opaque and white as the ice of a deep northern winter. He was holding Kairaithin back; that, too, was obvious.

But Tehre saw several less obvious things as well. She saw that, though Beguchren was battling the griffin mage, his attention was really elsewhere. His strange icy eyes hardly turned toward the griffin; he was searching instead through the roiling, dust-laden sky for something else. Or someone else. A different griffin? Tehre guessed. Another griffin mage? Or something else?

And Lord Bertaud also seemed distracted or worried—well, anybody would be *worried*, yes, but in fact anybody would be terrified, and he did not seem terrified at all. He was not crouching under the violence of the winds, as she was. He was standing, his hands at his sides, his head back, watching Kairaithin. Sometimes he stared up at another griffin as it passed more closely than usual, flashing into view and then disappearing again into the fiery winds; the only time Tehre saw him flinch was at the swift approach of a gleaming white griffin, so pure a white that it might have been carved out of alabaster and then brought to burning life. It slashed all along the hillside, so low the long feathers of its wing tips might have brushed the sand if it had stroked downward. But its wings tilted before it touched the sand, and it angled sharply up and away—actually, feathers must be made of a peculiarly strong and flexible material or they would surely break against the force of the air when any feathered creature turned like that—

Tehre was recalled to the moment as pillars of twisted rock forced their way abruptly through the sand behind Kairaithin, and to either side; the desert trembled and rumbled as the stone tore its way free from the sand and out into the violent wind, which shrieked and moaned as it was cut by the sharp edges of the rock. She could feel the grinding movement of those contorted pillars where she sat—no, she realized: She could feel the movement of the pillars that were rising behind them. The griffin mage was building a circle of twisted pillars to enclose them all. That could not be good. She stared at Gereint for an instant; he seemed no better. Beguchren did not seem able to keep Kairaithin from making the pillars. Tehre got unsteadily to her feet and made her way over to Bertaud's side, catching his arm to steady herself as the ground shook again.

"Do you understand this?" she asked him when he glanced distractedly down at her. She had to half shout to be heard over the battling winds and grinding stone. "You—in Feierabiand—did you—did they—"

The foreigner put an arm around her to steady her as the ground shuddered. He shook his head. "Nothing like this happened in Feierabiand! Not that I saw! Kairaithin killed a lot of cold mages, he said, but I didn't see it!"

"Beguchren was always the strongest of our cold mages!" Tehre peered through the veiling sand and dust that obscured the desert. "I don't understand what he's doing—I don't understand what he did to Gereint—it looks like he's battling Kairaithin, but I'd take oath half his attention's on something else, only I don't know what!"

"He's searching for Kes," Bertaud said, grimly, but almost too low for her to make out his words. "He's searching for Kes!" he repeated, when she shook her head. "A girl—one of ours—he made her into a fire mage, a fire-healer; she's why the griffins don't have to fear ten thousand soldiers—if your king had sent so many, and I saw only a few hundred down there, I think!"

The griffins had made a human girl into a fire mage? Tehre stared at Bertaud, but he seemed perfectly serious.

The desert cracked open at their feet, knife-edged stone ripping free of the sand to slice the dust-laden wind into shrieking ribbons; both Tehre and Lord Bertaud staggered backward. Tehre would have fallen except Bertaud caught her, and then he slipped and might have fallen himself except she braced her whole strength to support him, and with one accord they flung themselves, stumbling, toward Beguchren. They knelt down there in the relative calm behind the cold mage, beside Gereint, where the ground was steadier and where they might be protected from the worst of the violent winds. The mage did not pay them any heed—neither, more disturbingly, did Gereint.

She asked Bertaud, "He made her into a fire mage? A human girl? He made a creature of earth into a creature of fire? Didn't it hurt her terribly? Didn't she *mind*?"

Bertaud, hunkering down to one knee between Tehre and the scattered sparks that came down the wind, shook his head. "Not after it was done, I believe. You have to understand . . . once you're a creature of fire, once you understand fire and take it into your heart, the country of fire is very beautiful."

She supposed that might even be true, though at the moment the desert seemed anything but beautiful—fierce, worse than fierce—savage, even murderous. But if you were a creature of fire, she supposed it might seem different.

"Your Beguchren is trying to find Kes, I think," Bertaud said, while Tehre was still trying to understand how a human woman might be made into a creature of fire. "He wants to kill her, I suppose! He might want to kill Kairaithin, but that isn't important—but it would change everything, if the griffins didn't have Kes—if they didn't have her, I expect your king would send ten thousand soldiers to destroy them all—he'd want to destroy the country of fire entirely and reclaim not only Melentser for his own, but all the northern desert—he's ambitious, is the Arobern—"

Tehre supposed this was true. At the moment, destroying all the griffins and reclaiming this burning desert for earth seemed a fine idea to her, but Lord Bertaud sounded terribly grim. His face had gone tight and hard, and the expression in his eyes was bleak. He said something else, too low for Tehre to understand. Then he glanced at her and said more clearly, "Everything depends on your Beguchren's strength, and Kairaithin's—Kairaithin told me once that in the desert, he was stronger than Beguchren—"

"Oh," Tehre said, surprised. Pieces of a puzzle she'd barely glimpsed in outline fell suddenly into place. She said with conviction, "Beguchren's made Gereint into a mage, and now he's using Gereint's strength to support his own. Gereint would have had plenty of strength to give, I expect—"

Bertaud was shaking his head. "Wait, wait, he did what?"

"As Kairaithin made your Feierabianden girl into a fire mage," Tehre said patiently, surprised he hadn't grasped this at once. "It's not quite the same thing—in fact, it should be much easier. I wonder if it takes a maker who's already got a little magecraft woven through his gift? Or if any maker can be made into a mage? I wonder if *I* . . ." She stopped. It was a disquieting idea.

Another griffin came slanting out of the fire-streaked wind and landed neatly on the sand by Kairaithin, and another after that. The first was large, not as massive as Kairaithin, but heavy and muscular: a powerful griffin with golden eyes and bronze feathers; the feathers of his wings were bronze streaked with copper and gold and his lion rear a dark bronze gold. The second, smaller, griffin was a rich gold-stippled brown.

On the back of the smaller griffin perched a human girl, only even without Bertaud's explanation, Tehre would never have mistaken her for anything human. She was fine boned, small, pretty—but she looked even less human than Kairaithin had when he'd taken human form. She seemed spun out of white gold and fire; her eyes were filled with fire; bright little tongues of fire flickered in her pale hair and ran down her bare arms. She was smiling, a dangerous expression that was also somehow joyous. She slipped down from the brown griffin's back to stand between it and Kairaithin, but she left a hand buried in the feathers of its neck.

Beguchren, frowning, took one step forward. Ice rimed his white eyes and his hands; ice glittered on the sand where he'd set his feet and sparkled in the air around him; near him, the dark of the desert night was lit by a pearly light that sparkled with frost. He took another step.

Kairaithin folded his heavy black wings, a gesture that somehow seemed contemptuous, and tilted his head downward so that his savage beak pointed at the burning sand under his feet. The other griffins swayed forward, their wings still half spread; the bronze one snaked its head out low and hissed. Kes tossed her head, dropped her hand away from the brown griffin's neck, and stood straight, smiling.

Behind them and to either side, a net of fire spun itself between one stone pillar and the next, and the next, and the next after that: a tight-woven web of fire wound itself around the griffin mages and Beguchren, and around Tehre and Bertaud where they knelt beside Gereint. All around the circle flames sprang up, burning tall and smokeless, white and gold and blood crimson, columns and sheets of fire that towered straight up toward the sky in a sudden, shocking absence of wind.

Beguchren took one more step forward, and a broad, nebulous bolt of mist and frost speared out toward—not Kairaithin, Bertaud had been right—toward Kes.

The girl did not move. But she did not need to. The attack never touched her. Fire rose up and swallowed the cold mist and absorbed it, and then burned higher, reaching out to engulf Kes entirely. Any normal human girl would have burned alive in that fire. Kes stood amid the flames, her smile never faltering, her body blurring into fire and then reshaping itself out of fire once more.

"They're all mages," Bertaud said quietly, to himself as much as to Tehre. "Kairaithin's brought some of his young students into their power—including Kes. I don't think your Beguchren can match them, however much power he's taken from your friend."

Tehre shook her head, wanting to deny this, but actually she thought he was right. The frost surrounding Beguchren had closed in around him, and she doubted the mage was contracting his power of his own accord. His face was taut and strained. He bowed his head and lifted his hands, but the spear of ice he shaped out of his need flung it-self only halfway toward the human fire mage before the fierce heat of the surrounding fire trapped it and it dissolved back into the air.

Beguchren made a low sound, lifting his head again. In his frost-white eyes was frustration and anger and the terrible knowledge of failure, and Tehre found herself holding her breath in sympathy—she leaped to her feet and ran to him, in her mind a confused idea of telling him to make her into a mage, to use her power, she was ready to argue, *I have more strength than you'd think. Use it. Use me.* But the thought came too late and she had no chance to make the offer: Even as she reached Beguchren, his eyes rolled back and he folded slowly to his knees and then to the sand. She caught him, went down with him, sup-ported his head on her knee, setting her hand against his face as she tried to determine whether he'd actually died or only collapsed—he was cold, cold as ice to the touch, but she found a weak pulse beating against the fine skin of his throat.

But she already knew it didn't matter: If the mage still lived, he wouldn't for long. She could feel the ferocity of the surrounding desert without even looking up.

Then she looked up.

The fire woven between the stones had begun to die—or, not die, but ebb slowly back into the sand and the wind. The stone pillars stood like plinths of hot emptiness against the sky; far above, an unseen griffin cried out, a high, wild shriek, fierce and exultant. The sound sent icy prickles down Tehre's spine. Kairaithin and his companions, lit by their own fire, were still visible, and that was worse than the unseen griffins in the air above.

Kes was laughing, delight in her eyes, in her face. She said to Kairaithin in a light, fierce voice that was nothing like the voice of a human woman, "This was a night for victory and the living fire!"

And we shall finish the victory, lest we dishonor the night that has given it to us, agreed the griffin mage, his voice slicing not quite painfully around the edges of Tehre's mind.

Kes shook off fire as an ordinary woman might shake drops of water off her hands. Then she flung herself onto the back of the brown griffin, which dipped its wings to make room for her to mount. The griffin was laughing too, not aloud, but joy blazed from every line of its slender body. It hurled itself aloft, the girl bending low over its neck, and the fiery wind blazed around them both, the darkness opening to let them through.

The bronze griffin said to Kairaithin, its voice terrifyingly eager, *Shall we end this?* It swayed forward a step, its wings flaring, the rising wind hissing through the feathers with a deadly sound. Tehre thought it might simply bite Beguchren's head off and she crouched defensively down over the mage. Though probably that would simply prompt the griffin to bite *her* head off instead . . .

"No," said Lord Bertaud. He stood up, walked quietly to stand beside Tehre, dropped a hand to touch her shoulder. But he did not look at her. He was looking only at Kairaithin. He said flatly, as though he really thought the griffin would care what he said, "It's not acceptable to Feierabiand that Casmantium be destroyed."

Is it acceptable to you that the country of fire be destroyed? asked the griffin mage, his voice terrible with contained anger. *Is it acceptable to you that the People of Fire and Air be destroyed?*

"No," said Bertaud. "Find another way."

Kairaithin's wings flared; he flung his head up, his terrible beak snapping shut with a horrifying, deadly sound. *If there is no other way?*

"There must be," Lord Bertaud insisted, but to Tehre he looked grim and ill, as though he thought maybe there was not.

The griffin mage caught fire from the wind, drew fire from the sand, sent fire running in a thin loop around the circle of pillars. He was going to kill them all, Tehre thought; whatever alliance existed between the griffins and Feierabiand, he was going to burn them all to ash, she and Lord Bertaud and Gereint, and below them all those men with their useless spears, and then the griffins were going to ruin the rivers on which all of southern Casmantium depended and laugh as the country of earth withered . . . She said, "No," and stood up, lowering Beguchren gently to the sand. Everyone was staring at her, but she barely noticed. All her attention was on Gereint, who was unchanged, tucked down against the sand, not quite unconscious, but certainly not aware. Alone of them all, he had noticed neither battle nor defeat and was now innocent of their imminent death.

His strength had been taken by Beguchren. But he hadn't been injured. He was only weak. If he regained his strength, he'd be a mage, probably. Untrained, of course. That hadn't mattered to Beguchren. The king's mage might even have found it an advantage. It wouldn't be an advantage now. But still . . . Tehre knelt beside Gereint, laid a hand on his shoulder, and spun off some of her own strength, feeding it to him as a healer might support an injured man. She'd watched her mother do this, and although she'd never done it before herself, it seemed easy enough. She had told Beguchren the truth: She was stronger than she looked; she could draw strength from her gift, plenty to spare.

Under her hand, Gereint's shoulder tensed. His head came up. Awareness came into his eyes. He looked first up into her face. He was pleased to see her: that, first. Then surprised. Then frightened, as memory and thought came back to him. He looked past her, then to Lord Bertaud, whom he did not know. He dismissed him, looked farther. Saw Beguchren, lying abandoned and insensible on the sand. The fear was replaced by anger, and then, as he turned his attention instead toward Kairaithin and the other griffin, by grim revulsion. Tehre stared at him. She had understood the surprise, the fear, the anger. But the depth of loathing she saw in Gereint's eyes astonished her. Or, no. Hadn't somebody . . . probably Andreikan Warichteier . . . said something about a violent antipathy between mages of earth and mages of fire? And Gereint was a mage now.

Not taking his eyes off of Kairaithin, he got to his feet, and Tehre jumped up and backed away, suddenly not certain whom, or what, she'd woken from an exhausted stupor and brought back into the desert night.

CHAPTER 14

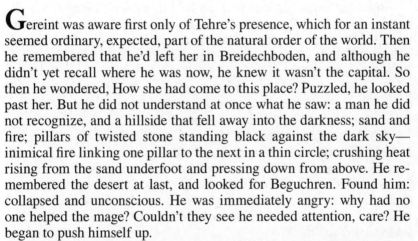

Gereint was aware first only of Tehre's presence, which for an instant seemed ordinary, expected, part of the natural order of the world. Then he remembered that he'd left her in Breidechboden, and although he didn't yet recall where he was now, he knew it wasn't the capital. So then he wondered, How she had come to this place? Puzzled, he looked past her. But he did not understand at once what he saw: a man he did not recognize, and a hillside that fell away into the darkness; sand and fire; pillars of twisted stone standing black against the dark sky—inimical fire linking one pillar to the next in a thin circle; crushing heat rising from the sand underfoot and pressing down from above. He remembered the desert at last, and looked for Beguchren. Found him: collapsed and unconscious. He was immediately angry: why had no one helped the mage? Couldn't they see he needed attention, care? He began to push himself up.

Then he finally saw the griffins, and the anger he'd felt on Beguchren's behalf flared into a cold white fury laced with loathing. Memory crashed back with an almost physical shock, and he found himself on his feet, glaring toward the creatures, outraged by their very existence. If he'd known how to attack them, he would have done it then. Though, an instant later, it occurred to him that Beguchren *had* known how to fight them and *he* was lying helpless on the sand. And if the king's own mage had been defeated, what chance did an ignorant, untrained new-made mage have in any battle? He hesitated, caught between furious antipathy and an awareness of his own helplessness.

Then Tehre caught his hand.

Startled out of his anger, Gereint stared down at her. She was tiny, covered with red dust, her hair singed and her hands blistered from the fire that scattered from the wind. Her mouth was set in determination, her eyes snapping with forceful thought. She did not seem frightened at all. She looked exactly as she always did when absorbed by a difficult problem: intense and absorbed and distracted. She said quickly, "Either the griffins will destroy Casmantium, or we'll destroy them, and we don't have the strength to stop them, but there's another way, there really is—as long as you'll help me, are you a maker at all, anymore?"

"I—" began Gereint. He meant to say, *I'm a stranger to myself. I don't know what I am.* Only Tehre did not wait for him to say anything at all.

She put her other hand on Gereint's arm, whether to steady herself or to somehow balance her gift against his unskilled mage power or to take back some of the strength she'd given him or even to give him more of her strength; he couldn't tell.

But what happened was nothing he'd thought of. Instead, the pillars nearest at hand shattered. Shards of knife-edged stone whirled into the night. Then the farther pillars broke, and the ones after that, all around the circle. Tiny fragments flew like arrows, large pieces fell to the sand with massive, dull impacts. The fire between them died; the griffins were gone—no, the smaller one was gone; the massive black one had merely shifted back a short way. It called up a fiery wind; the desert trembled; stone shifted underfoot.

"I'll break the desert itself," Tehre warned breathlessly. "I'll make a crack right across this hillside, a crack that goes down so far the molten fire under the sand drains down into the darkness under the mountains. I can do it. I can do it, so back away! Get your people away! Gereint, the mountains, I can feel them looming over there, all that stone; raw stone is just waiting to be shaped into masonry, don't the stonecarvers say that?"

That was all the warning she gave him before she broke the mountains.

It should have been impossible. It was certainly a feat beyond any maker Gereint had ever heard of, yet completely unrelated to anything he could imagine doing with magecraft. But Tehre had certainly done it *somehow*. Though the mountains were far away and invisible in the darkness, he heard them go: the three on the right and the two on the left, and maybe others more distant still; a heavy grinding roar so immense it went beyond any measurement of sound and became a physical presence in the night. It went on and on, fathomless: a huge booming roar of stone falling, pounding against more stone, grinding inexorably downhill.

"Help me make a wall," Tehre ordered breathlessly, standing on her toes to shout into Gereint's ear. "They're falling, but they're not falling *right*, I can tell, the pieces are scattering all down the hillsides, they need to be a *wall*—"

No, it wasn't a wall she had made, not yet. It was an avalanche, and it was huge. Gereint tried to use his maker's sense of materials to track what Tehre had done, but he couldn't. He reached after his gift for making, after the familiar awareness of materials that waited to be shaped, but that awareness was gone; there was nothing left. The loss was like the loss of a hand, of his eyes, but in place of the maker's awareness was something else, a more direct awareness of power and force and strength, an awareness of movement and the chance that something would go one way and not another.

Not just the near mountains, Gereint thought. Tehre had pulled down half the mountain range, by the sound and the feel of it. She had broken free the granite at the heart of the mountains and called the stone down from the heights toward the dry track of the great river— toward them all. He shouted back to Tehre, over the roar of approaching stone, "You should have *warned* me—"

"How long do you think I should have waited?" Tehre had closed her eyes, letting her maker's awareness guide her. She said urgently, her eyes still closed, "I can break the pieces into blocks as they come, but I can't get the blocks to fall where they need to go. There're too many and they're too heavy and coming too fast—"

Everything was *too heavy and coming too fast*. Gereint shut his eyes and tried to think about being a pivot in the world, a point of focus where forces balanced. It was surprisingly easy to think of himself that way. He could *feel* the grounded power of the hundreds of men below the hill, surprisingly steady, like springs of water welling up through the sand. He could feel the deep strength of earth and stone, behind or beyond the quick, foreign balance of fire; it underlay the new desert and rose, he thought, somehow *through* the men.

And beyond desert and fire and men and earth, he perceived the rushing stone and earth of the avalanche. He felt the shattered, thundering stone as a gathering rush of power—not a maker's sense at all, not something he could touch or hold, not something that spoke to him of potential shape and form, but *something*.

Something suddenly caught up all the strength of earth Gereint could perceive, power right at the edge of his perception, stripped that power out of the men who had dared the desert, and through them pulled strength right out of the earth beneath the fiery sands and set it loose in an unfocused whirlwind.

Gereint, stunned, nevertheless caught up the freed power and bent its path. He let it slam through the world not as it wished to run, a wild and uncontrolled outflow across all the hills, but channeled into a narrow strip—was dimly aware of another focal point in the world that balanced against his, that supported him—the avalanche tore its way through the desert sand and piled itself up all along the western shore of the dry river, stretching north to south and then bending away to the west in a wide strip of . . . blocks, he realized at last. Not raw stone mixed with gravel and dirt and desert sand, but huge rough-edged granite blocks that Tehre had shaped out of the mountains, without chisel or mallet or the thousand years of labor it should have taken her. He opened his eyes, looking for her.

Tehre was sitting now at his feet, near the limp shape of Beguchren. She had one hand on the fallen mage's shoulder, but her head was bowed over her drawn-up knees and her eyes were closed. She was not looking at Beguchren, Gereint knew. She was watching the cracking stone with her inward maker's eyes, encouraging it to break along the lines she wanted, with something greater than the skill of any ordinary builder or engineer. Coaxing the blocks to fall into position even far to the west, supported by the enormous power Gereint had caught and made, in turn, available for her.

Gereint glanced over at the stranger, who was standing, oddly, beside the black griffin mage. Down by the dry river, he could dimly make out Amnachudran's company—not with his eyes, he realized eventually, but with some new strange sense. He thought the men still lived . . . He was not certain. The griffins had not destroyed them. The dimness was a function of what he had done himself, was still doing. He thought they had not died when magecraft had suddenly seized on their strength and through them on the strength of the earth. But he was not certain.

The griffins were gone out of the wind, out of sight . . . He was aware of them, a tug against his attention, flame-edged monsters with no proper shape, pulling the natural strength of earth in thoroughly unnatural directions . . . but high, distant, not at the moment dangerous. Save for the griffin mage. He stared that way, torn, hesitating to go down toward the wall Tehre was building because he did not want to have the griffin at his back, knowing he did not have the skill or experience to do proper battle—

"Go on," shouted the stranger over the gradually lessening crash and rumble and roar of the avalanche. "Go! Kairaithin won't fight you!" His Prechen was fluent, not exactly accented, but with a foreign touch to it: He was Feierabianden, Gereint realized, and guessed that he might actually be able to speak for the griffin—and he had come with Tehre, and she had not seemed to think of him as an enemy. And now he said the griffin mage would not fight? If he had the strength and training and the *time* to fight the griffin, Gereint would never have trusted that assurance. But he could feel the wall still crashing into place far to the west, and there was no time.

He took a step down toward the riverbed, paused impatiently, and moved himself through a fold of space to stand beside the great wall. Above him and all along the wall, he could feel blocks break free, roll and crash down from the stony heights, pirouette, and slam into their proper positions. That was Tehre's task.

But a deep steady vein of magecraft ran through him now, and he had a task of his own. He laid his hand against the rough face of the wall and made it heavily itself, made the block of stone more thoroughly stone, anchored it solidly to the rock that underlay the new desert and to the blocks that surrounded it. There was no moisture in the air. But the griffins' desert was too new to have burned the memory of water out of the land. The river at his back, dry as it was, remembered water, remembered the rushing, unpredictable force of the spring flood and the slow, deep, easy wash of the summer. He let that memory bend around him, flow from memory into the moment, laid the memory of water and ice into the stone under his hands and between that block and the next and the next. He turned, trailing the tips of his fingers across the stone, walked slowly upriver, setting the memory of living water and the solidity of the earth deeply into the wall as he walked.

He did not know how long he walked. He was not only walking but letting himself blur through distance, moving higher and higher into the mountains, the dry Teschanken to his right and the wall to his left. He became aware, gradually, of a presence paralleling his path on the other side of the wall. It was a fiery presence, powerful . . . It laid fire and the memory of fire into the wall on its other side. Gereint's first impulse was to fight that foreign magecrafting, but . . . the memory and training of a maker could not help but understand the balance and symmetry implicit in that working. Earth and water on this side of the wall, fire on that; it would be, he thought, a wall that would forever lock the country of fire away from the country of earth.

At least so far as the wall reached. He wondered how far it ran, how many mountains Tehre had shattered, how many blocks she had coaxed into shape and position . . . *That* was not any simple gift. No. *I'm something of a maker, a builder, an engineer, a scholar*, she had said. She had not said, *And something of a mage*. But Beguchren had wanted Gereint because he'd seen a streak of hidden magecraft in his gift; Gereint understood that now, because he had seen the same touch of magecraft in Tehre, only clearer and stronger, he suspected, than his had ever been while he was a maker.

The wall trailed off at last, high in the mountains. The blocks here were smaller and narrower, and then smaller still, until there was only ordinary unshaped stone underfoot and the clear sky of afternoon overhead, and nothing to balance and anchor and layer with memories of earth and water and ice . . . Gereint pulled his awareness slowly out of the stone. It took him a moment to remember his own shape, to remember he was not granite. Then he found he stood by the shore of a lake so immense that he could not see the other side. Curious, he tried to span the lake with his new awareness of space and movement . . . Even then, he could not find its opposite shore, only mist and glittering frost that reached from the surface of the water to the clouds above. The wall held any touch of fire back from it and from the rivers it fed, and at his right hand the Teschanken poured in an icy cataract down from the infinite bowl of the lake and away toward the country of men.

"This is not a place for the People of Fire," said a hard, austere, weary voice, enunciating clearly to cut over the noise from the river. The griffin mage came around the low end of the wall to stand on the shore of the lake. He wore the shape of a man. But Gereint would never have mistaken him, even for an instant, for a man. He was horrified the creature should have come here, to this place, where the magic of earth and water lay so close to the ordinary world that one might almost waver between them. It was a terrible place for a creature of fire.

He shifted back a wary step, groping after magecraft, after memories of ice.

"Be still, man. Peace," said the griffin. His tone, though weary, was also sardonic and edged with dislike. "You do not wish to do battle against me, even here in this place of water and earth."

This was true. Gereint could feel the appalling force of the griffin mage flaring barely out of sight behind the shape he wore. The griffin *felt* old: ageless in the same way that Beguchren had seemed ageless. Gereint did not doubt the depth of the griffin's skill, or his strength. He most definitely did not want to fight him. He knew he would lose. He said nothing.

"The Safiad's man, the representative of Feierabiand . . . he argued the wisdom of sealing this wall from both directions," the griffin said. "I agreed, and reached after a new wind, and called it down from the heights. The great wind that shatters stone . . . Your little maker has surprising strength. You lent a great deal to the effort. But not enough to build a wall along all the border between our two countries."

Gereint groped after coherence. "You . . . helped her? *You* helped us?" It seemed too ridiculous a suggestion even to put into words.

"I helped you," agreed the griffin, drily mocking. "Were you not aware? To build the wall, and then to seal the wall from our side as you did from yours. Walls are not a thing of my people. But this one . . . this one may serve us. Perhaps the man of Feierabiand had the right of it. A wall may serve better than war. I am told that Feierabiand would turn against the people of fire, raise up its mages and arm its soldiers with cold metal and ice, did we bring Casmantium to ruin. I am told that even Linularinum would enter the war that would result."

This was a new thought, but, "It would," Gereint answered the griffin mage's sardonic tone. "I hadn't thought . . . but of course it would. Feierabiand would have to renounce its alliance with your people, and Linularinum would have to support Feierabiand. We all . . ." He did not quite know how to phrase the thought.

"Belong to the country of earth; just so," agreed the griffin. "And we do not. A truth my people had perhaps not sufficiently considered. Thus, I decided it would be best to ride this new wind all the way to its end. Especially as I saw no other alternative." He turned, gestured back along the long endless structure of the wall. "This remains unsealed along half its length." He considered briefly and then added, harshly amused, "More than half."

Gereint didn't answer. He had a strong feeling that the griffin was concealing something, or at least failing to mention something important. That the reason the griffin mage had chosen to set his strength alongside Gereint's on the far side of the wall . . . was complex and dangerous and either inexplicable in human terms or else something the creature had no intention of explaining. But he could also see that the griffin was right about the wall: It was unfinished. The task needed to be seen through all the way to the end. And for whatever reason, the griffin meant to complete it. But he was appalled by the idea of doing over again the labor they had just completed.

"Though, if you lack the strength—" the griffin mage began, his tone edged with contempt.

Shaken by loathing, Gereint said sharply, "I'll manage my side. See you do the same!" And he flung himself away from the lake, with its mysterious shores hidden by its shifting mists, and back through a fold in the world, to the place where he had started the work of sealing the wall. It was easy: as easy and natural as making had once been for him; a step and the world tilted and swung around him, and another step and he stood again by the river, below the hillside where Beguchren had challenged the griffins. The hills were empty now. Neither men nor griffins remained. But water ran clear and sweet in its rugged channel, finding its way around the odd, twisted red cliff that had blocked its old path. Delicate green shoots were already poking up along the river's new channel, from good earth only lightly disguised by a thin covering of red sand.

Now, in daylight, Gereint could see the broken mountains. Some of the broken mountains. He could see where the three closest mountains had stood. The earth was nearly level there now, the broken and torn ground between the more distant mountains and the wall showing where the avalanche of stone had come down. Gercint shook his head, looking at the miles-wide trail of devastation that marked the path of the avalanche through the stark emptiness of the desert. If there had been forest or pasture left there, the avalanche would have destroyed it as certainly as the desert had done. And if he had looked over the wall, he knew he would find similar destruction. How many mountains must be leveled to build a hundred miles of wall? Two hundred miles? All the closest mountains, he concluded, and probably some of the more distant mountains had been hauled down as well . . . Tehre would never have had the strength to do this, not even with the power he had found for her. More than ever, Gereint was aware that he did not want to fight the griffin mage. He was unwillingly, bitterly, grateful to the Feierabianden lord for persuading the griffin to throw his immense strength behind Tehre's effort, and now behind his own.

He knew the griffin was there now. On the other side of the wall. Waiting. He could almost feel the creature's fierce, patient scorn. *If you lack the strength* . . . Gereint set his teeth and turned back to the wall.

CHAPTER 15

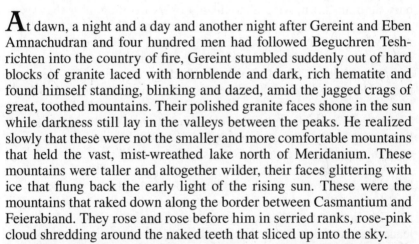

At dawn, a night and a day and another night after Gereint and Eben Amnachudran and four hundred men had followed Beguchren Teshrichten into the country of fire, Gereint stumbled suddenly out of hard blocks of granite laced with hornblende and dark, rich hematite and found himself standing, blinking and dazed, amid the jagged crags of great, toothed mountains. Their polished granite faces shone in the sun while darkness still lay in the valleys between the peaks. He realized slowly that these were not the smaller and more comfortable mountains that held the vast, mist-wreathed lake north of Meridanium. These mountains were taller and altogether wilder, their faces glittering with ice that flung back the early light of the rising sun. These were the mountains that raked down along the border between Casmantium and Feierabiand. They rose and rose before him in serried ranks, rose-pink cloud shredding around the naked teeth that sliced up into the sky.

Behind him, he knew without turning, ran a hundred miles of wall. Two hundred miles. More, maybe. Blocks of stone a spear-cast wide and three high wound along a path all across northern Casmantium. On the far side lived fire and the hot wind, the merciless sun and burning sands . . . The griffin mage was there, opposite Gereint, a fierce presence that blazed and flickered with fire. But, though Gereint tried to gather the remnants of his strength to meet the challenge he half expected, the griffin did not intrude into the country of earth.

On this side, the mountain was glazed with ice. Mist condensed in the cold that radiated from the wall, curling in wisps and streamers along the powerful earth. The ice and the heavy earth denied fire, resisted any incursion of fire. But, though any ordinary griffin might be

held by the wall, Gereint suspected it would not stop the griffin mage if
he bent his strength against it. Though surely this dawn had found the
griffin as exhausted and worn as Gereint . . .

Perhaps it did, for suddenly Gereint could tell that the griffin mage
was gone. Away into the brilliant inimical desert, to rest amid the red
sands and burning winds—he was welcome to them. Gereint longed
for his own place of rest and silence. He rested his hands on the frozen
wall, bowed his head, stretched his awareness wearily back along the
long, long span of stone, and let the world fold itself around him. And
found himself standing, for the third time, in the courtyard outside
Eben Amnachudran's house, surrounded by the scents of cut hay and
horses, apples, and, somewhere close at hand, warm bread fresh from
the oven. The familiar, homey scents, the ordinary bustle of men and
women about their ordinary business, the natural warmth of an ordinary autumn dawn, were all suddenly overwhelming after the desert
and the griffin and the wall. Gereint folded up his knees and sat down
right where he stood, on the very doorstep of Amnachudran's house,
lacking even the strength to look for the fragrant bread.

Amnachudran found him there. He did not speak: only Gereint's
name. He put a hand under Gereint's elbow, urged him wordlessly to
his feet, and brought him to a room paneled in pine and oak. Lady
Emre, her face shadowed with worry, brought him bread dripping with
butter and honey. Gereint ate three bites of the bread and then found
enough strength and awareness to ask, "Tehre?"

Amnachudran and his wife exchanged a glance. "She's fine. She's
here," Lady Emre assured him. "She'll be glad to know you are—you
are here. Shall I send for her?"

Gereint shook his head. "Later." He set the bread down on its plate,
leaned his head against the back of the chair, and was instantly asleep.

He woke early in the morning on the next day, having slept around an
entire day and night. He knew exactly how much time had passed; a deep
awareness of time and place seemed an odd and unexpected offshoot of
magecraft, more welcome than some. And he woke rested, and clear-
headed, altogether a better awakening than his last in this house . . . Eben
Amnachudran sat in a high-armed chair by the room's window, gazing
out at his orchards. His expression was quiet, thoughtful, still touched
with the weariness and strain of the past days. His elbows were propped
on the windowsill and his chin rested on his laced fingers; in one hand
he held a quill pen, its feather brushing his mouth and cheek. On a table
by his elbow rested a large leather-bound book, laid open to a map of
northern Casmantium, with notations in black and red ink fitted into its

margins. Also on the table, of more immediate interest, rested a plate of honey cakes and a platter with tea things.

Gereint cleared his throat. "That's a copy of Berusent, isn't it? You're not getting honey on the pages, I trust?"

Amnachudran swung around, smiling. "Gereint. Good morning! We were beginning to fear you might never wake on your own—I half wanted to try to bring you back to 'this hither shore of dreams' myself, you know, but Emre was adamant that you should be let sleep till you woke. How are you? Can you sit up? Can you hold a cup? The pot's a good one; it keeps tea hot and fresh for hours. I don't know how you usually drink it, but I thought it best to put plenty of honey in this." Rising, he poured steaming tea and brought the cup and the plate of cakes to the bedside table.

Gereint propped himself up against the pillows. He found himself smiling. "I always seem to be waking up in your house . . ."

"After prodigious feats deserving of the very best tea." Amnachudran handed him the cup, watching to be sure he could hold it without spilling the scalding liquid.

Gereint drank the tea all at once, like medicine, and allowed the scholar to take back the cup and pour it full again. The tea was indeed very sweet, much sweeter than he ordinarily took it, but this morning he welcomed the rich sweetness. He ate a cake, licked honey off his fingers, and asked suddenly, "Tehre?"

"Perfectly well. Asking for you. She argued, along with me, that we should try to wake you, but Emre overruled us both, no doubt wisely. She was worried about you. She said you hadn't anything like your ordinary strength to start—and we all could see what you'd done to the wall. Tehre's friend Lord Bertaud insists it runs the *entire* length of the griffins' desert?"

"From the great lake high in the north, along the Teschanken, and then west along the border right to the western mountains. Lord Bertaud? That is the Feierabianden lord?"

"Yes. A very useful sort of friend for Tehre to have made, I gather."

Gereint shuddered at the memory of the griffin mage, but he said, to be fair, "The griffin said the Feierabianden lord persuaded him to seal the wall with fire on his side."

"Yes, so I understand." Amnachudran poured a cup of tea for himself and sipped it slowly. "We are very fortunate Lord Bertaud was sufficiently concerned to insist on coming north. And very fortunate my daughter insisted on accompanying him. I'd never have thought— well, parents are the worst judges of their children's skill, as they say. But among you all, we managed to claim something very like victory.

I'd not have imagined that, watching the griffins ride that burning wind of theirs toward us. But I admit, I didn't believe the wall could run all the way to the western mountains."

"I didn't exactly use my own strength to seal it. I used mine, but also the deep strength of earth." Gereint paused, looked more closely at Amnachudran's face. "And the strength of your men. Isn't that right? Your strength . . . but you seem well enough . . ." He could not quite bring himself to ask the question he wanted to ask.

"Hardly anyone actually died," the scholar answered, not needing to hear the question. "Fortunately, once the desert withdrew, Emre brought nearly everyone remaining in the household to find us and bring us home."

Gereint imagined the lingering death that would otherwise likely have claimed the men whose strength he'd so ruthlessly used. He swallowed.

"What you did was necessary. You saved us all," Amnachudran said gently, watching his face. "You and Tehre. And Beguchren Teshrichten. And even that griffin mage, once the Feierabianden lord persuaded him to help rather than hinder . . ."

"Beguchren tried to explain to me about making earth more . . . I don't know. More itself. The earth holds so much power . . . I could never have done it with only my own strength." Gereint paused, then added, "It's true about the griffin. He used his own strength, but he also channeled the fierce strength of fire. He said he helped Tehre build the wall . . . He helped me seal it." Though it was hard to believe a creature of fire would speak any sort of truth. "Maybe Beguchren—" He paused. Put the cup he held down on the bedside table. Asked, trepidation running through him like ice, "Beguchren?"

Amnachudran hesitated. "Asleep," he said finally. "We think."

The cold mage was asleep. But asleep in a way that worried Gereint enormously. He seemed shrunken among the bedclothes, lost amid the blankets and pillows. He had never been anything but slight, but now the flesh seemed to have melted away from his body. The fine bones of his face stood in stark prominence; his eyes had sunk into shadowed hollows; he was deathly pale. Gereint thought he looked far closer to death than to waking.

Lady Emre sat in a high-backed chair close beside the bed, her hand resting lightly on the blankets close by Beguchren's face. She looked drained and weary, and she had lost a good deal of the comfortable plumpness Gereint remembered. But her smile, as she sprang to her feet and came to greet him, had all of its accustomed, lively warmth. "Gereint!" she exclaimed. "Back among us! You see, I told Eben to let you sleep, and here you are! You look quite wonderful! Though you need feeding up, I can see. You're still far too thin. Eben, you must remember to tell the cook—oh, he's not back yet, that's right. Well, then, let's remember to tell whoever's in the kitchen to make something fortifying for noon."

Gereint smiled back at her and forbore to mention her own strained look. She had not asked anything about the battle or the griffins or the wall, for which he was grateful. He cast an inquiring look at the still figure on the bed.

"Yes, poor man," Lady Emre agreed. She moved back to the bedside and frowned down at the small figure of the mage. "I don't know. I thought he would wake, but as you see, he hasn't."

"Which didn't reassure us about you," put in Amnachudran.

Tehre came in hurriedly, catching herself on the door frame when she stumbled in her haste. "Gereint! I thought I heard your voice." She came to him unselfconsciously and took his hands, tilting her head back to gaze up at his face. "You look good. More at home in your mind and heart than I thought you'd be. I was worried about you. But you've adjusted to the magecraft you enfolded within your self, haven't you? That's splendid. Did you run that ice and mist all the way to the western mountains, then? I told my father there'd be no point to sealing that wall along only half its length."

It was so like her, Gereint thought, to make an instant and correct judgment about him, mention and dismiss it in the same breath, and shift at once to a technical question. He smiled down at her. "I can't believe you broke half a mountain range and built a wall *two hundred miles* long. Do you know, the blocks right up in the western mountains are just as big and well-formed, and just as neatly placed, as the ones over here by the river? I don't see how magecraft could do anything like that, so I guess you're truly a maker and not a mage, but I've also never heard of any feat of building that could even *begin* to touch that wall."

Tehre blushed and looked down, suddenly shy. "Oh, well . . . I'd never have had the strength to run the blocks so far without the power you found for me. And actually I think it might have been Kairaithin who did the last bit, up by the western mountains. I don't think I did that. And maybe Beguchren . . ." She glanced uneasily over at the small, still, pale form tucked into the middle of the bed. "I think maybe he helped. Mages might not be makers, but I think he put his strength into getting the blocks to land right. I think he gave me the strength of the earth. I think . . ." She hesitated, then finished in a rush: "I think that's what happened to him: I think he used himself up by making himself a channel between the deep magic of the earth and me."

Gereint followed her gaze. "Yes. I think that's right. *Someone* pulled the power of earth up through the men, and I don't think it was I . . . I thought I knew why he wanted those men to come with us. Maybe I guessed right, but I didn't guess everything. I would never have thought it was even *possible* to do that."

"It was evidently as hard on him as on any of us," Amnachudran said.

Gereint continued to gaze at the still, small form of the mage. "Oh, yes."

"You recovered," Lady Emre said optimistically. "Perhaps he will, too. All of you collapsed except Tehre." She gave her daughter a proud glance.

"It didn't take *strength* to actually bring down the mountains, you know," Tehre explained modestly. "Just an understanding of how things break." She turned to Gereint. "You know, I figured something out up there when I was helping the mountains break into proper blocks." She leaned forward, her eyes lighting now with enthusiasm, her voice rising as her tone gained intensity. "If you take the force with which a material is pulled under tension, call that the stress to which you subject the material, and how far the material is stretched by that tension, call that the strain, then the ratio of stress to strain gives you a very simple measure of the material's stiffness, do you see?"

"Yes . . ." Gereint thought he might, more or less.

"Well, it turns out that when you run a thin crack through a material, what happens is there's a tremendous increase in the stress right at the tip of the crack because the stress has to go around the crack and it just piles up at the tip. And the finer the crack, the greater the increase, do you see? You can calculate it—it's the stress times a factor, I think the factor must be something like double the square root of the length of the crack divided by the radius of the tip of the crack. If you calculate it like that, you can see right away why a crack through any stiff material would have a critical length and after that length, the crack would run, and *that's* why stiff materials like stone can't take any tension to speak of, do you see?"

"Well, I'll just leave you children alone, then," said Lady Emre, casting her gaze upward. But she was laughing at the same time, though wryly. "I'll go find your Lord Bertaud, Tehre, my dear, and let him know our friend Gereint's awakened. You can find me in the library, probably, in the unlikely event you want me." She dropped a fond kiss on the back of Tehre's neck, patted Gereint's arm, and went out.

Gereint nodded absently, but he was too delighted by Tehre to really notice her mother's departure. "Fascinating," he told Tehre, sincerely.

"And *useful*. I can visualize what you mean, more or less, I think. You figured that out right there, with fire scattering in the wind and wrapping around that circle of pillars? Tehre, you amaze me."

Tehre blushed and glanced down. "Oh, well . . . I ought to have worked it out long before. Only I didn't until I started breaking the pillars . . ."

"So you reached up to the mountains, started tiny cracks in the stone, and then applied tension."

"It took hardly any tension," Tehre said earnestly. "That's the whole point. But applied in the right directions. And a *lot* of cracks, of course."

Gereint couldn't stop smiling. "Of course."

"I'll show you—" But she stopped, her enthusiasm fading.

"It's all right," Gereint said gently. "Beguchren was right, though for reasons I don't think he anticipated. It's all right."

"You don't mind?" But Tehre saw or guessed the answer to that question and went on immediately so he wouldn't have to answer it: "You can't undo it? Make yourself over again, in reverse?"

"No," Gereint said. "A maker can remake himself. But a mage's skill isn't in making. It's like shattering a sword or breaking a mountain into blocks: You can't change your mind later and put the material back the way it was to start."

"No," Tehre agreed in a small voice.

"That's true for everything of importance," Eben Amnachudran said quietly. He laid his hands on his daughter's shoulders and looked over her head at Gereint.

Uncomfortable, Gereint turned away and went to stand by the bed, gazing down at Beguchren. He asked, not looking up, "Your lady wife couldn't help him?"

Amnachudran came to stand beside him, Tehre moving up on his other side. The scholar said, "We all collapsed at the end, of course, but that was just a matter of rest. Tauban was torn up by a blow from a griffin—almost the only real casualty we suffered—though, if that counts, Ansant managed to catch a spear in the thigh, somewhere in the most confused part of the . . ." He paused. "Exercise. Beguchren Teshrichten protected us, exactly as he said he would."

By the scholar's tone, he'd believed they would all die. Gereint nodded, without comment.

"Emre could handle all that. But this"—Amnachudran gestured to the still figure amid the pillows—"this she couldn't touch, and rest doesn't seem to be doing it, either. I thought I might; I thought it might be some sort of symbolic injury—to the will, perhaps, or the heart or the self. But . . ." His voice trailed off.

Gereint stared down at the small form of the mage. Then he glanced sideways at Tehre. "You were right. He caught the strength of the deep earth and bent it around his own strength and handed it off to you and me. I don't think he's injured. Not even symbolically. But I think he emptied himself down to the very dregs of his will and heart and self . . ." He laid one hand gently on Beguchren's arm. It was painfully thin.

Closing his eyes, Gereint sent his mind groping after the mage's awareness and memory and self. He found nothing but emptiness . . . But within that emptiness, the deep magic of earth and stone, which filled the world, so that actually there was no emptiness anywhere. Beyond that deep magic lay an aching cold, as familiar to him as his own hands and mind . . . He glimpsed years scrolling out endlessly, faces and voices he remembered . . . He realized only slowly that they were not faces or voices *he* remembered. This cold magic was not something familiar to *him*. And at the beginning, the blank drifting emptiness had not been *his*.

So he reached out to find that sense of emptiness, and into it he poured all the memories he'd caught out of the dark. He tried to fill it with the essential, intrinsic awareness of earth and stone and cold and mist . . . that slid away from him, but his mind caught eagerly at memory. No. Not *his* mind. A woman's face, fair and smiling; a man's face, dark and angry. A voice that spoke his name. Not *his* name, but . . . It was hard to tell which name was his by right, which heart, which mind, which self . . . The music of a spinet, winding through a familiar house; the music of a harp, notes drifting up to the sky . . .

Gereint pulled himself painfully free of memory, up into that measureless, empty sky, and found himself blinking and dazed, in a small, warm room with the warm autumn breeze blowing the curtains at the window, with Tehre on one side and her father on the other. He remembered Tehre at once, but it took a moment for him to recall Eben Amnachudran's name.

On the bed before them, Beguchren drew a breath and opened his eyes.

Beside Gereint, Amnachudran made a small sound. Tehre didn't. She backed quietly away and ran out into the hall. Gereint knew she'd gone to summon her mother and fetch tea, and since Beguchren needed both, that was eminently practical.

The mage's white brows drew together. His eyes were no longer ice pale. They were the powerful dark gray of pewter, of storm clouds, of the last beat of dusk before full dark . . . Gereint blinked, realizing at precisely the same moment as Beguchren himself that the man was no longer a mage. He felt Beguchren's shock reverberate through his own mind. That deep awareness of earth, the awareness that Gereint had learned in the desert while firc fell out of the dark wind and the wild cries of griffins echoed overhead—*He* still held that awareness, like an extra sense, like an extension of his very *self.* But Beguchren did not. It had not been merely weakened. It was gone. Burned out by fire, used up by merciless need . . .

He did not say anything. There seemed nothing to say. Except he did not let Beguchren fall back into the waiting emptiness, which for a moment he was afraid he might try to do. He made him sit up instead, arranging the pillows behind him, took the tea Tehre had brought, and himself held the cup to Beguchren's lips.

"Is he well, now?" Amnachudran asked nervously—asking Gereint and not Beguchren. He leaned around Gereint, reached to take Beguchren's thin wrist in his hand, set his thumb over the beating pulse, and paused. He was, Gereint surmised, enough of a mage to understand, if belatedly, what had happened.

"He's perfectly fine," Gereint said flatly, his tone daring Beguchren to contradict him even in the privacy of his own mind.

Beguchren's storm-gray eyes closed. But his mouth crooked. He said nothing, but lifted a hand to demand, wordlessly but stubbornly, that Gereint give him the cup.

Equally wordless, Gereint set it into his hand.

Beguchren lifted the cup, sipped, and lowered it again with determined steadiness.

Gereint took it just as the other man's hand began to tremble. He said quietly, "There is a wall stretching from the cold lake above the Teschanken down along the river, and then west all the way to the far mountains. It is sealed with ice and earth on this side, and with fire on the other. The rivers are flowing with clean water again, and the country of fire won't overreach itself again."

Beguchren nodded, very faintly. He whispered, "I'll sleep now."

"A little more tea first," Gereint said gently, and folded Beguchren's smaller hand around the cup, steadying it for him to lift and then lower once more.

Lady Emre hurried in with a plate of cakes, Tehre's Lord Bertaud trailing diffidently behind her. Gereint did not appreciate the crowd, but he took the cup away again, broke the cake, and put a sticky fragment in Beguchren's hand. "Eat that," he said. "Eat it, and then you can sleep. But promise me you'll wake." He paused and added, with a measure of ruthlessness that surprised even himself, "You owe me that."

Beguchren's brows drew together, but he did not deny it. He nodded again, very slightly, and fell asleep sitting up, with the bit of cake dissolving on his tongue.

Very much as Gereint had done, Beguchren slept through the day and then the whole of the following night. And very much as Gereint had, he woke in far better command of himself. No one had to bully or coax him into eating honey cakes, and then porridge and eggs and cold sliced beef. He spoke to Gereint for a long while—or Gereint spoke to him: Beguchren wanted to know everything that had happened after his own collapse. Gereint could not, of course, tell him anything about most of that. Tehre filled in the part she knew, and her father described, though only in very restrained terms, the confusion and terror that had beset the company down by the river.

"Until the mountains broke, and the great stone blocks came spilling down from the heights, and the wall built itself all along the river," he said, his eyes dark and amazed with memory. "And we all fell, then, just fell where we stood—that was you, my lord, of course. Emre says she found us there at dawn. She and the other women carried us all out of a desert that was, she tells me, already trying to be good, ordinary earth, through breezes that carried the scents of warm grass and damp leaves. Before they'd got us two miles, the river came pouring down its bed . . . It's not quite the same bed," he added as an aside to Gereint. "I've been to look at it. The nearer mountains were so broken and leveled, it's a wider, shallower river now when it reaches this country. Where the water strikes the wall, do you know, it freezes? Cold mists roll over its surface . . . I don't know. It's no river you'd think to fish from, now."

"Farther south, it will seem more familiar," Beguchren said quietly.

"Well, lord, I'm sure that's true, and probably just as well. I'm not sure anyone would want to put a boat out in the river amid that mist."

Beguchren nodded, his storm-gray eyes unreadable. "And this Feierabianden lord? Lord Bertaud, yes?"

"Bertaud son of Boudan," Tehre put in quickly. "He helped us, helped me . . ."

"Yes?"

"The griffin mage told me he helped build and seal the wall because of Lord Bertaud's influence," Gereint added.

Beguchren's expression became even more inscrutable.

Tehre traded a glance with her father, which Gereint found impossible to decipher. "I'll find him, ask him to speak with you," she suggested.

"Please do," Beguchren said softly, and sent everyone else away so that he might speak to the foreign lord alone.

"Though I don't know why," Tehre told Gereint later. "Bertaud said he only asked perfectly normal, straightforward things. Just what happened."

Bertaud? Gereint thought. Tehre was so informal with the foreign lord? She called him by name like that, without even thinking? But he said only, "Perhaps he was simply tired of being attended by a crowd, and I don't blame him."

"Perhaps that's so," Tehre agreed, and began absently to sketch equations containing the square root of the ratio of crack length over the radius of crack tip, or so Gereint supposed. She was, she'd said, trying to work out whether you indeed simply doubled that value in her stress calculations, or whether the multiplicative factor merely *approximated* two. And she thought there was some small additive factor as well . . . Gereint left her to it. At least any Feierabianden lords who happened to wander by would probably find the calculations even more impenetrable than he did himself.

The day after that, Beguchren got up from his bed and made his way through the halls and out into the courtyard, speaking to no one save for a polite murmur of acknowledgment to an astonished man-at-arms at the front gate. The man-at-arms hurried to tell Eben Amnachudran, and Amnachudran told Gereint, and Gereint found Beguchren sitting, pale and exhausted, underneath a big old apple tree. He was leaning against its knotted trunk, his face tipped back toward the leafy branches, his eyes closed, looking so ethereal it seemed strange the light breeze did not carry him away.

The tree had recovered well from the brief encroachment of the desert wind. Sweet golden apples hung thickly overhead. Their fragrance drifted in the quiet air. Amid the grasses, windfall apples buzzed with wasps too busy to notice or resent the intrusion of men.

"You don't need to fetch your own, you know," Gereint said, sitting down beside Beguchren. "The children brought plenty right into the kitchens."

The smaller man smiled wryly, not opening his eyes. After a moment, he said, "It's just as well. I think I could neither climb the tree for the hanging fruit, nor chase away the wasps from the fallen."

"You're stronger. You think you can walk back to the house from here?"

"Oh, yes. In a little while. After I sit here for a few moments . . ."

"Shall I leave?"

"It doesn't matter. Stay, if you wish."

They sat in companionable silence for a time. Eventually, Gereint ventured, "The Arobern will value you anyway, you know," and then flushed, immediately realizing how stupid that sounded.

Beguchren mercifully didn't even open his eyes, much less respond.

After a while, Gereint gathered his nerve and tried again, more simply and directly. "I'm sorry. I'd give it back to you, if I could. I suppose you can't make yourself back into a mage as I did? Recover magecraft through the side door, as it were?"

"No. I'm not a maker." Beguchren paused, and then added, "We both lost what we valued, I suppose. It's fair enough. It's not that different from what I did to you. In reverse."

"It worked."

"Not in anything like the manner I'd intended. Nor at the price I'd prepared to pay. Not even in the same *coin* I'd prepared to pay." He suddenly sounded exhausted. "Thus the world teaches us humility."

"But it still worked."

". . . true." There was a small silence. Beguchren said, "I suppose I'll become accustomed to it, in time."

In much the same way that a man might become accustomed to being blind and deaf. Just so. Gereint did not answer. He stood up after a moment, reaching high into the branches for a couple of apples. He had a belt knife, but it was too large and clumsy a thing to peel apples with. If he'd still been a maker, he could have coaxed the knife to exceed its design, encouraged it to hold the sort of edge such delicate work demanded . . . He cut each apple in quarters, cored them, and handed half the pieces to Beguchren without trying to peel them. They sat under the tree and ate the apples, surrounded by the quiet autumn sunlight and the buzzing of wasps. In the distance voices called, indistinct but cheerful.

"I believe I can probably walk back to the house now," Beguchren said. He glanced at Gereint, half smiling. "And if I can't . . ."

"I'm sure that won't be necessary." Gereint got to his feet and offered the other man a hand up.

Beguchren made it back to the house on his own feet. But once they were back in the house, he shook his head quietly as Gereint turned toward his room. "I'll speak to Eben Amnachudran. And Lady Emre."

Gereint said, puzzled, "You can do that from your bed—"

"No," said Beguchren. Quietly but definitely.

By which Gereint understood that Beguchren did not want to *chat* with Amnachudran or his wife. He wanted to talk to them in some more formal place than a bedroom, in some more formal capacity than that of their guest. And since he was no longer a mage, that most likely meant he wanted to speak to them as a king's agent. "Likely they'll be in Amnachudran's office," he guessed, and hailed a passing servant with the query.

Both Eben Amnachudran and his wife were in the office-music room. Amnachudran was, of course, at his desk and surrounded by books, but somewhat to Gereint's surprise, Lord Bertaud was also leaning over the desk. Both men were poring over a large open book bound in pale linen and illustrated all around the text with dragons and griffins in gold and red and black ink. Tehre was a few steps away, gazing down at a sketch of a bridge and absently rolling a quill pen between her fingers. Lady Emre was seated, as she had been the first time Gereint had seen her, at her spinet. This time she was playing, her expression abstracted. The music was a northern children's song, very simple and plain. In Lady Emre's hands, it recovered the charm that too great familiarity might have stolen from it and became not merely plain, but elegant.

But she lifted her hands from the keys, turning with everyone else when Gereint and Beguchren came in. Amnachudran moved hastily to pull chairs around for them. Beguchren sank into his with a slight nod, but Gereint merely drifted a step away to lean his hip against the edge of the big desk, watching curiously.

"I'll leave tomorrow morning," Beguchren began. "So if I may trouble you, honored sir, for the loan of a carriage and driver? Thank you." He paused and surveyed them all. The cool authority of his tone and manner could be estimated, Gereint thought, by the lack of overt protest at the idea of his traveling. The effort that matter-of-fact coolness cost him was less easy to estimate.

"I am grateful for all your efforts over the past days," Beguchren continued. "On my behalf, and in the Arobern's voice, I thank you. We can only imagine how else events might have unfolded. With, to be sure, the most profound gratitude that we need imagination to view those events." He gave them each a slight nod and said to Lord Bertaud, "I am quite certain the king will wish to thank you personally for your assistance. I hope you will accompany me back to the court in Breidechboden?" He accepted the Feierabianden lord's murmured assurance with another nod.

Then Beguchren leaned back in his chair, took a breath, turned his storm-gray eyes to Eben Amnachudran, and added, "The only question that remains to be settled before my departure, then, is this: Was it you yourself who removed Gereint Enseichen's brand? Or was it your lady wife?"

There was a deep, deep silence. Gereint hadn't seen that coming at all. But, he gradually realized, Amnachudran had. The scholar looked shocked by the question, but he did not, somehow, look *surprised*. He stood with his palms flat on his desk, his head slightly bowed, not looking at any of them. After a moment he lifted his head and glanced at his wife. Lady Emre looked stricken. Her eyes were on Beguchren, not on her husband; she shook her head very slightly in a motion that might have been disbelief or might have been a plea, and either way was probably involuntary. But she did not say anything or make any overt gesture.

Amnachudran said at last to Beguchren, "My lord, it was I."

Beguchren inclined his head. "Then I will have to ask you, also, to accompany me tomorrow."

"Of course," said Amnachudran, just a little stiffly.

No one else said a word. Tehre opened her mouth, but her mother half lifted a hand and shook her head quickly, and, to Gereint's surprise, Tehre closed her mouth again without making a sound. Her eyes snapped with anger, but then narrowed, and Gereint knew she was thinking hard. He wished he knew what conclusion she might come to. He himself felt torn between wanting to exclaim to Beguchren, in outrage, *How can you?* and at the same time wanting to plead with Amnachudran and the rest, *He's the king's agent; what else can he do?* He said nothing at all.

CHAPTER 16

The Arobern received them, two days after their return to Breidech-boden, in an intimidating room large enough for thirty men to gather, a room that held enough large, heavy, ornately carved chairs to accommodate all thirty as well as a single massive and ornate desk. The king had heard the whole account from Beguchren, or so Gereint surmised. Certainly Beguchren had gone to him at once on arriving in the city. No one else had; no one else had been invited to.

Gereint had stayed, of course, at the Amnachudran townhouse, with Tehre and her father, and Sicheir, who, he gathered, had gone on to Breidechboden with the king's agent after Tehre had defied the agent to go north. The other party to that defiance, Lord Bertaud, alone among them presumably not at personal risk of the king's displeasure, had returned to whatever apartment within the palace was allotted for his use. Tehre had received two messages from the Feierabianden lord, one each day, and returned three of her own, which was only natural. Gereint set his teeth against any ill-considered comment he might have made about this correspondence.

There had been no word from either Beguchren or the king until at last, and to everyone's unspoken relief, the command to appear for an audience had been brought by an extremely elegant royal chamberlain. The waiting had been difficult for Eben Amnachudran and his children, Gereint knew. But if any of them had said a word about their nervousness, it had not been to Gereint.

The king was not seated at the desk, nor in the room at all, when the chamberlain ushered them within. This was not a surprise; he would hardly have arrived early to wait for suppliants to come before him. No; they had been sent for and had come, and now would wait the king's pleasure. Nothing rested on the desk save an elegant gold-and-crystal four-hour sand timer, turned recently, so that perhaps half the sand had run through to the bottom glass. Gereint hoped the sand did not mark the wait they were expected to endure: Two hours might not realistically be long to wait for a royal audience, but at the moment it seemed an intolerable span of time.

Though the room was not without interest. Blue-and-teal abstract mosaics rippled all along three of the walls, high up, near the ceiling, which was painted pale blue with flying larks. The remaining wall held only a large painting framed with long velvet hangings of blue and violet, showing Breidechboden from above as a lark might see it. The light that poured across the painted city possessed a crystalline clarity, as though the city had been created in just the instant the painting captured and had not yet begun to age. It occurred to Gereint, for the first time but with a curious sense of inevitability, that the artist was certainly Beguchren Teshrichten himself.

Gereint found the room, as a whole, rather alarming. And yet . . . it might have been far worse. It might have been a formal audience hall, all porphyry columns and vaulted, echoing marble, with a chill to it that bit worse than any northern midwinter. This room, though it fairly radiated authority, was not nearly so formal, and the chamberlain who guided them invited them all to enter with an expansive gesture that suggested welcome rather than command. It was not the sort of reception they might have expected from an angry king. But it was a little hard to estimate what sort of reception it actually *was*.

Lord Bertaud was already present. Gereint could not decide whether the foreigner's earlier arrival was accidental or meant to indicate something, or, if it was deliberate, what it was meant to indicate. Probably he was reading too much into mere happenstance.

Tehre went at once to greet the Feierabianden lord, Gereint and Eben Amnachudran and Sicheir following more slowly. Tehre's father had been very quiet and inward for the days of the journey from his house to Breidechboden, and after their arrival in the capital he had become quieter still. But there was a new quality to his silence now. Gereint understood that, or thought he did. He believed the Arobern would forgive any of them anything, as well he ought to—he *believed* that—but the king was well known to despise corruption or vice or any dishonesty in his appointed judges. So Gereint did not know, none of them knew, exactly what the king would do.

The Feierabianden lord had a smile for Tehre; rather too warm a smile for any foreigner to direct toward a Casmantian lady, was

Gereint's impression. The nod of greeting he himself gave the man was perhaps a little stiff. Neither of them spoke; it did not seem a place or moment for idle conversation, and what could they possibly say? But the foreigner offered in return a gesture that seemed oddly poised midway between a nod and a bow, and the same to Eben Amnachudran. Amnachudran inclined his head in response, glanced briefly at his daughter, and drew breath as though he might speak. But then he said nothing.

"You may all sit," the chamberlain told them, arranging chairs in a loose semicircle by the desk. "You, honored sir—you, sir—you, sir—Lady Tehre, if you wish—over here, my lord, if you would be so kind."

No one ventured to protest these arrangements, which placed Lord Bertaud a little away from the rest and in a distinctly more ornate chair. Gereint's chair was close enough to Tehre's that he might have held her hand, and he was tempted to, save any such gesture would have been thoroughly inappropriate under the circumstances. Not to mention the eye of her father.

The entrance of the king interrupted Gereint's thoughts, which was perhaps as well.

The Arobern, as was his widely reputed habit, was not wearing court dress. He was dressed only a little more elaborately than a soldier, in black, except his belt was sapphire blue and his buttons, probably, were sapphire in truth. He wore around his throat the thick gold chain of the Casmantian kings, and around his left wrist a wide-linked chain of black iron.

Beguchren Teshrichten walked not behind the king, like a servant, but beside him, like a friend. Beguchren might, next to the dark bulk of the Arobern and with the smooth fineness of his face, have looked rather like an elegant, wealthy, arrogant child. But despite the strain and weariness that still clung to him, there was too much authority in the tilt of his fine head to support that illusion, and far too many years in his storm-dark eyes. Those eyes met Gereint's, unfathomable as ever, but he did not even nod, far less speak.

Everyone rose hastily, even the Feierabianden lord, but the Arobern turned a big hand palm upward to signal that no one need kneel, and then turned the gesture to a casual little wave that invited them all to resume their seats. The courtesy made Gereint uncomfortable.

Beguchren settled quietly into a particularly ornate chair set next to the heavy desk, rested his hands on the arms of the chair, and gazed at them with impenetrable calm.

The Arobern did not sit but leaned his hip against the polished edge of the desk, crossed his arms over his chest, and surveyed them all. When his forceful, dark gaze crossed Gereint's, Gereint wanted to flinch and drop his eyes; a slave's impulse, or the deference any Casmantian owed his king, or the impulse of a guilty man? It felt oddly like guilt, though he knew very well he had nothing for which to atone. He set his jaw and stared back.

"I believe," the Arobern said, in his deep, guttural voice, "that I have the tale plain and clear. Does anyone believe it necessary to add to the account my agent Beguchren Teshrichten has given to me?"

No one appeared to, though Gereint could not stop himself from glancing at Amnachudran.

"So," said the Arobern. He turned to the Feierabianden lord, inclining his heavy head. "Lord Bertaud, you spoke for Casmantium before the representative of the griffins. Their mage, yes? It was your word that caused the griffin mage to align his power with ours in the building of that wall. That is so, yes?"

Lord Bertaud hesitated for a long moment. At last he said quietly, "It was a little more complicated than that. Sipiike Kairaithin himself favored the solution Lady Tehre devised. I know he set himself against the will of his own king to support the building of that wall. We—you owe him a debt, which I doubt you will ever have an opportunity to repay. But I hope you'll keep in mind, Lord King, that at the end, not every griffin strove for the destruction of your country."

The Arobern paid the foreign lord careful attention. When the foreigner had finished speaking, he answered, "As you say so, Lord Bertaud, I will remember it. I know well your people, and you particularly, have forged a much greater understanding with the griffins than Casmantium has ever managed, despite all our long experience."

Lord Bertaud inclined his head. "Perhaps it's our lack of violent history that allows Feierabiand to approach the People of Fire and Air more, ah—"

"More productively," suggested Beguchren, quietly. "I think it's clear that earth mages, particularly cold mages, should not determine policy when dealing with the . . . People of Air and Fire. Certainly the counsel of mages is suspect in that regard, and so I've advised my lord king."

Lord Bertaud looked startled and satisfied in approximately equal measure. He said after a moment, "I'm . . . that is, I think perhaps you may be correct, Lord Beguchren, and I'm very much hopeful that this, ah, caution, may lead to a better outcome along the border between earth and fire. If, ah . . ."

"If the wall should fail," Beguchren completed the thought. He turned his head, regarding Gereint, one pale brow lifting. He said, not quite a question, "As it should not, however."

Gereint shook his head uncertainly. "I don't think so, my lord. I don't—I can't well judge, but I don't think so."

"It should last for a long time," Tehre put in earnestly. "Quite a long time, really. It's structurally very sound. Because of how wide it is, you know. Width and weight always stabilize a wall—"

The Arobern smoothly interrupted what might have become a detailed digression on the nature and stability of walls. "Lady Tehre," he said formally, "Casmantium is amazed by your skill and prowess as a builder and an engineer. Casmantium and I are grateful for your insight and your skill, laid down at great risk and in despite of my command." His manner became less formal and more expansive. "Which, hah, I think I might forgive! My agent Detreir Enteirich was most alarmed at your defiance and the defiance of Lord Bertaud, but I have assured him that, under the circumstances, he need not be concerned at his failure to complete the charge I gave him."

From her air of startlement, Gereint rather thought Tehre might have genuinely forgotten about this incident herself. Lord Bertaud's mouth crooked in a wry smile.

The king, too, looked amused, as though he also suspected Tehre had forgotten. "I think I will send you west, with your honored brother and with Lord Bertaud if he will agree, to where my engineers and builders are working on my new road," he told her. "I think you have ideas for bridges and roadwork. And more than ideas, I think! You are not any ordinary maker, hah? My friend Beguchren tells me that we need a new word to describe what you are: not a mage, but not exactly a maker. You and he can decide. But I will send you west, and send my agent Detreir Enteirich with you, to ensure my engineers know to regard your views with respect."

Tehre had flushed, but her face was alight with enthusiasm. "Oh, yes! I have this wonderful idea for a new kind of bridge; it has—well." Surprising Gereint, she cut herself off and said merely, "I'm sure it will work. Nearly sure." But then she frowned, suddenly cautious. "Oh! But the Fellesteden heir, what *is* his name? I don't know, maybe he—it's possible he might—"

"I think Casnerach Fellesteden will not further trouble you or your family," the king assured her, smiling affably and somehow almost as fiercely as a griffin. "So you will go west. That is good." He turned at last to Gereint. "And you, Gereint Enseichen. What should I say to you?"

Gereint knew he had flushed. He truly had no idea how to respond. The king's gaze was uncomfortably intense when it was aimed precisely at him, Gereint found.

The Arobern said, "So we gain at very least a respite, maybe for years, maybe for our generation. Maybe for an age. And you did this for us."

This was unanswerable. Gereint managed a small nod.

"I am very satisfied with your work in the service of my friend Beguchren Teshrichten, and of Casmantium—that is, my service. Beguchren hoped you would do well for him. Neither of us, I think, understood how well you might do. Or under what circumstances. Or at what cost."

Gereint shook his head. "The cost wasn't mine. Not really. Not in the end." His eyes met Beguchren's, and he looked away again at once. He said to the Arobern, "It wasn't any of my doing that put me in a position to stumble into a way to be useful. I know that very well. I'm grateful Lord Beguchren's foresight and courage brought us all through that night of fire." He met Beguchren's eyes again, this time deliberately. "If not quite as we expected, still we came through to the dawn."

"As you say," the Arobern said, as gently as his gravelly voice permitted.

Beguchren bowed his head a little, and there was a pause.

Then the Arobern said, turning to the last of them, "Eben Amnachudran, your role, also, I have heard described. I commend your decisiveness and your steady courage in those days of fire. And through that last night. And your kindness to my friend Beguchren, among all the men who fell under your care."

Amnachudran, rather pale, bowed his head. He began to speak, but stopped.

The Arobern's heavy brows lifted. He asked, "What penalty should attend a judge of mine who interferes with a proper *geas* in defiance of my law and then conceals that interference? And what difference should it make if that same judge should comport himself creditably during a crisis in the days following that crime?"

Tehre sat frozen, her hand touching her mouth. Lord Bertaud looked quietly aside, not to intrude on this Casmantian matter. Beguchren was, as always, calmly inscrutable. Gereint didn't know what he showed—nothing, he hoped. Yet, at least. It took an effort to say nothing, to leave Eben Amnachudran to answer that accusation alone.

Amnachudran lifted his head. "No difference, of course. The law is very clear that one honorable act does not clear dishonor from an earlier act. As I knew very well." He got to his feet, took one step forward, and sank to his knees. "Lord King, when I chose to break your law, I should have resigned my judgeship. Instead, yes, I tried to hide what I had done. I ask for mercy."

"Do you so? Now?"

Amnachudran flinched just a little, but visibly. "Lord King, you'll say I should have come to you then if I would ask for mercy. That to plead for clemency only after one is caught is nothing honorable. That's true. Of course I should. And I'm aware, as Touchan Dachbraden points out, that any judge renowned for mercy must also be renowned, in precisely equal measure, for injustice. I know it. I don't argue it."

The Arobern went around the massive desk, took a velvet pouch from a drawer, and poured out into his broad hand two familiar silver *geas* rings. They chimed together as they slid into the king's hand, delicate and horrifying. The king stirred them with one blunt finger and they chimed again, more quietly. With his new mage's awareness, Gereint found he could actually *see* the cold magecraft woven into the rings, like a filigree of frost laid over the silver.

The king said to Amnachudran, "Justice might be to set the *geas* on the man who unlawfully interfered with its binding on another. What say you, my judge?"

Amnachudran had gone dead white. He began to answer, and stopped as Gereint's hand closed hard on his shoulder. Tehre, with a self-control that amazed Gereint, still said nothing at all, but waited to see what he would do and what the king would do. Her eyes were brilliant with anger and fear.

Gereint had found himself on his feet and beside Amnachudran without thinking. Now he took an instant for thought, reached the same conclusion the back of his mind seemed to have made first, and said sharply, allowing himself the sharpness, "If I served Beguchren Teshrichten, I should have those rings. You said I might melt them down or throw them in the river, whatever I chose. You said that. But there are other rings, I suppose. I'll beg you not to use them, Lord King. If I am owed anything at all, I'll beg you for mercy for my friend."

Tehre leaped to her feet and said fiercely, "If *I* am owed anything, then *I* will beg for mercy for my father. And I *am* owed, Lord King! You said you were grateful! And you should be!"

The Arobern considered her, bright and intense and tiny, with the light shining gold in her hair and her eyes snapping with passion. His expression was hard to read. He drew breath to respond.

Before the king could speak, Beguchren rose, effortlessly drawing all eyes. His manner impeccably elegant and formal, he went over to where Eben Amnachudran knelt and stood for a moment looking down at him.

Then Beguchren turned to face the king, standing on Amnachudran's other side, his small hand resting on the kneeling man's shoulder in an echo of Gereint's gesture. When Beguchren looked at the king, it was with a confidence no one else could possibly share; even, perhaps, with a trace of humor. He said gently, "Lord King . . . I, too, beg you for mercy for this man. Not for justice, for one need not plead for justice from a just king. But for clemency for a man who has served you; for the father of a lady who has served you well; for the friend of my student Gereint Enseichen, who has served you well. And for my sake, because I ask you."

Student? Gereint thought, startled. He glanced sidelong at Beguchren's face, but there was, of course, nothing to read there.

"Well," said the Arobern, a little blankly. And then, "I meant to offer clemency, you know, my friend."

"I would have thought so," answered Beguchren, smiling his slight, impenetrable smile. "But as I am the architect of this moment, I wished to be quite certain of the resulting . . ."

"Edifice?" suggested the Arobern. "Or artwork, hah?"

"If you like." Beguchren glanced down again at the kneeling Amnachudran. "I'm grateful for your assistance," he said to him softly. "And your kindness, and that of your lady wife. On my own behalf, not the behalf of Casmantium entire."

Eben Amnachudran lowered his head in quiet gratitude and then lifted his gaze once more to the king's face. He did not speak.

"A king who is renowned for mercy," said the Arobern, with heavy irony, "must also be renowned in equal measure for injustice." He paused. No one moved. The king said, "Eben Amnachudran, no judge of mine may disregard my law with impunity. I therefore declare that you are no longer a judge."

Amnachudran's mouth flinched slightly, but he nodded.

"However, yes, I think the *geas* would not be a suitable punishment for you, and anyway, I have said I would be clement." He dropped the silver rings carelessly to the polished surface of the desk and went on: "You dislike the *geas,* I think. Not only for yourself; you dislike it generally. I think it serves its purpose. But recently it has occurred to me that sometimes it may be too harsh a penalty for one man or another, or applied under questionable circumstances. It has occurred to me that I might appoint an agent of mine to investigate possible abuses of the *geas*. To determine whether there may be some men—and women—who might have been bound unjustly, or who might reasonably apply"—his mouth twisted slightly—"for clemency. But this work would take a long time, yes? I do not have an agent I can spare to this work." He paused.

Then he took a carved bone disk from the same pouch that had held the *geas* rings. Unusually, the token was dyed in two tones: sapphire on the spear-and-shield face, rich purple on the tree-and-falcon side. The king tossed the token upward and caught it without looking. He said to Amnachudran, "You might undertake this work for me, do you think so? It would take you away your home, from your family; it would require you to travel widely and spend prodigious effort. So this is not a reward I give you. But it is clemency, I think, yes?"

"Yes," Amnachudran whispered. He cleared his throat and said more loudly, "Yes, Lord King. I thank you for your generosity."

"Hah." The Arobern tossed the disk upward once more, caught it. Held it out to Amnachudran. "Take it," he commanded.

Gereint put a hand unobtrusively under the older man's elbow to help him to his feet, but once he was up, Amnachudran walked forward on his own, steadily, to take the dyed token from the king's hand. The king tipped it into his palm, closed a powerful hand around Amnachudran's fist as he took it, and said sternly, "The task will require a man of careful judgment. That is important. Not too merciful, not too harsh. Yes?"

Amnachudran bowed his head. He did not answer hastily, but only after a moment, and in a low, serious tone, "My Lord King, I will try to be worthy of your trust."

"I think you will be," said the Arobern, and let him go. Then he scooped up the *geas* rings with a sudden motion and held them out to Gereint, who took them. The rings burned in his palm with an odd cold life, not quite like anything he had ever perceived.

"They are yours," the king said gravely. "Did I not say they would be?"

"I believe I might be able to teach you how to unweave the magecrafting," Beguchren said, equally serious. "It would be a useful exercise."

Gereint crushed the first response that came onto his tongue into a polite and restrained, "I'm sure there will be other exercises that will prove as useful." He, in his turn, tossed the rings to Tehre.

She caught them out of the air as neatly as though she had known from the first precisely what he would do. She was smiling. It was a brilliant smile, edged with irony. "Silver's not the same as stone," she told him. "I don't think the same calculations exactly apply."

"Do you need them?"

"No," Tehre said. "There's another equation for metals; I've just now worked it out." And she tossed the rings into the air. The light glittered on the silver, and on the frost that wove like lace across the metal . . . and, with a delicate shivering music like the shattering of tiny bells, the rings dissolved into a glittering dust that scattered across the Arobern's polished desk.

The destruction of the symbols of slavery was, in a strange way, more dramatic than freedom itself had been. Gereint felt his mouth curving into an involuntary smile, probably, he suspected, with an edge of concentrated lunacy beneath it. "You'll have to teach me that equation."

Tehre gazed back at him with cautious, pleased surprise that only barely overlay the intensity beneath. "I'll teach you *all* the equations. If you like."

Gereint could not stop smiling. He wondered how long it might take to erase that caution from her eyes. Not so long, perhaps, with some dedicated effort. He said, "All of them? I'm sure that will take a long time. Years, I expect. But I can't think of a better way to spend years." And he crossed to her side and, as he had wanted to do almost from the beginning, folded her small hand in his large one and looked down into her eyes.

Tehre flushed, and laughed, and glanced at her father and the king . . . but then she tilted her face up to gaze at Gereint, put her other small hand halfway around his—all it would reach—and said, teasing, but serious as well, "It might take forever. Because when you've learned all of them, I'll invent more."

"The philosophers say numbers are infinite," Gereint said with deep satisfaction. "So there's no reason we should ever run out."

"Go away," the Arobern said, amused. "Enjoy your infinite equations, and if some of them apply to the building of mountain roads and high bridges, all the better." He gestured dismissal to them all.

Gereint lingered to give Beguchren a long look, afraid he might well feel himself abandoned. Beguchren smiled. This time, to Gereint, the smile did not seem entirely inscrutable, but amused and even pleased; avoiding bitterness, he suspected, with a deliberate effort. Gereint nodded to Beguchren, then turned to Eben Amnachudran with an apologetic little tilt of his head that said, *I know I should have asked you first*, but was not very sincere about the apology. There was nothing but approval and relief in the smile the king's newest agent returned. And at last Gereint spared the Feierabianden Lord Bertaud a glance of acknowledgment that he tried not to let be smug, and received in return a quiet, sincere nod that almost made him repent the smugness, not that he could restrain it.

But he didn't speak to any of them. He only said, "Bridges," to Tehre, and she, trying not to smile and failing spectacularly, nodded with a pretense of solemnity that fooled no one and answered, "Bridges. We definitely need to study bridges," and pulled him with her out of the room and the palace and the court entirely, back into the brilliant light of the world.

LAW OF THE
BROKEN EARTH

This one's for Dad, who makes sure all the hardware in my life keeps running so that I don't have to be distracted by leaking pipes, oil changes, clogged filters, or any of the myriad nuisances that beset everyone not so lucky in their relatives. Thanks, Dad!

PROLOGUE

Mienthe did not remember her mother, and she was afraid of her father—a cold, harsh-voiced man with a scathing turn of phrase when his children displeased him. He favored his son, already almost a young man when Mienthe was born, and left Mienthe largely to the care of a succession of nurses—a succession because servants rarely stayed long in that house. If Mienthe had had no one but the nurses, her childhood might have been bleak indeed. But she had Tef.

Tef was the gardener and a man of general work. He had been a soldier for many years and lost a foot in a long-ago dispute with Casmantium. Tef was no longer young and he walked with a crutch, but he was not afraid of Mienthe's father. It never crossed Mienthe's mind that *he* might give notice.

Despite the lack of a foot, Tef carried Mienthe through the gardens on his shoulders. He also let her eat her lunches with him in the kitchen, showed her how to cut flowers so they would stay fresh longer, and gave her a kitten that grew into an enormous slit-eyed gray cat. Tef could speak to cats and so there were always cats about the garden and his cottage, but none of them were as huge or as dignified as the gray cat he gave Mienthe.

When Mienthe was seven, one of her nurses started teaching her her letters. But that nurse had only barely shown her how to form each letter and spell her own name before Mienthe's father raged at her about *Good paper left out in the weather* and *When are you going to teach that child to keep in mind what she is about? A sight more valuable than teaching a mere girl how to spell*, and the nurse gave him notice and Mienthe a tearful farewell. After that, Tef got out a tattered old gardener's compendium and taught Mienthe her letters himself.

Mienthe could spell Tef's name before her own, and she could spell *bittersweet* and *catbrier* and even *quaking grass* long before she could spell her father's name. As her father did not notice she had learned to write at all, this did not offend him.

Tef could not teach Mienthe embroidery or deportment, but he taught Mienthe to ride by putting her up on her brother's outgrown pony and letting her fall off until she learned to stay on, which, fortunately, her brother never discovered, and he taught her to imitate the purring call of a contented gray jay and the rippling coo of a dove and the friendly little chirp of a sparrow so well she could often coax one bird or another to take seeds or crumbs out of her hand.

"It's good you can keep the cats from eating the birds," Mienthe told Tef earnestly. "But do you mind?" People who could speak to an animal, she knew, never liked constraining the natural desires of that animal.

"I don't mind," said Tef, smiling down at her. He was sitting perfectly still so he wouldn't frighten the purple-shouldered finch perched on Mienthe's finger. "The cats can catch voles and rabbits. That's much more useful than birds. I wonder if you'll find yourself speaking to some of the little birds one day? That would be pretty and charming."

Mienthe gazed down at the finch on her finger and smiled. But she said, "It wouldn't be very useful. Not like speaking to cats is to you."

Tef shrugged, smiling. "You're Lord Beraod's daughter. You don't need to worry about being useful. Anyway, your father would probably be better pleased with an animal that was pretty and charming than one that's only useful."

This was true. Mienthe wished she was pretty and charming herself, like a finch. Maybe her father . . . But she moved her hand too suddenly then, and the bird flew away with a flash of buff and purple, and she forgot her half-recognized thought.

When Mienthe was nine, a terrible storm came pounding out of the sea into the Delta. The storm uprooted trees, tore the roofs off houses, flooded fields, and drowned dozens of people who happened to be in the path of its greatest fury. Among those who died were Mienthe's brother and, trying to rescue him from the racing flood, her father.

Mienthe was her father's sole heir. Tef explained this to her. He explained why three uncles and five cousins—none of whom Mienthe knew, but all with young sons—suddenly appeared and began to quarrel over which of them might best give her a home. Mienthe tried to understand what Tef told her, but everything was suddenly so confusing. The quarrel had something to do with the sons, and with her. "I'm . . . to go live with one of them? Somewhere else?" she asked anxiously. "Can't you come, too?"

"No, Mie," Tef said, stroking her hair with his big hand. "No, I can't. Not one of your uncles or cousins would permit that. But you'll do well, do you see? I'm sure you'll like living with your uncle Talenes." Tef thought Uncle Talenes was going to win the quarrel. "You'll have his sons to play with and a nurse who will stay longer than a season and an aunt to be fond of you."

Tef was right about one thing: In the end, Uncle Talenes vanquished the rest of the uncles and cousins. Uncle Talenes finally resorted to the simple expedient of using his thirty men-at-arms—no one else had brought so many—to appropriate Mienthe and carry her away, leaving the rest to continue their suddenly pointless argument without her.

But Tef was wrong about everything else.

Uncle Talenes lived several days' journey from Kames, where Mienthe's father's house was, in a large high-walled house outside Tiefenauer. Uncle Talenes's house had mosaic floors and colored glass in the windows and a beautiful fountain in the courtyard. All around the fountain were flower beds, vivid blooms tumbling over their edges. Three great oaks in the courtyard held cages of fluttering, sweet-voiced birds. Mienthe was not allowed to splash in the fountain no matter how hot the weather. She was allowed to sit on the raked gravel under the trees as long as she was careful not to tear her clothing, but she could not listen to the birds without being sorry for the cages.

Nor, aside from the courtyard, were there any gardens. The wild Delta marshes began almost directly outside the gate and ran from the house all the way to the sea. The tough salt grasses would cut your fingers if you swung your hand through them, and mosquitoes whined in the heavy shade.

"Stay out of the marsh," Aunt Eren warned Mienthe. "There are snakes and poisonous frogs, and quicksand if you put a foot wrong. Snakes, do you hear? Stay close to the house. *Close to the house.* Do you understand me?" That was how she usually spoke to Mienthe: as though Mienthe were too young and stupid to understand anything unless it was very simple and emphatically repeated.

Aunt Eren was not fond of Mienthe. She was not fond of children generally, but her sons did not much regard their mother's temper. Mienthe did not know what she could safely disregard and what she must take care for. She wanted to please her aunt, only she was too careless and not clever enough and could not seem to learn how.

Nor did Aunt Eren hire a nurse for Mienthe. She said Mienthe was too old to need a nurse and should have a proper maid instead, but then she did not hire one. Two of Aunt Eren's own maids took turns looking after Mienthe instead, but she could see they did not like to. Mienthe tried to be quiet and give them no bother.

Mienthe's half cousins had pursuits and friends of their own. They were not in the least interested in the little girl so suddenly thrust into their family, but they left her alone. Uncle Talenes was worse than either Aunt Eren or the boys. He had a sharp, whining voice that made her think of the mosquitoes, and he was dismayed, *dismayed* to find her awkward and inarticulate in front of him and in front of the guests to whom he wanted to show her off. Was Mienthe perhaps not very clever? Then it was certainly a shame she was not prettier, wasn't it? How fortunate for her that her future was safe in his hands . . .

Mienthe tried to be grateful to her uncle for giving her a home, but she missed Tef.

Then, late in the year after Mienthe turned twelve, her cousin Bertaud came back to the Delta from the royal court. For days no one spoke of anything else. Mienthe knew that Bertaud was another cousin, much older than she was. He had grown up in the Delta, but he had gone away and no one had thought he would come back. Only recently something had happened, some trouble with Casmantium, or with griffins, or somehow with both, and now he seemed to have come back to stay. Mienthe wondered why her cousin had left the Delta, but she wondered even more why he had returned. She thought that if *she* ever left the Delta, she never would come back.

But her cousin Bertaud even took up his inheritance as Lord of the Delta. This seemed to shock and offend Uncle Talenes, though Mienthe was not sure why, if it was his rightful inheritance. He took over the great house in Tiefenauer, sending Mienthe's uncle Bodoranes back to his personal estate, and he dismissed all the staff. His dismissal of the staff seemed to shock and offend Aunt Eren as much as his mere return had Uncle Talenes. Both agreed that Bertaud must be high-handed and arrogant and vicious. Yes, it was vicious, uprooting poor Bodoranes like that after all his years and *years* of service, while Bertaud had lived high in the court and ignored the Delta. And flinging out all those people into the cold! But, well, yes, he *was* by blood Lord of the Delta, and perhaps there were ways to make the best of it . . . One might even have to note that Bodoranes had been regrettably obstinate in some respects . . .

Since the weather in the Delta was warm even this late in the fall, Mienthe wondered what her aunt could mean about flinging people into the cold. And how exactly did Uncle Talenes mean to "make the best" of the new lord's arrival?

"We need to see him, see what he's like," Uncle Talenes explained to his elder son, now seventeen and very interested in girls, as long as they weren't Mienthe. "He's Lord of the Delta, for good or ill, and we need to get an idea of him. And we need to be polite. Very, very polite. If he's clever, he'll see how much to everyone's advantage raising the tariffs on Linularinan glass would be"—Uncle Talenes was heavily invested in Delta glass and ceramics—"and if he's less clever, then maybe he could use someone cleverer to point out these things."

Karre nodded, puffed up with importance because his father was explaining this to him. Mienthe, tucked forgotten in a chair in the corner, understood finally that her uncle meant to bully or bribe the new Lord of the Delta if he could. She thought he probably could. Uncle Talenes almost always got his own way.

And Uncle Talenes seemed likely to get his own way this time, too. Not many days after he'd returned to the Delta, Lord Bertaud wrote accepting Talenes's invitation to dine and expressing a hope that two days hence would be convenient, if he were to call.

Aunt Eren stood over the servants while they scrubbed the mosaic floors and put flowers in every room and raked the gravel smooth in the drive. Uncle Talenes made sure his sons and Mienthe were well turned out, and that Aunt Eren was wearing her most expensive jewelry, and he explained several times to the whole household, in ever more vivid terms, how important it was to impress Lord Bertaud.

And precisely at noon on the day arranged, Lord Bertaud arrived.

The family resemblance was clear. He was dark, as all Mienthe's uncles and cousins were dark; he was tall, as they all were tall; and he had the heavy bones that made him look sturdy rather than handsome. He did not speak quickly and laugh often, as Uncle Talenes did; indeed, his manner was so restrained he seemed severe. Mienthe thought he looked both edgy and stern, and she thought there was an odd kind of depth to his eyes, a depth that somehow seemed familiar, although she could not put a name to it.

Lord Bertaud accepted Uncle Talenes's effusive congratulations on his return with an abstracted nod, and nodded again as Uncle Talenes introduced his wife and sons. He did not seem to be paying very close attention, but he frowned when Uncle Talenes introduced Mienthe.

"Beraod's daughter?" he asked. "Why is she here with you?"

Smiling down at Mienthe possessively, Talenes explained about the storm and how he had offered poor Mienthe a home. He brought her forward to greet her lord cousin, but Lord Bertaud's sternness frightened her, so after she whispered her proper greeting she could not think of anything to say to him.

"*Manners*, Mienthe," Aunt Eren sighed reproachfully, and Uncle

Talenes confided to Lord Bertaud that Mienthe was not, perhaps, very clever. Terre and Karre rolled their eyes and nudged each other. Mienthe longed to flee out to the courtyard. She flushed and looked fixedly at the mosaics underfoot.

Lord Bertaud frowned.

The meal was awful. The food was good, but Aunt Eren snapped at the maids and sent one dish back to the kitchens because it was too spicy and she was sure, as she repeated several times, that Lord Bertaud must have lost his taste for spicy food away in the north. Uncle Talenes worked smooth comments into the conversation about the brilliance with which Bertaud had handled the recent problems with Casmantium. And with the griffins, so there *had* been something to do with griffins. Mienthe gathered that Feierabiand had been at war with the griffins, or maybe with Casmantium, or maybe with both at the same time, or else one right after the other. And then maybe there had been something about griffins again, and a wall.

It was all very confusing. Mienthe knew nothing about griffins and couldn't imagine what a wall had to do with anything, but she wondered why her uncle, usually so clever, did not see that Lord Bertaud did not want to talk about the recent problems, whatever they had exactly involved. Lord Bertaud grew more and more remote. Mienthe fixed her eyes on her plate and moved food around so it might seem she had eaten part of it.

Lord Bertaud said little himself. Uncle Talenes gave complicated, assured explanations of why the tariffs between the Delta and Linularinum should be raised. Aunt Eren told him at great length about the shortcomings of the Tiefenauer markets and assured him that the Desamion markets on the other side of the river were no better. When Uncle Talenes and Aunt Eren left pauses in the flow of words, Lord Bertaud asked Terre about hunting in the marshes and Karre about the best places in Tiefenauer to buy bows and horses, and listened to their enthusiastic answers with as much attention as he'd given to their parents' discourse.

And he told Mienthe he was sorry to hear about her loss and asked whether she liked living in Tiefenauer with Uncle Talenes.

The question froze Mienthe in her seat. She could not answer truthfully, but she had not expected her lord cousin to speak to her at all and was too confused to lie. The silence that stretched out was horribly uncomfortable.

Then Uncle Talenes sharply assured Lord Bertaud that of course Mienthe was perfectly happy, didn't he provide everything she needed? She was great friends with his son Terre; the two would assuredly wed in two years, as soon as Mienthe was old enough. Terre glanced side-long at his father's face, swallowed, and tried to sound enthusiastic as he agreed. Karre leaned his elbow on the table and grinned at his brother. Aunt Eren scolded Mienthe for her discourtesy in failing to answer her lord cousin's question.

"I am happy," Mienthe whispered dutifully, but something made her add, risking a quick glance up at her lord cousin, "Only sometimes I miss Tef."

"Who is Tef?" Lord Bertaud asked her gently.

Mienthe flinched under Aunt Eren's cold glare and opened her mouth, but she did not know how to answer this question and in the end only looked helplessly at Lord Bertaud. Tef was Tef; it seemed impossible to explain him.

"Who is Tef?" Lord Bertaud asked Uncle Talenes.

Uncle Talenes. shook his head, baffled. "A childhood friend?" he guessed.

Mienthe stared down at her plate and wished passionately that she was free to run out to the courtyard and hide under the great oaks. Then Uncle Talenes began to talk about tariffs and trade again, and the discomfort was covered over. But to Mienthe the rest of the meal seemed to last for hours and hours, even though in fact her lord cousin departed the house long before dusk.

Once he was gone, Aunt Eren scolded Mienthe again for clumsiness and discourtesy—Any well-bred girl should be able to respond gracefully to a simple question, and why ever had Mienthe thought Lord Bertaud would want to hear about some little friend from years past? Anyone would have thought Mienthe had *no* sense of gratitude for anything Talenes had done for her, and no one liked an ungrateful child. Look up, Mienthe, and say, "Yes, Aunt Eren," properly. She was much too old to sulk like a spoiled toddler, and Aunt Eren wouldn't have it.

Mienthe said *Yes, Aunt Eren*, and *No, Aunt Eren*, and looked up when she was bidden to, and down when she could, and at last her aunt allowed her to escape to the courtyard. Mienthe tucked herself up next to the largest of the oaks and wished desperately for Tef. Speaking his name to her cousin had made her remember him too clearly.

Six days after Lord Bertaud's visit, not long after dawn, a four-horse coach with the king's badge in gold scrollwork on one door and the Delta's in silver on the other arrived at the house unannounced. It swished around the drive and pulled up by the front entrance. The driver, a grim-looking older man with the king's badge on his shoulder, set the brake, leaped down from his high seat, opened the coach door, and placed a step so his passenger could step down.

The man who descended from the coach, Mienthe saw, did not fit the image implied by its elegance. He looked to be a soldier or a guardsman, not a nobleman. By his bearing, he was well enough bred, but no one extraordinary. But he wore the king's badge on one shoulder and the Delta's on the other. Mienthe did not move from the window seat of her room. She was curious about the visitor, but not enough to put herself in her uncle's way.

She was surprised when Karre put his head through her door a moment later and said, "Father wants you. In his study. Hurry up, can't you?"

Mienthe stared after Karre when he had vanished. Her heart sank, for whatever Uncle Talenes wanted, she already knew she would not be able to do it, or at least would not be able to do it properly, or would not want to do it. Probably he wanted to show her off to the visitor. Mienthe knew she would look stiff and slow and that Uncle Talenes would regretfully tell his visitor that she was not very clever. But Karre called impatiently from out in the hall, so she reluctantly got to her feet.

She was not surprised to find the visitor with Uncle Talenes when she came into the study, but she *was* surprised at Uncle Talenes's expression and manner. Her uncle liked to show her to his friends and talk about what he would do with her father's estate when she married Terre, but this time he did not look like he had brought her in to show her off. He looked angry, but stifled, as though he was afraid to show his anger too clearly.

In contrast, the visitor looked . . . not quite oblivious of Uncle Talenes's anger, Mienthe thought. No, he looked like he knew Uncle Talenes was angry, but also like he did not mind his anger in the least. Mienthe admired him at once: *She* never felt anything but afraid and ashamed when Uncle Talenes was angry with *her.*

"Mienthe? Daughter of Beraod?" asked the visitor, but not as though he had any doubt as to who she was. He regarded Mienthe with lively interest. He was not smiling, but his wide expressive mouth looked like it would smile easily. She nodded uncertainly.

"Mienthe—" began Uncle Talenes.

The visitor held up a hand, and he stopped.

Mienthe gazed at this oddly powerful stranger with nervous amazement, waiting to hear what he wanted with her. She felt suspended in the moment, as in the eye of a soundless storm; she felt that her whole life had narrowed to this one point and that in a moment, when the man spoke, the storm would break. But she could not have said whether she was terrified of the storm or longed for it to come.

"I am Enned son of Lakas, king's man and servant of the Lord of the Delta," declared the young man. "Your cousin Bertaud son of Boudan, Lord of the Delta by right of blood and let of His Majesty Iaor Safiad, bids me bring you to him. He has decided that henceforward you will live with him in his house. You are to make ready at once and come back with me this very day." Looking at Uncle Talenes, he added warningly, "And you are not to fail of this command, on pain of Lord Bertaud's great displeasure."

"This is outrageous—" Uncle Talenes began.

The young man held up a hand again. "I merely do as I'm bid," he said, so sternly that Uncle Talenes stopped midprotest. "If you wish to contend with this order, Lord Talenes, you must carry your protest to the Lord of the Delta."

Mienthe looked at the stranger—Enned son of Lakas—for a long moment, trying to understand what he had said. She faltered at last, "I am to go with you?"

"Yes," said Enned, and he did smile then.

"I am not to come back?"

"No," agreed the young man. He looked at Uncle Talenes. "It will not take long to gather Mienthe's things," he said. The way he said it, it was not a question but a command.

"I—" said Uncle Talenes. "My wife—"

"The lord's house is not so far away that you will not be able to visit, if it pleases you to do so," Enned said. He did not say that Mienthe would visit Uncle Talenes's house.

"But—" said Uncle Talenes.

"I am to return before noon. We will need to depart in less than an hour," said the young man inflexibly. "I am quite certain it will not take long to gather Mienthe's things."

Uncle Talenes stared at the young man, then at Mienthe. He said to Mienthe, within his voice a note of conciliation she had never before heard, "Mienthe, this is outrageous—it is insupportable! You must tell the esteemed, ah, the esteemed Enned son of Lakas, you will certainly stay here, among people who know you and have your best interests close at heart—"

Mienthe gazed into her uncle's face for a moment. Then she lowered her gaze and stared fixedly at the floor.

Uncle Talenes flung up his hands and went out. Mienthe heard him shouting for Aunt Eren and for the servants. She lifted her head, giving the esteemed Enned son of Lakas a cautious glance out of the corner of her eye.

The young man smiled at her. "We shall leave them to it. Where shall we wait where we will be out of the way?"

Mienthe led the way to the courtyard.

Enned son of Lakas admired the huge oaks and trailed his hand in the fountain. Mienthe stood uncertainly, looking at him, and he turned his head and smiled at her again.

His smile lit his eyes and made Mienthe want to smile back, though she did not, in case he might find it impudent. But the smile gave her the courage to ask again, "I am not to come back?"

"That's as my lord wills," Enned said seriously. "But I think it most unlikely."

Mienthe thought about this. Then she turned and, going from one of the great oaks to the next, she stood on her toes, reached up as high as she could, and opened the doors to all the cages one after another.

The birds swirled out and swept around the courtyard in a flurry of sky blue and delicate green, soft primrose yellow and pure white. The palest blue one landed for a moment on Mienthe's upraised hand, and then all the birds darted up and over the walls and out into the broad sky.

Mienthe lowered her hand slowly once all of the birds were gone. When she nervously looked at Enned, she found that although he was looking at her intently and no longer smiling, his expression was only resigned rather than angry.

"Well," he said, "I suppose I can pay for those, if Lord Talenes asks."

Uncle Talenes did not ask. He was too busy trying to persuade Mienthe that she really wanted to stay with his family. Aunt Eren tried, too, though not very hard. Mienthe looked steadfastly at the floor of Uncle Talenes's study, and then at the mosaic floor of the entry hall, and then at the gravel of the drive. When Enned asked her if everything was packed that should be, she nodded without even glancing up.

"Well, you can send back if anything is missing," Enned told her, and to Uncle Talenes, "Thank you, Lord Talenes, and my lord sends his thanks as well." Then he handed Mienthe formally into the coach and signaled the driver, and the horses tossed up their heads and trotted smartly around the sweep of the drive and out onto the raised road that led through the deep marshlands into Tiefenauer.

Mienthe settled herself on the cushioned bench and fixed her gaze out the window. A bird called in the marshes—not the little brightly colored ones from the cages, but something that sounded larger and much wilder.

"You will like the great house," Enned said to her, but not quite confidently.

"Yes," Mienthe answered obediently, dropping her eyes to her folded hands in her lap.

"You cannot have been happy living with your uncle, surely?" Enned asked, but he sounded uncertain. "Now we are away, will you not speak plainly to me? My lord did not mean to take you away from a house where you were happy. He will send you back if you ask him."

Mienthe turned her head and stared at the man. "But you said he would not send me back?" Then, as Enned began to answer, she declared passionately, "I will never go back—I will run into the marshes first, even if there *are* snakes and poisonous frogs!"

"Good for you!" answered Enned, smiling again. "But I think that will not be necessary."

He sounded cheerful once more. Mienthe looked at her hands and did not reply.

The great house was not what she had expected, though she had not realized she expected anything until she found herself surprised. It was not neatly self-contained, but rather long and rambling. It occupied all the top of a long, low hill near the center of town. It had one wing sweeping out *this* way and another angled back *this* way and a third spilling down the hill *that* way, as though whoever had built it had never paused to think what the whole would look like when he had designed the parts. It was made of red brick and gray stone and pale cypress wood, and it was surrounded by sweeping gardens—not formal gardens such as at her father's house, but wild-looking shrubberies with walks winding away into them.

The house was huge, but nearly all the windows were tight-shuttered, and there was nothing of the crowded clamor that should have occupied so great a dwelling. Mienthe remembered that her lord cousin was supposed to have dismissed all the staff. She would have liked to ask Enned about this, but she did not quite dare. The coach swept around the wide drive and drew to a halt, and the driver jumped down to put the step in place. Enned descended and turned to offer Mienthe his hand.

Lord Bertaud came out of the house before they quite reached it. He looked tired and distracted. Behind the tiredness and distraction was that other, darker depth that Mienthe could not quite recognize. But his expression lightened when he saw her, and he came down the steps and took Mienthe's hands in his.

"Cousin!" he said. "Welcome!" He smiled down at her with every evidence of pleased satisfaction. The darkness in his eyes, if it had been there at all, was hidden by his smile. Mienthe blushed with confusion and nervousness, but her cousin did not seem to mind, or even notice. He said to Enned, "There was no trouble?"

"Not at all," Enned replied cheerfully. "I enjoyed myself. What a pity all your orders cannot be such a pleasure to carry out, my lord."

"Indeed." Lord Bertaud released one of Mienthe's hands so he could clap the young man on the shoulder. "Go help Ansed put the coach away, if you will, and settle the horses, and then come report to me."

"My lord," Enned answered, with a small bow for his lord and another for Mienthe, and turned to hail the coach's driver.

Lord Bertaud drew Mienthe after him toward the house. "You will be hungry after your journey. I had my men wait the noon meal—I am afraid we do not have a cook as yet. Indeed, as yet we have few servants of any description," he added apologetically. "Of course you must have a maid, and I have arranged interviews for tomorrow, but for the moment you must make do with Ansed's wife. Edlis is her name. I am sure she will not be what you are accustomed to, cousin, but I hope you will be patient with her."

Mienthe, who was not accustomed to any but the most grudging help with anything, did not know how to answer.

Lord Bertaud did not seem to mind her silence, but led her into the house and down a long floor. The floor was not decorated with any mosaic tiles. It was plain wood. Though the boards were clean, they were not even painted, and they creaked underfoot. He told her, "You may explore the house after we eat, or whenever you like. I have put you in a room near mine for now—all the house save part of this wing is shut up at the moment, but later you may certainly choose any room that pleases you."

They turned a corner and entered the kitchens, which were wide and sprawling, with three ovens and four work counters and a long table in front of two large windows. The windows were shaded by the branches of overhanging trees, but open to catch any breeze. The door to an ice cellar stood open, with a cool draft rising from it, and only one of the ovens glowed with heat. It was immediately obvious that there was no proper kitchen staff, for the meal was being prepared by a man who looked like a soldier.

"Yes," said Lord Bertaud, evidently amused by Mienthe's expression. "I did not want to hire a cook you did not like, cousin; the cook is almost as important as your maids. So it's camp cooking for us today, I fear."

"Well, my lord, I think we've managed something better than camp fare," the man said cheerfully. "Nothing fancy, I own, but a roast is easy enough, and you can always tuck potatoes in the drippings. And I sent Daued into town for pastries." The man nodded to Mienthe politely. "My lady."

Mienthe hesitantly nodded back.

"We will all eat in the staff hall today, with perfect informality," declared her cousin.

"Yes, my lord," agreed the man, and poked the roast with a long-handled fork. "This is so tender it's near melted, lord, so we can serve as you please."

"Half an hour," said Lord Bertaud, and to Mienthe, "I think you will like to meet my new gardener. I hired him just two days past, but I'm quite pleased. Just step out through that door and I think you will find him working in the kitchen gardens, just here by the house."

Mienthe stared at her cousin.

"Go on," Lord Bertaud said, smiling at her. "Tell him that everyone will be eating in the staff hall, please, cousin. In half an hour, but if you are a little delayed, no one will mind."

This all seemed strange to Mienthe, but then everything about her cousin seemed strange to her. When Lord Bertaud nodded firmly toward the kitchen door, she took a cautious step toward it. When he nodded to her again, she turned and pushed open the door.

The gardener was sitting on a short-legged stool, carefully setting new ruby-stemmed chard seedlings into a bed to replace long-bolted lettuces. Though his back was toward Mienthe, she knew him at once. She stopped and stared, for though she knew him, she did not believe she could be right. But he heard the kitchen door close behind her and turned. His broad, grizzled face had not changed at all.

"Mie!" Tef said and reached down for the crutch lying beside his stool.

Mienthe did not run to him. She walked, slowly and carefully, feeling that with any step he might suddenly turn into someone else, a stranger, someone she did not know; perhaps she only imagined she knew him because the smell of herbs and turned earth had overwhelmed her with memory. But when she reached the gardener and put a cautious hand out to his, he was still Tef. He rubbed dirt off his hands and put a hand on her shoulder, and pulled her into an embrace, and Mienthe tucked herself close to his chest and burst into tears.

"Well, now, it was an odd thing," Tef told her a little later, when the brief storm had passed and Mienthe had washed her face with water out of his watering jug. "This man rode up to my house four days ago. He asked me was I the Tef who'd used to be a gardener for Lord Beraod. I said yes, and he asked me all about the old household."

"And about me," Mienthe said. Four days ago, so Lord Bertaud must have sent a man to Kames almost as soon as he had left Uncle Talenes's house. So he must have been thinking even then about bringing her to live with him in the great house. That decisiveness frightened Mienthe a little because she still had no idea *why* her cousin had brought her to live with him.

"Yes, Mie, and about you, though not right at first. I could see he'd been working around to something, but I didn't rightly know what, and then after I knew what, I'd no idea of why. But I couldn't see what harm it would do to answer his questions, so I told him."

"Yes, but what did you tell him?"

"Well, the truth! That your mama died when you were three and your father barely noticed you except when you got in his way; that Lord Beraod had a temper with a bite to it and couldn't keep staff no matter he paid high; that you had twenty-seven nurses in six years and hardly a one worth a barley groat, much less a copper coin; and that—" He paused.

Mienthe looked at Tef wonderingly. "What?"

"Well, that I'd let you follow me about, I suppose," Tef said gruffly. "So this man, he said Lord Bertaud, Boudan's son, had come back to the Delta and meant to be lord here, only he needed staff, and would I want to come be a gardener at the great house? I said I wasn't any younger now than I was then, but he said Lord Bertaud wouldn't mind about that. And then he said the lord would be sending for you, Mie, so I gave my house to my nephew's daughter and packed up my things, and, well, here we are."

Mienthe thought about this. Then she asked, "But *why* did he send for me?" and waited confidently for the answer. It never occurred to her that Tef might not know.

Nor was she disappointed. Tef said briskly, "Well, that's simple enough, I expect. You know the old lord, Lord Berdoen that was your grandfather, you know he was a terror, I suppose, and rode his twelve sons with a hard hand on the rein and whip, as they say."

Everyone knew that. Mienthe nodded.

"Well, Lord Boudan, your cousin's father, he had just the same cold heart and heavy hand as the old lord, so they say. Anyway, Lord Boudan, he sent his son to serve at court—that was while the old king was alive, but by all accounts, Prince Iaor liked Bertaud well and kept him close. So even after Lord Boudan and then the old king died, Lord Bertaud didn't come home—not but for flying visits, do you see. He'd hated his father so much he couldn't stand any part of the Delta, is what I'd guess, and so he stayed on at court. And he still is close to the king, from what they say about this past summer: They say Iaor sent your cousin as his envoy to Casmantium after that trouble this summer, did you hear about that?"

Mienthe shook her head uncertainly, meaning that if her uncle had said anything about it at the time, either he hadn't said it to her or she hadn't been paying attention.

"Well, I don't know much about it, either, but there's been talk about it around and about the Delta because of your cousin's being our right lord, do you see? And some folk say one thing and some another, but I guess there was some kind of problem with griffins coming over the mountains into Feierabiand early in the summer, but it all had to do with Casmantium somehow, which *that* part makes sense, I guess, since everybody knows that's where griffins live, up there north of Casmantium. And Lord Bertaud was important in getting it all to come out right, somehow, and then the king sent him to Casmantium after it was all over, to escort the young Casmantian prince to our court as a hostage—"

"Oh!" said Mienthe, startled, and then put a hand over her mouth to show she was sorry for interrupting.

"Well, that's what they say, though how our king made Casmantium's king send him, I'm sure I don't know. He must be about your age, I guess. The young prince, I mean."

"Oh," Mienthe said again, feeling intensely sorry for the displaced Casmantian prince. "I suppose he was sad to leave his home and go somewhere to live with strangers?" She supposed he might even have been sorry to leave his father, too, though that required some imagination.

Tef patted her hands. "Oh, well, Mie, a boy that age might be ready for an adventure, maybe. And you know, our Safiad king's a decent sort by all accounts. Anyway, I've barely seen your cousin to speak to, you know, but somehow I don't think he'd be the sort to lend himself to anything that wasn't right and proper."

"He seems kind," Mienthe whispered.

"He does that. Anyway, besides about the young prince, I heard tell of something about a wall in Casmantium, but I can't rightly say I know what that was about, except it was about the griffins again and likely needed some kind of mageworking to build. They say the Wall is a hundred miles long and was built in a single night, but I don't know as I believe even the greatest Casmantian makers and builders could do that. Not even with mages to help."

Mienthe nodded.

"Well, your cousin's no mage, but I guess he built that Wall, or maybe had it built, somehow. Whatever he did, he came out of it with honors from both the Casmantian king and our king, which you can maybe guess or else our king wouldn't hardly have sent his own men to serve Lord Bertaud here in the Delta, would he?"

Mienthe wondered again why her cousin had come back.

"Oh, well," said Tef, when she asked him. He paused, picking up a clump of dark earth and crumbling it thoughtfully in his fingers. "You know, Mie, I think maybe Lord Bertaud was hurt somehow in all that mess this summer, and don't fool yourself, if there was any kind of battle, I'm sure it was a right mess. They always are. Or maybe he was just tired out. I wonder if maybe he . . . well. What I think is, when it came right to it, when he found he needed a place to shut himself away from everything and just rest, somehow he found himself thinking of the Delta. It's in his blood, after all, however hard a man his father was."

Mienthe nodded doubtfully. "But—" she began, and then exclaimed, "Oh!" as she suddenly understood something else. "*That's* why he dismissed all the staff here—because he'd hated his father's house so much and didn't want anyone here who'd been here when he was a boy! Is that why?"

"I should think so. He's allowing the staff to reapply, but the word is, only the younger staff have a chance to come back—it's just what you said, he doesn't want anyone here who reminds him of those bad years. And that's why he sent for you, do you see, Mie? Because he saw you in your uncle Talenes's house and you reminded him of himself, that's what I expect happened, and he decided to rescue you just as the king once rescued him."

"Yes . . ." Mienthe said softly. She could see this was true, that it must be true. Her heart tried to rise up and sink both at once. From being afraid that she would not be able to please her cousin and that he would send her back, she found herself afraid that she would not be able to please him and that he would be disappointed in her. Her famous, important cousin might not be sorry he had rescued her, but he would be sorry he had rescued *her.* That he had not found a girl who was clever and pretty graceful—someone he could be proud of having rescued. Tears welled up in her eyes, and she rubbed her sleeve fiercely across her eyes—she never cried, and here she was weeping twice in an hour!

In an hour. Mienthe jumped to her feet and said, "He said half an hour!" and then she *really* wanted to cry, because here she had barely arrived at the great house and already she was letting her cousin see how careless and stupid she was—

"Hush, Mie, it'll all be well," Tef promised her, patting her foot because he couldn't reach her shoulder. "Do you think he didn't know we'd get to talking? Hand me my crutch, there's a sweet girl, and don't cry."

If you are a little delayed, no one will mind, her cousin had said, Mienthe remembered, so maybe Tef was right. She tried to smile, but still said anxiously, "But we should hurry. To the—to the staff hall, he said."

"The staff hall it is, then," Tef agreed, climbing laboriously to his feet.

CHAPTER 1

Six years later

Tiefenauer, largest town of all the wide Delta, was a place of broad
streets and ancient cypresses and swamp oaks. Wooden boardwalks lay
beside all the important streets, allowing passersby to keep out of the
winter mud that sometimes flooded even over the cobbles. Deep drain-
age channels ran underneath the boardwalks, so that only the greatest
storms of spring and fall would flood the town. Even so, winter and
spring and fall were the seasons when Tiefenauer bustled with energy
and life.

In the summer, when the days grew long and the air hung motionless and heavy, the town became as somnolent as the air. Flowers of
purple and red tumbled from every balcony, and it seemed that every
house in Tiefenauer had at least one balcony. Fat bumblebees hummed
placidly among the flowers, and all the people of Tiefenauer hung out
little pots of sugar water to attract the large purple-backed humming-
birds, and the little red-throated ones, to their balconies. Larger birds
darted among the branches of the great trees and nested in the streamers of moss that festooned them.

Years ago, Tan had lived in Tiefenauer for one long, lazy summer
that stood out, jewel-bright, in his memory. He wished fervently that it
was summer now. The Delta was seldom so terribly cold, but it surely
seemed cold enough. He knelt, shaking and half frozen, in the dirty
straw of his cell, and tried not to laugh. There was nothing the least
amusing in his situation, except that it was so utterly, perfectly ludi-
crous.

He said to the prison guard—a brawny young man with broad

shoulders, big hands, and, currently, an expression of grim distaste, "I suppose everyone begs you to carry messages to their friends and promises rewards for the favor. But does everyone ask you to take a message to the lord himself? Not even a message. Just a name. I swear to you, he'll know that name. I swear to you, he'll want to see me. He *must* see me. It's—"

"Desperately important, I know," interrupted the young guard. He gave a scornful, uneasy jerk of his head. "Of course it is. But they're busy up in the great house. Anyway, it's against the rules. That's enough for me! Do you think I want to be stuck down in this pit forever? I'll warn you, though, don't trouble offering a bribe to Jer when he comes on duty. He'll take your money and give you nothing for it."

"If I had anything to bribe either of you with, I'd risk it," Tan assured the young man. "Unfortunately, all I can offer is a promise that if you take my name up to the great house, you'll not remain a prison guard."

"Because I'll be a prisoner myself?" the guard said, not quite as naive as he looked. "Indeed, I would be in your debt, esteemed sir. I said, it's against the rules." He half turned, preparing to go on with his rounds.

Tan longed to pound his hands against the floor and shout. But it wouldn't help, and anyway he was too tired. He made himself speak softly instead. "Well, I'm sure that's a comfort to you. When I'm found murdered in this cell, I hope you will wonder how far you are responsible. But you won't need to reproach yourself, will you? You'll know you followed the *rules*."

The guard turned back, frowning. "I think you're safe enough in our keeping."

Tan laughed out loud. "You think, what? That I'm some thief or common thug? I'm asking you, begging you, to take my name to the Lord of the Delta himself, and you think I'm a *thief*? Is that what you think?"

The young guard opened his mouth, shut it again, turned his back, gave Tan an unsettled look over his shoulder, and walked out. The door slammed behind him with disheartening finality, leaving Tan alone in the dark and cold. Tan pressed his hands over his eyes. Perhaps a little less sarcasm, a little more humility? If he had not learned a measure of humility tonight, he surely never would.

He eased himself back to sit against the wall. The stone was dry enough, but cold. It seemed to suck the warmth right out of his bones. After a moment he hunched away from it and huddled into the straw. The window of his cell admitted, at the moment, nothing past its bars more alarming than the chill air of earliest spring and little curls of mist. Tan wondered how long it would take for Linularinan agents to track him to this cell. How they would laugh, to find him so stupidly trapped, and by his own people! And then someone would throw a poison dart through that window or, much worse, bribe the prison guards to release him into their hands. And after that . . .

It was appalling that only the basic integrity of a young prison guard who didn't break the rules might protect him from his enemies. He knew, of course, that no such integrity could possibly protect him well enough.

The outer door swung back suddenly, letting in the bright swinging light of lanterns and the heavy tread of boots. Tan straightened, then got to his feet and tried to look intelligent and at least somewhat respectable. The young guard had come back, and with him was the officer of the watch: a powerful man with a harsh, brutal face.

"Well?" he said to Tan.

"Esteemed Captain," Tan said immediately, and bowed.

"You don't consider our protection here adequate, is that right? You've got *special* enemies, that's what I hear. You think you'll fare better if your name goes up the hill, do you?"

"If you please to send it, esteemed sir, and I swear to you it will be recognized."

The captain looked Tan up and down with obvious distaste. "You're safe enough here, I assure you, so you may set your heart at rest on that account."

Tan bowed his head and said nothing.

"Huh. A prodigal cousin, are you? Got in bad company and came dragging home to beg pardon and payment of your debts from the lord?"

"If you like," Tan agreed obligingly. He tried to look dissolute and repentant.

"You think Lord Bertaud will be happy to hear your name, do you? Not likely! Theft, brawling, murder: What else do you drag at your heel? You think the lord will pardon all that for whatever blood you might have in common?" The captain sounded like he doubted this. He said with grim satisfaction, "You think he wants some bastard half cousin up at the great house *now*, with the king's household in residence? If you had the sense of a turnip, you'd hope no judge had time for you until next month, after the king's gone back to Tihannad, if you hope for mercy from Lord Bertaud."

Tan gazed at the captain. He said slowly, "King Iaor is here?"

"You didn't know?" This time, the captain sounded honestly astonished. "Earth and sea, man, where have you been the past six years? It's that long since His Majesty began breaking his annual progress in the Delta for a month or more! Ever since Lord Bertaud came home." He looked grimly pleased to crush Tan's hopes.

"If Bertaud doesn't know my name, Iaor will," Tan declared at once, hoping it was true.

The captain scowled. "*Lord* Bertaud, man, and *King* Iaor, man! Let us have some respect!"

Tan bowed apology. "I beg your pardon, esteemed Captain. I meant no disrespect." He tried to remember a name that both Bertaud and the king might recognize.

"Well," the captain said, looking at him hard. "And what name is it that they'll know, up at the great house?"

"Teras son of Toharas," Tan said, hoping that this was true.

"Huh." The captain turned his head and fixed the young guard with a cold eye. The young man straightened his back and swallowed. "Since you and the prisoner are both so concerned for his safety, you can stay on after your shift and keep an eye on him," said the captain. "Without extra pay, of course." He walked out.

The young guard looked morosely at Tan. "Thank you so much. I ought to beat you bloody."

"Your captain may yet send my name up the hill," Tan said softly. "That chance is worth any beating. So is your watchful presence here. Did you think I did not mean my warning to you? You may well have saved my life tonight." He bowed his head, adding formally, "I am in your debt, and you may call upon me." He looked up again, smiling, and added, "For all you may not find such a promise very impressive just at this moment. What is your name, if I may be so bold as to inquire?"

The guard seemed warily impressed, and not very inclined to carry out his threat. He hesitated for a moment and then said, "Tenned. Son of Tenned."

"Tenned son of Tenned. I thank you." Tan bowed. Then, as the young man did not seem likely to carry out his threat, Tan sat down in the straw, wrapped his arms around his body, and tried not to shiver the last of his strength away. Tenned's presence was indeed a comfort and a safeguard. Tan might even dare to rest, if he were not so cold.

Tenned regarded him for a long moment. Then he set his jaw, hooked his lantern to a hook high up in the wall, and left the room.

But he came back in mere moments with a threadbare blanket and a hard roll stuffed with sausage, both of which he tossed wordlessly through the bars to Tan.

Despite his surprise, Tan caught the food and the blanket. A flush crept up the guard's face when Tan stared at him, making him seem younger still. Tan shook his head. "Truly, you need a place in some other company. You are too kind to be"—he gestured at the walls of his cell and, by extension, at the prison entire—"here."

The guard crossed his arms uneasily across his chest and glanced away. But he said in a low voice, "Maybe, if the captain doesn't send word up the hill . . . maybe I'll go after all. At noon." He gave Tan a hard look. "If the captain lets me off duty at noon. That's a double watch. He'll set up to three extra, if he's angry enough. He did that to a new guard last week, when he let a prisoner get his keys."

Tan might have wished Tenned to be careless enough to let Tan get his keys, but this seemed most unlikely. He contented himself with nodding sympathetically.

But at two hours past dawn, the guard captain came back himself, with a pair of extra guards and a set of slender keys. The stamp of their boots woke Tan, who sat up and then got to his feet, laying aside the blanket with a nod of thanks to Tenned.

"I don't know as anyone recalls your name, mind," the captain told Tan. "Maybe they're only interested. But you're to go up and they'll take a look at you, at least. *I* wouldn't care to miss it. I'm taking you up myself."

Tan looked over the two guards the captain had brought with him and shook his head. "You should have more men."

The captain lifted his eyebrows. "What? That tough, are you?"

"Not for me. Six men, at least. Ten would be better. You should detail half to keep their attention outward."

For a long moment, the captain was silent. Tan wondered whether he had at last succeeded in impressing the man with his sincerity, if nothing else. Or, given the captain's harsh, expressionless stare, whether he had at last succeeded in offending the man beyond bearing. The man had shoulders like an ox; he could undoubtedly deliver a ferocious beating if he decided a prisoner was being deliberately insolent. "Not that I'd try to instruct you in your business, esteemed Captain," Tan added, trying his best to look respectful.

But the captain only said at last, to one of his men, "Beras, go round up everyone who's free and tell 'em meet us at the front gate. Tenned. Unlock that cell." He shot Tan an ironic look and threw the young guard a set of manacles. "Chain the prisoner."

Tan put his hands out cooperatively, hoping to get Tenned to chain his hands in front of his body rather than behind. From the deepening irony of the captain's expression, the man recognized that old trick. But he said nothing, and Tenned did indeed allow Tan to keep his hands in front.

The great house stood, in fact, on a long, low hill—low, but the only hill for half a day's travel in any direction, the Delta not being re-nowned for hills of any kind. The house was itself essentially long and low, though one wing had two stories and one round tower at the edge of the adjoining wing stood two stories higher than that. The tower was windowless. Tan wasn't quite certain what that said about the character of the man who had commanded it built.

The house had been built by a succession of Delta lords, each add-ing to it primarily by building out into its grounds rather than upward. One wing of the house had originally been stables—but very fine stables—and another had once probably been a mews, from the look of the extremely broad windows. The current stables and mews and ken-nels were just visible, far around the side of the house. If Tan had seen them earlier, he might have guessed that the king was in residence, both from the general busy atmosphere and from the fineness of the horses. The guard captain appeared to be heading for a door over in that general area.

The captain had, in the end, surrounded Tan with nine guards and had ordered five of them to forget the prisoner and watch the streets. Half a dozen crows flew overhead, cawing harshly. They flew ahead of the little procession and over the rooftops to either side. Another crow perched on the captain's shoulder, tilting its head this way and that, its bright black eyes intelligent and alert. It seemed the captain had an af-finity for crows. At the moment, Tan could hardly imagine a more use-ful affinity, though he'd have preferred to have a larger flock looking for trouble. Though, even so, it didn't seem likely anyone with a bow could stay hidden on a roof with even a few crows flying watchfully near. Even a man who could whisper to his arrows and make them turn to strike their target had to aim somewhere *near* where he wanted them to strike.

The captain followed the flight of his crows with a frowning look, then turned his attention back to his prisoner. Perhaps he suspected some ruse on Tan's part. Tan would have been happy to have a ruse in mind, but he did not. Perhaps it was better so. As his trouble last night had so clearly demonstrated, he might in fact be safer in chains and surrounded by guards than he would have been slipping quietly through the city on his own. Especially with royal guardsmen set all about the great house.

"Here we are," the guard captain said to Tan as they came up to a narrow, plain door set in the side of a plain, windowless building. "I see we had enough crows after all—and two or three guards would have been sufficient, after all."

"Unless the force you displayed deterred my enemies," Tan suggested blandly. "Esteemed Captain."

The captain looked at him fixedly for a moment. But then he merely put out one massive hand and shoved the door open. It was not locked. They shed half the guards and all the crows as they went through it, and through a barren entryway, and at last into an unadorned reception room that contained nothing but a small table and one chair.

The chair was occupied. Bertaud son of Boudan—so Tan supposed—looked up. His gaze was intent and mistrustful, but not, Tan thought, actually hostile. At least, not yet. The young man Tan remembered from the court at Tihannad had grown into a solid, self-assured lord. He'd come to look a good deal like his father, which must surely gall him. But there was an interesting depth in his eyes, and lines around his mouth that Tan did not remember. Tan wondered how he had come by that compelling intensity.

Tan went to one knee before Bertaud's chair, rested his bound hands on his other knee, and bowed his head for a moment. Then he lifted his head and looked Bertaud in the face. Their eyes met. Bertaud's look became searching, then questioning. He drew breath to speak.

Before he could, Tan said quickly, "Hair darker than yours. Longer than yours, tied back with a plain cord. Ten fewer years, forty extra pounds, and no sense of style. A ring on my left hand—"

"A beryl," Bertaud said. He straightened in his chair, frowning. "Set in a heavy iron ring. You were before my time." He meant, before Iaor had made him lord of the king's own guard. "I remember you with Moutres." Lord Moutres had held that post of trust for Iaor's father and then, for some years, for Iaor.

Rising, Bertaud came forward to examine Tan more closely. "How do you come here?"

"Ah . . ." Tan hesitated. He asked cautiously, "Do you know . . . what I did for, um, Moutres?"

Bertaud frowned again. "Not in detail."

"The king knows—"

"His Majesty is otherwise occupied."

There wasn't a lot of give in that flat statement. Tan paused. Then he said, "I've just come across the bridge. From Teramondian. I was too closely pursued to get across the river farther north; I was forced to run south and even so I hardly made it out of Linularinum. But now I understand that His Majesty is here after all, so that's well enough. If he'll see me. Or if you will, my lord, but *privately*, I beg you."

Bertaud simply looked at him for a long moment. Tan tried to look like an earnest servant of the king rather than a desperate fool who'd put a foot wrong in the Linularinan court and run home for rescue. After a moment, Bertaud said, "Teras son of Toharas, is it? Is that the name I should give to the king?"

Tan hesitated. Then he surprised himself by saying, "Tan. You may tell His Majesty it is Tan who has brought him a difficult gift."

"Son of?"

Tan shook his head. "Just Tan." He was prepared for either suspicion or scorn, depending on whether the lord took him for insolently reticent or the son of a careless father. He certainly did not intend to lay out any explanations. Especially as both answers obtained.

But he saw neither suspicion nor scorn. Lord Bertaud only inclined his head gravely. "So I shall inform the king," he said, gave the guard captain a raised-eyebrow look, and left the room.

The captain stared down at Tan and shook his head. "Huh."

Tan bowed his head meekly and composed himself to wait.

After a surprisingly short time, however, the door swung open once more. Bertaud came in first, but stepped aside at once and personally held the door.

Iaor Daveien Behanad Safiad, King of Feierabiand and, more or less, of the Delta, clearly did not keep any great state when he visited Tiefenauer. He had brought no attendants nor guardsmen of his own; he wore no crown and no jewels save for a ruby of moderate size set in a heavy gold ring. But nevertheless, even if Tan had never seen him before, he would have known he was looking at the king.

King Iaor was broad, stocky, not overtall. But he held himself with more than mere assurance, with a presumption of authority that was unquestionably royal. Tan took a breath and waited for the king to speak first. But the king glanced impatiently toward the door, so Tan gathered they were in fact still waiting for someone—perhaps the king was not without attendants after all.

Lord Bertaud was still holding the door, with an air of amusement as well as impatience. A hurried tread was audible, and then a stocky, broad-shouldered young man of perhaps eighteen entered hastily, escorting a girl about his own age, trim-figured and pretty in a straightforward way, wheaten hair caught back with a ribbon.

"I beg your pardon, cousin," the young woman said hastily to Bertaud, then bit her lip and turned to the king. "It's my fault Erich's late—I asked him where he was off to in such a hurry and then I made him bring me. If you—that is, if you don't mind? Please?" She glanced sidelong at Bertaud.

"Mienthe—" began Bertaud, in a tone of exasperated affection.

"The fault was entirely mine," declared the young man, who must be, Tan realized, Erichstaben son of Brechen Glansent. Or, as the Casmantians would have it, Prince Erichstaben Taben Arobern, first and only son of Brechen Glansent Arobern, *the* Arobern, King of Casmantium, currently a hostage at the court of King Iaor. Though the Casmantian prince certainly did not seem to feel his status as a hostage. He said to Iaor, in a deep voice that carried a guttural, clipped accent, "Your Majesty, if you will pardon my forwardness—"

"*If* you please—" began Bertaud sternly.

King Iaor held up a hand and everyone stopped.

A reluctant smile crooked Bertaud's mouth. "You won't permit me to scold them?"

The king said drily, "If Erich is to attend us here, then I can imagine no possible reason your cousin should not." He gave the pair a long look and added, "Though if I send you away, I shall expect you to go without argument."

Both Erich and Mienthe nodded earnestly.

The king returned a grave nod. Then he looked at Tan for a long moment, his expression impossible to read. Then he said, "Teras son of Toharas?" To Tan's relief, his voice held recognition and a trace of amusement.

"I've gone by that name," Tan said, a little defensively. "Not for some time, I admit."

"No," agreed the king. "Though I recall it. But it is your own name that brought me to hear you." He sat down in the chair and raised his eyebrows. "Well? I understand you meant to come to me in Tihannad? You are far out of your way."

"Fortunately, so is Your Majesty," Tan said smoothly. He glanced around at the clutter of guardsmen. "You'll want to speak to me privately. Or more privately than this, at least." He thought he should ask the king to send away the Casmantian prince and Bertaud's cousin, but he also thought Iaor would refuse. And at least he could be almost entirely certain that neither of them could possibly be a Linularinan agent.

King Iaor tilted his head to one side and glanced at Bertaud. Bertaud nodded to the captain. "You and your men may wait outside." When the captain glowered in disapproval, he added, "If you would be so good, Captain Geroen."

The disapproval became outright mulishness. "No, my lord. With His Majesty right here, *and* your lady cousin?"

"We know this man," Lord Bertaud said patiently.

"You don't, my lord, begging your pardon. You might have done once, but now he's been in Linularinum, hasn't he? For ears, isn't that

so? And this is a man my guardsmen took up for mayhem and murder!
He had two bodies at his feet when they found him, and him unmarked!"

Bertaud's eyebrows rose. The king sat back in the chair, crooking a
finger across his mouth. Erich grinned outright, but Mienthe looked
solemn and a little distressed. The guardsmen all stared at their captain
in horror.

The guard captain said grimly, "My lord, neither you nor His Majesty
nor Lady Mienthe will be left alone with a dangerous prisoner while I'm
captain of the prison guard. Nor I won't resign. You can dismiss me, if it
please you. But if you do, if you've any sense, my lord, you'll call for
someone you trust before you talk to this man. Dessand, maybe, or Eniad.
Or some of His Majesty's men." He glared at Bertaud.

"I think," Bertaud said gently, after a brief pause, "that you had
better stay with us yourself, Geroen."

Captain Geroen nodded curtly.

"Then, if you will free the prisoner's hands, and dismiss your
men—"

"Nor you won't loose those manacles, my lord, not without you
keep more than one man by you! No, it won't do him any harm to wear
iron a bit longer."

This time the pause stretched out. But at last the lord said, with
deliberate patience, "Perhaps you will at least permit me to dismiss
your men?"

Geroen set his jaw. His heavy features were not suited to apology,
but he said harshly, "I'd flog a man of mine for defiance, my lord, of
course I would. I'll willingly take a flogging on your order, just so as
you're alive to *give* the order! I beg your pardon, my lord, and beg you
again not to take risks that, earth and *iron*, my lord, *are not necessary*."

Tan was impressed. He rather thought the guardsmen had all
stopped breathing. He knew they had all gone beyond horror to terror.
If he'd meant to try some move of his own, this would surely have been
the moment for it, with all attention riveted on the captain. Alas, he had
no occasion to profit from the distraction.

"Captain Geroen, you must assuredly dismiss your men, if you are
going to corrupt their innocence with so appalling an example," Bertaud said at last, after a fraught pause. "You may do so now."

The captain made a curt gesture. His men fled.

"I think," Bertaud said drily to the king, "that this is all the privacy
we will be afforded."

The king was very clearly trying not to smile. "Your captain's
loyalty does you credit, my friend." He transferred his gaze from Ber-

taud to Captain Geroen. "Of course, without discretion, loyalty is strictly limited in value."

There was nothing Geroen could say to that. He set his heavy jaw and bowed his head.

"So," Iaor said to Tan, his tone rather dry, "perhaps you will now tell us the news you've brought out of Linularinum."

Tan glanced deliberately at Prince Erichstaben, at Lady Mienthe.

"I think we need not be concerned with Erich's discretion," King Iaor said.

"Certainly not with Mienthe's," Bertaud said crisply.

Tan sighed, bowed his head, and said, "I'm one of Moutres's confidential agents, as you no doubt recall, Your Majesty. I don't know whether you knew that I've been in Linularinum, in Teramondian, at the old Fox's court? Been there for years, doing deep work, do you understand? And I won something for it. I got Istierinan's private papers."

"Istierinan Hamoddian?" King Iaor asked sharply.

Tan tried to look modest. "Why, yes. Himself. He was a little upset, as you might imagine. I got out of Teramondian two steps in front of his men. I'd intended to run for Tihannad, but they clung too close to my heel. By the time I got to Falle, they were only half a step behind, and less than that by Desamion." Tan stopped, lifted his chained hands to rub his mouth. After a moment, he went on in a lower voice, "Earth and stone, I thought they had me twice before I made it across the river—" He stopped again. Then he took a hard breath, met the king's eyes, and said, "They came across the river after me."

"*Did* they?" King Iaor leaned forward, gripping the arms of the chair. "How did they *dare*?"

"I don't know, Your Majesty. That surprised me, too, the more as they must have known you were here. Not a mark on me, Captain Geroen says. Earth and stone, every hair I own should be white after the past days. They pressed me hard enough I was barely able to keep upright by the time a brace of earnest guardsmen caught me standing flat over a couple of bodies in an alley. Caught in the street by the city guard! Moutres wouldn't be the only one to laugh himself insensible, if he knew. But," and Tan gave Geroen a little nod, "if they hadn't picked me up, I don't know that I'd have lasted the night. And if Captain Geroen hadn't set an extra guard on me last night, and put half his men around me to bring me up here, the whole effort might have been wasted."

The king slowly leaned back in the chair again. "Well, no surprise that the city had a restless night. What were these papers you stole?"

"Oh, everything," Tan said briskly. "Lists of Istierinan's agents, and lists of men he suspects are ours. Lists of men who aren't agents, but dupes and useful fools, and of men who have been bribed. Comments about Linularinum's own nobility and men of substance, which ones Ist-ierinan is watching and which ones he thinks susceptible to bribes, and which ones are susceptible to blackmail—the notations there made fas-cinating reading, but the list of *our* people is even better."

The king blinked. The Casmantian prince, young Erichstaben, looked, for the first time, as though he wondered whether he should be present to hear this. Mienthe's gaze was wide and fascinated. Bertaud asked, "He had all that out in plain sight?"

"Locked in a hidden drawer, my lord, and all in cipher, of course. Three different ciphers, in fact. I broke them. Well, two of them. I al-ready had the key for one."

"I see. And where are these papers now?"

"He didn't have them when he was picked up last night," Geroen declared.

"I destroyed them, of course. After I memorized them."

"You memorized them," Bertaud repeated.

"I have a good memory."

"I see."

"I'll give it all to you, now." Tan glanced from Bertaud to the king and back. "Today. Right now, if you'll permit me. I'd suggest at least a dozen copies to be sent north as well, to both the winter court in Tihan-nad and the summer court in Tiearanan. Any couriers who go openly by the road had better have fast horses and plenty of nerve, but Linulari-num must *not* imagine they've stopped that information getting out. It's very good His Majesty is here. Now that I'm in your hands, that should stop Istierinan's agents flat where they stand, no matter their orders."

"Yes," said Bertaud. "I see that." He hesitated, glancing at the king. Iaor made a little gesture inviting him to proceed. Bertaud turned back to Tan, regarding him with narrow intensity. "A secure room," he said aloud. "With a desk and plenty of paper. And at least one clerk to assist you. You will permit a clerk to assist you?"

"Of course, my lord." Though Tan didn't much care for the idea. Nevertheless, he knew he would not have the strength to write out all the copies as swiftly as it had to be done. He said smoothly, "Anyone you see fit to assign the duty."

"We'll want guards," Geroen put in grimly. "All around the house, not just the spy and his clerks. And in the stables. And around the cou-riers. And the couriers' equipment." He glanced at King Iaor. "I'll ask His Majesty to set his own guardsmen all about his household."

"And I shall see they coordinate with yours," the king said to Bertaud, who nodded thanks.

"I'd ask for Tenned son of Tenned as a guard. And food," Tan put in with prudent emphasis. "And wine. Well watered," he added regretfully. He would have liked to add, *and a bath*, only truly he did not want to take that much time. He was intensely grateful that both Bertaud and Iaor seemed able to grasp the concept of urgency. If not of perfect discretion.

"All of that, yes. Very well. Free his hands, Geroen." The lord's tone brooked no argument. "I want you back with your men and on the job. You may leave this man to me. That *is* an order."

The captain's shoulders straightened. "Yes, my lord."

The paper was crisp and fresh, the quills well-made, and the clerk glum but quick and with a fair hand—no surprise, as he looked to have Linularinan blood. There were no windows in this room. Three guards were posted outside each of its two doors, and Tenned son of Tenned inside the room, looking alert and nervous. Bread and soft cheese occupied a separate table, and wine cut half-and-half with water.

The clerk was horrified at what Tan wrote out for him to copy. "I shouldn't know any of this," he protested. "Earth and stone, I don't *want* to know any of this!"

Tan looked him up and down. "Are you trustworthy? Discreet? You don't babble when you're in your cups, do you? You're loyal to Feierabiand?"

"Yes!" said the clerk hotly. "No! I mean, yes! But—"

"Then you'll do, man. Would you tell Lord Bertaud he should have selected a different man? Did you make these quills?"

"Yes . . ."

"Good quills. Now be quiet and let me work." Tan let himself fall into the cold legist's stillness that let him bring forth perfect memories. That stillness didn't come quite so easily as he'd expected—well, he was already tired. And distracted—he'd need to write an analysis to accompany these lists—later, later. No thought, no fretting, just memory. He let the quill fly across the paper.

He rose out of that trance of silence and speed much later to find Bertaud himself sitting at the table beside the clerk, writing out a copy in his own hand. He blinked, surprised—and then groaned, aware all at once of his aching hand and wrist. And back. And neck. In fact, he ached all over, far worse than usual. Pain lanced through his head, so sharp that for a moment he was blind. How long *had* he been working?

Even his eyes felt gritty and hot. Tan laid the quill aside and pressed his hands over his eyes.

"That's everything?" Bertaud asked.

Tan had very little idea what he'd just flung onto paper. But he shouldn't have stopped unless it was. He opened his eyes and peered blearily down at the stack of pages. "I think so. It should be." He shuffled rapidly through the papers. Everything seemed to be in order. Except— "I need to write a covering analysis. Broken stone and black iron! I don't think I have the wit of a crow left at the moment." He leaned back in his chair, stretching. Every bone and ligament in his body seemed to creak. Well, he'd had the bare bones of an analysis in his head since he'd left Teramondian. And the quill was still flowing with ink. Better still, with ink that resisted smudging. Sighing, he picked up the quill once more. The headache stabbed behind his eyes, and he couldn't keep from flinching. But the analysis still needed to be written. After that he might be able to finally put the quill down and *sleep.*

Bertaud silently passed him more paper and looked through the just-finished lists. His eyebrows rose, and he shook his head. He passed half the lists over to the clerk, taking the other half to copy himself. He could at least work quietly, for he did not harass Tan with questions, but left him alone to try to bludgeon coherent phrases out of his exhausted mind and fair script out of his stiff fingers. The little sleep he'd gotten in the prison seemed days past . . . He finished at last, tossed down the quill, and blew on the ink to dry it.

Bertaud took the analysis without comment, read it through once quickly, then again more slowly. Then he gave Tan a long look.

"The ink isn't smudged?" Tan asked blearily. "I didn't transpose two phrases or lose half a paragraph?" His gift shouldn't allow such mistakes, but he was so tired . . .

"No," Bertaud said. He sat down again and began to copy out the document. He said absently, not pausing in his task, "You need rest, I know. I'll send you to your bed shortly. Before I do, take a moment and think. Is there anything else I should tell Iaor when I bring him this?"

Tan rubbed his hands hard across his face. Then he poured himself some watered wine—well, he reached for the decanter, but Tenned was there before him and handed him a glass without a word. Tan nodded to the young guard and tried to collect his thoughts while he waited for Bertaud to finish the copy he was making and give the original to the clerk.

Then he said, "Tell His Majesty the whole lot could be false, deliberately put in my way to mislead us. One always has to remember that other men are also intelligent," he added to Bertaud's startled look. "But

I don't think that's the case here, not from the way Istierinan stirred up all Linularinum and not from the feel of the information. Still, you might tell the king . . . remind him that the politest smile still hides teeth, and that no Linularinan smiles without calculating which way fortune is tending. All the rest is"—he waved a hand—"contained there."

"Yes," said the lord. He rose with his set of papers. And, after a moment of thought, gathered up an equal pile of blank pages, which he made into an identical packet. Tan nodded his approval.

"Twelve more full copies, and hand them out as they're finished," Bertaud said to the clerk. He added to Tan, "I've sent half a dozen couriers out already, for Tihannad and Tiearanan, but four of those were carrying blanks and the other two only had partial copies. I'll send some of these with couriers, mostly across country, and some with soldiers. And I've arranged to send a couple out in, hmm, less-conventional hands."

Tan inclined his head again, satisfied with all these arrangements. "And I?"

"You'll stay here in my house. You need time to rest and recover." Tan nodded.

"My steward here is Dessand. Eniad is captain of the king's soldiers quartered in Tiefenauer. Geroen you have met—"

"What, he's still a captain of the guard?" Tan said in mock astonishment. "You didn't flog the hide off his back?"

The lord smiled. "I did worse than that. He's no longer merely a captain—he's *the* captain now. I made him captain of the whole city guard. I'd been looking for a replacement for the post. Geroen will do well, I believe."

Tan believed it, too. He scrubbed his hands across his face again, then pushed himself to his feet, all his joints complaining, and looked at young Tenned.

"Bath and bed, says my lord," the guard said earnestly, answering all of Tan's hopes. "Or supper first, if you like. Whatever you like, esteemed sir." He gave Tan an uncertain look. "Teras son of Toharas? Or is it, uh, Tan?"

Lord Bertaud lifted an amused eyebrow.

For once, Tan honestly could not think of a single reason to claim a false name. Istierinan's men knew very well who he was and would not care what name he used. And to the people on this side of the river, it should matter even less. "Tan will do," he told the young man. "A bath, bed, supper . . . I can't think of anything better. You'll attend me?"

"Yes . . ." Tenned did not quite seem to know whether he thought this was a better assignment than standing guard in the prison or not.

Tan smiled. "Well, you look strong enough to catch me if I collapse on the stairs rather than making it all the way to that promised bath. Good. Hold high the lamp, then, and light well the path!"

The young man nodded uncertainly, clearly missing the reference. Lord Bertaud, however, caught the allusion. He smiled, though a little grimly.

Tan grinned and declared, "Wishing no one any ill in the world, my lord! Or no one who ought properly to be on this side of the river. By now, Istierinan's agents will have realized it's far too late to stop all that"—he waved a vague hand at the growing stack of paper—"from getting out, and away home they'll go, feathers well ruffled and plucked. Then all good little boys will sleep safe in their beds, which is just as well." He paused, suddenly realizing that he was speaking far too freely. "Bed," he muttered. "Yes. Tenned—"

"Esteemed sir," the young man said, baffled but polite, and held open the door for Tan.

He had, later, only the vaguest memories of the bath or of finding a wide bed swathed in linen and lamb's wool, in a warm room lit by the ruddy glow of a banked fire and smelling, oddly enough, of honeysuckle. He must have felt himself safe, or else he was exhausted beyond caring, because he sank into the darkness behind the fire's glow and let the scent of honeysuckle carry him away.

CHAPTER 2

Mienthe had been feeling odd for days: restless and somehow as though she ought to be doing something urgent. But she had no idea what that should be. Before King Iaor had brought his household to Tiefenauer, she had longed to travel north to meet them. She'd *longed* to leave the Delta, which was not a new feeling, but something was different about it this spring. It seemed both stronger and more urgent this year, and she didn't know why. She'd expected the feeling to go away after the king arrived. Yet, even after the great house was filled to the roof tiles with Iaor and Niethe and the little princesses and all their attendants—and Erich—the restlessness had lingered. Mienthe didn't understand it. Usually the best month of the year was the one in which the king and his family and Erich visited the Delta.

Erich had been a stocky, rather small boy of twelve when King Iaor had compelled the King of Casmantium to send him to Feierabiand. As a guarantee of civility between the two countries, Iaor had said. Erich was supposed to stay in Feierabiand for eight years. Mienthe supposed King Iaor thought that was long enough to make his point.

Erich had come to the Delta with Iaor every year since the king had begun making his annual progress through the south of his country, so he and Mienthe had met when they were children. Mienthe had been new to the great house, uncertain of her cousin, shy of strangers, frightened of King Iaor and all his retinue. Erich had been new to Feierabiand, awkward with the language, excruciatingly conscious that he was supposed to honorably represent his father and country, and glad to find one person in the great house he didn't need to be wary of. They'd become friends at once.

The year after that, during the awful period of Tef's illness, Bertaud had asked Iaor to send Erich to the Delta, and the king had permitted him to come. Mienthe had been so grateful. Erich had not been at all shocked at Mienthe's grief for a man who had not even been kin, a man who had been only a servant; indeed, it had been Erich who had persuaded Bertaud to let Mienthe help dig Tef's grave, even when her hands blistered and bled. She had been so grateful.

Now the eight years of Erich's residence in Feierabiand were almost past. He was eighteen now. He'd changed a great deal since last year's visit. Last year, he'd suddenly become taller than Mienthe. But though he'd come into his height, he'd been as angular and ungainly as one of the storks that nested on the rooftops of the town. His hands had seemed too big for his bony wrists and his elbows had stuck out and he banged into the furniture and dropped plates. But this year he seemed to have turned all his growth into brawn. He'd filled out and got some weight on his bones, and he now looked very much the young man and not a boy at all.

He would be nineteen in midsummer, three weeks before Mienthe's birthday, and the year after that he would turn twenty, and then he would go home. Mienthe didn't like to think about that. She was almost certain his father would never let Erich come back to Feierabiand, and almost as certain that her cousin Bertaud, reluctant as he was to leave the Delta, would never again find it necessary to visit Casmantium.

She could ask Bertaud whether she might accompany the king's household when King Iaor left Tiefenauer. Erich would like that—*she* would like that. Or she thought she would. She ought to. Bertaud might let her go, even if he refused to leave the Delta himself. She wanted to ask him for permission—or at least, she felt as though she *ought* to want to ask him. But somehow the idea of joining the king's progress didn't exactly feel right. Mienthe had wanted so badly to go north just a day or so ago, but now she just didn't. Neither feeling made any sense!

Probably it was just the spring making her so restless. Probably it was watching the swallows dip and whirl through the sky and fly north, toward the higher country where they nested.

She found that she welcomed the distraction that her cousin's astonishing new guest had brought. She even found herself at once disposed to like him—even though she'd seen him only during that first strained interview, and even though he had clearly not wanted her there. She'd liked him and been glad he'd made it safely to the great house, for all he'd seemed to bring an echo of violence and fear with him. And of course, it had been fortunate he'd come to the Delta, since he'd found the king so much faster than if he'd gone to Tihannad.

Tan had an air of having *lived*, of having been out in the world. She liked that, even given just the little glimpse she'd had of him. She'd liked the slightly mocking quirk to his mouth when he'd said, *I have a good memory.* She had admired the way he'd spoken with such confidence to the king and to her cousin, even though he was clearly exhausted and maybe even a little frightened.

She would never have guessed, if she'd seen him in town, that he was actually Feierabianden. He looked pure Linularinan. No doubt that had been very helpful to him in his . . . profession. One expected Casmantian people to be broad-boned and clever with their hands; some of the artisans in town were Casmantian and one could spot them a mile away and by torchlight, as the saying went. The folk of Linularinum weren't quite so distinctive, but they were born with contract law and an inclination for poetry in their blood to go along with their straight brown hair and their prim expressions. That was what people said. There were plenty of people with mixed blood along the river, especially in the Delta, but Tan didn't look like he'd been born of mixed blood. In fact, he looked *exactly* like Mienthe's idea of a Linularinan legist, except not as old and stiff as most legists. And friendlier. And, oddly, less secretive.

Well, again, that was probably because he was a spy. He could probably look friendly and openhearted and honest no matter what he was thinking or feeling. Probably seeming sincere was part of being a confidential agent. You seemed ordinary and normal and people told you things. That wasn't very nice. Probably Mienthe should be cautious of trusting him. But she didn't feel cautious. She felt concerned. They said Tan had written out all the information he'd brought and then collapsed in exhaustion. He'd been either asleep or unconscious for two days now, which could happen when somebody overused his gift. Nevertheless, Mienthe felt strongly that she should go look in on him, make sure he was well. That was foolish. She'd already looked in several times this very day, once this very afternoon. Of course he was perfectly well.

Nevertheless, she found herself wandering restlessly toward his room, even though she had no real business to take her in that direction.

"Mie!" said Erich as she passed the kitchens—of course he had been in the kitchens—and swung out the door to stride along beside her. He handed her a sweet roll, wrapped in paper to keep the honey and butter from dripping onto the floor. "Where are you going?"

Mienthe hesitated.

"To see if the spy is awake," Erich said cheerfully. "Yes, I thought so. You should let me come."

"I ought to ask one of my maids to come," Mienthe muttered. "I meant to, Erich, truly, but Karin wasn't handy just now."

"And Emnis might worry and fuss," Erich said comfortably. "So she might. I will go with you. Wait a little and I will get a plate of sweet rolls. Nobody would be surprised if you brought the spy some rolls." His voice was deeper and somehow grittier than it had been even last year, which was when his voice had finally broken. His slight accent seemed to have become a little more pronounced with that change.

"He's probably still asleep—"

"If he's woken up, he will no doubt be glad of the rolls," Erich said, shrugging. "I don't mind going to look. If he's still asleep, *I* will be glad of the rolls. You eat that one, Mie. You're too thin." He turned and disappeared back into the kitchens, coming back almost at once with a generous plateful of rolls.

Tan was still asleep, but Captain Geroen, sitting in his room with his legs stretched out and a glower on his coarse-featured face, was glad to see the sweet rolls and didn't question Mienthe's right to look in on the spy.

"I never thought a legist could wear himself out with a quill like a soldier on a forced march," the captain said. "Makes me glad to be a speaker and not a legist. Even aside from liking crows better than just their feathers." He gave the bed a disgusted scowl.

"You think he's all right, though?" Mienthe asked. She trusted her cousin's judgment, but she wasn't certain she liked the guard captain. He frightened her a little. Erich didn't seem frightened, but then he wouldn't. He leaned in the doorway and ate another roll himself.

"I should think so, lady. Just exhausted." The captain gave the bed another disgusted look, but this time Mienthe thought she could see concern hiding behind his grim features. "With more than the effort of lifting a quill, to be fair, from what he said of his past days. No, he'll be up and about—"

Tan shifted, moved a hand, made a wordless mutter of protest, opened his eyes, tried to sit up, and groaned.

Captain Geroen wiped honey off his fingers with the cloth that had been draped over the plate, stalked over to the bed, and put a surprisingly gentle hand under Tan's elbow to help him sit up. Then he poured some water into a glass, set it on the bed table, stepped back and glowered at the spy, fists on his hips. "Stiff, are you?"

Tan glanced past the captain to take in Mienthe's presence, and Erich's beyond her. He seemed half amused and half dismayed to find his room so crowded. But he nodded thanks for the water and said to Geroen, with a deliberate good humor that had more than a slight edge of mockery to it, "Well, I see Bertaud—forgive me, let us by all means be respectful, I mean to say *Lord* Bertaud—didn't flog the flesh off your bones. What astonishing leniency!"

The captain looked embarrassed, an expression that sat oddly on his heavy features. "He's not much for the post and the whip, is our lord. But I did think he might dismiss me."

"After the shocking example you set for your pure-minded naive young guardsmen? I should hardly be astonished he found a more suitable penalty."

"Hah. He told you about that, did he?"

"He did. I admit I'm surprised to find you here watching me sleep. Flattering though it is to be the focus of your personal attention, I should imagine the new captain of the entire city guard might have one or two other matters of almost equal consequence to absorb his attention."

When he put it that way, Mienthe was surprised, too. But Geroen only lifted a heavy eyebrow at Tan. "I have been attending to them, as happens. And then I came back to look in on you. Just how long do you think you've been out?"

Tan leaned back against the pillows, looking faintly disturbed. "I see. How long, then?"

Mienthe said anxiously, "You worked right through that whole day and collapsed well after dark. That was fifty hours ago, more or less."

"So a good morning to you, esteemed sir!" said Captain Geroen drily. "We were beginning to wonder whether you'd ever wake again or just sleep till you turned to stone, and the bed linens around you."

"Ah." Tan seemed slightly stunned. "One would think I'd had to write out all eighteen copies myself. No wonder I'm so—" He turned his head toward the plate of rolls Mienthe still held and finished plaintively, "So close to collapsing a second time for want of sustenance. Lady Mienthe, are any of those, by chance, for me?"

Mienthe laughed. "All of them, if you like! And we can send to the kitchens if you'd like something else." She handed the tray to Captain Geroen to put on the bed table, where Tan could reach them. "We should go—I'm sure you want to eat and wash and dress, and I should tell my cousin you're awake—"

Tan waved a sweet roll at her. "Lady Mienthe, you are a jewel among women. Sit, please, and tell me all that has happened in the past two days—or at least, if anything important has happened, perhaps you might mention it to me? Any official protests from Linularinum? Alarms in the night? Has Istierinan presented himself to Iaor with a demand for my return?"

Mienthe couldn't help but laugh again. "No!"

"Good," said Tan, and bit with enthusiasm into the roll.

"I'll go," Geroen said. "I should report." He gave Erich a significant look.

Erich gestured acknowledgment. "I'll stay," he assured the captain.

"Good to have that settled," Tan said cheerfully.

He wasn't at all as Mienthe had expected. Bertaud had told her that spywork was hard and dangerous, and that good spies saved a lot of soldiers and should be respected. And Erich had pointed out that everyone knew Linularinum had lots of spies in Feierabiand, so really it was only fair that Feierabiand have some in Linularinum.

Mienthe supposed that spywork must be frightening and dangerous and difficult. It must be hard to find out secrets and sneak away with them—Mienthe had a vague idea that spies slipped through darkened rooms and found secret ledgers in locked desks, and thought she would die of fright if she tried to sneak around that way. But worse than that would be making somebody trust you when you knew all the time you were going to betray their trust. *That* would be hard. Unless you really didn't like the person you were betraying, but then pretending you did would be worse still. She had wondered what the kind of man who would do that might be like. Tan wasn't at all what she had imagined.

"Tan . . ." Mienthe said curiously, wanting to hear him speak again, to see whether she could hear any deceit in his voice.

"Esteemed lady?"

Mienthe asked, "Do you never tell anybody the rest of your name?"

"Not often," Tan said mildly. He didn't seem in the least offended or embarrassed, and there was nothing secretive or deceitful in his manner, even when he was explaining straight out that he kept secrets. He said, "I've offended people, you know. There are plenty of people I'd prefer not know my mother's name."

"Oh. Of course." Mienthe was embarrassed that he'd needed to explain that, and embarrassed again because he'd said he didn't want to give his *mother's* name. She guessed his father must have been careless. She didn't know what to say.

Erich said, rescuing her, "His Majesty said he doesn't think he's ever had a confidential agent bring him such a coup, and for all the difficulty it will cause him, he is glad to have a way to set the Fox of Linularinum at a disadvantage."

Tan gave Erich a thoughtful look. "I'm sure that's so, Prince Erichstaben. Yes, I suppose now he has a considerable advantage over both his neighbors."

That was barbed, but Erich didn't seem offended. He only said mildly, "I don't mind. Anyway, I'm going back to Casmantium in two years."

"Are you?" Tan said, with just the faintest edge of doubt in his tone.

Mienthe started to say something sharp, she didn't know what, but Erich said, his tone still mild, "You've been in Linularinum too long, maybe."

After a moment, Tan laughed. "Perhaps."

Mienthe looked at him, puzzled.

"Ah, well," Tan said to her. "You'd think Feierabiand would be closely allied to Linularinum, wouldn't you? We share a common history and a common language, which you'd think would make us far more like one another than either of us is like Casmantium, and there's quite a lot of shared blood along the river and down here in the Delta." He gave Erich a little nod and went on, "But in some ways, I think Casmantium is far more Feierabiand's natural ally. We're alike in our straightforwardness and love of honesty, which aren't qualities Linularinum admires."

There was an odd, wistful tone to his voice when he said that last. Mienthe said, "But you loved Linularinum, didn't you? And then you had to leave it. I'm sorry."

She seemed to have taken Tan by surprise. For a long moment, he only gazed wordlessly at her. But then he said slowly, "I suppose you've heard all your life, living on the border as you do, about Linularinan haughtiness, how the people of Linularinum look down on the people of Feierabiand as so many unlettered peasants. About how secretive and sly they are, and how they never use one word when they can fit in several dozen. And there's some truth to that. They love poetry—"

"Oh, I know!" Mienthe exclaimed, and then blushed because she had interrupted. But Tan only lifted a curious eyebrow, so she said, "I think everyone on both sides of the bridge reads Linularinan epic romances. All the girls in the great house read them—I read them, too. All we can get, I mean. They're wonderful fun."

Erich rolled his eyes, but Tan grinned. "All the girls in Teramondian read them, too: high birth or low, court ladies or merchants' daughters. Their mothers pretend indifference, but I've noticed even quite elderly matrons will correct your smallest errors if you refer to even the most recent epics."

And Tan had actually tested that, Mienthe guessed, just to amuse himself or purely out of habit. She didn't know whether that was entertaining or a bit frightening.

"But anyone from Linularinum will go beyond the popular epics. Especially in the court, people would rather quote something flowery and obscure—especially obscure—than simply say anything right out."

"Oh." Mienthe tried to imagine this.

"It's true they're secretive and love to be clever, but half the time when they're sneaking around trying to out-maneuver someone, they're actually arranging something kind for a friend. They like to surprise people, and they don't brag about it when they've been generous."

He almost made her admire secrecy, though it had never before occurred to her that that might be an admirable quality. "Are they kinder and more generous than we are, then?"

"Oh . . . no, I don't think so. But much less straightforward about both friendships and enmities. It's true what they say, that no one smiles in Linularinum without first calculating which way fortune is tending. But it's also true—this is a Linularinan saying—that the politest smile still contains teeth. You can't guess whether a man is your friend or not by whether he smiles at you."

"They sound very different from us," Mienthe said doubtfully. She wondered if this could actually be true. Though she'd heard that saying.

"In some ways. And in other ways, that perhaps matter more, they aren't different at all."

Mienthe nodded. She was even more certain now that he had loved Linularinum. She looked for something to say that might ease his sense of loss, but couldn't think of anything. Probably a Linularinan woman would be able to think of something subtle and obscure and, what had he said? Flowery. Something subtle and obscure and flowery to make him feel better. She didn't seem to be as clever as a Linularinan woman. She said merely, which was true but neither subtle nor clever, "I'm sorry for your loss. I don't suppose you'll have a chance to go back to Teramondian now."

Tan said after a moment, "It was bound to come to this eventually. That it was *that* day, right then, when all the pieces suddenly fell into order . . . Well, the years do shatter in our hands, and cut us to the bone if we try to hold them."

Mienthe could not imagine wanting to hold on to the past. Then she thought of Tef, and after all understood exactly what Tan meant. Erich, too, nodded.

"So tell me how I came to be so fortunate as to find Iaor here before me," Tan said to him, deliberately breaking the moment.

Erich shrugged. "*His Majesty,*" he said with some emphasis, "likes to see his country. And he likes to leave the cold heights and come down to the Delta before the heat of summer."

"Eminently sensible," murmured Tan, with a quirk of one eyebrow.

"I've always thought so," Erich agreed with a grin. "We chase the spring, and by the time we reach Tiearanan, we find the ice gone from the mountains and the flowers blooming."

"Yes, but it's more than that," Mienthe put in, "because they say His Majesty never guested in the Delta until Bertaud came back. Everything—" She stopped abruptly, having come surprisingly close to adding, *Everything changed when my cousin came home.* How strange that she should have begun to say something so personal.

"The Fox never leaves Teramondian, I think. I think perhaps I prefer His Majesty's"—and here Tan lifted a wry eyebrow at Erich, who grinned back—"inclination to see the whole of his country."

Mienthe nodded. "From here, King Iaor takes his household along the coast to Terabiand, then back north along the Nejeied River to the summer court in Tiearanan."

"Lingering in Terabiand if there are any reports of late snows in the mountains," put in Erich.

"Yes, so the whole progress takes about two months, sometimes more, doesn't it, Erich? I've always wanted to go along . . . My cousin doesn't want to spend so long away from the Delta, I suppose," Mienthe added a little doubtfully.

"He doesn't care to travel?"

"Oh, before, he went everywhere in Feierabiand, I think," she said. "And to—" *Casmantium*, she had meant to say, but that had been after Casmantium had tried to annex part of Feierabiand, when her cousin had escorted Erich from his father's court to Iaor's and she didn't want to say that. She said instead, "I think he likes to stay closer to home, now."

"Of course," Tan murmured.

Mienthe realized suddenly that Tan really had known about the progress, but had simply wanted to get them talking freely. And she had—much more than usual. She gave him a narrow look, wondering whether to laugh or be angry. "You're very good at that, aren't you? I think I understand why you're such a good spy. Confidential agent, I mean."

Tan looked surprised. Then he laughed and opened his hands in a gesture of contrition. "Habit," he said apologetically. "One I'll have to break, now I'm no longer an agent—certainly not confidential. Forgive me, esteemed lady."

Mienthe thought it would be very difficult to break a habit of getting people to talk to you, and doubted Tan really meant to try. And the other half of that habit must be not talking too much yourself, at least not about anything important. That must be hard, learning to say things, but nothing that mattered. She'd certainly been carrying more than her share of the conversation so far, which wasn't at all usual for her, and hadn't been her intention, either.

Perhaps guessing her thoughts, Tan said lightly, "I do know some north Linularinan poetry, including a couple of romantic epics you might not have heard this far south. I could write them out for you, if you like."

Mienthe straightened, excited and happy at this generous offer, even though he'd obviously made it partly to turn the subject and partly to flatter her because she was Bertaud's cousin. But she hardly meant to turn the offer down, no matter why he'd made it. She said quickly, "Oh, could you? Of course you could—you have a legist's memory. That would be wonderful, truly! And it would be something quiet you could do, when I know you're still tired." She hesitated, remembering that he was a guest, and still recovering from injury or exhaustion. "If you're sure you don't mind?"

"Not in the least," Tan said cheerfully. "Whom should I ask for paper and quills?"

"Oh, I'll send you all the things you'd need," Mienthe assured him. She jumped up, but then hesitated. "I know you only just came out of a legist's trance. Of course you need to rest. I'd understand if you've worn your gift out for the next little while—I didn't mean to ask you to write things for me if you're too tired or anything—"

"Not at all," Tan assured her with perfect good cheer. "An unhurried little task like this is just what I need to limber my gift and memory and fingers all up again."

"If you're sure," Mienthe said. But he did look tired now, she thought. "But *I'm* sure you should rest. I'll tell the kitchens to send up a real tray, shall I?" There were only crumbs on the plate that had held the rolls.

"A wonderful idea," Tan agreed, and let his head rest against the pillows.

"Though I should go find Bertaud first," Mienthe added doubtfully, once she and Erich were in the hall. There were two guardsmen in the hall, which she found did not surprise her.

"Go," agreed Erich. "I'm sure Geroen passed the word along, but yes, go. I do not mind to go back by the kitchens."

Mienthe grinned and let him go. But once she was alone, her steps slowed. She was, she decided, thinking back on it, not quite as pleased at Tan's offer as she ought to have been. How strange it was, to be a little bit suspicious of every single thing a man said! She found herself wondering if Tan was trying to make a good impression on her, and then wondering if asking herself that question meant he wasn't succeeding, and then asking herself whether it was fair to be suspicious of a man who had, after all, risked his life to bring Feierabiand important information. Or fair to worry about whether Tan was being altogether honest with her, when, after all, she never did know whether *anyone* ever was. Except her cousin, of course.

Her steps quickened as she suddenly found herself eager to talk to Bertaud. She wanted to ask him whether he liked Tan, whether he thought he ought to like him, whether he trusted him—was it possible to like somebody you didn't trust? Was it *proper* to allow yourself to like somebody you didn't trust?

Though the great house had hardly been built to loom over the town, some parts of it were set rather high, and then the whole house was on a hill—not a high hill, but the highest Tiefenauer offered. The solar was nearly as high up as the tower room, but in every other way it was the antithesis of that windowless chamber, being long and narrow and very nearly nothing but windows. It was much too hot in high summer for anyone but a particularly determined cat, but it was perfect in the winter and early spring, especially at sunset, for almost all of its windows looked west. One could look right out over the rooftops of Tiefenauer to the flashing ribbon of the river, the bridge leading in a fine and delicate arch over to Linularinum. Away to the north, the marshes were a dusky emerald with occasional glints of diamond brilliance where the sunlight struck through the dense trees to the still waters beneath. To the south, visible on clear days, the infinite sea stretched away, muddy and opaque where the Sierhanan River emptied, clear sapphire farther out.

Mienthe had expected Bertaud to be in company with King Iaor, with maybe half a dozen attendants besides. But her cousin was quite alone. He was sitting in a high-backed chair drawn up close to the windows. There was a book open on his knee, but he wasn't reading it. He was gazing out over the city, past the city, at the clouds piling up over the sea, purple and gold against a luminous sky, crimson in the west where the setting sun turned the sea to flame.

He did not see Mienthe at once. She watched him in silence for a moment. The brilliant light showed her fine lines at the corners of his

eyes, deeper lines at the corners of his mouth. He looked older in
this light, only . . . not exactly older. Her cousin looked, Mienthe
thought, as though something had recalled to him some grief or hard
memory.

Then, though she was standing motionless, he must have heard her,
for he turned his head. The golden light of sunset seemed to fill his
eyes with fire, and yet behind the opaque veil of fire, they were dark.
Even bleak. Some of the other girls Mienthe knew who also liked epic
romances would have instantly spun a tale of love and loss to explain
that bleakness. Mienthe didn't think what she saw had any such simple
explanation. She didn't understand her cousin's unspoken sorrow, yet
somehow she recognized it. She stood mute in the doorway.

Then the setting sun touched the surface of the sea, the angle of the
light coming in through the windows changed, and the moment passed.

"Mienthe," Bertaud said, rising to greet her. With the light now at
his back, it was impossible to make out his expression at all.

Though Mienthe listened carefully, she could hear neither grief nor
loneliness in his tone. She said, "Tan's awake, did Geroen tell you? I
went to see him." She'd been a little worried that her cousin might not
approve, but he only nodded and invited her, with a gesture, to take a
chair near his.

"What did you think of our spy?"

"Oh . . ." Mienthe tried to think how to answer. "He has enough
charm, when he wants to. I think he must have been a good spy."

"Indeed. He's resting now, I suppose? Well enough. I'll want to
speak with him tonight. Or possibly Iaor will. Or perhaps both of us."

Poor spy, to have both the king and her cousin looming over him at
once.

"I left orders for one of Geroen's men to attend him at all times. I
want him to stay close for a few more days, and I don't think I necessarily trust that man to obey any command he'd rather conveniently
forget."

Her cousin was smiling a little as he said this last, but Mienthe
thought he wasn't really amused. He wasn't used, she decided, to having
to doubt whether anybody would obey him, and he didn't like having to
wonder.

Mienthe nodded and started to speak, but then stopped. The sun
was nearly down, flashing flame-red against the flat horizon where sea
met sky. Other than that distant blaze, the world had gone dark. The
dark and hidden depths of the marshes rolled out beyond the city;
nearer at hand, the earliest stars glimmered into sight to meet the
warmer glow of lanterns and lamps in the streets below. Bertaud took a

taper from the desk, struck it to life, and stretched up to light the lamps that hung from the ceiling on bronze chains.

And outside the windows of the solar, a sudden blackness moved against the sky. It spread out, bulking enormous—not a bird, no bird would be so large, but certainly not clouds across the sky; it moved too fast and looked all wrong for that. She held her breath, half expecting it to crash against the windows—shattering glass would fly everywhere— she took a step back in fearful anticipation. But then the dark shape, if she'd really ever seen it at all, dwindled and disappeared.

Mienthe took a step closer to the windows, blinking, wondering whether she'd actually seen something or merely imagined it.

Behind her, Bertaud made a wordless sound that held an extraordinary combination of astonishment, longing, intense joy, and anger.

She turned. There was a man in the solar with them. A stranger. He was much older than Mienthe—older than Bertaud, she thought, though she did not understand why she thought so. His black hair was not streaked with gray and his eyes were ageless, but Mienthe was sure that he was actually much older than he looked. He had an austere, proud face and powerful deep-set black eyes. His clothing was all of black and a red as dark as dying coals.

And there was something strange about his shadow. It wasn't just the flickering light of the lamps: The shadow itself flickered with fire; it was *made* of fire, but with eyes as black as those of the man who cast it. And it was the wrong shape—not the shape of a man at all, but Mienthe could not have said what form could have cast it. She took another involuntary step back, expecting the rugs and drapes and polished wood of the solar to blaze up in flames. But the shadow seemed to contain its fire, and nothing else burned. Then the man turned his head, glancing at her with a strange kind of indifferent curiosity. Mienthe saw that although his eyes were black, they, too, were filled with fire. She stared back, feeling pinned in place with shock and terror, like a hare under the shadow of a falcon.

Then Bertaud took a step forward. He said sharply, "Kairaithin. Anasakuse Sipiike Kairaithin. Why have you come here?"

The stranger turned his attention back to him, and the moment passed.

Beneath the sharpness, Bertaud's voice shook. But not, thought Mienthe, in terror. Whatever strong emotion gripped her cousin, it was not fear. Nor had Bertaud moved—say, to step in front of her. He did not pay her any attention at all. Rather than feeling hurt or overlooked, Mienthe found this reassuring. The man—the mage—whoever he was, he had to be a mage, though she had never heard of any mage who cast a shadow of fire—but he could not be so dangerous if her cousin, who clearly knew him, did not think Mienthe needed protection.

Bertaud did not wait for an answer, but said, his tone changing, "You look tired. You look . . . older. Are you . . . are you well, then?" His voice had dropped, the anger replaced by . . . worry? Fear? Mienthe wasn't certain what she heard in his voice. "Did it harm you, crossing the Wall?" Bertaud asked. And then, "But how *did* you cross it?"

The man—the fire mage, Kairaithin—tilted his head, somehow a strange motion that made Mienthe think of the way a bird moved; it had something of that quick, abrupt quality. Mienthe saw that his shadow was a bird's shadow, only too large and feathered with fire, and not altogether the shape of a bird. She blinked and at last recognized what creature cast that kind of shadow—she couldn't believe she'd been so slow to understand. This was not a man at all, not at *all*. He was a griffin. The human shape he wore just barely disguised the fact, and only for a moment.

The griffin said, "The answer to all your questions is the same answer."

His voice was as outrageously inhuman as his shadow: pitiless as fire and with a strange timbre, as though his tongue and throat were not accustomed to shaping the sounds of any ordinary language. He stood very still, watching Bertaud. Not as a falcon watches a hare, Mienthe thought, but she was not sure why she thought it was different, or why she thought the stranger was . . . not exactly afraid, but wary.

Bertaud, too, stood unmoving. Mienthe thought he had recovered from his astonishment, but she thought he was bracing himself against some message he would not welcome. He said, "What is that answer?"

"The Wall has cracked," the griffin said. Then he was still again, watching Bertaud.

Bertaud clearly understood this very well. "Tehre's Wall?" her cousin said, not a question, but in clear dismay. "How?"

"I do not know. It should have stood for a thousand years, that making," answered the griffin—Kairaithin, Anasakuse Something Kairaithin—and how did her cousin come to know his name? Or the names of any griffins?

Bertaud said, "I thought it would."

"Yes. Something disturbed the balance, which should have been secure. The Wall has cracked through twice—in the east where the lake lies high in the mountains and then again in the higher mountains of the west, near where the mouth of the lake called Niambe finds its source."

Bertaud took a step forward. "Is it a problem with the wild magic, then? Does that interfere with the mageworking?"

Kairaithin moved a hand in a minimal gesture of bafflement. "Perhaps. The wild magic has lately trembled, yes. Something has troubled it. Or so I felt as I came through the heights. Though why, then, have both the wild magic and the maker's magic woven into the Wall changed this spring, now, at this moment?" He did not attempt to answer his own question, but only stood still again, watching her cousin.

"So you came here to me," said Bertaud, and stopped. There was an expectation in his silence. He was waiting . . . he expected something from the griffin mage. Something specific. Something, Mienthe thought, that he did not really want to receive, or hear, or know. And the mage expected something from her cousin as well.

"Twice, you have tasked me with my oversight when I did not warn you of an approaching storm," said Kairaithin. "This time I think it best that you know what comes. This wind that approaches now . . . it will be a savage wind. If the Wall does not hold, as I think it will not, then my people will come down across the country of earth in a storm of fire." There was neither apology nor regret in his tone as he said this. He simply said it. But there was an odd trepidation hidden behind the fierce indifference of his voice. He was afraid of what Bertaud might say or do, Mienthe realized. She blinked, not understanding this at all. She didn't understand why a griffin fire mage—a griffin mage so powerful he could take on human shape and draw himself right out of air and the sunset light—should be afraid of anyone. Certainly not why he should be afraid of her *cousin*.

"Why would they?" asked Bertaud. "How can they? Six years ago, you said that if your people fought mine without quarter, yours would be destroyed. How has that changed? Discounting what—what might prevent them. You have not told them about that?"

"No, nor dare I. Everything I told you six years ago remains true," Kairaithin said sharply. "Save this one thing: My people now count among their treasures the fire mage Kereskiita Keskainiane Raikaisi-piike. Kes. My *kiinukaile* Opailikiita Sehanaka Kiistaike remains her first *iskarianere*, but Kes has also taken Tastairiane Apailika as a second *iskarianere*."

"Tastairiane!" Bertaud exclaimed, flinching from a name he evidently recognized.

"Even so. Kes has come entirely into her power. She has become fierce and forgotten the earth from which she was taken. She calls for a wind of fire and a brilliant day of blood, and though I would speak against her, I have no allies among the People of Fire and Air."

Bertaud said, "Even without allies, Sipiike Kairaithin, can you not turn that wind, no matter how strong the storm, and find another for your people to ride?"

"You mistake me," said Kairaithin. And, after a moment, "Do you not understand me, man? When I say I have no allies, I mean I fly alone. The Lord of Fire and Air no longer regards my opinion. He has not since I supported the building of the Wall. He does not understand . . . none of my people understand . . . why, on that night of fire, I chose to turn the wind we had brought down against Casmantium. He believes I deliberately caught defeat out of a wind that should have carried us to victory."

There was a pause. Then Bertaud said quietly, "No. I did not know." And, after a moment, "I am sorry, Kairaithin. I would do the same again. But I'm sorry the cost of what we all did that night fell on you."

The griffin mage shrugged off his sympathy. "It has mattered little. While earth and fire were divided, the People of Fire and Air had little need for my strength. Now that the Wall's protection is failing, they still need not regard me." The griffin mage paused. But then he said, his voice not precisely gentle, but so low Mienthe had to strain to hear him, "I would I had found a different wind to call, these six years past, when the cold mages of Casmantium first struck against my people. This one has come about into a different quarter than I ever intended. I see only two directions in which it may lead: the destruction of your people or the destruction of mine. I would choose neither. But I do not see any wind that can carry us in any direction but toward disaster."

"But—" said Bertaud, and stopped.

"Yes," said the griffin. "I am at fault. I am twice at fault. If I had properly judged the wind as I called it up six years ago, I would have guessed what storm it might become. If I had understood that, I would have seen plainly that I should have killed you, there in that desert we made with such bitter cost. Now the chance is gone and I do not know what to do. So I came here to you, though you did not call me. Will you hold me?"

Bertaud did not answer at once. At last he said, "No," and hesitated, glancing down. And then looked up once more to meet Kairaithin's fierce gaze. "Not yet. Not if I can avoid it—How long will the Wall stand, can you guess?"

The griffin mage shrugged. "Not long, unless the balance between fire and earth and the wild magic is restored. And, as I do not know what disturbed it, I cannot guess how it might be restored. I have studied the weakness in the Wall over these past days. I have considered the lengthening and branching of the cracks. I do not think it will hold long. Five days?"

"Five!" Bertaud exclaimed.

"Or six. Or ten." Kairaithin lifted a hand and dropped it again in weary uncertainty. "I do not think it will hold longer than ten days, if it holds so long. And what will you do when it breaks, man?"

Bertaud did not answer.

Mienthe had an idea the griffin might have said something else, something more, only she was in the room, listening. His black eyes shifted to consider her. She flinched and tried not to back away, though she couldn't have explained why she thought it would be a bad idea to back away.

Kairaithin turned his gaze back toward Bertaud. "This is . . . your mate? Your child?"

"My cousin," Bertaud said. Then added, "My *iskarianere*—I think that would do." He moved to stand next to Mienthe, put an arm around her shoulders. Not exactly protectively. Even now, it did not seem to occur to him that she might need protection. Now she had at last drawn the griffin's attention, Mienthe found this extremely reassuring.

"She is yours. I shall not harm her. I have no inclination to harm her. Do you understand me, man?"

"Yes," Bertaud said.

Mienthe wondered what he'd understood that she had missed. This did not seem the moment to ask.

"What will you do?" asked Kairaithin.

"I don't know. Warn Iaor. Go north. Wait to see what happens to the Wall. What will you do?"

"I?" There was a slight pause. "I will seek an alternative wind, though I do not yet perceive any faintest whisper of any breeze I should wish to call up. And I will wait for you to call me. Call me, man, before you call any other. Shall I trust you so far?"

"Just so far," Bertaud said, rather more grimly than seemed reasonable for such an answer.

The griffin mage inclined his proud head. His black eyes blazed with fire and something else less identifiable; even the black eyes of his fiery shadow burned. Then he was gone.

Mienthe took a step away from Bertaud and looked at him incredulously.

"Mienthe—" her cousin began, then dropped into a chair, bowed his head against his hand, and laughed. There was little humor in the sound. He laughed as though he did not know whether he should weep.

Mienthe went to him, put her hand on his shoulder, and bent to rest her cheek against the top of his head. She did not speak.

After a while, Bertaud stopped laughing. He put a hand up to cover hers, where it still rested on his shoulder, and said, "It will be . . . everything will come right, in the end." He did not say it as though reassuring a young child, nor did he say it with the foolish confidence of a man who believes that a peril must surely be averted simply because he wishes it will be. He said it like a hope. Like an entreaty to the future.

"Yes," said Mienthe, because that was what he needed her to say. She took his hand in hers, tucked her legs up under her skirts, and sat on the floor beside his chair as she had used to do when she was a child. She leaned her cheek against his knee, saying nothing more.

For a long time they sat like that, while the last glimmers of fire-tinged light faded in the west. The lamplight in the solar turned the window glass into an opaque mirror and showed Mienthe her face and her cousin's. She thought she looked shocked, but that Bertaud looked desolate.

"You seem . . . very calm," Bertaud said at last, his eyes meeting hers in the glass.

Mienthe did not know what to say. She was surprised he thought so.

"Do you know . . . did you understand . . ." But her cousin did not seem to know how to finish either sentence.

"He was a griffin," Mienthe said in a small voice. "You knew his name . . . you knew him. He came to warn you about danger. About a fire mage who is your enemy. About danger to the Wall—the Wall in Casmantium, the one you helped to build."

"Tehre's Wall. Yes. But I didn't help build it. I was only there when it was built." Bertaud paused. He added, reluctantly, Mienthe thought, "Maybe my presence convinced Kairaithin to help build it."

"He is a griffin and a mage," Mienthe said, trying to get this all straight in her mind. "He helped you six years ago when the griffins came into Feierabiand. You stopped us battling them and made them our allies. And then he helped you again when you—when the Casmantian Wall was built. Between fire and earth, he said. Between the . . . the griffins' desert and the country of men? He is your friend . . ." She hesitated, feeling strongly that the word did not exactly apply. But she did not know what other word to use. She repeated, "He is your friend, and he has suffered for it."

"I think he has," Bertaud said. He sounded tired and disheartened.

"And now the Wall is going to break? And there will be a . . . a war between fire and earth? I thought . . . I never heard anyone say that the griffins were dangerous to us. Only maybe to the northern towns of Casmantium, up close to where the desert lies."

"Yes," said Bertaud. "No. It's a little more complicated than that."

He clearly did not want to explain. Mienthe said cautiously, looking up at him, "And the griffin mage, he thinks you might do something again. As you did six years ago? What *was* it you did?" The lamplight sent golden light and uncertain shadows across her cousin's face, so that his shape seemed to change as she gazed at him: First he seemed wholly a creature of ordinary earth, and then, as the light shifted, half a creature of fire.

"Nothing I ever want to do again," he said succinctly, and got to his feet. Then he just stood for a moment, looking down at her. He asked, "What did you think of Kairaithin?"

Mienthe, too, rose to her feet, not very gracefully from her place on the floor. She wondered what her cousin wanted her to say. That she liked his friend? But she couldn't say she did. That she appreciated what the griffin mage had done for him? But she had no clear idea what that had *been*. She said at last, "He is very . . . very . . . He frightened me. But his shadow is beautiful."

Bertaud smiled at her, the weariness she saw in him seeming to lighten a little. "Did you think so? He frightened you, that's reasonable. But he didn't terrify you. Good."

Mienthe nodded uncertainly. "But what will you do now?"

"Now?" He paused, seeming to consider. Then he said, with evident reluctance, "I suppose now I had better speak to Iaor. I suppose we will ride north."

Mienthe felt very young and ignorant. She wanted to ask her cousin about the Wall, about the griffins. She wanted very badly to ask again, *But what was it that you did?* And she wanted to ask again, *What will you do now?* But it was very clear he was evading all questions like those. To protect her? Or because, as Mienthe suspected, he did not know the answers himself? She said instead, humbly, "May I come with you to see the king? I would like—I would like to know what you will do."

Bertaud looked distractedly down at her, half his attention already turning toward what he would tell the king. Or maybe to memories of the past: memories of fire and the Casmantian Wall. But after a moment he nodded. "Yes. Come. If I go north, Mie, you'll stand in my place as the Lady of the Delta."

Mienthe stared at him.

"So you must certainly hear what Iaor and I decide to do," finished her cousin, and touched her shoulder to urge her toward the door.

Niethe daughter of Jereien, known since her marriage as Niethe Jereien Safiad Nataviad in the most formal, old-fashioned style, was a lovely and charming woman who was much younger than King Iaor. Indeed, she was not so very much older than Mienthe. Queen Niethe enjoyed being queen, loved her royal husband, doted on her little daughters, and loathed travel with a deep passion. She detested the mud of winter and the dusty summer, she hated rain, and she said the bright sun gave her headaches and made her skin freckle. She insisted on wearing unsuitable clothing and then complained of wrinkles and stains. She would not ride a horse, but then found fault with the closeness of her carriage.

But Niethe, who accompanied her husband on his annual progress only because she hated being parted from him even more than she hated travel, clearly had not expected to arrive in Tiefenauer only to have the king bid her an almost immediate farewell. This taxed even the queen's good humor, though normally she accepted the broad demands on her husband's attention with perfect amiability.

"It can't be helped," King Iaor told her apologetically. "I'm certain you will be perfectly safe here, and far more comfortable than possible on a fast ride north."

Even though the queen smiled and nodded, she somehow gave the impression she had turned her back on him. With a flounce.

Mienthe tried not to laugh. Really it was nothing to laugh at. If Bertaud and King Iaor thought the breaking of the Wall was so dangerous they would not even wait for dawn, but would ride for Tihannad this very night, then there was nothing at all to laugh at. Niethe knew it, too, or she would really be angry rather than merely teasing Iaor in order to make him think she was not frightened.

What was really odd was that Mienthe felt no desire at all to go north herself. It was just as well, since Bertaud would never have allowed her to come—no more than Iaor would allow Niethe to come—but she was surprised she had no urge to ask for permission whether her cousin would grant it or not.

Erich, of course, *was* going with the king. He came over to Mienthe, leaned his hip against the low table near her, and said lightly, "So now I have at last a chance for swift journeys and brave exploits. I'll cover myself with glory and when next we meet, I will tell you all my tales of bright valor, do you think so?"

"Of course." Mienthe smiled up at him. "I'll expect that of you—brave exploits and bright valor, and only very little exaggeration."

"I never exaggerate!" Erich informed her in lofty tones. "Well, only a very little." He hesitated, lowered his deep voice—it was easier for him to boom than whisper, now—and asked, "You know? Why we—why your lord cousin is going north?"

"The griffins," said Mienthe, deliberately vague. "And the Wall."

"Yes," agreed Erich. He frowned at Mienthe. "My father said—

this was years ago, but I remember, Mie. He said your country would regret the alliance it made with the griffins. Creatures of earth should not make common cause with creatures of fire. We are too much . . . ah. Too much opposed. He said nothing good would come of it."

Mienthe tilted her head. "Well, your father shouldn't have pushed us to make common cause, then, if he had such strong opinions on the matter."

"No," Erich growled, with rather more force than Mienthe had expected. "He should not have. To be fair, he did not expect any such outcome because no one in Casmantium would think to make that alliance."

"We don't have your bad history with griffins," Mienthe suggested.

Erich nodded. "Yes. The bad history. Your lord cousin, he has a good history with the griffins, is that so?"

"Yes, I think he does," Mienthe said, guardedly, because she could not quite see where the Casmantian prince was going with this.

"He said so. I hope so," Erich said. He looked at Mienthe for a long moment, the expression in his dark eyes very sober. "But you should remember, you should always remember, a creature of earth should not trust a creature of fire. You will remember this, Mie? If the griffin your cousin says is his friend comes here again to speak to you?"

Mienthe was astonished. "I can't imagine why he would. He doesn't know me—he's not *my* friend."

"He made a human girl into a fire mage. Your honored cousin said so. He spoke of it, he and the Safiad."

By *the Safiad* he meant King Iaor, as *the Arobern* meant the King of Casmantium. Even after six years in Feierabiand, Erich liked to use the occasional Casmantian turn of phrase. He might do this to deliberately set himself apart; the prince was not above reminding others that he was Casmantian and royal. But Mienthe thought he simply wished to remind himself of his true heritage and nationality, in moments when he felt himself in danger of forgetting. She wondered what tricks a girl might use to remember her heritage after a griffin turned her into a fire mage. And how well those tricks would work. And for how long.

She said slowly, "I knew that, I think. I had forgotten. And I did not know it was *that* griffin who did it. Bertaud—" She stopped, not wanting to say out loud, *My cousin did not tell me that; he never talks even to me about what happened six years ago.*

"That griffin, he saw you when he came to speak to your honored cousin. Maybe he might come back. He took that other girl, before. Maybe he will come here to look for you."

That seemed very unlikely.

"If he does," Erich said, taking her hand in both of his—her fingers vanished entirely between his enormous hands. He looked intently into her face, "If he does, Mie, remember that a creature of earth should never make common cause with a creature of fire. Never. Promise me you will remember."

"Of course I'll remember," Mienthe assured him, an easy promise to make as she knew very well nothing of the kind would come about. "I'll be careful—truly, Erich. But you'll be the one in danger, which is why you'll get to do all the brave exploits. All I'll get to do here is attend the queen and the little princesses and wait for you to send me news."

The prince's mouth crooked. "Attending those little girls *is* a brave exploit." He stood up and stood for a moment gazing down at her. His eyes held a question, but Mienthe did not know what question she saw there.

But the arrival of the little princesses in person, brought in quickly to make their farewells to their father, interrupted Erich before he could speak, if he meant to.

The older of the princesses was called Karianes Nataviad Merimne Safiad. She was nearly five years old, plump, pretty, cheerful, and kind-hearted; everyone said she was very like Niethe's mother. The littler princess was Anlin Nataviad Merimne Safiad, a child who already, at three, showed her father's strong will and determined temper. Both little girls ran to say good-bye to Erich after speaking to their father. He had been at the Feierabianden court all their lives and, not having a clear idea about just what a hostage was, they thought he was their brother. Erich called them his little sisters once removed and let them tease him into the most impossible mischief.

Erich threw Anlin up into the air and then caught her again, repeating the procedure at once with her older sister. "Oof!" he said, pretending he might not be able to lift the five-year-old. "Have you grown more just over these few days?"

Karianes laughed, but then pouted. "Do you *have* to go?"

"I have to, yes, but Mie will be here."

The little girls gazed at Mienthe with doubtful expressions. A year was a long time to such small children, and they were clearly uncertain whether they should like to trade Erich for Mienthe. Then Anlin said, "You gave me a kitten."

Mienthe smiled, surprised the child had remembered; the last time the princesses had visited the Delta, Anlin had been only just talking. Even surrounded by her nurses and her mother's ladies, she had seemed somehow alone to Mienthe. And one of the stable cats had had kittens the right age. "Yes," she agreed. "A black one with white feet and a white nose."

"He wanted to come," declared Anlin. "But Mama wouldn't let him."

Mienthe had very little idea how to talk to children. "Traveling is hard on cats," she said sympathetically. "I'm sure he'll be waiting for you at home."

"He wanted to come," Anlin repeated, scowling. "He told me he did."

"Maybe she has an affinity to cats, like Tef?" Mienthe said to Erich. She was pleased by the idea, almost like finding such a gift in the child would be a tribute to Tef's memory. But then maybe the child simply had a vivid imagination. She *was* very young for any gift to come out.

Erich shrugged, but looked a little envious. Affinities for particular animals, common as dirt in Feierabiand, were fairly rare in Casmantium— just as the people of Feierabiand usually were smaller and fair, where those of Casmantium were broad and dark. Erich thought the ability to speak to an animal was a very exotic sort of gift, much more interesting than the making and building that were common gifts in his own country. Mienthe thought she wouldn't complain if she had even the most common gift in the world, but both Erich and she were well past the age when gifts usually came out.

The princesses' nurses swept down then to carry them back to their beds, and there was a general movement of the king's party toward departure. Erich pressed Mienthe's hands quickly in his and said, "Remember your promise!" She nodded, and he strode quickly away without looking back.

Bertaud strode over to take Mienthe's shoulders and look down at her in earnest concern.

"You'll be well," Mienthe told him. "You'll find something to do, even if the Wall breaks." Her tone sounded odd even to her own ear, midway between a plea and a command.

Her cousin said swiftly, "Of course I will. And you'll be safe here."

That was a command, to the world if not to Mienthe. She nodded.

"I'll send you news if I can, if there's any to send. And I'll return as swiftly as I may," Bertaud told her. "Mienthe—" He stopped.

Mienthe waited.

"If Kairaithin comes here, if he comes to you," her cousin said, and paused again. Then he said quickly, "If he comes, I think you should probably trust him. Especially if he says he comes from me. If he says so, it will likely be true. Do you understand?"

"No," Mienthe said honestly. "I don't think I understand anything. But I'll remember."

Her cousin barely smiled. "Yes, well. Very well. Remember, then, and that will do. I doubt he'll come. I'm sure he'll have no reason to come here. All the trouble will be in the north." He hesitated another moment, gazing at Mienthe as though he wanted to be certain he'd be able to recall her image perfectly, forever. Then he released her and spun to stride after Iaor.

Mienthe watched him go. If this were a romantic epic, she would disguise herself and sneak along with Bertaud and the king. Of course, if this were a romantic epic, then Erich and she would be certain to have amazing adventures and save Feierabiand—or more likely, both Feierabiand and Casmantium. They would fall in love and part tragically, he to be King of Casmantium and she to be just another Delta lady. They'd never see one another again because, no matter how good the road between the two countries was in the real world, that was how romantic epics ended: tragically.

Mienthe sighed. There was no point in counting over the thousands of reasons it wouldn't work out like that even if she did sneak herself into her cousin's party, which, of course, she couldn't.

Even though it was so late, Mienthe thought she might just slip past Tan's room quickly and assure herself he was safe and well. He would be asleep—she knew that—but she was somehow uneasy and knew she wouldn't be able to sleep herself until she'd glanced in and made certain that he was well. She didn't understand this. But she knew it was true. She didn't even go to the window to watch Bertaud and Erich and the rest ride away. She went straight to Tan's room.

The hallway outside the room was empty, but Mienthe didn't think anything of that; she'd forgotten that Captain Geroen had been told to have his guardsmen attend Tan. It wasn't the absence of the guardsmen that alarmed Mienthe. Yet she abruptly became certain, even as she walked quickly toward the door, that something was wrong. She took hold of the doorknob with a peculiar sense that the door might not open to Tan's room at all—that it might open to anything and any location *except* that room. But when she swung it cautiously back, there was the room after all. The sheets of paper and jars of ink were still laid out in good order on the bed table, but the bed was empty. The whole room was silent and empty.

Or not quite empty. Geroen's young guardsmen were sitting on the floor, against the wall, pale and insensible. But Tan was not there.

Yet Mienthe found she knew where he was, just as surely as she knew, without looking, which way was down or where her own hands were.

She knew Tan was unconscious. She knew he was nearby, but getting rapidly farther away. She knew he was heading west, toward the river and Linularinum. And she knew something else: that she would never manage to persuade Geroen she knew anything at all.

She was right about everything but the last.

CHAPTER 3

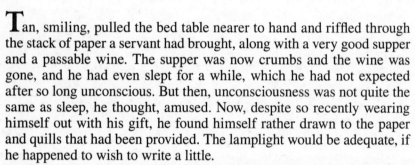

Tan, smiling, pulled the bed table nearer to hand and riffled through the stack of paper a servant had brought, along with a very good supper and a passable wine. The supper was now crumbs and the wine was gone, and he had even slept for a while, which he had not expected after so long unconscious. But then, unconsciousness was not quite the same as sleep, he thought, amused. Now, despite so recently wearing himself out with his gift, he found himself rather drawn to the paper and quills that had been provided. The lamplight would be adequate, if he happened to wish to write a little.

It was good paper, thick and heavily textured. Well-made paper like this was a pleasure to work with; it wouldn't let ink smudge or fade. The array of inks was also impressive. The blue was a good, deep color like distilled Casmantian sapphires, the green fresh and bright as springtime, the purple dusky and rich.

He thought that a young woman of the Delta was unlikely to know, but would probably like, Anariddthen's newest cycle, all sweet love and desperate loss and brave heroism, and an ending that was, contrary to most romantic epics, at least ambiguous rather than tragic. It would please pretty little Mienthe, he decided. He was clear already that any-one who wished Lord Bertaud's goodwill might well give some thought to pleasing his cousin.

The Anariddthen—yes, Tan decided. Not only would young Mienthe probably like it, it also could be taken in pieces of a sensible size. There wasn't much chance he'd fall into the legist's trance and wear his fingers to the bone trying to reach the end in one session. Yes. The Anariddthen would do very well. Green ink, Tan thought, for the beginning. He picked up a green quill—made from a parrot's feather, he presumed, and very handsome it was, if not the sort of quill a professional would care to be seen using for serious work. But perfect for a light romance. He dipped it into the matching ink, and found himself standing alone, chilled half to death, in a cavernous building filled with dim shadows and dusty cobwebs.

There had been no sense of transition at all. Tan's shocked gasp and sharp twitch backward were natural, but ill-advised: He discovered that his ankles were chained together and his wrists chained to his ankles by coming too hard against the limits of the chains, losing his balance, and falling. And then he discovered that another chain was around his neck, this one running high aloft to the distant ceiling of the building. With his hands chained, Tan could not catch himself: The chain about his neck slipped through a steel ring and he was suddenly strangling. It took a terrifying moment of breathless, off-balance struggle to regain his feet, and even then he had to toss his head sharply to get the strangling chain to run back through the slip-ring so he could catch his breath.

His throat felt bruised where the chain had closed around it. For an instant he could not help but picture what would have happened if he'd fallen with a little more force and crushed his windpipe, or if he hadn't been able to get back to his feet and had simply hung there, strangling— The images went beyond vivid to visceral, and he shut his eyes for a long moment and devoted himself to breathing. Slow, steady breaths. He was not going to panic and give himself to his enemies . . . to Istierinan, to be plain, and what was Istierinan doing with a pet mage running his errands? What mage would it even be? None of the court mages at Teramondian served or worked with or even liked Istierinan, so far as Tan knew. Obviously he had missed something. Evidently something important.

Tan knew very little about magecraft, but obviously Istierinan couldn't have stolen him out of the Delta's great house and tumbled him into this place through a blank moment of time unless he had a Linularinan mage working with him. But, earth and iron, why had the Linularinan spymaster gone to such trouble to do it? Istierinan risked offending not just Feierabiand but *the Lord of the Delta* by stealing Tan out of *his own house*? Even when it was patently too late to stop the stolen information from getting out? It was incredible.

Although, on the other hand, Tan had to credit that Istierinan had clearly managed the trick. Perhaps so silently that Lord Bertaud would not be able to take official offense? At least, so silently that Istierinan could *tell* himself that the Lord of the Delta wouldn't be able to take offense? Tan ran that question backward and forward in his mind even while he turned most of his attention toward examining his situation and his prison. He wasn't injured. Not even bruised, save where the chain had closed across his throat when he'd fallen. Istierinan and his people had taken some care, then, that he not be harmed. Yet. But his shirt was gone, and his boots. No wonder he was cold. His skin prickled with the chill. Or maybe with fear.

He tried to bury the fear beneath rational thought and a practical attention toward possible escape. The building seemed to be a warehouse. Or a barn. A barn, yes. That loft had probably held bales of hay or straw, and those rot-riddled boards over there had probably once outlined neat stalls. Though the table near at hand was new, obviously brought in recently. Like the chains and their bolts. An old disused barn, then, freshly tricked out for its new and far more questionable role. Too far from the city, he was certain, for passersby to hear shouts.

Well, and come to that, why was Istierinan not already standing at that nice new table, with all the tools he might require laid out for use? Was he simply waiting for fear and cold and exhaustion to wear Tan down? The scene, one had to admit, was quite adequately set for the purpose. The slip-chain was a nice touch. How long could a man stay on his feet when collapse would mean strangling? A long time, Tan thought, but not forever, and when he died, his death would be, in a way, something he'd done to himself. Yes, that was the kind of subtlety that would appeal to Istierinan.

Tan had spent nearly seven years making a place for himself, or for the man he had pretended to be, in the old Fox's court in Teramondian. Even before that, he had spent other, earlier, years living out other false lives in one part or another of Linularinum. He had done it because he loved Feierabiand, and because . . . well, for many reasons that had seemed good at the time. He had resented Linularinan arrogance and high-handedness; that had been part of it. He had feared what might eventually come about if the Linularinan king and court were allowed to disdain Feierabiand. And he had enjoyed the game of spycraft and his own skill at it. An agent operating in deep cover lived a life of slow, tedious deception that flashed with lightning-lit moments of brilliant terror, and Tan would not have traded those moments for a life-time of secure prosperity.

Thus, for years Tan had walked the knife's edge of deception, as they said. The knife in that saying was understood to be laid as a bridge across disownment—for spies, if caught, were very seldom owned by their masters—and death. And he had done it even though, in those years, he had learned to love Linularinum as well as Feierabiand.

Every confidential agent struggled with questions about loyalty and treachery. These were questions with which Tan had years ago made his peace. It had helped that he never felt any love for the old Fox, Mariddeier Kohorrian, who paid far too much attention to cleverness and the strictest possible interpretation of the law and not nearly enough to justice. But it had helped even more that in those last years, as he'd gained Istierinan's trust, he'd also learned to hate him. The Linularinan spymaster had seemed to Tan to embody everything he disliked about the Linularinan people while specifically eschewing all their admirable qualities. He was not merely deceitful but falsehearted, not merely justifiably proud of his own skills but contemptuous of those owned by others, and slyly cruel even when he seemed overtly kind.

Maybe silence and cold was exactly the vengeance Istierinan had in mind. Maybe no one would come to question Tan, not even to watch or gloat. An uncomfortable idea, in its way worse than, well, other ideas. Maybe Istierinan was employing time itself as a subtle weapon as well, forcing Tan to suffer from the contradictory fears that someone would come and that no one would. Time to try to escape and fail, to wear out his strength to no avail, with the strangling chain waiting all the while to tighten when he could no longer keep his feet . . .

At the moment, however, Tan definitely was not desperate enough to wish for the arrival of his enemies. He turned his head, shuffled as far around as the chains would allow, inspecting the warehouse more closely. No windows, no visible door. The slanted golden light of late afternoon filtered in through missing boards high in the roof. The building was not, then, in good shape. He should be able to break a way out, if he could get out of the chains.

Which did not seem likely. The barn might be decrepit, but the chains were new and well-made, and they'd been bolted to a floor that seemed depressingly sturdy. No signs of wood-rot underfoot, no. Above . . . when Tan tensed the muscles of his neck and cautiously put pressure on the chain around his throat, he could feel no give to the boards above. Nor, when he tried standing on his toes and ducking, could he loosen the slip-chain enough to get his head through. He thought, briefly, about trying to jerk the neck-chain loose. But it would be unfortunate if he accidentally crushed his own windpipe instead of breaking the chain. Istierinan would laugh himself stupid when he finally arrived.

Tan stood quietly for some time, thinking and letting his eyes roam aimlessly about the barn, hoping for inspiration. None came. He found himself shivering and, as he had no other protection, tried to pretend that he wasn't cold. Far too many little breezes and gusts could make their way through the cracks and gaps and the spaces left by missing boards. Spring it might be, but only just, and even in the Delta, it was too cold to go without boots or shirt. The light dimmed . . . overcast? Tan doubted the roof of this barn would prove tight against wind and rain. A chilly rain would be perfect to complete this situation. Though, as he had no water, he might soon be grateful for even the most bone-chilling rain. Or was it dusk? It seemed too early. But he did not, after all, know how long ago he had been captured. Hours? Days? He surely should be thirstier, if it had been so long.

He tried again to break loose the bolts that held him chained—he'd already decided the chains themselves were hopeless. Nothing. He then tried, briefly, to work his hands out of their shackles. His hands were long, his wrists not overthick. But the steel shackles were too tight. Even if Tan broke the bones of his hands and fingers, there would still be the shackles on his ankles. Hard to deal with those if his fingers were broken. Though if he could only get the slip-chain off, he might count that a net gain. If he was sufficiently desperate. Not yet.

He could try shouting. He knew very well no decent, uninvolved person would be near enough to hear him. On the other hand, if ene-mies were nearby, *they* would hear him. They might even come. That was an uncomfortable uncertainty. So not yet for shouting, either, then. Though possibly soon . . .

Then, somewhere out of sight, a door creaked open and thudded closed. Enemies were coming, after all. It was a mark of Istierinan's cleverness that Tan was almost glad to hear them. He straightened his shoulders and turned his head. Boots thumped hollowly across the floor, more than one pair. Dust rose into the air. Someone coughed. Torchlight wavered, red as death.

The Istierinan whom Tan had known, Istierinan Hamoddian, son of Lord Iskiriadde Hamoddian, had passed himself off as a careless court dandy, a man with wit and wealth, but no interest in or connec-tion with serious matters. Dissolute and reckless, though undoubtedly clever. The sort of man admired by younger sons who admired profli-gacy for its own sake and were likely to die young in some foolish stunt or quarrel.

But Istierinan Hamoddian was showing Tan a very different face now. Not only was he dressed as plainly as any ordinary traveler, but his long, bony face, usually expressive, was blank and still. Very little remained to suggest the self-indulgent courtier Tan remembered. Here, for this role he was playing now, he had not troubled to color the gray out of his hair. No wonder, Tan thought, that he had customarily done so, for the silver at his temples made him look not only older but far more serious. Istierinan's mouth, always ready to crook in ironic humor, was set in a thin line. His wit wasn't hidden, but altered out of all recognition to a kind of grim acuity. His deep-set eyes, though shadowed with weariness, held a cold resolution. Tan wondered, distantly, how many of Istierinan's young admirers would even recognize him now.

Istierinan was carrying nothing. But the two burly men he'd brought with him held cudgels as well as torches, and one of them carried a leather satchel that might contain anything. Tan tried, unsuccessfully, not to imagine the sort of tools it probably held.

Istierinan stopped perhaps six feet from Tan, looking at him without speaking.

Tan stared back, equally wordless. He considered, briefly, pretending innocence and demanding what Istierinan meant by this abduction. But the spymaster did not look in the mood for such pretense, thoroughly ruined in any case by Tan's convoluted flight out of Linularinum to the Delta. No innocent man could have made it, or would have known how to even try, and no clever repartee could possibly disguise the fact.

Nor did Istierinan seem inclined toward any sort of game or indirection. He simply looked at Tan for a moment longer and then asked abruptly, "Where is it? Do you still have it yourself? If you've passed it on, to whom?"

These all seemed odd questions, when Tan had stolen information rather than any object. He said cautiously, "What, it?" Not altogether to his surprise, Istierinan merely glanced impatiently at one of his thugs. The man lifted a muscled arm. Tan kept his gaze on Istierinan, not the thug. He said quickly and sharply, "Well, here we are, very like Redrierre and Moddrisian, and just as unlikely to come to a satisfactory conclusion, do you think? Be sensible, man! I'll answer any question you ask, but if you want answers, you'll have to ask clearly! I swear I don't know what you mean."

The spymaster didn't even blink. The thug stepped forward, walked around behind Tan, and hit him: a hard, twisting blow to the kidney. Gasping, Tan stumbled and sagged—then found the slip-chain cutting off his air. He tried to straighten and the thug kicked his feet out from under him. Then all of them just stood and waited while Tan struggled, strangling, to get back to his feet. He made it at last, tossing his head hard to loosen the chain and sucking in great lungfuls of precious air.

"Where is it?" Istierinan repeated in a level voice. "Do you still hold it yourself? If you do, then return it, and this can be over swiftly. Or otherwise, if you will not. Or have you given it away? To whom? The Lord of the Delta, likely not." He made a small movement, dismissing this possibility as though he and Tan both knew it was foolish. "But perhaps one of his people might have been able to take it? Well?"

Tan shook his head. "Lord Istierinan, I'm afraid this is going to be a long night. Because I truly do not know what you are talking about! I took nothing returnable. Everything I stole was set down in plain ink and has long since been carried away out of the past into the future—" He stopped as the Linularinan spymaster stepped across to the table and began to take things out of the satchel.

To Tan's astonishment, what he was laying out was bottles of ink and little bundles of quills. Tan almost laughed in sheer surprise. Quills and ink! Whatever Istierinan had in mind, Tan was definitely glad to see legist's tools rather than the other sort. But what did the Linularinan spymaster have in mind?

"Well?" Istierinan said to Tan. Not ominously. He'd taken a quill out of the packet, and ran it now through his fingers. His tone was more one of . . . weary exasperation, if Tan was any judge. The spymaster made a small gesture down toward Tan's feet. "You would have more trouble keeping your feet, I imagine, with broken toes. Or *missing* toes. Or whatever. There are so many possibilities."

"I'm sure you're right," Tan agreed smoothly. "There's surely no need to test the question, if you would only be plain. Lord Istierinan, what is it you *want*?"

"Want?" Istierinan took a small step forward, his calm cracking to show—what? Anger, yes, but not merely anger: There was something else underneath the rage. Fear, even terror, tightly leashed, and something else—desperation? Despair? Istierinan might well lose his position because of what Tan had done to him—probably would, probably should, maybe already had—but Tan had not thought the old Fox of Linularinum would go so far as to torture and destroy a spymaster who failed him. But he could not at the moment imagine what other fear could render Istierinan so desperate now.

Or had the King of Linularinum *not* sent Istierinan after Tan after all? Maybe Istierinan was here on his own, in one last effort to regain the king's favor and his old place in the Fox's court? No, that didn't seem likely—Tan's thoughts were interrupted in their circular flight by Istierinan himself taking a cudgel from one of his thugs and slamming it down toward one of his feet. Tan jerked his foot out of the way and Istierinan changed the strike to a sweeping sideways blow against his knee.

The *crack* of wood against bone was horrifying even before the pain hit, and then the cudgel swept around to threaten the other knee, and Tan tried to get out of the way of the blow, lost his footing completely, and found himself once again strangling helplessly, only this

time the agony from his broken knee overwhelmed the terror of suffo-
cation, briefly. Then the lack of air forced even the pain into the background, and at last he made it back to his feet—his foot—but then
immediately fell again as some of his weight came onto his bad knee in
a red explosion. He made it up once more, somehow, and fought to keep
his balance—he dreaded a blow against the other knee, though he told
himself, with what rationality remained to him, that surely Istierinan
did not mean to kill him, not yet. Though a second blow against the
first leg would not be much of an improvement.

But Istierinan did not strike him again, waiting instead for Tan to
regain his balance and his breath. When Tan swayed, flinched from the
red rolling pain, and nearly fell again, the spymaster put the tip of the
cudgel against Tan's chest to steady him. "So," he said softly. "Will you
continue to insist that this night be long?"

Tan tried to focus on the question, on Istierinan's face. The haze of
sweat and tears and nauseating pain got in the way. He blinked, blinked
again, and managed at last to put the pain aside enough to spare some
attention to the spymaster. Istierinan was now leaning on the cudgel
like a walking stick. If he'd been playing the court dandy, he would
have probably looked urbane and sophisticated. Here in this disused
barn, no one could have mistaken his ruthlessness.

"Are you listening to me? Are you capable of thought?"

Tan shook his head, not in denial, but trying to clear his mind.
Even that motion somehow jarred his leg. Tears of pain came into his
eyes; a wave of faintness threatened his balance. At Istierinan's impatient wave, one of the thugs stepped forward to support him.

"Would you care to sit down? Agree to return . . . what you stole, and
you may. One way or the other, you will return it, or at least release it,
before dawn. Give it to me now and I will even let you go, no more
harmed than you are now. I will sign any binding contract you care to
dictate," he added, as Tan's eyebrows rose in wordless incredulity. He
took a small but rather fine leather-bound book out of his satchel, gave
Tan a significant look, and set the book down on the table, precisely cen-
tered. Then he removed the top from one of his bottles of ink, picked up
a quill, and gave Tan another look, even more significant. Tan stared at
him, hopelessly bewildered.

"Or if you no longer have it, tell me to whom you gave it," Istierinan
snapped. "I will at least make this night a short one."

Tan wanted to ask again what *it* was, but was afraid of what Istierinan might do if he seemed to be defiant. The thug, responding to another of Istierinan's gestured commands, released Tan and stepped
back, punctuating the spymaster's demand with a clear illustration of

what the rest of the night would be like if Tan continued to be obdurate. Tan tensed the muscles of his neck, trying to let the slip-chain carry some of his weight. This was not a successful endeavor. He tried to think. This was also not a very successful endeavor. Istierinan was still waiting. Tan opened his mouth to agree, at least to get Istierinan to release the slip-chain, let him sit down, if only for a moment until the spymaster understood that Tan really could not do as he demanded— even a brief respite would be a very good thing—

There was a shout, and the sound of running steps coming rapidly closer, a lot of men by the sound, and then almost at once the deadly whip of arrows through the cobweb-strewn space under the vaulted roof of the barn and more shouts.

Istierinan whirled, shocked, and then hesitated, taking a step toward Tan. Another shout echoed in the close space, and more arrows flew—better aimed this time, so much better that Tan belatedly realized that the first volley had been meant merely to frighten the spymaster and his men and drive them away from their prisoner. Istierinan realized that, too, and that, chained as Tan was, it was going to be impossible to take him with them in their flight. He snatched up the torches instead and flung them down, shadows whirling and surging as the flames whipped through the air.

Tan expected Istierinan to kill him, since he couldn't keep him. To his surprise, the spymaster spun and reached for the book instead. But an arrow sliced the air not an inch from his hand and then another cut across his forearm, loosing a red spray of blood—Istierinan made a sound between a gasp and a scream, jerking involuntarily away, but even then he did not run. But another arrow struck him in the back. One of his men caught him up as he collapsed, and carried him away at a run, not at all discommoded by the burden.

Then Tan's rescuers were arriving—men in plain clothing without badges or identifying marks, but with very businesslike weapons. Most of them went straight past Tan, hurrying cautiously into the echoing reaches of the barn, but a small group of men stopped to collect the abandoned torches and, very much to Tan's relief, two came to get him free. Tan was not altogether astonished to find Geroen among those who stayed near at hand, but he was speechless to glimpse the slender figure of Mienthe stretching up on her toes to peer over the captain's shoulder.

"Can't you stand?" growled Geroen, coming to look Tan up and down. "Your knee, is it? Sepes, get that chain off from around his neck. Why's that other one still on his hands? What do you mean, you've no key? Earth and iron! What do you need a key for? Didn't anybody ever teach you to pick locks?"

Tan blinked, wondering whether he could have heard this right, but then the captain quite matter-of-factly produced a set of lockpicks and bent to examine the shackles. "Not any locksmith's best work," he added after a moment, straightening as the wristbands snapped open—then caught Tan's arm in a hard grip as Tan swayed and added, "None of that, now! Here, Keier, keep him upright, will you, while I get these other shackles—" He grunted down to one knee to work on the ankle chains.

Tan clung to Keier, but he stared at Mienthe, still baffled by her presence. Like the men, she was wearing plain, sturdy clothing—boy's clothing, in fact, very practical—but no one could have mistaken her for a boy. Her hair hung down her back in a heavy plait, and her delicate bones were much too fine for a boy's. Though admirably composed, she was clearly frightened. She was breathing quickly, her face was pale, and her hands were balled into fists, probably to hide their shaking. On the other hand, she neither babbled nor spooked nervously at every distant sound, the two most common failings of young men on their first assignments in enemy territory. Instead, she walked forward to peer curiously at the things laid out on the table. One of the men guarding her immediately collected a torch and obligingly held it for her. Picking up a quill, she ran the long feather through her fingers. Then she flipped open the book to gaze at its pages. Her brows drew together in puzzlement.

"He can't walk on that," Geroen said to one of his men, oblivious of or indifferent to Mienthe's interest in the things the Linularinan spymaster had abandoned. "You and Sepes, carry him. Jump to it, now, do you think we've got all year for this?"

"Wait—" Tan began, nodding toward the table.

"Shut up!" Geroen ordered curtly. "Do you *know* how much trouble you've caused? I'll give you a hint for free! Not near as much as there'll be if we're caught this side of the river. Keier—"

"Tan, can you . . ." Mienthe looked at him in concern, her voice trailing off. She closed the book again and tucked it back in the abandoned satchel, so that was all right. And she began to collect the inks and quills as well. The instincts of a spy, Tan thought, to take away anything odd for later perusal at leisure. He was almost amused despite the brutal circumstances, but he was glad to see someone had the right impulse, since Geroen clearly did not.

"I'm well, I'm well," Tan assured Mienthe, through his teeth because he had to choke back a groan of pain as he tried to take a step. The attempt proved ill-advised. "You have that book safe, all those things?"

"Yes—"

"You, and you." Captain Geroen pointed a thick finger at two of his men. "Get him up and out. Lady, if you will, this is not the time to dither about looking at—Did you find anyone?" he interrupted himself to demand as some of his men reemerged from the far gloomy reaches of the barn. And, to the reluctant shakes of their heads, "Too much to expect, I suppose. Lady—"

Mienthe said meekly to Geroen, "Yes, Captain, of course. Is everyone here? Wasn't there any sign of the, um, the men who . . ."

"Nothing but shadows and starlight as far as we could see," said one of the men who'd gone after Istierinan. He added a little defensively, "Once they were out of this building, there were a thousand places to hide, and there's not much moon tonight."

"It's not likely a lot of Delta guardsmen off the streets will find Istierinan Hamoddian or his men," Tan put in. "Those weren't some petty street-thugs, Geroen. That was the Linularinan spymaster. He might have been struck by an arrow, but those men he had won't be fools. Although you might have taken them by surprise, you aren't likely to take them up now."

Geroen grunted, scowling at any possible excuses. But he didn't order his people after Istierinan, either. He said instead, "Nor I wouldn't want to. Last thing we need here, another spy! You men, get *our* spy out of that chair. Our way's still clear, is it, Jerren?"

Tan wondered, briefly, what kind of animal Jerren bespoke. Something that could see in the dark, presumably. Rats? Owls? But then the two young men the captain had assigned to him lifted him up and he lost all interest in any questions other than *How far to the river?* and *How long till I can lie down?* and, impolite but honest doubt: *So do you have a half-skilled healing mage anywhere in Tiefenauer?*

The barn proved to be set to one side of an abandoned farmyard, not far from a decrepit house. A stretch of briars and poison ivy and other coarse brush indicated an abandoned pasture, and a timber fence in ill-repair outlined a rutted gravel road. It was not quite raining, but heavily overcast, with a fine mist blowing on the wind.

A lot of horses came up out of the brush. In the dark, the sound of their hooves crunching through the undergrowth took at least a year or two off Tan's life, until he managed at last to make out their riderless state. Strangely, the animals moved all together, not one straying away from the herd—ah. Of course some of Geroen's men would be able to speak to horses; living in Linularinum, Tan had become less accustomed to everyone and his cousin having that sort of gift, but there was a lot of Feierabianden blood in the Delta.

"You can't hardly ride with that leg," Geroen began.

"I'd rather ride than walk, and I'd drag myself along by my teeth to get out of this place," Tan assured him. "Just get me up on a horse and I'll stay there, I promise you."

Though this claim was true in its essentials, getting up into the saddle of even the most patient beast proved even less entertaining in practice than Tan had envisioned. But he was up at last, and they were all moving.

Tan had opted to allow his bad leg to hang loose rather than try to get his foot into the stirrup. Now he rapidly decided that had been a mistake—though he knew any other decision would have been just as agonizing—yes, and falling off would be even worse, though at the moment, *even worse* was something of a theoretical construct. He braced himself against swirling dizziness with a hand on the pommel and tried not to scream or sob or throw up, all bad for his reputation as well as inconvenient when trying to run away.

He'd have liked to sink into blind misery and just endure while Geroen's men got him home. In fact, he rather felt that he deserved to. He could hardly kick his horse to get it up beside Geroen's, but when the captain came past him, he managed to gather enough shards of control and rationality to ask, "How far to the border? What do you figure are the chances of meeting the wrong sort of patrol between here and there? Are these all the men you have?" There were nineteen men, Tan knew, some distant part of his mind having made an automatic count. Nineteen men and Bertaud's little cousin. Not the sort of force he could quite imagine facing down, say, a company of regular Linularinan soldiers under Istierinan's command. Even if they had any right to try, which they arguably didn't, on this side of the river.

"Not far," Geroen said briefly. "But too far, if we run into the wrong sort of trouble. Can you canter?" He gave Tan a close look. "Never mind! Even a trot would have you off in a trice, a blind crow at midnight could see that."

Tan could hardly deny it. He wondered just where Istierinan might have got to, and with whom, and in command of what resources. And just what their chances were of finding out the answers to all those questions. Far too good, he feared.

Mienthe rode over. Even in the dark, anyone could see that she was tense, excited, worried, determined, very young, and, most of all, decidedly female. Why, why, why had Geroen brought her? If they did encounter any regular Linularinan soldiers, it would be blazingly obvious she was somebody important. The Linularinan authorities would have every reason to believe the Delta had deliberately sent her to lend formal authority to some nefarious purpose, and what would Bertaud say if they got his cousin taken up by enemy soldiers on the wrong side of the river?

But she was still self-possessed, and she still had the leather satchel over her shoulder, Tan was relieved to see. She said, to Tan but mostly addressing Geroen, "Tan, I'll get up behind you." Then, as the captain began to protest, "No, it only makes sense! I'm the only one here light enough to let the horse carry two at speed, and I can keep him from falling. Then we can make better time, and if you only have one horse to guard rather than two, won't that simplify everything in case of, well, in case?"

It would, unquestionably. Though Tan also had an uncomfortable vision of the horse stumbling at some unforgiving moment, with both of them falling, to yield twice the disaster they'd otherwise face. Even so . . .

"Over you get, then," Geroen said gruffly. Tan couldn't tell whether he was also suffering from a too-vivid imagination. He sounded ill-tempered enough either way.

Mienthe slid across from her horse to Tan's without even dismounting. She sat close behind him, her thighs bracing his, her small hands firm on his hips. He immediately felt much more secure in the saddle. The horse's gait smoothed out as it, too, recognized the steadiness of its second rider. Under other circumstances, Tan would have enjoyed having the girl behind him. He tried to think of an appropriate quotation for this sort of situation—he knew there was one—but the agony radiating from his knee not only ruined his memory but also ensured, very decisively, that he'd be thinking no impure thoughts about Lord Bertaud's cousin.

Geroen waved, and the horse lunged forward into a canter along a road they could only barely see; one had to just trust the horses knew where they were putting their feet. "It's not far to the river," Mienthe said to Tan. She didn't quite shout, although nervous excitement made her speak much more loudly than necessary. That was as well, as Tan was tending to lose words and phrases among the waves of pain that beset him.

Tan was certain they would find a company of Linularinan soldiers between them and the river, yet they met no one. This astonished him, until he remembered Istierinan falling with an arrow in his back. They passed half a handful of travelers on the road, so they would be remembered, but Tan could not bring himself to care. They found no one waiting when they finally waded out of the marshes proper and into the mud at the river's edge, which was his sole concern.

"There's a ford?" Tan muttered when he'd realized they'd stopped. He squinted blearily out across the wide expanse of water. For all the sluggish current, the river looked deep here. The water looked like pewter in the dim light, stark angular silhouettes of cypress knees black against the slow-moving glimmer.

Then he watched incredulously as one clumsy but solid-looking rowboat and then another were drawn out of the hidden darkness behind the cypress knees. All that way along the road and then through the marshes, and they'd come out at the riverbank just where the rowboats had been hidden? His opinion of Geroen, already fairly solid, rose another notch.

And he was very, very glad there were boats. Though he was not entirely certain he would be able to make it down from this horse without collapsing into unconsciousness and then into the black swamp mud. Drowning in a foot of water! *There* would be a stupid death. Though, no, of course, he realized muzzily. Mienthe was right behind him. She would drag him out . . . A guardsman reached up to help Tan down, and he found he'd been right about at least one thing: Black unconsciousness was indeed waiting for him. The last thing he was aware of was Mienthe's sharp exclamation of dismay as she snatched at his arm.

CHAPTER 4

Mienthe had been frightened from the moment she'd realized that Tan was missing and that, with Bertaud gone, she was the only one who could possibly order a raid to get him back. But she had not been utterly *terrified* until she realized she had actually managed to persuade Geroen not only to obey that command, but to take her with him.

Then, once they were committed, Mienthe had been terrified she'd lose her sense of Tan's position and that she wouldn't be able to find him after all. She was terrified they'd run into a Linularinan patrol and have to either run or fight, neither option at all desirable. She was terrified they'd find Tan and be unable to get him back, or find he'd already been killed. Right at the end, before they'd found the barn, she'd even thought that she might just be wrong about what she thought she knew. The conviction that she knew Tan's position was very strong, but once that doubt had occurred to her, it had crept persistently about in the back of her mind no matter how she tried to ignore it.

But then they had found Tan after all, and there hadn't been a lot of Linularinan soldiers, and Tan *had* still been alive—though what had been done to him was brutal, and getting away again was a nightmare.

Then Mienthe had been terrified they'd be caught by Linularinan troops after all, or guardsmen, or spies, or whoever had been in that barn with Tan. But then they'd found the boats, and Tan had fainted, which made getting him across the river much less awful, even though by that time the mist had changed to a cold and very unpleasant drizzle.

And no one had tried to stop them, which amazed Mienthe. She suspected Geroen was also astonished at how lucky they'd been, though he was so gruff it was hard to tell. She was still amazed she'd managed to persuade him that yes, really, she *did* know where Tan was, but no, she *couldn't* explain it to anybody else. But when she'd insisted, instead of ignoring her, Geroen had said, in an extremely neutral tone, "Well, lady, I hadn't heard you'd gone for a mage, but it could be useful now and no mistake."

Mienthe couldn't believe she really might be developing mage power and she was a little ashamed of letting Geroen think she was. But she certainly hadn't tried to stop his arranging the raid. And she'd agreed with him about informing the queen—or at least, she'd agreed with him that the queen shouldn't be informed. Mienthe hadn't wanted to argue with Niethe or her royal guardsmen, and neither, apparently, had Geroen. Instead, they'd agreed that they should move fast. And they had, so fast they'd very nearly got to Tan before his Linularinan enemies had got him across the river. But not quite.

But to Mienthe's intense gratitude, the captain hadn't quit even then, but had instead pulled success right out of the teeth of looming defeat.

Now they were back in Feierabiand and it wasn't even dawn yet, which seemed incredible. She supposed Bertaud and the king must be most of the way to Sihannas by now, and knew nothing at all about what had happened to Tan or what she had done, which seemed in a way even more incredible.

Tan was more or less conscious again, which was unfortunate. Mienthe, riding in the cart next to him, flinched every time the cart jarred across an uneven cobblestone. Tan himself seemed beyond flinching for anything so minor. It had nearly stopped raining, but it was still impossible to tell whether the moisture beading on his face was rain or tears. Mienthe thought Tan was definitely due his share of tears, all things considered.

But there was the great house at last. Unfortunately, the house wasn't waiting for them quietly, as Mienthe had expected and hoped. The lanterns, set high on their tall poles, blazed through the gardens and before every door. Lamps glowed in every window, and the main doors stood wide open to the chill darkness of the streets, and there were Delta guardsmen and royal soldiers everywhere.

Captain Geroen set his jaw, not quite looking at Mienthe where she sat in the cart. "Her Majesty got it out of my officers where we'd gone, I suppose."

Biting her lip, Mienthe nodded. Geroen was right. Queen Niethe must have found out where they'd gone, and even if she approved the result of what they'd done, she might be really angry at their lack of . . . finesse. Even if she wasn't, she would certainly tell King Iaor all about it. Possibly worse, either Niethe or the king would unquestionably tell Bertaud.

But she said optimistically, trying to sound firm and decisive, "This is the Delta, and her Majesty isn't the Lady of the Delta. With Bertaud gone, I am. He said so." She hesitated. That had *sounded* firm, hadn't it? She wished she felt the truth of the statement with half that firmness. But she continued, "So if I approved our, um, raid, then even the queen hasn't anything to say about it. Or not much." But she couldn't help but add, "I think."

"Huh," said Geroen, clearly not reassured.

"I had hoped she wouldn't find out," Mienthe admitted in a smaller voice. "I suppose she'll tell Iaor. And Bertaud."

"I suppose she will," Geroen agreed glumly, clearly not looking forward to facing her cousin. "Likely your lord cousin will break me right back to prison guard when he finds out about this. If he doesn't toss me in a cell myself."

Mienthe shook her head, though privately she wondered whether Geroen might be right. If they'd been clever and quick enough, they would have recovered Tan *before* the Linularinan spymaster had got him across the bridge. Then they wouldn't have needed to charge off through the marshes and across the river on a wild and completely illegal raid of their own. Bertaud might be really furious, especially with Geroen, because the captain had let her come on the raid.

Mienthe said stubbornly, "Linularinum started it. And I had to go along, or we'd never have managed. Besides, by the time he finds out, it'll be so long ago, maybe . . . Anyway, we *did* get Tan back. And we didn't get caught."

"Both matters of the greatest importance," Tan put in from the bottom of the cart, not opening his eyes. His voice was barely audible, but his tone had recovered a thread of mocking humor. "Be a pity to stop here and let all that effort go to waste."

Geroen grunted a laugh, signaled the cart's driver to stop, swung off his horse, and offered Mienthe a hand down from the cart.

The queen, followed by a scattering of staff and servants, came out the open doors at just that moment. She stood for a moment, staring at them. Then she came down the steps and made her way over to the cart. The queen took Mienthe's hand, to her immense relief seeming not so furious after all. Her pretty mouth set as her glance encompassed Tan's pale, pain-drawn face.

"A smashed knee," Geroen said briefly, not quite meeting the queen's eyes.

"I'd never have lived through the night if not for this rescue," Tan

managed in his thread of a voice. Mienthe hoped the queen would remember to mention *that* to her husband, as well as the rest.

"I asked for your staff to send for a mage skilled in healing as soon
as I understood where you'd gone," Queen Niethe told Mienthe. She
touched Tan's throat, then his forehead. She frowned down at him. "Already fevered—well, the mage will see you right, and for that I'm truly
grateful." She turned to wave at the hovering servants.

Iriene was the only mage in Tiefenauer skilled in healing, and she
was in fact skilled at no other kind of magecraft. But she was a very
skillful healer indeed. Folk came from all over the Delta to see her.
Mienthe had seen Iriene repair a terribly broken elbow once when one
of the upper-house maids' child had fallen out of a window; she could
surely fix Tan's knee. And the queen had already sent for her. A tension
Mienthe hadn't quite realized she'd felt eased.

Tan, closing his eyes again, whispered, "A mage is better than a
miser when health is more valued than gold," which sounded like a
quote, though Mienthe didn't recognize the source.

"That's the only injury?" Niethe asked, looking searchingly at
Mienthe. "You're well?"

"Yes—"

"Well, good! But there's no credit to your guard captain for that," the
queen said, and stared at Geroen, who lowered his eyes wordlessly. Not
in the least appeased, Queen Niethe said in an unforgiving tone, "You
took *Bertaud's little cousin* across the river into Linularinum, risking
who knows what mayhem *and* a cross-border incident? I can't imagine
what Iaor will say! And you, Mienthe! What *can* you have been thinking? I would hardly credit it, save you standing here covered in swamp
mud!"

Geroen could hardly answer this, so Mienthe did. "Your Majesty,
Captain Geroen didn't take me across the river," she said, trying not to
let her voice tremble. She made herself meet the queen's eyes. "*I* took
him. And I'm sorry if His Majesty will be angry, but I'm the Lady of
the Delta while my cousin is away, so how could I let Linularinan
agents kidnap people right out of the great house? And we did get Tan
back."

The queen stared at her, taken very much aback.

Mienthe knew she'd flushed. Her heart was beating too fast. Despite her brave words, she knew the king, and probably Bertaud, would
indeed be angry. And she knew she was the one who deserved their
anger—she'd taken Bertaud's authority on herself, and whatever he'd
said, she wasn't at all certain she'd had the right, not really.

She also knew that none of the risks they'd taken would have been necessary if she'd only kept Tan safer to begin with, or moved faster to get him back—she'd known where he was from the moment he'd been taken, and they'd *still* had to go into Linularinum to get him? If she'd only been faster, not only would they have avoided any potential trouble with Linularinum, but Tan wouldn't have gotten hurt.

"Well," Niethe said, now sounding a little doubtful, "if you stopped those sly Linularinan agents from doing their malicious work on this side of the river, that's well done, at least." She smiled suddenly. "I won't scold you, Mienthe. Maybe you're right. I imagine your cousin will have one or two things to say when he returns, however!"

Mienthe imagined so, too, more vividly than Niethe could. She tried to smile.

Behind the queen, the mage Iriene came out onto the porch, took in the crowd with one comprehensive, unimpressed glance, and said sharply, "Why are you all dithering about in the damp? Get this injured man somewhere clean and warm, and everyone else get out of the way, if you please! Do we have a litter? Well, what are we all standing about for, then? You"—she stabbed a finger at some of the queen's attendants—"get a litter and get that man inside. Jump!"

In all the Delta, Iriene daughter of Iriene was not only the mage most skilled with healing magic but also the one least impressed by rank, wealth, or authority. Only learning impressed her, so Bertaud had told Mienthe, and only if it had to do with healing. She paid so little attention to anything else that Mienthe suspected she might not even know who Niethe was. If she knew, it wasn't stopping her commanding the queen's own guardsmen, who, after only the quickest glance at Niethe, were indeed jumping to obey the mage.

"Gently, there!" exclaimed Iriene, hovering over Tan as he was transferred from cart to litter. She scowled ferociously down at him, waving a sharp hand through the air as though trying to brush away a cloud of gnats. "Well, *that's* strange—" she began, but then her breath puffed out in exasperation as someone staggered and jolted the litter. Instead of finishing her thought, she reached out with one hand and laid her fingers on Tan's leg above the knee. Tan gasped and then sagged all over as the pain abruptly eased.

"So that's in hand," Niethe said as the mage and her party passed indoors. She turned her head, frowning. "Very well. Captain . . . Geroen, isn't it?"

Geroen ducked his head. "Your Majesty."

"I trust you'll be able to keep hold of him this time? I'm quite certain that Iaor would not approve of a repetition of this night's exercise."

"Yes, Your Majesty. No, indeed. I'll go see to that, then." The guard captain hesitated fractionally, glancing at Mienthe. "If I've your leave to do so."

"Yes," Mienthe said, surprised. "Of course. Go on."

Geroen gave her a curt bow and followed Iriene and her retinue of litter-bearers.

"Mienthe . . . you're well, truly?" Niethe gave her a searching look. "I see you are. This"—the queen visibly edited any number of phrases such as *harebrained* and *madly foolish* out of her speech—"night's, um, work, was truly your idea? Just what *did* you all do? And how?"

"Captain Geroen would probably explain everything better," Mienthe said humbly. Everything seemed to blur together in her mind. Especially all that horrible ride back toward the river.

The queen smiled. "Well, you can tell me all about it *after* you've cleaned up and warmed up and had a chance to rest, Mienthe, lest you catch the ague and require Iriene's skills on your own account! Perhaps you'll join me for breakfast in the brown room, in, say, an hour? Two hours?"

Appalled at the idea that the queen might wait for *her*, Mienthe assured Niethe that an hour would be wonderful, ample, more than generous. Then she fled hastily to her room. She wanted a long, hot bath with lots of fragrant soap, and she wanted to wash her hair at least twice—she was sure there was swamp mud in it as well as on her clothing, she could smell the reek wafting around her every time she shook her head—and she wanted to wrap herself in warm towels in front of a roaring fire and let her maids comb out her clean hair. Then she wanted her warmest, softest robe and a cup of hot tea and a sweet roll with jam, and *then* she wanted to fall into her bed and sleep for about three days.

She thought she might at least manage a very quick bath and her hair.

"Your clothes! Your hair!" Karin, the youngest of her maids, exclaimed. The girl stared at Mienthe, laughing through her horror. "Let me call Emnis—do you want me to call her?" Emnis was Mienthe's senior maid. Mienthe started to answer, but Karin went on without waiting, "No, of course you don't; if she sees you like that, she'll never help find boy's things for you again *ever*. Did you know the queen was looking for you?"

"I saw her—"

"The *queen* saw you like that?"

Mienthe couldn't help but laugh at Karin's expression. "I think everyone was a little distracted by other things. I'm supposed to go join Her Majesty for a decent breakfast in an hour, or I'd be begging you to run down to the kitchens for me—even the bath could wait. Briefly. Did you hear we got Tan back?"

"Everyone's heard that, and that he's hurt." Karin rolled her eyes, her voice tart on her answer. "Half the household staff has him dying before another nightfall, and the other half thinks he'll be up dancing before dusk, but I don't think even the esteemed Iriene is quite *that* good a healer. But they *all* think he's terribly romantic! The injured hero, right out of an epic. You'd think *he'd* rescued *you* and not the other way around!"

Mienthe laughed again. "Oh, that would fit into an epic much better! What has Iriene said, have you heard?"

"She's still working on him, they say, so I guess he won't be dancing at dusk because she wouldn't take so long for anything simple! Let me help you off with that. There's hot water—I had them bring it as soon as we heard you'd come back—" The girl's voice trembled on that last and she fell abruptly silent.

"I'm sorry you were frightened," Mienthe told her gently.

"I'm never frightened. I'm just jealous because you got to go off on romantic adventures and I didn't." Karin effectively stifled any response Mienthe could make by pulling her shift suddenly over her head.

The water in the copper basin was still hot, for which Mienthe was grateful. Karin helped Mienthe take down her hair and step into the steaming bath.

"What do you want to wear? If Her Majesty will be at breakfast . . . Do you think the blue dress?"

Mienthe hesitated. "The queen has such lovely things even when she's traveling. And all her ladies . . . maybe the green?"

Karin laughed. "Oh, the green, then, by all means! I'll lay it out for you. Oh—here's Emnis, after all!" She kicked Mienthe's discarded clothing out of sight behind the door, handed Mienthe the soap, and slipped out toward the wardrobe, adding over her shoulder, "Maybe you could tell me, later, all the parts you leave out for Her Majesty?" She meant, after Emnis was no longer around to be horrified.

Mienthe's senior maid appeared in the doorway, clucking with mild disapproval over the state of Mienthe's hair, looking so perfectly ordinary that Mienthe found she could almost believe that nothing unusual had ever happened or ever would.

Emnis had been Mienthe's maid almost since she'd come to live in the great house. She wasn't especially pretty or at all clever, and she worried if Mienthe got mud on her skirts or under her fingernails, but she was kind and cheerful. She murmured all the time she was helping Mienthe wash her hair, a low-voiced sound as pleasant and almost as meaningless as the babble of a stream. Did Mienthe want the green

dress again, or the white one with the flowers on it, and did she expect
to go out in the gardens today, because then certainly not the white.
Did she want those new slippers with the pretty stitching on the toes?
Here, now, careful stepping out of the bath. Now, couldn't Mienthe
please settle down just for a moment so Emnis could dry her hair a bit
before she braided it and put it up, and no, there wasn't a trace of
swamp-smell left, for a mercy; earth and iron, you'd think Mienthe had
been swimming right through the swamps all night. Here, perhaps a
touch of this rose oil under her ears, just to be sure.

No, Mienthe thought. Of the whole household, Emnis was probably the one person who had the least curiosity about recent events and
the least inclination to gather and pass on rumors. It was restful. She let
Karin bring her the slippers with the stitching on the toes, then stood
for a moment looking at her maids and at the comfortable rooms
around her and thinking, really for the first time, that she might honestly have lost everything on last night's adventure. If there had been a
whole troop of Linularinan soldiers at that barn . . . or if they'd met
trouble on the ride home . . . If there had been a mage with the Linularinan spymaster, as it seemed there must have been, well, they hadn't
had a mage of their own—unless Mienthe herself—well, that seemed
just silly. But . . . anything might have happened. She'd known that, but
somehow she hadn't really *known* it until this moment after everything
was over and everyone was safe. She shivered.

"You're cold?" Emnis asked anxiously and patted Mienthe's hand.
"Your hands are cold!" she exclaimed, and went to get a long scarf of
dark green and gold that would go with Mienthe's dress.

Mienthe started to explain that she wasn't cold, exactly, only
shocked in retrospect by how . . . well, how thoughtless and, really, she
had to admit, how foolish she'd been. But then she didn't try to explain
after all. She just accepted the scarf and swirled it around her neck,
took a deep breath, and went to find the queen and breakfast.

Breakfast was soft-scrambled eggs and sweet rolls and cold thin-sliced
beef and ham and plenty of last fall's cider, hot and spiced and served
in enormous earthenware mugs. Mienthe was glad to see all of it, but
especially happy to see the cider, which warmed the last of the chill
from her bones. Already the long night seemed to have happened a
long time ago, or maybe to be the fragile echo of a dream. But the
queen was waiting for her to explain what she'd done, and why, and
how. The *how* seemed particularly obscure, now.

"Just begin somewhere and tell it in any order," Niethe advised her,
smiling. The queen must have allowed her ladies to breakfast earlier

and then sent them away, because she was the only person present at breakfast aside from Mienthe and the captain of her royal guard, whose name, Mienthe knew, was Temnan. *He* was not smiling. He was a stodgy man in his fifties, not at all the sort of person who would agree to make a spontaneous raid across the river on the spur of the moment.

Mienthe was grateful that at least the queen's ladies weren't present. She knew she would become tongue-tied and clumsy in that graceful company. The ladies would exclaim in horror and assure Mienthe that she'd been foolish and she wouldn't know how to answer. Maybe the queen had guessed that and sent them away to allow Mienthe to speak freely—though it was hard to imagine Niethe understanding the shyness that afflicted Mienthe in that company.

"How did you come to lose that spy, and how did you get him back?" the queen asked in a kind tone. "You've taught Linularinum to be a little more respectful, perhaps. Iaor will be glad of that, at least! But how ever did they get, ah, Tan out of this house in the first place?"

That was as good a starting place as any, though Mienthe had to admit she had no idea. Captain Geroen entered the small breakfast room while she was saying so, but before she had to try to explain her strange but definite knowledge of Tan's position. This was good, because she didn't know how to explain that, either.

Geroen had cleaned up and no doubt snatched a bite to eat in the kitchens, but he looked tired. Though he didn't exactly droop where he stood, he somehow gave the impression he would have liked to. He gave a little dip of his head and said, "First off, Your Majesty, my lady—Iriene sends down word that our Tan will get back on his feet again soon enough, though he'll likely walk with a cane for a day or two. She says she thinks lately her own strength hasn't been just everything it should be, but the knee's not as bad as it could have been and she thinks he'll recover completely."

Mienthe only just kept from clapping her hands like a child. "Wonderful!"

Geroen's mouth crooked. He gave Mienthe the merest shiver of a wink. "Eh, and the esteemed Iriene said quite a bit more about the stupidity of putting a man with that kind of injury up on horseback, and it was a wonder he didn't fall off and break his other leg, or his neck, which she said would have saved her a lot of bother and we might keep that close in mind next time."

Mienthe hid a smile behind her hand. She hadn't realized Geroen knew Iriene, but even the acerbic healer would surely not say that to someone she didn't know at all.

Geroen had turned back to address the queen. "It was magecraft,

Your Majesty. We know that right enough. Some Linularinan mage got their agents into the great house and stole the wits right out of my men's heads and wrapped Tan up in some kind of magecrafting so's he couldn't even yell out a warning and took him off. Only the lady, she knew all about it. I guess she's maybe going to develop mage-skill herself."

"Is she?" Niethe said, as astonished as if the captain had suggested Mienthe might change into a crow and fly away. She gazed at Mienthe with fascination, as though wondering whether she might suddenly turn the plates into crumbling loam or the polished glassware into budding flowers.

Mienthe blushed and said hastily, "I'm sure I'm not! We've never once had a mage in our family. Hardly any of my cousins are even gifted! I don't see how I *could* be a—a mage. I don't know anything about mages or mage-working or—or *anything*. I just knew . . . I knew what had happened, more or less, when I went back into Tan's room. I don't know. I just . . ."

"Well, Mienthe, ordinarily people *don't* just know such things," Niethe said reasonably.

"She told me she knew exactly where Tan was, direction and distance, and she made me believe it," Geroen said. "Nobody else did, or could, or I thought so, though I admit I maybe should have let that spy go before risking Lady Mienthe in Linularinum."

The royal captain snorted under his breath.

Geroen flushed slightly, but kept his eyes on the queen. "Well, but at first we thought maybe we could get him back without even crossing the river, and well, anyway, granting I never thought for a moment her lord cousin would approve, when that hope failed I thought we might risk a brief little excursion into Linularinum to get him out." Geroen paused again.

Captain Temnan drew breath to speak, but Mienthe leaped in before he could. "That was *my* doing, really." And then she went on, in her firmest tone, telling the rest of it so Geroen wouldn't try to take all the responsibility back on himself, as he clearly felt he ought to do. She explained how they'd crossed the river and found Tan. Geroen filled in some things she hadn't noticed about the barn and the people they'd surprised there, and the way Tan had been all chained up. Mienthe hadn't noticed the part about the slip-chain around his neck. She bit her lip and tried hard not to think about that, or about what might have happened if they'd been captured by the sort of people who would do things like that.

Temnan didn't look surprised by any of these details, but Niethe sat

back in her chair, looking rather grim and ill. Mienthe thought the
queen's imagination had taken much the same direction as hers on that
topic.

To distract them both from any such ideas, she quickly picked up
the story again. She explained about the strange things they'd found in
the barn, the book and the other things. "I looked at the book; I've
looked all through it, but every page is blank," she explained. "There
are inks in six different colors, and nine kinds of quills, but they all
look perfectly ordinary to me."

The queen nodded. "Well, *that* was well done, bringing all those
things away with you." Her tone implied that it might be the only thing
they'd done of which she wholeheartedly approved, though she didn't
actually say so. "I'm very certain the mages in Tiearanan will be most
interested in those items."

"But what do you suppose the Linularinan agents meant to do?"

Niethe lifted her hands in a pretty shrug and raised her eyebrows at
Temnan.

The captain of the royal guard tilted his head. "One would hardly
care to guess. Geroen, have one of your men fetch from her rooms the
items Lady Mienthe described and bring them here."

Geroen's face, Mienthe thought, was really a good one for a guard
captain: heavy-boned, rather coarse, and unusually hard to read. He
was probably good at pian stones; nobody would be able to tell from his
expression what stones he had in reserve. But she could see he didn't
like to be commanded by Temnan, royal guard captain or not. She said
hastily, "If you would be so good, Geroen."

Geroen nodded stiffly and stepped briefly out to give that order.

The queen said thoughtfully, "One ordinarily expects a legist to
draw up contracts. I wonder what contract these men had in mind for
Tan to write out? Well, and after Rachel Neumeier that?" She listened
intently and quietly, but once Mienthe had finished, she asked, "But
why did they pursue Tan with such dedication?"

"For personal vengeance?" suggested Temnan.

Mienthe looked doubtfully at Geroen. "Would you say so?"

The captain hesitated, then shook his head. "Lady . . . no. As you
ask me, I'd say no. I haven't questioned Tan, not seeing as he was in any
condition to answer, but that was an interrogation, is what I'd say, not
just some Linularinan fool indulging himself in a wild venture to get
himself a chance at his personal enemy. Tan did say . . . Let me see.
Something like, *That wasn't some petty street-thug; that was the Linularinan spymaster.* 'The' spymaster, he said, not just 'a' spymaster. He
called him by name. He said it was Istierinan."

"I remember that name—" Mienthe began.

One of Geroen's guardsmen came in before she could finish her thought, bending to murmur to the captain.

"Tan?" asked Mienthe.

"He's unconscious and expected to remain so for some time," Geroen reported, dismissing the man with a curt nod. "I'll give orders for my men to stay on close guard, but I don't know how those Linularinan agents got through my men the first time."

"I'll give my men orders to stand alongside yours," said Temnan, and added, his tone a trifle supercilious, "if you'll permit me, Captain Geroen, and if Her Majesty approves. I've men from Tiearanan who might notice magework if anyone starts anything of that sort."

Geroen hesitated for a bare moment, then nodded abruptly.

"To be sure," agreed Niethe.

Mienthe said, "I'll go sit with Tan—" but surprised herself with a jaw-cracking yawn before she could finish her sentence. She put her hand over her mouth and blinked suddenly blurry eyes.

"You will not," the queen said firmly. "I'm sure our guardsmen can keep him safe. *You* will go to bed, Mienthe, and no matter it's just past breakfast time. Sleep till noon, if you like—or till supper." She stood up, came around the table, and touched Mienthe's shoulder. "Rest well, and never fret. Now we're all alert, I can hardly believe any Linularinan agents will try a second time. Just to be certain, I believe I'll send a formal courier across the river, inquiring whether Linularinum has deliberately attempted to provoke Feierabiand. *That* should make them pause."

Mienthe thought it certainly would. She hoped whoever had tried to kidnap Tan found himself in deep water. "Good," she said, and got stiffly to her feet.

CHAPTER 5

Tan was desperately bored. The servants were fine about fluffing pillows, but not very accommodating when it came to providing books or writing materials or anything else that would give him reason to sit upright. Iriene had plainly given orders, which the servants had proved tiresomely determined to follow, that he was supposed to be lying flat, keeping his leg elevated on pillows, and sleeping. Since he had been sleeping all day, this left Tan bored, nervous, and thoroughly irritated.

He looked up at the sudden murmur outside the chamber. He could distinguish the voices of his guards, of course, but also that of a woman. A servant bringing a book or two after all, he hoped, and moved uncomfortably, wishing he could sit up properly.

But it wasn't a servant who came in.

"Mienthe!" Tan exclaimed. Then he was immediately embarrassed that he'd been sufficiently startled as to forget his manners—in fact, he was embarrassed he'd been surprised at all. Surely it was not in the least remarkable that Mienthe would come find him and assure herself he was mending. He said more moderately, "Esteemed lady," and pushed ineffectually at the bed linens, determined to sit up after all, whether or not Iriene would approve.

Refreshingly, Mienthe did not command him to lie down flat. Evidently she hadn't been told he was supposed to stay down. She helped him sit instead, arranging the pillows so he could be more comfortable. Then she drew a chair near the bed and perched on its edge, like a bird ready to take flight. "Your knee?" she asked anxiously. "Did the esteemed Iriene mend it? It hadn't been too badly damaged?"

"I'm told it will heal well, so long as I restrain myself from overusing it now," Tan assured her. "I have no notion why everyone seems to feel compelled to emphasize that latter clause."

Mienthe laughed, but her voice was strained, and Tan realized—he should have perceived it at once—that the young woman was not anxious over his well-being, or not *only* anxious over his well-being. Something had frightened her. Something else. He tried to imagine what might have frightened or disturbed Mienthe more than the thought of enemy spies and mages sneaking about her home and kidnapping people. His imagination failed him. "Esteemed lady?" he said cautiously.

"Oh, Mienthe, please!" she told him.

She wasn't flirting. Tan had nearly reached the conclusion that, impossible as it seemed, Mienthe didn't know *how* to flirt. She simply preferred informality and, in her straightforward way, said so. Tan smiled. "I suppose the events of last night ought to constitute an introduction. Not a proper introduction, perhaps, but thorough. So I suppose we might call one another by name, if you like, and then perhaps you might tell me what is troubling you?"

"Oh, well—" Mienthe eyed him cautiously. "Something else has happened. Shall I tell you, or do you need to rest?" She bit her lip. "You probably need to rest."

Not eager to be left again to lonely boredom, Tan declared, "I have been required to dedicate myself to nothing but rest all the long day. Be so kind as to tell me all." He lifted an expectant eyebrow at the young woman.

"Well . . ." Mienthe hesitated, though Tan thought she was merely trying to collect her thoughts rather than hesitating to tell him the news. He wondered what had possibly unnerved her. It was difficult to reconcile the collected young woman of the Linularinan raid with this diffidence. He tried to look encouraging.

"My cousin—" Mienthe began, but stopped. "I don't know . . . Do you know things?"

And how was a man to answer a question like that? Tan said, "Of course you shouldn't discuss with me anything your cousin told you in confidence," because it was important to establish a good, honest character if you wanted anyone to tell you their secrets, far less other people's secrets.

Mienthe nodded, but distractedly, as though she'd barely heard him. She declared, "You *expect* people to have lived their own lives before you ever met them!" Rising to her feet, she paced rapidly to one side of the little chamber and then back again.

"But sometimes it's a shock, to find out about those past lives," Tan suggested. He couldn't imagine what had happened. Something to do with her? With him? With someone else?

"Yes, exactly! I knew perfectly well my cousin did *something* to stop us fighting the griffins. And then something else when he was in Casmantium. But I don't know"—she flung her hands sharply upward for emphasis—"anything! Do *you* know about that? Especially about the Wall? The Wall in Casmantium, I mean, the one between the griffins and . . . and everybody else?"

· "We had reports, of course." Tan watched her carefully, trying to think what might have prompted these questions. "Those events six years ago were the subject of some speculation in the Fox's court, I believe. I wasn't . . . I'd barely arrived in Teramondian that year. My attention was all for trying to win a place at court. I'd have assumed the people of the Delta would follow their own lord's actions a great deal more closely than even the most interested of the old Fox's advisers."

"I was only twelve," Mienthe said, not really to him.

"What happened?" Tan asked patiently

"Oh . . . this griffin came to see my cousin. Did anybody tell you that?"

Tan was rendered, for once, utterly speechless. Whatever he'd expected the young woman to say, *that* hadn't been it. He cleared his throat, but then only waved weakly for her to go on.

"No one did? Well, you were sleeping all day, you said, and then I suppose everyone thought you shouldn't be troubled." She gave him an anxious look.

"Don't stop there!" Tan said, and laughed. "*That* would trouble me!"

"Oh . . . yes, I suppose." Mienthe smiled, too. "Anyway, yes. A griffin. A mage. A griffin mage, I mean. He wore the shape of a man, but . . . I didn't know griffins could do that. Not even their mages. Not that you'd have ever mistaken him for an ordinary man. Anasa—I don't remember his whole name. Something Kairaithin."

"A griffin mage." Only long practice allowed Tan to keep the disbelief out of his tone.

"Yes. Oh, yes. He was very—he was—you could tell. He helped my cousin six years ago, and he helped build the Casmantian Wall. I think," she added, somewhat more doubtfully, "I think he *is* my cousin's friend, but . . ."

"But he didn't just slip down from the griffins' desert to wish your cousin a pleasant evening," Tan prompted her when it became clear that the pause might lengthen.

"Well, I think he came to warn Bertaud that the Wall is going to break," Mienthe said, simply, as though she were in the habit of constantly providing amazing information in the most casual way.

"Ah." Tan hadn't seen *that* coming at all. He tried to think of everything he'd ever heard concerning the great Casmantian Wall. He knew that some Casmantian makers and mages had gotten together and built it in a day and a night and another day, or so the wonder of the making had been reported. He knew it was supposed to forever divide the country of fire from the country of earth . . . He gathered that "forever" had been a slight overestimation.

"He said the . . . the balance had been disturbed. Between earth and fire, he said. He said the Wall is—is cracked through. At both ends, I think he meant. When it breaks, something terrible will happen, and he said it will shatter in a few days or a few weeks—" Mienthe's voice was rising.

"But not tonight, I hope," Tan said, deliberately wry to offset any incipient hysteria. "So what did your lord cousin do about this?"

"Oh, he and the king went north, to look at the Wall, above Tihannad, you know . . ."

"Of course." *That* explained why her cousin had not stopped Mienthe from joining that little raid into Linularinum, which Tan supposed made the griffin's warning a good thing for him, if for no one else. He asked cautiously, "What disturbed the balance, did this griffin explain that? What terrible thing will happen if the Wall breaks?"

Mienthe shook her head, meaning she had no idea. "Only, I think, the griffins are very angry, and I think that if the Wall breaks, there will be a war . . ."

"Well, how many griffins can there be?" Tan asked reasonably. "It's hard to imagine there could be more than a very small war, after all."

Mienthe shook her head again. "I don't know . . . That wasn't what I thought he meant."

Had her cousin's visitor actually been a griffin? In human shape, Mienthe had said. But you would never mistake him for a man, she'd said. Why not? How could one tell? Especially if one had never encountered a griffin before at all, either in his true shape or disguised?

On the other hand, her cousin truly had, by all reports, been closely involved with the problems Feierabiand had had with griffins six years ago. He would certainly know a griffin when he saw one. And if anyone might find a griffin mage on his doorstep, it was likely Bertaud.

And if that much was true . . . He said at last, "Well, esteemed Mienthe, you've certainly given me a good deal to think over," which was true.

"But you don't know anything."

"Very little," Tan admitted. "Or very little about griffins. It's amazing how seldom the subject comes up in Linularinum—except as a consideration for determining what the King of Casmantium might do."

Mienthe drooped slightly with discouragement.

"Please don't rush out, however," Tan said quickly, afraid she might. "Perhaps you might try telling me everything *you* know about griffins. Lord Bertaud is your cousin. Perhaps you've learned a bit more than you think you have—"

"No, I don't think so. He never speaks of those things." Mienthe hesitated, and then added slowly, "He never has. Never. I think . . ." But she stopped, feeling perhaps that she had come too close to private things. She opened her hands in a shrug, then gazed down into her palms as though she might find the answer there.

Then she glanced up. "But . . . I'm so sorry. Here I am telling you all about the griffins and the Wall when there's nothing either of us can do about the trouble there. How are *you*? Do you do well enough?"

"Well," Tan said, trying not to laugh, "I'm here and not chained in some dismal barn on the other side of the river, so not only am I very well, I must also suppose no one's been able to get past your care of me. For all of which I am, I assure you, very grateful indeed. I shall hope we are not so distracted by this other problem that Istierinan is permitted a second opening."

"Oh, I'm sure Linularinum won't—"

Tan dismissed this assurance with a wave of his hand. "It obviously took a mage to get me out of this house. I am not confident what this mage might do next, if Istierinan insists. Istierinan Hamoddian can be uncommonly single-minded."

Mienthe looked at him expectantly. "So why *did* your Istierinan kidnap you at all, if you'd already finished writing everything out for Bertaud? Or did he not know you'd already finished?"

"After three days in the great house? He can't have not known." Tan paused. He rather thought Mienthe was clever, and he knew she had found him by some sort of odd magecraft. And he owed her a debt. And, besides that, he could think of absolutely no reason to keep this particular secret. So he said slowly, "Istierinan wasn't after vengeance—or not *only* after vengeance. He asked me where 'it' was. Whether I still held 'it' myself or had given 'it' away. Not to the Lord of the Delta, he said. He said maybe I'd been able to give 'it' to one of Bertaud's people."

"*Able* to give it," Mienthe repeated blankly.

"That's what he said. Very odd, yes. He wanted me to return what I had taken. I never could get him to tell me what I was supposed to have stolen. Nor did I have enough time to guess its shape from the pattern of his questions. Fortunately, to be sure."

"But you must know what it might have been?" Mienthe asked, leaning forward in intense curiosity.

Tan flung up his hands. "Nothing but information! Nothing I could return, even if I wanted to return it—no more than I could return spoken words to the past that existed before they were spoken."

"Well," Mienthe said reasonably, "Istierinan thinks you stole something else, doesn't he?"

Tan opened his hands in a gesture of bafflement. "Nothing occurs to me. Except that someone else took advantage of my, ah, of the confusion I caused, to steal something else. Something more tangible. And Istierinan thinks I stole it." Some lying dog-livered bastard was using Tan to conceal his own crime. Tan was offended, and then amused, since he hardly had any right to protest another man's dishonesty.

"Well, that's not good, if Istierinan is going to keep coming after you to try to get it back. And not good for anyone else, if he's willing to cross into the Delta and invade even our great house to get it," Mienthe observed, with some justice. "And with the king himself in residence! Or the queen, at least—I suppose Iaor was actually gone before they came after you. I suppose that might be why they thought they had a chance, right then; everything *was* confused, with everybody coming and going."

Tan thought about that, and about the scene in the barn, and about the agonizing but surprisingly uneventful flight back through the marshes and across the river. He said slowly, "Do you know, I wonder whether Istierinan is operating on his own in this. Mariddeier Kohorrian is a clever, ruthless man and a good king, and I don't think he would send agents to strike openly across the river into the Delta."

Mienthe made an interested sound.

Her eyes were quite pretty when she was so intent, Tan noticed— she was rather a pretty girl overall, but she didn't show herself off— indeed, she was so little given to flamboyance a man could simply look right past her.

She said, "Maybe he's the only one who knows something got stolen, and he's trying to keep it that way."

And, yes, she *was* clever. Tan cleared his throat. "Yes," he said. "That seems very possible." He began to smile. "And he thinks I have whatever was stolen, and so he let the real thief get away. Poor Istierinan!

Going after the wrong man is no way to win back the regard of the old Fox!"

"It won't seem nearly so amusing if he keeps coming after you," Mienthe observed tartly.

"No, I imagine not." Tan tilted his head, letting his smile broaden. "One might as well enjoy these little moments of irony, esteemed Mienthe. Appreciating the humor life presents to us is what keeps us young. What a lot it is presenting us with at the moment, to be sure. Griffins and mages, legists and spymasters—"

The door opened.

Mienthe rose with a slightly guilty air, though by the time she turned she had done a creditable job of putting on an air of innocent inquiry.

Tan made himself smile as well as he waited for the door to swing back far enough to show him their visitor. Probably it was not Istierinan or his pet mage—ah. Almost as frightening: Their visitor was Iriene herself.

The healer was frowning. That much did not surprise Tan at all.

"You," Iriene said severely, with only the briefest nod for Mienthe, "should be lying flat. I left strict instructions. In fact, as I recall, I gave *you* strict instructions. And here you are sitting up."

Tan rapidly considered and discarded half a dozen possible replies, from the flippant to the meek, and replied with almost no hesitation, "Truly, esteemed Iriene, I'd rather try standing and walking. One never knows what necessity might arise. Sitting upright seemed a reasonable compromise, besides being more respectful to Lady Mienthe."

Iriene gave him a hard stare and a short nod, acknowledging both the impudence and the possibility of sudden necessity. "Just so you understand that if you undo all my fine work through impatience, I won't bother finding the time to do it over again. It's not easy doing work that detailed, you know, even when I'm at my best. Which I'm not, lately, so don't push your limits or you might find them before you want to, you hear me?"

"Yes, esteemed Iriene," Tan agreed meekly.

"Esteemed Iriene—" Mienthe said hesitantly.

The healer-mage turned her hard look on Mienthe. "And don't you be fussing my patient," she warned.

"No, I won't—I haven't," Mienthe said, just as meekly as Tan had. "I don't think I have. But, Iriene, I wondered . . . that is, people think . . . people say . . . I must have found Tan by magecraft. But I don't think I have any mage power. I don't feel as though I do."

Iriene's gaze became inquisitive. She looked Mienthe up and down.

Then she shrugged. "You don't have the look of it to me," she said. "But I'm not the best one to ask, Lady Mienthe. I'm barely a mage myself—I heal. That's what I do. That's all I do." She paused, glanced at Tan, and shrugged again. "Him now. Events want to slip around *him*. Even I can see that."

"Events want to—?" Mienthe began.

"And what precisely does that mean?" Tan demanded at the same time, much more sharply.

Iriene said to Mienthe, "You don't see it?"

Mienthe looked closely at Tan, who found himself flushing under her regard. But then she only opened her hands in bafflement and said to Iriene, "No, esteemed healer, I don't think I see anything."

"Huh," said Iriene. "And that griffin who came to see your lord cousin. You were there when he was? You met him? That's right, is it?"

Mienthe nodded.

"And did you hate him, then?"

"*Hate* him," Mienthe repeated, clearly still baffled. "No, I don't think so. I thought he was frightening—and beautiful—and dangerous. But I didn't see any reason to hate him. I mean, he's my cousin's friend. Or something like a friend, I think," she added, with a finicky air of conscientious precision that made Tan want to laugh, though at the same time he appreciated it; so few people could manage to say anything at all with precision.

"Then I don't think you're rising into mage power," said Iriene. "I couldn't say what else might be coming along for you."

Mienthe gazed at her. "Do our mages detest, um, theirs?"

"Oh, yes. Passionately," Iriene assured her. "Overpoweringly. Not that I've ever seen a griffin mage, you know, but that's what I understand. Meriemne—that elderly mage in Tihannad, do you know her?—she wrote up a warning and sent it around after all that bother six years ago. She said the loathing earth mages feel for fire ruins their judgment when they encounter a griffin mage." The healer lifted a sardonic eyebrow as she added this last. "As though anything's likely to ruin *Meriemne's* judgment. Hah! I don't think so. Anyway, I don't suppose it's ever likely to matter, down here in these marshes, but I don't think you can be rising into mage power."

Mienthe nodded solemnly. Tan couldn't tell whether she was relieved or disappointed by this verdict. He said, "Esteemed Iriene, before you go, may I ask also about the odd book Mienthe—Lady Mienthe—brought back from Linularinum?"

"Oh, yes," Mienthe said, clearly much happier now that they weren't talking about her. "It had blank pages. All the pages were blank. Have you seen it? I think it's in my cousin's study—I could get it—"

Iriene held up a hand, shaking her head. "Books and such are matters for a legist, not a mage," she said firmly. "Healing's my business. Let me look at that knee of yours, esteemed Tan, and we'll see if you might be able to hobble down to a proper breakfast tomorrow morning, if not supper tonight. Though I warn you, you are not to attempt to walk without a cane, much less run, regardless of any unfortunate *necessities* that may arise."

"Queen Niethe's sending a formal protest across the river," put in Mienthe, before Tan could produce his own sharp response.

"Is she?" Tan was amused. "Yes, I imagine if the old Fox realizes that Her Majesty's taken official notice of Istierinan's indiscretions, he might very well haul Istierinan around on a close rein. And if he *hasn't* known, what a treat for him when he finds out."

Mienthe's mouth crooked. "I'm sure. So rest easy, if you please, and try not to press the esteemed Iriene's goodwill too hard, do you hear?"

Tan bowed his head, trying to present the very image of perfect docility.

Mienthe laughed and rose to her feet. "I'll leave you, then, but I hope I'll see you at breakfast tomorrow—if not supper tonight." She made a face. "Supper will be with the queen and all her ladies."

She did not actually say *And I'm going to hate every minute of it*, but Tan heard that in her tone, and no wonder. A girl with so little artifice, thrown in among all those court ladies? Even ladies of Feierabiand's court would not be short of artifice. Mienthe would be like a sparrow caged among canaries in that company. Though he was a little surprised he cared how the girl fared among the queen's ladies, Tan found himself wishing he could attend the supper himself. He could support Mienthe—he could be so subtle neither she nor anyone else would realize what he was doing, and yet make certain she did herself proper credit.

But he knew without asking that the healer wouldn't change her mind or her prescription for rest. Tan didn't protest Iriene's swift, ruthless examination—he wouldn't have dared, and anyway he, too, hoped to see Mienthe at breakfast. No doubt a passing urge for the young woman's company was quite well explained by boredom. And she was, after all, reasonably pretty.

Mienthe was sorry to leave Tan—he was so interesting, and he seemed clever, and she knew he must be terribly bored left on his own with nothing but orders to rest. But if she was the Lady of the Delta, it was her task to make sure her cousin's household was fit to entertain the queen without shaming the hospitality of the Delta, and she'd neglected that duty terribly.

Very soon thereafter she found she had developed a raging headache.

First Eris, the cook, had sent a kitchen girl running to say that the mutton had gone a bit off, and the morning's catch out of the sea had been disappointing, and could they possibly serve Her Majesty fish out of the marshes? And if not, whatever should they do? Did Mienthe know of any dishes Her Majesty particularly favored? Or disfavored? That they could actually prepare, nothing made of air and rose petals such as they made at court, no, and would plain cream pastries suit Her Majesty at all, could Mienthe guess?

As a deluge is foreshadowed by a single drop of rain, this first problem was followed by others from every corner of the house. The master of the stables sent a boy to inform Mienthe that the queen's favorite mare wouldn't be fit to ride for a few days as the animal had been kicked by another horse when the beasts had been turned out into the house-pasture, and could Mienthe possibly tell the queen herself so the staff wouldn't have to risk displeasing her? And then the upstairs maids sent a girl to tell Mienthe that in all the flurry of the previous night no one had remembered to cut flowers for the vases, and would the queen insist on flowers on her supper table tonight or might they possibly wait to cut some for tomorrow? And then the laundry maids reported that a cat had had her kittens right in the midst of the finest bed linens and now there weren't enough for all the queen's ladies, as Her Majesty had brought twice as many as they had expected, and what could they possibly *do* when there wasn't time to wash the linens before bedtime and all the shops in town were closed at this hour?

If Tef had still had charge of the great house's cats, that last problem would never have arisen. It was thinking of Tef that gave Mienthe the headache, she was fairly certain. She longed to go sit on his gravestone and plait grass stems and flowers into a bracelet as he'd shown her, and forget all about the queen and her ladies.

Instead, she told the kitchens that fish of whatever origin would be delicious, and she suggested they round the menu out with duck and agreed that the queen would assuredly love cream pastries.

Then she sent the boy back to the stablemaster with the suggestion that the queen, if she wished to ride out in the next few days, might like to try the paces of that pretty gray mare her cousin had just purchased— the animal had nice manners, didn't she? The stablemaster might make sure the mare was kept clean and perhaps the boys might braid ribbons into her mane. Or early flowers. The queen liked flowers and would undoubtedly find the gesture charming. Although Mienthe was quite certain, she assured the upstairs maids, that no one would mind doing without flowers on the dining table just this one evening.

Then she patiently sent two of the younger maids, along with one of the guardsmen, to rouse out the proper shopkeepers and buy new bed linens, instructing them to pay extra for the favor even if the shopkeepers didn't request it.

After that, Mienthe had the headache.

She would have liked to beg off from supper, but of course she could not do anything of the kind. She wished Tan could have come down for it, or if he couldn't, she wished she might simply have a tray in her room. The little princesses, not even needing broken legs to excuse them, were not present, their nurses having taken them away to have their suppers privately.

That left Mienthe and the queen, and the dozen or so ladies Her Majesty had brought along on this progress—indeed, twice as many as she ever had before. No wonder the maids were fretting about the linens. Nearly all of the ladies were older than Mienthe, and all of them wore more elaborate and stylish gowns, and more ostentatious and expensive jewels. And they all chatted with one another in an oblique way that, Mienthe thought, might fit right in at the Linularinan court, because she didn't understand more than a phrase here or there.

Mienthe smiled and nodded when anyone spoke to her, and fervently wished Tan were at the table. He would probably be able effortlessly to translate all those little barbed comments, even though he was more closely acquainted with the Linularinan court than the one in Feierabiand.

The fish was good, though, and the duck superb.

"How quiet you are this evening, Mienthe!" the queen said at last, gazing down the table. She spoke with warm good humor; if she even noticed the edged tone of her ladies' chatter, it wasn't apparent. She said, plainly intending to avoid any difficult topic, "Tell us all the gossip of Tiefenauer and of the Delta, do. Such a large and complicated family you have here! There must be all sorts of interesting frivolities and nonsense we might hear of, to lighten the hour."

Mienthe's smile slipped.

However, even the most interminable evening must end at last, and to Mienthe's great relief the queen professed herself weary before the sweet wine was poured. That allowed Mienthe to declare her own exhaustion and retire, if not altogether in good order, at least not in an obvious rout.

Breakfast would be better. Not only would Tan be there—probably—but also the queen would rise early and breakfast while most of her ladies-in-waiting yet drowsed. Even if Iriene didn't permit Tan to come, Mienthe could ask the queen about her daughters. Niethe could chatter on endlessly about her daughters, so that would work well, and Mienthe would not be required to do anything more demanding than nod occasionally.

Also, perhaps by then this truly ferocious headache would have cleared away.

Mienthe was very tired. She missed Bertaud suddenly and fiercely; she wanted to be able to run up to his suite right now and find him there. Oddly, she also wanted to visit Tan once more. That was odd and a little embarrassing—what if he thought she was flinging herself at him?—but it was true. She wanted to go up and see that he was still safe and well. She found she had turned, without consciously deciding she would, toward his room.

The headache pounded. Mienthe lifted a hand to press against her eyes and walked blindly down the hall and around a corner, down a short flight of steps and around another corner, and at last out a side door into the garden, where a shortcut might take her to the house's east wing by a shorter path. But then she lingered. The breeze tonight had much less of a chill to it; though it was not exactly warm, one could feel the promise of the coming summer in the air. She could hear, out in the darkness where the lamps did not cast their glow, the urgent piping of the little green frogs. Somewhere a night heron made its harsh croak and after a moment its distant mate answered. The headache eased at last, and Mienthe sighed and straightened her shoulders. She was very tired. But she still wanted to see Tan—at least to glance in on him and see that the maids hadn't forgotten him in the midst of this royal visit.

The headache returned between one step and the next, pressing ferociously down upon Mienthe as though it came from something outside her, something in the air or in the very darkness. Half blinded by it, Mienthe sat down right where she was, on the raked gravel of the path, and bent over, pressing both hands hard against her temples. She had never had such a headache in her life.

Mienthe reached out with one hand and, with her fingers, scraped a spiral in the gravel of the path. Something in the air or the darkness twisted about, echoing the shape she'd drawn; she felt its movement as it followed the spiral pattern. Her headache eased suddenly, then pounded with renewed intensity. She found herself on her feet, walking in a spiral, from the inside out. Something walked with her and behind her like a shadow. That was how it felt. It was her headache, or she thought it was. It wasn't part of her at all, but followed her as closely as her own shadow. Her actual shadow flickered out madly in all directions because of the house lanterns and the moon high above, but the thing that followed her stayed right at her heels. She drew a spiral in the gravel and the earth and the air, a spiral that opened out and out and out. The thing that followed her followed the spiral, followed it farther than she had drawn it or could draw it, ran in a spiral out into the night and dissipated like mist.

In the house, someone shouted. Then someone else. Someone was speaking. His voice echoed all through the house and the grounds, but Mienthe could not understand the words. No, not speaking, exactly, there was no actual voice. But someone was doing something *like* speaking, and the whole house seemed to bend around to listen to that person. Only that person's voice, or whatever, twisted around in a spiral that opened up and out, its power dissipating. The house seemed to shudder and settle firmly back upon its foundations.

There was more shouting. Someone ran out of the house, past Mienthe, too far away for her to see anything about him; his shadow trailed at his heel, strangely constant in its direction despite the multitude of lanterns. He vanished into the lamplit city below the hill, his shadow tucked up close behind him. Someone else followed the first man. Several more people, pelting through the garden in different directions. Mienthe stepped back out of the way, pressing close to the wall of the house. It stood solidly at her back, a warm, strangely solid presence—why *strangely* solid? How should a house be but solid? Mienthe rubbed her hands across her face, trying to think. Her mind felt sluggish as mud. Within the house was an uproar that reminded her of the wild tumult that had swept through the house one autumn when a hurricane had come off the sea and lifted the roof off half a wing.

But her headache was completely gone.

The Linularinan agents had tried again to come at Tan. Mienthe, her thoughts still confused and slow, got that clear only gradually. They'd tried to come and go unseen, as they had before—to steal Tan away without sound or breath or any sort of fuss. They nearly had. They'd slipped through the gaps between the Delta guardsmen and the royal guardsmen like mist in the night.

Mienthe felt horribly embarrassed. Bertaud had left her his authority, hadn't he? That made it her duty and responsibility to protect Tan, and she'd so nearly failed. She could imagine, far too easily, how disappointed Bertaud would have been in her if she'd let Linularinan agents kidnap a man *twice* from his house. She'd meant to check with Geroen about how all his men had sorted out with the queen's, but she'd forgotten, and then her forgetfulness had nearly cost Tan—everything, probably, Mienthe guessed.

"I'm sorry," Mienthe told Tan, once everything seemed to have been sorted out and peace had descended once more on the house.

Tan, seated on a couch in the queen's sitting room—well, in Bertaud's sitting room, made over for her royal presence—raised his eyebrows at her. There was an air about him of somewhat affected theatricality, as though the attitude was one he put on for his own amusement and that of his companions, not to be taken seriously by any of them. This dramatic air was aided by the cane someone had found for him, a handsome thing of carved cypress wood with a brass knob on the top, the sort aged gentlemen might carry. Mienthe's own father had carried one, and had always given the impression he might hit the servants with it, though he never had.

Tan folded his hands atop his cane and gazed over it at Mienthe, in exaggerated astonishment. "You're apologizing to me? For what? A second timely rescue?"

"You shouldn't have *needed* a second rescue!" Mienthe exclaimed.

"You're quite right! I certainly shouldn't have." Tan's tone was light, but then he hesitated and went on in a lower voice, "I'd picked up a quill. I was only going to write out some small thing, poetry for you, maybe—I don't know quite what I had in mind. I think now—in fact, it now seems abundantly obvious—that it's my legist gift Istierinan's mage is using. Somehow. I think he finds me when I touch a quill. I have no notion how, but then I'm not a mage. But if you hadn't provided a second rescue, I'd likely have needed nothing after my misjudgment but a timely funeral, and more likely have had nothing but a muddy hole in the swamp, at that."

The queen, seated in the room's most delicate and expensive cherrywood chair, leaned her chin on her palm and let them argue. She looked less frightened than Mienthe had expected, but thoroughly exasperated. Half a dozen of her ladies hovered around her, whispering behind their hands to one another, looking uncertain and worried and far less sophisticated and ornamental than they had a few hours earlier. The rest of the court ladies, to Mienthe's considerable relief, were not in evidence; they had been replaced for the moment by several grimvisaged royal guardsmen who did not speak at all. They looked exactly as embarrassed about the failure of their guard as she felt about her own lack of forethought.

The door across the room opened, and Geroen came in. Iriene came with him, which was a little bold of her, since that brought her into the queen's presence when she hadn't been sent for. Mienthe decided she didn't care.

Geroen gave the queen a low bow and turned, quite correctly, to Mienthe as the Lady of the Delta. "Lady," he said stiffly. "There's no sign of any of those dog-livered Linularinan cowards anywhere in the city. Not that my men seem overdependable in setting eye or hand on them. But the esteemed Iriene agrees."

"Not that I might know," the mage said, wryly acknowledging her own lack of power.

"I think Istierinan's mage must be uncommonly skilled," Tan murmured. "How else would it be possible to come and go so silently in so crowded a house? Never mind so boldly," he added, with a nod to the queen.

"We'd all be glad to know how they could be so bold," Geroen growled.

Niethe was silent for a moment. Then she touched a graceful hand to her temple for a moment, dropped her hand, and asked, "How exactly did we send those . . . those dog-livered Linularinan cowards . . . on their way?"

"Lady Mienthe did it," Geroen growled. He gave Mienthe a quick look. "The esteemed Iriene says."

"I?" asked Mienthe uncertainly.

"You did," Iriene said crisply. She was looking at Mienthe with something like sympathy, but without doubt. "I don't understand it, but I'm sure."

"I don't . . ." Mienthe hesitated. She rubbed her forehead, searching for . . . something. The memory of pain? The echo of a shape she had drawn into herself, into the earth? "I don't . . . I don't truly know. I don't think . . . I don't think I *did* anything, exactly. There was something strange, something about shadows, and spirals . . ."

"You most certainly did do something. You did magecraft. I saw it." Iriene's voice had gone oddly gentle. "You sat down on the path and drew in the gravel, and the Linularinan working tangled up in the shape you drew and spun away and out."

Mienthe stared at the mage. Iriene had said she couldn't be a mage because she didn't hate her cousin's griffin friend. And she didn't *feel* at all like a mage. And yet . . . yet . . . she supposed she didn't really know how a mage was *supposed* to feel. And if she'd done magecraft, didn't that mean she *had* to be a mage? She said uncertainly, "No one in my grandfather's family has ever been a mage. Hardly any of us are even gifted . . ."

"Well, you will be the first, then," Iriene said practically. "Perhaps you have it from your mother."

Mienthe stared at the mage. She had never been able to recall the least detail about her mother. Tef had described her for Mienthe long ago, when she'd wondered with a child's curiosity about the mother she'd never known. A pale little mouse of a woman, he had said, always tiptoeing about in terror of drawing the attention of some stalking cat. A woman with colorless eyes and delicate bones and a pretty voice, though she seldom spoke. She had been afraid of Mienthe's father. Mienthe understood that perfectly, but she wished now that she could remember her mother.

"Fortunate for us, wherever you have it from!" declared the queen, speaking for the first time in several moments. She studied Mienthe with a lively curiosity that made Mienthe feel rather like a fancy caged songbird. "You must have a great deal of natural talent, surely, to notice this skillful Linularinan mage and know without training or study how you might expose and dismiss him. And you truly had no least inkling of your power?"

Mienthe truly had no least inkling of it now, except she couldn't deny that she seemed to have somehow used it. She began to answer the queen, found she had no idea what answer to give, and stopped.

"We all have an inkling of it now!" said Tan. "I would kiss your hands and feet, esteemed Mienthe, except I would have to rise, so I hope you will excuse me. How very splendid you are! An ornament to the Delta, to the city, and to your cousin's house!"

Somehow this excessively flowery speech settled Mienthe where the queen's warm approval had only worried her.

"I don't know about ornaments," Iriene said, with a lowering glance toward Tan, "but it seems to me that broad events are tending to pivot here, that this year the Delta has become a linchpin for the world. I suppose that's Mienthe, too, or else those Linularinan mages. I don't know. Everything looks strange."

"It's not me!" Mienthe said at once. She thought she might understand what the mage meant about pivotpoints and linchpins, and this made her almost more uncomfortable than being accused of being a pivot-point herself, because she could see that no one else in the room understood at all.

"I don't know," Iriene said doubtfully. "It seems to me it *is* you, lady, but then everything looks strange in this house right now. I could

almost think it was him"—she nodded toward Tan and finished—"
except if anybody's at the heart and the hub of whatever's moving in
the Delta, lady, it should be you and not some nice young Linularinan
legist."

Tan tilted his head, looking curious and amused at this character-
ization.

Mienthe understood the amusement. So little of that description
was actually true. How very strange and uncomfortable, to be aware
that someone's appearance was deliberately cultivated and thoroughly
false. She wondered whether Tan could possibly be at the heart and hub
of all these recent events. That seemed much more likely than that she
was. She said aloud, "It isn't *me* they're trying to kidnap."

"That's true," said Geroen, and glowered at Tan. "What was it you
brought away with you from Linularinum, huh? What *did* you steal
from the old Fox's house?"

Tan opened his mouth as though to say, as he had said all along,
Nothing. But then he looked suddenly extremely thoughtful. He said
instead, "Esteemed Captain . . . I'd have said I took nothing from
Mariddeier Kohorrian save information. But it's clear Istierinan believes I took something more, ah, tangible. He must indeed hold this as
an adamant conviction. I thought . . . I had concluded that someone
else was using my, ah, my work to disguise his own theft. But before
this, I would not have said the Fox's spymaster could so easily be led
astray by mere clouds of obfuscation. Certainly not to acts of war."

"War!" exclaimed Queen Niethe, and then, as she realized this was
obviously the case, looked sorry she had spoken.

Tan politely pretended not to notice the queen's embarrassment.
"The Linularinan actions can hardly be seen in a less serious light.
Only King Iaor's generosity will allow it to be cast otherwise—if he is
generously inclined."

"To be sure—yet he will surely wish to be generous—no one can
want a *war*," the queen said earnestly.

"Anyone would suspect, from the actions of his agents, that the Fox
is in fact inclined toward war," Tan said, and looked around at them all.
"But I have observed Mariddeier Kohorrian closely for better than six
years, and I would swear he is never pointlessly aggressive. He might
wish to reclaim the Delta, so often held by Linularinum and not by
Feierabiand—"

Everyone nodded, fully aware of the Delta's complicated history.

"But he is not as, ah, forcefully acquisitive by nature, as, say, the
Arobern of Casmantium. I still suspect Istierinan is acting alone and
without Kohorrian's knowledge. But if the Fox himself is directing

these activities, I believe it is with some restricted object, and not with any desire to provoke His Majesty to answer directly."

From Geroen's pessimistic glower, he was not confident of this assessment. Queen Niethe, on the other hand, seemed to have been rather too thoroughly reassured. Mienthe suspected that this might be because the queen simply did not want to believe that anything very dramatic was likely to happen. Niethe thrived in her wellordered life and hated uproar and all disarray.

Mienthe herself thought that Tan would not have put his conclusion quite so firmly if he was not confident, but she also wondered just how infallible his judgment was. He'd thoroughly underrated the Linularinan spymaster's determination, evidently. And the Linularinan mage's ability to find him. Whom else might he have underrated? But she said only, "If either Kohorrian or Istierinan acts to gain a limited object, then that must be recovering the thing they believe you stole. I think it would be nice to know what that thing is supposed to be."

"It certainly would," Tan said fervently. "I would try to write it out, assuming it's a legist-magic of some sort, only after, well, everything, I confess I'm afraid of what Istierinan's mages might do if I pick up a quill."

"Nothing," the queen said firmly. "Not while we are all alert and watching—not while *I* am actually here in this room, surely, do you think?"

Mienthe did not find herself confident of this.

"I'll just write out the briefest line—I'll see what comes to me," Tan promised. He looked sidelong at Mienthe. "If you will permit me? It's your house—and you I've depended on, all unknowing, for rescue. Twice, now. Shall I risk a third time?"

"Perhaps not," murmured the queen, gazing at Mienthe with concern.

"Lady Mienthe?" Tan asked.

Mienthe wanted to refuse, but somehow, with Tan seeming to expect her to bravely agree, it was hard to say no. "Well," she said, not entirely willingly, "I want to know, too. All right. All right. Geroen, could you bring Tan a quill and a leaf of paper, from the desk over there?"

Captain Geroen handed Tan a long black feather, which he ran through his fingers. Nothing happened. Tan smiled reassuringly at Mienthe, dipped the quill in the bottle of ink Geroen wordlessly held for him, and, for lack of a proper table, set the paper on his knee.

Mienthe fell asleep before the ink touched the paper. She fell asleep sitting up, with her eyes open. That was how it seemed to her. She dreamed about a thin black spiral that glistened like ink. It was a different kind of spiral than the one she'd drawn earlier. This kind of spiral led inward and down to a concentrated point rather than rising and diffusing outward. She closed her eyes and followed the spiral down and down, and in, and farther in . . . She blinked, words writing themselves in spidery black script against the emptiness of her inner vision. Though the writing itself was black, colors bloomed behind the script: emerald and dark summergreen, primrose yellow, rich caramel gold and brown, the blues and slate colors of the sea. The fragrance of honeysuckle and spring rain filled the air, and behind those fragrances, the heavier, more powerful scents of new-turned earth and sea brine.

She could not read even a single letter of the words she saw. Nor did she hear them. Though they seemed real and meaningful, they were not at all like spoken words. But she knew what they said. Or she knew, at least, that part of their purpose was to close tight and hold hard, and yet another part was to flex and move against pressure, only all those concepts were wrong—Mienthe didn't mean "hold" or "flex" or "pressure," or even "purpose." It was very strange to have concepts in her mind that she couldn't actually grasp.

Then Mienthe found herself blinking once again at the ordinary sitting room. Tan was sitting with his head bowed against his hand, his face hidden. He made no sound, but obviously he was in some distress, though she did not know exactly why. There were no marks of any kind on the paper that rested on his knee.

Iriene was staring at both of them. "Well," she said. "Well . . . that was no ordinary mageworking, was it? It wasn't anything I recognize. How strange. Was that legist-magic?"

"Yes," said Tan, not looking up. "Though it wasn't anything I recognize, either."

"Oh," said Mienthe. "Legist-magic? That explains the words, and why they're written out rather than spoken, and I suppose it also explains why I couldn't read them—because I'm not a legist."

"Words?" asked the queen, puzzled.

"Written?" said Iriene, at nearly the same time. "Did *you* see something, Lady Mienthe? What did you see?"

"*Purposeful* words?" asked Tan, looking up at last.

"But surely you saw them, too?" Mienthe asked him. "You're a legist—didn't you understand them?"

Tan touched his forehead gingerly with the tips of two fingers, as though not perfectly certain the top of his head was still attached. "I don't . . . nothing's very clear . . . I wonder *what* Istierinan had hidden in that study of his? Something that only a legist could take, and not even quite realize he'd taken it?"

"Oh!" Mienthe jumped to her feet and was through the door before she'd even realized that she'd forgotten to take proper leave of the queen. But the book was right there on the shelf where she had known she would find it. The fat little book with its expensive leather binding and its thick, heavy, blank pages, with no sign that anybody had ever written a single word in it.

Mienthe found she had no difficulty imagining thin, ornate writing filling the book, black and spidery across all its fine pages. She only wondered what the writing might have said.

CHAPTER 6

Tan recognized the book, of course—recognized it at last not merely as the blank-paged book Istierinan had brought to that memorable interview in the barn, but from before that as well—from that last rushed day and frantic night in Teramondian, when everything had suddenly fallen into order and he'd slipped past Istierinan's watchful eye and into his private study. Years of work used up in that one night, years of moving in all the right circles to gain knowledge of disaffected younger sons and yet with all the right steps to gain the trust of their weary fathers as well . . . Tan had not in the least minded acting as one of Istierinan's close-held Teramondian agents. He'd gradually established himself as one of Istierinan's most useful agents in the Fox's court, and that night he'd poured out every last drop of credit he'd ever gained. But he'd judged it worth the cast, and so it had been.

And now here this one small book was again, which he had hardly noticed at the time. Not that it was poorly made. It was, in fact, superior workmanship all through: top-quality paper that would take ink beautifully, a tooled leather binding. He was afraid to touch it himself in case that, too, might serve as a trigger for Istierinan's mage—and surprised again by the blaze of anger he felt at being forced to such timidity. But he asked Mienthe to page through the book for him. He watched in growing unease as the young woman turned one blank page after another. Finally he asked her to shut the book again.

Queen Niethe, curious, held out her hand, but one of her ladies took the book instead and held it for her so the queen would not touch it. That seemed a wise precaution to Tan, though he doubted it was necessary. Nevertheless, a weak-minded fear of the book ironically filled him now, when it was too late to evade whatever magic it had contained.

He had looked at this book and evidently taken the writing out of it, and he did not even remember what it had said. It was some trap Istierinan had left for a thief or a spy, and he had fallen into it. The writing in the book had got into his mind. Of course it had. Where else would it have gone? What had it done to him? What might it be doing still? No doubt it had rendered him vulnerable to Istierinan's mage—no doubt he was still vulnerable—and who knew what Istierinan might be able to do to him through it? Tan wanted to run in circles, screaming. Only years of hard-held discipline, a disinclination to look like a hysterical fool in public, and his injured knee allowed him to stay sitting calmly in his chair.

He said, trying for a calm tone, "I'm only surprised I did not recognize it at once. But I had other things to think about when Istierinan was, ah, making inquiries." He hesitated. Then he admitted, "This book was in Istierinan's study, on a shelf with a few others and a trinket or three and several jars of ink. I glanced through it . . . it wasn't set apart. I didn't think it special. I suppose I thought it might contain the key to a cipher or such, but . . ." He stopped.

"But it was blank?" Mienthe said.

"No . . ." Tan said absently. Why *had* he concluded that this little book held nothing of interest? Not because its pages were empty; at the time, it had held writing. But he had no memory now of *what* writing it had held. That . . . that was unexpected. Both the current state of the pages and the failure of memory. Tan could read a dozen books in quick succession and afterward give a very close approximation of what each had said; a fine memory for written language was part of the legist gift. He rubbed his palms on his sleeves as though he had touched something unclean and looked at Iriene.

The mage, frowning, held her hand out for the book. The queen's lady gave it to her.

The mage ran her fingers across the leather of the book's binding, opened it to touch the fine, thick, unmarked paper within, closed it again, held it briefly to her lips, shook her head, and declared, "I can't tell a thing about it, but I don't think it's ever held any kind of magecraft."

"Of course not," Tan said, just as Queen Niethe asked, "Oh, but surely it must have, esteemed Iriene?" and Mienthe said in a surprised tone, "But that can't be right," and Captain Geroen snapped, "Of course it has! Why else would Linularinan agents be so interested?"

Everyone stared at Tan.

Tan cleared his throat. But, since he was committed, he also said, "It's a legist's book. Or it was. It held law. Written law—law a master-legist set down stone-hard. Binding law. Until I read it. I wonder if any legist reading this book would have stripped the words out of it, or if it was something about me? My gift?"

From their expressions, Tan rather thought that neither the queen nor any of the guard officers in the room understood what he was saying. Geroen gave a wise, knowing nod, but that was only bluff, Tan could see. The queen looked honestly blank—well, likely she had little to do with any legists or legist-magic. Iriene at least knew that the legist gift was not the same as magecraft, but Tan took leave to doubt whether the healer knew much more than that.

Mienthe, now . . . Mienthe had taken the blank book back into her hands. She, too, had nodded, but in her case, and not really with surprise, Tan thought what he'd said might have actually made sense to her. She was stroking her fingertips across one of the book's empty pages, her expression abstracted.

What law was it, that Tan now held? He could feel nothing foreign or unfamiliar set into his mind . . . Would he feel it? Or had it simply restructured his mind and he had not even noticed? *There* was a pleasant thought!

But whatever the book had done to him, whatever he'd done to it, he knew with a profound certainty that he did not want to touch it again himself.

A guardsman came in, hesitated for a moment just inside the door, and finally came over to murmur to Captain Geroen. The captain's expression, from stern, became thunderous. He bowed his head awkwardly to the queen, begged Mienthe's pardon with a vague word about seeing to his duty, and went out. Queen Niethe seemed to think little of his going, but Tan found himself meeting Mienthe's eyes, a common thought of Istierinan and secretive Linularinan agents occurring, he was certain, to both of them. Tan had, once again, this time knowing the risk, set his hand to a quill. Who knew what Istierinan's mage might have done in that moment?

"Not twice in the same night," murmured Mienthe, aloud but more or less to herself. "Not once we are alarmed and alert. Surely not."

"No," Tan agreed, but heard the doubt echo behind his own words.

Queen Niethe glanced from one of them to the other, but said nothing. They were all silent for a long moment and then another, waiting for any alarm to ring through the house. But there was nothing. The queen said at last, "No, indeed. Of course not." She rose with practiced, stately grace and said to Iriene, "So the mystery has begun to be solved, has it not? We know about the strange book and the legist's magic in it; we know why the sly Linularinans have become so bold; we are alarmed and alert. There is nothing more to do tonight?"

Iriene did not quite like to declare one way or another, but thought they might send the book to Tiearanan, where the best mages in Feierabiand studied and wrote and crafted their work. Or maybe they should look for a skilled legist who might know what a book like this one had held?

Tan did not say, *You will hardly find a legist more powerfully gifted than I am on this side of the river,* though he might have, and rather tartly. It was true that he would not mind another competent legist's opinion, but he doubted the competence of any Feierabianden legist that might be found. Linularinum for law; everyone knew that, and it was true.

But he did not object. He collected his cane and his balance, rose, bowed his head courteously to the queen, and retired so that she could, as she so clearly desired, speak privately to her own people: to Iriene if she saw any point to it, and to her own guardsmen and perhaps to whatever ladies and advisers she most trusted.

Mienthe must not have been one of those, for she took the queen's words as a dismissal as well and rose, tucking the book under her arm, to accompany Tan. Well, she was young, and Lady of the Delta rather than a constant companion in the Safiad court, undoubtedly loyal to her cousin more than to the queen. On reflection, Tan was not astonished that Queen Niethe did not keep the girl close now. At least she did not seem to take her dismissal as a slight.

Then Mienthe gave him an anxious, sidelong look, and Tan realized that in fact she had deliberately excused herself from the queen's presence in order to stay close to him—that she did not trust any protection Iriene could provide, that she did not trust the guardsmen, no matter how alarmed and alert they might be. She had rescued Tan from his enemies twice, and felt keenly the responsibility of both those rescues. He was surprised he had not understood at once. He felt a sudden, surprising warmth of feeling toward this young woman, so earnest and so astonishingly ready to assume deep obligations toward a chance-met stranger who was not even truly one of her own people.

Mienthe, unaware of the sudden shift in Tan's regard, tapped the empty Linularinan book against her palm, glanced quickly up and down the hall, and said hesitantly, "I'm—that is, I have a comfortable couch in my sitting room." She had clearly forgotten her own authority in this house, for she did not make this suggestion into an order, but ducked her head apologetically as she offered it. "You might . . . I know you have your own room upstairs in the tower, and I'm sure that is probably perfectly safe for you, now. But I wonder if you might rather . . . a couch where no one at all knows to look for you . . . where

I would be able to see you myself . . . I know it's not really a proper suggestion . . ."

The windowless tower room seemed now, in Tan's reflection, rather less like a refuge and more like a trap. A couch in a room where no one would expect to find him, a last-minute offer no one had overheard, from this young woman who'd shown such a gift for extracting him from the hands of his enemies . . . That seemed very practical. He was not too proud to say so. He said, which was even the truth, "I think it's a very proper and brave suggestion, from the Lady of the Delta to a guest who's under her protection. I'll accept, lady, and thank you for the consideration."

Mienthe looked relieved. She nodded her head to show him the way. "I was going to ask one of my maids to bring tea, but maybe it would be better not to let the kitchen know where you are, either. Though my maids are discreet. I think."

In Tan's experience, maids were never discreet. He didn't quite know how to say so. He could hardly suggest young Lady Mienthe invite him to stay unchaperoned in her own rooms.

"Karin can be discreet," Mienthe said, in the tone of one coming to a necessary conclusion. "She chatters, but that's all just show for the young men. She won't talk about anything important."

Tan said nothing.

"I swear I won't tell," the young maid Karin promised solemnly when Mienthe told her that Tan might be spending the night on a couch in her sitting room. She was a buxom girl with an outrageously flirtatious manner. "Not even my string of lovers," she added at Tan's doubtful glance, and winked. Oddly, Tan felt the girl might actually be telling the truth about her discretion, if not her string of lovers.

Mienthe made Tan take the best couch and settled in a cane chair, tucking her feet under her skirts like a child. "Well," she said, looking at Tan, and stopped, clearly not knowing what to say, and small blame for that.

The maid had settled, more or less out of earshot, across the room on the hearth of a fireplace. She busied herself with some sort of needlework, pretending, in the immemorial way of maids everywhere, not to listen.

"So," Tan said, low enough that the maid might not overhear, "and are you rising into mage power, Lady Mienthe?"

"No!" said Mienthe at once, but then hesitated. "I don't know. I don't think so. How can one tell?"

Tan, not being a mage himself, had no idea.

"And you?" Mienthe said. "Do you feel anything? Have you, since you found that book?"

Tan had to admit he could not tell. "It's all very . . . very . . ."

"Alarming? Well, but exciting, too, don't you think? It could have been anything, couldn't it? Well, anything valuable," Mienthe amended. "Something that your Istierinan would be desperate not to lose. Something to do with the magic of language and law. Maybe you'll be able to speak all languages now, do you think? Wouldn't that be wonderful? Erich tried to teach me Prechen, but I couldn't get more than a word or two to come off my tongue. Or maybe you'll be able to tell when someone is speaking the truth, or when they're writing a contract with intent to deceive. It stands to reason a legist would put only some wonderful, strong magic in a book, doesn't it? Only he didn't expect another legist with such a strong gift to get it out again, did he? Only then you did." Mienthe paused, staring at Tan in speculation.

Tan tried not to smile. He liked her optimism, and hoped she was right, and hesitated to say anything that might reveal his own terror of what his mind might now contain.

Somewhere, distantly, there was a shout. Indistinct with distance, but definitely a shout. Mienthe jumped up in alarm, and Tan reached for his cane.

There was a firm knock on the door before he could get to his feet. A guardsman opened it, leaned in, and said, "Lady Mienthe?" He looked a little embarrassed, but determined—the very picture of a man driven by orders to a forwardness that was not his by nature. It was Tenned son of Tenned, which amused Tan even under these circumstances. "You do find yourself on duty at the most fraught moments," he commented.

"Yes," said the young guardsman in a harassed tone. "Nothing like this ever happened before you came to Tiefenauer. I don't think I'll ever complain of boredom again."

"What *now*?" Mienthe asked.

"Esteemed lady—" Tenned began, but paused. Then he said, out in a rush, "Captain Geroen says he's getting reports from riverside, they say there's an awful lot of activity across the river, and Captain Geroen wants to undeck our half of the bridge, and send men to watch all the fordable parts of the river upstream and down, and muster the men. And the other captains, as were in command of the different divisions before Lord Bertaud appointed Geroen above them all, they don't want to do any of that, they say it's a fool who sees smoke from one campfire and declares the whole forest is burning. And the captain of the royal guard, Temnan, you know, he wants to send after the king to see what he should do—"

"*That's* a fool," Tan murmured. "Indecisiveness is the worst of faults in a captain—other than shyness, and that *send after the king* could be a sign of either. Or both. I don't know what influential family the king would be accommodating to have promoted a fool to a captaincy, but I wonder if this is why he left the man behind?"

"To guard his *queen*?" Mienthe objected. "And his daughters?"

"He can't have expected anything to happen . . ."

"I'm sure Temnan is perfectly competent," Mienthe declared, but her eyes hid worry.

"However that is, Captain Geroen, he sent me to find you, esteemed lady, and beg you come and tell him he can undeck the bridge—"

"That can't be necessary," said Mienthe, rather blankly.

The bridge between Tiefenauer in the Delta and Linularinan Desamion had never been a truly permanent sort of bridge of stone and iron; the history of the Delta was too complicated. It was a timber bridge, which meant that rotted timbers had to be replaced from time to time, but also meant that either side could undeck the bridge if times became suddenly uncertain.

"Lady—" Tenned began.

"Esteemed Mienthe—" Tan said at the same time.

Mienthe held up her hand to quiet them both. Possibly Tan's comment about indecisiveness was echoing in her ears, because she said to the guardsman, "Go tell Captain Geroen to give whatever orders he sees fit about the bridge, and about setting sentries around Tiefenauer. Mustering the men—isn't that something we sometimes drill? Don't I recall my cousin ordering a muster once just to see how fast the guard could respond?"

"Four years ago, yes, lady," said Tenned respectfully. "Just after I joined."

"We could do that now. Couldn't we? But in the middle of the night? Maybe we ought to wait for morning?"

"The captain—"

"I'll come speak to Captain Geroen," Mienthe decided. "But I think—wait a moment." She caught up the blank-paged book and darted with it into the other room. But in only a moment she was back again, breathless, the Linularinan book gone. "All right, let's go," she said to Tenned, and waved at Tan to accompany her.

"Kohorrian cannot possibly be planning to march troops across that bridge!" the captain of the royal guardsmen was—not quite shouting,

Tan decided, but very nearly. "Earth and iron, man, you'll have Her Majesty in fits to suit your own silly humors! Are you a guard captain or a little girl, to be afraid of moving shadows in the night?"

Geroen simply stood with his head down and his eyes half shut, in much the same attitude he might have shown in a storm. He seemed otherwise unmoved by the other's vehemence. Next to Temnan's polished courtier's grace, Geroen looked decidedly lower-class, mulishly stubborn, and even rather brutish. But he also looked like the very last man to be moved by tight nerves and silly humors.

"I'm not entirely certain we can be perfectly confident of what the old Fox may and may not do," Tan put in smoothly, in a tone of polite deference. "And, after all, though the move must naturally prove unnecessary, I'm certain the city guard will profit from a little exercise."

"What is Her Majesty's opinion?" Mienthe asked.

"The queen has long since retired for the night," Temnan said stiffly, by which Tan understood that he was not so confident of his own position that he wanted to risk the queen's overriding him. Not that Tan was in the least interested in the queen's opinion, personally. He glanced sidelong at Mienthe, wondering how to convey a suggestion that, at least tonight, they might best take any warnings very seriously.

Mienthe did not seem to need to hear this advice from anyone. She kept her gaze on the royal captain's face, lifted her chin and said, "Well, though I should be glad of Her Majesty's opinion, in the Delta my cousin's opinion is foremost."

"I've sent after His Majesty and Lord Bertaud—"

Mienthe continued as though the captain had not spoken, "And since my cousin is not here, I will decide what we will do." Tan, standing close behind her, was aware that the young woman's hands were trembling. She had closed them into loose fists to hide the fact. From Temnan's stuffed expression, he did not realize Mienthe was nervous— but he did know that she was right about where authority rested in the Delta, and that he'd been in the wrong to try to overrule Tiefenauer's own captain.

Mienthe turned deliberately to Geroen and said, "Do as you see fit to guard the Delta and the city and this house. We will say it was a practice drill, if nothing comes of it. Do as you think best in all matters, Captain Geroen, and then come and explain to me what kind of activity it *is* that you think you've seen on the other side of the river and what you think it means."

The captain gave her a firm, satisfied nod. "Lady."

"Very well." Mienthe looked around once, uncertainly, as though hoping to see good advice carved into the walls or the ceiling. She said,

"I wish—" but cut that thought off uncompleted. She looked at Tan instead. He gave her an encouraging nod and no suggestions at all, because she was already doing exactly as he'd have advised her. She looked faintly surprised, as though she'd expected argument or advice and was a little taken aback to receive only approving silence.

Mariddeier Kohorrian, the Fox of Linularinum, might or might not have desired soldiers bearing his badge and wearing his colors to march across the bridge, but someone—Istierinan Hamoddian, or someone he was advising—had indeed pulled together a surprisingly strong muster and pointed it toward the Delta. Geroen brought Mienthe that news almost before they'd gone—not back to Mienthe's rooms to wait, but to the solar, the one room in the entire great house that offered the best view of the city.

It should have been a quiet view, a peaceful night in the city. But there were lanterns everywhere, and torches and bonfires down by the river. Men moving in the streets, some with aimless confusion, but many quickly and with purpose.

Geroen brought descriptions of what he'd done with the city guardsmen, how he'd arranged them—along with a grim assurance that the eastern half of the bridge had been successfully undecked and bowmen placed on the rooftops to be sure the Linularinan troops could not easily redeck it from their side.

"But they want to," the captain told Mienthe, without any satisfaction at being proved right. "They've tried twice, under shields."

Mienthe said, voicing the common shock, "I can't believe it. I can't believe they're really trying this. How can they *dare*? Are you sure?" Then she waved this away, embarrassed. "Of course you are, of course—I can't believe it, but I believe *you*."

"None of us can believe it, but there it is." Geroen didn't sound panicky, or even excited. He sounded, Tan decided, rather more morose than anything else. There was a scrape across one cheek and his shoulders were slumped with weariness, but he met Mienthe's wide-eyed gaze with commendable straightness. He said, "Now, that lot trying to cross on the bridge—they'll have a hard time getting the job done, too hard a job if you take my meaning, and it's my opinion they're just meant to draw the eye."

"What?" Mienthe did not, in fact, quite seem to take captain's meaning.

"Ah, well," he said, more plainly. "I can't see as any sensible man would start up a war over some fool magic book, but it looks a great lot like maybe someone over there's maybe not sensible. If it was me and I meant to do a right job of it, then I'd be sliding around through the marshes and never mind the bridge until I could get control of both ends of it, do you see?"

Mienthe nodded. "Go on."

"Well, so I've got men watching, but not enough, my lady. I want to rouse out anybody as ever's been in the militia and send them out to watch, if you'll give me leave. And south, right down at the river mouth, because if it was me over there, I'd be thinking about loading up a few ships and tucking around that way—"

"You've sent a strong mage down to the sea to wake the wild magic, I suppose," Tan said quietly.

"I did that, for which I hope you'll give me leave, Lady Mienthe, because I ought by rights to have asked before I did any such thing, but—"

"You sent for Eniad of Saum," Mienthe guessed.

Geroen looked a little embarrassed, as well he might, having made the broad decision to involve other Delta cities in Tiefenauer's trouble. "You did say as I should do as I saw fit, my lady."

"No, you were right to send to Saum," Mienthe said quickly. "I'd have told you to, if I'd thought of it. Eniad of Saum is just who we'll want to send the sea wild and close our harbor—all the harbors, I suppose, just in case—well, in case. How long ago did you send your man?"

"Oh . . . right after you said I might, Lady Mienthe. And I sent over to Kames with word that maybe there could be some trouble, and up along the Sierhanan, thinking it would be best to have the whole Delta alert, just in case."

"Just what you should do," Tan said quietly, as Mienthe was starting to look doubtful about just how broad the captain's actions had been.

Mienthe glanced at him, then looked back at the captain and nodded. "All right. And what else?"

"Oh, well . . . that royal—" Geroen visibly edited what he'd first intended to say, continuing only after a perceptible pause, "The esteemed captain of Her Majesty's guard, he's sent men of his north as fast as they can ride, after His Majesty, and that's all very well, but he's not proved willing to let any man of his stand duty more than half a stone's throw from Her Majesty, which is all very well, but I'm not having him stand like a stone statue with his—anyway, begging your pardon, my lady, but I'm not having it. I want those men of his used for something better than house ornaments, and I thought maybe you might see your way to asking Her Majesty about that, my lady."

"Yes," said Mienthe, nodding. "I can do that." She was clearly relieved to be given a task that she understood, one within her proper bounds. "Very well. I'll speak to Temnan, but I'm not sure you'll get any of his men, because I'm going to wake the queen. I think Her Majesty should leave the Delta—tonight, at once." She hesitated. "That is, if you think . . ."

"Yes, my lady," Geroen said stolidly. "I think that's well advised."

Mienthe nodded quickly, relieved. "But maybe she'll spare at least a few of her guardsmen to help us here." She turned to Tan and went on, her tone a mix of justifiable incredulity and wonder, "All of this for you?"

"I don't see that it can be," Tan said hastily. "Truly, Mienthe— esteemed lady, I mean; forgive me. But whatever was in that book, it cannot possibly have been sufficiently important to justify, well, all this."

"It must be," Geroen disagreed. "If Linularinum's willing to start a war over you, then they obviously think you're important enough to justify it, eh, or they wouldn't, would they? And they have, and what else do you think could have brought them to it?"

"The griffins' Wall," Mienthe suggested, and lifted her hands in a little shrug when they looked at her. "Well, I mean, suppose Linularinum learned about the Wall cracking even before we did, maybe, and Mariddeier Kohorrian thought if Iaor and Bertaud were distracted enough in the north, maybe he could try to interfere down here in the Delta? And maybe he's just decided to use Tan as an excuse? Is that possible?"

Tan honestly did not think it could be. "Kohorrian is a little too clever to try anything quite so blatant, I think. Not when he must know how little the Delta would welcome any attempt to forcibly change its allegiance."

"I don't know," said Mienthe, and then to Geroen, "I wonder if you might be able to send a man of yours across to the Linularinan force? With a wand, I mean." She meant a white courier's wand, which in this context would show a request for parley. "He could ask what it is they want. He could try to find out whether the man behind this is that enemy of Tan's, Istierinan, I mean, or whether it's someone else, or whether Mariddeier Kohorrian himself is provoking us, and why. Or, at least, why he says he's doing it. I'll write a letter for a man to take across."

"Yes, good," Geroen agreed. He rubbed his face with a big hand, blinking wearily. "I should have thought of it myself. At the very least it may set those Linularinan bastards back a bit by their heels. Begging your pardon—"

"Good. Good. All right. Send me someone, then, and Tan, would you see if there's paper in that desk? Or, no, I don't suppose you'd better touch any legist's things—"

"No," agreed Tan, startled at the sharp anger he felt at that casual statement. *I don't suppose you'd better touch any legist's things.* He hid the anger, put it down: how stupid, how unreasoning a reaction. The sort of emotional reaction that could get a man killed, if he wasn't able to set it aside. He was indeed sensibly afraid to use his gift; Mienthe was quite right. It wasn't her fault anyway, but Istierinan's. He closed his eyes for an instant and took a breath, then clambered to his feet and came to lean over the young woman's shoulder. "Perhaps I will be able to suggest some phrasing you might use."

"Yes, please. Geroen, find someone to act as courier, please, and find a white wand for him. I'm sure my cousin has some in his study. And do send word at once if anything happens, will you? And send someone else to tell the queen's captain I want to see him."

The captain braced his shoulders back. "Yes, my lady."

But they never had a chance to send the letter, nor even to speak to the captain of the royal guardsmen. Mienthe's idea to write a letter had been a good one, and there ought by rights to have been time to write out a dozen fair copies if she'd been so inclined.

But Istierinan, or someone, had evidently sent men upriver and across the Sierhanan by boat long before he'd begun making threatening gestures toward the bridge. Linularinan soldiers must have crossed into Feierabiand, along some quiet, dark stretch of river where no one was watching—maybe the Linularinan commanders had sent a small force across first to establish a bridgehead and stop any warning being sent south, because it was from the north and east that Linularinan soldiers first made their way into Tiefenauer.

"This night has been past imagining! How I wish Bertaud was here!" Mienthe said passionately when they had this last news. She stared in despair at Tan.

Tan shrugged helplessly, not pointing out that the night was far from over even yet. But he said, "Though it might be as well if your lord cousin was here, Lady Mienthe, you're doing well enough on your own."

Mienthe stared at him, but Geroen himself flung open the door and strode in before she could say anything, if she meant to.

Her Majesty, Geroen informed them, had agreed that she and her daughters should withdraw at once, north toward Sihannas. Niethe wanted Tan and Mienthe to come with her. Tan agreed that the queen's withdrawing was a fine idea, but he said at once, "But not with me in her party. No."

Mienthe met his eyes, and he knew she agreed with him: He must not accompany the queen's party, in case they were all wrong and the Linularinan force was in fact moving solely because of Tan.

Tan said, "You, however, should certainly go with the queen."

"Oh," said Mienthe, appearing very much surprised by this idea. "No, I can't possibly. No, I'll stay here. It's only right—"

"It's only foolish," growled Geroen. He glowered at Mienthe.

Mienthe lifted her chin. "I can't possibly abandon Tiefenauer. I'm staying."

Geroen glared at her even more furiously. "Out of the question!"

"I won't—I'll—" began Mienthe.

"Anyway, Her Majesty's ordered you to make ready, so if she says you're going, you're going," Geroen said with clear satisfaction. "Better tell your maids. I'll tell them in the stables to get horses ready for you and your women."

Tan tapped his cane gently against the floor, waited a beat to collect both Geroen's and Mienthe's attention, and said gently, "Captain Geroen, you are captain of the Tiefenauer guard and therefore Lady Mienthe's servant. You are not her lord cousin, to bid her come and go."

Geroen flushed. He opened his mouth, but shut it again without speaking.

Mienthe, having recovered something of her ordinary poise, said firmly, "My maids may certainly go north, Captain, but Queen Niethe will assuredly reconsider her command to me." She was furious. Her eyes snapped with anger and determination. "I'm quite certain that Her Majesty will not be comfortable commanding the Lady of the Delta. I will not abandon the Delta or Tiefenauer or this house, Geroen; not for your urging or the queen's command. I'm certain my cousin would agree."

Geroen glared wordlessly at the young woman, then gave Tan a grim look. "Well, *you*, I guess, won't give me such trouble, so you think which way you want to ride out," he snapped, and strode out before either of them could argue.

Tan shook his head, trying not to laugh. "That's an uncommonly determined man, is my opinion. I've no astonishment he was slow of promotion and tended to be assigned hard duty—night captain of the prison guard, indeed! He's hardly a courtier, is he?"

Mienthe gave Tan a long look. Then she did laugh. "You like him, don't you? I'd think you'd prefer men who were, what, subtle and obscure and quoting poetry . . ."

Tan smiled back at her. "Ah, well . . . I like a man who knows his mind and his duty, and it's novel to meet one who doesn't give a thought to arranging his words prettily. One can understand his frustration."

The young woman shook her head and insisted, "Yes, but, Bertaud would perfectly well understand that I can't leave." But her tone was uncertain.

Tan wondered who had taught her to doubt herself. It seemed to him she needn't. Not at all to his astonishment, later in the stableyard, while everyone sorted out horses and baggage by the light of torches and lanterns, Mienthe continued her steady refusal of all invitations and exhortations and, eventually, commands to the contrary.

Queen Niethe thought Mienthe's stubbornness was perfectly exasperating and terribly dangerous and possibly illegal, but, as Mienthe was not shy of pointing out, Tiefenauer was not merely another Feierabianden town. Neither the queen nor the captain of her guard nor even Geroen quite dared put Mienthe on a horse by force, especially after she said flatly that they'd have to tie her hands to the pommel to make her stay in the saddle.

Tan was not actually surprised that the young woman could hold with such firm purpose to her refusal, though he saw that everyone else was, possibly excepting Captain Geroen. He gazed after the queen's retreating party with an obscure feeling of satisfaction, though when he caught Mienthe's gaze he shook his head in mock dismay. "So sad!" he exclaimed. "There they all go, and us left behind bereft."

Mienthe gave him a distracted glance—then looked again, more carefully. "Should you be standing on that leg?"

Perceptive girl. Tan had thought his grip on his cane was subtle. Evidently not. Rather than pretend he hadn't been leaning heavily on the cane, he smiled and said, "This leg does insist on joining me, even in locations bereft of chairs. The esteemed Iriene is not here to scold me, fortunately. I'm sure I'll soon be seated. On a horse, unfortunately, but we all have one or another burden to bear."

Mienthe stared at him, and then laughed—a little grudgingly, but she laughed.

"Ah, look," Tan said, tipping his head to indicate she should turn, "here are some of those earnest young men of Geroen's—Tenned, my friend, and how does this fine night find you?"

The young guardsman in question, in company with another of the same kind, ran an exasperated hand through his hair and then glared at Tan, perhaps mimicking Captain Geroen. "I'd thank you twice over, esteemed sir, to get into the house and out of our way." He looked at

Mienthe and added in a far more conciliatory tone, "And you, my lady, if you would be so kind."

Tan threw an exaggerated glance around. "Anybody might be out here," he said in a low, urgent voice. And then, speaking in a normal tone, "Unfortunately, that's even true." He hesitated and then looked at Mienthe. "Esteemed lady—"

"Yes," Mienthe said, meeting his eyes. "You should leave, of course. Tenned and Keier can go with you." She gave the two young guardsmen a stern look. Neither of them objected.

"Not north," said Tan.

"No," Mienthe said distractedly, and might have gone on, but a distant ringing, clashing sound cut her off. For a long moment, everyone in the stableyard stood perfectly still, listening.

"There's fighting to the south," Tan said, which they all knew. "And the west, of course. I'll go east."

Mienthe hesitated an instant and then came unexpectedly to take Tan's hands and look seriously into his face. "Be careful, Tan. Be careful, don't take chances, be quick, be safe! Go to my father's house, it's just north of Kames. Use my name—Keier, they'll know you in Kames, won't they? Tan—" She pressed his hands in hers and then let go. "You'll be well. See to it that you are. You still need to write out some Linularinan court epics for me, eventually. I'll expect it, do you hear?"

"I'll look forward to it," Tan said, bemused and oddly pleased. "And you, don't take foolish risks, esteemed Mienthe. I need someone who will properly appreciate Linularinan court poetry."

Mienthe managed a smile and then turned to run inside. Tan would not have laid odds on what Mienthe might do. Too brave for her own good, and then a deep sense of personal responsibility . . . He discovered that he was personally concerned for her safety, a good deal more so than he'd have expected, and blinked in surprise.

But the young woman, and the great house, and the city entire, would likely be safer after Tan was safely away. He looked at Tenned and Keier.

"We'll get on the road at once, esteemed sir," said Tenned, indicating a waiting horse. "East should be safe enough, but if you'll pardon me, I think we should hurry—"

The distant sounds of battle underscored his words.

"I suspect you're right," Tan agreed, and limped rapidly toward the horse one of the grooms held. He even allowed Tenned to help him mount, when ordinarily he would not lightly have let anyone see such evidence of his weakness.

But as they rode out of the stableyard, he could not help but glance back over his shoulder at the great house, defiantly lit with lanterns beside each door and lamps in each window. He wondered at which window Mienthe was standing, watching everyone ride away. She would have guardsmen all around her, and perhaps one or another servant too loyal or elderly to flee the house. Tan knew that. But somehow he pictured her standing alone, with the lamplight catching in her eyes and glowing through her wheaten hair, and the dark violent night pressing against the glass before her.

CHAPTER 7

Two rivers ran out of Niambe Lake: the little Sef, which fed into the great Sierhanan, whose width divided Feierabiand from Linularinum; and the larger and more southerly Nejeied, which ran right down the middle of Feierabiand all the way to Terabiand on the coast.

Two rivers likewise fed the lake. One, the upper Nejeied, had its source in the high, distant mountains of the far north, beyond Tiea-ranan. But the other river, the one that came down to the eastern tip of the lake, had no name. That river came down out of the wicked teeth of the mountains where men seldom ventured. There was no reason to brave that place, for if a man did, with enormous difficulty, crest the difficult pass where the river ran, he would look down only into the savage desert where griffins flew on a fiery wind and no man could live.

There, at the top of the world, among the high, jagged peaks where the nameless river had its source, stood a cottage. It had been built below the sky and above the world, in a small, level place surrounded by tilting planes of stone and ice. It was solidly made of rough stone, chunks of pale granite mottled with dark hornblende and darker iron ore; the chinks and cracks between the stones were sealed with packed moss and ice. Within, the cottage was plain but surprisingly comfortable, not least because of a fire that burned continually, with neither fuel nor smoke, in a ring of stones in the middle of the floor. This had been a gift from the desert, a contained fragment of fire that would probably continue to burn even when time had long since reduced the cottage to a heap of tumbled and broken stones.

Above the cottage, the polished, ice-streaked granite faces of the mountains raked up into the sky, so that on bright days light was thrown back and forth above the thatched roof. On those days, with sunlight striking at every angle through the clear air, mist rose from the ice to wreathe around the cottage.

The true source of the river was invisible among the sharp peaks and the drifting mist and the clamor of cold, brilliant light, but a silver thread of moisture ran down the stone beside the cottage. This narrow stream fed a tiny alpine meadow surrounding the cottage, as it fed a string of similar meadows on its meandering route down toward the lake that was its eventual destination. The trickle of water sparkled with more than ordinary brilliance in the sun, and in fact it sparkled more than any water had a right to even when the clouds piled up thick around the tips of the mountains, for the nameless river carried something of the wild magic of the mountains down from the heights.

There was little snow this high in the mountains, for the air was too dry. Even so, ice glittered in the shadow of the cottage. Yet the meadow seemed like a cup into which the brilliance and warmth of the sunlit afternoon had been poured, so the meadow was not, in fact, so terribly cold.

A dozen small, hardy brown hens and one white-feathered cock pecked around the cottage, taking advantage of the relative warmth. A long-legged goat with a tawny coat stood in the sun and gazed, with a meditative expression, into the empty vistas below the cottage. Above the cottage, clinging to a broken edge of stone and singing in a voice that rose through the still air like sparks from a bonfire, perched a bird.

The bird was about the size of a common jay, the gray-and-black jay that sometimes ventured up to these high meadows. But this bird was not a jay, nor anything like one. It was feathered in fire. Its head was orange, with black streaked like ash above its black eyes. Its breast was gold, its wings orange and crimson, the long trailing feathers of its tail crimson and gold. When it sang, its throat vibrated and sparks showered down across the ice that glittered on the stone below its perch. When it flew, which it did suddenly, darting high into the sky and then down again and away to the east and north, flames scattered through the air from the wind of its wings.

The bird did not come to the cottage every day. But sometimes, especially on afternoons such as this, when the air was brilliant and still as glass, it came to sing for him. Jos, who had few visitors, liked to think the bird scattered luck as well as fire from its wings. He regarded any day on which it appeared as a lucky day. And he thought, pausing with his hands full of grain to throw out for the hens, that luck would be a good thing, today.

Far down below the cottage, yet well within sight, stood one end of the Great Wall. Jos thought of it that way: the Great Wall. It was impossible not to set that kind of emphasis on it, if you looked down upon it on every clear day. The Wall dominated his world, even more than the jagged peaks of these wild mountains. It was made of massive granite blocks carved out of the heart of a mountain . . . more than one mountain, for this Wall wove its way from this place to the other end that anchored it, two hundred miles or more to the east. South of the Great Wall lay the wild wooded hills and great fertile plains and rich, crowded cities of Casmantium, where Jos had been born. To the north lay the desert.

The griffins' desert was nothing in size compared to Casmantium, but from Jos's vantage, looking down on both simultaneously, this was not perceptible. The desert ran down the far slopes of the mountains and then away farther than sight could discern: red sand and knife-edged red stone; molten light thick as honey and heavy as gold; winds that hissed with sand and flickered with fire. The northern face of the Wall, its desert side, burned with a hard, brilliant flame so bright it was painful to look directly at it. The other face . . . on the side of earth, the Wall was glazed with ice and veiled with mist. Above the Wall, all the way to the vault of the sky, the air shimmered, for the Wall was more than a physical barrier. It barred the passage of any winged creature of fire or earth as thoroughly as it barred those that were land-bound.

At two points, where the Wall had cracked through, massive clouds of white steam billowed up into the sky.

Judging by the amount of steam, the cracks had not gotten any worse today, Jos estimated. Or not much worse. Was that luck? Or had Kes found something better to do on this day than pry at the cracks, try to pull down the Great Wall, try to burn through to the country of earth? He peered carefully into the burning sky above the country of fire, but he could see no griffins riding their hot, dangerous winds. Perhaps they had all allowed those winds to carry them back into the heart of their own country. Perhaps Kes had gone with them. Perhaps Kes had called up that wind, a wind that would lead her adopted people away from the Wall that constrained them . . .

More likely the griffins had simply caught sight of a herd of fire-deer and allowed themselves to be distracted. Most likely they would come back soon. If not before sundown, then probably tomorrow.

And even without Kes or her companion mages pushing at the Wall, Jos thought the cracks would probably get worse. He was almost certain they had been worse this dawn than last night's dusk. Damage that worsened overnight was probably not due to the griffins' mages.

Jos only wished he knew what had caused the damage in the first place, what was still causing more damage every day. And, of course, he might wish as well that knowing what had caused the problem would let him see how it might be fixed. That was a separate issue.

There was a ripple in the air, a shift in the light, and Kairaithin was suddenly present, lying on the high winds, far above. His shadow swept across the meadow, brilliant and fiery-hot.

In his true form, Anasakuse Sipiike Kairaithin was a great-winged griffin, not the most beautiful griffin Jos knew, but one of the greatest and most terrible. He was a very dark griffin. Black feathers ran down from his savage eagle's head and ruffled out in a thick mane around his shoulders and chest. His black wings were edged and barred with narrow flickers of ember-red. They tilted to catch the wind, shedding droplets of fire into the chilly mountain air. His lion pelt was a shade darker than crimson, his talons and lion claws black as iron.

The chickens scattered beneath his fiery shadow, squawking in desperate terror, heads ducked low and wings fluttering. The goat, wiser than the chickens, bolted straight through the door into the cottage where it would, judging from past experience, crowd itself under the bed.

Jos tilted his head back to watch the griffin come down through the thin air—air imbued with the natural, wild magic of the mountains and the river. No griffins but this one could come to this place. That was why the Wall had been allowed to end down below: because it ran out into thin, cold air and wild magic inimical to griffin fire, and no griffin could simply pass around its end. Except this one. Anasakuse Sipiike Kairaithin seemed to have no difficulty going wherever he chose, whether in the country of fire or the country of earth or this wild country that belonged to neither.

Kairaithin landed neatly in the middle of the tiny meadow. Heat radiated from him. In his shadow, the delicate grasses withered. But in the rest of the meadow, flowers opened and tilted their sensitive faces toward the griffin's warmth as toward the sun.

Jos said mildly, "If you would come in your human form, I would not need to spend hours prying the goat out of my house and collecting terrified chickens."

Kairaithin tucked himself into a neat sitting posture like a cat, tail curled around his eagle talons. He tilted his head to one side, the mountain light glancing off his savage-edged beak as off polished metal. He said, *Have you other pressing amusements with which to occupy your hours?*

A joke. At least, Jos thought that question had probably been intended as a joke. Sometimes griffin humor seemed a little obscure to an ordinary man. He said after a moment, "Well. Little enough, I suppose, except for watching the Wall."

The griffin's eyes were black, pitiless as the desert sun or the mountain cold or a fall from a bitter height. But they could glint with a kind of hard humor. They did now. The griffin said, *One hopes observing the wall is not an activity that calls for your constant attention.*

Jos said straight-faced, "I suppose I might be able to spare an hour from my scrutiny." Then he added, much more tentatively, "The damage seems very little worse today than it did yesterday. Do you think perhaps the cracks through the Wall are becoming more stable?"

The griffin did not answer this, which might mean that he was uncertain or might mean that he thought not, but probably meant that he did not wish to dwell on a false hope. He asked, *Kes?*

"She has not come today." To the endmost block, Jos meant, the block that anchored this end of the Wall—the block that was most seriously cracked. Once, he would have meant, *She has not come here to speak to me.* He did not have to say that, now. Now, she never came to the cottage or to Jos. She ventured up into the mountains only to cast fire against the Wall, to try to shatter the stone or throw it down.

Opailikiita Sehanaka Kiistaike? Ashairiikiu Ruuanse Tekainiike?

Ruuanse Tekainiike was a young griffin mage, hardly more than a *kiinukaile*, a student. Griffins might be students for a long time or a short time, and became full mages and no one's subordinate, as Jos understood it, simply by waking up one morning and declaring themselves masters. Ruuanse Tekainiike was not a student because he admitted no master, but he was in no way Kairaithin's equal. He did not worry Jos at all. Or very little.

Opailikiita was different. Opailikiita was a young griffin as well; she, too, was nothing like as powerful as Kairaithin, though Jos had reason enough to respect her power. But, much more important, she was a particular friend to Kes. *Iskarianere* was the griffin term for it— like sisters. Jos knew the word, though he was aware he had only a dim idea of its true meaning.

But then, as Jos also knew, griffins had only the dimmest idea of human concepts like *friendship* and *love*. He said, "Not them either."

Kairaithin was silent for a time, gazing down from the little meadow toward the Wall. The sun had slid down past the tips of the highest mountains, so that great shadows lay in the valleys in the lee of the mountains. The temperature was already falling—or would be, if not for Kairaithin's presence in the meadow. Alpine bees made their determined way from flower to flower, taking advantage of the warmth the griffin had brought into their meadow. Jos wondered whether the griffin's presence was, on balance, useful or detrimental to the meadow. He might shed warmth and light all about, but those grasses and flowers his shadow had burned would be a long time recovering.

Of course, if the Wall shattered, a little patch of burned grasses in a high meadow would be very far from the worst problem they would all face.

Bertaud son of Boudan is coming here, said Kairaithin, still gazing downhill. *Your king is coming with him.*

"Here?" Jos was dismayed—then he asked himself, Why dismay? On his own account, or merely at the thought of his silent mountains being overrun by the king and his company? Either way, he smothered that first sharp reaction and asked instead, "Why? I mean, what do they expect to do?" Something useful? He could not imagine what.

The griffin's long lion-tail tapped once, twice, on the ground at his feet. Though he had been acquainted with Kairaithin for some years, and on tolerably good terms for several of those years, Jos could not guess whether that movement signified annoyance or satisfaction or nervousness or predatory intent or something else entirely. When Kairaithin spoke, he could recognize nothing in his voice but a strange kind of patient anger, and that had informed the griffin for as long as Jos could remember—since the Wall, indeed. Which Kairaithin had helped to build, after which he'd been cast out by his own people. Jos knew little more about it than that, for the griffin had never spoken of it. But he thought he understood Kairaithin's anger. What he did not understand was the patience.

I carried word to Bertaud son of Boudan, Kairaithin said. *I, as though I were a courier, bearing a white wand and the authority of your king.*

The idea of the griffin as an official Feierabianden courier made Jos smile. He turned his head to hide his expression. In Feierabiand, nearly all the royal couriers were girls of decent but not high birth; they tended to form a tight-knit alliance, married one another's brothers and cousins when they retired from active service, and brought up their daughters to be couriers as well. And they were all, that Jos had ever met, passionately proud of their calling. However Kairaithin viewed the service he had performed—and it seemed both a wise and a very small service, to this point—Jos thought he understood the griffin well enough to be certain he was not *proud* of it.

Jos wondered whether Kairaithin was, in fact, ashamed of his role in building the Wall, whether he was ashamed of once again defying the will of his people in carrying word of the damage to the Wall to human authorities. If he were a man rather than a griffin, that was a question that Jos—Jos in particular, all things considered—might even have found a way to ask him. But even when he wore the shape of a man, Kairaithin was nothing like a man. Jos could not imagine a way to pose such a question to the fierce, proud, incomprehensible griffin, whatever shape he wore. He said instead, "When will they get here?"

The griffin turned his narrow eagle's head to look at Jos.

He was angry, Jos realized. The griffin's black gaze was so powerful he half expected the granite of the mountain to crack and shatter under that stare. Jos stopped himself from taking a step backward by a plain act of will. It helped that he was sure—well, almost sure—that the griffin was not angry with *him*.

Soon, said Kairaithin. *Within the hour.*

"Oh." Jos hadn't realized that when the griffin said King Iaor and Lord Bertaud were coming, he meant *right now*. He glanced uncertainly around the meadow, down the slope where riders might come at any moment around the corner of the mountain. He did not know what Kairaithin had in mind, but he was almost completely certain that he did not want to meet the king or Bertaud or anyone in their party. "I could go . . . I could go somewhere, I suppose." Though he did not know where. He would need the shelter of the cottage at dusk . . .

You will stay here. You will speak for me, said the griffin.

Jos stared at him. "I will? What would I possibly say?"

What occurs to you to say. But Kairaithin paused then, and Jos realized he was not as arrogant as that command had made him seem; that he was, in some way, actually uncertain. He said, *Bertaud son of Boudan knows me . . . as well as any man. But you have gazed down at that Wall from almost the time it was made, and you know it well. And you know Kes.*

"Not anymore," said Jos grimly.

As well as any creature living. Better, I believe, than I. In some ways, better even than her iskarianere. *I wish you to explain what you know to the king of men and to his people. It is better for a man to speak to men.*

The belief that the King of Feierabiand would listen to *Jos*, of all men living, showed a certain wild optimism coupled with a complete lack of understanding of the way men made decisions. Or possibly, Jos realized bleakly, it showed an accurate assessment of how dangerous matters were, that Kairaithin considered that, regardless of all else, the King of Feierabiand would indeed feel himself compelled to listen respectfully to a Casmantian spy—an ex-Casmantian spy, a traitor to his own king, a man who had betrayed his own people for the sake of a

Feierabianden girl. And—to cap the tale—a man who had then not even managed to keep the girl.

Iaor Daveien Behanad Safiad was not an overtall man, nor overbroad, nor did he care to make an excessive display, except now and then and to produce a specific effect, at court—usually at his more formal summer court, in high northern Tiearanan. Or so Jos had heard, long ago, when he had heard everything from everyone. Then, poised at a small, neat inn at Minas Ford, on the road that led from Terabiand on the coast up the length of Feierabiand to graceful Tiearanan, he had been so placed as to hear and overhear both the most urgent tidings from the indiscreet servants of important lords and merchants and the most trivial gossip from farmers' wives and the servants of courtiers. Though Jos was generally quiet himself, other men tended to speak freely in his presence. This was a natural gift that had served him well . . . until the time came when he had been commanded to definitively act against Feierabiand, and chose not to. For Kes's sake.

He hardly remembered the state of mind and heart that had driven him at that time.

But he remembered Iaor Safiad, who, though he was not an exceptionally big man and though he made no great display, nevertheless drew the eye. And he remembered Lord Bertaud, the king's servant and friend, whom Jos had once gone out of his way to mislead regarding the number and disposition of the griffins that had come into Feierabiand . . . None of that had ended in any way as Jos or his master in the Casmantian spy network had expected. No. Events had unrolled down a different path. Because of Kes. Who now was still driving events, and still in no manner anyone could have foreseen.

Jos strongly suspected that neither King Iaor nor Lord Bertaud had forgotten him, or the role he had played—the role he had tried to play. No more than he'd forgotten them.

And Kairaithin thought he could speak to those men?

Jos stood in front of his cottage, his arms crossed uneasily across his chest, watching the riders come around the curve of the mountain. Kairaithin lounged near at hand, his great catlike body curved in a comfortable, relaxed pose against a shining granite cliff. Above him, sheets of ice became, under the griffin's influence, plumes of mist. Jos was grateful for his supportive presence, but he knew that Kairaithin's relaxed pose was an illusion—though it was a good pose and he was not quite certain how he could tell it was false. Nor did he understand the griffin's tension. Kings and lords, all the formal titles of men, what did they mean to a griffin? To one of the most powerful of all griffins; a griffin mage who, exile or no, undoubtedly still cast even his own former students thoroughly in the shade?

Nevertheless, Jos knew that Kairaithin was tense. The knowledge made him anxious in his turn. He had had a lot of practice, once, in masking his thoughts and emotions from the eyes of men. He hoped he had not lost the knack of it.

Iaor had brought only half a dozen men, besides Lord Bertaud. Well, that was reasonable. They had come merely to look at the Great Wall, Jos presumed, and getting an army up into these rugged mountains would be a nightmare. If it could be done at all. This broken rock where the nameless river had its birth might be called a pass, but that was nearly a courtesy term rather than a strictly accurate description. One could get horses less than a third of the way, and to get all the way up to this high meadow, even mules needed considerable luck, shoes made specially by the best makers to provide better grip, and perfect weather. Jos tried to work out the logistics that would be required to bring an actual army through these mountains and gave up at once. Definitely a nightmare.

Probably King Iaor hoped that *looking* was all he and his people would be required to do. They would come up to this vantage, look down at the Wall, and worry over the cracks where the steam plumed out into the air. But then they would find that the cracks after all grew no worse. That the damage, whatever had caused it, had ceased. That the Wall would after all hold for a hundred years, or a thousand, and that no one now living would need to concern himself about the antipathy between fire and earth because the two would not, in this age, come actively into conflict. That was probably what they hoped. Jos had no conviction that they would discover any such happy outcome. He certainly could not give them any reassurance.

The riders slowed as they breasted the crest of the path—if one could call that rugged cut through the stone a path—crossed the silver thread of the stream, came single-file into the little meadow and up to the cottage, and reined in their mules. The mules were too tired and too glad of the meadow to object very strenuously to Kairaithin's presence, though the goat, wiser or not as weary, had not ventured from its hidden nook beneath the bed.

King Iaor had changed very little, was Jos's immediate judgment, but Lord Bertaud had changed a great deal.

The king had grown perhaps a touch more settled, a touch more solid—that was how Jos described the quality to himself. More solid in his authority and his confidence. Though by no means an old man, Iaor Safiad had been king now for some decades and had grown by this time comfortable with his kingship. He had married just before the . . . trouble, six years ago. Jos knew nothing of recent events at the Feierabianden court, or any court, but looking at the king now, he was willing to lay good odds that the Safiad's marriage had prospered. He had that air of satisfaction with himself and with life, though rather overlaid just now by weariness and unease.

King Iaor was a hard man to read, kings having as much need to conceal their thoughts and emotions as spies. But to Jos, as the king gazed down at the Wall and the plumes of steam rising from it, he looked tired and a little disgusted, as though he found the possible failure of the Wall a personal provocation. That, too, was the reaction of a man with a family as well as the reaction of a king who was concerned to protect his people.

Then Iaor pulled his gaze from the imposing, disturbing sight below to give Jos a little nod of recognition and acknowledgment.

Jos nodded back, not bowing because this was not his king. He said formally, "Your Majesty," which was the proper form of address in Feierabiand.

"Jos," said the king in a neutral tone. His gaze shifted to the griffin lounging near at hand. "Anasakuse Sipiike Kairaithin. What have we here?" He nodded down the pass toward the Wall.

Kairaithin did not answer, leaving Jos to speak—a man to speak to men, indeed. Jos said, "The plumes show where the Wall is cracked through. The cracks appeared some days ago." He was embarrassed to admit that he did not know precisely how many days. In these latter years, he had become unaccustomed to counting off each passing day according to the proper calendar and found the habit difficult to reacquire. He said instead, which was perhaps more to the point, "The fire mages on the desert side have been trying to split the Wall open along those cracks. Not Kairaithin. Two young griffin mages. And Kes." He glanced at the somber Kairaithin, whose student the girl had been, then turned his gaze back at the king, who had known her, briefly, when she had been human. Or mostly human.

King Iaor lifted an eyebrow, but it was Lord Bertaud who spoke. "She has become wholly a creature of fire, then." It was a statement rather than a question, and there was an odd note to the lord's voice, a note that Jos did not understand. He gave Lord Bertaud a close look.

Where the king had grown a bit more solid and comfortable over the past years, Jos thought that Lord Bertaud had grown darker of mood and more inward. There was a grimness underlying his manner and tone, not something born of the anxieties of the moment, Jos thought, but something that had been shaped out of a deeper trouble or grief. Some grief of love lost, or some private longing deferred? Or something less recognizable? Jos saw the deliberation with which Bertaud avoided meeting Kairaithin's eyes, and wondered at it. *I carried word to Bertaud son of Boudan*, the griffin had said. Why to Bertaud?

Jos knew very little about Lord Bertaud; nothing about what the man had done with himself after those strange and difficult events six years ago. He had not been curious about the world for years. He had, indeed, been determinedly incurious, and it left him uncomfortably ignorant now.

In the early years, when she had still remembered dimly what she had been, Kes had come sometimes to tell him about her life among the griffins. She had described to Jos the beauty of fire and the empty desert, and sometimes she and Opailikiita had carried him high aloft through the crystalline fire of the high desert night. It had been beautiful, and Jos had longed for wings of his own, that he might ride those high winds himself. But Kes had never been very interested in the human world even when she had been human, and after she became a creature of fire she cared even less for the affairs of men.

In those years, and from time to time even now, it was Sipiike Kairaithin who brought Jos the odd tidbit of news from the human world. Certainly it had been Kairaithin who had explained how and why the Great Wall had been made, though never why he had bent his strength against his own people to help build it. The griffin had mentioned Bertaud now and again, however, and Jos understood, or thought he had understood, that Kairaithin stood as something of a friend to the man—as much as a griffin could befriend a man. He had envisioned a relationship something like the one he himself shared with the griffin: ill-defined, perhaps, and awkward to explain, but a relationship nevertheless.

But what he saw in Bertaud, when the lord let his gaze cross the griffin's, was something he did not recognize at all.

She has become wholly a creature of fire, the lord had said. Jos looked at him for another moment and then answered slowly, "Well, lord, yes, I fear so. She has forgotten her past, or I expect she remembers it like a dream, maybe. She's a mage now. The most powerful fire mage in the desert, I imagine—excepting Sipiike Kairaithin." He gave Kairaithin a little nod.

"I see." Bertaud was looking at Jos now. His tone had become almost painfully neutral.

Jos tried not to wince. He kept his own tone matter-of-fact. "Tastairiane Apailika is her *iskarianere* now. She's listening to him, I guess, and she's trying to break the Wall from the far side. And she will, too, eventually, if she keeps prying at those cracks."

"Tastairiane," said King Iaor. "That white griffin. The savage one."

"Yes," said Jos, not adding that all griffins were savage. Anyway, the king was, in every way that mattered, right about Tastairiane.

"Little Kes has become that one's friend?"

"Friend" was not precisely correct, and though Kes was far from large, no one who met her now would say "little Kes" in anything like that tone. But Jos merely said, "Yes," again, because this, too, was enough like the truth to serve. He added, "She and Tastairiane Apailika are alike in their ambition to see the desert grow, I think, and alike in their scorn for all the country of earth. The Wall was well and wisely made"—and how he wished he'd been there himself to watch that spectacular making!—"but now it's started cracking, it won't hold long, not with fire magic striking through against the earth magic on the other side. Do we know what caused the cracks in the first place?"

King Iaor looked at Bertaud, who looked at Kairaithin. The griffin said nothing, only the feathers behind his head ruffled a little and then flattened again. Bertaud glanced uneasily away and said, "We've discussed this. We have an earth mage in our company, though under strict orders to keep hold of himself. But his first thought is to wonder whether the wild magic of these mountains, allied to ordinary earth magic but not of it, might possibly work against the magecraft set in that wall." He cleared his throat and added to Kairaithin, "You might discuss this with him, if both of you can bear to, well, speak to one another." He cleared his throat again, ducked his head a little, and finished, "We did send a message to Casmantium. To the Arobern, and his mages, and most particularly to Tehre Amnachudran Tanshan."

Lady Tehre was the Casmantian maker who, along with the last remaining cold mages of Casmantium, had been responsible for raising the Wall. Jos had got a brief sketch of those events from Kairaithin, but only a rough one. From the significant glance Bertaud gave the griffin mage, Kairaithin might have left out a good many details.

Of course you have, the griffin said, without any inflection in the smooth, dangerous voice that slid around the edges of their minds. *I will speak to the earth mage, as he is here and perhaps may understand the southern side of the Wall. But if this making does not stand*—he meant the Great Wall, of course—*it is difficult to imagine what more Casmantian strength can do.*

This was hard to argue, and for a long moment they all stood in silence.

"Well," said King Iaor, glancing around at them all and then looking away, down toward the Great Wall and the rising billows of steam where the magic of earth met inimical fire, "at least we are here, where all these events are unrolling before us. We must be grateful for fair warning and a chance to prepare, or else we would all be standing in the south with no idea what might be coming down on us and no opportunity to influence events at all." He looked at Kairaithin. "We are grateful for that. And for any other assistance you might see your way to offering."

The griffin said nothing.

After an awkward moment, the king added to Jos, "If you would be so good, I think we would welcome a chance to speak further—of Kes, and Tastairiane Apailika"—he stumbled only a little over the name, awkward for a human tongue—"and of what you think might happen if that Wall breaks."

"Yes," said Jos, without enthusiasm. He had no idea what would happen if the Great Wall shattered, or what they would be able to do about it in the event. But he said, "I have little. But there is a fire, at least, and if Kairaithin would be good enough to take the shape of a man, we may all be able to fit under my roof." If they could get the goat out from under the bed, they would also be more comfortable, he did not add. And wondered whether he might be able to send a couple of the king's men to find the scattered hens.

But even that thought was not quite enough to make him smile.

CHAPTER 8

Mienthe had been glad to see the queen and her little daughters heading out of Tiefenauer. She was relieved to know they would soon be safe in Sihannas. But she'd never for an instant intended to leave the town herself. She didn't understand why anyone had supposed she would flee. Even if she wanted to—and she was willing to admit to herself that maybe she did—she couldn't. How could she? She was sorry Bertaud would worry when he heard she had refused to leave Tiefenauer, but he would understand. She thought he would. She was fairly certain.

Anyway, by the time her cousin heard about Linularinum's boldness, she hoped that Tan's enemies would have learned that he had escaped them. Then the Linularinan force would go away again and she could send her cousin *that* word, which would be much better than having him just hear that Tiefenauer was under attack.

Anyway, Bertaud must be in the mountains now, as hard as he and the king had intended to ride. He might be looking down at the Wall right now. Then he would have other things to worry about than herself or even the Delta.

As few as five days for the Wall to break, that's what the griffin mage had said. Maybe as many as ten, but maybe as few as five. Four, now. Or even three, by the coming dawn. But maybe as many as seven, she reminded herself. And anyway, the Wall wasn't *her* concern. Bertaud would fix the Wall. He would get his griffin friend to help him and put things right.

And after he did, she wanted him to find a message waiting for him that assured him she was safe and the Delta was safe and the Linularinan force had once more withdrawn to its proper side of the river.

She hoped she would be able to send him that message. She thought she would. Anyway, she doubted she was personally in any danger. No matter how enraged Tan's enemies might be, they would undoubtedly think backward and forward before doing harm to the Lady of the Delta.

No. She was safe enough. *Tan* was the one who, Mienthe thought, might face pursuit and danger; Tan, who despite any other suggestions he might have made, was clearly the Linularinan objective. Or one objective, at least, for it did not seem reasonable that such an outrageous Linularinan action had *only* Tan in mind. Though, indeed, in recent days, Mienthe had lost confidence in caution or good sense or even clear sanity on the Linularinan side of the river.

Mienthe stood in the unlit solar, looking out across the gardens and the town but following Tan cross-country in her mind. The road to Kames was rougher and narrower than the river road, deeply rutted by traffic in the muddy spring, despite all that makers had done to build the road properly. And the countryside was cut through by numberless streams and sloughs and even a small river or two. A man couldn't ride fast on that road, never mind how skilled a rider he might be or how good the horse.

She wanted urgently to know Tan was safe—she even almost wished she'd gone to Kames with him. At least she wished she *could* have. She could have made sure he was welcomed by the staff at her father's house. Sighing, she turned away from the windows, went out into the lantern-lit hallway. There were three guardsmen there, assigned to stay with her while this strange night played itself out. She wanted to ask them what was going on out in the town, but of course they would know no more than she. Less, since they hadn't been gazing out the solar windows. Unless— "Has there been news?" she asked them.

They shook their heads. "We'd have sent any messages on to you anyway, my lady," one of them said. "But there's nothing. Only what we knew already. There's fighting. But so far as we know, for all they caught us by surprise, we're still holding them on the other side of the square."

Mienthe nodded.

"We'll send immediately if there's any other word," the guardsman promised her.

"Yes," murmured Mienthe, and went back into the solar. She opened one of the windows and let in the chill of the night air and the distant sound of shouting and battle. Closer at hand there was almost no sound at all: The few remaining servants were keeping close and quiet, as though if they were very still, danger might not find them. Though in fact there was another faint sound, like someone singing . . . Well, no, that was ridiculous; the sound was nothing like singing, but then Mienthe did not know how better to describe it.

The sound was getting louder, too, though it was still very faint. It might not be at all like a melody, but it was also not the sort of pattern-less sound the wind might make whistling past thin leaves or knife-edged grasses. It wound up and around, up and around, up and around.

Mienthe found that she was trying to follow the sound, only it turned and turned back on itself, wound itself higher and higher . . . She could not actually hear it; it had become too high and faint to be heard. Only she could *feel* it, turning and turning, and that was when she realized at last that she was somehow listening to some kind of mageworking. That she had been listening to it for some time, and that she'd somehow been wound up in it herself. She could no longer see the shine of lamplight against the glass of the windows, or the dim shapes of the town outside, or the stars above, or the sparks from the torches guardsmen carried out in the gardens. In fact, she could not see even her own hands, though she thought she lifted them and opened and closed them before her eyes. She might have been sitting in a chair, or standing, or lying in her own bed, dreaming. She could not tell. She could see nothing, hear nothing. There was only the dark, winding tight all about her, and the sound that was not exactly a sound and that she could no longer hear.

Young people who discovered the mage gift waking in them went to high Tiearanan to study, those who found in themselves the neces-sary dedication. That was not all of them, not nearly. Mienthe had known one boy, a servant's son. When the boy, whose name was Ges, had been about twelve or fourteen, his mother had shown Bertaud a kitchen spoon made of delicate, opalescent stone and nervously ex-plained that it had been ordinary wood until her son had stirred soup with it, and now look! Bertaud had run his fingers over the spoon and asked the boy whether he had indeed changed it, and Ges had an-swered, even more nervously, that he didn't know but he was afraid to touch anything else. He'd said that he thought he'd started to hear the voices of the earth and the rain—the earth spoke in a deep, grinding mutter, he said, and the myriad voices of the rain flashed in and out, glittering.

Mienthe had been jealous of the boy, not because of the spoon or even because he could hear the voices hidden in the rain, but because he'd gone to Tiearanan. Her cousin had given Ges money, and more to his mother, and sent a man of his with them, and though the man and the mother had returned to the Delta before the turning of the year, the boy had not. Mienthe supposed he was a mage now—or maybe still studying to be a mage, because his mother had said they studied for a long time and she didn't know how any boy could have the patience for it, but that Ges had seemed to like it. But then, he'd always been a quiet, patient sort of boy, she'd added, with understandable pride.

Mages—young people who woke into magecraft and then actually decided to be mages—studied for years to learn how to use their power, and here Mienthe was, trapped in the dark, with a single high-pitched note winding up around her, and neither teachers nor time to study.

She did not panic. Or maybe she did panic. She had no way to run in circles, and no way to hear herself if she screamed, so how could she even tell? There was nothing in the dark with her except the inaudible whining note—other people heard the glittering voices of the rain, and here she was with nothing but this unpleasant mosquito-whine. That seemed almost funny, though not really.

Mienthe followed the sound she almost heard because it was the only thing she could follow and she could not think of anything else to do. She could not have said how she followed it, because she had no sense of actual movement. Nevertheless, she pursued it up and around, up and around, up and around. She found herself curving in a tight inward path. It wound infinitely tight, she knew. It would never, ever let her out . . . she might have panicked then. She wanted to panic, but she still had no way to scream or flail about or cry, so instead she fled back the way she had come, down and around, down and down further still.

The sound deepened and deepened. Mienthe found she could *see* it, running before her, a narrow, faint ribbon of glimmering light—well, it was not light and it did not glimmer, but it was like that, in a way. It widened, and widened again. Mienthe could not see her own body, she could not see anything but the ribbon of light, but she imagined herself running, her legs moving, her arms, the impact of her feet on the road, the wind of her own motion against her face.

The ribbon widened and widened, and opened; Mienthe skidded down it at a great rate so that she began to be afraid of falling, of the height from which she might fall, of where she might fall to, only she was more afraid of stopping, of being trapped motionless within the confines of the path. Though it was not very confining, anymore. It had widened so far it seemed to encompass the world. Its faint light surrounded her, pale as the glimmer of moonlight on pearl, and then she saw that a faint light *did* surround her, that it *was* moonlight, and with a tremendous sense of motionless, forceless impact, she found that she was standing once more in the night-dark solar, with the windows open before her and moonlight pouring through her hands and the breeze chilly against her face.

There was no whining spiral wrapping itself around her, no blind darkness. Only the ordinary night, and the sounds of men calling to one another and of distant battle. But in a way, she almost thought she could still see that rising ribbon of light twining through the darkness, and the deep hum the spiral had made still echoed somewhere—she could not tell whether she was only remembering the sound it had made or whether she was still truly hearing that sustained note that was not quite music. Or, if she was still hearing it, whether that was only in her mind or actually out in the world.

Blinking, she set her hands on the windowsill and shook her head. She tried to decide whether she'd ever truly heard—seen—experienced that strange magecrafted spiral at all. Whether she'd drawn it into the night air herself, or . . . No, she knew, even as the thought occurred to her, that *she* hadn't drawn this spiral.

A Linularinan mage had drawn it. Someone who had meant to trap her in his crafting? She was afraid that might be so. Tan's enemies might not have known she existed earlier . . . Could that have been only the previous night? Everything had been happening so fast, and nothing that happened made any sense. Except that maybe the Linularinan mages had discovered her, or had realized that she was their enemy, or had decided that they needed to clear her out of their way before they renewed their search for Tan. *That* made sense.

Mienthe took a breath that was half a sob and pushed herself away from the window.

The guardsmen who had previously been in the hall were gone, replaced by three others. Mienthe wondered whether the shift had been about to change when she'd stepped out earlier or whether she had been caught in that magecrafted spiral much longer than she'd thought. Though it couldn't have been *so* much longer, or she supposed it would not still be night. Unless it was some other night? No—it couldn't have been that long, or the guardsmen would surely look a great deal more disturbed. She felt relieved but also surprised, as though it would really have been easier to believe that days had passed. Or weeks. Or years.

"I'm going outside," she said abruptly.

"My lady—" the senior of the guardsmen protested, but Mienthe went past him without pausing and ran down the stairs, taking them two at a time like a child, and thrust open the door that led to the gardens and, past the gardens, to the stables and mews.

She stopped there, right outside the door. The clamor of battle seemed much closer—much too close—she could make out individual voices shouting within the clamor, hear the thudding of horses' hooves on cobbled streets, see the flash of swords through the shrubbery. A single arrow rose in a long, high arch, its wicked steel point shining like a chip of ice in the moonlight. The long smooth track of its flight caught Mienthe's eye and she watched it rise, seem to hesitate at the apex of its flight, and then fall. It sliced through the air with a high, singing sound and, by some singular chance of battle, buried itself in the garden earth directly before Mienthe's feet. She stared down at the humming feather-tipped shaft and thought how oddly like the hum of the spiral its whistling flight had sounded.

"Lady!" one of the guardsmen said urgently, catching hold of her arm. "Lady—"

"Yes," Mienthe said dazedly.

"You can't stand here in the garden!" the guardsman said. "It's not safe!"

This was abundantly clear, yet Mienthe resisted his pull. She did not even know why. She began to speak, but then did not know what to say. Somewhere near at hand, men were shouting. Somewhere even closer, someone screamed, a high, agonized, bewildered sound.

"It was a horse, that was only a horse!" said the guardsman when Mienthe flinched and gasped. "But it might be *you* next time, lady! You can't stay here!"

Mienthe stared at the man. If she'd meant to flee Tiefenauer, she should have gone with the queen. She'd thought the Linularinan commanders would send someone to the great house. She'd thought . . . It was hard to remember what she'd thought. But it certainly hadn't occurred to her that Linularinan mages might specifically attack *her*. And if they did—*if* they did—she turned suddenly and looked east, as though she could see right through the town and the surrounding marshes and past the rivers and upper woodlands, right to Kames at the very edge of the Delta. Where she had sent Tan. Where, she found herself convinced, his Linularinan enemies would pursue him. Even there.

And she would not be with him. She would not be there to counter any Linularinan mage who found him. Because the Linularinan mages had found her here, and if their first attack had failed, then they would only try again. Unless the ordinary swords the Linularinan soldiers carried killed her first.

Mienthe caught her breath, shook free of the guardsman's grip on her arm, and ran for the stables.

There were no horses there. "They took them all—the town guard needed them," said the senior guardsman, looking sick with dismay. "We didn't know—we didn't know you'd need them, my lady."

Mienthe stared at him. She said at last, "How could you have known? Where's Geroen?"

The guardsmen did not know.

"East," said Mienthe. "East. I'll go on foot." She took a step that way and found the three guardsmen falling in around her. She started to protest, but then did not know why she should object. And then she did: If the Linularinan mages found her again, she knew she would not be able to protect these men. But she could not send them away. She needed their help, and besides, they would not go.

There was fighting immediately to the south and west of the great house, and more than a few disturbing sounds to the north, but the east seemed relatively clear. The cobbled streets were narrow and dark, well suited to barricades, and there were plenty of barricades. The Delta had always been pressed between Linularinum and Feierabiand; a large proportion of all the male townsfolk belonged to the militia, or had, and most of the rest were willing to fight. Even some of the women would fight: Plenty of upper windows held a woman with a bow, over-looking her husband or son in the streets below.

And the people recognized Mienthe, which surprised her—they would look at her guardsmen and then at her, and then they would haul back an overturned cart or some other part of a barricade to let her through. At first she thought they would be dismayed to see her fleeing the great house, but instead they nodded to her and smiled grimly and promised her that those Linularinan bastards, begging her pardon, would have a hard time getting through *these* streets.

Mienthe hoped they were right, but she couldn't believe how quickly the Linularinan soldiers, however careless their fathers might have been, had pressed through the town to come to the great house. She thought she could almost *feel* them, or someone, behind her: a dark, looming, seeking presence that pressed hard at her back, hum-ming with power. She thought they knew where she was—she found herself terrified, certain that if she looked over her shoulder she would find someone there. When one of her guardsmen put a hand on her arm, she whirled, only the tightness of her throat keeping her from a scream.

"There's some Linularinan company up ahead there," whispered the man, not so much to Mienthe as to the other two men. "Hear that? That's not townsfolk up there."

Mienthe realized he was right. Up ahead, where the town gave way to farms on the drier bits of land and marshes between the farms, there was a low sound of men moving. A lot of men, moving through the darkness, coming into the town from the east. Muttered curses as they moved without a light over rough ground and muddy roads . . . The east should have been clear, but some clever Linularinan officer had thought to send a force around this way, either to block Tan's escape or to flank Tiefenauer's defenders. Mienthe found she had no doubt that the Linularinan officers knew about Tan, or at least that someone in Tiefenauer might break for the east and that they should stop him. It occurred to her that they might even have caught him—no. She took a breath and let it out again, slowly. Tan was, she knew, well away, far to the east. If this Linularinan company had been sent around to the east to stop him, it had gotten to its position too late.

But not too late to block *her.*

The senior of the guardsmen touched her arm again and jerked his head to the right, *This way.* Mienthe followed him down a narrow lane until he stopped in a doorway. The door was locked and no one answered the guardsman's cautious rap, but the doorway was in deep shadow and offered at least a little shelter. "Likely they'll go on past," whispered the guardsman. "Likely they won't search too close—only enough to be sure there's not a great lot of militia or guardsmen ready to come after them and stick them in the back. But then, we're obviously guard, and that means you're obviously a lady, and I don't know what they'd do if they found us."

The guardsman was probably thinking the Linularinan soldiers might take Mienthe as a hostage, but what Mienthe thought was someone in that company might recognize her as the one who had rescued Tan from their hands. She had a vivid, awful picture of coming face-to-face with Tan's particular enemy, Istierinan. He would . . . if he caught her, he would . . . She had no idea what he might do, and she didn't want to find out.

The guardsman must have read some of this in her face because his expression became, if possible, even more grim. He said, "You two, lead them off if they come this way. My lady, if you will please come with me." He led Mienthe farther down the lane. "There'll be a side street or alley," he muttered to her. "We'll get around them in the dark. Even if they do spot us, they'll not look too close. A man and a woman fleeing the town, that's nothing to draw attention. Here, lady, watch your step."

Mienthe was well past worrying about a little mud. The street was too narrow for the moonlight to provide any illumination; it was too dark to see even the cobbles of the street. It was so dark there was a constant risk of running headlong into an unexpected wall, but she

could hear—she thought she could hear—the tramp of soldiers entering the town. The sounds echoed oddly in the narrow streets so that it
was hard to tell their direction and distance, but she was sure it was
soldiers. Boots, mostly, and the unidentifiable sounds of a lot of men
moving in company, but occasionally also the ring of shod hooves.
That was bold, but then maybe the Linularinan soldiers had a few
people who could speak to horses in that company; the gift wasn't possessed *only* by the folk of Feierabiand, any more than straight light
brown hair was possessed only by the people of Linularinum. But the
sound of hooves made her check and turn her head, wishing *she* had an
affinity for horses and could call one away from those soldiers.

"Lady!" whispered the guardsman, realizing Mienthe had paused.
He, too, was all but invisible in the darkness.

Mienthe took a step forward.

Light bloomed beyond the guardsman, lamps carried high on poles
so that their light shone out before the approaching soldiers—another
company, or part of the same one, but either way wholly unexpected.
The guardsman spun around, his hand going to his sword and then falling away because there were far too many soldiers to fight. But then he
drew after all, setting himself in the middle of the narrow lane.

"No!" Mienthe cried, understanding that the guardsman meant to
delay the Linularinan soldiers just that small time that might let her
escape, and understanding as well that if he fought, he would die. "No!"
she said again. "Don't fight them!" Then she whirled and fled back the
way they had come, hoping that once she was clear, the guardsman
would let himself surrender, knowing that if she stayed he would certainly fight, and anyway she did not dare be captured herself.

Behind her, swords rang. Before her, the darkness offered not
safety—there was no safety anywhere—but at least some measure of
concealment, at least until she ran into the other company of Linularinan soldiers. She looked for a way to get away from the lane, to slip
away sideways. She tested one door and then another, but both were
locked and no one came when she pounded her hand against the doors.
She dreaded every moment that she might see the shine of lamplight
off the painted wood of the buildings and the damp cobbles, or hear the
sounds of approaching soldiers. Above, the moonlight slid across the
shingles of the roofs.

Ahead of her, Mienthe heard the flat sounds of boots on the cobbles. Light shone dimly, not yet near, but coming nearer. Behind her,
she was almost certain she could hear more boots. She stopped, looked
quickly about, and then leaped for a handhold on the windowsill of a
house. The window was shuttered tight, but she got her foot up on the

doorknob of the house and hauled herself upward. The windowsill provided her next foothold, and she tried hard not to think about falling—she would break her ankle on the cobbles and then she would certainly be caught—the moonlight picked out the details of the upper story of the building, but also mercilessly revealed Mienthe to anyone who glanced up from below. The upper windows were also shuttered, but besides the balcony there was a trellis with vines. The vines would never hold her weight, but she thought the trellis might, and anyway she could not find any other foothold.

Below her, the two companies of soldiers approached from opposite directions. They would meet almost directly below her, and then how long would it take someone to look up? Mienthe gingerly committed her weight to the trellis. The sweet scent of the flowers rose around her as she crushed the vines. It seemed to her that the fragrance alone would draw someone to gaze upward, and on this clear night there was no hope of clouds to veil the moon. Mienthe tried not to make a sound as she pulled herself upward, got first a hand and then a knee onto the balcony railing—the railing had seemed sturdier before she needed to balance on it. She laid one hand flat against the rough wood, reached upward with her other hand, and felt along the edge of the roof.

Below her, someone suddenly called out.

Mienthe didn't glance down. She was obviously a woman. Would they shoot a woman when they didn't even know who she was? Or, if there was a mage with them, would *he* know who she was? Then they might shoot her—or just climb after her—probably a soldier would think nothing of this climb. Mienthe gripped the edge of the roof with both hands and scrambled to get her foot up to the top of the trellis. For a sickening moment she thought she would lose her hold and fall. Her arms trembled with the strain. Then she got a proper foothold at last, kicked hard, heaved, and managed to haul herself up to the roof.

The roof tiles proved more slippery underfoot than Mienthe had expected. She made her way up the slope of the roof as quickly as she dared and then over the peak and down the other side. Behind her she could hear soldiers scrambling up the wall after her, and then a loud ripping, tearing sound as—she guessed—the trellis pulled away from the wall under their greater weight. The crashing noises and curses that followed were gratifying, but how long would it take the rest of the soldiers to get out of the lane and around to the other side of the buildings? So long that Mienthe would be able to get down and run for some other hiding place? What hiding place, that they could not immediately find?

Reaching the edge of the roof, she indeed found a handful of soldiers there before her, along with a mounted officer. Two of the soldiers had bows, but it was the officer on the horse who frightened her. Without even thinking about it, Mienthe crouched, ripped up a heavy tile, and flung it down. Though she had not stopped to aim, the tile sketched a wide curving path through the air and hit the man in the face.

The Linularinan officer crumpled backward off his horse, but Mienthe, in flinging the tile, lost her precarious balance, staggered sideways, tried helplessly to catch herself on the empty air, and fell off the roof.

She did not have time to cry out, but also she did not exactly fall, although she did not know what other word she could use to describe what happened. It was as though she followed the same curving path along which she had thrown the tile; it was as though she rode a sense of balance she had not recognized until she fell along an invisible current in the wind or an unseen ribbon of moonlight. There was no time to be amazed. She fell, and then she was standing on the muddy ground next to the startled horse. The animal shied violently, only Mienthe caught his rein and flung herself into the saddle, wrenched his head around, and let him go.

Only one soldier tried to catch her, and he missed his grab for the horse's rein. The horse's shoulder struck him and flung him aside, and then Mienthe was past, weaving through the maze of the town's last scattered buildings and then pounding along a muddy moonlit road, heading out into the marshes and sloughs of the wide Delta.

She did not look back. If anyone followed her, she did not know it.

Mienthe did not stop again until near dawn, after putting miles of tangled, difficult country between herself and Tiefenauer. She had not kept to the road but headed straight for Kames. Or, at least, straight for Tan. She knew exactly where he was. Despite everything, she felt a great lightening of her spirits to know that he was far away to the east and that she was heading toward him. She found it difficult to imagine how she had let him ride east without her, almost impossible to picture herself heading, now, either north after the queen or back toward Tiefenauer.

The ordinary night sounds of the marshes surrounded her: the rippling splash of a stream, the rattle of the breeze through reeds, the rustle of leaves and the creak of leather as her tired horse shifted his weight. Above, the moon stood low over the dark shapes of the trees. To either side, water glinted like metal. Mienthe was cold, shivering; she could not feel her feet and her fingers were cramped on the reins. No one else was in sight, and though she held her breath and listened, she could not hear any voices calling.

Birds called, though, sharp trills and buzzes and one rippling little
song that rose and rose until it seemed it must go beyond sound to silence, but after the song had climbed as high as it could go, it tumbled
down again in a burst of notes. Mienthe knew the bird that made that
song. It was a little speckled brown bird with a yellow throat. Though
she could not see it in the undergrowth, she realized that she could see
branches against the paling sky and that dawn had arrived.

There was a raw chill in the air. Though she worried a little about
the smoke, Mienthe made a small fire. Steam rose from her clothing
and boots. The boots, which had been good ones, ankle-high and embroidered around the tops, were undoubtedly ruined. She hoped they
would be wearable for a little while yet; a day at least, until she reached
her father's house in Kames. She did not know what she would find
there. She did not actually expect a welcome, or, unexpectedly determined as Tan's enemies seemed to be, much safety. But she thought she
might at least hope for dry boots.

Now, on her own and more or less safe, she had time to think—too
much time and far too much solitude for her peace of mind.

She wondered where the queen and the royal party might be. Safe
in Sihannas? She wondered about Tan. How far in front of her was he?
Would he find her father's house—would he be safe there until she
could come? Would *she* be safe until she got there?

If there was a Linularinan mage behind her, he was probably much
better trained than Mienthe. Only stubbornness and luck had got her
out of that strange magecrafted trap in Tiefenauer, and then more luck
had kept her from falling right into Linularinan hands when she toppled
off that roof. She hoped the guardsmen she had left behind were all
right. She did not know enough to guess whether the two might have
gotten away, or whether the Linularinan soldiers might have spared the
one who had set himself in their way to guard her flight.

Where, she wondered, was the Linularinan mage now? As soon as
the question occurred to her, Mienthe was certain he was somewhere
close by, far too close—just out of sight—probably hidden at the edge
of the tangled undergrowth on the far side of the stream, looking at her.
Telling herself that this was unlikely to the very edge of impossibility
did no good at all. Mienthe stood up, peering intently back across the
stream, but she could see nothing. Birds called: long liquid trills and
rattling buzzes and a sweet three-note song that sounded like someone
calling *mock-e-lee, mock-e-lee.*

There was, Mienthe gradually realized, no one there. The birds
would not be singing so freely if anyone was hidden there—and no one
was, anyway. A Linularinan mage would hardly have crept after her by

himself and hidden to watch her. How silly she had been, to feel one might have! The conviction was fading—it was gone, and Mienthe could not even really remember how it had felt to be so certain. A ridiculous certainty! No mage would be slipping about by *himself*, and she could hardly fail to notice a whole Linularinan company stomping through the marshes after her. And the Linularinan mage, whoever he might be, could not really be *very* powerful, or Mienthe would never have been able to wind herself backward out of his magecrafted trap.

There was nothing to fear. Any sensible person could see that there was nothing at all to fear in the marshes, however damp, or in this clear spring dawn, no matter how chilly or uncomfortable. She told herself this, firmly, and as she cast one final uneasy glance across to the west, the sun came up above the trees and the moon became pale and transparent against the brightening sky, and then it was full day. At last. The last of her nervousness lifted like mist, warmed away by the sun. She rose stiffly and, having nothing better, rubbed the horse's legs down with handfuls of coarse marsh grass. The animal deserved better of her than muddy grasses and a tired pat, but she had no grain to give him. At least he seemed to have no serious cuts or bruises.

She could see no sign of pursuit, no suggestion that any Linularinan in the wide world had ever defied the proper bounds of his country to cross into Feierabiand. Indeed, now that her earlier fear had eased, Mienthe found it difficult to believe that any Linularinan soldiers had actually crossed the Sierhanan at all. She felt as though she had probably dreamed everything of the past night. She thought she might awaken at any moment to find herself in her own room, lilac-scented lanterns glowing in the predawn dimness and the gentle sounds of the stirring household around her. It was hard to believe that she was already awake, that she really was cold and muddy and in desperate need of hot water and soap and tea, and that the great house lay miles and miles behind her.

No maid called her name, and neither hot water and soap nor tea appeared, alas. Only the horse shifted restlessly across the damp hillocks of mud and grass, his hooves crunching through the winter's litter and leaving deep marks in the muddy ground. Mienthe sighed, climbed to her feet—her joints creaked—and went to investigate whether there might be a bit of hard bread in the saddlebags.

There was no bread, but there was a little cloth bag of dried apples and another of tough jerky. Mienthe ate the jerky and fed the apples to the horse, and after that felt rather more cheerful. The horse, a big sorrel animal that looked as though he had Delta blood in him, pointed his ears forward and seemed a little more satisfied with the morning as well, even when Mienthe put on her wet boots, kicked out the fire, and lifted herself—rather awkwardly, with neither mounting block nor helpful groom—back into the saddle.

The horse picked his way slowly among broad-boled trees in woodlands that did not seem ever to have known an ax, lipping at leaves and the grasses that grew in sunny glades among the trees. While the horse might breakfast on leaves, Mienthe was not finding the jerky she'd eaten a wholly adequate breakfast with which to face the long day. And her feet slipped and chafed inside her clammy boots.

It was all rather disheartening.

Mienthe kept as far as possible to drier ridges, which provided brief, welcome respites from the mud of the lower-lying regions. Her boots had begun to dry at last, but water came chest-deep on her horse in some of the unavoidable marshy areas. Mienthe kicked her feet out of the stirrups, tucked her feet up, and stubbornly kept riding east, until at last she found herself emerging from the shadows of the marshes and riding down a final bank onto the broad, hard-beaten surface of a true road, and lying before her, in the brilliance of a clear afternoon, the wide brown width of the lower branch of the Sierhanan River.

She encouraged her horse to trot. He did not want to do that, laying his ears flat and jigging sideways when she tried to make him, and after the night and day they had had Mienthe could hardly blame him. But the horse was good-tempered enough to lengthen his stride into the fast, swinging walk that was almost as fast as a trot would have been, the walk that made Delta horses so desirable as plow animals. That was good enough. Mienthe did not really want to sit a jarring trot, anyway.

There were plenty of hoof marks and the tracks of wagons and carts in the packed earth of the road, and Mienthe practiced in her mind the sorts of things she might say to startled folk she might pass, to explain her solitude and muddy, bedraggled appearance: *I barely got out of Tiefenauer in front of Linularinan soldiers . . . I had to cross through the marshes.* Perfectly true. Yet she did not feel she had any ability to explain what had really happened, what still might be happening. She could visualize merchants or farmers rolling their eyes: *Chased out of Tiefenauer by Linularinan mages, were you?* Mienthe knew she simply did not have the ability to make anybody believe anything of the sort. Especially not while her horse and skirts and boots were caked with mud, and her hair straggling down her back—she could not look less like a granddaughter of old Berdoen and a cousin of the Lord of the Delta.

But there were few other travelers, and although they gave Mienthe curious, sidelong glances, none of them stopped to speak to her. She passed the occasional farm-track, and from time to time pasture fences ran along the road for some way. Sometimes big, flat-faced white cattle gazed at her incuriously from behind those fences. Tall shaggy farm dogs watched suspiciously as she passed, in case she should be a swamp cat or a cattle thief, but they did not come out to the road.

This branch of the Sierhanan, like the northern branch, was cleaner and wider and better for traffic than any of the smaller Delta rivers. Boats ran along with the current—flatboats, mostly, heading downstream; now and again a keelboat being heaved back upstream by a team of oxen. But the keel road was on the other side of the river and the drovers much too far away to call to or see clearly.

For the first time, it occurred to Mienthe that even when she found her father's house, the staff there might not know her. Certainly they would not be able to see in her the nine-year-old child she had been . . . Would any of them even have known her when she *was* nine? A sudden, vivid memory of Tef, in the cutting garden gathering flowers for the house, came into her mind. She could almost make herself believe he would be at her father's house, living still. Tears prickled behind her eyes.

She would have felt so much more that she was riding to her proper home if she had really expected to find Tef there waiting for her. She couldn't think of her father's house as her home at all. It occurred to Mienthe that she did not even know exactly where her father's house actually *was*. Well, she knew that it was set on the river a little north of Kames proper, so she must go right past it if she kept on south on this road, but would she recognize its drive when she came to it? She experienced a sudden conviction that this was impossible, that she would not, that she would have to ride all the way into Kames and ask there for directions, like a beggar hoping for generosity from some relative who had a place at the house as a maid or stablemaster . . . She flushed and checked her horse, looking indecisively left toward the river, and then right, up the low wooded hill that ran up away from the river . . . and there were the gates.

She somehow knew the carved wooden posts at once, and the wrought-iron bands that spiraled around them; she knew the graveled track that led between avenues of great oaks and how it would curve through neatly kept woodlands to the wide gardens surrounding the big house. Though she would have said she had no clear memory of any of this from her childhood, she knew it all. She checked her horse and sat for a long moment simply staring at the gates and the graveled drive. She did not feel excited or happy to have come back to this house; was she simply too tired? But she did not even feel very relieved to have arrived. She must be much more weary than she had thought.

Or more frightened of the reception she might meet.

As soon as she thought of this, Mienthe knew it was true. She knew the people in that house would not recognize her. She wondered if they would even admit her. They might think she was an impostor who was trying to mock them and steal things to which she had no claim. Or they might think she was a madwoman who claimed to be Berdoen's granddaughter and Beraod's daughter and Bertaud's cousin because . . . because . . . Mienthe could not quite imagine why anybody would claim to be Beraod's daughter. Probably that was because her memories of her father were a little too vivid . . .

But Tan would be there, and *he* could tell them who she was. Mienthe found she had no doubt that he was there. That was a heartening thought. She lifted the reins, clucked to the horse, and rode up the curving drive, between the oaks and through the woodlands, and out into the gardens in the last light of the day.

The gardens were not as well-kept as she remembered them, and the house was smaller, and down the hill the river blazed through the trees as though the slanting evening light had set the water afire. Someone called, and someone else answered, and there was a sudden confusion of movement and voices and faces. Suddenly nothing was familiar, and Mienthe tried to speak to an older man who had come out to hold her reins but could not think of anything to say. She wanted to dismount but was afraid to, although she did not know why she should be afraid— she told herself she should not be—she knew she was being foolish—

And then a familiar voice said, "Mienthe!" and Tan was beside her horse, offering her a hand to dismount. His was the only familiar face she saw. She took his hand gratefully and slid down from her horse with a sense that she had, after all, come at last to a place of safety, a place she knew.

CHAPTER 9

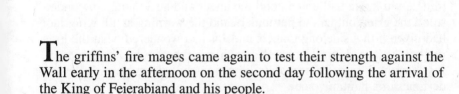

The griffins' fire mages came again to test their strength against the Wall early in the afternoon on the second day following the arrival of the King of Feierabiand and his people.

King Iaor Safiad was not there to see them. After that first icy, brilliant night, the king had taken nearly all his people and gone away again, down the difficult mountain path. He would rouse his people and make them ready—his men, of course, but most especially his mages: the earth mages of Tihannad and all those in high Tiearanan. And he would set all the smiths of both cities to make arrowheads and spearheads infused with the most solid earthbound magecraft possible. So he had said, after looking down upon the cracked Wall and consulting the young earth mage he had brought, and Lord Bertaud, and Anasakuse Sipiike Kairaithin. He had not asked Jos for his opinion, but Jos had not disagreed.

"It might hold a hundred years like that, I suppose," the king had said, not with any great conviction. "But it might break tomorrow, and then where will we be?" Then he had added, a touch more hopefully, to Kairaithin, "You are certain your people intend to come down upon Feierabiand if they can break that Wall? *We* have never offended them—or I had thought not. I had thought we had become something like allies . . ."

Had you thought so? Kairaithin had asked him. *Well, something like, perhaps, for that brief moment caught out of time. But fire cannot truly ally with earth, king of men. That wall will not shatter along all its length; it will break here, at this end, where its balance has been disturbed and where it comes hard against the mountains. If the People of Fire and Air will come past its barrier, they will do so here, in this wild country, and thus they must strike into Feierabiand and not against Casmantium.*

"But—" the king had protested.

"Tastairiane Apailika makes no distinction among the countries of men," Lord Bertaud had put in, in a low voice. "He never has. And he likes killing and blood."

Tastairiane Apailika means eventually to burn all the country of earth, Kairaithin had said. *He is determined to leave nothing but fire in all the world, with the brilliant sky above and the world empty of everything but fierce wind singing past red stone.*

"We won't permit that," Lord Bertaud had said. His voice had still been low, but Jos had heard odd notes of grief and anger and warning mingled in it. He had understood the anger and he'd thought he understood the grief, but he did not understand the warning at all. King Iaor had given him a sidelong glance, and Jos had wondered what the king might have heard in his voice. Kairaithin had not looked at him at all. Jos thought the griffin probably did not know how to hear all the undertones of a human voice.

"Indeed, we will not," King Iaor had agreed, and at dawn the next day he had taken his very silent and subdued earth mage—struck dumb by the near edge of the desert or by the Great Wall or by the enormous, contained threat of Kairaithin himself, for Jos had not heard the young man utter a single word that day or all that night—the king had taken his earth mage and the rest of his retinue and gone down again from the mountain pass to Tihannad, to make what preparations seemed possible and practical.

Lord Bertaud alone had stayed to watch the Wall. He, with his mule and another, and Jos, and the goat, and the frightened chickens, rather crowded the cottage. The rear part of the building, built out in a simple lean-to, had provided ample room for one goat but was hard put to accommodate two mules as well. Their ears brushed the rough stones when they lifted their heads and they seemed rather inclined to eat the thatch. Fortunately, the goat and the mules were willing to be amicable even in their crowded quarters. Perhaps the memory of the griffin lingered even once Kairaithin had gone, so that the presence of any other creature seemed more welcome to all three animals.

In the griffin's absence, the white cock and all but one of the hens had crept back at last to their roost, attached as it was to the cottage and providing the only reliable warmth in all the mountains. Jos was sorry about his missing hen, though. She had not been one of the most reliable layers of the flock, but he did not like to think of her lost in the cold. He gave the remaining birds an extra handful of grain to help them forget their fright, watching carefully to make certain the larger hens did not keep the smaller from the grain. Such small concerns occupied him when he did not want to go back into the main part of the cottage.

Once the king and his people had gone and the immediate subject of the Wall and its possible shattering had been exhausted, Jos did not know what to say to Lord Bertaud. Once, Jos had had the gift of speaking easily, of drawing out anyone to whom he spoke, of putting anyone he met at ease. Somewhere during the past six years, he had lost all those skills. Now he did not know how to speak to anyone but the echoing mountains and one griffin mage exiled from his own people.

Nor did the Feierabianden lord seem to know how to speak to Jos. He had too much natural tact, it appeared, to ask anything like, *So, how have you lived? How has it been for you here in these mountains, belonging neither to fire nor to earth?* Far less would he ask any such question as, *How long was it before Kes forsook your company for that of Tastairiane?* And if Lord Bertaud—thankfully—possessed too much delicacy to ask any of those questions, Jos certainly did not intend to volunteer answers.

Or it might have been that Lord Bertaud simply despised Jos too much to speak to him, aside from the commonplaces necessary in such close accommodations. Though Jos would have liked to ask about the world below the mountains, he did not care to invite any rebuff by asking questions. He did not speak. Nor did Lord Bertaud. So it was a silent day that stretched out after King Iaor had departed. There was only the clucking of the hens to break the quiet, and the song of a hardy finch or two that had come bravely up from the lower meadows, and the muted hum of the bees, and the ceaseless winds above that always sang with more or less violence through the heights.

And after the long day, it was a silent evening, and later still a deathly quiet night. The dawn that followed was cold, of course, as every dawn was cold in these mountains. But the stream did not freeze. It seldom froze even in the depths of the most savage winter; its own inherent wild magic kept it running freely across the clean stone when any sensible water would have turned to shimmering ice and frozen mist.

Jos filled his single pot and made tea from his small store. He was glad to see Lord Bertaud's saddlebags still held some good bread and hard cheese, and some dried beef, and a handful of last fall's wrinkled apples. As it happened, Jos did have two mugs, for occasionally Kairaithin took the form of a man to visit him and then the griffin mage liked tea—or perhaps was simply amused to go through the motions of human hospitality; Jos was never confident he understood the griffin's motivations in even so simple a matter. But there were two mugs. He added sugar and a pat of goat's-milk butter to the tea in each mug and handed one, steaming, to his . . . guest, he supposed. For a sufficiently flexible understanding of the word.

Bertaud set out the bread and other things, and took the offered mug with a nod that seemed civil enough. He took the chair nearest the fire, less inured than Jos to the chill that seemed to creep through the stone walls of the cottage. There was actually an abundance of chairs—four, recalling the days when Kes and Opailikiita and Kairaithin had all occasionally come to visit Jos. Opailikiita had never, so far as Jos knew, taken human shape, but in those days he had thought it best to be prepared in case one day she might.

Instead, Kes had gradually lost her own human form, in every sense but the least important, and had ceased to visit the cottage. Jos had more than once thought of flinging two of the chairs down from the heights, letting them shatter on the stone below. He did not know whether it was hope or apathy or sheer blind obstinacy that had held him back from doing it.

"Is it all Tastairiane Apailika?" Lord Bertaud asked at last. He was not looking at Jos. He was staring into the fire. If he had noticed that the fire burned ceaselessly without wood or coal, he had not commented. Perhaps he had not noticed. A lord would not be accustomed to building up or maintaining his own fires. And he seemed much absorbed in his own thoughts. He asked again, "Is this Tastairiane, all this determination to defeat the Wall? Without him, would the People of Fire and Air so passionately desire to burn their way across the world?"

He, too, spoke of the Wall with the slight pause and distinct emphasis that Jos felt the Great Wall deserved. And, Jos noticed, the lord called the griffins by the name they called themselves without hesitation, without even appearing to think about it. He thought once more of how Kairaithin had said, *I carried word to Bertaud son of Boudan*, and again he wondered what the relationship between the two comprised.

But he did not know the answer to the lord's question, and only shook his head.

Lord Bertaud looked Jos in the face for a moment and then suddenly got to his feet and turned away, the sharp motion of a man who could not bear to sit still. He said harshly, "I cannot—they cannot be permitted to do as they wish to do." Going to the cottage's single tight-shuttered window, he put back the shutters with quick, forceful motions and let in the cold, brilliant morning light. Then he stood perfectly still for some time, gazing out. From the direction of his gaze, he was staring down toward the Wall.

The pale dazzling light that poured in through the open window was welcome, the harsh cold much less so. Jos opened his mouth to say, *Close the shutters, man, are you mad?* but then, watching the Feierabianden lord, he did not speak. The constraint he felt was, he realized, due far less to his fear that Lord Bertaud would take offense than to his surety that the lord would not even hear him. Jos thought the other man was so deeply absorbed in his own thoughts and fears that he would not have heard the crash and roar of an avalanche coming down from the frozen heights. For the first time, it occurred to Jos that the lord's enduring silence might be due to his own distraction and worries and not to any distaste or scorn he felt for his company.

After a moment, Jos went to stand behind Lord Bertaud and look over his shoulder. The Wall glowed in the morning light, but the light that struck it from either side was entirely distinct. On the desert side, the molten sunlight poured down from a savage white sky that seemed oddly metallic. The light on that side of the barrier seemed to pool against the barrier of the Wall, thick as honey, pressing against the huge granite blocks as though it possessed actual body and weight. On the other side, ice flashed and glittered in a pale, thin brilliance that came down from the high, blue vault of the heavens, carrying no warmth at all.

From both sides, light seemed to gather and pool in the cracks in the Wall. Light ran down from the cracks like liquid; steam billowed up from them, glowing in the sunlit air, gradually dispersing as it rose into the sky.

And the griffin mages flicked abruptly into view high against the white-hot brilliant desert sky and plunged downward like striking falcons, crying in their high, fierce voices.

Ashairiikiu Ruuanse Tekainiike, youngest and most arrogant of the fire mages, burned in fiery metallic colors, bronze and gold with flickers of blazing copper. Opailikiita Sehanaka Kiistaike, a smaller and more graceful griffin of gold-flecked brown, carried Kes on her back. Even at this distance, the girl was visible as a streak of white and gold against the darker, scorching colors of the griffins.

They blazed downward without pause, straight toward the burning sands of the red desert, far too fast. But at the last moment before they would have struck the sand, they blurred into wind and light and reshaped themselves, at rest and laughing beside the towering Wall. At

least Jos imagined they were laughing—at least Kes would be laughing, and the griffins blazing with their fierce silent humor, so like and
yet unlike the humor of men.

Kes stepped forward and laid her hands on the Wall. Fire blazed up
at her touch, licking in rich, blazing sheets up the side of the wall. Fire
found the longest, deepest crack and poured into it, filled it, pried at it.
Great white clouds of steam plumed upward. Jos could hear, in his
mind if not in truth, the hiss of fire meeting ice. He fancied he heard
the stone shift and crack under the assault of the flames; he imagined
he could even hear the powerful magic of making and building that
had been woven into the Wall groan with the strain as it tried to main-
tain the cohesion of a Wall that suddenly wanted to explode into a
chaotic storm of shattered, knife-edged shards of granite and crystal.

Beside Jos, Lord Bertaud uttered a low oath. He had stepped back
in shock at the deadly plunge of the griffins, and now, recovering himself, he gripped the cold stone of the windowsill and stared downward.
His expression was odd. Jos had seen creatures of fire many times, but
was still struck anew each time by their ferocity and beauty. He was
not surprised by Bertaud's shock. What he did not understand was the
intensity of grief and longing hidden behind the man's hard-held calm.

Bertaud spoke at last, his tone flat with the effort it took to contain
his emotions. "Tastairiane Apailika is not there."

"If the Wall breaks, I'm sure he'll come," Jos said. He kept his
voice light, dry, inexpressive.

Nevertheless, something in his tone must have caught Bertaud's attention, for the lord turned his head, his glance sharp and, at last, attentive. But what he said was, "I'm sure he will. When he does . . ." But
his voice trailed off, and he did not complete this thought. He turned
instead, caught up his fur-lined coat, and stepped across to the door. He
fumbled for a moment with the cold iron of the latch and the stiff
leather of the hinges, then thrust the door open and stepped out into the
chilly light of the morning.

Jos followed, though his coat was nothing like as good. He found
Lord Bertaud standing out in the middle of the meadow, scowling
down through the brilliant freezing air toward the distant Wall. His
arms were crossed over his chest. Despite his forbidding expression
and solid stance, something about his attitude struck Jos not as aggressive but as defensive, even hesitant. But when he spoke, he did not
sound hesitant at all. He sounded sharp and commanding, every bit the
court lord.

He did not speak to Jos, however. Instead, he called out into the
crystalline silence of the heights, "Kairaithin!"

At once, as though the griffin had been waiting for that call, fire blurred out upon the meadow. Anasakuse Sipiike Kairaithin drew himself out of fire and air and the piercing stillness of the mountains. For that first moment, he wore his true form: fierce black eagle head and feather-maned neck and chest, black-clawed red lion rear, his eyes blazing with fiery darkness. Then his wings beat once, scattering fire through the air, and closed around him like a cloak as he reared up and dwindled to the shape of a man. But the black eyes he turned toward them were unchanged, strange and unsettling in the face of a man, and his massive winged shadow stretched out behind him with the same fiery black eyes.

He said, his tone unreadable, "I am here."

Lord Bertaud gave an uneasy little nod, but now that the griffin mage had come, he did not seem to know what to say.

Jos came forward, with a deferential glance for Lord Bertaud and a welcoming nod for the griffin. "Kairaithin," he said, and gestured down the slanting, jagged pass toward the Wall. "What shall we do? Shall we go down and speak to them?"

"They will not hear you," the griffin mage answered, his tone strangely bleak. He glanced at Bertaud, half lifting a hand. But when he spoke, it was to Jos. "I will take you down to them, if you wish. But a day of blood and fire is coming, and I see no way to prevent it. Only to turn it in one direction or the other. But whether it turns right or left, still there will be blood and fire."

Jos waited a moment, but still Lord Bertaud did not speak. So he asked, "If your king and the fire mages you trained and all your people call for a wind to carry them to that day of fire, why should you want to turn it?"

He thought at first that Kairaithin would not answer. The griffin mage did not look at him, but glanced once more at Bertaud and then down toward the wall. But Kairaithin said at last, "If the People of Fire and Air try to ride that wind, they will find an unexpected storm which carries all before it. They believe the earth alone will burn, but fire and earth alike will be torn asunder."

Bertaud still said nothing, but somehow Jos found that his very silence commanded attention. He looked from man to griffin and, with a spy's trick to encourage others to speak, refused to say anything himself that would disguise or slip over the palpable tension that sang between them.

"You should go down to the Wall," Kairaithin said abruptly. His black gaze was on Bertaud's face, but he was speaking to Jos. He said, "You should go speak to Keskainiane Raikaisipiike. Kes. Perhaps she will hear you. Neither Opailikiita Sehanaka Kiistaike nor Ruuanse Tekainiike are important. Kes calls their common wind and sets its direction. If Kes is turned toward a different wind, all the mages of fire will turn, and the Wall may yet stand."

"I have spoken to her," Jos protested. "You know she will not listen to me." Then he paused, because Kairaithin did know that. Jos belatedly understood that Kairaithin wished to speak to Lord Bertaud and did not want Jos to overhear what they would say to each other. He looked from one of them to the other, seeing that Lord Bertaud, too, understood Kairaithin's intention.

Bertaud did not seem surprised by this, however. He stood looking aside, down toward the Wall, his shoulder turned toward both Jos and Kairaithin. His expression was closed and forbidding. Jos thought the man was not angry, or upset, or even frightened—he would have understood any of those emotions. He did not understand what he saw in that set, rigid face. He did not understand the strange relationship between the Feierabianden lord and the griffin mage, but he was abruptly certain that it was somehow important.

Jos wanted to argue, insist upon staying here by the cottage. He wanted badly to know what the other two had to say to each other that they did not want him to overhear. But no argument of his would matter if Kairaithin did not choose to hear him. Kairaithin could simply take the Feierabianden lord elsewhere if he wished to speak to him privately. Or if the griffin mage commanded Jos to leave, Jos had no power to defy him.

But Lord Bertaud said unexpectedly, "We might all go down to the Wall, perhaps. We might all speak to Kes. I'm curious to see her." He glanced at Jos. "If you say she has forgotten us, forgotten the country of earth, then of course I believe you. But even so, I would like to speak to her."

Jos found he wanted to know what the Feierabianden lord might find to say to Kes—and what answer Kes might give him. He nodded wordlessly.

Bertaud turned back to Kairaithin. "Those young griffins, they were your students, were they not? Have you so little influence with them now? Or have they sufficient strength to challenge you? I admit, that would astonish me."

Kairaithin did not answer at once. He regarded Lord Bertaud with close attention, as though wondering, as Jos was, what might lie behind these comments. But he said at last, "Neither Ruuanse Tekainiike nor Opailikiita Sehanaka Kiistaike could challenge me. You might well be astonished at such a suggestion. But your Kes has become in all truth

Keskainiane Raikaisipiike—her intimates may perhaps still call her Kereskiita, the little fire-kitten, but she is no more a kitten."

The griffin mage looked for a moment down along the broken stone of the pass, at the white fire that blazed around Kes and poured away from her to tear at the crack in the Wall. But at last he added in a low voice, "Well, I thought that one day she might challenge me. That day has long since come. I should never have made that human child into a creature of fire. Though that was not the greatest of errors I made six years ago." He glanced back at Bertaud and away again.

Bertaud said quietly, even gently, "We can none of us turn time to run back, nor say what would have happened if we had acted other than we did. We all do as best we can. Who is to say that we would not have come to this in the end, your people and mine, whatever we did?"

After an almost imperceptible pause, the griffin mage answered. "Not to this. Not without the wind I called up. Not without Kes." He paused again, very briefly, and corrected himself. "Keskainiane Raikaisipiike."

Bertaud looked down toward the pass. "Even now, I can't think of her by any name but Kes."

Jos wanted to say, *Speak with her for five minutes together, and you will learn to.* But he kept silent, not wishing to stop either of the others from speaking further if he wished.

Besides, even Jos, who had spoken to her not so long ago, still thought of her by the human name she had long since ceased to use.

"We will go down," Kairaithin said, and on that word shifted them all out of the bright airy heights and straight down into the powerful desert.

For the first moment, the heat was welcome, even pleasant. Jos found his numbed fingertips and his ears thawing instantly. He had almost forgotten what it was like to be really warm. This heat spread through him, unknotting muscles in his back and neck, so that he relaxed and stretched and stood straight.

After that one moment, the desert heat rapidly became excessive, and then overwhelming. The red sands were alive with delicate flames that flickered upward with every motion and then subsided, ebbing like water. The air sparkled not only with red dust but also with sparks of fire that settled downward as flecks of gold. The wind was hot and gritty and bone-dry. The very sunlight was entirely different here than it ever was in the country of earth: It hammered down upon them, brazen and heavy.

Kes turned. The young griffin mages turned with her: Opailikiita Sehanaka Kiistaike, as dependably good-humored as any griffin ever could be, the rich brown of her feathers flecked and stippled with gold, slim and beautiful. A pace to the rear, Ashairiikiu Ruuanse Tekainiike, dark bronze and gold, his eyes brilliant gold and his temper far less certain.

Kes herself looked less human even than Kairaithin, for where the griffin mage had deliberately put on human form as a mask and a convenience, Kes was not making any pretense of being human. Only her shape was human. She seemed to have been formed out of white gold and alabaster and porcelain; she glowed from within as though white fire flowed in her veins. Maybe it did. Fire filled her hands and poured down her arms, pale fire scattered from her hair when she turned to look at them. Fire glowed in her eyes, pale and brilliant and terrible. Her shadow, flung across the red sand, was as molten as her eyes.

She was smiling, an expression that expressed nothing human. She looked happy, even joyful, but hers was a dangerous joy that held nothing of ordinary affection or gentleness. She said, "Jos!" and came to take his hands.

Jos was absurdly flattered that she would speak to him first, that she would come to greet him before she even acknowledged Kairaithin, much less Bertaud. Though he knew she spoke to him first partly as a deliberate slight against Kairaithin, though he knew she had her griffin *iskarianere* now and never thought of him, he could not help but find the pleasure in her voice flattering. But he stepped backward as she came toward him. He could not help but step back, for the fire that filled Kes, unleashed as it was now, would burn him to the bone and she had plainly forgotten this.

She realized this an instant after he did, and stopped. The white fire that burned so bright in her did not exactly fade, but it ebbed lower and lower, until standing near her was not quite so much like standing near an oven. She reached out to him again, and this time Jos let her take his hands. Her fingers did not seem exactly human in his; they were slender and graceful, exactly as he remembered, but holding her hands was like holding the hands of an alabaster lamp shaped like a woman. She said again, not gently or cheerfully, but with a kind of pleased possessiveness, "Jos."

He knew perfectly well that she spoke to him and ignored Kairaithin in this pointed way in order to deliver a subtle affront. He knew this. But it did not stop his heart from coming into his throat in the most foolish and childish way. He said, "Kes," and found he could not say anything else.

"Why do you wish to break the Wall?" Lord Bertaud asked her, very simply and directly, when Kairaithin did not speak.

Kes released Jos's hands, turning to gaze at the Feierabianden lord. Her smile had grown somehow both more brilliant and sharper-edged. She was wilder than a griffin, less fierce but more capricious, less high-tempered and passionate but more whimsical. Or so she seemed to Jos, who had known her when she was a human girl and then while she had been made from a creature of earth to one of fire and then afterward, when the fire had taken her completely. She said, "Why should any such constraint be allowed to stand? It is an offense against all the country of fire. Besides, Taipiikiu Tastairiane Apailika wishes the Wall to be broken, and why should I not please him if I can, now it has been cracked through?"

"Tastairiane?" said Bertaud, as though even saying the name hurt him.

"You recall Tastairiane Apailika? He is my *iskarianere* now," said Kes. She spoke with pleased amusement, but the edge to her humor was sharp enough to cut to the bone.

"Yes," said Bertaud in a low tone. "I had heard so."

"Had you? Well, one would never predict what word might be carried on some errant wind," Kes said, and laughed.

It was a cruel laugh, like no sound she would ever have made when she was human. Jos winced from it. He knew, none better, how pitiless the griffins were by nature, but pitilessness was not the same as cruelty, and it hurt him to hear that note in her voice.

Bertaud said, not as though he expected Kes to understand or believe him but as though he felt driven to speak despite this, "If griffins turn once-for-all against men, if it should come to true battle, Kes, I promise you, no one will win. Least of all the People of Fire and Air." He hesitated and then added, "Even you, swift as you are to heal the injured, even you cannot bring a griffin back to life after he has been killed."

Kes only laughed, shaking her head in dismissal of this warning. "Oh, no. You're mistaken. You're entirely mistaken. If I'm swift enough, no injury need be mortal."

"You cannot be so swift, not when thousands upon thousands of men draw together to face a mere few hundreds of griffins—"

"I can be as swift and attentive as I must be," Kes answered with perfect confidence. She reached out to lay her hand on the Wall. Fire ran up along the great blocks, playing over her wrist and hand. The flames were ruddy where they rose from the red sands, but white where they crossed her hand. She smiled.

"Kes," said Kairaithin. "Keskainiane Raikaisipiike."

"*Siipikaile*," said Kes, turning to face him directly for the first time. *Teacher*, that was. But she pronounced the word with a mocking edge, and met his powerful black gaze without the slightest flinch. Her eyes were filled with fire, black and gold and paler gold, set in a face that might have been carved of porcelain. Jos remembered when Kes had had eyes of a pale grayed blue, like water. He tried to remember when they had turned to fire. Not at once, he thought. Not in those early years, when they had built his cottage and kindled the fire that burned within it. There had still been a touch of humanity about her in those days. But the last of it had burned away a long time ago.

Neither of the young griffin mages flanking her acknowledged Kairaithin at all. They would not, Jos knew. No griffin would speak to Kairaithin, from what he had said about flying alone. Brawny, powerful-shouldered Ruuanse Tekainiike crouched down a little; the feathers of his neck and chest, feathers that might have been beaten out of bronze and inlaid with gold by some master metalsmith, ruffled up with a stiff rattling sound. He looked brutal and dangerous, but he did not meet Kairaithin's eyes. He was not a match for his former teacher and no one, least of all Tekainiike himself, mistook it.

Opailikiita was a question. Opailikiita Sehanaka Kiistaike . . . she had been Kairaithin's student long before he had stolen Kes from the country of earth and made her into a creature of fire. Slender and small, her beauty was subtle rather than flashy. She was more powerful than she seemed to any first glance. Jos had once known her rather well. When Opailikiita turned her head to avoid looking at Kairaithin, Jos suspected it was not acknowledgment of his superior strength that made her look aside. He thought it was regret for what her old teacher had lost. Or at least some griffin emotion similar to regret; some emotion hotter and more violent than mere regret. A sort of angry grief, perhaps.

Kairaithin would not be goaded, neither by the scorn in Kes's voice nor by the overt indifference of his former students. Perhaps he truly did not care. He said, "You understand less than you believe," but when he took a step forward and lifted a hand, it was not to remonstrate with Kes, as Jos at first thought. Instead, he struck at her with a wholly unexpected blaze of power that burned right through her and hurled the rest of them violently aside.

Kes shredded into fire and air under that blow. She did not even have time to cry out. Opailikiita did, the harsh scraping shriek of an enraged griffin. She flung herself fearlessly at Kairaithin, who merely called up a hard wind that threw her aside, tumbling her over. Young Tekainiike, also shrieking, reared back in shock and then leaped into the air, his wings thundering as he strove for height—fleeing, to Jos's shock, who would not have expected any griffin to fly from such a battle.

Jos had also shouted aloud in shock and grief. He had been flung to his hands and knees, for even the glancing edge of Kairaithin's power was like the blow of a smith's hammer. Half blinded by flying wind and whirling sand, conscious of the furious griffins above and about, he could not even crawl out of the way. He was aware of Kairaithin rearing up, of his human shape exploding to match his immense shadow, of black feathers raking the air above him; he was aware of fire cracking across the sky and of the flaming wind roaring down from the high, hard sky—

Then Bertaud seized Jos by the arm. He had been the first of them all to regain his balance, and the only one among them to make no sound. Jos had a fleeting realization that the other man might actually have guessed that Kairaithin might strike at Kes, for he had evidently been ready for it. Now he dragged at Jos, who with the other man's help managed to regain his feet; they both ducked away from the violence of wind and fire, their arms over their faces to guard against the rushing sand.

"You knew—" Jos began, shouting over the fury of wind and griffins, but then coughed and could not continue.

He did not know what answer the Feierabianden lord might have made, for the other griffins came then, rushing down out of the storm; the harsh desert sunlight struck off their wings and flanks as off bronze and copper and gold. The ferocious light flamed on their knife-edged beaks and talons and glowed in their eyes. Behind them, the sky turned crimson with driving sand, and below them fire fell like rain from the wind of their wings.

In those first moments, Jos thought that all the griffins in the world had come to avenge Kes. Then he realized both that only a double-handful of griffins were actually plunging down that fiery wind toward them—though that seemed enough and to spare—and that Kes did not need to be avenged. Kairaithin had not succeeded in his aim.

At least not yet. A streak of white and gold fire poured itself through the wind, shaping itself back into the form of a human woman. Kairaithin, beautiful and terrible, rearing huge against the sky, the wind of his power roaring through his black wings, struck at her again. Again she shredded away into fire and wind. She could not answer him, or would not, or at least she did not. She fled. But Kairaithin used his strength to block her flight, pinning her against the Wall and dragging her ruthlessly back into shape. He meant to kill her—to destroy her—she could not match him. Jos made a wordless sound but did not know he had tried to leap forward until he found Bertaud blocking his way, the other man's grip on his arm so fierce even Jos could not break it. He wanted to hit him. He stopped instead, leaning forward, his fists clenched.

Kiibaile Esterire Airaikeliu, the Lord of Fire and Air, the king of all the griffins, swept down out of the sky. His immense power came before him like a motionless hurricane—Jos did not know how else to express it. All other power flattened out before him, crushed to stillness. The wind itself died; the air cleared of its red haze of dust; the flames that had blazed up from the desert sands died.

On all sides, the struggle quieted. Kairaithin settled back slowly to the ground, folding his great wings. Kes, looking tiny and helpless and frightened, drew herself slowly away from the Wall and turned to face them, one hand still braced against the fire-washed stone for support. The Lord of Fire and Air landed near her, his gold-and-crimson mate on his other side and the savage white Tastairiane Apailika beyond her. Ruuanse Tekainiike, looking much younger and smaller in such company, came down warily near them. The young griffin mage had not fled after all, Jos realized belatedly, but had gone to bring the king and his company to this place.

And now that the king was here, Kairaithin had lost. There was no more mockery in the look Kes gave him, but rather wary respect. But even the greatest griffin mage could not threaten her again, not—

Kairaithin, who had turned to face the Lord of Fire and Air, flung a slender blaze of power like a knife at Kes. He did not even look at her; his blow took everyone by surprise, most of all Kes. It was a thrust of such power and strength that it passed right through the forceful stillness the king of griffins had imposed, and unable to block or answer it, she leaped away. But anyone, even Jos, could see that she was nothing like fast enough.

Everyone moved in a blaze of speed and fury: Opailikiita with a blaze of magecraft of her own to block Kairaithin's blow, the Lord of Fire and Air casting himself forward to protect Kes, the king's mate lunging after him, Tastairiane and a half dozen other griffins flinging themselves simultaneously against Kairaithin. And Kairaithin *was* overset by their combined force, but only momentarily, for he was a very powerful mage and neither Tastairiane nor any of his own former students could match him.

But though the griffin mage was forced back, and back again, until he was pinned against the Wall himself, his blow had found its mark. There could be no mistake on that account, for even Jos and Bertaud, out of place as they were, felt the reverberation of power and loss and destruction echo and reecho through the desert. It happened very swiftly, but there was a whirl of blinding sand and fire and an explosion of red dust, and then a single hard, savage cry of fury and anguish, and then, suddenly, stillness.

But it was not the same stillness that the king had imposed.

At first, even after the griffins drew back, Jos thought Kairaithin had after all managed to achieve his aim. He thought that Kes had been destroyed. Even though the woman he had known had ceased to exist years ago, grief rose up into his throat and choked him. He started to step forward, blindly, wanting at least to look down at her body, or at least at the ebbing fire and white sand and flecks of gold that she might have left if she had been too little human to leave a body.

As he had before, Bertaud stopped him. Jos started to knock the other man's hand away, and then stopped, for he saw with astonishment that again, though he could not imagine how, Kairaithin had missed his mark. Kes was still alive. She was standing beside Opailikiita, her hand buried in the soft feathers of the slender griffin's neck, staring at Kairaithin. Her expression was very odd.

It took Jos much longer than it should have to realize that the Lord of Fire and Air had taken Kairaithin's blow in her place, and that in her place he had been destroyed. He understood this only when the red-and-gold griffin who had been the king's mate, crouching low to the desert sand, gave another loud cry, of such despair and grief and fury that Jos was frozen speechless and motionless by it, as a mouse might be frozen among its tangled grasses by the scream of a stooping falcon.

Everyone seemed equally frozen, griffin and human alike. Kes was holding one hand out to where the king had been. Red dust sifted through her slender fingers. She looked stricken. Beside her, almost as close as Opailikiita, Tastairiane Apailika stood so still he might have been hammered out of white gold. His fiery blue eyes blazed and his immense wings were half spread, the feathers like the flame at the white-hot heart of a fire.

The red-and-gold griffin who had been the king's mate—her name was Nehaistiane Esterikiu Anahaikuuanse—flung herself abruptly into the brilliant air and exploded violently into flaming wind and red sand, and was gone.

For a long, long moment, no one else moved.

At last, Tastairiane Apailika turned his savage, beautiful, white-feathered head and looked deliberately at Kairaithin.

All the lesser griffins fell back and away, as though at a signal. Kairaithin came a pace away from the looming Wall and stood, outwardly impassive but, to Jos's practiced eye, looking weary and heartsick and very much alone. The black feathers of his neck and shoulders ruffled up and then smoothed down again. His great wings were nearly furled. He turned his head to look at Kes—no. At the place where the Lord of Fire and Air had died, where now nothing remained but drifting red dust and flickers of fire. He did not look at Kes herself. Nor did he look at the white griffin who stood near her.

But Tastairiane Apailika looked at him. The white griffin said in a smooth, deadly voice that sliced across their minds like a knife, *Kiibaile Esterire Airaikeliu is gone. Nehaistiane Esterikiu Anahaikuuanse is gone. Who will challenge me?*

From the depth of silence that followed, it appeared no one would.

The shining white griffin continued to regard Kairaithin. He was poised with supreme grace and confidence, wings angled aggressively forward. The hot sunlight blazed off his terrible beak as though striking edged metal. He lifted one eagle's foot clear of the sand, his talons glinting like silver knives.

In contrast, Kairaithin clearly did not want to fight. He still looked dangerous—nothing could stop his looking dangerous. Jos did not think he was exactly afraid, for fear was not something griffins understood. But he looked as though, if he were to challenge Tastairiane Apailika now, he would lose. And he looked as though he knew it.

The Lord of Fire and Air has gone into the fire and the air, the white griffin said. His tone was not exactly triumphant, but it held pride and strength and something more, an awareness of his own strength, and a willingness to command. He said, *I am become the Lord of Fire and Air. Will any challenge me?*

All the other griffins shifted, not exactly rushing to put themselves at Tastairiane Apailika's back, but reorienting themselves around him. They accepted him as their lord, Jos saw, and he saw that even Kairaithin felt the new power and confidence in the white griffin, that he could not help but respond to it, for all he was unalterably opposed to the other.

Kes said, in her smooth, light voice that was so nearly the voice Jos remembered, "Lord of Fire and Air! What wind will you call us all to ride?"

Tastairiane Apailika turned to her and said, *Break the Wall.*

"I will break it," said Kes. She looked at Kairaithin. She was not laughing now. She reached out with great deliberation to set her palm against the burning stone, in a gesture that was very clearly a challenge, and a challenge that she very clearly knew her former teacher could not take up.

Come, said the new Lord of Fire and Air, to Kairaithin. There was a new depth and power to his voice. Tastairiane Apailika had come fully into his strength. Something about declaring himself had done that for him, or else something in the recognition of the other griffins. He commanded Kairaithin again, *Come here.*

Kairaithin seemed to shrink back and down—not very much, not even with any perceptible motion. But Jos saw very clearly that the griffin mage had nothing left with which to defy the new king of the griffins: neither strength nor pride nor even the certainty that recently had sustained him.

Then Bertaud, with a courage and presence of mind that astonished Jos, walked across to Kairaithin's side. He turned there, setting one hand on the black-fathered neck, and regarded Tastairiane Apailika with an expression Jos could not read at all.

Well, man? the white griffin asked him impatiently.

Bertaud began to answer him.

What answer the Feierabianden lord might have made, Jos could not guess, but he did not have a chance to speak. Before Bertaud could utter even a single word, Kairaithin, with more decisive speed than Jos had imagined he could yet command, swept him up, and Jos with him, and took them with him, away from the Wall and out of the desert entirely.

The world tilted and turned, and raked away behind and beyond them, and they were standing abruptly on solid stone. They stood now in the mountains, in a high, clear morning above Tihannad, with Niambe Lake shining beside the city.

The city lay below them, quiet and peaceful, with no sign of any impending peril. Here and there bright-coated skaters raced along the lake's edge where the ice was still firm enough to be trusted, but little wavelets rippled across the middle of the lake. Mist rose from the lake into the cold air. Out in the town, threads of darker smoke made their way gently up into the sky.

It was almost impossible, in this place, to really believe in the desert, or in griffins, or in the Wall that had so briefly held fire from the country of earth and that was now so near failure.

Kairaithin had taken on human form again, perhaps because he had brought them to a place of men. He stood now with his head bowed and his eyes closed, as though he had used up the last of his strength in bringing them here. Perhaps he had, for when he took a step, he swayed. Catching his arm to steady him, Jos looked at Bertaud in alarm.

The Feierabianden lord was not looking at him, nor even at Kairaithin. He was staring down at Niambe Lake and at the city, his expression closed and forbidding, his mouth set hard. He said abruptly, "We will go down to the king's house."

Jos only nodded.

"Unless you have another suggestion to offer? Or to force upon us?" Bertaud said to Kairaithin, with a coldness that astonished Jos.

But the griffin mage did not respond in kind. He did not seem offended, or even surprised. He only nodded in weary acquiescence and gestured for Bertaud to lead the way down from the shoulder of the mountain to Niambe Lake, and thence to the king's house in Tihannad.

CHAPTER 10

The road through the mountains from Minas Ford in Feierabiand to the town of Ehre in Casmantium was the greatest road in the world. Mienthe had not seen every road in the world, but she was certain none could rival the one through the pass above Minas Ford. The very best Casmantian makers and builders and engineers—Mienthe was not quite certain of the proper bounds of any of those terms, in Casmantian usage—had been years in the building of this road, which even now was not quite completed.

In some places, Casmantian builders had cut the road back into the sides of the mountains; in others, they had swung it right out over wild precipices, supporting the great stones with ironwork and vaunting buttresses, rather as though they were building a massive palace. Sometimes bridges seemed to have been flung across from one high place to another just out of the builders' exuberance. The longest gaps had been spanned by tremendous iron arches from which were suspended the most amazing bridges, hung on iron chains. All her life, Mienthe had heard of the splendid skill of Casmantian makers and builders. Now she decided that she had never heard even half the truth.

With this new road, it was possible to ride straight through the pass without ever picking one's way far down a mountainside into a steep valley and then laboriously climbing back up the other side, as the old road had required. It was even possible for a long train of heavy wagons to cross straight through the pass, with never a perilous turn around the narrow shoulder of some mountain where a cross-footed mule might drag an entire unfortunate team off some terrible cliff. It was not, unfortunately, always possible for a few travelers mounted on swift horses to swing wide around such a heavy train of wagons.

Mienthe stood up in her stirrups, trying to peer ahead over the long train of wagons making their slow, cautious descent around a long curving angle of a mountain. She was quite certain her horse could have taken that same descent at three times the speed and been up around this mountain and up the next rise as well, and across the bridge dimly visible far ahead, all before these wagons would reach the lowest turn of the road and begin the next ascent.

"There will be room at the bottom to get around them," Tan said, his expressive mouth crooking with amusement.

Mienthe thought his unfailing good humor about the minor discomforts and irritations of their journey might eventually become unbearably provoking. There was some irony in that, since Tan was the one who had argued against making this particular journey at all. After alert guardsmen had reported possible Linularinan agents in Kames, asking questions about the house and grounds, Tan had wanted to go straight north as fast as he could ride, drawing the most persistent and dangerous Linularinan agents away with him. But Mienthe had worried that his enemies might also have already got ahead of him, waiting for him to run north and right into their hands.

With a quite terrifying quirk of humor, Tan had been very much inclined to oblige them. "The day I can't outwit and outrun an ordinary shaved-penny spy or two, Linularinan or otherwise, I'll retire from the game and take up turnip farming," he had said, with altogether too much complacency for his own good, in Mienthe's opinion.

Mienthe had wondered aloud just how many of those shaved-penny spies might actually be Linularinan mages. That had blunted the edge of Tan's amusement. Then she had asked him how many times he meant to put her to the trouble of rescuing him, and that had done for the rest.

"You should be glad to see me go north," he had said. "I can get past anyone Istierinan has in my way, Mie, and then let him try the skill of his mages against the mages of Tihannad. I know you're longing to get back to Tiefenauer. You should let me go."

Mienthe hadn't been convinced that any such flight would succeed. But she was afraid for Tan to stay in her father's house in Kames, doubly afraid now that they were both certain Istierinan knew where he was. At the same time, she knew exactly which unexpected direction they could take that would lead them straight to safe shelter.

"The Arobern is on good terms with my cousin," she had pointed out. "And however bold your Istierinan is here, he won't lightly try his hand in Casmantium, do you think? You can take shelter with the

Arobern, I'm sure he'll have no objection, and then once you're out of Linularinum's reach, surely Istierinan will pull his people back. Kohorrian will probably even apologize to Iaor for any *misunderstandings*."

Tan had stared at her. "There are times, Mie," he had said at last, "when your utterances blossom out with a most peculiar complexity, as the flowers of some wondrous country. Some might consider a confidential agent who delivers himself over to a foreign king not merely foolish, but actually treasonous, you know."

"The Arobern won't do anything like that!" Mienthe had protested, shocked.

"Anyway, isn't the information you carry nearly all about Linularinum? What does it matter if Casmantium has it, too?"

Tan had had to admit that this was a point.

Mienthe had argued, "We don't know I can protect you from Linularinan mages, but we know I *have*. I'm afraid to ask you to stay here and afraid to see you go north alone. But I think if we can get through the pass into Casmantium, we'll both be safe."

"We?" said Tan, sounding both startled and for once quite serious. "Out of the question, Mie—"

"I'm not leaving you for Istierinan!" Mienthe had insisted, thoroughly exasperated. "Nor staying here to wait for him myself. You could even be right about being in danger from a foreign king! But I'm Bertaud's cousin and the Arobern's friend, and that changes everything. I'm going."

"Well," Tan had said after a moment, "I know how stubborn you are, and—" He had paused and then added, his manner suddenly almost serious, "I admit, Mie, I would find your company a welcome reassurance, under the circumstances. But your cousin is probably going to kill me for putting you in such danger."

The thought occurred to Mienthe that, though plenty of people might find her company welcome, no one, not even her cousin, had ever said he found her company *reassuring*. She did not know what to say to that. But in the end, she and Tan, and a handful of guardsmen, and the maid from Kames whom her steward had demanded she take with her for propriety's sake, had all headed east and not north.

Mienthe had not even known she'd had a steward, though she supposed she'd have guessed if she'd ever thought about it. She had never wanted to hear about anything to do with her father's house or her inheritance. But, after all, someone had to look after her father's house and see that it remained in good repair, and keep an eye on the land to prevent too much clandestine wood-cutting or poaching or grazing.

She supposed Bertaud had approved the man; at least he seemed competent and reliable. A little too forceful, perhaps, when insisting that Mienthe have a female companion.

Not that the maid was with her now, which Mienthe actually did regret. But they had lost two of the guardsmen finding out just how swiftly the Linularinan agents had moved to surround Kames. After that, Tan had given up any idea of heading north, and Mienthe had insisted that the maid be left in a little village along their way, with the other guardsman to keep the woman safe and eventually see her back to the house at Kames. Propriety and appearances were all very well, but the maid had been rather too old for a fast journey, and frightened by the close pursuit they'd encountered.

After that, by common accord, Mienthe and Tan had skirted any larger village or small town they'd passed and slipped right by the rebuilt Minas Ford in the fading light of evening, camping in one of the recently deserted engineer's camps right in the pass itself. And now they were here, entirely out of Feierabiand, in these mountains that belonged to no country at all. And they did not even have any clear certainty about whether they were truly riding toward shelter in Casmantium, far less whether they were riding toward allies.

But, though Mienthe did not know how likely they were to find friends in Ehre, she knew that if they turned back, they would find enemies behind them. And she was certain that the King of Casmantium, once he knew she was Bertaud's cousin and Erich's friend, would be very polite. She was certain he would offer the hospitality of his court and that he would not harass Tan at all, even if he learned that Tan had been one of King Iaor's important confidential agents, which she supposed they would have to tell him. At least, they would have to explain their presence somehow.

No, she was confident of the Arobern's courtesy and hopeful of his goodwill. She even wondered whether he might lend her a few men . . . say, a company . . . to see them safe back through the pass and north to Tihannad. Even this did not seem unlikely.

But how far was it, from the mouth of the pass at Ehre to the Casmantian capital city?

Tan did not know the answer to this when she asked him. "I can tell you every distance in Linularinum, from Dessam in the far north right down to Desamion," he said, and shrugged. "But I never expected to visit Casmantium. I don't even speak Prechen. I don't suppose . . . ?"

Mienthe didn't, either, aside from a few laborious words. She could say *Please* and *Thank you*, and she thought she could manage *My cousin is Bertaud son of Boudan, Lord of the Delta*, which might be very much to the point. But she did not know how to say anything as complicated as *Linularinum has invaded the Delta and their agents are trailing us, or at least Tan, because he accidentally stole some powerful legist-magic out of a special book, so we need to see the Arobern right away.*

She wondered whether Linularinan agents had actually dared come after them into the pass. She glanced uneasily over her shoulder. But the road behind them was clear all the way up the long sweeping curve of the mountain they had just descended, and beyond that she could not see.

"We're well ahead, I'm quite certain, even if Istierinan has the nerve and resolve to send a man of his right to the very doorstep of Brechen Arobern himself," Tan said.

He meant this to be comforting. It would have been more so, except he'd said something very like it before. That had been just prior to the loss of the two guardsmen. But Mienthe did not comment. She merely nodded and wondered whether, once they got past the wagons, they might possibly be able to beg or bribe the men driving the mule teams to slow to an even more deliberate pace and block anyone coming behind them.

As it happened, once they reached the wide gap at the bottom of the slope, the muleteers drew politely to one side to allow swifter travelers past. When Mienthe—very tentatively—put her request to the drivers, they seemed oddly eager to assure her they would be very slow on any upward stretch, and assuredly did not care to have any overbold travelers startle their mules by coming up alongside when there clearly wasn't room.

It dawned on Mienthe, rather too slowly, that the muleteers thought she was with Tan in a very specific sense. They thought that she must have slipped away from her father, or maybe from her proper husband. Mienthe, horrified and offended, wanted to correct them. Before she could, Tan caught her eye and her hand and proceeded to encourage the muleteers' assumption by putting on an understated air of nervous, half-embarrassed smugness that would have got the idea across to men far less romantically inclined. The muleteers grew even more amused and accommodating. Mienthe smiled until her face hurt.

She was too angry to speak to Tan when they at last left the wagons behind and rode up the next neatly angled slope of the road.

"It's very convenient for them to assume—" Tan began once they were well away.

"I know," Mienthe said through her teeth.

"It's only practical—"

"I know!" said Mienthe, and put her hood up to make it clear she did not want to be mollified.

They did not speak again until they reached the middle of the pass, with its welcoming public house and stables and twelve lamps glowing along the road on either side to lead weary travelers in out of the cold.

The public house was set up on a low place where mountains climbed away in serried ranks in all directions. The mountains, glittering with ice, were rose-pink and gold where the late sunlight slanted down across them; the shadows between and behind them were violet, and the road running away toward the east seemed picked out in gold where it twisted up across the face of the nearest. Where the road flung itself across a chasm, high above, the iron bridge looked like a stark black thread.

The public house had a stable behind and two long wings, one angling in from the east and the other from the west. These met in the middle in a handsome square-cornered three-story building of dressed stone with carved wooden doors and real glass in the windows, blazing gold in the light. The whole was substantially larger than her father's house, much more elegant than the great house in Tiefenauer, and a great deal more elaborate than anything Mienthe had expected to find in the middle of what was still, despite the fine new road, a rugged mountain pass.

Mienthe, wordless, gazed down and up and around in amazement.

Tan said in a low voice, "Would we might rise on eagle's wings, mount above the heights where the rising sun strikes music from the stone, and fall again through the silence that is song."

"Oh," said Mienthe softly. And after a moment, "If there's a poem that catches an echo of this"—Mienthe opened her hands to the surrounding mountains—"then someday you really must teach it to me."

Tan nodded. But he also said, "We might be wiser not to stay at that inn."

Still stunned by beauty, Mienthe hardly understood him for a moment. Then she did, and, unreasonably, resented it. She said grimly, "Of course," and nudged her horse forward again. She wondered if Tan thought they could get all the way through to Ehre without stopping. She knew she couldn't.

"There must be good places along the road for a cold camp," Tan said, not quite looking at her. "I'm sure travelers used to have to camp three or four nights from one side to the other, or many more than that for slow wagons such as those we passed. I should think the builders will have let their road encompass some of those old campsites."

"Yes," said Mienthe.

"I'm sorry—"

Mienthe snapped, "For what? Of course we can't stop there. You're perfectly right."

"For being right," Tan said gently. "It hasn't happened often of late, Mienthe; do grant me my one moment of reasonable competence in these days of striking idiocy. I do think we oughtn't stay there, but I hope we may stop for supper."

"Oh," said Mienthe, in a much smaller voice. She felt she ought to apologize as well, but wasn't sure for what, or how. She said merely, "All right."

The public house offered hot spiced wine and roasted kid, soft flatbreads, a compote of dried apples and raisins, and little cakes dripping with honey, "Which my wife makes them special," said the host, a big man from Feierabiand, with a generous belly and a booming laugh. "With honey from her sister's bees, down near Talend. The bees there, they make a special honey from the trees that flower at midsummer, dark as molasses. Good to keep off illness, they say it is, and good especially to sweeten a dark heart, not that that matters to *you*, esteemed lady, eh?"

He winked down at Mienthe, clearly assuming, just as the muleteers had, that she was with Tan. At least Tan did not suggest to him that they were running away together. Not where Mienthe could hear him, anyway. She tried not to wonder what he told the host to explain why they were not staying the night at the house.

But at least the host also told them of a cold campsite a little more than an hour's ride up the east side of the pass.

Even so, Mienthe was certain for some little while that the lowering dusk would catch them still abroad on the road. Certainly the host's estimate seemed a little over-optimistic, or else he'd been thinking of riders with fresh horses, or at least riders coming down from heights rather than trudging upward.

They had lanterns. The road was, after all, good. She tried not to be frightened by the mere idea of riding up the twisting length of any mountain road, no matter how fine the road or how bright the lanterns.

But at last they came up a rise that had been, by the worn and rugged look of it, part of the old road, simply incorporated into the new. Then they crossed one of those improbable iron bridges and came onto a section of the road where the stones were so new and fresh they looked all but polished, and beyond that the new road ran again into a section of the old. "Yes," Tan said, gesturing away down the rugged slope that fell away from the road, "you can see where the old road plunged way down into that valley and then crawled slowly back up to this height."

Mienthe nodded obediently, although she was far too cold and tired to appreciate how much effort the new road had saved them, just so long as it had. But then they turned along a long switchback and came out at last, with the last of the slanting light, onto a broad flat place that had plainly been used as a campsite for many years. A cliff reared out a tight little nook, just right to keep off the weather, and circles of fire-stones were laid ready before the cliff. There was even a neat stack of firewood against the cliff, which someone must have gathered with considerable labor, because even the small twisted trees of the heights were rare so high.

Mienthe arranged wood with numb fingers and struck a fire while Tan unsaddled the horses. He did not hobble the beasts, which were as tired and cold as their riders and very willing to be led into the nook. He was limping, Mienthe saw; he had been only very slightly lame in Kames, but he'd used himself hard on their flight and the limp was much worse now. She was immediately worried, and then resented the necessity of worry, which she knew very well was unfair. But there was nothing she could do if the half-healed knee had been reinjured—nothing either of them could do, this side of Ehre. So she worried. "Your leg?" she asked Tan.

"It will do," he said, and stopped limping, which made Mienthe feel guilty and more resentful still. Even worse, Tan did not seem to notice her bad temper.

She got up and went herself to pour out handfuls of grain for the horses and check their feet. At least there were few other camp tasks, as simply as they were traveling. Tan settled by the fire and stretched his leg out carefully, with a saddle under his knee.

Mienthe wrapped herself up in a blanket and tucked herself, not too close to Tan, between the cliff wall and the fire where the reflected warmth would, she hoped, eventually thaw her fingers and toes. She was acutely aware of his presence. And of the absence of the maid. And of the silence and solitude that surrounded them. She did not know what to say, but found herself suddenly unable to look at him.

"Tomorrow should see us out of the pass and down at least to Ehre," he said, throwing another branch on the fire. His tone was utterly prosaic.

Mienthe nodded, staring fixedly into the fire.

"I could bring you something to eat—"

She shook her head and leaned her head back against the cliff.

Then she lay down right where she was, closed her eyes, and opened them what seemed mere moments later to a spectacular dawn.

Clouds had piled up in the east, rose-pink and deep carmine and gold. The sun, rising behind the clouds and among the teeth of the mountains, flooded the valleys between the peaks with a streaming pale light that seemed almost solid enough to touch. To either side of the road, the luminous faces of the mountains glowed gold and pink with reflected light; ice streaked the high jagged tips of the mountains with crystalline fire. Violet and indigo shadows stretched out below the mountains, and the iron bridge, a surprising distance below their campsite, gleamed like polished jet.

"Good morning," Tan said, smiling rather tentatively at Mienthe from beside the fire. He was heating pieces of last night's roasted meat on sticks over the coals and folding them into flatbreads, and it was the savory smell of the dripping fat that had woken her.

Mienthe found herself suddenly and unexpectedly happy. It might have been the clarity of the air and the brilliance of the light, or the deep warmth that had built up around her through the night from the fire, or the feeling of safety. She had not realized how frightened she had felt, or for how long, until she woke secure in this stony nook high above the world, with no company but Tan and the horses. Somehow, in the bright light of the morning, it no longer seemed nearly so strange or worrisome to be alone in the mountains with only Tan for a companion.

She sat up, then got to her feet, shook out her traveling skirt and rubbed her face with her hands—Tan had put out a bowl of water and even a surprising bit of soap, so she could wash her face like a civilized person. Then she knelt down by the fire while Tan saddled the horses and rolled up the blankets. She didn't even feel guilty about letting him do all the work. He looked wide awake and energetic, like he'd been up for hours, and he was hardly limping at all. Besides, there wasn't a great deal of work involved in cleaning up their camp. So she peacefully ate the hot meat and exactly half of the honey cakes out of the packet. The honey *was* very good, spicier and somehow wilder than the honey from Delta wildflowers.

"We'll be out of the pass and in Casmantium by noon," Tan said, leading her horse up to her and offering her the reins. "Shall we lay odds on it?"

Mienthe couldn't help but laugh. She laid Tan odds of three to one that they wouldn't reach the far end of the great road before midafternoon, because that way she couldn't lose—at least, she would rather lose than win.

"Your knee is better?" she remembered to ask.

"A night's rest was all it required. It'll be well enough as long as I leave the stirrups long," he assured her.

He sounded so very sincere that Mienthe wondered if he was actually concealing a good deal of pain, but so far as she could see he looked calm and relaxed, without any of the visible tension of pain. So in the end she simply nodded and guided her horse out of the sheltered nook and up the long curve of the road that led east.

There was room to ride abreast, and for a while they did. But neither of them spoke, and after a little while, Tan fell back behind Mienthe. She did not mind. She liked the illusion that she was riding alone between stone and sky, the morning light pouring through the cold air around her, the granite glittering in the sun and the clean wind against her face. She could imagine she was the only living creature within a hundred miles—and her horse, of course. The horse also seemed cheerful this bright morning, moving willingly along with a long stride, its head up and its ears pricked forward.

This road truly was wonderful, Mienthe decided. She enjoyed its long spiral climb around the curve of a mountain and the artful way it doglegged up a narrow pass between two broken crags, with the sky an amazingly dark blue above and the mountains luminous with reflected light. She enjoyed the sharp thrill of crossing a graceful bridge spanning a gulf between two narrow spires. The chasm must have been at least four hundred feet long—she counted her horse's strides to make that estimate and, turning at the end to look back at the bridge's graceful, narrow length, wondered whether it was the longest bridge in the world and what magic of making kept it from collapsing down into the gulf.

The road climbed and climbed, and then they came up and around a particularly steep and awkward turn around a dramatic cliff that raked against the sky. Mienthe immediately understood exactly why the engineers had designed the curve as they had, despite its awkwardness. As they came around the last sharp turn, they found the whole world spread out unexpectedly before them in one long eastward sweep of stone and sky, down and down and dizzyingly down, until they could see the green of trees far below, and the town of Ehre, its high wall and wide streets and granite houses faintly blurred by a haze of smoke and distance.

Mienthe had checked her horse without noticing, and now she turned to Tan and smiled.

He gazed back at her, not smiling himself. Indeed, he looked rather pale and serious. Mienthe had not realized until that moment how ner-

vous Tan was about entering Casmantium, about delivering himself
into the Arobern's hands. But he only said after a moment, lightly,
"Casmantium before noon, as I said. No doubt it shall tremble at our
coming. What were those odds?"

As it would not be kind to notice his anxiety, Mienthe laughed and
said, "It's farther than it looks, I believe, and noon's not so far away. I
think I'll win our wager yet—which is good, as you know perfectly
well it was three to one!"

She patted her horse on the neck and nudged it forward, in no particular hurry—not that she would mind losing the wager, but because
she found herself oddly reluctant to arrive at Ehre, and thus in Casmantium, with the freedom and peace of the mountains behind them.

They came down out of the mountain pass and rode through the great
iron gates, the gates that marked the border of Casmantium, exactly at
noon, when the sun stood precisely overhead and all shadows were as
small and unobtrusive as they ever could be. On the mountain side of
the gates, the paving stones of the mountain road ran broad and smooth
up into the pass behind them. Before them, on the other side of the iron
gates, the road was narrower and made simply of pounded earth, with
plain timbers to keep it from washing too badly when streams fed by
melting snow came down from the mountains in the spring. Ehre, west-
ernmost town of Casmantium, stood with its imposing square stone towers rising up behind its high stone walls, less than half a mile farther on
down this ordinary road.

They had actually come to the iron gates a scant few minutes before noon, but Tan caught Mienthe's reins and held her back until they
could tell by the shadows of the gates that the sun stood precisely at
noon. Then he led her horse through the gates onto Casmantian soil
and solemnly offered Mienthe three coins. It was absurd, of course, but
she nevertheless gave him one back. Then they traded again, so that
both of them were back where they'd begun. She tried not to laugh,
but it was impossible not to smile. It was hard to remember the fear
that had dogged their steps for those last days. Mienthe did not know
what they would find in Ehre, but she was at least confident it would
not be Linularinan agents.

After they passed through the iron gates, she turned once more to
look wistfully back up the long sweep of the road behind them. The
achingly brilliant blue of the sky stretched infinitely far, above gray
and silver mountains that shaded away to violet as they rose to meet the
sky. Mienthe could make out the narrow thread of the road, snaking its
way up and up until the narrow thread of it tipped at last over a curve

high above. She sighed and began to turn away for the final time, toward Ehre and the last long stretch of their journey. But then she paused, her attention caught by the movement of tiny black figures high above, coming slowly over that last high curve. They were so far away and so tiny that she probably would not have seen these other travelers at all except they paused, gazing down from the crest of the road as she and Tan had done, and as they paused there they were clearly silhouetted against the brilliant sky.

Though she knew other travelers must use the great road, though she knew there was no reason to suspect those barely visible flecks were anything sinister or anything to do with them at all, she nevertheless found her pleasure in the day instantly quenched, as swiftly as a smothered candle flame. "Tan," she said.

He turned, following her gaze up to the high curve of the road, and stilled. He said at last, deliberately calm, "The road is open to anyone, after all."

"Yes," said Mienthe, and heard her own voice come out small and tight.

"There's no reason to think they're anything to do with us."

"No," Mienthe agreed.

Tan gave her a level glance and added, still in that calm tone, "But we might ride on, even so. We might ride straight through Ehre and be well out in the countryside by dusk, do you think?"

"Yes," said Mienthe. She had hoped to rest in some pleasant public house in Ehre. She didn't say so, but only pressed her horse into a swinging trot toward the walls of the town, so near at hand.

But she could not believe, now, that those walls would offer anything but an illusion of safety.

Mienthe had thought Ehre a small mountain town, larger than Minas Ford, no doubt, for all the building that had been done at Minas Ford and Minas Spring in the past years, but still far smaller than Tiefenauer. Certainly Ehre had not seemed very large from above, but it was intensely busy; busier and far more crowded than she had expected. She thought it was probably a market day, for farmers with empty carts were passing in and out of the stone gates that pierced Ehre's walls. Well, mostly out, for they'd clearly disposed of their produce earlier in the day. But plenty of other people were going in or coming out. Not merely ordinary folk, either, but an astonishing number of fancy carriages and riders dressed not for the practical necessities of travel, but in finely dyed linen with lace at their wrists and delicate embroidery, and fancy rings for the men or bangles for the ladies. Mienthe thought she wouldn't have been able to wear so fine an outfit for an hour on the road without snagging a thread or ripping the lace.

"Do you suppose there's a spring fair?" Mienthe asked Tan. "Or perhaps the lord here is celebrating the birth of an heir?"

Tan had a thoughtful, wary look on his face, but it fell away almost before Mienthe had noticed it, and he smiled and shrugged with every evidence of good humor. "Perhaps a fair," he agreed. "It's useful. I much doubt anyone will look twice at strangers passing through." He touched his reins to direct his horse toward the gates that led into the town.

At first Tan's prediction seemed accurate. There were guardsmen at those stone gates, but they seemed unconcerned about travelers and simply waved everyone through after a brief exchange of words. Mienthe knew that they would do the same for herself and Tan, but she could not help feeling as though the hunted, anxious days just past must show somehow. She felt very strongly that the guards would stop them and demand knowingly, *And just what brings you to Ehre, eh, esteemed lady? Bringing trouble at your heel, are you? Linularinan agents, is it?* And while she wanted to explain about all of that to the Arobern, she certainly did not want to be taken for a hysteric or a madwoman by provincial guards here in Ehre.

She wished that Bertaud was here with her—visiting Casmantium wouldn't be frightening at all if her cousin were with her—even if he'd come bearing news of trouble and disorder in Feierabiand, everyone here would respect him and believe everything he said. She had been desperately eager to arrive in Ehre, but now she looked anxiously sideways at Tan, riding beside her on the road. He did not look in the least concerned about the guardsmen. Mienthe did not for a moment believe his confident pose. She wished she did.

But they could hardly go back through the pass.

The guardsmen asked, without much interest, what business had brought them to Ehre. Tan, with a discretion Mienthe thoroughly approved, did not go into any details. He gave his name as Teras son of Toharas and did not give hers at all; he merely said that they were on their way to Breidechboden—he pronounced the name quite creditably—with an important message from Lord Bertaud of the Delta to King Brechen Glansent Arobern.

They had agreed he would say so much, because Tan said that complicated lies were difficult to put over properly and Mienthe had suggested that she might well pass for a courier; that, indeed, after their recent hasty days of travel across country with never a decent chance to pause at any civilized house or inn, she would be hard put to look like a respectable lady. She had flatly refused, this time, to allow Tan to imply they were fleeing together from an outraged husband.

But after that nothing in the encounter followed any outline either of them had envisioned.

"You plan to go to Breidechboden?" one of the men said, in accented but quite accomplished Terheien. His gaze, from bored, had become intent. "You wish to speak to the Arobern for the Lord of the Delta?" He did not sound, as Mienthe would have expected, doubtful. He simply gave Tan a long look and Mienthe a polite nod and said, "I am glad to save you many miles. The Arobern is not in Breidechboden. He is here."

"Here? In Ehre?" Mienthe said blankly, before she could stop herself. She had meant to leave all the speaking to Tan, but in her startlement she had forgotten.

"In Ehre. Yes," said the guardsman. "This is good news, yes? Because you bring an important message. You do not have a wand?"

He meant the white wand Feierabianden couriers carried. Mienthe shook her head mutely, mindful of what Tan had said about complicated lies. She said, trying to sound confident but finding her voice coming out small and nervous, "But I do carry an urgent message, esteemed sir."

The guardsman gave a little nod. "I will escort you to the king myself, honored courier, and bring him word you have come. From the Delta, as you say you are sent by the honored Lord of the Delta." He was watching them closely, Mienthe realized, in case they had lied and the news he gave them was actually very bad news indeed.

But when she met the man's eyes, he smiled deferentially and ducked his head, and she saw he did not think they had lied at all. He thought she was probably a true courier, that she did bring word of some kind to his king, and that Tan was her proper escort. Though Mienthe *did* carry an important warning and *did* urgently want an audience with the King of Casmantium, she felt oddly like an impostor under the regard of the guardsman. She tried not to let this show.

"It's good news indeed, esteemed sir," Tan said with smooth sincerity. He drew his horse aside with hardly a hesitation, nodding to Mienthe to precede him. He, too, had understood the conclusion the guardsman had drawn and now played precisely to that conclusion. Mienthe thought probably Tan would be best pleased to step out of view, play the role of servant and protector. He would tuck himself in her shadow so that everyone would see and remember only her. She understood why he wanted to do that, so even though she found the attention of the guardsmen uncomfortable, she nodded and rode ahead of both men into the town.

It occurred to her before they had gone very far that they were going to see the King of Casmantium and that, much worse, he was actually going to see *them*. She wondered what her hair looked like— she had not managed to wash it since Kames—and might there be visible dirt on her face? Though the mountains had been clean stone and ice, mostly. But her traveling skirt was terribly crumpled, and once she discarded her coat, she was almost certain she would find a grease mark on her blouse from the previous night's dinner. She wondered whether they might really need to go *straight* to the Arobern. Might the guardsmen let them stop at some inn or public house, first? One with decent bathing facilities and a laundry?

But a sidelong glance at their escort told her how little hope there was of such a stop. They were accompanied by several guardsmen, not merely the one who had said he would escort them, though that one was clearly in charge. He looked very serious and determined. If Mienthe and Tan had wanted to break away and lose themselves in Ehre, this would have been inconvenient. As it was, except that her sudden burst of self-consciousness made her wish for a little less efficiency, the presence of the guardsmen was very convenient indeed. The streets were terribly crowded and Mienthe had no idea in the world where she was going. But the guardsmen cleared a way for them, guiding them around in a confusingly circular path that seemed to lead them strangely out of the way if they meant to go, as Mienthe had assumed, toward the center of the town.

Just as she started to wonder very seriously where exactly the guardsmen were taking them, the streets suddenly opened up and there before them was a very large stone fortress, a building not without a certain grace, but obviously intended far more for defense than for beauty. There was no evident garden, only a small courtyard of raked granite grit, with stables to one side and one massive tree on the other.

"The governor's palace," said their guide. "The Arobern is there now. I will show you where to wait and then I will take word to the king's . . . ah, the word is . . . the king's chamberlain, yes? Forgive me; I am clumsy with your language."

"But you speak Terheien very well," Mienthe said.

The man ducked his head again. "The honored courier flatters my poor skill," he said politely, and swung down from his own horse to hold hers.

Mienthe dismounted. So did Tan, though no one held his horse for him. He kept a grip on his horse's saddle, Mienthe saw, and his mouth tightened with pain as his weight came down on his bad leg. She gave him a worried glance, to which he returned only a short nod. He let go of the saddle and took two deliberate steps away from his horse, hardly limping at all, though Mienthe did not like to guess what that effort cost him.

The door to which the guardsman brought them was a plain one, set out of the way, well around the palace from the main doors. It opened onto a narrow hall, but the rugs on the stone floor were good ones, and the walls paneled in carved wood. At the end of the hall was a surprisingly pretty receiving chamber, furnished with clear attention to elegance and style. The floor was stone, with rugs of violet and blue to muffle the cold and noise. The furnishings were all wood save for the small tables, which were each topped with a sheet of polished granite. A bronze statue of a leaping stag stood in one corner, and a pewter tree with silver leaves and little birds of copper and black iron in another. There were no windows, but lamps of copper and glass hung from the paneled ceiling, and porcelain lamps stood on the tables.

"I will leave you here," said the guardsman, speaking to Mienthe. "I will tell the chamberlain. I will be very clear. I think the Arobern will send for you quickly, but I will tell them to send tea. You will wait? This is acceptable?"

"Yes," said Mienthe, wondering what he would say or do if she said *No*. She said helplessly, "But my hair—" and stopped, blushing in embarrassed confusion.

The corners of the guardsman's mouth twitched uncontrollably upward before he tamped his lips out straight again. He said very firmly, "The King of Casmantium is accustomed to receive urgent news from couriers and agents. Honored lady."

"Yes," Mienthe said, though not with nearly the firmness the man had managed. She told herself it was perfectly true. The guardsman bowed, rather more deeply than she had expected, and went out. None of the guardsmen stayed in the room with them, though she was not at all surprised to see two of them stop outside the door—there was only one door—with a patient attitude that suggested they might be there for some time.

"Your hair looks perfectly charming," Tan told her, without the hint of a smile, after the door had closed. "There's a tiny bit of ash on your chin, just—" He brushed his thumb across his own chin.

Mienthe scrubbed her face vigorously with her sleeve, sighed, and looked around. At least there were chairs, nice ones with thick cushions. She thought hot tea sounded wonderful, especially if it came with cakes or sweet rolls, and she thought even more strongly that Tan should sit down. She sank into the nearest chair herself, by way of example, and said, "I suppose the Arobern really is here."

"Yes," agreed Tan. "For a brief time, I was afraid our friends there might be taking us somewhere other than to the king, but now I rather suspect they are royal guardsmen and not merely local men who prefer soldiering to farming." He lowered himself slowly into a chair, not grimacing at all, and carefully stretched his leg out before him.

Mienthe did not ask about his knee, since the way he moved told her everything she needed to know. Anyway, she had some hope he would be able to rest it properly now. She asked instead, "You do intend to tell the king who you are, don't you? If he will see us, I mean? Because I don't know how to explain everything without explaining that." She considered for a moment and added, "I don't know how to explain *anything* without explaining that."

"If the Arobern actually sends for us, I suppose he must have the entire wretched story from top to toe," Tan said, not as if the prospect pleased him. He tilted his head against the back of his chair, closed his eyes, and let his breath out, slowly.

"I hadn't known—" Mienthe began worriedly, and stopped.

"I had no difficulty until I tried walking on it," Tan said, not opening his eyes. "I'm sure it will soon be better. You will do me the favor of not mentioning the problem to anyone."

"No, of course I won't," Mienthe promised, though she couldn't decide whether this request—or command—was based on any practical consideration or merely on Tan's habitual unwillingness to let anybody know the truth about anything.

There was a sound at the door, and she turned, thinking of the promised tea. But the sound did not presage a tray-bearing servant, but rather an elegant man in lavender and gray who bowed his head briefly to Mienthe and said, in smooth, perfect Terheien, "The Lord King Brechen Glansent Arobern is pleased to grant you audience, esteemed lady, and you, sir, if you will please accompany me."

The King of Casmantium looked very much as Mienthe had expected.

Bertaud had never spoken to her—not even to her—of the summer of the griffins, nor of his months in Casmantium that had followed. Mienthe had clearly understood, as so few people seemed to, that whether he had achieved some sort of triumph or not, whether or not he was honored for whatever he had done, her cousin had suffered somehow in that year and did not like to think of that time.

She had once believed, with a child's natural romanticism, that he had probably fallen in love with a Casmantian woman and she had broken his heart. Later, it had occurred to her that this was, perhaps, a simplistic explanation. Also, she had come to understand that her cousin's grief, whatever its source, was in some way deeper—no, not deeper, that wasn't fair. But then perhaps somehow *broader* than the grief that afflicted men who were merely unlucky with a woman. Though this assessment was based largely on the lovesick and forlorn men who trailed behind her maid Karin like a line of goslings piping piteously behind a swan—well, that was a silly image, but anyway, perhaps comparing Bertaud to her maid's hopeless collection of would-be lovers wasn't quite fair.

Whatever the source of his distaste for the subject, she had never asked her cousin any questions about that time. Even as a child, she had very well understood how someone might wish to forget the past. Or, if the past could not be forgotten, at least to keep from dragging through unpleasant memories. She had been wordlessly determined that, with her, Bertaud might speak or keep silent, exactly as he wished.

But that had not stopped her deep curiosity to know everything about her cousin and what he had done. After he had brought her to live with him in the great house, she had admired him enormously and had longed to know all the details about every admirable thing he had ever done. She had asked his guardsmen, and the servants, and she had once found the nerve to ask King Iaor, and although no one knew everything, she had learned by heart the bits they all knew and had made up stories to tell herself that explained the parts they did not know.

But she would have known the King of Casmantium anyway, because he looked so much like his son, Erich. When she saw Brechen Glansent Arobern, she almost felt as though she recognized him. It was odd to think that he could have no idea who she was.

The Arobern was a big man, burly as well as tall, who looked more like a professional soldier than a king, except for the sapphire and amethyst buttons on his shirt and the heavy gold chain around his throat. He wore unornamented black and had a black-hilted sword slung at his side, and as his close-cropped hair and heavy beard were also black, he made rather a grim, aggressive impression, which Mienthe supposed was purposeful. Certainly it was effective. His jaw was heavy, but his deep-set eyes, glinting with wit as well as forceful energy, prevented him from looking dull or brutish. She would have been afraid of him, except she saw him through Erich's memory as well as her own eyes, so she saw kindness and generosity in his face, as well as aggressive energy.

The king sat in a plain chair of polished granite, in a room that was not large and yet managed, with its violet-draped walls and thick indigo rugs and the sapphire-blue glass of its lanterns, to seem ostentatious. Though there were other chairs in the room—plain wood—everyone else in the room was standing.

There were several guardsmen and servants, but there were also some few people who were clearly more important than these attendants. Close by the king's side, leaning casually against the back of the stone chair, stood a slight, fine-boned man with perfectly white hair. Mienthe immediately recognized this man. Bertaud might not like to speak of Casmantium, but both King Iaor and Erich had described him to her. Though King Iaor had disliked him, Erich had told her that while he was impossible to deceive, he was also wise and kind. *He's the only man in Casmantium who isn't a little afraid of my father*, Erich had said. *When he's kind to you, it isn't because you're a prince.*

This was Beguchren Teshrichten, who, Erich said, had been a mage but who, so King Iaor had said, had somehow lost his magecraft— used it up or burned it out, or the griffins had burned it out when they defeated him. *Something* had happened to him, but King Iaor had not been clear about exactly what that was.

But Lord Beguchren *looked* like a mage. Despite his white hair, at first she did not think he was very old. Then she looked again and was not sure, because his opaque pewter-gray eyes somehow seemed ancient. He was a very small man, no taller than Mienthe herself—if anything, he was a little shorter than she was. Despite his small size, the impenetrable calm in his pewter-dark eyes made Lord Beguchren rather intimidating, especially because he was also thoroughly elegant. There was delicate white embroidery on his white shirt, which had buttons of pearl and just a little lace at the wrists—Mienthe, who was not ordinarily much interested in fine clothing, instantly longed for a gown made by his tailor—and there were very fine sapphires set in the silver rings on three fingers of his left hand.

Behind this man and a little to the side stood a man who was so much taller that he made Beguchren Teshrichten look as small as a child. He had broad shoulders and big hands and a strong, bony face that was not exactly handsome. Yet he owned, Mienthe could not help noticing, a lanky, raw-boned masculinity that was, in its way, more striking than ordinary handsomeness.

The tall man was also particularly perceptive: For all Tan was working to stay quietly in the background, the greater part of his attention was definitely fixed on Tan and not on Mienthe. She wondered how Tan had caught his interest so quickly and definitively. The tall man did not seem to wish to stare, but he looked again and again at Tan with quick, covert glances, each time looking away at once. Mienthe frowned at him. He noticed it after a moment, took a deep breath, closed his eyes for a moment, and then gave Mienthe a carefully attentive look and a smile. She did not find his gaze aggressive like the Arobern's nor unfathomable like Beguchren's, but curious and even friendly. If not for his strange reaction to Tan, she would have thought it the look of a warmhearted man who wished to believe the best of every stranger. But there *was* that reaction, so she did not know what to think.

Beside the tall man stood a small, delicate woman with lovely molasses-dark hair and great natural poise. By the way she rested her hand possessively on his arm, she was clearly his wife. There was no sign of warmth or friendliness from her, but there was no hostility, either. Her gaze was, Mienthe decided, professionally intent and curious. She did not seem to share her husband's fascination with Tan, but gazed steadily and analytically at Mienthe. It was the sort of look Mienthe expected from a mage. Probably she *was* a mage, whether Lord Beguchren was or not. For all her cool dispassion, Mienthe was absurdly glad to see another woman in the room.

Mienthe wanted to look at Tan, but he was a step behind her. So after a moment, since there was plainly nothing else to do, she walked forward, offered the Arobern a very small bow—he was not her king, so although she longed to be able to ask someone, she thought it must be wrong for her to do more. Then, straightening, she waited for the king to address her.

The Arobern nodded back, very grave and regal. He said without preamble, in strongly accented but understandable Terheien, "You did not send me a wand, but I think you are a courier. From the Delta, I am informed. Also from the Safiad, yes?"

Mienthe stared at him for a moment. She remembered Tan saying, *I suppose he must have the entire wretched story from top to toe.* But she did not know how to begin.

Then Tan breathed in her ear, "Whose cousin are you? Well?"

Mienthe blinked. She took a deep breath and said, her voice only wavering a little, "Lord King"—she thought that was the correct Casmantian form of address—"Lord King, I am not precisely a courier. But it is true I carry a warning from the Delta. From my cousin. I'm—my name is Mienthe daughter of Beraod. Bertaud son of Boudan is my cousin. He—I—I know you are an honorable man and a strong king. So I came to you, because there is trouble in the Delta and I did not know where else to go."

There was a pause, during which the King of Casmantium looked hard at Mienthe. He did not smile or nod, and for a moment she was afraid he did not believe her. Then he stood up and inclined his head to her, and she saw that though she had taken him by surprise, he did not doubt her. She supposed few people dared lie to him. Certainly not with the rather alarming Beguchren Teshrichten by his side.

"A chair for Lady Mienthe," the Arobern commanded, and waited for one to be brought over before he dropped back into his own chair. He made a broad gesture that dismissed most of the guardsmen and nearly all of the servants. Then, once the room was more nearly private, he said, "I have had word from the Safiad. That is why I came to Ehre, so that couriers from Feierabiand could come to me more swiftly. Now you say you are come directly from the Delta, not from the Safiad but on your own account? Tell me your warning."

It seemed an unbelievable tale when Mienthe laid it out, which she tried to do in order, from Tan's appearance in Tiefenauer carrying secrets he'd stolen from the Linularinan spymaster, straight on through his kidnapping right out of a guarded house by that same spymaster and then the immediate invasion of the Delta by Linularinan soldiers. It sounded unbelievable even to her. She stumbled embarrassedly through an explanation of how she'd found Tan, of how she might be waking into the mage gift, though she didn't feel like she was becoming a mage, but really she did not know what becoming a mage felt like—here, though no one interrupted, Beguchren Teshrichten and the tall man exchanged a significant look, and Mienthe stopped.

"Go on," said the Arobern, with an impatient frown for his own people.

Mienthe hesitated for a moment, but when no one else said anything, she went on to describe the book, the one with the empty pages, that the Linularinan spymaster had brought with him from Teramondian. She looked again at Tan in case he should want to explain about the book. He only nodded at her again, so she explained how they thought Tan must have taken some powerful legist-working or law out of the book and how the Linularinan spymaster, or someone, seemed amazingly determined to get it back.

Mienthe looked from one to another of her audience, unable to gauge what anybody thought of any of this. She said uncertainly, "And then when we thought we might go north, Tan and I, we were afraid we might find Linularinan agents before us. They won't *stop*. I don't know if King Iaor knows all this yet, though some word must surely have got north by this time. But I don't know whether he's free to respond to Linularinum's provocation, because of the griffins. You do know about that? That's what was in the message you were sent, isn't that right? A mage of theirs, named Kairaithin, I think, brought word that the Wall, the Great Wall my cousin helped build, that it was cracked through. But was there anything about Linularinum in that message?"

"No," said the Arobern, looking at her.

"Well, then I bring you that word," Mienthe said simply. "We don't know why they are so horribly determined, but we think—that is, I think—"

"We," said Tan quietly, the first time he had spoken.

Mienthe nodded, grateful for his support. "Maybe it's not so, but we think it's something to do with the book and the magic of law it held, and we think there were Linularinan agents still behind us in the pass. Maybe three hours behind? Just at the crest of the mountain when we had reached the iron gates. Though it might not have been—that is, honest travelers might also have come behind us by chance."

The Arobern looked at Mienthe for a moment. Then he studied Tan for a much longer moment. At last he said to Beguchren Teshrichten, "What do *you* say, hah?"

The small man gave his king an impenetrable look and then glanced up at the tall man with the quirk of one frost-white eyebrow. He asked, "Gereint?"

The tall man looked carefully at Mienthe and then glanced at Tan, though he looked away again at once with a slight wince. He took a deep breath, shrugged, and said to Beguchren, his voice exactly as deep and gravelly as Mienthe had expected, but somehow not harsh, "I don't know whether the honored lady is a mage. I'm looking right at her and still I can't tell. I told you how oddly magecraft has been behaving of late. That may be interfering with my perception. I look at the honored lady and sometimes I think she's a mage and sometimes I think she's nothing like a mage." He glanced at Tan once more and away.

"But the man?" Beguchren Teshrichten said patiently.

"Oh, well . . . the man. I don't think *he's* a mage; that's not what I'm seeing. But forces are not simply bending around him as they bend around a mage." Gereint pointed one powerful finger at Tan, who flinched just perceptibly. "Forces—events—every chance in the whole world is twisting, distorting, and folding right *there*. I've never seen anything like it. I've never heard of anything like it. I can't think of a single passage in Warichteier's *Principia* or any other book that refers to anything remotely like it. I certainly can't do the phenomenon justice, not being a poet, but if you'll forgive a poor attempt, I'd say it's as though this man here is the hinge around which the whole age is trying to turn."

This time Beguchren lifted both eyebrows. Then, while everyone else, including Tan, stared at his tall friend who had come out with such astonishing statements, he gave the Arobern a significant look.

The Arobern said to Mienthe, "Three hours behind you, hah?" Then he turned to one of the guardsmen, the one who had escorted Mienthe and Tan through Ehre, and commanded, "Set a guard on the iron gates. At once, do you hear? I wish to see anyone who comes through those gates. I wish to see these travelers personally, you understand, whoever they might be. And set a stronger guard on all the gates into Ehre—be quick to do that. Anyone who seems perhaps a little out of the ordinary, you understand? Men who are neither merchants nor farmers nor of any trade you can name. Look at these people for me, and send me word if you have any doubt what you have caught in your net."

The guardsman bowed without a word and went out quickly.

The Arobern got to his feet. Mienthe jumped up immediately, not to stay seated while the king stood, and looked anxiously at Tan. Practiced as he was at showing only what he wished to show, he looked faintly stunned. Mienthe thought his expression was sincere. She certainly thought he had every reason to look stunned.

To Mienthe, the king said, "Honored lady, I will ask Lady Tehre Amnachudran Tanshan to grant you the hospitality of her household, if this is agreeable to you and if Lady Tehre will permit me the liberty."

The tiny woman had been staring, with everyone else, at Tan. Now she transferred her interested gaze from Tan to Mienthe and said, in nearly accentless Terheien, "Yes, I am pleased to make such an offer. That will do very well." She smiled, a sharp expression but not unkind, and added, directly to Mienthe, "I'm sure you wish to wash and shift your clothing. If I haven't anything to suit you, I've got some cloth we can easily run up into a nice gown—I've been considering cloth lately. Working with cloth is more complicated and interesting than you'd think. Of course everything is fine if you apply any tension straight along the threads, and cloth distorts symmetrically if you apply tension at forty-five degrees to the angle of the warp and weft threads, but what I can't make out is the equations that allow you to predict the degree and kind of deformation if the tension is applied at some intermediate angle—"

Gereint broke into this discourse without the least surprise or fuss, "Tehre, if you please, I imagine Lady Mienthe would like to have something to eat at a civilized table while you find appropriate clothing for her." He added to Mienthe, "I think I am able to assure you, Lady Mienthe, that no Linularinan agent, mage or otherwise, will trouble your rest in *my* household."

Mienthe nodded, trying not to laugh. *Tehre's Wall*, the griffin had said to her cousin. So Lady Tehre had made that Wall. Mienthe found she was not at all surprised. She wondered what sort of protections might surround a household that included Lady Tehre and her husband. Very secure ones, probably.

Then she realized the king had not said he would send *Tan* with Lady Tehre, and hesitated, wondering whether she should say something, or ask, or protest.

Before she could speak, the Arobern said to Tan, "You, I wish to give into the hands of my friend Beguchren Teshrichten and my mage Gereint Enseichen. Will you permit this?"

For once, Tan did not seem to have any smooth response to hand.

CHAPTER 11

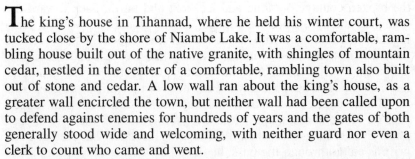

The king's house in Tihannad, where he held his winter court, was tucked close by the shore of Niambe Lake. It was a comfortable, rambling house built out of the native granite, with shingles of mountain cedar, nestled in the center of a comfortable, rambling town also built out of stone and cedar. A low wall ran about the king's house, as a greater wall encircled the town, but neither wall had been called upon to defend against enemies for hundreds of years and the gates of both generally stood wide and welcoming, with neither guard nor even a clerk to count who came and went.

But the gates of Tihannad were guarded now, and all but hidden by the crowd of folk waiting to be admitted. Jos saw at once that very few folk were leaving, or at least not heading south; all efforts were bent toward getting in.

Lord Bertaud paused when he saw the crowded roads and the press at the gates, his eyebrows rising. He might have been wondering, as Jos certainly was, whether the folk pressing into Tihannad expected walls of stone and timber to defend against griffins who rode upon the wind. Though perhaps it was not the walls themselves but the lake so near those walls that was expected to ward away fire. Perhaps it even would.

"I would have thought Tiearanan would be the retreat of choice," Bertaud commented, gazing down toward the press at the gates. "Though perhaps it is, for those who are able to climb that steep road at speed. These may be local folk who fear they may not come swiftly enough to any more-distant shelter."

Jos only nodded distractedly, and Kairaithin did not even seem to hear these comments. After a moment, Bertaud shrugged and led the way down across the slope of the mountain toward the town.

For a few minutes, they walked in silence. Jos thought about the wall, and a little about Kes, but that was too painful and he tried to think about other things—anything else—only then he thought, *So here we are, walking down toward Tihannad,* and that was such a strange, uncomfortable thought that he hardly knew what to do with it. Six years alone in the high mountains had surely unfit him for human company, and what would he possibly do now in a clamorous town? A *Feierabianden* town crowded with fearful farmers who hoped their walls or their lake would protect them.

Lord Bertaud would hardly have brought Jos trailing at his heel to any purpose. Only the exigency of the moment had compelled Kairaithin to shift them all, and he had brought them here. But though that was well enough for Lord Bertaud, Tihannad was no place for Jos.

His steps slowed, and then stopped. He looked uncertainly up into the broken country of stone and ice, east and north, back toward the high pass and his abandoned cottage. His fire would burn without ceasing, but would his goat and all the foolish chickens know how to make their way from meadow to meadow along the silver length of the nameless river, down to warmer country and better pastures? The goat, perhaps, he thought, but probably not the hens or the vain white cock.

But he could hardly make his way back up through that rugged pass on foot and alone and without anything at all in the way of supplies. Even if he could, when the Great Wall finally shattered and the griffins came through the pass, he doubted whether they would spare anything they found in their way, man or goat or bird. Probably they would tear every stone apart from every other stone merely with the fiery wind of their passage.

Kairaithin, too, had halted. He had followed Jos's gaze, up and east and north, but there was nothing a man could understand in his eyes. Jos wondered what the griffin mage was seeing. Not these mountains, nor a small abandoned stone cottage. Fire, and the Wall, and the red dust where the king of the griffins had lunged forward just that little bit too fast . . .

Jos regarded the griffin mage with worry. Kairaithin did not seem to have recovered his emotional balance, whatever that properly comprised, from the brief, shocking battle by the Wall. He seemed stunned, perhaps by his failed attempt to destroy Kes; or by his awareness that the Great Wall must surely break; or, most likely of all, from the awareness that the king of the griffins was dead and that Kairaithin himself had killed him.

Jos had expected Kairaithin to leave them here above Tihannad once he had brought them here, to let them make their own way down to the lake and into the town. He had expected the griffin mage to take himself away alone to some deserted bit of desert where he might think or curse or worry or consider the new span of his options, or whatever it was that a griffin might do at such a moment of personal loss. He had little idea what that might be, but he did believe that Kairaithin felt the king's death as a personal loss, and far more bitterly for how it had happened.

Instead, the griffin mage had followed the men down along the side of the mountain toward the lake, as though, Jos thought, he simply could not imagine where else he might go. Now, standing with his face raised to the high mountains, his expression closed and still, he looked, for the first time, not only drawn and weary but also old.

Then Lord Bertaud looked over his shoulder and impatiently snapped at both of them, "Come!"

Jos flinched, more in startlement than in alarm. But, after all, where else could he go? He took a step after the Feierabianden lord.

But, to his surprise, Kairaithin also flinched and lowered his head and came, like a servant or a dog. Jos had not precisely expected a flash of anger or offended pride; he had not thought about that command or its tone enough to expect anything. But he was deeply shocked by the weary compliance he saw in the griffin mage's bowed head.

It seemed to shock Bertaud as well, for he turned quickly and came back toward them—toward Kairaithin, because he was not looking at Jos. He began to reach out a hand as though he would touch the griffin mage, grip his arm or his shoulder. But then he stopped and his hand fell back to his side. But the intensity of his gaze seemed to compel a response from Kairaithin, who lifted his head and met Bertaud's eyes.

They stood on the cold windswept stone of the mountain, the two of them, Feierabianden lord and griffin mage, as though for that moment they were the only two living creatures in the world. Jos could not understand what he saw between them. He thought it was neither friendship nor enmity, but perhaps some strange kind of understanding that owed something to both.

Bertaud said quietly, "I beg your pardon."

"You need not," Kairaithin answered. He bowed his head again, and this time Jos saw that he did this with a kind of deliberate effort, yet not precisely unwillingly. He said, "Everything I have done has led to this moment. All the important choices fell to me, and I was wrong, and wrong again, and all that has come or will come now is due to my lack of foresight."

"No," said Bertaud at once, forcefully. "Six years ago, if you had not made Kes into a creature of fire, everything that you feared for your people would have happened exactly as you foresaw it. Your diminished people could never have faced both Feierabiand and Casmantium, and it would have come to that eventually. Those Casmantian cold mages were determined to destroy you all, and they would have done it. I believe they would, if not right at that moment, then very soon—"

"I should have foreseen what a weapon I made, when I made Kes—"

"You did! Of course you did! Why should you mind giving your people a potent weapon? It was me you didn't foresee, and how could you have? How could anyone have?"

"You call *griffins*?" Jos exclaimed, utterly shocked by this sudden realization—Feierabiand for calling, yes, very well, but calling *griffins*?

Then, as both Bertaud and Kairaithin turned toward him, he understood just how foolish he had been to cry this realization aloud to the listening mountains. Six years alone had been too many—he would never have exclaimed aloud when he'd been practicing proper spycraft, no matter how shocked he'd been—he took a step back.

Kairaithin, his mouth tight, the expression in his black eyes unreadable, began to lift his hand.

Jos took another step back, knowing there was no point to it, no flight possible, nothing to say. He had in one flashing moment—too late—understood what it would do to the griffins to know that they could be commanded like dogs, and understood as well that no one in the world knew they could be, except those standing here on this mountain above Niambe Lake. It was impossible that any oath of silence could possibly satisfy Kairaithin. He took a hard breath, straightened his shoulders, and looked the griffin mage full in the face. He saw no mercy there. He did not expect to, for he knew that mercy was not something griffins understood. He found himself thinking of Kes, beautiful and inhuman and just as merciless as a griffin. He tried to think of her, instead, as she had been years ago, when she had been merely human. He could remember, though with some effort, the shy, graceful girl who had shunned company—though not his—and liked to run barefoot in the hills. He shut his eyes to better hold her image before his mind's eye.

"No!" snapped Bertaud.

Jos opened his eyes.

The griffin mage had stopped, his hand only half raised. He was looking at Bertaud.

"He won't speak of it." Bertaud did not look at Jos, only at Kairaithin. "It's not his fault he realized. We were careless—I was careless. But he's accomplished at keeping secrets, and he'll tell no one. Whom would he tell, and to what purpose?"

"He will cry it from the rooftops of your human town; to everyone and in every direction of the wind he will call it out. He will do it to compel you to act."

"*Events* will compel me to act! Unless we find another choice! Another wind to ride, not one that rises from anything that has yet happened!"

"Great secrets are always safest if no one knows them—as anyone accustomed to secrets is well aware!"

Jos couldn't quite keep from flinching. For a long moment they all stood in silence. Jos did not move. He tried not even to breathe. But Lord Bertaud and the griffin mage were glaring at each other; for the moment they both seemed to have forgotten him.

He found himself turning over this new and shocking revelation in his mind—Lord Bertaud could call griffins, so he could command them to cease their attack, only he did not want to command them. Because—and if Jos had not been so closely acquainted with griffins over the past year, he would never have understood this—because they could never accept being commanded. The knowledge that they could be called to heel by a man would *destroy* them—in fact, if they knew that it was possible for a man to command them, they would probably become even more determined to kill everyone and tear down all the country of earth.

Several odd comments he had not quite understood, from both Bertaud and Kairaithin, suddenly fell into place.

He said suddenly, without truly knowing beforehand that he was going to speak at all, "What if you get Tastairiane by himself? What if you demonstrate to *him* what power you hold? No, better, not merely a demonstration and a warning; what if you simply command him to turn away from this wind, to bid Kes leave be the Wall, to keep his people in their desert?"

Both Lord Bertaud and Kairaithin turned to stare at him. Jos tried not to flinch—he had not exactly meant to make himself the renewed focus of their common attention, only the idea had occurred to him—likely he had not understood properly—there was probably some very good reason that wouldn't work—

Bertaud said at last, "Kairaithin?"

"A dangerous wind," the griffin mage said, not looking at him. He was looking at Jos, but now with something like his accustomed fierce power in his fiery black gaze. "As goes the Lord of Fire and Air, so go the People of Fire and Air. If Tastairiane Apailika is filled with fury and despair, then fury and despair will burn through the country of fire. But . . ."

Bertaud said nothing. Jos thought he was probably trying not to exclaim, *Well, that's all right, then!* Though perhaps not. Jos had lived in Feierabiand for many years, more than long enough to know how violently a man who could call an animal hated to do anything to harm that animal. How much more intense would that revulsion of feeling be if you could command not animals, but a fierce and beautiful people? A people who would surely die if they knew they were constrained, either in violent resistance or simply in outraged bursts of fire and sand?

"But no king is eternal," said Kairaithin, continuing his earlier thought. "At some time in the future, Tastairiane Apailika will no longer be the Lord of Fire and Air, and at that time, so long as the People of Fire and Air remain, another king might set a new and better direction." His eyes were on Bertaud's. He said, "I do not know how I may come at Tastairiane Apailika, or how I may bring him alone to you. But I will try. If you give me leave."

Lord Bertaud said flatly, "Go."

Kairaithin blurred away into the air and the cold sunlight, and was gone.

Bertaud stood rigid for a moment, looking at nothing; at the slant of the cold light across the lake, perhaps. Then he shuddered and rubbed his hands across his face, and looked up at last at Jos.

Jos did not speak. He did not know what to say.

"Your suggestion might prove a good one," Bertaud said at last. "I thank you. I certainly bear you no ill will. But I don't know whether I should have stopped him. You understand the price of forbearance? You must *never* even imply that there is a shadow of a chance that you might ever tell *anyone*—you must swear to me you will *never*—"

"I understand," Jos assured him fervently. "I promise you, lord." He hesitated. Then he said, "You know I don't hate them? I'm afraid of them, but I don't hate them and I don't want them destroyed, and I don't know how many other men could swear to that, but I can. I do. I'll tell no one, lord. I do swear it. I'm sorry I ever guessed, except as it may let Kairaithin take down that bastard Tastairiane. I wouldn't be sorry if *he* were destroyed."

"Earth and stone." Bertaud rubbed his face again, then looked up and nodded. "Very well. I accept your word and your promise. *Keep* it, man. You may. In the end, if I must, I'll reveal it myself."

Of course he would. So long as . . . "Kairaithin cannot find a way to slip sideways around this . . . affinity of yours and kill you himself?"

Jos tried not to sound too diffident. "To him, that must surely seem an acceptable solution, lord?"

Bertaud laughed, without much humor. "I'm confident he wishes he had when he had the chance. No. It's too late now for him to reach after *that* wind. He can't approach me without my awareness, and I'm alert to the possibility, I assure you." He gazed down toward Tihannad for some time in silence.

Jos supposed the Feierabianden lord knew the measure and limits of his own gift. Nevertheless, he resolved to stay near him if he could, so he might at least cry a warning if Lord Bertaud was mistaken.

Bertaud nodded to Jos at last and led the way that last little distance down to the lake and then along the lakeshore road to the gates of Tihannad and, with some difficulty, through the crowd that pressed forward. But once at the gate, the men there recognized him, of course.

"Begging your pardon, but it's the king's orders, my lord, because of the trouble in the south," an officer of the guardsmen told Bertaud. "Everyone to be let in, but we're to direct them as best we may. Everyone's taking in one or two families, and the king's ordered temporary shelter set up for the rest—"

"Trouble in the *south*," Bertaud said. He and Jos exchanged a baffled look.

"So they say, my lord," said the officer. "Couriers have been riding in and out all today and yesterday, until one would expect them to wear out their wands as well as their horses. His Majesty is in his house, so far as we've had word here, and I'm sure he'll be glad to see you, my lord, if you'll go up. I'm sure we can find horses for you and your companion—"

"Thank you," said Lord Bertaud, with a shake of his head that suggested, not that he was rejecting the offer, but that he had no more idea than Jos what might have happened in the south. "Yes, we would be glad if you could find an extra beast or two. *Where* in the south, do you know?"

The officer gave Bertaud a close look and lowered his voice. "Ah, my lord, I'm sorry if I'm the first to tell you so, but what we hear is those sly Linularinan bastards have crossed the river into the Delta, taking advantage of what they hope will be trouble here. I don't know as whether that's true, my lord. You should ask at the king's house—"

"Yes," Bertaud said, in a blank tone.

King Iaor received them without formality, in a large, plain room with five tables, where at the moment maps were spread out on all but one of the tables and pinned up on three of the walls. The king was attended

by two of his generals and by the captain of his personal guard, and by
another man for whom Bertaud spared a sharp look.

"Yes, my queen is returned, and my daughters, thankfully all safe,"
said the king, evidently in explanation of that man's presence. He
opened one hand in a curt gesture, signaling that they need not bow or
stand otherwise on ceremony. "They are come weary and bedraggled,
but safe. Earth and iron, if I had known we rode on *campaign*, I would
hardly have invited them to accompany me! Tell me that they will be
safe here." He cocked his head at Bertaud, who wordlessly shook his
head.

"No?" said the king, and gestured for two of his attendants to unroll another map on the only clear table. He said, "One may possibly
expect Tihannad itself to be protected by the intrinsic magic of the
lake . . . we do expect so. Nevertheless, I think I will send the queen
and my little girls north to Tieararan. If there is trouble from any direction, it will surely come there last."

"And from what direction do we expect trouble? From what other
direction," Bertaud amended. "From the south, is it? What is this I hear
about Linularinum coming across the river into the Delta?"

The king nodded sharply. "Would I was able to deny that word! But
I fear it is true enough. Niethe herself tells me she fled only just in time.
Bertaud, I regret that I must inform you that your cousin Mienthe in-
sisted on remaining in Tiefenauer."

Lord Bertaud stood very still, as though he had received a blow
and was waiting to feel the extent of the damage.

"Likely she is perfectly safe. Kohorrian will surely not allow his
men to pillage, least of all your own house in your own town. He will
not wish to offend the Delta so seriously—"

"He has offended me," Bertaud said. His voice had gone quiet and
hard, with an undertone of ferocity nearly as dangerous as a griffin's.

"Well, he has assuredly offended me!" snapped the king, and
slammed a fist down without warning onto the nearest table. "My Niethe, *my little girls*, riding night and day through dangerous sloughs
and along animal trails, because Kohorrian thinks if we are sufficiently
distracted in the north, then he may make as free as he likes with the
south! We shall find a way to sort out this trouble with the griffins, I
trust we shall, and then we shall assuredly ride south and explain
clearly to Kohorrian the depths of our offense."

"May we find it so," said Bertaud grimly.

Iaor nodded. "There is word that Linularinan forces are active west
of the Delta as well, over toward Minas Ford and Minas Spring. Nevertheless, we believe that the greatest part of his ambition, whatever ill-

conceived notion informs it, concerns the Delta itself. I should send you south—"

Bertaud opened his mouth, but then closed it again without speaking. Clearly he longed to take a fast horse and as many men as the king would give him and ride south as fast as he could go. But, thought Jos, even more clearly he knew that if the Wall above Niambe Lake shattered, he would need to be right here, right *here*, where the griffins must come through the narrow pass and pass by the lake. He could not possibly ride south, not on any account, not even if his pride were scored beyond bearing at this extraordinary Linularinan insult, not even if he had a wife and a dozen children in Tiefenauer and far less if his greatest hostage to the exigencies of war were a mere cousin, with which in any case the Lord of the Delta was reputedly well-endowed.

"So I am to gather you have no good word to bring me?" Iaor asked, regarding Bertaud narrowly. "Advise me, my old friend, and we shall consider what we may best do."

Lord Bertaud took a slow breath. Another.

Jos wanted to say, *You cannot possibly go south*, only Bertaud would not likely welcome advice he knew already, nor Jos's temerity in offering it. He said nothing.

"As you permit me," Bertaud said at last. "Yes, send Niethe and the girls to Tiearanan. Then, my king, take what force you have gathered and ride south yourself. See to the Delta. Reprimand Kohorrian. Leave me a small force here. If the Wall breaks and the griffins come through the pass—and I think it likely will, and so they may well—in this exigency, my king, trust me to turn them, with such allies as I am able to persuade. Or if I cannot turn them, then nothing can, and as that is so, your armies will be better occupied elsewhere."

From the king's blank expression, this was not the advice he had anticipated. He met Bertaud's eyes in silence. There was something between them, Jos guessed; something difficult of which this moment reminded them both. But neither man spoke of it. The king only asked at last, "Shall I trust your judgment in this? Do you trust your own judgment in this?"

"Yes," said Bertaud, his tone flat. "As I beg you will, my king."

"Ah." The king glanced around at his maps, down at the nearest. Up again. He glanced questioningly at Jos.

"He does well enough with me," Bertaud said. He offered no explanation, as he had offered none in all this tangled implication and half-truth.

However, the king asked for none. He only nodded and glanced again down at the map. Then he looked up again. "My generals"—he nodded right and left at the sober, quiet men who attended him—"have been gathering men this past day. They will be able to ride the day after tomorrow, or possibly the day after that. Perhaps with me, perhaps with you, perhaps with neither of us. I will wish to hear in more detail of what you have discovered regarding the Wall and the griffins; we will both wait for further news from the south. Then we will decide, in all good order, what we shall do."

"My king, I can desire nothing but what you desire," Lord Bertaud said formally, and bowed.

Jos was already certain that, whatever the king wanted and whatever he thought was important, the final decision would place Bertaud firmly in the path of any incursion of griffins through the northern pass. It was absolutely essential that the decision fall out that way, and so Lord Bertaud would say whatever he must, do whatever he must, to be certain it did.

But he was also certain that unless Kairaithin said and did whatever *he* had to, in order to ensure a private meeting between Lord Bertaud and Tastairiane, and quickly, quickly—before the Wall shattered—no good outcome was even vaguely possible, whatever men and the kings of men might arrange among themselves.

CHAPTER 12

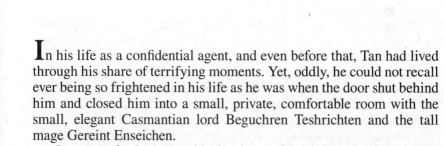

In his life as a confidential agent, and even before that, Tan had lived through his share of terrifying moments. Yet, oddly, he could not recall ever being so frightened in his life as he was when the door shut behind him and closed him into a small, private, comfortable room with the small, elegant Casmantian lord Beguchren Teshrichten and the tall mage Gereint Enseichen.

It was perfectly reasonable for the confidential agent of one country to be afraid if he fell into the power of a different country. Certain obvious events were likely to unfold from that point. But an awareness of that fact did not explain Tan's fear, and he knew it did not.

Mienthe had insisted on staying close by him, which Tan considered very nearly heroism as it meant she must postpone her bath. He had considered prompting her to go with the Casmantian lady, as the Arobern clearly wished. Compliance with the Arobern's wishes might well have been tactically the wiser course. But, though he was ashamed of the depth of his own need for her support, he was too grateful for her presence to make any effort to send her away.

Because he was ashamed and angry as well as frightened, Tan said sharply, "Well, Lord Beguchren, as there is no great need to dissemble, shall we be plain? You mean to pry open my mind and heart and discover what is written there. Is that not true?"

Mienthe, shocked and distressed, took half a step forward, but Lord Beguchren only gave Tan a slight, imperturbable smile, tipped his head toward a chair drawn up near a wide fireplace, and said mildly, in smooth, unaccented Terheien, "If you will sit, we will make an effort to discover whether or not that will be necessary."

Tan did not move.

"He is frightened," said the tall man. Gereint Enseichen. His tone was matter-of-fact, utterly lacking in censure. He added wryly, "You have this effect on ordinary men, my lord. I well remember our own first meeting." As he spoke, he rearranged the chairs in the room so that four of them formed a neat rectangle in front of the fire, a porcelain lamp hanging behind each. Then he settled in one of the chairs, folding up his long limbs with every sign of satisfaction. "Honored lady, if you will?" he said to Mienthe, indicating one of the remaining chairs, and, "My lord? Honored sir?" he added, nodding toward the others.

The white-haired Casmantian lord was not quite smiling, but nevertheless he looked amused. He said mildly, "Well, but I was constrained by a royal command to terrify you, Gereint," but he also moved to take the indicated chair.

"You terrified me for a great long time after that," the mage said. "You still do." He did not sound in the least terrified, but rather warmly affectionate.

Tan saw very clearly that the two men, however different they might seem, were close friends. For some inexplicable reason, he found this reassuring. And he did not want to frighten Mienthe by letting her see his own fear.

She laid a tentative hand on his arm. "You probably should sit, do you think?"

Tan's knee *was* making itself a trifle obvious: A long, slow ache had spread from the knee all the way up and down his leg. He gazed for a moment at Mienthe's anxious, earnest face and then found himself able to walk forward, almost without limping, and take his place in the appointed chair. The stiffness of his movements owed nothing to his bad knee. He did not understand why he could not mime relaxation, amiability, dense stupidity . . . He had drawn one mask or another across his own manner for so long that he would have thought the exercise had become effortless. But all masks seemed far out of reach today. He said sharply, to the mage, "What is it you see in me? What do you mean by saying that, what, events turn around me?"

"A very good question," agreed the Casmantian mage amiably. He regarded Tan with great curiosity for a moment, then looked away, wincing slightly. He told the fire, "One certainly understands why mages have no difficulty tracking you. It's quite a remarkable effect, when you try to examine it closely."

"I wish I—" Lord Beguchren began, but cut that thought short.

"As do we all," said Gereint Enseichen, in a tone both wry and deliberately brisk.

Mienthe gazed at him for a moment, then at the elegant Lord Beguchren. She started to speak, then visibly changed her mind about what she meant to say and said instead, "Whatever Tan is, *I* can't be a mage. Isn't that right? I don't see anything strange when I look at him. And my cousin said I couldn't be a mage because I didn't hate his friend. Kairaithin, I mean. The griffin mage."

Lord Beguchren regarded her thoughtfully. "If I remember your story correctly, after you were forced to flee Tiefenauer, you went directly to your father's house at Kames, to which you had directed the honored Tan. Why did you go there, rather than north to find your lord cousin?"

"Well, I . . . I don't . . ." Mienthe frowned. She opened her hands in a gesture of bafflement. "I don't . . . I don't really know why. Only . . ." She shook her head and looked back at Tan, her brows drawing together in puzzlement.

"You were drawn to find the honored Tan in Linularinum, after Istierinan Hamoddian had taken him; you found him without difficulty; and then again you were drawn after him to Kames. Gereint? You do not believe the lady is a mage?"

The tall man sat forward, turning so he could study Mienthe without looking also at Tan. He tilted his head in polite curiosity. "Perhaps you may have a very weak mage power, Lady Mienthe. That might explain why you have found yourself drawn toward the honored Tan without being exactly aware of what draws you, and also why you were able to endure the presence of a griffin mage without distress."

Mienthe nodded uncertainly.

Tan said sharply, not uncertain at all on this point, "Whatever gift or power the lady holds, I can assure you, it is hardly *weak*."

"Thus the world insists on defying our expectations," Lord Beguchren murmured. He steepled his hands, regarding both Mienthe and Tan over the tips of his fingers. "The lady holds a powerful gift, but nothing a mage can recognize. Though your presence, honored Tan, distorts the world, we are told that you are not yourself a mage." He paused, his expression becoming even more bland and unreadable. "Mages do not ordinarily devote great attention to the work of ordinary gifts. Possibly this has constituted an oversight."

"So, now?" Tan challenged him.

"I, too, have directed only scant attention to the gift of law," the elegant lord said softly. "A regrettable neglect." He paused, but then went on, speaking directly to Tan, "While the lady's gift is interesting, it is yours that appears to require urgent attention. Your current condition has clearly come about not because of the working of any actual magecraft, but because of the great influence of the legistwork you have taken into yourself. The conclusion to which we are guided by events is that very influential factions within Linularinum are so distressed by the fact that they have lost this work that they are willing to provoke Iaor Safiad to war to regain it." He paused.

Tan said quietly—he could manage a quiet, civil tone if he concentrated—"I suspect Istierinan—or, yes, I know, possibly some faceless, nameless Linularinan faction—knew that your Great Wall had cracked through. So they wagered that King Iaor would be compelled to commit his strength in the north, giving them a relatively free hand to act in the south."

"And yet," murmured Lord Beguchren, "if I were a clever Linularinan spymaster, I should have assumed that the goodwill established six years past between Feierabiand and the griffins might possibly hold. That Wall was not built because the griffins intended to strike against *Feierabiand*. Why would any Linularinan faction, no matter how prescient, have guessed that the breaking of the Wall would draw peril down across Feierabiand rather than Casmantium?"

Tan had no answer to this.

"I think," Lord Beguchren said quietly, "that we have perhaps gone as far as ignorance can carry us. I think perhaps it is time to seek a clearer understanding of this book and the work it contained. I think it will after all be necessary to, as you so neatly put it, open your mind and heart and discover what is written there."

Mienthe said uncertainly, "If you'll permit it, Tan?"

And if he would not, Tan had no doubt that Lord Beguchren would compel him. That would horrify Mienthe. And to what point, when the Casmantian lord was so clearly correct? But he still could not make himself speak.

Lord Beguchren, though undoubtedly aware of Tan's sharp terror, said mildly to Mienthe, "He is aware there is no other reasonable course open to any of us. He was aware of it from the first."

Mienthe was, Tan regretted to see, indeed beginning to look horrified. He reached out toward her and managed to say with a quite creditable imitation of calm, "That's true. That's true, Mie."

Mienthe, unmollified, jumped to her feet and came over to stand behind him. Placing her hands on his shoulders, she glared at the Casmantian lord, looking young, small, unkempt with hard travel and, Tan thought, also quite courageous and resolute. He was distantly amused at his own appreciation of the young woman, grown more and more acute through the recent days. How foolish to allow himself to feel any attraction whatsoever toward Lord Bertaud's cousin under these circumstances! Or, to be sure, under any circumstances.

"Of course you must stay with him, Lady Mienthe," conceded Lord Beguchren, so gracefully that one was hardly aware he was making a concession. He gave Gereint Enseichen a glance that combined inquiry and command.

The tall mage unfolded himself from his chair with a slightly apologetic air, as though he knew he tended to loom and wished not to alarm anyone. Nevertheless, he alarmed Tan, who gripped the arms of his chair.

"Only if you're certain," Mienthe declared, color high in her face, glaring both at the mage and at the inscrutable Lord Beguchren beyond him.

Tan would in fact have been glad to refuse if refusal had been possible. But he was well aware that the Casmantian lord would not in fact allow defiance, and even more clearly aware that the disorder resulting from any attempt to stop this could not serve anyone. Least of all Mienthe. He reached up to lay his own hand over one of hers and concentrated on producing an expression of mild acceptance.

The mage took the one step necessary, reached out with one big hand, and touched Tan's cheek with the tips of two fingers.

Tan had thought he'd prepared himself for the mage's intrusion, but he found he had not begun to imagine what that intrusion would be like. No kind of preparation could have been sufficient. Gereint Enseichen sent his mind slicing through every mask Tan could put in his way, striking ruthlessly past every illusion of calm acceptance and through the shock and fury and terror beneath, laying open the privacy of mind that Tan cherished more than affection or honor or any other quality that he might have claimed to value more highly.

Tan would after all have fought this incursion, if he had been in any way able to fight it. He could not. Memories shifted rapidly before his mind's eye, a confused blur of images and emotions, with anger and fear underlying them all, so that even memories of his childhood, of the house by the river, of his mother's face became colored by dark flashes of rage. He cried out . . . would have cried out, but he had no voice. His first sight of Teramondian whirled by him, of the Fox's court, of Istierinan . . . He had liked Istierinan on that first encounter, as nearly everyone liked him on first acquaintance, even those who did not approve of the dissolute face he showed the court; not many ever saw his other face . . .

He saw Istierinan's study, all his traps and locks and codes defeated. The wild, reckless pleasure of that morning swept through him again . . . He had got past all the Linularinan spymaster's defenses and now everything was open to him, defenseless, save for the trifling exercise of getting away again. The thought of Istierinan's white-hot rage when he discovered Tan's depredations made him laugh. He turned, took a small, thick book off a shelf.

He had not planned to take it. It had not caught his eye. He did not know why he had reached for it. He only found it in his hand as though it had come there by some odd chance of the day. He hardly paid it any mind even as he flipped it open, glanced down at a random page—

He was standing somewhere warm and close and not in any way Istierinan's study. His throat felt raw; his eyes burned as though he had been working all night by the poor light of inadequate candles, writing out some complicated, tight-binding contract with a thousand codicils and appendices; his leg ached ferociously from hip to foot. He was violently angry.

Mienthe was clinging to his arm with both hands. Tan nearly struck her—he might have hit her, except the Casmantian mage grabbed his arm.

Turning in the mage's grip, Tan hit him instead, hard, a twisting blow up under the ribs. It was the sort of blow a spy learned for those scuffles that might happen in the shadows, where no one involved had the least interest in the civilized rules of proper encounters.

Big the Casmantian mage might be, but he was not a brawler: He collapsed to one knee with a choking sound, his arms pressed against his stomach and side. Tan stared down at him. He felt strange: half satisfied and half appalled and entirely uncertain about what had just happened. The only thing he remembered with perfect clarity was hitting the mage. A powerful Casmantian court mage, it gradually occurred to him. In front of his friend, the even more powerful Lord Beguchren. And in front of Mienthe. Whom he'd possibly come near striking as well.

"Appalled" began to win out over "satisfied" as his anger ebbed at last. Tan looked up cautiously.

Mienthe was standing several paces away, her hands over her mouth, staring at him. Lord Beguchren had one hand on her arm, having drawn her back out of Tan's way. His expression was unreadable.

At Tan's feet, the Casmantian mage began, with a pained noise and some difficulty, to climb back to his feet. Tan cautiously offered him a hand, more than half expecting a stinging rebuff. He knew he should offer an apology as well—he searched for suitably abject phrases, but his normal gift for facile speech seemed to have deserted him.

But the mage accepted his hand, levered himself upright, touched his side tenderly where Tan had hit him, and cast a distinctly amused glance toward Lord Beguchren. He said to Tan, "How very gratifying that must have been. All men so provoked should have such recourse. Though I'm grateful you did not have a knife to hand."

Tan did not know what to say.

Gereint glanced once again at Lord Beguchren, turned back to Tan, and added, in a far more formal tone that nevertheless still held that unexpected note of humor, "Though my actions were unpardonable, may I ask you nevertheless to pardon them?"

Tan managed a stiff, reluctant nod.

The tall mage inclined his head in formal gratitude. Then he sighed, limped back to the grouping of chairs, lowered himself into one with a grunt, and stared into the fire for a long moment without speaking, presumably ordering his thoughts. Or the images and impressions he'd taken from Tan's heart and mind.

Tan closed his eyes for a moment against a powerful urge to hit him again, possibly after finding a knife. It was the urge of a fool. A hot-hearted, intemperate fool. He tried to put it aside, dismiss the anger, assert a more reasoned calm. In the event, unable to force calmness on his heart or nerves, he settled for what he hoped was a composed expression. But he did manage to give Mienthe a brief smile that he hoped was reassuringly natural, and walk with an assumption of calm across to take his place in one of the other chairs. Mienthe followed, though hesitantly, and Lord Beguchren came to lean on the back of the fourth chair, regarding them all with bland patience.

Gereint Enseichen looked up at last. He turned first to Tan. "I give you my promise," the mage said formally, "that I shall not speak to any man, nor for any urging, of anything I glimpsed in your heart. Can you trust me for that?"

As a rule, Tan did not trust anyone for anything. But if he'd had to wager on the big mage's essential honesty, he would have felt reasonably confident of collecting his winnings. This helped a little. He produced a second nod, not with great goodwill, but a trifle less stiffly, and looked at the fire so that he would not have to look at anyone else.

"Possibly an overbroad promise, under the circumstances," Lord Beguchren observed. His tone was unruffled, but with an almost imperceptible bite behind the calm.

"No. The little that I glimpsed of the book is not, ah, does not—" He lifted a hand in frustration at the limits of language.

"Lacks emotional context," Tan said tonelessly. He did not look around, but kept his gaze fixed on the fire. There was a pleasant smell in the room from the mountain cedar in the fire. He tried to fix his mind on that.

"Yes, well put. Exactly." The mage paused.

"You only glimpsed a little?" That was Mienthe. She sounded disappointed and decidedly offended. "You did that, that—you did whatever that was to Tan, and you didn't even see anything?"

"Even a fleeting glimpse may reveal a great truth," Lord Beguchren said quietly.

"There was a book," the big mage said slowly, and in a tone that suggested he was not certain even of this. "There *was* a book . . . or a working that *looked* like a book. Tan . . . the honored Tan . . ."

Tan said curtly, not lifting his gaze from the fire, "Now we are so well acquainted, I think we need not be overly concerned with formality."

This produced an uncomfortable pause. Then Gereint Enseichen said, "Tan, then. Tan had, I think, something like an affinity for that book. I wonder whether any of the rest of us would have had that book fall into our hands, if we'd been in that room? I think not; I do think it unlikely."

"I believe it is Andreikan Warichteier who discusses the various meanings of 'affinity' in magework and among the various natural gifts," Lord Beguchren commented.

"Warichteier has one discussion of the subject," Gereint agreed. "And I believe Entechsan Terichsekiun developed a theory of affinity and similarity, though not in exactly this context. I don't know of any philosopher who described a marked affinity between a piece of legistwork and a legist—but I'm not as familiar with Linularinan philosophers as I should be."

Tan shook his head. He asked after a moment, managing a more natural tone than he had expected, "We knew there was a book; that's no great revelation. Did you manage to glimpse anything at all *in* the book?" He hesitated, almost believing he might remember—but no. There was nothing. He rubbed his forehead, frowning.

"A word. A line perhaps." The Casmantian mage frowned as well. "I couldn't read it."

Tan dropped his hand and gave the mage a cold stare. "Of course you cannot read Terheien as well as you speak it. We might have considered that earlier."

"Ah," said the mage, with a quick gesture of apology. "No, in fact that should not signify in such an exercise—not so long as *you* understood what you read."

"You are not a legist," Lord Beguchren murmured.

Everyone looked at him.

"*Gereint* is not a legist," the small, elegant Casmantian lord repeated. "That was legistwork and nothing, perhaps, meant for other eyes. What does the legist gift encompass?" He paused, looking expectantly at Tan.

"Law," Tan said, since it was clearly expected of him, though everyone knew this. "Especially written law. Contract law. You do have legists in Casmantium."

"Yes," agreed Lord Beguchren. "Not as Linularinum has, however. You look very Linularinan yourself, you know. You are Feierabianden by conviction, perhaps, rather than by birth?"

"Does it signify?" Tan snapped.

Mienthe said quickly, "There's thorough mixing of blood along the river, you know, Lord Beguchren. Especially in the Delta."

"Yes," the Casmantian lord repeated. His expression was unreadable, but a subtle intensity had come into his voice. He tapped the arm of his chair very gently. "You are a very strongly gifted legist," he said to Tan. It wasn't a question. "The legist gift has to do, as you say, with written law, contract law. They say one should count one's fingers after signing a Linularinan contract—"

"And the fingers of your children and grandchildren in the next generations. So they do." Tan was not pleased to have that old censorious line recalled. He said, "In Linularinum, tight contracts are admired; in Feierabiand, and Casmantium as well, no doubt, signatories frequently have more concern with how contracts can be broken than with how they may most advantageously be kept."

"Even the most ambitious Casmantian merchant would probably say, 'How they might be most *honorably* kept,'" Lord Beguchren said. "But then, Casmantium is not a nation of legists." Perhaps fortunately, he held up a hand to forestall Tan's first, intemperate response. He said patiently, "What I am trying to say, perhaps with less grace than I might, is that a mage, most especially a Casmantian mage, is not likely to immediately grasp the more complicated elements of legist-magic. What was in that book was law—written law—contract law, and well set about with the strongest possible legist-magic. I doubt whether Mariddeier Kohorrian would provoke Iaor Safiad over any specific contract, however important. I greatly doubt whether Istierinan Hamoddian would so vehemently pursue a confidential agent who stole from him long after the stolen information had been passed on, if the only other item stolen were a specific piece of legal work, no matter how elegant."

"Well?" Mienthe asked. "So it was some sort of important magic Tan took. We knew that already! But meant to do what? We still don't know! We haven't gotten anywhere!"

A terrible binding, Tan thought. An immensely strong legal binding, something the kings of Linularinum needed to bind their courts or their country to order. Or something else, something worse. Something that would undoubtedly do terrible things to any careless legist strong enough, and unfortunate enough, to accidentally lay his hand on it. Particularly a legist who had deliberately deceived and betrayed the Linularinan king and court.

"Indeed, this remains an excellent question," said Lord Beguchren at last, still very softly. "To discover what Linularinum has lost and we might have gained . . . Gereint. Do you suppose you might find, somewhere in this house, a decent quill and a book of blank paper?"

Gereint shook his head. "My lord, forgive me; I have evidently not been clear. I believe that very book, as well as the writing it contained, is an integral part of the work." He looked at Tan. "I feel certain— please tell me plainly if I am mistaken—but I feel certain that you cannot possibly write out any part of that work save you have the book itself to write it in."

Tan turned this idea over in his mind. He saw . . . he thought he saw . . . at least he thought it was *possible* that he saw a faint glimmer of how to do that sort of work. One would make a book that was not precisely a book, or not *only* a book; one would write in it with quills that were not ordinary quills, cut with special care to pick up precisely the right kind of ink . . . One would take this book and write in it using words that were not ordinary words, language that was not everyday language, the sort of language that could not be spoken, for it was meant only for the eye and hand and mind of another legist . . .

"But it's true I'm not a legist. Perhaps my understanding is not correct," said Gereint.

"No," Tan said absently, and then glanced up. "No," he repeated with more decision. "No, I think your understanding is without fault. I think only a legist could make a book like that, and only if he knew precisely what work he wished that book to encompass. And I suspect Istierinan made this thing, or at least I think he believes he can make it over, if once he reclaims both that book and me."

"But," Mienthe said, looking from the mage to Lord Beguchren in some distress, her hands clasped urgently in her lap, "but the book, we don't have it with us. It's in Tiefenauer!"

"Then Istierinan Hamoddian has undoubtedly reclaimed it, and lacks only our friend, here"—Lord Beguchren nodded toward Tan— "to reclaim the work entire."

"Oh," said Mienthe quickly. "No, I don't think he does have it, unless he could find it by—by magic, you know. I hid the book in my room. I don't think Istierinan will find it. Not even my maid has ever

found my hiding place, and you know how maids find *everything*."
Then the young woman ruined this confident assertion by adding, with
sudden doubt, "I think."

The corners of Lord Beguchren's eyes crinkled with humor, and
Gereint Enseichen tilted back his head and laughed out loud.

But Tan had never felt less like laughing.

There was a quiet rap on the door, and a servant—no, a guardsman—
entered. The man ducked his head in apology and said to Lord Beguchren, "Begging your pardon, my lord, but the Arobern bids me inform
you that a Linularinan agent has been captured. He requests you will
come." The man's eyes went to Mienthe. "He asks whether his honored
guests will be pleased to come as well."

Mienthe was not surprised to find that there had indeed been several
Linularinan agents behind herself and Tan in the pass, but even though
she was not surprised, she was still horrified. They had been so close
behind—she could not help but think, *What if we had not been able to
get around the mule wagons? What if we had decided to stay the night
in the guest house? What if we hadn't woken early this morning?*

The Arobern's guardsmen thought there had been three agents altogether. Two, it seemed, had been killed. But the third man had been
properly and thoroughly apprehended. Once his advisers and guests
were ready, the Arobern signaled his guardsmen and they brought their
prisoner forward and flung him down before the Arobern, on his knees
on the cold stone floor.

The man caught his balance, his bound hands flat against the floor,
and then straightened his back and lifted his head. He was very obviously Linularinan: He had not only the sharp face, with narrow eyes
and angular cheekbones and a long nose; the straight light brown hair,
and the graceful hands with rings on his long fingers; but also, despite
his current position, the indefinable air of superiority.

He did not fight the guardsmen, but flung back his head, glaring up
and to both sides and then focusing on the king—no, not on the *king*,
but beyond him, on Tan. Tan returned only a bland look, but the Arobern
scowled.

The man abruptly transferred his glare to the king and snapped,
"You have no idea what you have there! You can have no idea, or you'd
immediately repudiate him and give him into my hands!"

The Arobern said, his deep voice as mild as he could make it,
"Maybe. Maybe that's right. So tell me what he is, and maybe I will give
him to you, yes?"

Tan raised one eyebrow and smiled, very slightly. It was the most extraordinarily insulting smile. Mienthe wondered how he *did* that, and whether she might be able to learn how.

The captive swelled with outrage, but he did not fling himself forward or rant wildly. He glowered, at Tan and at the Arobern, and then, craning his head around, at Gereint Enseichen. "*You* should know I speak the truth!" he said to the tall mage.

Gereint Enseichen gave a mild shrug. "I know events are in sweeping motion. I know that chance and opportunity turn around this man." He nodded at Tan, but without taking his eyes off the prisoner. "I know Linularinum is responsible."

"Linularinum! Responsible!" cried the man, and stopped, breathing hard. Collecting himself, he said in a more moderate tone, "Is it the proper owner of a jewel, or the thief who steals it, who is responsible for the man who covets and kills for it once it is out in the world?"

"Neither," said Lord Beguchren. His light, cool voice drew all their attention; his gray eyes effortlessly held those of the prisoner. He moved a step forward, out of the Arobern's shadow. "It is the man who does murder who is responsible, and neither the jewel's owner nor the thief. Or would eminent scholars and philosophers argue otherwise, in Linularinum?" He paused for a heartbeat and then went on, even more quietly, "And who is responsible for what some strange and powerful legistwork might do? Or might fail to do? The legist who created the work with quill and ink and his mastery of language? The mage who hid it out of the view of ordinary men? The king who guarded it from one age to the next?"

"It's too perilous to have out in the world!" shouted the Linularinan prisoner. He tried to get to his feet, but the soldiers hastily caught his shoulders and held him from rising.

"Of course it is," murmured Beguchren, catching and holding his gaze. "What is it, man? What is this thing that is so perilous for anyone but a Linularinan to hold?"

The prisoner stared at the small, elegant Casmantian lord in very much the way a bird was said to stare at a serpent. He said in a quick, sharp tone, "Do you not understand? Not even yet? This was a working against—for—it was a working of natural law. Do you not perceive the terrible distortion of the world around this thief, as the world seeks the proper bindings of law? Do you not understand what desperate peril we are in, now the strands of natural law are breaking?"

"The *proper* bindings of law," murmured Lord Beguchren.

The prisoner sat back on his heels and stared at Beguchren, furious, his bound hands raised in urgent supplication. "You must understand. A thousand years ago, we founded the age by binding into place the laws of earth and fire, and pressing aside the unbounded wild magic of mountains and forest. And then that fool"—he glared furiously at Tan, who looked merely blandly attentive—"that *fool*," the Linularinan prisoner repeated, "undid half our bindings in a day. The rest will break in time. And you *shelter* him? From *us*? Give him to me—for all of us. Let us recast our bindings, if any legist of our age has such power—will you leave the law of the world unsettled and wild?"

"The law of the world," Lord Beguchren repeated. He still spoke quietly, but his tone had become biting, cold as the gray heights of the mountains, and his storm-gray eyes were dark with fury. He took a step forward and said, "The laws of earth and fire, do you say? Gereint has described to me a certain strange quality he has recently found echoing behind the magecraft he has tried to work. We had assumed this strangeness was due to the cracking of Tehre's Wall. Now I wonder whether both the breaking of the Wall and this disturbance to mage power might be due instead to a common cause." He paused and then added, his voice dropping even further, "I wonder why Linularinum seems so untroubled by the threat the griffins pose to all our countries? Certainly Mariddeier Kohorrian seems perfectly ready to distract and weaken Iaor Safiad, and this at a time when one would expect him to see the necessity of supporting Feierabiand against griffin-fire."

The Linularinan agent did not answer.

"Indeed . . ." said Lord Beguchren. "Indeed, one might almost wonder why it is that *Casmantium* has endured the continual threat of fire, why it is that Feierabiand's border with the desert has now and again been breached and is now threatened again, and yet *Linularinum* has never seen so much as a grain of red sand blowing in the wind. Fire stays well clear of Linularinum. It always has. I wonder why that is? Just how have the legists of Linularinum written their binding law, this law that their clever kings have owned from the beginning of the age, and have hidden from the rest of us?"

"Only *we*—" said the prisoner, and stopped.

The Arobern, whose grip on the arms of his granite throne had tightened until his knuckles whitened, stood up at last. He seemed to loom massive as the mountains. The expression in his deep-set eyes went well beyond rage.

The Linularinan prisoner flinched back from the king, for which Mienthe did not blame him at all. She would have backed away herself except she could not move. But then the prisoner abruptly reached down with both his bound hands, sketching a swift line of writing on the stone floor with a fingertip. The letters that followed his tracing finger were sharp, angular, jagged things, nothing like ordinary letters.

They were black, but not the shining black of fresh ink. They were a strange, bodiless, empty black, as though the man were carving narrow but bottomless cracks right into the stone, so that the blackness at the heart of the earth showed through.

To Mienthe, it seemed that the whole world abruptly tilted sideways. She did not lose her balance; it was not that sort of tilt. But everything seemed to stutter and pause, and the cracks ran swiftly out across the stone and yawned wide—she thought someone was shouting and someone else was cursing and someone else was screaming, or maybe that was all the same person. She seemed caught in a timeless moment that did not contain alarm or movement, around which urgent sound pressed but into which it did not intrude. She seemed to watch the empty black letters slashed into the stone lengthen; they sliced out like knife cuts toward Tan. But Mienthe felt neither frightened nor rushed. She seemed to have all the time in the world to move; indeed, she seemed to be the only person in the world who was moving, or who *could* move. She stepped dreamily through the slanted world to intercept the black writing before it could reach Tan, and stooped, and drew a spiral on the floor to catch the sharp letters. Then she straightened and stood quietly, watching.

The black letters reached her spiral, and rushed into it, and the deep-cut writing swept down and around and around and down and disappeared into the depths of the earth, and the polished stone closed over the place where they had been, and suddenly time, too, rushed forward, and the world slammed back toward its ordinary level with a tremendous silent crash. Mienthe staggered.

Before she could fall, Tan caught her elbow with one strong hand, steadying her until she could recover her balance. He was not looking at her, however, but at the Linularinan agent—a mage, Mienthe realized belatedly. Or, no, with that strange writing, a legist, of course. Then she followed Tan's gaze, and found it did not matter, not for any immediate practical purpose. In startlement or terror or outrage, one of the prisoner's guards had cut his throat. A great wash of crimson blood ran across the stone, filling the deep-carved letters the agent had drawn into the stone and trickling across the floor of the hall.

There was no sign, now, that the carved letters had ever sliced out toward Tan. But there was a crystalline spiral set directly into the stone a step away from where he stood with Mienthe. It was no wider than a man's hand at its widest diameter: A perfect spiral of smoky quartz set right into the polished granite, turning and turning inward until the fine pattern in its center became too fine to see. Tan glanced down at this spiral, his brows drawing together in bemusement. Then he looked at Mienthe. There was no surprise in his face. He only gave her a little, acknowledging tip of his head: *Did it again, didn't you?* As though he'd have expected nothing less. Mienthe blushed.

The Arobern, too, stared at the spiral for a moment. Then he turned his head to look at the dead man and the blood, and at last at the guardsman who had killed him.

The man ducked his head in uncertain apology and came forward to offer the hilt of his bloody knife to the king. "If I was wrong—" he began and stopped, swallowing. Then he drew a quick breath and met the Arobern's eyes. "Lord King, if I was wrong, then I beg your pardon."

The Arobern shook his head. He reached out to touch the knife's hilt, but he did not take it; instead, he folded the guardsman's fingers back around the hilt. "He meant his blow for my guest, a man under my protection. I would not like to have my protection fail. Your blow guarded my honor, and I thank you for it."

The guardsman, looking much happier, bowed his head and backed away. Other men came deferentially forward to take away the body and clean up the blood. There was a surprising amount of blood. Mienthe tried not to look. She stared down at the crystalline spiral she'd drawn instead, though it pulled at her eyes and made her dizzy. It was still better than looking at the blood.

"It was *your* blow that protected me," Tan said to Mienthe in a low voice. "So I'll thank *you* for that."

Mienthe shook her head. She rubbed her foot cautiously over the spiral. It gleamed dully, a spiral of ordinary smoky quartz that might have been there since the stone was carved and carried into this house and laid down to be part of the room's floor. Tears prickled unexpectedly in her eyes, and she blinked hard. "I do things," she whispered. "I feel things, and I don't know why or how. There's something in me that makes me do things, but it isn't me and I don't know what it is."

Tan shook his head and, to Mienthe's surprise, took her hand in both of his. "It's you," he said. "It's all you. You simply have a gift you haven't yet recognized. But it's guiding you well, Mie, don't you think? You've done all the right things so far, and which of the rest of us can claim as much? Until you learn to recognize and understand your gift, you might simply try trusting it—and yourself—a little."

Mienthe stared at him. Then she tried to smile.

"Quite so," said Lord Beguchren, approaching unexpectedly. "One does wonder what sort of gift you hold, Lady Mienthe, but it seems one might do far worse than trust it." He knelt to trace the quartz spiral with one fingertip. Then, rising, he lifted a frost-white eyebrow at her.

He was still very angry, Mienthe knew that. Although she knew he was not angry with her or with Tan, she did not know what to say to him. She did not know what she thought about anything. She was shaking and found she couldn't stop. Tan put his arm around her shoulders, and she leaned against his solid weight gratefully.

The Arobern had been glowering down at the bloody granite and the crystalline spiral. Now he turned abruptly and said to Gereint Enseichen, "Assist my guardsmen, if you please. If there is another Linularinan agent in Ehre, I think this may be a matter of some urgency. Also see to the safety of your own household. I will assuredly ask you and your lady wife to extend hospitality to my guests."

"Yes," agreed the tall mage, inclining his head. He smiled reassuringly at Mienthe and went out.

The king said, to Mienthe and Tan and Lord Beguchren, "Come."

Mienthe thought drearily that the Casmantian king was going to want to go over everything again, and she knew she didn't want to. This day had been unpleasant enough living through it just once. Tears pressed again at her eyes. Tan tightened his arm around her shoulders, and she thought of his voice asking tartly, *Whose cousin are you?* She straightened her shoulders, blinked hard, lifted her head, and followed the Arobern.

The king guided them no farther than down a short hall, to a much smaller and less formal chamber with thick rugs on the floor and cushions on the chairs. He waved to the chairs without ceremony and said shortly to Lord Beguchren, as soon as they were all seated, "Well?"

The small lord hesitated. Then he opened his fine hands and said, "From what that . . . person . . . described, I surmise it is possible to reorder the natural law of the world to a degree I would have previously believed impossible. I surmise that the honored Tan may be able to effect such a change."

Tan said sharply, "It would be pleasant to think so, no doubt." He was rubbing his knee, an absent, unmindful gesture that was utterly out of character. Mienthe guessed by that how very disturbed he was by everything that had happened. She rose from the chair she'd just taken and went to lean on the back of his chair, resting her hand on his shoulder. The muscles were rock-hard under her touch. But he looked up at her and managed a small nod.

Lord Beguchren only said smoothly, "If Tehre's Wall shatters, then an effort to alter and bind natural law might seem suddenly very wise indeed, no matter with what doubt any of us may now regard the prospect. It does not seem wholly beyond the bounds of possibility that the honored Tan might be able to, if I may be forgiven the term, 'rewrite' a certain element of the natural law of the world. A small element, a trivial item that would not disorder the world to any great extent . . . I wonder, for example, whether he might be able to use this book and the work he holds himself to more thoroughly subordinate fire to earth."

There was a pause. Tan did not look at the Casmantian lord, or at the Arobern. He looked at Mienthe. She thought he needed something from her, but she had no idea what he wanted her to say and could only gaze back at him.

There was a subdued cough at the door, and a guardsman said apologetically, "Lord King, forgive me. We have had another messenger through the pass. A courier—a royal courier, from Feierabiand."

The Arobern scowled but laughed at the same time. He waved an impatient hand. "Of course I will see the courier. At once." He threw a harried glance around the room, ran a broad hand through his short hair, and said to Mienthe, to the rest of them, "Of course you must stay. You must all stay."

The courier was a young woman, no older than Mienthe, who looked just as tired as Mienthe felt and twice as travel-ragged. She glanced at the rest of them, but was clearly too weary to be curious and turned at once to the Arobern, bowed, and held out her white courier's wand.

"Yes," said the Arobern. "I will assuredly hear you. What message does Iaor Safiad send to me?"

"Lord King," said the courier in a faint voice, then took a breath and continued more strongly, "His Majesty Iaor Safiad sends me to say to you: He believes the Wall will not hold, that it is impossible it should hold, and that as it is the fifth day since the warning was given, we are even now within the period of greatest peril. He bids me say: The griffins have a new king who is furious and intemperate. This king of theirs scorns men and detests all the country of earth. His Majesty says that the king of the griffins will not likely stop in Feierabiand. He warns you to look east as well as north and guard the passes through the mountains." The woman stopped, swallowed, and added in a faint voice, "That's all. Will there be a response?"

The Arobern said, "Honored courier, I must consider. If there is a response, I will tell it to you in the morning. Go. Rest. My household will see to your comfort."

The courier bowed once more—she staggered a little as she straightened—and allowed herself to be led away.

Mienthe stared at the Arobern, stricken and wordless.

"My friend," the Arobern said to Beguchren Teshrichten, "what is in your mind?"

The elegant lord inclined his head. He said, "Here in this extremity, where fire threatens to burn across all the world, an unlooked-for weapon has flung itself into our hands." He met Tan's eyes and went on, quietly, "You are pursued. You have enemies. Well, so do we all. It seems to me we may well consider how we may confound all our enemies at once, and if we also forever shift the balance between earth and fire to favor earth, is that not also very well?" He turned to the Arobern. "Shall we not send agents to recover this book? Shall we not bring it here and see what the honored Tan might make of it?"

"What say you?" the king said to Tan.

Before Tan could answer, Mienthe said quickly, "But—" She stopped as everyone looked at her, but then remembered Tan saying, *You might try trusting yourself a little,* and went on, "But, Lord King, if you will pardon me, is it wise to send a small number of men through the pass, when we have no idea what they might find? Even if Linularinum doesn't have its own agents in the way, which I'm sure it does, wouldn't it take a terribly long time for men to go all the way to Tiefenauer and then come all the way back here? From the—the word about the Wall and the griffins, can we take so much time?"

The Arobern tapped his fingers on the arm of his chair. "Very well! What do you wish me to do?"

"I want you to send an army into Feierabiand!" Mienthe declared. "You have one; of course you do, with all the, the warnings flying back and forth across the mountains! So you have an army ready, haven't you, and here it is, right at the mouth of the pass, just where we need it to be! I want you to send an *army* through the pass and press back the Linularinan forces and confound their mages and make a safe road for Tan to go *himself* back to Tiefenauer—and me, of course—and then we can get the book and see how useful it might be."

Tan was staring at her, looking appalled by this idea. "A wise man does not leave be the hart at bay to pursue a glimmering fantasy by moonlight, nor forsake his house of stone to build a palace of sunbeams," he said, with some force. "I admire your boldness, but you cannot possibly set all your hopes on—"

"I'm not!" exclaimed Mienthe. "If the Arobern sends an army to the Delta, then at least Linularinum will be out of the Delta, which is one thing we want." She turned back to the Arobern himself. "And if you do that, then you'll have an army in place to help block the griffins before they can come into Casmantium, which has to be something you want, and if Lord Beguchren is right about that book and about Tan, then we can stop the griffins entirely, and we all want that, don't we? So why not do everything at once?"

There was a slightly stunned pause.

The Arobern himself broke it, rising to pace several strides away and then turn and come back. He moved with sharp energy, glowering at Mienthe with uncommon ferocity. "I thought of exactly what you say, yes?" he growled. "But you have forgotten: I cannot take men through that pass and march them through Feierabiand, because Iaor Safiad has my son in his court and within his reach! Do you think he will stop to ask me what I do, when he sees the spears of my soldiers flashing in the sun?"

The Arobern flung himself back down in his chair and scowled around at them all. "I could send that girl back to Iaor Safiad, yes, and ask him politely if he would permit me to bring a few thousand men marching through southern Feierabiand. Except there is no time! Who knows whether the griffins have already come through the high pass and down against Tihannad? Nor will Safiad trust me or what I might do! Later, when he sees I kept faith with him, that will be too late!"

"You have another son now," Lord Beguchren said very quietly.

"A babe in arms does not replace my first son!"

Mienthe stared at both men, utterly horrified. She exclaimed, "But King Iaor would never harm Erich! I don't care if—if Erich is supposed to be a hostage against you, it doesn't matter what you do, he would never touch him!"

"He is a king!" shouted the Arobern, lunging back to his feet. "He will do what he must!"

Mienthe jumped to her feet to face the King of Casmantium and shouted back, "He won't!" She found she was glaring as fiercely as the Arobern. "Who knows King Iaor better, you or I? He's spent a month out of every year in the Delta, in my cousin's house, and every year he's brought your son with him. He treats him like his own son! When little Anlin fell off her pony last spring and broke her wrist, it was Erich who carried her back to the house and sat up with her all night and told her stories so she wouldn't cry! He told her about the time he broke his arm falling off the roof of your palace in Breidechboden, and she made him promise that someday when she visited Casmantium he'd show her just where. He made her promise she wouldn't climb out and fall from the same place!" Mienthe stopped. Then she finished with dignity, "It doesn't matter what you think. King Iaor is honorable and kind and he might have taken your son as his hostage, but when it comes to the moment, he won't touch him."

The Arobern was gazing at her now with a very strange expression. "My son has stayed in your house for a month out of every year?"

Mienthe nodded uncertainly.

"You must know him now better than I do."

Mienthe opened her mouth and shut it again. She said at last, "He's a great deal like you, I think. Only not so hot-hearted. He loves you and Casmantium, but . . ."

"But he has learned to love Feierabiand and the Safiad as well," the Arobern said heavily. "Yes. That is what the Safiad meant to teach him, and better that than . . ." His voice trailed off. "It is true that I have gathered a small army here. It is also true that I have thought of taking this army of mine through the pass. I would be glad to keep any war on the west side of the mountains, away from my own country. But . . ."

"You are a king," Lord Beguchren said quietly. "You will do what you must."

CHAPTER 13

An hour before dusk, the Arobern and all his people came out of the western mouth of the pass and found themselves slowly descending the lower slopes of the foothills and approaching the soft new green of the spring pastures spread out below.

Beguchren found the long rolling view of Feierabiand's gentle countryside . . . troubling. He knew those foothills and pastures, for this was the identical view that had greeted that other Casmantian army six years ago, when the Arobern had come for the first time into Feierabiand. Then, his ambition had been conquest. He had intended to use the griffins as unwilling, ignorant weapons against Feierabiand. The cold mages of Casmantium . . . Beguchren and all his brethren . . . had hardly cared whether the king's plan succeeded. *They* had intended the ultimate destruction of all the griffins.

If the Arobern had not been so ambitious . . . if the cold mages of Casmantium had not encouraged him in his ambition . . . then, very likely, the griffins would have kept, within reason, to their desert isolation. The slow battle between fire and earth would have continued as it had from the beginning of the age: inconclusive and wearying, but never ruinous.

Casmantium would still have its cold mages. Beguchren would not have been required to consign each of his long companions to the cold earth. The Great Wall would have been neither built nor broken.

Beguchren himself would still have his mage-sense and his power.

This was not a new thought. Only the regret and grief had become suddenly more piercing in the face of the green Feierabianden spring, with its soft breeze and gentle warmth.

Beguchren looked for signs of the stark desert the griffins had

made here among the gentle hills and farms of Feierabiand. Looking
down from this height, those signs were not obvious even to his experienced eye. But below and over to the south, the grasses were different:
longer and harsher and strangely wiry. And there was a faint reddish
cast to the land underlying those grasses. There were no trees in that
area, except someone had apparently planted some young oaks and
elms; the saplings stood in rows much too neat for trees that had
sprouted naturally. Farther away, almost at the edges of visibility, stood a
twisted, jagged tower of stone. The sunlight caught on it oddly, with a
bloodred glimmer that turned its sharp edges almost translucent. Beguchren bowed his head, fixing his gaze instead on the mane of his horse,
on his own fingers gripping the reins.

"My friend," said the Arobern, and Beguchren drew a hard breath
and looked up again.

The king had drawn up his horse, so that Beguchren had come up
beside him. Their eyes met in a perfect understanding of shared guilt
and regret. But neither of them would speak of the past, the Arobern
because he was determinedly focused on the present and Beguchren
because he was far too intensely private a man.

Leaning on his pommel, the Arobern gestured down the slope,
west and a little south. "The ford is there, with its good bridge. The
bridge is still there, I think. It was repaired when the rebuilding of the
town began."

Beguchren nodded. Of course the king would know for certain
about the bridge—he would have had reports from his agents about
every bridge and ford that would allow men to cross all the rivers in
Feierabiand.

"So," the Arobern said gravely. Lady Mienthe, her legist companion at her heel, had come up on the king's other side and was looking
at him questioningly; he turned toward her and went on, "We will assume the Wall yet holds. Perhaps it does." It had been seven days since
the griffin mage had brought his warning to Lord Bertaud. Perhaps the
Wall held, and if it did not, still there was little they could do other than
ride for the Delta and try an unexpected sideways blow against the griffins.

"We will cross the Nejeied," continued the Arobern. "We will go
across the country, straight toward Tiefenauer, at least until we are
closer." He had been practicing, as he managed the difficult Feierabianden names with only a little clumsiness.

"Yes?" Lady Mienthe said uncertainly.

The Arobern glanced sidelong at Beguchren and said, "If the Wall
is broken, then Iaor Safiad will stay in the north. But if it still holds,

then he may come south. If he comes, what will be his road? Will he
ride down along the Sierhanan, straight for the Delta but always risking
that he may find Linularinan soldiers have crossed the river and gotten
in front of him? Or that he may find an attack coming from any direction, if Linularinum has crossed in force and laid a trap for him?"

"No," said Beguchren, as the Arobern clearly wished to have all
these tactical considerations laid out for the lady. "If the Safiad moves
south, he will come down along the Nejeied this far. His options are
wide, once he is here. He could cross west toward the Delta if he finds
the Linularinan assault his greatest concern, as I imagine he hopes; or
continue down the Nejeied toward Terabiand if for some reason he
thought that wise; or if his hopes fail him and he suddenly discovers
Linularinum to be the least of his concerns, he might go south along
the Sepes River to Talend and have the forest at his back when he faces
the griffins. He might even, in extremity, retreat with his men into the
pass. I imagine that the griffins would care for that even less than they
would like the forest."

"That is also what I think," said the Arobern, and paused. From the
king's grim expression, and from the way his gaze rested for a long moment on Lady Mienthe's face, he was probably trying to imagine what
he might say to King Iaor, if they happened to find him on the road
down there, on the other side of the bridge.

"We will go down to the bridge," the Arobern decided. "Lady
Mienthe—" He frowned at her, though not unkindly. "You must speak
to the people there and bid them to be calm."

"They will know they cannot fight us," Lord Beguchren said,
watching her face. The lady was clearly thinking of how frightened her
folk would be when they saw thousands of Casmantian spears flashing
through the dust raised by thousands of Casmantian boots. He said,
"They may scatter up and downriver, however, with the most disturbing tales of Casmantian invasion. You might persuade them to send a
second lot of messengers after the first, in the hope that we may not
encounter too much difficulty as we move farther into Feierabiand."

"We will move too swiftly to encounter difficulty," the Arobern
declared. "If Iaor Safiad comes upon us, we will hope he will listen to
us with both his ears. I will send that little courier north today, this
very hour, explaining what we are about and asking his pardon for our
boldness. Lord Beguchren, I will ask you to stay here, athwart the
likely road, so that if the honored courier does not reach the Safiad, you
may meet him here."

Lord Beguchren, unsurprised, inclined his head in acceptance of
this command. "I am honored by your trust," he said quietly, and to

Lady Mienthe, who was looking openly surprised, "It is a mage you will need with you in the west."

"And it's a smooth tongue the lord king will need here in the east," said Tan, unexpectedly, for he had rarely spoken to any of them on this ride, and had assiduously avoided both Beguchren and Gereint. His tone now was stiff. But he went on, glancing from one of them to the next and ending with an earnest nod toward the Arobern, "King Iaor may even believe that you deliberately act together with Mariddeier Kohorrian, and that you have some plan for dealing with the griffins after you've finished partitioning Feierabiand between you."

Beguchren gave the legist a considering nod and agreed, "Indeed. I shall hope that in such exigency, I will be able to clarify matters."

The Arobern grimaced and then looked keenly at Mienthe. "The Safiad knows you well, hah? Your cousin is his friend as well as his adviser and a lord of his court. Maybe I should leave you here also. Then you would be safe and also you could speak for me to your king. Maybe that would be clever, yes?"

"No—no, it wouldn't!" said Mienthe, plainly horrified. "I have to go west! I need to be in Tiefenauer! Or," she amended, "at least, I need to be with Tan." She said this as she might have said *The sky is blue* or *Water runs downhill*. As though it were a flat statement of such obvious truth that no one could possibly dispute it.

Tan said, a snap of temper in his voice, "I should hate to go west without Mienthe. It isn't your mage who's so far turned away three Linularinan attacks against me."

Lady Mienthe looked at Tan with surprise and pleasure, as though she hadn't expected his support. But, when the Arobern began stubbornly to speak again of her safety, it was to Beguchren she turned for help. Though Beguchren had to acknowledge, without modesty, that if the young woman was not confident of her ability to carry her own point, she could not have chosen better in looking for one who both could and would argue for her.

He said, "Your feelings have been remarkable of late, have they not, Lady Mienthe? Both in their strength and then in their direction. We are assured that you are not a mage. However, even so, I think it very likely that you perceive the turn and tilt of the world." He paused.

Mienthe stared at him blankly. She clearly had no idea what it would be like to perceive forces, balances and events pivoting, and just as clearly doubted that she felt any such thing.

But Beguchren was confident of it.

He turned gravely toward the Arobern. "Lord King," he said formally, "I must advise against your suggestion, reasonable and wise as it seems. I believe the honored Lady Mienthe should return to Tiefenauer with the honored Tan, with all reasonable alacrity."

"Huh. I thought only to keep you safe—" the Arobern said to Mienthe. He glanced at Beguchren and shrugged. "But very well! You will assuredly go west, honored lady."

Beguchren said to his king, "I will speak for you to Iaor Safiad. I swear to you, I will not permit any harm to come to your son."

"I depend upon it," the Arobern growled. "I cannot give you many men, nor can I give you Gereint Enseichen. I will leave you—hah!—I will leave you Lady Tehre. *She* will make the Safiad listen to your voice. You must make him understand he must not press carelessly forward, that I have not set myself against him, that he must not interfere with me." The king paused.

"I understand you very well," Lord Beguchren said gently.

"Of course you do," agreed the Arobern, and swung around, waving for his officers to come hear his commands.

Iaor Safiad, if he left Lord Bertaud in Tihannad to find such accommodation with the griffins as he might—and Beguchren wished the Feierabianden lord joy of the effort—would very likely race south to meet the Linularinan offense. Beguchren remained convinced that the Safiad would come down the Nejeied. From Minas Ford, he could angle west toward Kames and from there strike directly toward Tiefenauer, exactly the route the Arobern had taken. True, there were poor roads and farmer's tracks all the way. But going that way, whatever Linularinan troops one might meet would lack support from across the river. This was what Beguchren thought the Safiad would do, thus driving straight against the rear of the Casmantian army, quite possibly leading to a very unfortunate outcome. Thus the urgent necessity of preventing him from pursuing any such course.

But if Iaor Safiad chose to ride south along the Nejeied at all, he would certainly have in mind the broad, open countryside west of Minas Spring, where the little Sepes divided from the larger Nejeied. This was the ideal place to rest his men and the fine Feierabianden horses.

Thus, this was where Beguchren set his own men, just past dawn on the day following their arrival in Feierabiand. He arranged them right across the middle of the open land, where the last of the precipitous hills leveled out to gentle pasturelands before reaching the river. It was a stupid position if he had meant to offer serious battle, especially with so few men. If he had actually intended to fight the Safiad, he would have wanted to arrange his men a fraction more northerly, where the narrow road lay between woodlands on the east and the river on the west. He would have set archers in the woods, so that Iaor Safiad would have been forced to bring his men through withering fire in order to come at his lines of spearmen. So his officers—two captains, each with a half-strength company—earnestly told him, unnecessarily. They and Lady Tehre had joined Beguchren under the awning of his tent, to look over the lines once more and review the plan.

"The point is not to fight," Beguchren said gently, "but to hold Iaor Safiad from pursuing the Arobern in error. Or committing other acts in error." Lady Tehre looked blank, which probably indicated that she was considering something entirely unrelated to what Beguchren had just said. But both the captains nodded, even more earnestly than they had explained how their men should be arranged. They were not stupid men. They knew very well the possible error to which Beguchren referred.

"But how are we to hold the Safiad if we cannot fight him?" the senior captain asked. "And should we not *prepare* to fight wholeheartedly, in case all else fails? Or, if all else fails, are we to prepare to yield this ground and our men and allow the Safiad through?" He plainly did not much care for this idea.

"We would much prefer not to yield," Beguchren conceded. "One fears that events in the Delta may become altogether too delicate to allow even the best-intentioned interference from without. Possibly Iaor Safiad will give me his word to allow our king a free hand, but I think that unlikely."

Both captains nodded; one of them laughed grimly.

Beguchren barely smiled. "Just so. So we shall prefer to delay Iaor Safiad past the likelihood of any great interference. We should prefer to hold him entirely. But we will first show him a face that may make him pause to reflect, rather than merely gather his forces for an assault. We shall assuredly not draw the first bow." He glanced from one man to the other and added without emphasis, "Indeed, you may warn your men that I will personally see to it that any man who shoots without the command is bound under the *geas*."

Lady Tehre looked up at that, suddenly attentive, frowning. Both captains paled. "No one will draw without leave," the senior said earnestly. "We assure you, my lord."

"Indeed, I am certain of it," murmured Beguchren. "Now, if we should be *compelled* to fight, we shall hope Lady Tehre may compensate for our poor disposition of forces."

The captains glanced at each other and then, with the greatest respect, at Lady Tehre. They were northern men; that was one reason the Arobern had left them with Beguchren. They had seen the Great Wall.

"Well, but," said Lady Tehre, worried, "there is no stone here to break; the mountains are a great distance away. I think too far."

The lady was perched on a camp chair, her hands folded demurely in her lap, a few strands of her dark hair curling down beside her face. She looked fragile and feminine and markedly more beautiful than she had six years ago. Marriage to Gereint had suited her very well.

She said now, "I can tear up the road under their horses, to be sure, my lord, but that wouldn't be enough to stop them, do you think, if they are determined? This soft black soil is very deep here along the river. I don't now what I could do with it." A tiny crease appeared between her fine eyebrows as she slipped into a maker's reverie. "Soft earth might actually *flow*, in a sense, rather like very thick molasses," she murmured. "I wonder . . ."

Beguchren left the lady to consider how deep soil might flow like a liquid and said to the captains, without the slightest fear he would distract her, "I expect the Safiad to make his appearance, in considerable force, quite soon. Today, tomorrow, most likely not so late as the day after. Suppose he approaches this very afternoon. If we cannot halt him entirely, I think we must delay him at least three days." After that, if the Wall had held so long, it would probably break. At that point Iaor Safiad would have to forget about the Delta and set his men against the griffins. If that happened, Beguchren intended to support the Feierabianden king with his own men. Provided he had any left, which he would not if he had been forced to use them in battle. He did not intend to have events come to that.

He said merely, "We do not wish our king to find himself pressed from the rear when he has urgent matters to which he must attend elsewhere. We most particularly do not wish him forced to engage Iaor Safiad personally. Given the possibility of unfortunate errors attending that sort of engagement, even if they had been previously avoided."

Again, both captains nodded. One of them murmured, "No, indeed, my lord," in a fervent tone that made Beguchren suspect the man had young sons of his own, and sufficient imagination to flinch from the picture this statement called to mind.

"We shall hope, however, to persuade the Safiad to hold using nothing more forceful than moral suasion," Beguchren said firmly, and dismissed the captains. As they drew away, he overheard one of them murmur to the other, "Well, my lord is the man for moral suasion, if anyone is," and the other answer, "He might bid the river flow backward and have it comply, but an offended king is likely to prove harder to turn than a river."

This summed the situation up tolerably well. Beguchren, too, would have much preferred not to be forced to depend wholly on his own personal persuasiveness. Lady Tehre was a weapon, but it was not weapons that would win this particular argument—not if it could be won at all.

He could not help but recall, as sometimes he did rather too vividly, that once his usefulness to his king had not been limited to the fluency of his tongue and the persuasiveness of his arguments. Sighing, he rose—stiffly, for he was no longer a young man—and, leaving Lady Tehre to contemplate the possibilities inherent in this gentle pastureland, went to once more look over the arrangements he had made.

The King of Feierabiand rode south along the river road and out into the broad pastureland just after noon. Scouts had warned Beguchren, so he had his men properly drawn up. The formality of their disposal made the thinness of their lines all the more apparent, which was not accidental. Nevertheless, they made a fine, aggressive display, with all their neat uniforms and their helms polished and their spears neatly parallel. The spear-and-falcon banner of the Casmantian king flew over their heads, sapphire and purple.

Only the officers were on horseback, and they would dismount if the Feierabianden troops rode forward, for there were certain to be horse-callers among the Feierabianden ranks. No Casmantian, whether soldier or officer, could possibly trust himself to even the best-trained horse. The long Casmantian spears, made by the best weaponsmiths in the world, were meant to compensate for this Feierabianden advantage. Ordinarily they might do so, though today, with so few men, and those arranged in long lines rather than a powerful defensive block, they would never compensate sufficiently if it came to battle.

Iaor Safiad had clearly had scouts of his own out ahead of his main force, for he did not seem surprised by what he found in the open country along the river. His men filed off the road and formed up in their own lines, broader and far thicker than the Casmantian lines, for this was the Safiad's main force, all that could be gathered hastily. Feierabiand was accustomed to having an uneasy neighbor on either side, and so that was a large proportion of all the male population, townsmen and farmers alike. The Feierabianden army might possess relatively few professional soldiers, but its militia was large, experienced, and swiftly available. And mounted. Feierabiand was proud of its horses and knew very well what a powerful advantage they possessed in their mounted companies. They rode to battle with other creatures as well: Hawks and even eagles perched on more than one shoulder, and the birds were greatly outnumbered by mastiffs with powerful shoulders and even more powerful jaws.

To be sure, though Beguchren might lack horses and dogs, he did have Lady Tehre by his side, and she was a weapon more to be valued than any number of spears. He asked her, "How much are we outnumbered, do you think?"

"Hmm?" The lady was mounted on a pretty bay mare. She wore a practical traveling dress with split skirts, a set of copper bangles around one wrist, and an abstracted expression. "Not much above four to one," she said, glancing casually across the field. "Four and a fraction, I believe. About four and a tenth. You know, I don't believe there's much to do with all this deep soil after all."

"Oh?" said Beguchren.

"No, I think the thing to do is snap all their bows. Or perhaps their arrows. The bows themselves are quite resilient to breaking, you know, especially at these cool temperatures, but they will very likely break if the arrows are broken just as their strings are released."

"Ah," said Beguchren.

"Although the timing in that case would certainly need to be very precise, even if they shoot in volley," Lady Tehre added reflectively. "Perhaps it would be better to think about—"

"Please do nothing at all until it is quite clear that the Feierabianden force is actually attacking," said Beguchren. "And I would greatly prefer it if, in that case, you do as little as seems consistent with a reasonable possibility of success."

The lady's gaze sharpened. After a moment, she smiled. "I understand," she said.

Beguchren returned a small smile of his own, confident that for all her apparent absentmindedness, she did.

He rode out alone across the field toward the Feierabianden lines— rode, because it showed both confidence and peaceable intent to ride a horse within distance of the Feierabianden horse-callers, and because the Casmantian commander could hardly walk on foot across the mud and grasses, and most of all because he needed the horse's height and beauty to make a proper show. The horse was a particularly fine white mare, not large, but pretty and elegant, with blue ribbons braided into her mane and tail for the occasion. Beguchren wore white to match her, embroidered with blue and set about with pearls. Together they would make a brilliant show, which was one skill Beguchren still owned, for all he had lost.

Iaor Safiad sat his own horse, a plain bay with good shoulders and

powerful quarters and not a single ribbon, in the center of the Feierabianden lines. He did not ride out to meet Beguchren. Nor, which might
have been more likely, did he send any man of his to ride out. He brought
his horse forward only a few paces and then waited, compelling Beguchren to come all the way to him.

The King of Feierabiand was not as big a man as the Arobern, but
he owned a kingliness all his own, and he had grown into his power as
he had aged. His lion-tawny hair was just becoming grizzled, but he
was one of those men, Beguchren thought, whose personal force would
only deepen with time.

At the moment, the Safiad's expression was stern and his mouth
tight with anger. A difficult audience, Beguchren judged. But he had
not expected otherwise.

The Feierabianden officers were spread out, each to his own company, and so far as Beguchren could judge, the king had not brought
any court advisers with him. But beside the king and a little behind sat
a young man on a fine black horse, a thickset young man with black
hair and dark eyes and the unmistakable look of his father. He carried
neither bow nor spear, but he had a sword at his side; a good, plain
weapon and no courtier's toy. He met Beguchren's eyes with a serious,
uneasy intensity.

Beguchren was already well within arrow-shot. He came within an
easy spear cast and then rode closer still, until he was very close; close
enough to be easily heard without shouting. Then he drew up his mare
and simply sat for a moment, meeting the furious stare of the King of
Feierabianden.

"Beguchren Teshrichten," the king said at last, bare acknowledgment with no courtesy to it. But he had reason to be angry.

"Iaor Daveien Behanad Safiad," Beguchren answered, inclining his
head in grave respect.

Iaor glared at him and lifted a hand, gesturing from left to right
across all the field and the men arranged in their lines there. "What is
this? Well? Brechen Glansent Arobern gave me his word he would be
amicable, and now I find *this* in my way? What will he have of me?"
He glared at Beguchren and then jerked a hand sideways to indicate
Prince Erichstaben. He said, even more furiously, "I am aware he has a
new young son; has he forgotten the one he gave to me? Does he believe my patience is without limit?"

Beguchren bowed his head in the face of the king's anger. He said
softly, "The Arobern indeed has hope of your patience, Iaor Safiad, but
he does not believe it to be limitless. He asks, if you please—"

The Safiad slammed a fist down on his own thigh, reining his horse back sharply when it flung up its head and jolted forward a surprised step.

Prince Erichstaben, breaking into the moment with a sense of dramatic timing that might have been his father's, moved suddenly. He had not appeared shocked or frightened at the Safiad's threat, but had given Beguchren an involuntary glance that repeated the king's question, only with real anxiety to it: *Has my father forgotten me?* But he did not ask that question aloud. He did not speak at all.

Instead, the prince stripped off his sword belt with quick movements, slung his sword over the pommel of his saddle, swung one leg over his horse's shoulder, and slid down to the ground. Then, having collected all eyes, he walked forward to stand by the Safiad's horse. He took the king's reins and himself steadied the horse, absently patted its shoulder, and at last lifted his head to look up at the king. He did not speak, but his open, honest look spoke for him quite clearly and very well matched the courage and dignity of his gesture. Then he glanced at Beguchren and bowed his head, waiting.

The prince's gesture could not have been better suited to Beguchren's purposes if he had directed the boy through every instant. It changed everything about how Beguchren meant to proceed, for he had expected that he would need to slip every word he spoke past the Safiad's outrage. But Prince Erichstaben had created a silence in which any word spoken would carry several times its normal weight, and in which any gesture, too, would carry more than usual weight and force.

Beguchren carried no sword of his own to give up, not even a knife, so he could not quite match the prince's gesture. But he twisted his reins about the pommel of his saddle and swung down to the ground, came forward a measured few steps, and sank down to one knee. He said clearly and steadily, "Lord King, Brechen Glansent Arobern remembers every oath he swore to you and repudiates nothing. He sends me to beg you hold your hand and your temper and your men." He deliberately touched his fingertips to the muddy ground and then to his lips in the gesture of eating dirt, met the king's eyes, and said, "I do not know how to beg more abjectly." He was satisfied to see that Iaor Safiad, taken aback, appeared at a loss for any answer.

Turning to the young prince, Beguchren added, with all the forceful sincerity at his command, "Your father has not forgotten you. However events fall, whatever these perilous days bring, he begs you believe that you have been always in his thoughts. He declares, with great passion, that no new babe can replace his firstborn son."

Prince Erichstaben's expression lightened. Though he still did not speak, he bent his head in an admirably dignified nod of acceptance and gratitude.

Beguchren shifted his gaze back to the Safiad. He said, "My king acknowledges that you hold the life of his son in your hand, but entreats you to hold." And then, once more directing his words to the prince, "I beg you will believe that only the hard necessity of a king could have driven him to risk you."

Iaor Safiad found himself constrained by Beguchren's meek humility on the one hand and by Prince Erichstaben's honest bravery on the other. He opened his mouth to speak or perhaps curse, but then only drew a hard breath. He said at last, still harshly but without the bright-lit fury of those early moments, "Get up, then—up, I say!—and tell me why the Arobern has committed this offense against my borders—for the second time!—and why I should hold."

Beguchren rose as quietly and smoothly as he could. He did not remount his horse, deliberately using his own slight size to further constrain the Safiad to a civilized restraint. He said, "The cousin of your lord Bertaud came to my lord king. Lady Mienthe daughter of Beraod. Through the pass she came, to Ehre, with a companion who gave his name first as Teras son of Toharas to the royal guardsmen and to my king only as Tan."

He had captured the Safiad's attention. Though the king did not speak, his curt gesture indicated that Beguchren should continue. So he outlined the alarming news the lady had brought them: Linularinum on the one side and griffins on the other and confusion throughout; the strange determination of Linularinan agents to reclaim the legist together with whatever mysterious working he had stolen. He drew, without allowing himself to flinch, on his understanding of mages and mageworking to describe the way events were bending wildly around Tan, and his own guess about the legist gift and what Tan had stolen, and what that theft might mean for them all.

He did not mention Lady Mienthe's odd gift or power, for fear the king's very familiarity with the young woman might lead him to discount her. But he gave an honest and almost complete account of the reasoning that had led the Arobern to come west, and their fear that the Safiad, though rightfully outraged, might perhaps err in his anger and prevent the recovery of the legist book. "If the Wall does not hold and griffins ride their burning winds across Feierabiand," he said quietly, "then we may all wish most fervently we had bent our efforts toward this work of legist-magic that might subordinate them."

The king lifted a skeptical eyebrow. "You think this is possible."

Beguchren met his eyes. "I think it likely," he said gently. "And who would know better than I?"

He had used that phrase many times in his long life, generally to good effect. Even here in this foreign country he saw the words go home and belief settle in the king's eyes.

The Feierabianden king said in a low tone far removed from his earlier anger, "I have heard a good deal of you, to be sure," and then paused.

Not for any reason would Beguchren have broken into that considering pause. He stood with his back straight and his hands open at his sides, his eyes steady on the king's face, waiting.

Prince Erichstaben waited also, his hand still resting on the neck of the king's horse. He did not look again up at the king, however, for pride forbade any faintest suggestion that he might ask for mercy, either for his father's sake or on his own account. There was tension in the set of his broad shoulders; nothing to wonder at with the recent vivid demonstration of a king forced to a hard necessity he would never have chosen freely. From that tension, Beguchren saw that the prince thought it was possible that the Safiad might still reject everything Beguchren had said and every plea he had made. But he also saw trust and even affection in the placement of the prince's hand on the neck of Iaor Safiad's horse.

The Safiad glanced down at the Casmantian prince. His expression was closed and cold, but only a man with a heart of stone could have been unmoved by the young man's quiet courage. Beguchren was not at all surprised when the king said, in the low tones of a man making an admission, "We should neither one of us forgive the other for such an act, nor for compelling it."

Beguchren bowed his head in acknowledgment.

The Safiad eyed him without enthusiasm. "Your king has presumed on my good nature, Lord Beguchren. He has greatly presumed. I am not in the least amused by his presumption, nor by your own effrontery. Nor is my patience endless. Get your men out of my way."

His head still bowed, Beguchren dropped again to one knee.

"Well you may beg," the Safiad said sharply. "It is indeed effrontery! You do not have men enough there to hold me. Well?"

"Lord King," Beguchren said, with a perfect humility that would surely have made the Arobern laugh out loud, "I am commanded in the strictest terms to see that the Arobern remains free to act, on your behalf and for us all. I beg you will forgive my effrontery and be so gracious as to permit me to obey my king. Only your generosity can redeem my honor. If you command me again, I shall have no choice but to comply, for, as you say, I have few men. I would never wish to compel a lady onto a field of battle, nor would the lady Tehre Amnachudran Tanshan wish to be so compelled. She would much prefer to ride north with all speed and see to her Wall; she was greatly distressed to hear of the damage that has come upon it."

The Safiad looked momentarily taken aback by this combined threat and offer. Then he actually laughed—a grim laugh, but with something like real amusement. "Get up," he said. "Get up, Lord Beguchren, and draw back your men. Set them in some less provocative order, and we shall discuss the matter. That is your pavilion down by the river? We shall retire to it and consider what we may do."

"Lord King, I shall do everything exactly as you command," Beguchren said smoothly, and rose.

CHAPTER 14

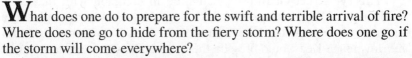

What does one do to prepare for the swift and terrible arrival of fire? Where does one go to hide from the fiery storm? Where does one go if the storm will come everywhere?

Casmantian for making, as the saying went, and to be sure, Feierabianden makers were neither so common nor so skilled as those of Casmantium. But it was humbling to see with what dedicated hearts the makers of Tihannad bent to their tasks. Especially when everyone in the city, and they themselves, must suspect their efforts would in the end prove inadequate.

One would not look to Feierabiand for the best of makers, but still, it is makers one needs before battle. Certainly horses and hounds would be by no means so useful against griffins as they might be against men. So what makers Tihannad possessed were wearing the skin off their fingers shaping arrow shafts and putting decent edges on spear points. Feierabianden mages did not know how to tip arrows with points of ice, but even in Feierabiand a weaponsmith could make spears that would resist breaking and arrows that would turn in the air to seek blood.

"Not blood," Jos told the harassed weapon-makers, having sought out the weapons-hall, which was crowded and clamoring. "Have your arrows seek fire. And see if you can get them to resist burning."

"It's not so easy to make *wood* resist *burning*," the head of the king's weapon-makers snapped impatiently, but he had fires kindled through the weapons-hall so the makers could keep their enemy more clearly in mind. Before Jos left the hall, he saw the man run a long gray-fletched shaft through his hands and then cast it into a fire, and when he lifted the arrow out again it was only smoking and not charred.

"That was well done," Lord Bertaud said to Jos when he heard of it. "I would dearly wish to have a hundred Casmantian makers here, and a dozen cold mages, but even advice may help. Have you any other suggestions for our makers?"

Jos wished he could say, *Oh, yes, only do this and avoid that and victory will be ours!* But he could only shake his head.

Bertaud nodded, unsurprised, and shifted a lamp over toward his maps. It was not yet dusk, but the room had only an east window and the light failed early this time of year.

He had been considering the lay of the land above the lake and before the precipitous hills, where they expected the griffins to come out of the broken country of the pass. "They will not care for those wild heights," he said absently, not really to Jos. "Nor for the magic carried by the gathering river and held by Niambe Lake."

This was true. Griffin-fire had little in common with that cold, wild magic. Their hot winds would blow only weakly through those mountains and near the lake. That could not possibly compensate for the advantage Kes would provide the griffins, however, not to any real degree. Jos did not say so. He did not have to. They both knew it.

"We will arrange our men here and here, I think," said Bertaud, tracking figures on a map. "Archers here and over along here. The griffins must come this way and that will force them to pass through this killing ground, here."

Griffin mages could burn arrows in the air, and Kes would heal any injured griffins before they could fall. Jos made no comment.

Lord Bertaud gave him a look. "Yes," he said. "But my officers will expect us to arrange ourselves as though we may do something useful. If the main body of men is here, then it will not seem strange if I set myself with a small, picked force"—he traced a line forward, right into the mouth of the pass—"here."

Jos nodded. "You don't think you can hold them all?" he ventured.

The Feierabianden lord did not look at him. "The pass will force them down and keep them tight-packed. I think I will be able to hold them all. But if I am wrong, I think it would be as well if we have our men arranged so as to be some use."

Jos nodded again.

"Tastairiane will be in the forefront of the attack, I imagine, and if I can stop him, that will at least cast the rest into confusion."

"Kes will stay far out of arrow reach. And out of your reach?"

"I can't—she isn't—" Bertaud stopped.

"She'll be riding Opailikiita, I guess."

"And if I can't compel Kes, I should be able to compel Opailikiita.

Yes. She has always been very careful to keep Kes far out of reach of any stray arrow, but the mountains may force her to fly lower, closer to the ground. And closer to me. I may be able to force Opailikiita to turn against Kes. That will allow our arrows to do useful work against the rest of the griffins." The lord did not look happy about this. There was a strained note in his voice, rather as though he were discussing his potential ability to impale children.

Jos nodded again, silent.

"I know," Bertaud said, looking up suddenly to meet his eyes. "I know it must be done, and better the griffins are destroyed than Tihannad, and after us all the country of earth. But—"

"I—"

Bertaud slammed his hand down on the maps he had been studying. He did not shout, but said almost in a whisper, "*Don't* . . . tell me you understand."

Jos caught himself, barely, before he could take a step backward. "No, lord. I beg your pardon."

The Feierabianden lord stared at him for another moment, his eyes narrow and his color high. Then his gaze fell, and he flung himself into a chair and rubbed his hands tiredly across his face. "Forgive me."

"There's nothing to forgive, lord," Jos said earnestly. He hesitated. "Kairaithin?"

"If he could bring me Tastairiane, or bring me *to* Tastairiane, he surely would have done it by this time, don't you think?" This began as a cry of despair, but ended as a question that pleaded for reassurance. "Do you think so? *Could* there still be time for Kairaithin to succeed? If he will try, in the end, and not merely delay and delay and hope I am overwhelmed in the end—"

"Until the last seconds run through the glass, there's still time."

Lord Bertaud laughed bitterly. "Ah. Thank you."

"It's an aphorism because it's true," Jos said gently, and heard the gentleness in his own tone, and was surprised by it. He had not realized until that moment that he thought the other man fragile.

"Well," said Bertaud, and hesitated, glanced around with an air of uncertainty that suddenly firmed into decision, and called into the air, "Kairaithin! Sipiike Kairaithin!"

The griffin mage came to that call, whispering out of the air like swirling ash. He drew darkness around himself as he came, rising to his feet out of black feathers and the sullen glow of a quenched fire. His shadow smoldered, brighter than either the lantern light or the pale daylight lingering outside the windows; the wooden floor under his feet smoked and charred.

Jos had never known the griffin mage to command his own power so ill. He wanted to exclaim, to remind Kairaithin to rule himself. Then the griffin turned his human face toward them, and they both saw the livid mark that ran across his cheek, and the way he held one arm tucked close to his body. Jos forgot what he had meant to say, and Lord Bertaud came to his feet, asking sharply, "Was that Tastairiane? Are you all right?"

"I am not defeated!" Kairaithin said fiercely. "Do *not* call me, man! Do you not understand I am doing all I can? Let me go!"

Bertaud lifted his hands in a helpless gesture of distress and grief, and the griffin shredded at once into the thin light, black feathers crossing the light like shadows, gone once more.

For a long moment, neither man moved or spoke. Then Bertaud laughed with no humor at all and pressed a hand across his eyes.

Jos said, "If he cannot get to Tastairiane Apailika . . ." He stopped.

"Do you know . . ." Bertaud began, and paused. But then he went on, speaking in a low voice. "He said once he would tell her. Kes. About me. About what she did, when she used fire to heal me, about how she'd woken this . . . gift . . . with her fire. He said the truth would do more than any lie to keep her from healing other men with fire; that she would understand she must never risk another man coming into this cursed affinity."

This explained a good deal. Jos only nodded, allowing the other man to talk, as he clearly needed to. It might be the only useful service he could actually provide, listening to secrets Lord Bertaud could not tell anyone else.

"He can't have done, of course. Or she would never support Tastairiane in this. And now it is too late. He'll never be able to come at her now, no more than he can come at Tastairiane himself."

Jos said quietly, "I suppose he saw, as the years turned on, how little she came to care for men. So he thought it was unnecessary to warn her not to heal men with fire. He thought, *Great secrets are always safest if no one knows them.* And he thought she would never care to heal a man so again. Even—" *Me*, he had meant to say, but that would sound hopelessly bitter. He did not finish the thought aloud.

"You're Casmantian. Not much chance you'd find yourself waking with any affinity, I imagine, no matter how much fire Kes poured into you. Though—" Lord Bertaud hesitated, and then finished a little grimly, "I suspect Kairaithin would have killed you if she'd ever happened to heal you with fire, just to be certain of it."

Jos winced a little. He had come to consider Sipiike Kairaithin as something almost like a friend. But he thought the lord was right. "I sprained my ankle once," he recalled. "That was during my first winter in the mountains. Kairaithin brought me splints . . . Kes did not come, not for several weeks. I wonder whether Kairaithin prevented her. He did not want to tell her this secret, but he would not risk her healing me . . . How does a fire mage heal a creature of earth?"

Bertaud only shrugged. "Go," he said. "Rest, if you can. This is, what, the ninth day since Kairaithin brought his warning? And Kes is still using her strength against the Wall, I'm sure. I imagine the last grains of sand are running through the glass. If Kairaithin cannot come against Tastairiane tonight or tomorrow, I think we will discover what will happen when unquenchable fire runs against unyielding stone."

Clearly the Feierabianden lord wished to be alone. Jos bowed and withdrew, leaving Lord Bertaud to pore once more over his maps. He could not imagine there was much chance of rest for either of them.

Jos walked slowly toward his room, an antechamber in Lord Bertaud's own apartment, through the dim light of the hallway. He was thinking of Kes. She had been in the back of his mind without ceasing all through these weary days, and was only more so now.

For all her fierce power, she knew so little. She knew nothing at all of what her adopted people would meet on this side of the pass . . . He thought of Bertaud saying, *He can't have told her.* What a pity! And how ironic for a man who had once been a spy to think a secret too close-kept. But if she knew . . . if she knew . . . This one particular secret would do best if one more person knew it, if Kes knew it. Kairaithin could not come close to her, no. Her *iskarianere* Tastairiane Apailika, Lord of Fire and Air, would see that no enemy could come close to her.

But even the Lord of Fire and Air could not hold a fire mage from going where she would; no, not even if it occurred to the powerful white griffin to constrain her. Likely it would not occur to him, for griffins did not lightly accept or impose any constraint on one another. Kairaithin might not be able to reach Kes. But, though Kes might be wary of Kairaithin, she would not fear *Jos*. If she wished, she could come to him. And then he could tell her this dangerous secret. He had sworn silence—but Lord Bertaud, from what he'd said a moment earlier, would plainly release him to tell *Kes*, if he could.

Probably she would not come. But if she did, he could tell her what awaited her adopted people on this side of the pass. Then she would at last understand why the People of Fire and Air must not strike into Feierabiand—no, nor against any part of the country of earth. Then she would refuse Tastairiane's command to break the Wall, and all the coming storm might yet be averted.

Jos turned on his heel and headed, not toward his room, but toward the stairs. Up and up again, from the busy areas of the house to the upper hallways where no one went but servants, and up again, the remaining flight to the slanted door that led out to the roof. Not a very high roof, for the kings of Feierabiand did not care for tremendous ornate palaces such as those the kings of Casmantium built. But nevertheless above the town and out in the free air, where a creature such as Kes might come.

It was just dusk, a propitious moment because fire mages moved most easily through wind and light at dusk. Even Kairaithin preferred to come and go at dusk, especially if he moved out into the foreign country of earth. Jos was not certain that Kes *could* shift herself from the country of fire and right across the wild mountains into the country of earth. Especially with the Wall in her way. Nor was he sure that she *would* come, even if she heard him, and he was not confident even of that.

But he called her. He called her by the name she had owned when she was human, and then by the beautiful, complicated name she owned now: Kereskiita Keskainiane Raikaisipiike. He gazed up at the earliest stars, glittering cold and distant in the luminous sky, and dropped the long graceful words off his tongue as though he were reciting poetry.

And Kes came. Like a white star falling to the earth, like lightning called out of the sky, like a stroke of fire through the dark; the breeze shifted from the north to the east, and strengthened, suddenly carrying a scent of hot sand and molten air, and Kes shaped herself out of the wind and walked forward across the shingled roof. She moved as though she barely touched the roof, as though she might walk straight up into the sky if she ceased to pay attention to where she placed her feet. Her shadow, dim in the dusk, glowed like the last of the sunset. Her eyes, turned toward him, were filled with fire.

Jos stood still, watching her come. His heart had twisted the moment he'd realized she had actually come to his call, and it felt tight and painful still. He could feel the beat of his pulse in his throat. She walked toward him, smiling her fierce, beautiful smile, her eyes blazing with life and fire, and he forgot for that first moment why he had called her and what he had intended to say.

"Jos," she said. Her voice was light and quick and joyful, but behind the joy was something else, a strange wistfulness that was more nearly something he could recognize. There was no cruelty to her voice now— nor any kindness, but that he could endure, so long as the cruelty had gone out of her. She held her hands out to him.

She had settled her fire, contained it; he could touch her without danger. So he took her hands in his and looked down into her lovely, inhuman face. He said, "Kes."

"You called me," said Kes. "I came . . . I wished to see you one more time." Her ethereal white brows drew together slightly in puzzlement. "I heard your voice, and I wished to come," she repeated, speaking slowly, as though she found this curious.

"Kes," Jos said again. And then, with dawning fear, "One more time?" He had closed his hands too tightly on hers. She did not flinch from his grip, but he realized the strength of his grip and flinched on her behalf, opening his hands.

She did not draw back. She did not seem even to realize he had let her go. "I broke the Wall," she said simply.

"This past noon, when the sun struck down with all its power. Only a very little is destroyed, but that part was the anchor that locked the Wall tight against the wild mountains. The pass is open to fire now. At dawn we will call up the fiery wind. Tomorrow will be a day for blood and fire."

She did not speak, as Jos might have expected, with joyful delight. Instead her voice held an odd kind of wistfulness. She tilted her head to look at him, a quick, almost birdlike motion. She said, "I might take you away. Not into the pass. Somewhere the People of Fire and Air will not come . . ."

"They will come everywhere, eventually. Or they would. Kes—" Jos wanted to touch her face, run his thumb along the angle of her jaw. He did not let himself reach out, but said urgently, "Kes, I'm so glad you came. You don't know what will happen. A day of fire and blood, you say, but it's a day that will quench all fire. Bertaud—Lord Bertaud, whom you know—do you not realize he holds an affinity for griffins?"

For a long moment, Kes did not seem to understand what he had said. Then she did not believe him. "A creature of earth?" she cried. "An affinity for the *People of Fire and Air*? You speak fables and sunbeams, your words are as the ash that crumbles when the wind touches it! That cannot be true. It is not true. How could it be true?" She took a step back from him. Another. Cried even more sharply, her tone more plainly human than he had heard it for years, "How can you tell such lies?"

"You woke the gift in him yourself, when you used fire to heal him," Jos told her urgently. "No one knows but Sipiike Kairaithin. Think of Kairaithin and tell me it's all sunlight and ash! Think of what Kairaithin has done over these past years and what he has refused to do and tell me it's a lie!"

The fire within Kes brightened, and brightened again, so fiercely that Jos had to take a step away himself. But Kes did not disappear into the wind. She had become a burning figure of white gold and porcelain, but she did not go.

"Kes!" he said, and made himself step forward again. "If the griffins come riding their wind of fire out of that pass tomorrow, they will *all* find out. Do you understand? Do you understand what that will do to them?"

"Yes," said Kes.

"You must stop them. It's Tastairiane Apailika driving this wind, isn't it? You can go to him tonight—tell him—"

"I can't *tell* him!" cried Kes.

"—tell him you've changed your mind, you won't support this attack against Feierabiand; you can tell him something—tell him you remember your sister. *Do* you remember your sister, Kes? I'm sure she hasn't forgotten you. It's just the same this time as six years ago! All the power is in *your* hands. Tell Tastairiane you won't support him and that we're prepared, that if griffins come through that pass tomorrow, they'll face ten thousand arrows and a thousand spears, and you won't be there to make his griffins whole when they're struck down—"

Kes shook her head. "He will never stop now. Not now that the Wall is broken. He will never stop, and even if I tell him, he won't believe it can be true, he'll think you lied to me. Or if he believes it, he'll be so angry—it's Bertaud, you say? Lord Bertaud son of Boudan who has this affinity to fire?"

"Yes—" Jos said, and realized as he spoke—too late!—that he should never have given her Bertaud's name. She shredded into a blazing white wind, and Jos stared, appalled, for far too long a moment before he flung himself for the stairs.

Bertaud was still in the map room when Jos hurled himself through the door, and still alive, which Jos had not expected; it must have taken Kes a moment to find him—well, she did not know the Feierabianden lord well and *he* had not been fool enough to call her name out across the winds.

But she was there before Jos, even so. She was walking forward when Jos slammed open the door and ran in, panting in great heaving breaths. She had her hand out in almost a friendly manner, and Bertaud was not alarmed—or not alarmed enough. He was just standing there, not even backing away, far less running for the door—not that running would help; the air prickled with living fire. In a moment the house itself would blaze up, the maps and furnishings and the underlying structure itself, and Lord Bertaud would burn like a tallow candle at the center of that conflagration.

Jos could not get enough breath to shout a warning, but Bertaud took in his precipitous arrival and then seemed to see for the first time the white fire prickling across Kes's outstretched hand. He caught the edge of the map table and flung it over to block her way; worse than useless, for the papers caught fire as they spilled across the floor. Kes put her foot on the fallen table and stepped across it, so lightly it did not even wobble, but flames licked out across the wood—white flames, pale gold at the edges, burning with an intense heat that seemed likely to set the air itself on fire. Bertaud tried to shout, but the burning air drove him back, choking, his arms across his face.

Here at the edge of the room where Jos stood it was not so unendurably hot, and so Jos took a quick hard breath and shouted, "Kairaithin! Anasakuse Sipiike Kairaithin!" His voice, rough and half-strangled with heat and terror, fell flat and dead against the brilliant air. He lunged forward over the burning table and caught Kes's uplifted hand in his, dragging her back and swinging her around. He looked into her face, and he could not recognize anything he saw in those golden eyes. The fire that filled her burned his hand and arm, but to his astonishment she caught her fire back away from him after that first instant, containing it, so he did not instantly die for his temerity.

Then Kairaithin came. The eastern wall went up in a fierce blaze, and Kairaithin strode out of that sheeting flame as though he were coming through a door and took in all that was happening in one swift, summing look.

For one horrifying instant, Jos thought the griffin mage might simply lend Kes his own terrible power and rip fire out of the air through the whole house. Then his furious black gaze locked on Bertaud's, and although the man was coughing and could not speak, all the flames flattened sharply toward the floor, flickering madly, and went out, exactly like candle flames blown out from above.

"Kairaithin—" said Kes. Her tone was urgent, remonstrating. She stretched her free hand out toward her old teacher.

"Kairaithin!" Bertaud said in a much different tone, though just as urgently, and tried to catch his breath through the coughing.

"No!" cried Jos. He knew the Feierabianden lord meant to command the griffin mage to kill Kes—he knew he should even agree, he knew very well he should agree, but he couldn't, not even now. He had not let go of Kes, not even yet, and now he jerked her back to put himself between her and Kairaithin. He shouted furiously to the griffin mage, "Get her *out* of here, get her as far away as you can, and *keep* her away! Don't you see, that will do, that will be enough, if she isn't there even that bastard Tastairiane won't press through the pass without her—" He ran out of breath, coughing helplessly; his chest burned and agony radiated from his hand all the way to his shoulders and he knew, he *knew* he hadn't said enough, hadn't said it *right*, he'd never been a man with a gift for words—

Then Kairaithin, with no expression Jos could read, called up a hard-driving wind right through the walls of the house, a wind shot through with wild darkness and rushing sand and flames, and that wind whirled all around them and swept them up, and the world tilted out from underneath them, and Lord Bertaud was left behind in the map room and the king's house as the griffin flung himself and Kes and Jos away into the wind.

CHAPTER 15

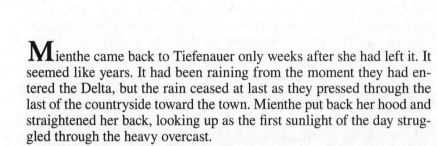

Mienthe came back to Tiefenauer only weeks after she had left it. It seemed like years. It had been raining from the moment they had entered the Delta, but the rain ceased at last as they pressed through the last of the countryside toward the town. Mienthe put back her hood and straightened her back, looking up as the first sunlight of the day struggled through the heavy overcast.

They were coming into Tiefenauer not from the east, but more from the south. The Arobern had taken them around that way so they could come up the coast road. "We turn only a little out of our way, and this road is better for marching, especially in the rain," he had said, with no explanation of how he came to know the quality of the roads in Feierabiand and the Delta. "And we do not wish to come without warning upon the Linularinan troops in the town."

Mienthe had been surprised.

"We do not wish to astonish and overwhelm them," the Arobern had explained. "We wish them to see us coming so that they may back out of our way. If they do not back away, *then* we will overwhelm them."

But he had seemed to expect the Linularinan forces to retreat. Mienthe was surprised by this, too. After all, Linularinum had shown itself amazingly determined. The Arobern certainly could not look for any additional support from Casmantium, whereas the Linularinan forces on this side of the river must have everything they needed.

"That is all true," agreed the Arobern. "And Gereint Enseichen thinks as you do, that we may find Linularinum reluctant to give way. But, militarily, they must. This is all hostile country for them. Half the men all through this country are militia, or have been. We will have the favor of the countryside and the Linularinan forces only sullenness and flung stones."

It was true that the Casmantian king had asked Mienthe to go ahead and speak to militia officers at Kames, so they had acquired three good-sized militia companies. The militia rode under the command of the Arobern's professional military officers. Their combined force now flew not only the spear-and-falcon banner of Casmantium, but also the oak banner of the Delta and the golden barley and blue river of Feierabiand. Until the Arobern explained, Mienthe had not realized that he had purposefully set all those banners up where they could be seen.

And at first he seemed to be right: They met no stiff resistance, only from time to time they glimpsed Linularinan scouts or agents, and then as they pressed forward they would often find obvious signs of a larger force that had been encamped and had now withdrawn. A formal alliance approaching and a thoroughly hostile Delta population to press them: The Linularinan officers did not want to face that. They withdrew, and withdrew again. So there had been no fighting.

"It may be different when we come to Tiefenauer," the Arobern warned Mienthe.

"It will be, if they haven't found that book of theirs," agreed Gereint Enseichen. He gave Mienthe a nod, but really he was speaking to the Arobern. "They might not wish to fight, but I think they will, rather than give up the town where they know it hides."

"They won't have found it," Mienthe had answered with confidence, but the Casmantian mage only shrugged, and as they at last approached Tiefenauer, she gradually became much less certain. She brushed damp strands of hair out of her face, peering ahead for the first glimpse of the city. The sun fought its way through towering clouds, and the woods along the road looked heavy, thick with green shadows. The shadows were ornamented by flashes of yellow and crimson where a flowering vine tumbled down a great oak or a bird darted past. Mosquitoes whined in the heavy shade, and sapphire-winged flycatchers dipped and wheeled in the complicated sky overhead. The horses' hooves thudded dully on the packed wet earth of the road, and everywhere there was the sound of rushing water—it ran down the ditches on either side of the road and against the banks where the road had been built up through a slough; it dripped from leaves overhead and trickled through the wet leaves that carpeted the ground under the trees. The reins were stiff and cold in Mienthe's fingers.

"It always seems to be raining when I come back to Tiefenauer after any time away," Mienthe said aloud.

"If it were in the mountains, it would be snow," Tan answered with the ghost of a smile. He was riding at Mienthe's shoulder, his customary place through all these long wet days. He seldom spoke now. His attention seemed to be directed inward. But he had perhaps seen Mienthe's anxiety and so spoke lightly, to take her mind from her mood.

Mienthe was not willing to be cheered. "At least that would be pretty," she said. It seldom snowed in the Delta; usually there was only a cold gray drizzle for days on end. Mienthe liked snow. She thought wistfully of pretty, wintertime Tihannad. Up in the shadow of the mountains, there might even be snow this late in the spring. Bertaud was there now. As soon as she thought of him, she found she missed him terribly. Had he met his griffin friend again; had they discovered why the Casmantian Wall was breaking and how to stop it breaking right through? He must have heard now about the trouble in the Delta . . .

It occurred to Mienthe, for the first time, that her cousin might possibly be riding for the Delta right now; that he might have come before them, he might even be there at this moment. She had assumed that he would stay close by the king, and that Iaor Safiad would avoid the Sierhanan road, and that they would meet Lord Beguchren at Minas Ford and Beguchren would stop them, exactly as the Arobern had planned. But what if—? And then what would he do, when he saw what Mienthe had brought home with her? If he had even made it to Tiefenauer on that dangerous road . . . if Linularinan soldiers hadn't stopped him, hadn't . . .

"It's a pity your lord cousin is stuck away up in Tihannad and won't be waiting to scold us for our adventures and send for healers and hot soup and warm blankets," Tan said, having evidently guessed the trend of Mienthe's thoughts.

"You don't suppose . . . you don't think . . ."

"Never in life, Mie. Even if he's settled whatever difficulty it is with the griffins, he'd never be so lost to sense as to take the Sierhanan road."

Somehow this reassurance seemed more decisive and solid when Tan said it aloud than when Mienthe only whispered it to herself. She nodded, feeling happier, and then at last they came around the curve of the road and the woodlands fell away to wet pasturelands and unplowed muddy fields and scattered farmhouses. Farther on, the farms gave way to the outermost sprawl of the town, and beyond that they could just make out the city proper, all washed slate and painted cypress and gleaming cobbles. It took a surprising effort for Mienthe to suppress the strong urge she felt to lift her horse into a canter and race down the center of the road, straight for the great house.

That wild ride might almost have been safe. There was no sign of any Linularinan force. It occurred to Mienthe only after some moments that of course the Arobern had known the road was clear; he had scouts of his own way out, after all. She said tentatively to Tan, "Do you suppose the Linularinan soldiers have all gone back across the bridge?"

Tan flashed her a smile that was only a little strained. "We shall hope so."

He almost hoped they hadn't, Mienthe understood. Of them all, Tan was the least eager to arrive, while no one but she seemed to feel this driving need for haste. But . . . *Trust your gift and yourself*, Tan had said to her, and though Mienthe thought she was probably foolishly impatient, she looked for the Arobern so she could ask whether they might press their pace to something a little less deliberate.

"We'll make haste, yes, but slowly," the Arobern told her. His tone was absent, but kind. He looked past her as he spoke, watching the road, watching the empty farmlands, studying the town they were approaching. "I thought they might get out and away across the river, but now I think they are there in the town, those Linularinan enemies of ours, you see? This country"—he made a broad gesture that encompassed the woods behind them and the cleared land near Tiefenauer and the town itself—"it is too empty. This is not peace we ride into, but a silence of waiting—ah. Do you see? Now we will find out what is there."

A small group of men had come warily up to the edge of the road to meet them. Farmers, Mienthe thought, and maybe a tradesman or two from the town. They stared at the banners, especially the Delta oak. And they looked at her, as the Arobern drew his horse up and waved a broad hand, signaling Mienthe to put herself in the forefront of the company. She was a little surprised, but only momentarily, for the militia companies were clearly pleased by his gesture and the waiting men as clearly reassured by it. The militia dipped their banners to her. Mienthe hoped she did not blush.

The men stepped up on the road to meet her, nodding respectfully and glancing warily past her at the Arobern, waiting beneath the blue-and-purple Casmantian banner. Mienthe thought they would not recognize her, that they might not trust her, but instead one of the townsmen came forward another half step and said, "Lady Mienthe, you won't remember me, I suppose. I'm Jeseth son of Tamanes. A glazier. I did the windows of the solar up at the great house for your cousin. That was some years ago—"

"I do remember!" Mienthe exclaimed. She did. She recognized the man's broad, weathered face and kindly eyes and short grizzled beard;

seeing him here was like a promise of homecoming. She said, "You fixed my window, too, when I broke it." She had been fourteen, and bent on rescuing a fledgling green jay that had got its foot tangled in the flowering vines outside her room. The poor creature had dangled helplessly upside down, cheeping piteously, but Mienthe had freed it easily. She hadn't slipped and broken the window until its frantic parents had startled her, diving to protect their young one.

"I did," said the glazier, smiling at her. "You showed me the little bird, which the esteemed Iriene had just fixed its leg. You had a scratch on your cheek where its mama had pecked you, and lucky she hadn't got your eye."

Mienthe blushed.

"It's good to see you safe," said the glazier. His gaze went past her, to the Casmantian banner. "You *are* safe, are you, lady?"

Mienthe blushed again, but nodded firmly.

"Well, and it's a strong ally you've brought trailing home at your heel. Which that is an ally, is it?"

Mienthe nodded again and found her voice. "He is, and he will be—I was afraid to come back, afraid I would find Linularinan soldiers in Tiefenauer and Linularinan officers in the great house—"

"So you will, and so we came up to warn you, seeing as you might want recent word of the town and the river," said the glazier. He'd brought his gaze back to her face. "We've not known what to do, what with your lord cousin gone to Tihannad. Earth and stone, even if Lord Bertaud's trying to get back here right this minute, who knows what he might have run into? We've no word from him and none from the king, and every one of your uncles pulling in a different direction. Arguing like a pack of fighting dogs with one bone, they are, and not one as will give way to the rest. And now here *you* are, lady, cutting straight past that whole lot and bringing a *Casmantian* lord home with you! That'll make those Linularinan bastards sit up on their hind legs and take notice, and at the same time save a great lot of arguing among our Delta lords." He gave Mienthe an approving nod.

"That's Brechen Glansent Arobern himself," Mienthe said. She raised her voice and said to all the silent little group of listening men, "This is the Arobern himself, come as a friend to our king and to my cousin and to the Delta. He'll push all those Linularinan troops back across the river, whether they've got the bridge decked or have to swim, and too bad for them if all this rain's got the river up!"

The men cheered and laughed, nodding approvingly. One farmer called out, "The bridge isn't decked even yet, and let the lot of them be swept right out to sea on the salt tide!" and they cheered again.

Mienthe nodded and smiled, but she also said, "Well, all the Delta will have to help. Neither the Arobern nor his men know the marshes or our town, and assuredly we want to clear out the Linularinan troops as quick as we may, so we can polish up Tiefenauer and present it properly to my lord cousin when he comes back!"

"That's right!" said one man, and another, "Hear the lady!"

"So tell our ally your news, and we'll see what we have to do," Mienthe concluded, and waved up the Arobern, who gave her an approving nod, swung down from his horse, and strode up on foot to speak to the men. He was bareheaded and informal, speaking quickly in his rough, accented Terheien, making farmers and townsmen alike forget he was a king and nodding now and then, respectfully, toward Mienthe.

All along the column there was a general easing, men passing along flasks of watered wine and pieces of hard cracker. "We can do better than that by you," one of the Delta farmers broke off to say, and spoke to one of the Arobern's officers, after which a half dozen Casmantian soldiers and a good many Delta men went off down the farm lane.

Soon after that there were loaves of good bread, and cold roasted mutton, and baskets of fried chicken and hot buttered muffins, brought by the farmers' wives and by boys too young for the militia but eager to touch the vicious heads of real Casmantian spears. "Which we had word of your banners long since," said one woman cheerfully. "And then my Tamed brought word of yourself, lady, and glad we were to hear *that* word! *You'll* teach those Linularinan bastards they can't take us so light, begging your pardon, lady."

Mienthe smiled and nodded and murmured whatever seemed appropriate and cast longing glances down the road. "Can't we get *on*?" she begged the Arobern at last. The sun stood nearly directly overhead, and she found herself fretting like a caged bird with all the bright sky above calling out to her to *fly*.

"We don't want to rush the Arobern past what he thinks is wise," murmured Tan, which sentiment collected approving nods from the Casmantian officers.

"We might wish to heed the lady's sense of urgency," said Gereint Enseichen, winning a grateful smile from Mienthe.

"I think we can," said the Arobern. He looked sternly at Tan and then transferred that heavy frown to Mienthe. "We shall expect some resistance; we shall expect some fighting. You will both assure me that you will stay close by the honored mage, do you hear? You will not ride ahead, no matter this *sense of urgency*. You will not fall behind no matter that you feel you have cause for alarm. Yes?"

"Yes!" declared Mienthe, trying to press the king and the whole company into motion with sheer willpower. Her grip tightened on her reins; her horse jigged sideways and spun in an impatient circle when she checked him. She longed to let the animal go, kick him into a gallop, fling him straight ahead at the town that lay so quietly before them.

"Yes," muttered Tan, his eyes on the damp road, steaming now in the sun. He swung reluctantly into the saddle. When Gereint took a step toward him, he flinched and backed his horse several steps.

The mage paused and looked at Tan for a moment without speaking. Then he went, still in silence, to mount his own tall horse.

Tiefenauer was not a great city, with tall mansions of fine dressed stone and wide avenues paved with tight-fitted blocks of stone. Its streets were narrow and cobbled, its buildings tight-packed and mostly of painted cypress and oak. Cheap gray paint was favored in the poorer areas of the town because it was cheap, with dark red or tawny yellow for those who were more daring; white where families could afford to have their houses painted every year. The white buildings had shutters and doors of scarlet or bright green or sunny yellow, and vines with purple or crimson or orange flowers tumbling from their balconies.

In most of the town, homes were small and mostly set above equally small shops: tailors and cobblers and dressmakers all along one long, narrow street; furniture-makers and harness-makers and metalsmiths near the horse-market; butchers and sausage-makers in the south of town and fishmongers along the river; bakers and confectioners and apothecaries and all sorts of small crafts on the north side. In the middle of town was a wonderful fountain, three levels of falling water leaping from top to bottom with hundreds of green copper fish. Beside the fountain stood a huge oak, in the wide square where twice a week the market was raised, and beyond the square the low hill with the sprawling great house atop it.

It was in the square that the bulk of the Linularinan forces were set, and in the gardens around the great house. But there were Linularinan soldiers all through the town, occupying the apartments above the shops and making free of the shops themselves.

"But not too free," the townsmen had said, with the grudging air of men bound despite their wishes to be fair. The glazier had added, "They'll let anyone out of Tiefenauer who wishes to go, which is a good many. There hasn't been much looting and less wanton pillage and no firing the buildings. While I was still there—I have a business to look after, but I sent my wife to her cousin down near Saum—but while I was still in Tiefenauer myself, I saw the Linularinan officers flog one of their men for theft and," he said with a grim nod of satisfaction, "they hanged a man for raping a girl, as well they might."

"A gentle occupation. They don't want your folk to hate them for generations," the Arobern had said, which was obvious.

"They only want that book—and Tan," Gereint Enseichen had added. "They must know the book is there. And Lady Mienthe is right: They haven't found it. But I can't imagine what's prevented them. If it's a twentieth-part as obvious as Tan himself, a blind mage should be able to walk right to it."

"So perhaps it isn't a twentieth-part as obvious," Tan had said, an edge to his tone. "Shall we stand here discussing it from one noon to the next, or shall we get on?"

They had gone on. Mienthe had no idea what the Arobern planned to do about the Linularinan soldiers in the houses or the ones in the square; she hadn't been able to make herself pay attention. She knew that Tan was near her, but she was barely aware even of Gereint Enseichen, though the mage rode close on her other side. All her attention was focused on the great house, on the book, on the pressing need to get to it and do—something. She could picture the book clearly in her mind's eye, but she could not picture what either she or Tan or Gereint might *do* with it. But she could not think about anything else. Images of the book occupied nearly the whole of her mind. She could have drawn every curve and line of its decorated cover; she could have told out how many pages it contained. She felt the textures of leather and fine thick paper against her fingers. She thought if *she* had been looking for it, she would inevitably have gone straight to it, with the same certainty with which the river knew which way to go to reach the sea. And, of course, she *was* looking for it, and when she was at last permitted to go freely forward, she headed for it with exactly that certainty.

So Mienthe did not know what disposition the Arobern made with his men, or with the militia companies; she did not know what arrangements he came to with the townsmen and surrounding farmers or even whether there was fighting in the streets of the town once they arrived. She noticed vaguely that she had gone largely blind. Or not really *blind*. It was not a malady of the eyes, but of the attention. She would blink and find quite a large block of time lost. She knew they were outside the town and then that they were in it, between gray-painted buildings, in a narrow alley that smelled of warm rain and steaming cobbles and horse dung and baking bread, with the angle and quality of the light quite different. Then she blinked again and only the cobbles were the same, for the buildings were painted white and the smells did not include bread but did include the fragrance of tumbling trumpet flowers, and the shadows were long and the air much cooler. Yet she had no sense of passing time: All her sense of time seemed to have narrowed to a single pressing urgent *now*.

She lost track of Gereint Enseichen, only noticing occasionally that he had seized her wrist to hold her back. Once when this happened, she stepped sideways and around in a neat circle that took her out of his hold and let her walk forward again, only then she found that Tan had not come with her, so she had to turn back to find him.

She neither noticed nor remembered to wonder whether any of the Arobern's men or townspeople had come with her. Tan was the only person she really noticed, and then only in his absence. She needed him to come with her, and when the world bent around her and behind her then she knew he had paused. If he would not come with her, then she, too, was constrained to pause. In those moments she tried to find him, take his hand, pull him forward after her. But he resisted her tug.

There was shouting, she noticed vaguely. And then she thought so again; she did not know if time had passed or if she was still caught in the same moment, but the shouting seemed to have become more violent and nearer at hand. Tan was refusing to follow her. Mienthe blinked, confused by the sweep of motion and color all around them; nothing would resolve to sensible form. She turned her head, but nothing she saw made sense. But Tan had a hard grip on her hand, and the book was now very close, it was right over *there*. She closed her own hand on Tan's and pulled him hard, around and into a circle that led around the violent motion and through brilliantly colored shadows, and there was the book— She pulled back the rug and shifted the wardrobe out half a step, leaned into the gap, tapped firmly against the upper edge of one panel of the wood that decorated the wall, and the panel swung open just a crack, and she pried it open just that little bit farther and reached into the dark gap behind the panel and the book fell neatly into her hand.

And the moment crashed into time, or time expanded to engulf the moment, and Mienthe found herself standing in her own apartment, her own bedchamber, with the last of the afternoon sunlight slanting in through her window, and the smell of smoke and dust hanging heavy in the air, and, not so far away, a clamor of shouting and screaming and the clash of weapons. Startlement made her gasp, and then rising fear might have made her cry out in earnest, only when she whirled about she found Tan standing in the middle of her room with a finger held to his lips and an expression of stifled hilarity in his eyes.

For a long, stretched moment, Tan was absolutely certain that Mienthe, having brought them by some strange mageworking right past who knew how many Linularinan soldiers and straight into the great house and her own room, would at this inopportune moment recover her senses and cry out some word of triumph or even, given her dazed expression, astonishment. As he could quite clearly hear the loud, authoritative voices of Linularinan soldiers directly without the room, this would hardly serve.

He had, however, for the first time in days—for the first time since Ehre, indeed—a wild desire to laugh. He felt very alert, and tremendously alive, and terribly frightened. He tried hard not to laugh. He bit his lips instead, and held out his hand.

Somewhere near at hand, a soldier called out and another answered: a formal sign and countersign, by the sound, as was the Linularinan practice in uncertain territory. Mienthe's eyes widened at the sound. She glanced over her shoulder, hesitated one more instant, and then darted across the room to Tan. She clasped the book—the book for which they had spent so much effort—in both her hands. For a moment Tan thought she might fall back into that trance of movement and magic that had so recently held her. But then she blinked, life and awareness returning to her eyes, and instead offered the book to Tan.

He did not touch it, but took her by the elbow and nodded aside, at the farthest doorway that led out of this room, and raised his eyebrows.

"Yes," Mienthe whispered, and ran that way.

The doorway proved to lead straightaway into a tiny, windowless corner room that was probably meant to be a maid's room, but fitted out not with its own narrow bed and tiny dresser but with a neat little writing desk and shelves of expensive books and little keepsakes. An illustrated herbal lay open on the desk, undisturbed, as it had no doubt lain since they had all fled so precipitously from this house.

The tiny room was surely as far from enemy soldiers as they might well find themselves. Mienthe closed the herbal and set it aside, then placed the blank Linularinan book down on the desk. She ran a fingertip over the curves and loops of its tooled leather cover and then looked rather blankly at Tan.

"You know what to do," Tan murmured to her.

Mienthe only shook her head. "I thought I would," she whispered back—she did not know that a whisper carried better than merely a low voice, but it should not matter, back in this corner as they were. She looked frightened and uncertain, and that was much worse. She whispered, "I thought I would know what to do, but all I see now is a book! All the rest is like, like a dream—misty, fading—We're here, we *have* this book, and now I don't know *anything*—"

"Shh," murmured Tan, touching her shoulder to quiet her. "All will be well. Everything will be well. Shh. Let me just see this odd creation now. The key to our hope and all our enemies' desire, and yet it is so very small."

Mienthe did not recognize the quote, of course. She only nodded, looking uncertain.

Tan did not try to explain. He only began to reach out—then caught himself and nodded to the young woman instead. "Open it for me, will you, please, for all kindness."

Mienthe managed a nervous little smile and a nod, and flipped the book open herself. She flipped past several of the heavy, ivory-colored sheets, each as empty as a cloudless sky. She said, "Maybe if you were to write in it—if you were to have nothing in your mind, but only touch a quill to its pages—do you think you might write out what you . . . what you have? What you hold in your mind?"

"What passes for my mind," Tan murmured absently. "Perhaps."

"But I don't have any quills—"

Without a word, Tan extracted a packet of quills from an inner pocket, held it up with a minor flourish, and set it down by the book.

Mienthe turned another blank page, and another. She shook her head. "There's nothing. It's so strange. It's almost as though there was never anything here at all."

Tan made a wordless comforting sound, not really attending. He took a quill, a small but neatly made crow's feather, out of the packet and tested it on his thumb. The ink was black, a good, flowing ink without grittiness or stutters, contained within a well-made quill, exactly what one would expect from the Casmantian king's own mage. Or ex-mage. From Lord Beguchren Teshrichten, in either case, from whom Tan had acquired the packet of quills. He looked at the book, considering. But when he moved to touch it, to write in it, he could bring himself to do neither. He had a reasonless but intense dread of the book, especially of setting ink to its empty pages. He knew he could not possibly bring himself to write anything at all in it.

"Well?" Mienthe asked anxiously, forgetting to whisper.

Tan shook his head. He laughed, though quietly. "So far out and as far back, and what have we to show for all our weary steps? We are come not even to our beginning, but beyond that. We are looking over ground we shall have to recover to come back to the place where we began—"

"Write something!" said Mienthe sharply.

Tan shook his head again. "I can't. I daren't. I don't know how. This isn't a book, Mie, it's something else that's just in the *shape* of a book. If it's legistwork, it's nothing I recognize, not even now."

Mienthe's lips pressed together, and her jaw set in that determined expression with which she faced down mountains and kings. She said, "We'll take it back to Gereint Enseichen. All the way back to Beguchren Teshrichten, if we have to. *He'll* know what to do with it."

She did not suggest how they might get out of this house and back across town; well, more than likely she did not remember anything of the twisting, difficult route they'd followed to get in. Or how they'd still be trapped outside this house now, save for that strange spiraling path she'd drawn across light and shadow to bring them the last little way, at the end . . . She flipped the book shut with a sharp, decisive movement.

Tan said suddenly, the pattern leaping out at him for the first time, "There's a spiral on the cover."

Mienthe blinked, and looked.

Tan traced the pattern for her in the air, the tip of his finger hovering above the leather. There *was* a spiral, when one looked for it—or not just one, indeed, but several: interlocking spirals set into the patterned leather among the circumscribed arcs of circles and ellipses. Some of the spirals were raised and turned right, but at least one was concave and turned left.

Mienthe traced the first spiral herself, with no need to be cautious about touching the book. She said, "Earth."

Tan looked at her, wanting to ask what she meant, fearing to interrupt whatever inspiration she might have discovered.

"Earth," Mienthe insisted, and traced the next spiral, a smaller one that interlocked with the first and then twisted away in its own direction. And the next, small and twining about the second. "Fire," she said. "And wind." She found another, this one pressed deep into the rich leather. When she touched it, her fine eyebrows drew together in something like pain. "Oh. The wild heights."

"Mie—"

"Yes," the young woman murmured. She stood up, took the crowfeather quill out of Tan's hand, walked back into the apartment's main sitting room, swung chairs aside every which way, kicked aside a rug, and bent to draw a spiral right on the naked boards of the floor.

Tan wouldn't have interrupted for the world. He hauled a couch out of her way; then, after a moment's consideration, stood it on end and leaned it into the little writing room. Then he stood in the doorway, watching with tense fascination as Mienthe completed the first big outer circle and began to bring the spiral inward.

There was a faintly audible alarmed shout. Tan jerked his head up, listening. The shout was repeated, nearer, he was almost certain. Mienthe did not seem to notice, but Tan was afraid the alarm might very soon press itself on her attention. He wished he knew what drawing spirals on the floor was going to do, or, which might be a more urgent question, how long it might take to do it. He had no weapons, and no particular skill with them even if he found a sword tucked away among the gowns in Mienthe's wardrobe. Chairs propped under the doorknobs of the outermost apartment door and then the sitting room door were all very well, but would hold professional soldiers for no more than moments—Mie might have found inspiration somewhere, but nothing useful occurred to Tan, and the shouting was now distinctly closer—

"Tan!" Mienthe called urgently from the sitting room, having either forgotten the need for quiet or justifiably concluded the precaution was now no use. "Tan! Oh—there you are, good. Get in the center. No, *with* the book!" She pressed it into his hands and pushed him toward the middle of the spiral that now nearly covered the floor: A dozen long, perfectly smooth turns ran away from the wall toward the center of the room. The black lines glistened as though with fresh ink, but not the best-made quill in the world could ever have held so much or drawn out such a broad, heavy stroke. And then in the next moment the black lines did not look like ink at all, but like shadows, like deep cracks that cut straight through into the heart of the world. He tried to follow the spiral inward with his eyes but found the center hard to see, as though it was very far away. The illusion that the overall spiral led downward as it turned inward was very powerful, even though when he looked across it rather than along its curving length, he could see perfectly well that the floor was level.

"Don't cut across the line!" she added.

"Don't cut the line?" Tan muttered. He cast a glance toward the door, which someone had just struck a reverberating blow. "Mie—"

"What?" She did not seem to notice, not even when the door shook in its frame under another blow. She stared instead at the widely spaced curving lines of the spiral. Her expression was intent, not blank as it had been out in the town. But was the difference good or bad?

The door shook again, and the wood cracked.

"Tan!" said Mienthe, but not about the door, and how nice for her to be so caught up in her strange magic that she did not need to suffer fear. She pointed toward the center of the spiral.

With an effort, Tan turned his back on the door and, stepping firmly into the spiral, began to walk around the curving pathway it provided toward its center. He was careful not to touch the glistening black line with his foot, though he wondered, if he did, would the ink smear, or would he simply find his foot plunging through an open chasm toward the center of the earth?

Mienthe exclaimed, "Oh, *where* did I leave off the end?" but she sounded frustrated rather than frightened. Then she said, "Oh," sounding much happier. How nice one of them could be happy.

Despite her warning to Tan, she walked suddenly forward right along the line, placing one foot carefully in front of the next. The ink did not smear, nor did she fall. Despite the narrowness of the line and all her care, she walked quickly, so that she threatened to reach the center long before Tan. He did not know whether this mattered, but found himself hurrying to keep up, so that they walked shoulder to shoulder, Mienthe on the outside line and himself on the inside, keeping to the space between the lines.

The crashing at the door now seemed to linger oddly on the air; the sounds reverberated against the air as though from a great distance . . . Black sparks were falling away from Mienthe's feet. She seemed to be walking on a layer of translucent glass that lay across deep cracks . . . To Tan, she did not seem to have created those cracks, but rather to have *collected* them somehow, pulling them out of the very fabric of the world and arranging them in this orderly shape, but he could not have explained what he meant by this idea or why he thought so. He also thought the cracks were going down, down and in, even though when he remembered to glance up he could see that they were still in the room, that the world outside the spiral seemed unchanged . . . perfectly unchanged, as though frozen in glass, as a glassblower might lock a delicate flower or leaf into a glass weight, only it was as though the glass had turned inside out, so that everything outside it was locked into stillness and only within the spiral did motion and life remain possible.

But this was an illusion, for even as the strange idea occurred to Tan, the door flew soundlessly to pieces—well, not soundlessly; it was only that the crashing, splintering sounds did not seem important.

Linularinan soldiers surged into the room but then flung themselves aside rather than forward. Tan wondered what they saw; indeed, he wondered what *he* saw. Mienthe had come to the end of her line, and Tan to the open center of the spiral, but, though he stopped, she kept on, placing one foot neatly before the last. Though she had no quill or ink, the line drew itself out under her feet, or she drew it after her by the act of walking forward. Tan wondered whether he should follow after her, but he could not see how there was room for him to go forward—nor could he see how *Mienthe* found room to walk forward, only she made her own space as she made her own line. But Tan did not know how to do that.

Istierinan Hamoddian came through the door after the soldiers, who pressed back to give him room. Tan turned to gaze at Istierinan, across what seemed simultaneously an immense distance and the span of an ordinary, rather small room. The Linularinan spymaster looked old, much older than he had bare weeks ago. Old and ill. The bones of his face had become prominent, his eyes dark and hollowed, his hands skeletally thin. He was holding something—a quill, Tan saw, made of a white falcon's feather, its tip glistening with ink so dark a red it might almost have been blood. Then Tan blinked again and saw that it *was* blood.

Istierinan spoke—he was shouting: The tendons stood out on his throat. In a way, Tan could not hear him, or only dimly, as from a long way away. Yet if he thought about the sounds, he realized they were actually loud. "You don't know what you're doing!" he cried. "You don't know what you *can* do!" He started toward the entrance to the spiral, his white quill held out before him like a weapon.

At the same time, Mienthe faltered, but not because of Istierinan. "It's not enough," she said, her tone dismayed. "I can't finish it—the turns are too tight—it doesn't go deep enough—it's not right, I'm not doing it right, it's all wrong—"

"Ignorant child!" Istierinan was beside himself with fury and a terror so great it was almost exaltation. "Of course you're not! How could you? *Get out of it*, turn it around— *You!*" he shouted at Tan. "Give what you stole back to me now and I may *even yet* be able to set this right!" He strode forward, set himself at the entrance of the spiral, but then hesitated there, his breath coming hard, his hands shaking, gathering himself for that first step.

"You'll *never* set it right," Mienthe cried. "You can't, you won't, you don't even want to! Get out, get away!"

"Mie—" said Tan. "If you can't do this, if you can't do whatever needs to be done, then maybe—"

Mienthe turned to him. She was weeping with frustration and fear, and her voice was shaking, but even so she spoke with passionate conviction. "He can't! He set it up all wrong before; it was him, if it wasn't him then it was someone *like* him. I'm sure it was! And he didn't do it right! It's never been right, not from the first time it was ever set down!"

"Mie, *what* was set up wrong?"

"Everything!" Mienthe cried. "The law of the world! He's a mage as well as a legist! He hates fire, and if *he* writes the law down in that book, he'll write it all wrong!"

Istierinan stepped into the spiral, between the black lines.

Tan turned so as to meet him when he came around the last turn, but for all Istierinan's age and evident illness, he moved toward Tan like a superior swordsman might stalk toward a rank novice who's had the temerity to issue a challenge. Tan had thought he understood legist-magic. Now he knew he didn't understand anything, and the only thing he knew with perfect certainty was that he was afraid of the older man.

"I see the way it should go—if I could only *finish* it," cried Mienthe, but though she turned and tried to draw her spiral forward and inward and down, it was as though she leaned against something solid, tried to press herself forward through air that had become as sheer and hard and unyielding as glass, and not nearly so easily broken.

Without warning, fire blazed out of the air and into the outer reaches of the spiral, slapped against Mienthe's empty black line as against a physical barrier, and rose, towering to the ceiling.

Tan, staggering, dropped to his knees and tucked himself forward over the book he still held, as though it contained all his hope of life and sanity. But the fire did not rush into the center of the spiral at all; rather, it whipped outward around the curving lines of the spiral and roared out into the room. It sheeted past and over Istierinan, who staggered but did not burn.

Outside the spiral, the fire was much worse. Flames roared up the walls; the discarded chairs caught; flames licked across the boards of the floor. The soldiers fled.

Mienthe was screaming, Tan realized at last. He came up to one knee, twisting about to look for her, but she was untouched. She was crouched down upon the black line of the spiral, her hands pressed against her lips, shaking and white with terror, but never stepping away from the line she had drawn.

Someone else groaned, a deep, raw sound of agony, and the flames suddenly flattened low and flickered out. The walls and floor were charred, everything was charred except within the spiral, but there was no longer living fire anywhere.

A man stood near the entrance to the spiral. His posture was rigid, ungiving. His austere face was set in an expression of bitter resignation and anger. When he turned his head, taking in the room and Mienthe's spiral, his black eyes burned with power. Istierinan, straightening, stared at him with horror and loathing.

A little distance from him stood a big man and, tiny next to him, tucked half out of sight behind him, a pale, fragile girl. The man was gripping her delicate hand in his big one, gripping hard, by the clenched muscles of his forearm. But it was not the girl who had cried out with pain, but the man, and now he let her go, cupping one terribly burned hand in the other.

The girl looked dismayed. She came back toward the man, her steps quick and light.

"No," snapped the dark man. "Fool! Do you not understand yet what may wake when you use fire to heal a man?"

"He's right. He's right. You mustn't," said the big man, backing away from the girl, his face twisting with pain and with some strong, dangerous emotion.

"It's my fault, then!" cried the girl, and whirled away from them all, gathering herself as though she might spring away into the air.

"No," said the dark man again.

The girl whirled to face him. "Let me go!" she cried. "Kairaithin, let me go! If this is my fault, let me set it right! He cannot constrain *me*!" Her voice was high and light, furious and desperate and somehow not at all a human voice. And she *glowed*, Tan realized, as though she burned with her own internal fire. Flames flickered within the tangled gold-white hair that fell down her back; her eyes were swimming with golden fire.

"Get out!" roared Istierinan, his voice thick with fury. "Get out!"

"Impossible," said the dark man, Kairaithin, but to the girl. He took no more notice of the Linularinan spymaster than an eagle might have paid a furious songbird. Less. He said, still to the girl, "And untrue. Nothing that has happened is your doing. Though you may still pay the cost of it. As may we all." His taut posture had not eased; he tilted his head as though listening to the great wind that had brought them; as though listening to the roar of fire, or of some powerful music none of the rest of them could hear. His voice was strong, harsh, dangerous.

Like the girl, he was a creature of fire, Tan realized, though the fire that burned in him was darker and more powerful and far more tightly controlled. His shadow rose behind him, huge and wild and burning. It was not the shadow of a man, and at last Tan realized what he was, what he must be, for all he wore the shape of a man. *This* was the griffin who had come to Mienthe's cousin? *This* had brought the warning that had taken Bertaud and the king away to the north and left the Delta vulnerable to Linularinan machinations? Tan was amazed by the composure Mienthe had shown after meeting this creature.

The griffin mage turned suddenly, focusing all that dark, burning power toward Mienthe. She didn't quite manage composure this time, but flinched noticeably from the scorching heat of his stare. "It was *your* wind," he said harshly. "When I looked for a new wind to ride, it was *your* wind that swept across mine. And what direction do you mean for this storm you are calling?"

Mienthe flinched from the powerful Kairaithin, but in fact nearly all of her attention was on the pale-burning girl. She took a step toward her along her black spiral, holding out her hand. "It was *you* I needed all along!" she said. "Fire to balance earth! No wonder, no wonder— Was there a wind? Well, no wonder it brought you here!"

"No!" cried Istierinan. "Fool!" He did not leave the protection of the spiral, however, but turned and began to walk once more along the narrow passage between its black lines, toward Tan.

The pale girl said furiously to Kairaithin, paying no attention to either Istierinan or Mienthe, "It wasn't *my* wind! I know what wind *I* would call up!"

"Kes," said the human man. He spoke with difficulty, his voice ragged with pain, but his voice checked her where the others had only fed her fury. He said again, "Kes. You were a creature of earth, once. Try to remember. I know you remember a little, or you wouldn't have held your fire back for me—you wouldn't have thought of healing me— and you did think of it. You did. You had a sister whom you loved, do you remember? I know she hasn't forgotten you. Would you really call up a wind for Tastairiane Apailika, a fire to burn across your sister and her horses? Across everything you ever loved?"

Kes stood still, her golden eyes on the man's strained face. Her eyes held nothing human; her expression was unreadable. But she stood still, listening.

"Kereskiita," said the dark man, "the storm Tastairiane Apailika wishes to ride will carry the People of Fire and Air to destruction." He lifted a hand, pointed straight at Mienthe's black spiral. "Here is a different storm, when I had all but given up hope that any countervailing wind might arise. It is perilous and terrible, but surely set in a direction none of us had anticipated. It is too late to turn Tastairiane Apailika's wind. Call this wind, then, and let it burn!"

"Kes," said the man. He cradled his burned hand against his body and stared at the girl, his eyes purely human. He said again, "Kes."

"Jos," said the girl very softly. "I do remember." And, turning toward the spiral, she took a single step that suddenly whirled her around it and left her standing beside Mienthe.

Far too close, in Tan's opinion, but though he flinched violently, Mienthe reached out and laid her hand against the hand of the girl of fire, palm to palm. Nor did she jerk back as away from fire, but only looked into her face for a moment, her expression very serious.

"No!" shouted Istierinan again, his voice cracking in furious despair.

Mienthe lifted her hand from the other girl's, turned, and began to draw out her spiral: around and in, around and in. Kes turned in the opposite direction and began to draw a spiral of her own, this one a narrow line of white fire that turned outward, rising. Though they both sketched their parallel spirals on the same level floor, somehow the black spiral seemed to turn down and down, while the burning white spiral rose as it turned.

Tan saw at once what Mienthe had meant by fire balancing earth, for now Mienthe moved much more easily, with no sign that she had ever or would ever come against a limit to how tight she might make her spiral, how deep she might send it. And Kes moved as easily, every step as light as though she were actually rising as she went, walking away into the air.

Istierinan cried out, an articulate sound. He dropped to one knee and drove the tip of his white quill straight across the line of white fire. The quill caught fire and blazed up with a flame as white as its feather, and the red ink ran out of it, hissing as it came against Kes's fiery spiral, quenching the flame and leaving only the black chasm of the spiral Mienthe had drawn.

Mienthe cried out, sounding furious as well as terrified. Then Kes cried out as well, her voice as piercing and inhuman as the shriek of a falcon. Their two voices blurred together until it was impossible to tell one from the other.

Tan began to stride forward, out of the center of the spiral, toward Istierinan.

"No!" said Kairaithin urgently. "No, man!"

"Yes, come to me!" called Istierinan grimly.

Tan stopped, looking helplessly from the griffin mage to the Linularinan legist, and Istierinan stood up and ran the white feather of his quill through his fingers. The fire that had caught in its feather went out, and he laughed.

Kairaithin, with no expression at all, took one step forward and exploded violently into fiery wind and driving red sand. The power of that wind slashed across the double spiral with incredible precision, slicing past Mienthe and Kes, scouring away the bloody ink and whipping up the white fire, hardly disturbing Tan's hair as it whipped past him but driving against Istierinan with terrible force, tearing at his face and eyes, flinging him to his knees, ripping the white quill from his hands. But, though the quill blazed up once more, it did not crumble to ash but flew across the spiral like a burning arrow. It fell point-down at Tan's feet, its tip deep in the wood of the floor, its feather burning on and on with white fire, like a slim taper that would not gutter out.

The power in that same great wind, unleashed, allowed Kes, even as she screamed in grief, to raise her fragile white hands and send her spiral racing infinitely wide and high, until it cracked the edges of the world and broke against the dome of the sky. Mienthe cried out, and her spiral leaped forward in equal measure as though dragged along by the fiery spiral, only hers broke open the day and the dark and twisted in and down until it shattered the center of the earth.

"Write down the law!" Mienthe cried.

As in a dream, Tan opened the book. He bent and took up the burning white quill.

"Write down fire and joy!" said Kes. She seemed to have forgotten grief. She lifted hands filled with blazing light and shook fire out of her hair, laughing.

"Write down earth *and* fire," said Jos, leaning against a wall that was, amazingly, still standing. "Write down sorrow as well as joy."

"You must subordinate fire to earth!" croaked Istierinan through burned lips and broken teeth, trying blindly to get to his feet.

Mienthe only watched Tan, her expression grave and trusting.

There was no ink left in the quill, so Tan tore its sharp point across his own wrist. He wrote in his own blood, across a page that would take no other ink, a single word. The word he wrote was

AMITY

He wrote it plainly, with neither flourish nor ornament. The word sank into the page and all through the book. From the center of the earth to the dome of the sky, from one edge of the world to the other, the writing remade the law of the world.

CHAPTER 16

It was nothing a mage would have thought of. Everyone agreed about that one thing, later. Everyone, at least, who was a mage, or had ever been a mage. Certainly Beguchren Teshrichten said so, so Mienthe was sure it was true.

"It required someone with a remarkable, anomalous gift," he said wryly to Mienthe. "Casmantium for making, Feierabiand for calling, and Linularinum for law, but I've never heard of anyone waking into a gift such as yours."

"Istierinan Hamoddian was anomalous, too," Mienthe pointed out.

"But not at all in the same way. Have some of these berries. What a splendid climate you have here in the Delta, to be sure. Fresh berries so early! No, we quite well understand Istierinan, anomalous as he undeniably was. One doesn't think of a mage being able to sustain any natural gift; indeed, we are taught that bringing out the mage power smothers the inborn gift. Yet clearly there are and have been exceptions." Beguchren tilted his head consideringly. "Perhaps the legist gift is more amenable to magework than making or calling. One does rather hope that such persons are rare, generally not quite so powerful, and now inclined toward a certain humility."

They might very well be so inclined, Mienthe thought, considering what had happened to Istierinan. She had thought they ought to leave him for King Iaor to judge, or even send him back to his own king, but Kes had not been patient or forgiving with the man who was, or so she had seemed to feel, in some part responsible for her old teacher's death. When she had destroyed him, she had not left even ash. Nor, when it came to the moment, had Mienthe tried very hard to stop her. She had not confessed to anyone her deep relief at the death of Tan's enemy. But she was relieved. All she said aloud was, "I hope they are *very* rare."

They were in the Arobern's camp, set neatly to the east of Tiefenauer, separate and self-contained. The Arobern had thought it politic to keep all his people outside the town, lest anyone should have any impression he'd ever meant to conquer or hold it himself. Iaor Safiad himself had firmly and pointedly occupied the great house as soon as he'd arrived, two days after Tan had written his new law to govern fire and earth. Bertaud had not yet returned. Mienthe was almost certain her cousin was well—the king assured Mienthe he was well—but she longed to see him and be certain of it herself.

Iaor Safiad had not yet granted the Arobern an audience. He had sent only curt word refusing the Casmantian king leave to withdraw east toward the pass. He had, however, sent almost every available Feierabianden healer to the Casmantian camp, thus demonstrating that while he might be furious with the Casmantian king, he was at least willing to admit that the Casmantian soldiers had suffered on Feierabiand's behalf. Everyone assumed that Iaor was much angrier with the King of Linularinum than with the Arobern—everyone assumed he would, in due course, forgive the Arobern's presumption. The Casmantian soldiers, nodding wisely, muttered about royal pride; three or four young men had already wistfully asked Mienthe about the Safiad's temper. She had not known how to answer their questions.

Beguchren Teshrichten had not asked Mienthe about either king. He said instead, "One does wonder whether your gift would ever have stirred if Tan hadn't happened to break the law Linularinan legists long ago imposed on the world." Then he paused and asked, very gently, "How does Tan do, today? May I hope that there has been some improvement?"

Mienthe began to answer, but tears suddenly closed her throat and she found she could not speak. Blinking hard, she opened her hands in a gesture of wretched uncertainty.

"I believe he will come to himself in good time, child. Recovery from such events does take time. He overused his gift, I suspect." The mage paused and then said plainly but not unkindly, "He might have lost it. Used it up. Such things can happen, in great extremity."

As Lord Beguchren knew better than anyone. Mienthe nodded. She swallowed, rubbed her hand across her mouth, and managed to ask, "Is there anything you might suggest?"

Beguchren lifted his shoulders in a minimal shrug. "I'm certain you are already doing everything I might suggest. Warmth, rest . . . the company of a friend . . ."

"King Iaor made me leave." Mienthe blushed slightly, remembering the king's blunt impatience. *You're too thin, Mienthe. How will it help him if you wear yourself to bone and nerve? Go for a walk, go for a ride, see the sky, have something to eat, have a nap, don't come back here until dusk. Trust Iriene to watch over him. That's an actual royal command, Mie. Now go away.* Though she suspected that Iaor had not actually meant for her to ride down to the Casmantian camp and visit Lord Beguchren.

"Undoubtedly wise. It serves nothing for you to fall ill yourself. Once you are both entirely recovered, I wonder whether you might care to visit Casmantium." Beguchren picked up another cluster of berries between his finger and thumb and gazed at it. "How very like a string of garnets! You might like to wait until your berrying season is past, perhaps. But I would be pleased if you—and Tan, of course—would visit me in Breidechboden. I would like very much to investigate the precise nature of your gift. I believe it is certainly a gift rather than any form of magecraft. But certainly an exceedingly odd gift. I wonder what other odd gifts we may find emerging now that the world is no longer subject to the constraints placed on natural law by Linularinan mages."

Mienthe thought she would be perfectly ecstatic if her gift, whatever it encompassed, never woke again. Drawing that last double spiral had left her with a persistent and not altogether comfortable sense of increased depth in the world. Well, that was an odd and entirely inaccurate way to describe it. It was more as though everything in the world was now attended by a faint reverberating echo—well, not precisely an *echo*. Mienthe frowned and ate a berry. The sharp sweet-tart taste seemed just a little bolder or darker or more distinct than it should have. She put the berries down and sighed.

Beguchren said gently, "Is it so very unpleasant?"

"Oh . . . it's not *unpleasant*, exactly." In fact, Beguchren's curiosity almost made her curious herself. "What other anomalous gifts?" she asked. "You really think other people might—might—" She waved a vague hand.

"Have gifts similar to yours? Or perhaps unique to themselves? Certainly. Why not? You demonstrate the possibility, and I do not believe the new law will constrain such gifts." Beguchren regarded her with a calm, detached interest that, oddly, made Mienthe feel more comfortable with her strange gift rather than less. He murmured, "I would like to see what you might do in the high mountains. I suspect your gift may be as closely related to wild magic as to the ordinary magic of the earth—an odd notion, and yet I do suspect so. I am curious to see what you might do with the winds. And perhaps with the sea. One might well understand both the winds and the sea to contain"—he made a circular motion in the air—"circles and spirals. Yet we have ordinarily envisioned the sea as allied to earth and the winds as allied to fire."

"Have we?" Mienthe, distracted by an odd thought, had barely heard him. She said instead, "I wonder whether, if a mage's power smothers the inborn gift and if you're no longer a mage—" She stopped. Looked up, with some trepidation. She had not meant to wake old sorrows.

But Beguchren was smiling slightly. "It doesn't matter," he said. "But, yes. I wonder that as well."

"If you—" Mienthe began hesitantly.

A Casmantian soldier, ducking his head in apology as well as to clear the low tent roof, came in, and she broke off, trying to decide whether she was glad or sorry for the interruption.

"Lady," the young man said to Mienthe, and to Beguchren, "my lord, the Arobern asks you to attend him. Immediately, he says, if you will forgive me."

Mienthe jumped to her feet. "I should go—"

"Not at all," murmured Beguchren, rising more slowly. "We may well value your advice, Lady Mienthe. Please accompany me."

"The Safiad has sent for me," the Arobern told them both. He paced nervously from one end of his much larger tent to the other, then spun to glare at Mienthe. "What will he say? What will he do? I am certain Erich is safe—" *Nearly* certain, suggested the stiffness of the Casmantian king's shoulders. "But what will he demand? An apology? An indemnity? " His deep voice dropped further, into a rumbling growl. "A longer term for my son to be held as a hostage at his court? "

Mienthe had to confess that she could not guess. "He *ought* to thank you," she added, but cautiously, because no one but she seemed to think this at all likely.

The Arobern grunted, jerked his head *No*. "I offended his pride. Twice. No. Three times. Once in coming through the pass without leave—twice in leaving Beguchren to delay him on his road—a third time, worst of all, because he knows he must be *grateful* to me." The Casmantian king jerked his head again. "No. He will be *furious*." He prevented Mienthe from exclaiming how unfair this was by adding, in a low growl, "I would be."

"He will be more furious still if you do not come as he bids you," murmured Beguchren. The elegant Casmantian lord looked faintly amused, so far as Mienthe could read his expression at all.

"Yes. True." The Arobern ran a big hand through his short-cropped hair, looking harassed. "Come," he said to Mienthe abruptly. "*You*, come. An apology is well enough, if that will satisfy the Safiad's temper, but if your king demands a second term for my son in his court, *you* tell him he should be grateful to me!"

Mienthe could hardly refuse.

Iaor Safiad was in the solar, in a big, heavy chair with ornate carving on its legs and back. Normally that chair occupied Bertaud's personal apartment, but Mienthe was not surprised to see that the king had claimed it, for it *was* very like a throne. Especially the way Iaor sat in it: not stiff, but upright, with his hands resting on the polished brass finials that finished its arms. There were other chairs near his, but none were much like a throne, and no one was sitting in any of them. There were guardsmen at the door, but they only stared straight ahead, with the most formally rigid posture possible, and did not even seem to notice the Arobern. Or Mienthe, standing nervously in his shadow. She did not know why *she* should be nervous, except that the Arobern's nervousness had communicated itself to her during the ride up to the great house.

Only one other person was with the king: Erich. Prince Erichstaben Taben Arobern, who was standing, his back straight, his chin raised, and his face blank, at the king's left hand. The Arobern stopped when he saw Erich. His gaze went first to his son's face, shifted to take in the young man's height and breadth of shoulder with silent amazement, and rose again to his face with an unspoken but unmistakable hunger.

Erich lifted his chin half an inch higher and met his father's eyes for a brief, taut moment, then turned his face aside as though the effort of sustaining that intense contact had abruptly grown too great. He glanced instead at Mienthe and tried to smile, but it was not a very convincing effort and he gave it up at once.

The echo behind the tension in the room was so powerful that Mienthe found it difficult to endure. She stopped just inside the door and simply tried to breathe evenly, hoping she would not be called upon to explain anything to anybody.

Mienthe was not surprised the king had Erich with him. What surprised her was how very much the prince resembled his father. Erich lacked some of his father's bulk, but none of his height. And their expressions were alike, also. They even stood with the same upright pride. She had not realized how very alike they were until she saw them like this: together in good light.

At last the Arobern moved his gaze, as with an effort, to Iaor Safiad. He walked forward with a heavy stride and stopped a few steps away from King Iaor's chair, his hands hooked in his belt. Mienthe could not read his expression now. There was nothing simple or friendly in the way the two kings looked at each other. She almost fancied she could hear the ringing clash of swords when their eyes met.

The Arobern said, his grim voice touched with irony, "Well, Iaor Daveien Behanad Safiad. I find the second time much like the first. Perhaps someday I will come before you as something other than a supplicant."

Iaor Safiad answered, with a flash of temper, "Perhaps someday you will come into Feierabiand *without* an army at your back."

So everybody else had been right, Mienthe saw, and she had been wrong. Her heart sank.

But the Arobern only lowered his eyes, like a man laying down a sword. He said, "Yes. I did not wish to offend you. But I expected you would be offended. You have been patient. And generous beyond measure."

"You left me little choice but generosity."

"You had every choice. You took that one. I am grateful." The Arobern looked deliberately at his son, then turned his gaze back to King Iaor. He sighed heavily, came one step closer to the throne, and began to kneel.

"No," said Iaor, stopping him. He turned one hand, indicating one of the other chairs. "Sit, if you wish."

There was a little pause.

The Arobern, moving slowly, seated himself in the chair. He set his broad hands on his knees and looked at Iaor Safiad without speaking.

"Your son," said King Iaor, with deliberate emphasis, "has grown into a fine man. He should make any father proud. No doubt Lord Beguchren told you."

"Yes," said the Arobern.

There was another pause. Iaor broke it. "You took every chance," he said, with the same slow, deliberate emphasis. "I am grateful."

The Arobern bent his head just enough to show he had heard, then met the other king's eyes again with somber intensity.

"Shall we agree we are mutually indebted? And that we are not likely to find ourselves at odds during the lifetimes of our children? Feierabiand is glad to count Casmantium as an ally."

"Casmantium, the same."

Iaor nodded. He said grimly, "Then, as we are allies, I will tell you that I intend to send a courier to Linularinum. To Kohorrian's court. I will bid Mariddeier Kohorrian attend me here in Tiefenauer. Do you think he will obey my summons?"

"Ah." The Arobern leaned back in his chair. After a moment, he smiled. It was not a kind expression. "I will send a man also, is this what you intend? Perhaps a soldier, to stand behind your girl courier? And Lord Bertaud will send a man of his, am I to think so? Yes. Then, yes, Kohorrian will come. You wish me to leave a man of mine here also, to stand at your back when you scold Mariddeier Kohorrian?"

Iaor did not precisely smile in return, but there was a glint of hard humor in his eyes. "I thought you might be persuaded to leave me Lord Beguchren Teshrichten for the purpose."

"Ah." The Arobern tapped his heavy fingers on the arm of his chair. "I should be pleased to see Lord Beguchren turn his tongue against Mariddeier Kohorrian rather than against me. And, in truth, I should value his counsel. I consider that he owes me at least so much. What surety would you require?"

The Arobern's eyebrows rose. "From you? I would be ashamed to ask for any surety from you, Iaor Safiad. I will bid Lord Beguchren act as my agent in this matter. I think he may even be pleased by the task."

King Iaor briefly inclined his head.

The Arobern nodded in return, paused, and then asked, "And I? What will you have of me, Iaor Safiad?"

"I will expect you to withdraw from my country quietly and in good order. As, of course, you entered it."

The Arobern, regarding Iaor warily, made a gesture of acquiescence. "As soon as you give me leave to go."

"I give you leave." Iaor gripped the arms of his chair and rose. Then he paused, looking down at the other king, and added, "As a hostage one will not touch has no practical use, I will release your son. When you return to Casmantium, Prince Erichstaben may go with you." He added to Erich, in a much different tone, "I'll miss you, boy, especially when my daughters pester me to teach them dangerous tricks with their ponies."

The young man flushed, grinned, and answered, "Well, Your Majesty, and I'll miss the little girls! May I thank you, and beg you to make my apologies to them for leaving without bidding them farewell?"

"Perhaps I'll send them to Casmantium for a visit," Iaor said to him. "In two years. If your father approves." He gave the Arobern a hard stare.

The Arobern got to his feet and bowed, very slightly. "Of course, Casmantium would be honored to welcome the little Safiad princesses," he said formally.

Erich smiled, a swift, affectionate smile. He glanced at Mienthe and the smile became wry. But then he looked back at his father and the smile slipped altogether.

King Iaor crooked a finger at Mienthe and walked out.

Mienthe followed, all her nerves on edge. She hadn't said a single word, even to say good-bye to Erich. She wondered how soon the Casmantian force would leave—soon, probably, at dawn, perhaps—She wondered whether King Iaor would mind if she went out to the camp again, to bid Erich and his father farewell? Because the king was indeed very angry, she knew, for all he showed it so little. She might not have realized it, except that to her new perception, the echo of his anger filled the space around him like a dark mist.

The door closed behind them, and the king stood still for a moment in the hallway, breathing deeply. Then he turned to Mienthe—she tried not to flinch—and took her by the shoulders. "Mie," he said, smiling with forced good humor that did not touch his eyes. He let her go, but indicated with a nod that she should walk with him. "What I am considering—tell me, Mienthe, would you perhaps consent to escort my daughters to Casmantium in a few years' time? I believe I might not object to a possible connection between my house and the Arobern's, and my daughters are not so much younger than Erich. I do not like to ask Bertaud to go, but you seem on good terms—excellent terms—with the Arobern and his people."

"I'm sorry," Mienthe said, answering the most important part of this. "I mean, of course I will gladly do anything you ask me to do, but—Your Majesty, everything happened so fast, and I didn't know what else to do, but go through the pass. I'm sorry—"

The king shook his head, his taut anger easing at last. "No. No indeed, Mie. It was well done. You have done nothing which requires forgiveness. Nor has Brechen Glansent Arobern. You need not tell me so. I am perfectly aware of it."

Mienthe nodded, relieved. She asked tentatively, "What will you say to Mariddeier Kohorrian?"

"Ah." This time, when the king smiled, the humor did reach his eyes. "I have no idea. I will think of something. Beguchren Teshrichten may advise me." He glanced up and smiled suddenly, a much kinder expression. "And perhaps your cousin may have some ideas of his own."

"Regarding Mariddeier Kohorrian? I could indeed make several suggestions," said Bertaud.

Mienthe whirled around. Her cousin was walking quickly toward them down the hall. His voice, light and ironic, did nothing to hide the shadows of grief and loss in his eyes, but he was alive, and not obviously injured, and he was *here*.

Forgetting the king, forgetting every reason for grief and fear, Mienthe ran forward to embrace him.

Bertaud caught her up as though she were still a child, in a hug that threatened her ribs, then set her down and held her at arm's length, looking searchingly into her face. "Cousin! You are well?"

"Yes, I am, but you? Are *you* well? Are you—" Mienthe hesitated. "You heard . . . Kes told you about your friend? I'm so sorry, Bertaud." She was dimly aware that the king had quietly withdrawn to leave them together, and even more vaguely glad of it, but she had no real attention to spare for anyone but her cousin. He looked, she thought, desperately weary and grieved.

Bertaud bent his head. "She told me, of course. He unmade himself to give you the power you needed to remake the law of the world. Or so I gather. I gather you discovered a gift in yourself which is not quite like anything else in the world." He touched her cheek gently, smiling. "My little cousin!"

Mienthe was embarrassed. "I . . . it wasn't exactly me. I just did things that came to me to do. Tan was much braver. Jos was *very* brave. And . . ." She stopped.

"I'm very certain Kairaithin was glad to know that the wind his death called up was so strong as to overwhelm any other gathering storm. He always—he always was determined to get his own way in everything. And he nearly always succeeded. Most importantly—most importantly at the end."

Mienthe nodded. She asked tentatively, "Do the griffins . . . Was there a ceremony?"

"Not as we understand such things." Bertaud paused, then touched her arm, inviting her to walk with him. "Kes told me that the red dust had blown all through my house and across my gardens and lands, and she kindled a fire for me. A fire for memory, that will never go out . . . If you don't mind, Mie, I thought I might set it to burn next to Tef's stone."

A lump came into her throat. She had to try twice before she could say, "I think that would be the perfect place for it."

They walked out to the gardens side by side. Standing among the stones of generations, Bertaud solemnly tipped a single glowing ember out of a small earthenware pot beside Tef's low, polished grave marker. The ember flickered twice, and for just an instant Mienthe feared it might go out, but then flames crept up from it, pale in the afternoon light, and in moments a hand-sized fire was burning on the gravel by the stone.

"He rode a wind of his own choosing," Bertaud said quietly, and stood gazing down at the fire for one more moment, and then turned away at last.

They walked back toward the house in silence. It looked just the same as it had a month ago, to a casual glance. But if one looked more closely, one would see the scars of battle on the doors and the shutters, and cut into the earth of the gardens . . . The real scars were invisible. For all of them. Mienthe broke the quiet at last to ask, "How did you leave Kes?"

Bertaud glanced down at her, smiling a little. "Well, I think. Or well enough. Grieving, of course. They do grieve for their losses. Busy. She is helping Gereint and Tehre rebuild the Wall. Now the law of the world is solidly in place, it seems quite unimaginable that the Wall ever broke, until you see the shards scattered all across the desert and the mountains."

"They're rebuilding it?" Mienthe was surprised.

"Fire and earth are still foreign to one another, if not inimical. Besides, Tehre said she couldn't bear to leave the Wall shattered and broken. But this time they are building it with a gate. When I left, Tehre was explaining all about the different ways there are of building gates and why arches are superior to architraves, or something of the sort. I confess I wasn't paying close attention."

Mienthe smiled.

"Kes is as beautiful as ever, and no more human. But . . . less unfamiliar, somehow. It's strange watching her with Gereint. They remember the antipathy, and yet they don't remember how it *felt*. I think they may even become friends, in time. She is the most powerful fire mage in the world now, I imagine."

Mienthe would have been astonished to find otherwise. She nodded.

"So she has become Lady of the Changing Winds. That would have pleased Kairaithin, I think. His humor was not like that of a man, but he would have appreciated the irony. And . . . I'll never like Tastairiane Apailika. Nor will he ever have much goodwill toward any creature of earth, I'm sure. But he is her *iskarianere*, you know. He is willing to please her, and so he is now willing to be . . . if not friendly, at least forbearing. I think Kairaithin would appreciate the irony in that, as well."

Mienthe nodded again. She paused as they reached the door, her hand on the splintered wood, and asked tentatively, "How is Jos?"

Her cousin glanced down at her. "I offered him a place here. I told him that the Delta is a good place for exiles, even those without full use of both their hands . . . I think he will come. He owes me something, and of course we all owe him everything, and why should he not live near those of us who know it? He no longer needs to live close to fire, not when Kes can so easily step from one country to the other. I think . . . I am certain that she will not forget him again."

"I'll be glad to see her again from time to time," Mienthe said seriously.

Bertaud nodded. He pushed open the door of the house, but turned to look once more back over the gardens. He still looked weary and grieved, and yet Mienthe thought there was a difference to the sorrow she saw in him now. It seemed deep as the earth, yet she thought this grief was not the same as the grief that had haunted him through the years. This one, she thought, might in time be assuaged.

He turned again, gesturing for Mienthe to precede him. "And your Tan? How does he do now?"

Mienthe shook her head. "The same. Kes told you? Nothing has changed. I have been sitting by him . . . Iaor made me leave him for the day, but I'm sure it's all right if I take *you* up. Will you come?"

Tan lay, very still and pale among the bed linens, in the same tower room Bertaud had given him when they had feared he was still pursued by his enemies. Before they had known who those enemies were, or why they pursued him . . . it seemed so long ago. How astonishing, Mienthe thought, that it had been so short a time.

The room contained little clutter. Only the bed, and a small fire in its brazier, and a single chair framed by two small tables. The first of these held a jug of water and an earthenware cup, and the other a single glass vase from which tumbled the fragrant ivory flowers of honeysuckle in full bloom.

Iriene occupied the chair. The healer-mage was looking at Tan, though the abstraction of her gaze suggested she might not be seeing him. A heavy cloth-bound book was propped open on her knee. Geroen was leaning on the back of her chair with a patient air that suggested he might have been there for rather a long time.

Iriene did not look up when the door opened, but Geroen straightened as he glanced around—then saw Bertaud and stiffened. "My lord—"

Bertaud held up a hand to check him. "Captain Geroen. How is he?"

"There has still been no change?" Mienthe asked anxiously. She slipped across the room and hovered over the still figure on the bed. He was not breathing—oh, of course he was, only slowly and shallowly. He was so pale—"Iriene, is he worse? He's worse, isn't he?"

"About the same, I should say," the healer-mage answered judiciously. She got to her feet, nodded absently to Bertaud, and said to Mienthe, "He's steady enough, you know. Don't you fret over the next few hours. I don't think there's much likely to change any time soon. Not that we exactly want this to go on, but it can, you know, for quite a long time. I'll just go down to the kitchens and have them warm up some broth, shall I?"

She was not really asking permission. Mienthe nodded anyway and perched on the edge of the chair, gazing down at Tan's still face.

Her cousin came to look over her shoulder, frowning. "Lord Beguchren looked very much like this, after he . . ." He did not complete the sentence.

"He said you could use yourself up," Mienthe said in a low voice.

"Gereint broke Beguchren out of his long sleep."

Mienthe nodded. "He told me. But he said it wasn't just that Gereint was a mage, but that he was also his friend." Tan had been away in Linularinum so long, and he was so private a man. Iriene might have healed his knee, but she didn't know him at all . . . no one knew him at all. "Beguchren said this might not be the same. He said we should just wait," Mienthe finished softly.

Tan was so thin and pale, and he looked so cold . . . She took one of his hands in both of hers. His fingers were cold as ice. She said over her shoulder, "Geroen, would you please build up the fire?"

The captain silently added a pine log to the fire, so that its resinous scent blended with the fragrance of the honeysuckle. Then he said again, "My lord . . ."

Bertaud turned to him, raising his eyebrows.

"My lord," Geroen repeated more firmly. "I've prepared a full report for you. All the damage that was done—not much out in the town, not that that's to my credit, which I know very well. More to the house." He hesitated and then said, "I should never have let those Linularinan bastards get a foothold on this side of the river, as I know very well. All the harm we suffered—My lord, I acknowledge it's my fault and my failing—"

Mienthe looked up in astonishment, though she didn't let go of Tan's hand. "That's not true—"

"Certainly it seems unnecessarily simplistic," Bertaud said mildly. "Mie, you're well enough here? Will you send me word immediately in the case of any change, or tonight in any case? Captain Geroen, you must tell me all that happened in my absence." He took the captain's arm, turning him gently toward the door. "I shall assuredly be glad of your report. But let's not be too hasty in declaring where the fault lies, shall we?" He led the other man out, and the door swung gently shut behind them.

Mienthe immediately forgot them. She leaned forward, studying Tan's drawn face. He *was* still breathing. About the same, Iriene had said. Mienthe thought he was worse: more still, more fine-drawn, colder.

If this were an epic romance, she would sit by his bed until at last he wasted away—that was the phrase an epic would use: wasted away. *Wasted*, indeed. What a terrible waste Tan's death would be. Bertaud had said Jos had saved them all, and of course he had; and so had Kes, and Kairaithin; and the Arobern by his courage, and Iaor by his generosity; and so had she, and what a very strange thought that was. But most of all *Tan* had saved them all, by knowing at the last what law to use to bind the world *properly*.

In a romantic epic, she would have fallen in love with Tan, and now she would watch him slowly waste away, and then she would go fling herself to her death from the highest tower of the house. Not that even the highest tower of this house was very tall, and it was surrounded by gardens and not paving stones. Probably, even if she were such a fool, she would only break her leg or something. So the romances had every detail wrong.

Or nearly every detail.

A mage who was also a friend could break this stillness. Mienthe came closer to being a friend than anybody else, but she wasn't a mage. *I just did things that came to me to do*, she had said to Bertaud, and that was true. Nothing came to her now, though she would have welcomed an urge to draw a spiral, any sort of prompting toward anything that might help. But there was nothing, though she tried to clear her mind and heart invitingly. She had no idea how to coax Tan out of his deep silence.

She might find a quill, fold his fingers around it, and offer him a book with blank pages. The feel of a feather quill, the smell of paper— that might draw him out of himself. Except, not if he had burned out his gift. Mienthe thought; then the grief of realizing his loss might drive him further away into his silence rather than drawing him back into the world.

She leaned forward, reached out with one hand, and touched his cheek. "Tan," she said, and realized with a faint despair that she did not even know with any certainty whether that was his name at all. He lied so easily about who he was . . . He lied with his words and his voice and his face, and then told the truth with his own blood, drawn out on the page . . . She said her own name instead, because she knew that it, at least, was true.

His eyelashes fluttered.

Mienthe was too startled to move, or to speak again.

"Mienthe?" he whispered, in a voice as scraped and raw as though he'd bound new law into the world by shouting and not with a quill.

That broke her stillness. Mienthe laughed, and found she was weeping. As weak as his voice was, the echo behind it was very strong. In fact, the echo behind *him* was suddenly very strong. She knew at once, though she could not have said how, that he had not lost his legist gift, that he had not lost anything. In every way that mattered, he was still himself, and she was suddenly glad of the strange new perception that let her be certain of that. She said through her tears, "Tan! I'm here—so are you—we're safe, we've fixed everything, we're all done, we're home—Do you remember everything? Do you remember anything?"

Tan blinked, and blinked again, and turned his head to look at her. A slight crease appeared between his eyebrows, and he frowned. "Home?" he whispered. "Silvered by the tears of fall, jeweled by the touch of winter, quickened by the breath of spring, and nourished by the generous summer . . . Am I come home?"

"Yes," said Mienthe. She touched his cheek again, lightly, fearing to hurt him. "Oh, yes. Don't try to remember." Mienthe poured some water into the cup for him. Then she was doubtful whether he could sit up—whether she should try to coax him to sit up. Maybe she should shout down the stairs and send someone running for Iriene—

"I do remember," Tan said, in a hoarse but stronger voice. He moved vaguely to sit up. "Mienthe—"

"I was so frightened we'd lost you." She folded his hand around the cup, and added in a much lower voice, "That I'd lost you." She looked up quickly then, meeting his eyes.

Tan's mouth crooked, but he shook his head. "Your cousin—"

Mienthe was surprised. Then she smiled. "You saved us all," she said. "So did we all, but mostly you. Do you think my cousin doesn't know it?"

"That's not exactly as I remember it—"

"It's certainly how *I* remember it," Mienthe said firmly. "Tan—*is* that your name?"

He tilted his head a little to the side, but he did not look away. "That is my name. My mother's name is Emnidde. My father was, as they say, careless." He waited, seeming to hold his breath, though how she could tell she did not know, as shallowly as his breaths came.

"Tan," Mienthe said firmly. "Son of Emnidde. That will do, if you'll promise me to answer to it. I never again want to call you, and then realize I don't even know with certainty what name to call—"

Tan closed his eyes and leaned his head back against the pillows, and for a moment she was frightened. But he only whispered, "Whatever name you call, I'll answer to it."

"Will you?" Mienthe wanted to believe him. "Do you promise me you will?"

Tan barely smiled, his eyes still closed. "I promise you. I might lie to anyone else, Mienthe, but I'll always tell you the truth and I'll always answer when you call. Only promise you will call me."

He meant his promise, Mienthe realized. She could hear the deep, shadowy echo behind his voice, and she knew it was the shadow of truth. "Then sleep," she said gently. "Sleep. And when the dawn comes, I promise I'll call you." Then she sat quietly, very still and perfectly happy, her hand lying over his, and watched his breaths deepen again.

acknowledgments

Thanks to my agent, Caitlin Blasdell, whose insightful comments about my manuscripts always help me fix weaknesses that I should have spotted but missed; and to my editor, Devi Pillai, who not only tells me I'm "awesome," but also talked me into writing a trilogy when that wasn't initially what I had in mind.

meet the author

Rachel Neumeier started writing fiction to relax when she was a graduate student and needed a hobby unrelated to her research. Prior to selling her first fantasy novel, she had published only a few articles in venues such as *The American Journal of Botany*. However, finding that her interests did not lie in research, Rachel left academia and began to let her hobbies take over her life instead. She now raises and shows Cavalier King Charles Spaniels, gardens, cooks, and occasionally finds time to read. She works part time for a tutoring program, though she tutors far more students in math and chemistry than in English composition. Find out more about Rachel Neumei at www.rachelneumeier .com.

interview

Have you always known that you wanted to write novels?

I always made up stories in boring classes—as far back as I can remember. (Doesn't everybody?) And I was never interested in short stories. Novel length is the only length that works for me. Or longer! It was *hard* to learn to write *short* novels.

After a hard day of writing, is there anything you like to do in your free time?

It would be nice if I could read, which has always been one of my favorite things. But when I'm actually involved in writing a book of my own, I read very little fiction. I read nonfiction, or cook, or work in the garden, or take the dogs for a walk, or if I have a show or obedience trial coming up I might work on, say, teaching one of my dogs to stand beautifully or heel backing up or something. Of course, if I work with one dog, they all want in on the fun, so training sessions can take a while.

Do you have any particularly favorite authors who have influenced your work?

Certainly! I love Patricia McKillip and Robin McKinley. And Patricia Wrede, Diana Wynne Jones, CJ Cherryh, and Lois McMaster Bujold, in no particular order, and I'm sure I've missed a couple of my favorites. But I have to say that I can only hope Patricia McKillip has influenced my writing; I think she writes the most perfect stories, in the most beautiful language.

The connection between the desert and griffins is a unique take on griffin mythology. Where did you draw your inspiration from?

Nowhere. It just happened. I didn't have that connection in mind at all. I like griffins and wanted to do something with them, but I had no idea there was going to be a connection between griffins and fire. Then I wrote the very first paragraph, and boom, there it was, right out of a, so to speak, clear sky.

Do you harbor a secret preference for any one griffin?

Actually, yes, not that it's secret. Eskainiane, the griffin who at the end—well, that would be giving too much away, I suppose. But to me, Eskainiane really exemplifies what the ideal griffin should be—generous, joyful, passionate, courageous, even exuberant. We don't see too much of him, but he's the sort of griffin who would make you think, Hey, being a griffin might be pretty neat.

The subtle, earth-based magic is seamlessly woven into the fabric of Kes and Bertaud's world. Was this an idea you had from the outset or did it develop over time?

It was a necessary part of the structure of the world as soon as griffins became connected to fire. I immediately saw that fire should be intrinsically opposed to, or at least foreign to, something else, something human. The something else became earth. The exact nature of human magic developed and changed a lot over time, though, and is actually still changing now as I finish book two and think about book three.

What's in store for the next novel of the Griffin Mage series?

That would be telling! Oh, okay, it's set in the country of Casmantium, it concerns the ongoing problem of imbalance between humans and griffins, and it develops a different aspect of earth magic than we see in the first book.

Finally, what has been your favorite part of the publishing process?

You'd think it would be seeing the book actually on the shelf in real bookstores, wouldn't you? But actually, by the time the book hits the shelves, I'm pretty accustomed to the idea that it's going to. (Not that this isn't still a fine thing!) No, the *best* part is when you *first* hear that an editor at a good publishing house loves one of your books and is making an offer.

The funny part about LORD OF THE CHANGING WINDS is that I had *just* moaned to a friend that this book hadn't found a home and I was starting to be afraid it wasn't going to—twenty minutes later, I got the good news from my agent. That is a thrill that isn't going to get old anytime soon.